GREAT
GHOST
STORIES

CHANCELLOR
PRESS

t

Previously published as
The Mammoth Book of Thrillers, Ghosts and Mysteries (1936) by Odhams Press Ltd
Great Tales of the Supernatural (1991) by Chancellor Press

Reprinted 1992

This 2002 edition published by Chancellor Press, an imprint of
Bounty Books, a division of Octopus Publishing Group,
2-4 Heron Quays, London E14 4JP

ISBN 0 7537 0572 9

Printed in Great Britain by Mackays of Chatham

CONTENTS

ILLUSTRATIONS

THE DIVER

FOR some reason or other the B.B.C. are always asking me to tell a ghost story—at least, they don't ask me, they tell me I've got to. I say, " What kind of a ghost story ? " and they say, " Any kind you like, so long as it's a personal experience and perfectly true."

Just like that ; and it's cramped my style a bit. Not that my personal experiences aren't true. Please don't think that. But it's simply this : that when it comes to supernatural matters my luck hasn't been very good. It isn't that I don't believe in such things on principle, but I do like to be present when the manifestations actually occur, instead of just taking other people's word for them ; and, somehow or other, as I've said before, my luck has not been very good.

Lots of people have tried to convert me. There was one young woman in particular. She took a lot of trouble about it—quite a lot. She used to dra—take me to all sorts of parties where they had séances—you know the kind : table-turning, planchette, and so on—but it wasn't any good. Nothing ever happened when I was there. Nothing spiritual, that is. People always said :

" Ah, my boy, you ought to have been here last night. The table fairly got up and hit us in the face."

Possibly very wonderful—but, after all, the ground will do that if you let it.

Well, as I say, they took me to several of these parties, and we used to sit for hours round tables, in a dim light, holding hands. That was rather fun sometimes—it depended on who one sat next to—but apart from that, the nights they took me no manifestations ever occurred. Planchette wouldn't spell a word, and the table might have been screwed to the

13

floor. To begin with they used to put it down to chance, or the conditions not being favourable. But after a time they began to put it down to me—and I thought : " Something will have to be done about it." It's never amusing to be looked upon as a sort of Jonah.

So I invented a patent table-tapper. It was made on the same principle as lazy tongs. You held it between your knees, and when you squeezed it a little mallet shot up (it was really a cotton reel stuck on the end of a pencil) and it hit the underneath of the table a proper biff. It was worked entirely with the knees, so that I could still hold the hands of the people on either side of me. And it was a success from the word " Go."

At the very next séance, as soon as the lights were down, I gave just a gentle tap. Our host said :

" Ah, a powerful force is present ! " and I gave a louder —ponk ! Then he said :

" How do you say ' Yes ' ? " —and I said :

" Ponk ! " Then he said :

" How do you say ' No ' ? " And I said :

" Ponk, ponk ! "

So far so good. Communication established. Then people began asking questions and I spelt out the answers. Awful hard work ponking right through the alphabet, but quite worth it. I'm afraid some of my answers made people sit up a bit. They got quite nervous as to what was coming next. Needless to say, this was some years ago.

Then some one said :

" Who's going to win the Derby ? " (I don't know *who* said that) and I laboriously spelt out Signorinetta. This was two days before the race. I don't know *why* I said Signorinetta, because there were several horses with shorter names, but it just came into my head. The annoying thing was that I didn't take my own tip and back it. You may remember it won at 100 to 1 by I don't know how many lengths—five lengths dividing second and third. However, it's no use crying over the stable door after the horse has spilt the milk, and it has nothing whatever to do with the story.

The amusing thing was that when the séance was over various people came round to me and said :

" *Now* will you believe in spiritualism ? " " What more proof do you want ? " and so on and so forth. It struck me as rather rich that they should try to convert me with my own false evidence. And I don't mind betting you that if I'd owned up to the whole thing being a spoof, not a soul would have believed me. That's always the way.

I've told you all this to show that I'm not exactly dippy on the subject of spiritualism—at any rate, not the table-turning variety—very largely because it *is* so easy to fake your results.

But when something *genuinely* uncanny comes along— why, then I'm one of the very first to be duly thrilled and mystified and—what not. It's one of those *genuine* cases I want to tell you about. It happened to me personally. But first of all you must know that there's a swimming-bath at my club. Very good swimming-bath, too. Deep at one end and shallow at the other. There's a sort of hall-place adjoining it, and in this hall there's a sandwich bar—very popular. It's much cheaper than lunching upstairs. Quite a lot of people seem to gravitate down there—especially towards the end of the month. Everything's quite informal. You just go to the counter and snatch what you want and take it to a table and eat it. Then when you've done, you go and tell George what you've had. George runs the show, and he says "one-and-ninepence," or whatever it is, and that's that.

Personally, I usually go to a table in a little recess close to the edge of the swimming-bath itself. You have to go down a few steps to get to it. But you are rather out of the turmoil and not so likely to get anything spilt over you. It's quite dangerous sometimes, people darting in and out like a lot of sharks—which reminds me : a member once wrote in to the secretary complaining that the place wasn't safe—I shan't say who it was, but you'd know his name if I told you ; I managed to get hold of a copy of his letter. This is what he says, speaking of the sandwich bar :

" I once saw an enormous shark, at least five feet ten inches long, go up to the counter and seize a sausage roll— itself nearly four inches long—and take it away to devour it. When he had bitten off the end, which he did with a single snap of his powerful jaws, he found that it was empty. The sausage, which ought to have been inside, had completely vanished. It had been stolen by another shark even more voracious and ferocious than himself.

" Never.shall I forget the awful spectacle of the baffled and impotent rage of this fearful monster. He went back to the counter, taking the empty sarcophagus with him, and said : ' George, I have been stung ! '

" In order to avoid such scenes of unparalleled and revolting cruelty "—after that he is rather inclined to exaggerate, so I shan't read any more—I usually go late, when the rush is over and it's fairly quiet. People come and practise diving, and sometimes they are worth watching—and sometimes not.

That's the sort of place it is, and if you know of anywhere less likely to be haunted I should like to see it. Very well, then.

One day I was just finishing lunch when there was a splash. I was reading a letter and didn't look up at once, but when I did I was rather surprised to see no ripples on the water, and no one swimming about, so I went on with my letter and didn't think any more about it. That was all that happened that day.

Two or three weeks later, at about the same time, I was again finishing lunch, and there was another splash. This time I looked up almost at once and saw the ripples, and it struck me *then* that it must have been an extraordinarily clean dive, considering that whoever it was must have gone in off the top. One could tell that from where the ripples were— well out in the middle. So I waited for him to come up. But he didn't come up. Then I thought that he must be doing a length under water, and I got up and went to the edge of the bath to watch for him. But still he didn't come up and I got a bit worried. He might have bumped his head on the bottom, or fainted, or anything, and I saw myself having to go in after him with all my clothes on.

I sprinted right round the bath, but there was undoubtedly no one in it. The attendant came out of one of the dressing-rooms and evidently thought I'd gone cracked, so I went to the weighing-machine and weighed myself—eleven stone eight—but I don't think he believed me.

That was the second incident. The third came about a fortnight later. This time I saw the whole thing quite clearly. I was sitting at my usual table and I saw a man climbing up the ladder leading to the top diving-board. When he got up there he came out to the extreme end of the plank and stood for a few seconds rubbing his chest and so on—like people often do.

He was rather tall and muscular—dark, with a small moustache—but what particularly caught my eye was a great big scar he had. It was about nine inches long and it reached down from his left shoulder towards the middle of his chest.

It looked like a bad gash with a bayonet. It must have hurt quite a lot when it was done.

I don't know why I took so much notice of him, but I just did, that's all. And, funnily enough, he seemed to be just as much interested in me as I was in him. He gave me a most meaning look. I didn't know what it meant, but it was undoubtedly a meaning look.

As soon as he saw that he'd got me watching him he dived in, and it was the most gorgeous dive I've ever seen. Hardly any noise or splash—just a gentle sort of plop as though he'd gone into oil rather than water—and the ripples died away almost at once. I thought, if only he'll do that a few more times it'll teach me a lot, and I waited for him to come up—and waited—and waited—but not a sign.

I went to the edge of the bath, and then I walked right round it. But, bar the water, it was perfectly empty. However, to make absolutely certain—I mean that he couldn't have got out without my seeing him—I dug out the attendant and satisfied myself that no towels and—er—costumes had been given out since twelve o'clock—it was then half-past two—and he, the attendant, he'd actually seen the last man leave.

The thing was getting quite serious. My scarred friend couldn't have melted away in the water, nor could he have dived slap through the bottom of the bath—at least, not without leaving some sort of a mark. So it was obvious that either the man had been a ghost, which was absurd—who's ever heard of a ghost in a swimming-bath?—I mean the ideas's too utterly —er—wet for anything—or that there was something wrong with the light lager I was having for lunch.

I went back to my table and found I'd hardly begun it, and in any case let me tell you it was *such* light lager that a gallon of it wouldn't have hurt a child of six—and—I'm *not* a child of six. So I ruled that out, and decided to wait and see if it happened again. It wouldn't have done to say anything about it. One's friends are apt to be a bit flippant when you tell 'em things like that. However, I made a point of sitting at the same table for weeks and weeks afterwards, but old stick-in-the-mud didn't show up again.

A good long time after this—it must have been eighteen months or more—I got an invitation to dine with some people called Pringle. They were old friends of mine, but I hadn't seen them for a long time because they'd mostly lived in Mexico, and one rather loses touch with people at that distance. Any-

way, they were going back there in a few days, and this was a
sort of farewell dinner.

They'd given up their flat and were staying at an hotel.
They'd got another man dining with them. His name was
Melhuish, and he was, with one exception, the most offensive
blighter I've ever come across. Do you know those people
who open their mouths to contradict what you are going to
say before you've even begun to say it ? Well, he did that,
among other things. It was rather difficult to be entirely
civil to him. He was travelling back to Mexico with the
Pringles, as he'd got the job of manager to one of their properties. Something to do with oil, but I didn't quite grasp
what, my mind was so taken up with trying to remember
where on earth I'd seen the man before.

Of course *you* all know. You know he was the man who
dived into the swimming-bath. It sticks out about a mile,
naturally ; but I'd only seen him once before in a bad light,
and it took me till half-way through the fish to place him.
Then it came back with a rush, and my interest in him became
very lively. He was an American, and he'd come over to
England two months before, looking for a job—so he said.
I asked him why he'd left America, and he didn't hear ; but
it did seem fairly certain that he'd never been in Europe before.
So when we got to dessert I proceeded to drop my brick.

I said : " Do you mind telling me whether you have a
scar on your chest like this ? " And I described it. The
Pringles just stared, but Melhuish looked as if he were going
to have a fit. Then he pulled himself together and said :
" Have you ever been in America ? " And I said : " No,
not that I know of." Then he said : " Well, it's a most extraordinary thing, but I *have* a scar on my chest," and he went
on to explain how he'd got it.

Funnily enough, he'd gone in for high diving a lot when
he was younger, and taken any amount of prizes, and on
one occasion he'd found a sharp stake at the bottom of a river.
He gave us full particulars. Very messy. But what they all
wanted to know was how the—how I knew anything about
it. Of course, it was a great temptation to tell 'em, but they'd
only have thought I'd gone off my rocker, so I started a hare
about perhaps having seen a photograph of his swimming-club
in some newspaper or other. They caught on to that idea
quite well, so I left them to it.

The whole thing was by way of being rather a problem,
and it kept me awake that night. Without being up in such

matters, it did occur to me that it might be a warning of some kind. Is it likely that any one—even a ghost—would take the trouble to come all the way from America simply to show me how well he could dive? Of course not, and I sort of thought that a man who was in the habit of going in off the deep end and *not* coming up again was no fit travelling companion for any friends of mine. I'm not superstitious, goodness knows! Of course, I don't walk under ladders, or light three matches with one cigarette, or any of those things, but that's because they're unlucky—not because I'm superstitious.

Anyhow, in case the Pringles might be, I went round next day and saw them. At least, I saw her—he was out—and told her all about the apparition at the club, and so on. That did it. She fairly went off pop. It was a portent, a direct intervention of Providence; nothing would induce her to travel with Melhuish after what she'd heard—and all the rest of it.

I left her to carry on the good work. I don't know how she managed it, but the fact remains that the Pringles did *not* start for Mexico, as arranged, and Melhuish did.

And now you are expecting me to say that the ship in which he sailed was never heard of again. But that wouldn't be strictly true. He got to the other side all right. But the train in which he was travelling through Mexico had to cross a bridge over a river. A steel bridge, it was. Now some months previously there'd been a slight scrap between two local bands of brigands, in the course of which the bridge had been blown up.

When the quarrel was patched up the bridge was patched up, too, but not with the meticulous care it might have been. The result was that in the daytime, when the sun was hot and the steelwork fully expanded, it was a perfectly good bridge, but at night, when it was cold and the girders had shrunk a bit—well, it didn't always quite meet in the middle.

It so happened that the train in question tried to cross this wretched bridge at the very moment when it was having rather a job to make both ends meet—and it simply couldn't bear it. The middle span carried away and the engine and two carriages crashed through into the river, and fourteen people were killed. It was very sad about thirteen of them, but the fourteenth was Mr. Melhuish.

There must be a moral to this story, if I could only think of it; but I can't, so perhaps some of you can help me by suggesting one. . . .

THE GHOUL OF
GOLDERS GREEN

IT is fortunate that the affair should have happened to Mr.
Ralph Wyndham Trevor and be told by him, for Mr.
Trevor is a scholar of some authority. It is in a spirit
of almost ominous premonition that he begins the tale, telling
how he was walking slowly up Davies Street one night when
he caught a crab. It need scarcely be said that Davies Street
owes its name to that Mary Davies, the heiress, who married
into the noble house of Grosvenor. That was years and years
ago, of course, and is of no importance whatsoever now, but
it may be of interest to students.

It was very late on a winter's night, and Mr. Trevor was
depressed, for he had that evening lost a great deal more than
he could afford at the card-game of auction-bridge. Davies
Street was deserted ; and the moon and Mr. Trevor walked
alone towards Berkeley Square. It was not the sort of moon
that Mr. Trevor remembered having seen before. It was,
indeed, the sort of moon one usually meets only in books or
wine. Mr. Trevor was sober.

Nothing happened, Mr. Trevor affirms, for quite a while ;
he just walked, and, at that corner where Davies Street and
Mount Street join together the better to become Berkeley
Square, stayed his walking, with the idea that he would soothe
his depression with the fumes of a cigarette. His cigarette-
case, however, was empty. All London, says Mr. Trevor,
appeared to be empty that night. Berkeley Square lay pallid
and desolate : looking clear, not as though with moonlight,
but with dead daylight ; and never a voice to put life into the
still streets, never a breeze to play with the bits of paper in
the gutters or to sing among the dry boughs of the trees.
Berkeley Square looked like nothing so much as an old stage-

property that no one had any use for. Mr. Trevor had no
use at all for it ; and became definitely antagonistic to it when
a taxi-cab crawled wretchedly across the waste white expanse,
and the driver, a man in a Homburg hat of green plush, looked
into his face with a beseeching look.

" Taxi, sir ? " he said.

Mr. Trevor says that, not wanting to hurt the man's
feelings, he just looked another way.

" Nice night, sir," said the driver miserably, " for a drive
in an 'ackney-carriage."

" I live," said Mr. Trevor with restraint, " only a few
doors off. So hackney-carriage to you."

" No luck ! " sighed the driver and accelerated madly away
even as Mr. Trevor changed his mind, for would it not be an
idea to drive to the nearest coffee-stall and buy some cigarettes ?
This, however, he was not to do, for there was no other reply
to his repeated calls of " Taxi ! " but certain heavy blows on
the silence of Davies Street behind him.

" Wanting a taxi, sir ? " said a voice which could only
belong to a policeman.

" Certainly not," said Mr. Trevor bitterly. " I never
want a taxi. But now and then a taxi-driver thrusts himself
on me and pays me to be seen in his cab, just to give it a tone.
Next question."

" Ho ! " said the policeman thoughtfully.

" I beg your pardon ? " said Mr. Trevor.

" Ho ! " said the policeman thoughtfully.

" The extent of your vocabulary," said Mr. Trevor
gloomily," leads me to conclude that you must have been
born a gentleman. Have you, in that case, a cigarette you
could spare ? "

" Gaspers," said the policeman.

" Thank you," said Mr. Trevor, rejecting them. " I am
no stranger to ptomaine-poisoning."

" That's funny," said the policeman, " your saying that.
I was just thinking of death."

" Death ? " said Mr. Trevor.

" You've said it," said the policeman.

" I've said what ? " said Mr. Trevor.

" Death," said the policeman.

" Oh, death ! " said Mr. Trevor. " I always say ' death,'
constable. It's my favourite word."

" Ghoulish, I calls it, sir. Ghoulish, no less."

" That entirely depends," said Mr. Trevor, " on what you

are talking about. In some things, ghoulish is as ghoulish does. In others, no."

"You've said it," said the policeman. "But ghoulish goes, in this 'ere affair. One after the other lying in their own blood, and not a sign as to who's done it, not a sign!"

"Oh, come, constable! Tut-tut! Not even a thumb-mark in the blood?"

"I'm telling you," said the policeman severely. "Corpses slit to ribbons all the way from 'Ampstead 'Eath to this 'ere Burkley Square. And why? That's what I asks myself. And why?"

"Of course," said Mr. Trevor gaily, "there certainly have been a lot of murders lately. Ha-ha! But not, surely, as many as all that!"

"I'm coming to that," said the policeman severely. "We don't allow of the Press reporting more'n a quarter of them. No, sir. That's wot it 'as come to, these larst few days. A more painful situation 'as rarely arisen in the hannals of British crime. The un'eard-of bestiality of the criminal may well baffle ordinary minds like yours and mine."

"I don't believe a word of it!" snapped Mr. Trevor.

"Ho, *you* don't!" said the policeman. "*You* don't!"

"That's right," said Mr. Trevor, "I don't. Do you mean to stand there and tell me that I wouldn't 'ave 'eard—I mean, have heard of this criminal if he had really existed?"

"You're a gent," said the policeman.

"You've said it," said Mr. Trevor.

"And gents," said the policeman, "know nothing. And what they do know is mouldy. Ever 'eard of Jack the Ripper?"

"Yes, I 'ave," said Mr. Trevor bitterly.

"*Have* is right, sir, if you'll excuse me. Well, Jack's death was never rightly proved, not it! So it might well be 'im at 'is old tricks again, even though 'e has been retired, in a manner of speaking, these forty years. Remorseless and hindiscriminate murder, swift and sure, was Jack's line, if you remember, sir."

"Before my time," said Mr. Trevor gloomily.

"Well, Jack's method was just to slit 'em up with a razor, frontwise and from south to north, and not a blessed word spoken. No one's touched 'im yet, not for efficiency, but this new chap, 'e looks like catching Jack up. *And* at Jack's own game, razor and all. Makes a man fair sick, sir, to see the completed work. Just slits 'em up as clean as you or me might slit up a vealanam-pie. We was laying bets on 'im over at Vine Street only to-night, curious like to see whether 'e'd beat Jack's record. But it'll take some beating, I give you my word. Up to date this chap 'as only done in twelve in three weeks—not that that's 'alf bad, seeing as how 'e's new to the game, more or less."

"Oh rather, more or less!" said Mr. Trevor faintly. "Twelve! Good God—only twelve! But why—why don't you catch the ghastly man?"

"Ho, why don't we!" said the policeman. "Becos we don't know 'ow, that's why. Not us! It's the little one-corpse men we're good for, not these 'ere big artists. Look at Jack the Ripper—did we catch 'im? Did we? And look at Julian Raphael—did we catch 'im? I'm asking you."

"I know you are," said Mr. Trevor gratefully. "Thank you."

"I don't want your thanks," said the policeman. "I'm just warning you."

Mr. Trevor gasped: "Warning *me*!"

"You've said it," said the policeman. "You don't ought to be out alone at this time of night, an 'earty young chap like you. These twelve 'e's already done in were all 'earty young chaps. 'E's partial to 'em 'earty, I do believe. And social gents some of 'em was, too, with top-'ats to hand, just like you might be now, sir, coming 'ome from a smoking-concert. Jack the Ripper all over again, that's wot I say. Except that this 'ere new corpse-fancier, 'e don't seem to fancy women at all."

"A chaps' murderer, what!" said Mr. Trevor faintly. "Ha-ha! What!"

"You've said it," said the policeman. "But you never know your luck, sir. And maybe as 'ow thirteen's your lucky number."

Mr. Trevor lays emphasis on the fact that throughout he treated the constable with the courtesy due from a gentleman to the law. He merely said: "Constable, I am now going home. I do not like you very much. You are an alarmist. And I hope that when you go to sleep to-night your ears swell so that when you wake up in the morning you will be able to fly straight to Heaven and never be seen or heard of again. You and your razors and your thirteens!"

"Ho, they ain't mine, far from it!" said the policeman, and even as he spoke a voice crashed upon the silence from the direction of Mount Street. The voice belonged to a tall figure in black and white, and on his head was a top-hat that shone under the pallid moon like a monstrous black jewel.

" That there," said the policeman, " is a Noise."

" He's singing," said Mr. Trevor.

" I'll teach 'im singing ! " said the policeman.

Sang the voice :

> " *With an host of furious fancies,*
> *Whereof I am commander,*
> *With a burning spear*
> *And a horse of air*
> *To the wilderness I wander.*"

" You will," said the policeman. " Oh, you will ! "

> " *By a knight of ghosts and shadows*
> *I summoned am to tourney*
> *Ten leagues beyond*
> *The wide world's end—*
> *Methinks it is no journey !* "

" Not to Vine Street, it isn't," said the policeman.

" Ho there ! " cried the approaching voice. " Who dares interrupt my song ! "

" Beau Maturin ! " cried Mr. Trevor gladly. " It's not you ! Bravo, Beau Maturin ! Sing, bless you, sing ! For I am depressed."

> " *From Heaven's Gate to Hampstead Heath*
> *Young Bacchus and his crew*
> *Came tumbling down, and o'er the town*
> *Their bursting trumpets blew.*"

" Fine big gent, your friend," said the policeman thoughtfully.

> " *And when they heard that happy word*
> *Policemen leapt and ambled :*
> *The busmen pranced, the maidens danced,*
> *The men in bowlers gambolled.*"

" Big ! " said Mr. Trevor. " Big ? Let me tell you, constable, that the last time Mr. Maturin hit Jack Dempsey, Dempsey bounced back from the floor so quick that he knocked Mr. Maturin out on the rebound."

Mr. Trevor says that Beau Maturin came on through the night like an avenger through a wilderness, so little did he reck of cruel moons and rude policemen. Said he : " Good evening, Ralph. Good evening, constable. Lo, I am in wine ! "

" You've said it," said the policeman.

" Gently, my dear ! Or," said Mr. Maturin cordially, " I will dot you one, and look at it which way you like it is a far far better thing to be in wine than in a hospital. Now, are there any good murders going to-night ? "

" Going ? " said the constable. " I'm 'ere to see there ain't any coming. But I've just been telling this gent about some recent crises. Corpses slit to ribbons just as you or me might slit up a vealanam——"

" Don't say that again ! " snapped Mr. Trevor.

" By Heaven, what's that ? " sighed Mr. Maturin ; and, following his intent eyes, they saw, a yard or so behind them on the pavement, a something that glittered in the moonlight. Mr. Trevor says that, without a thought for his own safety, he instantly took a step towards the thing, but that the policeman restrained him. It was Mr. Maturin who picked the thing up. The policeman whistled thoughtfully.

" A razor, let's face it ! " whispered Beau Maturin.

" *And* sharp ! " said the policeman, thoughtfully testing the glittering blade with the ball of his thumb.

Mr. Trevor says that he was never in his life less conscious of any feeling of excitement. He merely pointed out that he could swear there had been no razor there when he had come round the corner, and that, while he had stood there, no one had passed behind him.

" The chap that owns this razor," said the policeman, emphasizing each word with a gesture of the blade, " must 'ave slunk behind you and me as we stood 'ere talking and dropped it, maybe not finding it sharp enough for 'is purpose. What do you think, Mr. Maturin ? "

But Mr. Maturin begged to be excused from thinking, protesting that men are in the hands of God, and God is in the hands of women and so what the devil is there to think about ?

Mr. Trevor says that the motive behind his remark at that moment, which was to the effect that he simply must have a drink, was merely that he was thirsty. A clock struck two.

" After hours," said the policeman ; and he seemed, Mr. Trevor thought, to grin evilly.

"What do they know of hours," sighed Mr. Maturin, "who only Ciro's know? Come, Ralph. My love, she jilted me but the other night. Therefore I will swim in wine, and thrice will I call upon her name when I am drowning. Constable, good-night to you."

"Now I've warned you!" the policeman called after them. "Don't go into any alleys or passages like Lansdowne Passage, else you'll be finding yourselves slit up like vealanampies."

Maybe it was only the treacherous light of the moon, but Mr. Trevor fancied as he looked back that the policeman, where he stood thoughtfully fingering the shining blade, seemed to be grinning evilly at them.

II

THEY walked in silence, their steps ringing sharp on the bitter-chill air. The night in the sky was pale at the white disdain of the moon. It was Mr. Maturin who spoke at last, saying: "There's too much talk of murder to-night. A man cannot go to bed on such crude talk. You know me, kid. Shall we go to *The Garden of My Grandmother*?"

At that moment a taxi-cab crawled across the moonlight; and the driver, a man in a Homburg hat of green plush, did not attempt to hide his pleasure at being able to satisfy the gentlemen's request to take them to *The Garden of My Grandmother*.

Mr. Trevor says that he has rarely chanced upon a more unsatisfactory taxi-cab than that driven by the man in the Homburg hat of green plush. By closing one's eyes one might perhaps have created an illusion of movement by reason of certain internal shrieks and commotions, but when one saw the slow procession of shops by the windows and the lampposts loitering by the curb, one was, as Beau Maturin pointed out, justified in believing that the hackney-cab in question was not going fast enough to outstrip a retired Czecho-Slovakian Admiral in an egg-and-spoon race. Nor were they altogether surprised when the taxi-cab died on them in Conduit Street. The man in the Homburg hat of green plush jumped out and tried to re-start the engine. He failed. The gentlemen within waited the issue in silence. The silence, says Mr. Trevor, grew terrible. But the taxi-cab moved not, and the man in the Homburg hat of green plush began, in his agitation, thumping the carburettor with his clenched fist.

" No petrol," he pleaded. " No petrol."

Said Mr. Trevor to Mr. Maturin : " Let us go. Let us leave this man."

" 'Ere, my fare ! " said the fellow.

" Your fare ? " said Mr. Maturin, with contracted brows. " What do you mean, ' your fare ' ? "

" Bob on the meter," said the wretch.

" My friend will pay," said Mr. Maturin, and stalked away. Mr. Trevor says that, while retaining throughout the course of that miserable night his undoubted flair for generosity, he could not but hold Beau Maturin's high-handed disavowal of his responsibilities against him ; and he was hurrying after him up Conduit Street, turning over such phrases as might best point the occasion and make Mr. Maturin ashamed of himself, when that pretty gentleman swung round sharply and said : " Ssh ! "

But Mr. Trevor was disinclined to Ssh, maintaining that Mr. Maturin owed him ninepence.

" Ssh, you fool ! " snapped Mr. Maturin ; and Mr. Trevor had not obliged him for long before he discerned in the quietness of Conduit Street a small discordant noise, or rather, says Mr. Trevor, a series of small discordant noises.

" She's crying, let's face it," whispered Mr. Maturin.

" She ! Who ? "

" Ssh ! " snapped Mr. Maturin.

They were at that point in Conduit Street where a turn to the right will bring one into a fat little street which looks blind but isn't, insomuch as close by the entrance to the Alpine Club Galleries there is a narrow passage or alley leading into Savile Row. Mr. Trevor says that the repugnance with which he at that moment looked towards the darkness of that passage or alley had less than nothing to do with the bloodthirsty policeman's last words, but was due merely to an antipathy he had entertained towards all passages or alleys ever since George Tarlyon had seen a ghost in one. Mr. Maturin and he stood for some minutes in the full light of the moon while, as though from the very heart of the opposite darkness, the lacerating tremors of weeping echoed about their ears.

" I can't bear it ! " said Beau Maturin. " Come along." And he advanced towards the darkness, but Mr. Trevor said he would not, pleading foot-trouble.

" Come," said Beau Maturin, but Mr. Trevor said : " To-morrow, yes. But not to-night."

Then did Beau Maturin advance alone into the darkness

towards the passage or alley, and with one pounce the darkness stole his top-hat from the moon. Beau Maturin was invisible. The noise of weeping abated.

"Oi !" called Mr. Trevor. "Come back, you fool !"

"Ssh !" whispered the voice of Mr. Maturin.

Mr. Trevor said bitterly : "You're swanking, that's all !"

"It's a girl !" whispered the voice of Mr. Maturin, whereupon Mr. Trevor, who yielded to no man in the chivalry of his address towards women, at once advanced, caught up Mr. Maturin, and, without a thought for his own safety, was about to pass ahead of him, when Beau Maturin had the bad taste to whisper, "'Ware razors !" and thus again held the lead.

She who wept, now almost inaudibly, was a dark shape just within the passage. Her face, says Mr. Trevor, was not visible, yet her shadow had not those rather surprising contours which one generally associates with women who weep in the night.

"Madam," began Mr. Maturin.

"Oh !" sobbed the gentle voice. "He is insulting me !"

Mr. Trevor lays some emphasis on the fact that throughout the course of that miserable night his manners were a pattern of courtliness. Thinking, however, that a young lady in a situation so lachrymose would react more favourably to a fatherly tone, he said :

"My child, we hope——"

"Ah," sobbed the gentle voice. "Please go away, please ! I am *not* that sort !"

"Come, come !" said Mr. Maturin. "It is us whom you insult with a suspicion so disagreeable. My friend and I are not of the sort to commit ourselves to so low a process as that which is called, I believe, ' picking up.' "

"We have, as a matter of fact, friends of our own," said Mr. Trevor haughtily.

"Speaking generally," said Mr. Maturin, "women like us. Time over again I have had to sacrifice my friendship with a man in order to retain his wife's respect."

"Ah, you are a man of honour !" sobbed the young lady.

"We are two men of honour," said Mr. Trevor.

"And far," said Mr. Maturin warmly, "from intending you any mischief, we merely thought, on hearing you weeping——"

"You *heard* me, sir !"

" From Conduit Street," said Mr. Trevor severely, where-upon Mr. Maturin lifted up his voice and sang :

" *From Conduit Street, from Conduit Street,*
  The street of ties and tailors :
  From Conduit Street, from Conduit Street,
  A shocking street for trousers."

" Oh ! " sobbed the young lady. " Is this chivalry ? "

" Trousers," said Mr. Maturin, " are closely connected with chivalry, insomuch as he who commits chivalry without them is to be considered a rude fellow. But, child," Mr. Maturin protested sincerely, " we addressed you only in the hope that we might be of some service in the extremity of your grief. I assure you that you can trust us, for since we are no longer soldiers, rape and crime have ceased to attract us. However, you do not need us. We were wrong. We will go."

" It was I who was wrong ! " came the low voice ; and Mr. Trevor says that only then did the young lady raise her face, when it was instantly as though the beauty of that small face sent the surrounding darkness scurrying away. Not, however, that Mr. Trevor was impressed altogether in the young lady's favour. Her eyes, which were large, dark, and charming, appeared to rest on handsome Beau Maturin with an intentness which Mr. Trevor can only describe as bold ; while her disregard of his own presence might have hurt him had he, says Mr. Trevor, cared two pins for that kind of thing.

" You see, I have not eaten to-day," the young lady told Beau Maturin, who cried : " But, then, we *can* help you ! "

" Ah, how do I know ! Please," the young lady began weeping again, and Mr. Trevor says that had he not hardened his heart he could not say what he might not have done. " Please, sirs, I simply do not know what to do ! I am so unhappy, so alone—oh, but you cannot imagine ! You are gentlemen ? "

" Speaking for my friend," said Mr. Maturin warmly, " he has been asked to resign from Buck's Club only after repeated bankruptcies."

" Mr. Maturin," said Mr. Trevor, " has in his time been cashiered from no less a regiment than the Coldstream Guards."

The young lady did not, however, favour Mr. Trevor with so much as a glance, never once taking her beautiful eyes from the handsome face of Beau Maturin. Indeed, throughout the course of that miserable night she admirably controlled any interest Mr. Trevor might have aroused in her, which Mr. Trevor can only account for by the supposition that she must have been warned against him. Beau Maturin, meanwhile, had taken the young lady's arm, a familiarity with which Mr. Trevor cannot too strongly dissociate himself, and was saying :

" Child, you may come with us, if not with honour, at least with safety. And while you refresh yourself with food and drink you can tell us, if you please, the tale of your troubles. Can't she, Ralph ? "

" I don't see," said Mr. Trevor, " what good we can do."

" Your friend," said the young lady sadly to Beau Maturin, " does not like me. Perhaps you had better leave me alone to my misery."

" My friend," said Beau Maturin, guiding her steps down the fat little street towards Conduit Street, " likes you only too well, but is restraining himself for fear of your displeasure. Moreover, he cannot quickly adapt himself to the company of ingenuous young ladies, for he goes a good deal into society, where somewhat cruder methods obtain."

" But oh, where are you taking me to ? " suddenly cried the young lady.

" To *The Garden of My Grandmother*," said Mr. Trevor bitterly, and presently they found a taxi-cab on Regent Street which quickly delivered them at the place in Leicester Square. Mr. Trevor cannot help priding himself on the agility with which he leapt out of that taxi-cab, saying to the driver : " My friend will pay."

But Mr. Maturin, engrossed in paying those little attentions to the young lady which really attractive men, says Mr. Trevor, can afford to neglect, told the driver to wait, and when the driver said he did not want to wait, to go and boil his head.

III

MR. TREVOR describes *The Garden of My Grandmother* in some detail, but that would be of interest only to the specialist. The place was lately raided, and is now closed ; and remained open so long as it did only with the help of such devices as commend themselves to those aliens who know the laws of the land only to circumvent them. For some time, indeed, the police did not even know of its existence as a night-club, for the entrance to the place was through two mean-looking doors several yards apart, on one of which was boldly inscribed the word " Gentlemen " and on the other " Ladies."

Within, all was gaiety and chic. From the respectable night-clubs and restaurants, all closed by this hour, would come the *jeunesse* of England ; and an appetizing smell of kippers brought new life to the jaded senses of young ladies, while young gentlemen cleverly contrived to give the appearance of drinking ginger-ale by taking their champagne through straws. Mr. Trevor says, however, that there was not the smallest chance of the place being raided on the night in question, for among the company was a Prince of the Blood ; and it is an unwritten law in the Metropolitan Police Force that no night-club shall be raided while a Prince of the Blood is pulling a party therein.

The young lady and our two gentlemen were presently refreshing themselves at a table in a secluded corner ; and when at last only the wine was left before them Mr. Maturin assumed his courtliest manner to beg the young lady to tell her tale, and in detail, if she thought its relation would relieve her at all. She thought, with all the pensive beauty of her dark eyes, that it would, and immediately began on the following tale :

THE TALE OF THE BULGARIAN GIRL

I am (she said) twenty-three years old, and although I once spent two years in England at a boarding-school in Croydon, my life hitherto has been lived entirely in Bulgaria. My father was a Bulgar of the name of Samson Samsonovitch Samsonoff, my mother an Englishwoman of the Lancashire branch of the race of Jones, and for her tragic death in a railway accident just over a year ago I shall grieve all my life : which, I cannot help praying, may be a short one, for I weary of the insensate cruelties that every new day opens out for me.

I must tell you that my mother was an unusual woman, of rigid principles, lofty ideals, and a profound feeling for the grace and dignity of the English tongue, in which, in spite of my father's opposition, for the Samsonoffs are a bitter proud race, she made me proficient at an early age. Never had this admirable woman a thought in her life that was not directed towards furthering her husband's welfare and to obtaining the happiness of her only child ; and I am convinced that my father had not met his cruel death two months ago had she been spared to counsel him.

My father came of an ancient Macedonian house. For hundreds of years a bearer of the name of Samson Samsonovitch Samsonoff has trod the stark hillsides of the Balkans and raided the sweet, rich valleys about Philippopolis. As brigands, the Samsonoffs had never a rival ; as *comitadjis*, in war or peace, their name was a name for heroism and of terror ; while as assassins—for the domestic economy of Bulgaria has ever demanded the occasional services of a hawk's eye and a ruthless hand—a Samsonoff has been honourably associated with some of the most memorable coups in Balkan history. I am well aware that pride of family has exercised a base dominion over the minds of many good men and women ; yet I do not hesitate to confess that it is with almost unbearable regret that I look upon the fact that I, a wretched girl, am the last and only remnant of our once proud house.

Such a man it was with whom my mother, while accompanying her father, a civil engineer, through Bulgaria, married. Nor did it need anything less than the ardour of her love and the strength of her character to seduce a Samson Samsonovitch from the dour dominion of the hills to the conventional life of the valleys. I loved my father, but cannot be blind to the grave flaws in his character. A tall, hairy man, with a beard such as would have appalled your English description of Beaver, he was subject to ungovernable tempers and, occasionally, to regrettable lapses from that moral code which is such an attractive feature of English domestic life. Ah, you who live in the content and plenty of so civilized a land, how can you even imagine the horrors of lawlessness that obtain among primitive peoples ! Had not that good woman my mother always willed him to loving-kindness, Samsonovitch Samsonoff had more than once spilled the blood of his dearest friends in the heat of some petty tavern brawl.

We lived in a farmhouse in what is surely the loveliest valley in the world, that which is called the Valley of the Roses, and whence is given to the world that exquisite essence known as attar of roses. Our little household in that valley was a happy and united one ; more and more infrequent became my father's demoniac tempers ; and, but for his intolerance of fools and cravens, you had taken the last of the Samsonoffs to be a part of the life of the valley-men, of whose industry, the cultivation of roses, he rapidly became a master.

Thus we come to the time which I now think of as two months before my mother's death. My father had attained to a certain degree of wealth, and was ever enticing my mother with dreams of a prolonged visit to her beloved birthplace, Southport, which is, I believe, a pretty town on the seaboard of Lancashire, and which I look forward with delight to visiting. While enticing her, however, with such visions, he did not hesitate to warn her that she must wait on the issue of his fanciful hobby, which daily grew on him ; for the last of the Samsonoffs had become an inventor of flowers !

You may well look bewildered. But had you known my father you would in some measure have understood how a man, of an extreme audacity of temperament, might be driven into any fanciful pursuit that might lend a spice to a life of intolerable gentility. Nor was that pursuit so fanciful as might at first appear to those of conventionally studious minds : my father had a profound knowledge of the anatomy of flowers ; and was in the habit of saying that he could not but think that the mind of man had hitherto neglected the invention and cultivation of the most agreeable variations. In fine, the tempestuous but simple mind of Samsonovitch Samsonoff had been captivated by the possibility of growing green carnations.

My mother and I were, naturally enough, not at all averse from his practising so gentle a hobby as the invention and cultivation of improbable flowers. And it was long before we even dreamt of the evil consequences that might attend so inoffensive an ambition. But my poor mother was soon to be rid of the anxieties of this life.

One day she and I were sitting in the garden discussing the English fashion-journals, when, silently as a cloud, my father came out of the house and looked towards us in the half-frowning, half-smiling way of his best mood. Tall and patriarchal, he came towards us—and in his hand we saw a flower with a long slender stem, and we stared at it as though we could not believe our eyes, for it was a green carnation !

" You have painted it ! " we cried, my mother and I, for his success had seemed to us as remote as the stars.

" I have *made* it ! " said my father, and he smiled into his beard, which was ever his one confidential friend. " Women, I have made it in my laboratory. And as I have made this I can make thousands, millions, and thousands of millions ! "

He waved a closely-covered piece of paper towards me. " My daughter," he said, " here is your dower, your heritage. I am too old to burden myself with the cares of great riches, but by the help of this paper, you, my beloved child, will become an heiress who may condescend to an Emperor or an

American. We will not lose a minute before going to England, the land of honest men, to put the matter of the patent in train. For on this paper is written the formula by which green carnations, as well as all previously known varieties of carnations, can be *made* instead of grown. *Made*, I say, instead of grown! Women, do you understand what it is that I have achieved? I have stolen something of the secret of the sun!"

"Samson, boast not!" cried my mother, but he laughed at her and fondled me, while I stared in great wonder at the slip of paper that fluttered in his hand, and dreamed the fair dreams of wealth and happiness in a civilized country Ah, me, ah me, the ill-fated excellence of dreams! For here I am in the most civilized country in the world, a pauper, and more wretched than a pauper!

Our preparations for removal to England were not far advanced before that happened which brought the first cruel turn to our fortunes. On an evil day my mother set out to Vienna to buy some trivial thing, and—but I cannot speak of that, how she was returned to us a mangled corpse, her dear features mutilated beyond recognition by the fury of the railway accident.

My father took his sudden loss strangely: it was as though he was deprived at one blow of all the balance, the restraint, with which so many years of my mother's influence had softened the dangerous temper of the Samsonoff; and the brooding silence he put upon his surroundings clamoured with black thoughts. Worst of all, he began again to frequent the taverns in the valley, wherein he seemed to find solace in goading to fury the craven-hearted lowlanders among whom he had lived in peace for so long. The Samsonoff, in short, seemed rapidly to be reverting to type; and I, his daughter, must stand by and do nothing, for my influence over him was never but of the pettiest sort.

The weeks passed, and our preparations for departure to England proceeded at the soberest pace. In England we were going to stay with my mother's brother, a saintly man of some little property who lived a retired life in London, and whose heir I would in due course be, since he was himself without wife or children.

My father, never notable for the agreeable qualities of discretion and reticence, soon spread about the report of his discovery of the green carnation. He could not resist boasting of it in his cups, of the formula with which he could always make them, of the fortune he must inevitably make. Nor did he hesitate to taunt the men of the valley, they who came of generations of flower-growers, with his own success in an occupation which, he said, he had never undertaken but at a woman's persuasion, since it could be regarded as manly only by those who would describe as manly the painted face of a Circassian eunuch. Thus he would taunt them, laughing me to scorn when I ventured to point out that even worms will turn and cravens conspire. Woe and woe to the dour and high-handed in a world of polity, for their fate shall surely find them out !

One day, having been to the village to procure some yeast for the making of a *yaourt* or *yawort*, which is that same Bulgarian " sour milk " so strongly recommended to Anglo-Saxon digestions, I was startled, as I walked up the path to the door, by the bruit of loud, rough voices. Only too soon was my fear turned to horror. One of the voices was my father's, arrogant and harsh as only his could be, with a sneer like a snake running through it. The other I could not recognize, but could hear only too well that it had not the soft accents of the men of the valley ; and when, afraid to enter, I peered in through the window, I saw my father in violent altercation with a man his equal in stature and demeanour—another bearded giant, as fair as my father was dark, and with the livid eyes of a wolf.

What was my horror on recognizing him as Michaelis the *comitadji*, the notorious and brutal Michaelis of the hills. The Michaelis and the Samsonovitch Samsonoffs had always been the equal kings of the *banditti*, and, in many a fight between Christian and Turk, the equal champions of the Cross against the Crescent. And now, as I could hear through the window, the last of the Michaelis was asking of the last of the Samsonoffs some of his great wealth, that he might arm and munition his troop to the latest mode.

My father threw back his head and laughed. But his laugh had cost him dear had I not screamed a warning, for the Michaelis with the wolfish eyes had raised a broad knife. My father leapt to one side, and taking up the first thing that came to hand, a heavy bottle of *mastic*, crashed it down like an axe on the fair giant's head ; and then, without so much as a glance at the unconscious man, and massive though the Michaelis was, slung him over his shoulder, strode out of the house and garden, and flung him into the middle of the road-way, where he lay for long moaning savagely with the pain of his broken head. I had gone to the aid of the wretch, but my father would not let me, saying that no Michaelis ever yet died of a slap on the crown and that a little blood-letting would clear the man's mind of his boyish fancies. Ah, if it had !

It was at a late hour of the very next night—for since my mother's death my father would loiter in the taverns until all hours—that his hoarse voice roused me from my sleep ; and on descending I found him raging about the kitchen like a wounded tiger, his clothes in disorder and showing grim dark stains that, as I clung to him, foully wetted my hands. I prayed him, in an access of terror, to tell me he was not hurt, for what other protection than him had I in that murderous land ?

" I am not hurt, child," he growled impatiently. " But I have been driven to hurt some so that they can never again feel pain."

They had ambushed him, the cowards, as he came home through the wood—as though a hundred of those maggots of the valley could slay a Samsonovitch Samsonoff ! My father had caught the last of them by the throat, and the trembling coward had saved himself by confessing the plot. It appeared that it was they who had persuaded the Michaelis to visit us the day before, inflaming his fancy with tales of the discovery of the carnation and of the great riches the Samsonoff had concealed about the house. And the Michaelis had come to our house not for part of my father's wealth but for all he could find, as also for the secret of the carnation, which he might sell at a great price to some Jew in Sofia—he had come to kill my father !

" And I, like a fool," cried my father, " only broke the skin of his wolfish head ! Girl, we must be off at once ! I have not lived in unwilling peace all these years to die like a rat ; and now that these weak idiots have failed to kill me Michaelis and his troop will surround the house, and who shall escape the wolves of the hills ? Now linger not for your clothes and fineries. Grigory Eshekovitch has horses for us at the edge of the wood, and we can make Philippopolis by the morning. Here is all our money in notes. Take them, so that you will be provided for should these scum get me. And the formula —take care of the formula, child, for that is your fortune ! Should I have to stay behind, your mother's brother in England is a good man and will probably not rob you of more than half the profits of it."

And so we came to leave our beloved home, stealing like

thieves through the darkness of a moonless night. How shall I ever forget those desperate moments ! Our farm lay far from any other habitation, and a long sloping lane joined our pastures to the extensive Karaloff Wood, a wood always evoked by Bulgarian poets of past centuries as the home of vampires and the kennel of the hounds of hell.

There, at its borders, Grigory Eshekovitch, a homely man devoted to our interests, awaited us with two horses ; and, although I could not see his face in the darkness, I could imagine by the tremor of his never very assured voice how pallid, indeed green, it must have been ; for poor Grigory Eshekovitch suffered from some internal affection, which had the effect of establishing his complexion very uncertainly.

" Have you seen any one in the wood ? " my father asked him.

" No, but I have heard noises," Grigory Eshekovitch trembled.

" Bah ! " growled my father. " That was the chattering of your own miserable teeth."

I wonder what has happened to poor Grigory Eshekovitch, whether he survived that hideous night. We left him there, a trembling figure on the borders of the wood, while we put our horses into the heart of that darkness ; and I tried to find solace in our desperate situation by looking forward to the safety and comfort of our approaching life in England.   Little I knew that I was to suffer such agonies of fear in this huge city that I would wish myself back in the land of wolves !

My dreams were shattered by a low growl from my father, and we pulled up our horses, listening intently. By this time we were about half-way through the wood ; and had we not known the place by heart we had long since lost our way, for the curtain of leaves between us and the faint light of the stars made the place so black that we could not even see the faintest glimmer of each other. At last my father whispered that it was all right, and we were in the act of spurring our tired horses for the last dash through the wood when torches flamed on all sides, and we stood as in the tortured light of a crypt in moonlight.

" Samson Samsonovitch," cried a hoarse voice, and like a stab at my heart I knew it for the voice of the Michaelis, " we hope your sins are not too heavy, for your time has come."

It ill becomes a girl to boast of her parent ; but shall I neglect to mention the stern fortitude, the patriarchal resignation, the monumental bravery of my father, how he sat his horse still as a rock in a tempest and only his lips moved in a gentle whisper to me. " Child, save yourself," said he, and that was his farewell. " I command you to go—to save yourself and my secret from these hounds. Maybe I too will get through. God is as good to us as we deserve. Head right through them. Their aim, between you and me, will be so unsure that we might both escape. Go, and God go with you ! "

Can you ask me to remember the details of the awful moment ? The darkness, the flaming torches, the hoarse cries of the bandits as they rode in on us, my father's great courage—all these combined to produce in me a state for which the word " terror " seems altogether too homely. Perhaps I should not have left my father. Perhaps I should have died with him. I did not know what I was doing. Blindly as in a nightmare I spurred my horse midway between two moving torches. The horse, startled already, flew madly as the wind. Cries, curses, shots seemed to sweep about me, envelop me, but terror lent wings to my horse, and the shots and shouts faded behind me as phantoms might fade in a furious wind. Last of all came a fearful fusillade of shots, then a silence broken only by the harsh rustle of the bracken under my horse, which with the livid intelligence of fear, did not stop before we reached Philippopolis in the dawn.

I was never to see my father again. Until noon of the next day I sat anxiously in the only decent inn of the ancient town, praying that some act of Providence had come to his aid and that he might at any moment appear ; when, from a loquacious person, who did not know my name, I heard that the last of the Samsonoffs had that morning been found in Karaloff Wood nailed to a tree-trunk with eighteen bullet wounds in his body.

I will spare you my reflections on the pass in which I then found myself. No young girl was ever so completely alone as she who sat the day through in the parlour of the Bulgarian inn, trying to summon the energy with which to arrange for her long journey on the Orient Express to England.

Arrived in London, I at once set out to my uncle's house in Golgotha Road, Golders Green. I was a little surprised that he had not met me at the station, for I had warned him of my arrival by telegram ; but, knowing he was a gentleman of particular though agreeable habits, it was with a sufficiently good heart that I rang the bell of his tall, gloomy house, which stood at the end of a genteel street of exactly similar houses.

Allow me, if you please, to hurry over the relation of my further misfortunes. My uncle had died of a clot of blood on the heart a week before my arrival. His property he had, of course, left to me ; and I could instantly take possession of his house in Golgotha Road. I was utterly alone.

That was four weeks ago. Though entirely without friends or acquaintance—for my uncle's lawyer, Mr. Tarbold, was a man who bore his own lack of easy conversation and human sympathy with a resigned fortitude worthy of more wretched sorrows—I passed the first two weeks pleasantly enough in arranging the house to my taste, in engaging a housekeeper and training her to my ways, and in wondering how I must proceed as regards the patenting and exploiting of the carnation, the formula for which I kept locked in a secret drawer of my toilet-table.

At the end of three weeks—one week ago—my housekeeper gave me notice of her instant departure, saying that no consideration would persuade her to spend another night in the house. She was, it seemed, psychic, and the atmosphere of the house, which was certainly oppressive, weighed heavily on her mind. She had heard noises in the night, she affirmed, and also spoke indignantly of an unpleasant smell in the basement of the house, a musty smell which she for one made no bones of recognizing as of a graveyard consistency ; and if she did not know a graveyard smell, she asked, from one of decent origins, who did, for she had buried three husbands ?

Of course I laughed at her tremors, for I am not naturally of a nervous temper, and when she insisted on leaving that very day I was not at all disturbed. Nor did I instantly make inquiries for another woman, for I could very well manage by myself, and the work of the house, I thought, must help to fill in the awful spaces made by the utter lack of companionship. As to any nervousness at being left entirely alone in a house, surrounded as it was by the amenities of Golders Green, I never gave a thought to it, for I had been inured to a reasonable solitude all my life. And, putting up a notice of " Apartments to Let " in one of the ground-floor windows, I set about the business of the house in something of a spirit of adventure natural, if I may say so, to one of my years.

That, as I have said, was one week ago ; and the very next day but one after my housekeeper had left me was to see my hardly-won peace shattered at one blow. I do not know if you gentlemen are aware of the mode of life that obtains in Golders Green; but I must tell you that the natives of that quarter do not discourage the activities of barrel-organs—a somewhat surprising exercise of restraint to one who has been accustomed to the dolorous and beautiful songs of the Balkan *cziganes*. It is true, however, that these barrel-organs are played mostly by foreigners, and I have been given to understand that foreigners are one of the most sacred institutions of this great country.

The very next morning after my housekeeper had left me I was distracted from my work by a particularly disagreeable combination of sounds, which, I had no doubt, could come only from a barrel-organ not of the first order and the untrained voice of its owner. A little amused, I looked out of the window—and with a heart how still leapt back into the room, for the face of the organ-grinder was the face of the Michaelis!

I spent an hour of agony in wondering if he had seen me, for how could I doubt but that he had followed me to England in quest of the formula of the carnation? At last, however, I decided that he could not have seen me, and I was in some degree calmed by the decreasing noise of the barrel-organ as it inflicted itself on more distant streets. London, I told myself, was a very large city; it was not possible that the Michaelis could have the faintest idea in what part of it I lodged; and it could only have been by the most unfortunate combination of chances that he had brought his wretched organ into Golgotha Road. Nevertheless I took the precaution to withdraw the notice of Apartments to Let from the window, lest yet another unfortunate combination of chances should lead him or his minions to search for lodging in my house.

The next day passed quietly enough. I went out shopping with a veil over my face, for reasons you can well understand. And little did I dream that the approaching terror was to come from a quarter which would only be known to the Michaelis when he was dead.

That evening in my bedroom, in a curious moment of forgetfulness, I chanced to pull the bell-rope. I wanted some hot water, had for the moment forgotten that the silly woman had left me, and only remembered it with a smile when, far down in the basement, I heard the thin clatter of the bell. The bathroom was some way down the passage, and I had reached the door, empty jug in hand, when I was arrested by the sound of approaching steps ! They were very faint, they seemed to be coming up from the basement, as though in answer to the bell ! I pressed my hand to my forehead in a frantic attempt to collect my wits, and I have no hesitation in saying that for those few moments I was near insane. The accumulation of terrors in my recent life had, I thought, unhinged my mind ; and I must that day have engaged a servant and forgotten it.

Meantime the steps ascended, slowly, steadily, exactly as an elderly servant might ascend in answer to the bell ; and as they ascended I was driven, I cannot tell you how, somehow past fear. Maybe it was the blood of the Samsonoffs at last raging in me : I was not afraid, and, without locking the door, I withdrew to a far corner of the room, awaiting the moment when the steps must reach the door. I must not forget to add that the empty jug was still in my hand.

Steadily, but with a shuffling as of carpet-slippers, the steps came up the passage : slowly the door was opened, and a gaunt, grey-haired woman in musty black stood there, eyeing me with strange contempt. Fear returned, enveloped me, shook me, and I sobbed, I screamed. The woman did not move, did not speak, but stood there, gaunt and grey and dry, eyeing me with a strange contempt ; and on her lined face there was such an undreamt-of expression of evil. Yet I recognized her.

I must tell you that my mother had often, in telling me of her brother, spoken of his confidential housekeeper. My mother was a plain-spoken woman, and I had gathered from her that the woman had exercised some vulgar art to enthral my poor uncle and had dominated him, to his hurt, in all things. At the news of this woman's death just before my mother's tragic end, she had been unable to resist an expression of relief ; and I, on having taken possession of the house a few weeks before, had examined with great interest, as girls will, the various photographs of her that stood about the rooms.

It was from these that I recognized the woman who stood in the doorway. But she was dead, surely she had died more than a year ago ! Yet there she now stood, eyeing me with that strange contempt—with such contempt, indeed, that I, reacting from fear to anger, sternly demanded of her what she did there and what she wanted.

She was silent. That was perhaps the most awful moment of all—but no, no, there was worse to come ! For, sobbing with terror, I hurled the empty jug at her vile face with a precision of aim which now astonishes me : but she did not waver so much as the fraction of an inch as the jug came straight at her—and, passing through her head, smashed into pieces against the wall of the passage outside. I must have swooned where I stood, for when I was again conscious of my surroundings she was gone : I was alone ; but, far down in the house, I could hear the shuffling steps, retreating, descending, to the foul shades whence she had come.

Now I am one who cannot bear any imposition ; and unable, despite the witness of my own eyes, to believe in the psychic character of the intruder, I ran out of the room and in hot pursuit down the stairs. The gaunt woman must have descended with a swiftness surprising in one of her years, for I could only see her shadow far below, on the last flight of stairs that would take her to the basement. Into that lower darkness, I must confess, I had not the courage to follow her ; and still less so when, on peering down the pitch-dark stairs into the kitchen, I was assailed by that musty smell which my housekeeper had spoken of with such indignant conviction as of a graveyard consistency.

I locked the door of my room and slept, I need scarcely say, but ill that night. However, in the cheerful light of the following morning, I was inclined, as who would not, to pooh-pooh the incredible events of the previous night ; and again pulled the bell-rope, just to see the event, if any. There was ; and, unable to await the ascent of the shuffling steps, I crammed on a hat and ran down the stairs.

The woman was coming upstairs, steadily, inevitably. As she heard me descending she stopped and looked up, and I cannot describe the effect that the diabolical wickedness of her face had on me in the clear daylight. I stopped, was rooted there, could not move. To get to the front door I must pass the foul thing, and that I could not summon the courage to do. And then she raised an arm, as though to show me something, and I saw the blade of a razor shining in her hand. You may well shudder, gentlemen !

When I came to, it was to find myself lying at the foot of the stairs, whither I must have fallen, and the foul thing gone. Why she did not kill me, I do not know. God will pardon me for saying that maybe it had been better if she had, for what miseries are not still in store for me ! Trembling and weak, I reached the door and impelled myself into the clear air of morning. Nor could the fact that I had forgotten my veil, and the consequent fear of the Michaelis, persuade me to re-enter that house until I had regained some degree of calmness.

All day long I wandered about, knowing neither what to do nor where to go. I am not without some worldly sense, and I knew what little assistance the police could give me in such a dilemma, even had they believed me ; while, as for the lawyer, Mr. Tarbold, how could I face a man of so little sympathy in ordinary things with such an extraordinary tale ?

Towards ten o'clock that night, I determined to return and risk another night in that house ; I was desperate with weariness and hunger ; and could not buy food nor lodging for the night, for in my flight I had forgotten my purse ; while I argued to myself that if, after all, she had intended to murder me, she could without any difficulty have done so that morning when I lay unconscious on the stairs.

My bravery, however, did not help me to ascend the stairs to my bedroom with any resolution. I stole upstairs, myself verily like a phantom. But, hearing no sound in the house, I plucked up the courage to switch on the light on my bedroom landing. My bedroom-door stood open, but I could not remember whether or not I had left it so that morning. It was probable, in my hasty descent. I tiptoed to it and peered in—and I take the liberty to wonder whether any man, was he never such a lion-heart, had been less disturbed than I at the sight which the light of the moon revealed to my eyes.

The Michaelis lay full length on the floor, his great fair beard darkened with his blood, which came, I saw, from a great gash behind his ear. Across him, with her back to me, sat straddled the gaunt, foul thing, as silent as the grave. Yet even my terror could not overcome my curiosity as to her actions, for she kept on lowering and raising her left hand to and from the Michaelis's beard, while with her right, in which shone the bloody razor, she sawed the air from side to side. I could not realize what that vile shape was doing—I could, and could not admit the realization. For with her left hand she was plucking out one by one the long hairs of the Michaelis's beard, while with the razor in her right she was slicing them to the floor !

I must have gasped, made some noise, for she heard me ; and, turning on me and brandishing the dripping razor, she snarled like an animal and leapt towards me. But I am young and quick, and managed just in time to reach the street door and slam it against her enraged pursuit.

That was last night.   Since then, gentlemen, I have
wandered about the streets of London, resting a little among
the poor people in the parks.   I have had no food, for what
money I have is in that house, together with the formula for
the green carnation ; but nothing, not death by exposure nor
death by starvation, would induce me to return to the house
in Golders Green while it is haunted by that foul presence.
Is she a homicidal lunatic or a phantom from hell ?   I do not
know, I am too tired to care.   I have told you two gentlemen
my story because you seem kind and capable, and I can only
pray that I have not wearied you overmuch.   But I do beg
you to believe that nothing is farther from my mind than to
ask, and indeed nothing would induce me to accept, anything
from you but the generous sympathy of your understanding
and the advice of your chivalrous intelligence.   My tale is
finished, gentlemen.   And, alas, am not I ?

IV

MR. TREVOR is somewhat confused in his relation of the
course of events immediately subsequent to Miss
Samsonoff's narrative.   During its course he had time, he
says, to study the young lady's beauty, which, though of a
very superior order, was a little too innocent and insipid for
his taste.   His judgment, however, cannot be entirely fair, for
such was the direction of the young lady's eyes that Mr. Trevor
could judge her by her features only.   As to the story itself,
Mr. Trevor says that, while yielding to no one in his liking
for a good story, he could not see his way to considering Miss
Samsonoff's notable either for interest, entertainment, or that
human note of stark realism which makes for conviction ;   and
while, in the ordinary way, a murderer was to him like a magnet,
he could not rouse himself to feel irresistibly attracted towards
the ghoul of Golders Green.   It was therefore with surprise
not unmixed with pain that he heard Mr. Maturin saying :
    " Ralph, we are in luck ! "
    " To what," Mr. Trevor could not entirely cleanse his
voice from the impurity of sarcasm, " to what do you refer ? "
But it was not without some compunction that he heard the
young lady sigh miserably to Beau Maturin :
    " I am afraid I have wearied your friend.   Forgive me."
    " My friend," said Beau Maturin gently, " is an ass.   In
point of fact, Miss Samsonoff, far from wearying us, you have
put us under a great obligation——"

" Ah, you are kind ! " the young lady was moved to sob.

" On the contrary," Mr. Maturin warmly protested, " I am selfish. I gather you have not been reading the newspapers lately ? Had you done so, you would have read of a murderer who has recently been loose in London and has so far evaded not only capture but even identification. So far as the public know through the newspapers, this criminal has been responsible for only two or three murders ; but this very night my friend and I have had private information to the effect that within the last few weeks twelve mutilated corpses have been found in various parts of London ; to which we must now, no doubt, add a thirteenth, the remains of your late enemy, Mr. Michaelis. But where *your* information," said Mr. Maturin gallantly, " is especially valuable is that the police do not dream that the criminal is of your sex. To my friend and me it is this original point that invests the pursuit——"

" Pursuit ? " Mr. Trevor could not help starting.

" ——with," said Mr. Maturin coldly, " an added charm. And now with your permission, Miss Samsonoff, we will not only return to you your formula, as to the financial worth of which I cannot entirely share your late parent's optimism, but also——"

" Also," Mr. Trevor said with restraint, " we will first of all call at Vine Street and borrow a few policemen."

" Oh yes ! " the young lady said eagerly. " We will be sure to need some policemen. Please get some policemen. They will listen to you."

" I do not find an audience so difficult to find as all that," said Mr. Maturin coldly. " The London police, Miss Samsonoff, are delightful, but rather on the dull side. They are much given to standing in the middle of crowded roads and dreaming, and in even your short stay in London you must have observed what a serious, nay intolerable, obstruction they are to the traffic. No, no, my friend and I will get this murderer ourselves. Come, Miss Samsonoff."

" But I dare not come with you ! " cried the young lady. " I simply dare not approach that house again ! May I not await your return here ? "

" The attacks of ten murderers," said Mr. Maturin indignantly, " cannot disfigure your person more violently than being left alone in a night-club will disfigure your reputation. Bulgarians may be violent, Miss Samsonoff. But loungelizards are low dogs."

Mr. Trevor says that he was so plunged in thought that he

did not arise from the table with his usual agility ; and the
first notice he had that Mr. Maturin had risen and was nearly
at the door was on hearing him waive aside a pursuing waiter
with the damnable words : " My friend will pay."

Without, the taxi-cab was still waiting. Its driver, says
Mr. Trevor, was one of those stout men of little speech and
impatient demeanour : on which at this moment was plainly
written the fact that he had been disagreeably affected by
waiting in the cold for nearly two hours ; and on Mr. Maturin's
sternly giving him a Golders Green direction he just looked at
our two gentlemen and appeared to struggle with an impedi-
ment in his throat.

Golgotha Road was, as the young lady had described it, a
genteel street of tall, gloomy houses. Mr. Trevor says that he
cannot remember when he liked the look of a street less. The
taxi-cab had not penetrated far therein when Miss Samsonoff
timidly begged Mr. Maturin to stop its farther progress,
pointing out that she could not bear to wait immediately
opposite the house, and would, indeed, have preferred to await
her brave cavaliers in an altogether different part of London.
Mr. Maturin, however, soothed her fears ; and, gay as a schoolboy, took the key of the house from her reluctant fingers and
was jumping from the cab when Miss Samsonoff cried :

" But surely you have weapons ! "

Mr. Trevor says that, while yielding to no one in deploring
the use of weapons in daily life, in this particular instance the
young lady's words struck him as full of a practical grasp of
the situation.

" Of course," said Mr. Trevor nonchalantly, " we must
have weapons. How stupid of us to have forgotten ! I will
go back to my flat and get some. I won't be gone a moment."

" That's right," Mr. Maturin agreed, " because you won't
be gone at all. My dear Miss Samsonoff, my friend and I do
not need weapons. We put our trust in God and St. George.
Come along, Ralph. Miss Samsonoff, we will be back in a
few moments."

" And wot do I do ? " asked the taxi-driver.

" Nothing," cried Mr. Maturin gaily. " Nothing at all.
Aren't you lucky ! "

The house which the young lady had pointed out to them
had an air of even gloomier gentility than the others, and Mr.
Trevor says he cannot remember when he liked the look of a
house less, particularly when the ancient brown door gave to
Beau Maturin's hand before he had put the key into the lock.

Mr. Trevor could not resist a natural exclamation of surprise.
Mr. Maturin begged him not to shout. Mr. Trevor said that
he was not shouting, and, without a thought for his own safety,
was rushing headlong into the house to meet the terror single-
handed when he found that his shoe-lace was untied.

He found Beau Maturin in what, he supposed, would be
called a hall when it was not a pit of darkness. A stealthily lit
match revealed that it was a hall, a narrow one, and it also
revealed a closed door to the right, by Mr. Trevor's elbow,
which he removed. The match went out.

" Quietly," said Mr. Maturin quite unnecessarily, for
Mr. Trevor says he cannot remember when he felt less noisy.
He heard the door to his right open, softly, softly.

" Is it you opening that door ? " he asked, merely from
curiosity.

" Ssh ! " snapped Beau Maturin. " Hang on to my
shoulder-blades."

Mr. Trevor thought it better to calm Beau Maturin's fears
by acceding to his whim, and clung close behind him as they
entered the room. The moon, which Mr. Trevor already had
reason to dislike, was hanging at a moderate elevation over
Golders Green as though on purpose to reveal the darkness
of that room. Mr. Trevor's foot then struck a shape on the
floor. The shape was soft and long. Mr. Trevor was surprised. Mr. Maturin whispered :

" Found anything ? "

Mr. Trevor said briefly that his foot had.

" So's mine," said Beau Maturin. " What's yours like ?
Mine's rather soft to the touch."

" And mine," said Mr. Trevor.

" They're corpses, let's face it," sighed Mr. Maturin.
" Making fifteen in all, With us, seventeen. Just give yours a
kick, Ralph, to see if it's alive. I've kicked mine."

" I don't kick corpses," Mr. Trevor was muttering when
he felt a hard round thing shoved into the small of his
back.

" Ow ! " said Mr. Trevor.

" Found anything ? " said Mr. Maturin.

Mr. Trevor said briefly that there was something against
his back.

" And mine," sighed Mr. Maturin. " What's yours like ?
Mine's rather hard on the back."

" So is mine," said Mr. Trevor.

" They're revolvers, let's face it," sighed Beau Maturin.

" They are," said a harsh voice behind them. " So don't move."

" I've got some sense, thank you," snapped Beau Maturin.

" Sir," said the harsh voice, and it was a woman's voice, " I want none of your lip. I have you each covered with a revolver——"

" Waste," said Beau Maturin. " One revolver would have been quite enough. Besides, my friend and I were distinctly given to understand that you were partial to a razor. Or do you use that for shaving ? "

" I use a razor," said the harsh voice, " only when I want to kill. But I have a use for you two."

The light was suddenly switched on, a light so venomous, says Mr. Trevor, that they had to blink furiously. And that must have been a very large room, for they could not see into its far corners. The light came from what must have been a very high-powered lamp directly above a table in the middle of the room ; and it was concentrated by a shade in such a way as to fall, like a searchlight, exactly on the two helpless gentlemen. Mr. Trevor says that Beau Maturin's handsome face looked white and ghastly, so the Lord knows what Mr. Trevor's must have looked like. Meanwhile their captor leapt from her station behind them, and they were privileged to see her for the first time. She was, says Mr. Trevor, exactly as Miss Samsonoff had described her, grey and gaunt and dry, and her expression was strangely contemptuous and evil as sin. And never for a moment did she change the direction of her revolvers, which was towards our gentlemen's hearts. Mr. Trevor says he cannot remember when he saw a woman look less afraid that a revolver might go off in her hand.

" Look down," she commanded.

" It's all right," said Beau Maturin peaceably ; " we've already guessed what they are. Corpses. Nice cold night for them, too. Keep for days in weather like this."

Mr. Trevor could not resist looking down to his feet. The corpses were of two youngish men in dress-clothes.

" They're cut badly," said Mr. Maturin.

" They're not cut at all," said the woman harshly. " I shot these two for a change."

" I meant their clothes," Mr. Maturin explained. " Death was too good for them with dress-clothes like that."

" Well, I can't stop here all night talking about clothes," snapped the woman. " Now then, to business. These bodies have to be buried in the back-garden. You will each take one. There are spades just behind you. I shall not have the slightest hesitation in killing you as I have killed these two, but it will be more convenient if you do as you are told. I may kill you later, and I may not. Now be quick ! "

" Lord, what's that ! " cried Mr. Trevor sharply. He had that moment realized a strange muffled, ticking noise which must, he thought, come either from somewhere in the room or from a room nearby. And, while he was never in his life less conscious of feeling fear, he could not help but be startled by that ticking noise, for he had heard it before when timing a dynamite-bomb.

" That is why," the woman explained with what, Mr. Trevor supposed, was meant to be a smile, " you will be safer in the garden. Women are but weak creatures, and so I take the precaution of having a rather large size in dynamite-bombs so timed that I have but to press a button to send us all to blazes. It will not be comfortable for the police when, if ever, they catch me. But pick up those spades and get busy."

" Now don't be rude," begged Beau Maturin. " I can stand anything from plain women but discourtesy. Ralph, you take the bigger corpse, as you are smaller than I am, while I take this little fellow on my shoulder—which will probably be the nearest he will ever get to Heaven, with clothes cut as badly as that."

" You can come back for the bodies when you've dug the graves," snapped the woman. " Take the spades and go along that passage. No tricks ! I am just behind you."

There was a lot of rubbish in that garden. It had never been treated as a garden, it did not look like a garden, it looked even less like a garden than did *The Garden of My Grandmother*. High walls enclosed it. And over it that deplorable moon threw a sheet of dead daylight.

" Dig," said the woman with the revolvers, and they dug.

" Do you mind if we take our coats off ? " asked Beau Maturin. Mr. Trevor says that he was being sarcastic.

" I don't mind what you take off," snapped the woman.

" Now don't say naughty things ! " said Mr. Maturin. " Nothing is more revolting than the naughtiness of plain women."

" Dig," said the woman with the revolvers, and they dug.

They dug, says Mr. Trevor, for a long time, for a very long time. Not, however, that it was difficult digging once one had got into the swing of it, for that garden was mostly dug-up soil. Suddenly Beau Maturin said :

" Bet you a fiver I dig a grave for my fellow before you."

" Right ! " said Mr. Trevor.

" Dig," said the woman with the revolvers, and they dug.

" *And*," said the woman, " I don't allow any betting in this house. So call that bet off."

" What ? " said Mr. Maturin.

" Dig," said the woman with the revolvers.

Mr. Maturin threw down his spade.

" Dig," said the woman with the revolvers.

Mr. Trevor dug.

Mr. Maturin said : " Dig yourself ! "

" Dig," said the woman with the revolvers.

Mr. Trevor brandished his spade from a distance. He noticed for the first time that they had been digging in the light of the dawn and not of the moon.

" And who the deuce," said Mr. Maturin dangerously, " do you think you are, not to allow any betting ? I have stood a lot from you, but I won't stand that."

" Dig," said the woman with the revolvers, but Mr. Maturin advanced upon the revolvers like a punitive expedition. Mr. Trevor brandished his spade.

" Another step, and I fire ! " cried the woman harshly.

" Go ahead," said Mr. Maturin. " I'll teach you to stop me betting ! And I hate your face."

" Oh dear, oh dear ! " the woman suddenly cried with a face of fear, and, lowering her revolvers, fled into the house.

Mr. Trevor was so surprised that he could scarcely speak. Mr. Maturin laughed so much that he could not speak.

" What's there to laugh about ? " Mr. Trevor asked. at last.

" It's funny. They've had us, let's face it. Come on, let's follow her in."

" She may shoot," Mr. Trevor cautioned.

" Shoot my eye ! " sighed Beau Maturin.

Once in the house, Mr. Trevor stopped spellbound. There were voices, there was laughter—from the room of the two corpses !

" They're laughing at us ! " said Mr. Trevor.

" Who wouldn't ! " laughed Beau Maturin, and, opening the door, said : " Good morning."

" You've said it," said the policeman. " Haw-haw ! "

" You'll have some breakfast ? " asked the woman with the revolvers.

" Please do ! " said Miss Samsonoff.

" *I shall not have the slighest hesitation in killing you.*"

" You *ought* to be hungry," said the taxi-driver with the Homburg hat of green plush.

" Look here ! " gasped Mr. Trevor. " What the blazes——"

" Haw-haw ! " laughed the policeman. " 'Ave a bit of vealanam-pie ? "

" Now, Ted, don't be rude to the gentlemen ! " said the woman with the revolvers.

" Quite right, mother," said Miss Samsonoff. " We owe these gentlemen an explanation and an apology——"

" And if they don't take it we *are* in the soup ! " miserably said the man in the Homburg hat of green plush.

" Now, you two, go and get cups and plates for the two gentlemen," said the woman with the revolvers to the two corpses in dress-clothes.

" Listen, please," Miss Samsonoff gravely addressed Mr. Maturin, " my name isn't Samsonoff at all but Kettlewell, and that's my mother and these are my four brothers——"

" How do you do ? " said Mr. Maturin, absently drinking the policeman's coffee, but Mr. Trevor is glad that no one heard what he said.

" You see," said Miss Kettlewell, and she was shy and beautiful, " we are The Kettlewell Film Company, just us, but of course we haven't got a lot of money——"

" A ' lot ' is good ! " said the policeman.

" My brother there," and Miss Kettlewell pointed to the wretched man with the Homburg hat of green plush, " was the director of an American company in Los Angeles, but he got the sack lately, and so we thought we would make some films on our own. You see, we are such a large family ! And the recent murders gave us a really brilliant idea for a film called *The Ghoul of Golders Green*, which, thanks to you two [1] gentlemen, we have completed to-night. Oh, I do hope it will be a success, especially as you have been kind enough to help us in our predicament, for we hadn't any money to engage actors—and we did so need two gentlemen, just like you, who really looked the part, didn't we, mother ? "

" But, my dear child," cried Beau Maturin, " I'm afraid your film can't have come out very well. Trevor and I will

---

[1] When the film was released by the Kettlewell Film Corporation, evidences of public favour were so notably lacking that it was offered to the Society for Presenting Nature Films to the Blind.

Surely, after the above exposure of the methods adopted, no further reasons should be sought for the so much deplored inferiority of British films.

look perfectly ghastly, as we neither of us had any make-up on."

"But it's that kind of film!" smiled Miss Kettlewell. "You see, you and your friend are supposed to be corpses who, by some powerful psychic agency, are digging your own graves—Heavens, what's that?"

There, at the open door, stood an apparition with a dreadful face. He appeared, says Mr. Trevor, to have some difficulty in choosing among the words that his state of mind was suggesting to him.

"And me?" gasped the taxi-driver hoarsely. "Wot abaht me? 'Angingabahtallnight! 'Oo's going to pay me, that's wot I want to know? There's four quid and more on that clock——"

Mr. Maturin swept his empty coffee-cup round to indicate the family Kettlewell.

"My friends will pay," sighed Mr. Maturin.

THE MURDER OF THE MANDARIN

"WHAT'S that you're saying about murder?" asked Mrs. Cheswardine as she came into the large drawing-room, carrying the supper-tray.

"Put it down here," said her husband, referring to the supper-tray, and pointing to a little table which stood two legs off and two legs on the hearthrug.

"That apron suits you immensely," murmured Woodruff, the friend of the family, as he stretched his long limbs into the fender towards the fire, farther even than the long limbs of Cheswardine. Each man occupied an easy-chair on either side of the hearth ; each was very tall, and each was forty.

Mrs. Cheswardine, with a whisk infinitely graceful, set the tray on the table, took a seat behind it on a chair that looked like a toddling grand-nephew of the arm-chairs, and nervously smoothed out the apron.

As a matter of fact, the apron did suit her immensely. It is astounding, delicious, adorable, the effect of a natty little domestic apron suddenly put on over an elaborate and costly frock, especially when you can hear the rustle of a silk petticoat beneath, and more especially when the apron is smoothed out by jewelled fingers. Every man knows this. Every woman knows it. Mrs. Cheswardine knew it. In such matters Mrs. Cheswardine knew exactly what she was about. She delighted, when her husband brought Woodruff in late of a night, as he frequently did after a turn at the club, to prepare with her own hands—the servants being in bed—a little snack of supper for them. Tomato sandwiches, for instance, miraculously thin, together with champagne or Bass. The men preferred Bass, naturally, but if Mrs. Cheswardine had a fancy for a sip of champagne out of her husband's tumbler, Bass was not forthcoming.

To-night it was champagne.

Woodruff opened it, as he always did, and involuntarily poured out a libation on the hearth, as he almost always did. Good-natured, ungainly, long-suffering men seldom achieve the art of opening champagne.

Mrs. Cheswardine tapped her pink-slippered foot impatiently.

" You're all nerves to-night," Woodruff laughed, and " you've made me nervous." And at length he got some of the champagne into a tumbler.

" No, I'm not," Mrs. Cheswardine contradicted him.

" Yes, you are, Vera," Woodruff insisted calmly.

She smiled. The use of that elegant Christian name, with its faint suggestion of Russian archduchesses, had a strange effect on her, particularly from the lips of Woodruff. She was proud of it, and of her surname too—one of the oldest surnames in the Five Towns. The syllables of " Vera " invariably soothed her, like a charm. Woodruff, and Cheswardine also, had called her Vera during the whole of her life ; and she was thirty. They had all three lived in different houses at the top end of Trafalgar Road, Bursley. Woodruff fell in love with her first, when she was eighteen, but with no practical result. He was a brown-haired man, personable despite his ungainliness, but he failed to perceive that to worship from afar off is not the best way to capture a young woman with large eyes and an emotional disposition. Cheswardine, who had a black beard, simply came along and married the little thing. She fluttered down on to his shoulders like a pigeon. She adored him, feared him, cooed to him, worried him, and knew that there were depths of his mind which she would never plumb. Woodruff, after being best man, went on loving, meekly and yet philosophically, and found his chief joy in just these suppers. The arrangement suited Vera ; and as for the husband and the hopeless admirer, they had always been fast friends.

" I asked you what you were saying about murder," said Vera sharply, " but it seems——"

" Oh ! did you ? " Woodruff apologized. " I was saying that murder isn't such an impossible thing as it appears. Any one might commit a murder."

" Then you want to defend Harrisford ? Do you hear what he says, Stephen ? "

The notorious and terrible Harrisford murders were agitating the Five Towns that November. People read, talked, and dreamt murder ; for several weeks they took murder to all their meals.

" He doesn't want to defend Harrisford at all," said Cheswardine, with a superior masculine air, " and of course any one might commit a murder. I might."

" Stephen ! How horrid you are ! "

" You might, even ! " said Woodruff, gazing at Vera.

" Charlie ! Why, the blood alone——"

" There isn't always blood," said the oracular husband.

" Listen here," proceeded Woodruff, who read variously and enjoyed philosophical speculation. " Supposing that by just taking thought, by just wishing it, an Englishman could kill a mandarin in China and make himself rich for life, without anybody knowing anything about it ! How many mandarins do you suppose there would be left in China at the end of a week ? "

" At the end of twenty-four hours, rather," said Cheswardine grimly.

" Not one," said Woodruff.

" But that's absurd," Vera objected, disturbed. When these two men began their philosophical discussions they always succeeded in disturbing her. She hated to see life in a queer light. She hated to think.

" It isn't absurd," Woodruff replied. " It simply shows that what prevents wholesale murder is not the wickedness of it, but the fear of being found out, and the general mess, and seeing the corpse, and so on."

Vera shuddered.

" And I'm not sure," Woodruff proceeded, " that murder is so very much more wicked than lots of other things."

" Usury, for instance," Cheswardine put in.

" Or bigamy," said Woodruff.

" But an Englishman *couldn't* kill a mandarin in China by just wishing it," said Vera, looking up.

" How do we know ? " said Woodruff, in his patient voice. " How do we know ? You remember what I was telling you about thought-transference last week. It was in *Borderland*."

Vera felt as if there was no more solid ground to stand on, and it angered her to be plunging about in a bog.

" I think it's simply silly," she remarked. " No, thanks."

She said " No, thanks " to her husband, when he tendered his glass.

He moved the glass still closer to her lips.

" I said ' No, thanks,' " she repeated dryly.

" Just a mouthful," he urged.

" I'm not thirsty."

" Then you'd better go to bed," said he.

He had a habit of sending her to bed abruptly. She did not dislike it. But she had various ways of going. To-night it was the way of an archduchess.

II

WOODRUFF, in stating that Vera was all nerves that evening, was quite right. She was. And neither her husband nor Woodruff knew the reason.

The reason had to do most intimately with frocks.

Vera had been married ten years. But no one would have guessed it, to watch her girlish figure and her birdlike ways. You see, she was the only child in the house. She often bitterly regretted the absence of offspring to the name and honour of Cheswardine. She envied other wives their babies. She doted on babies. She said continually that in her deliberate opinion the proper mission of women was babies. She was the sort of woman that regards a cathedral as a place built especially to sit in and dream soft domestic dreams ; the sort of woman that adores music simply because it makes her dream. And Vera's brown studies, which were frequent, consisted chiefly of babies. But as babies amused themselves by coming down the chimneys of all the other houses in Bursley, and avoiding her house, she sought comfort in frocks. She made the best of herself. And it was a good best. Her figure was as near perfect as a woman's can be, and then there were those fine emotional eyes, and that flutteringness of the pigeon, and an ever-changing charm of gesture. Vera had become the best-dressed woman in Bursley. And that is saying something. Her husband was wealthy, with an increasing income, though, of course, as an earthenware manufacturer, and the son and grandson of an earthenware manufacturer, he joined heartily in the general Five Towns lamentation that there was no longer any money to be made out of " pots." He liked to have a well-dressed woman about the house, and he allowed her an incredible allowance, the amount of which was breathed with awe among Vera's friends ; a hundred a year, in fact. He paid it to her quarterly, by cheque. Such was his method.

Now a ball was to be given by the members of the Ladies'

Hockey Club (or such of them as had not been maimed for life in the pursuit of this noble pastime) on the very night after the conversation about murder.   Vera belonged to the Hockey Club (in a purely ornamental sense), and she had procured a frock for the ball which was calculated to crown her reputation as a mirror of elegance.   The skirt had—but no (see the columns of the *Staffordshire Signal* for the 9th November 1901). The mischief was that the gown lacked, for its final perfection, one particular thing, and that particular thing was separated from Vera by the glass front of Brunt's celebrated shop at Hanbridge.   Vera could have managed without it.   The gown would still have been brilliant without it.   But Vera had seen it, and she *wanted* it.

Its cost was a guinea.

Well, you will say, what is a guinea to a dainty creature with a hundred a year ?   Let her go and buy the article.   The point is that she couldn't, because she had only six and seven-pence left in the wide world.   (And six weeks to Christmas !) She had squandered—oh, soul above money !—twenty-five pounds, and more than twenty-five pounds, since the 29th of September.   Well, you will say, credit, in other words, tick ? No, no, no !   The giant Stephen absolutely and utterly forbade her to procure anything whatever on credit.   She was afraid of him.   She knew just how far she could go with Stephen. He was great and terrible.   Well, you will say, why couldn't she blandish and cajole Stephen for a sovereign or so ?   Im-possible !   She had a hundred a year on the clear under-standing that it was never exceeded nor anticipated.   Well, you will discreetly hint, there are certain devices known to housewives. . . . Hush !   Vera had already employed them. Six and sevenpence was not merely all that remained to her of her dress allowance ;   it was all that remained to her of her household allowance till the next Monday.

Hence her nerves.

There that poor unfortunate woman lay, with her uncon-scious tyrant of a husband snoring beside her, desolately wakeful under the night-light in the large, luxurious bedroom —three servants sleeping overhead, champagne in the cellar, furs in the wardrobe, valuable lace round her neck at that very instant, grand piano in the drawing-room, horses in the stable, stuffed bear in the hall—and her life was made a blank for want of fourteen and fivepence !   And she had nobody to confide in.   How true it is that the human soul is solitary, that content is the only true riches, and that to be happy we must be good !

It was at that juncture of despair that she thought of mandarins. Or rather—I may as well be frank—she had been thinking of mandarins all the time since retiring to rest. There *might* be something in Charlie's mandarin theory. . . . According to Charlie, so many queer, inexplicable things happened in the world. Occult—subliminal—astral—thought-waves. These expressions and many more occurred to her as she recollected Charlie's disconcerting conversations. There *might*. . . . One never knew.

Suddenly she thought of her husband's pockets, bulging with silver, with gold, and with bank-notes. Tantalizing vision ! No ! She could not steal. Besides, he might wake up.

And she returned to mandarins. She got herself into a very morbid and two-o'clock-in-the-morning state of mind. Suppose it was a dodge that *did* work. (Of course, she was extremely superstitious ; we all are.) She began to reflect seriously upon China. She remembered having heard that Chinese mandarins were very corrupt ; that they ground the faces of the poor, and put innocent victims to the torture ; in short, that they were sinful and horrid persons, scoundrels unfit for mercy. Then she pondered upon the remotest parts of China, regions where Europeans never could penetrate. No doubt there was some unimportant mandarin, somewhere in these regions, to whose district his death would be a decided blessing, to kill whom would indeed be an act of humanity. Probably a mandarin without wife or family ; a bachelor mandarin whom no relative would regret ; or, in the alternative, a mandarin with many wives, whose disgusting polygamy merited severe punishment ! An old mandarin already pretty nearly dead ; or, in the alternative, a young one just commencing a career of infamy !

" I'm awfully silly," she whispered to herself. " But still, if there *should* be anything in it. And I must, I must, I must have that thing for my dress ! "

She looked again at the dim forms of her husband's clothes, pitched anyhow on an ottoman. No ! She could not stoop to theft !

So she murdered a mandarin ; lying in bed there ; not any particular mandarin, a vague mandarin, the mandarin most convenient and suitable under all the circumstances. She deliberately wished him dead, on the off-chance of acquiring riches, or, more accurately, because she was short of fourteen and fivepence in order to look perfectly splendid at a ball.

In the morning when she woke up—her husband had already departed to the works—she thought how foolish she had been in the night. She did not feel sorry for having desired the sudden death of a fellow-creature. Not at all. She felt sorry because she was convinced, in the cold light of day, that the charm would not work. Charlie's notions were really too ridiculous, too preposterous. No! She must reconcile herself to wearing a ball dress which was less than perfection, and all for want of fourteen and fivepence. And she had more nerves than ever!

She had nerves to such an extent that when she went to unlock the drawer of her own private toilet-table, in which her prudent and fussy husband forced her to lock up her rings and brooches every night, she attacked the wrong drawer— an empty unfastened drawer that she never used. And lo! the empty drawer was not empty. There was a sovereign lying in it!

This gave her a start, connecting the discovery, as naturally at the first blush she did, with the mandarin.

Surely it couldn't be, after all.

Then she came to her senses. What absurdity! A coincidence, of course, nothing else! Besides, a mere sovereign! It wasn't enough. Charlie had said " rich for life." The sovereign must have lain there for months and months, forgotten.

However, it was none the less a sovereign. She picked it up, thanked Providence, ordered the dog-cart, and drove straight to Brunt's. The particular thing that she acquired was an exceedingly thin, slim, and fetching silver belt—a marvel for the money, and the ideal waist decoration for her wonderful white muslin gown. She bought it, and left the shop.

And as she came out of the shop, she saw a street urchin holding out the poster of the early edition of the *Signal*. And she read on the poster, in large letters : " DEATH OF LI HUNG CHANG." It is no exaggeration to say that she nearly fainted. Only by the exercise of that hard self-control, of which women alone are capable, did she refrain from tumbling against the blue-clad breast of Adams, the Cheswardine coachman.

She purchased the *Signal* with well-feigned calm, opened it and read : " *Stop-press news. Pekin. Li Hung Chang, the celebrated Chinese statesman, died at two o'clock this morning.— Reuter.*"

III

VERA reclined on the sofa that afternoon, and the sofa was drawn round in front of the drawing-room fire. And she wore her fluffiest and languidest *peignoir*. And there was a perfume of eau-de-Cologne in the apartment. Vera was having a headache ; she was having it in her grand, her official manner. Stephen had had to lunch alone. He had been told that in all probability his suffering wife would not be well enough to go to the ball. Whereupon he had grunted. As a fact, Vera's headache was extremely real, and she was very upset indeed.

The death of Li Hung Chang was heavily on her soul. Occultism was justified of itself. The affair lay beyond coincidence. She had always *known* that there was something in occultism, supernaturalism, so-called superstitions, what not. But she had never expected to prove the faith that was in her by such a homicidal act on her own part. It was detestable of Charlie to have mentioned the thing at all. He had no right to play with fire. And as for her husband, words could give but the merest rough outline of her resentment against Stephen. A pretty state of things that a woman with a position such as she had to keep up should be reduced to six and sevenpence ! Stephen, no doubt, expected her to visit the pawnshop. It would serve him right if she did so— and he met her coming out under the three brass balls ! Did she not dress solely and wholly to please him ? Not in the least to please herself ! Personally she had a mind set on higher things, impossible aspirations. But he liked fine clothes. And it was her duty to satisfy him. She strove to satisfy him in all matters. She lived for him. She sacrificed herself to him completely. And what did she get in return ? Nothing ! Nothing ! Nothing ! All men were selfish. And women were their victims. . . . Stephen, with his silly bullying rules against credit and so forth. . . . The worst of men was that they had no sense.

She put a new dose of eau-de-Cologne on her forehead, and leaned on one elbow. On the mantelpiece lay the tissue parcel containing the slim silver belt, the price of Li's death. She wanted to stick it in the fire. And only the fact that it would not burn prevented her savagely doing so. There was something wrong, too, with the occultism. To receive a paltry sovereign for murdering the greatest statesman of the

Eastern hemisphere was simply grotesque. Moreover, she had most distinctly not wanted to deprive China of a distinguished man. She had expressly stipulated for an inferior and insignificant mandarin, one that could be spared and that was unknown to Reuter. She supposed she ought to have looked up China at the Wedgwood Institution and selected a definite mandarin with a definite place of residence. But could she be expected to go about a murder deliberately like that?

With regard to the gross inadequacy of the fiscal return for her deed, perhaps that was her own fault. She had not wished for more. Her brain had been so occupied by the belt that she had wished only for the belt. But, perhaps, on the other hand, vast wealth was to come. Perhaps something might occur that very night. That would be better. Yet would it be better? However rich she might become, Stephen would coolly take charge of her riches, and dole them out to her, and make rules for her concerning them. And besides, Charlie would suspect her guilt. Charlie understood her, and perused her thoughts far better than Stephen did. She would never be able to conceal the truth from Charlie. The conversation, the death of Li within two hours, and then a sudden fortune accruing to her—Charlie would inevitably put two and two together and divine her shameful secret.

The outlook was thoroughly black anyway.

She then fell asleep.

When she awoke, some considerable time afterwards, Stephen was calling to her. It was his voice, indeed, that had aroused her. The room was dark.

" I say, Vera," he demanded, in a low, slightly inimical tone, " have you taken a sovereign out of the empty drawer in your toilet-table? "

" No," she said quickly, without thinking.

" Ah ! " he observed reflectively, " I knew I was right." He paused, and added coldly, " If you aren't better you ought to go to bed."

Then he left her, shutting the door with a noise that showed a certain lack of sympathy with her headache.

She sprang up. Her first feeling was one of thankfulness that that brief interview had occurred in darkness. So Stephen was aware of the existence of the sovereign ! The sovereign was not occult. Possibly he had put it there. And what did he know he was " right " about ?

She lighted the gas, and gazed at herself in the glass.

realizing that she no longer had a headache, and endeavouring to arrange her ideas.

" What's this ? " said another voice at the door. She glanced round hastily, guiltily. It was Charlie.

" Steve telephoned me you were too ill to go to the dance," explained Charlie, " so I thought I'd come and make inquiries. I quite expected to find you in bed with a nurse and a doctor or two at least. What is it ? " He smiled.

" Nothing," she replied. " Only a headache. It's gone now."

She stood against the mantelpiece, so that he should not see the white parcel.

" That's good," said Charlie.

There was a pause.

" Strange, Li Hung Chang dying last night, just after we had been talking about killing mandarins," she said. She could not keep off the subject. It attracted her like a snake, and she approached it in spite of the fact that she fervently wished not to approach it.

" Yes," said Charlie. " But Li wasn't a mandarin, you know. And he didn't die after we had been talking about mandarins. He died before."

" Oh ! I thought it said in the paper he died at two o'clock this morning."

" Two a.m. in Pekin," Charlie answered. " You must remember that Pekin time is many hours earlier than our time. It lies so far eastward."

" Oh ! " she said again.

Stephen hurried in, with a worried air.

" Ah ! It's you, Charlie ! "

" She isn't absolutely dying, I find," said Charlie, turning to Vera : " You are going to the dance after all—aren't you ? "

" I say, Vera," Stephen interrupted, " either you or I must have a scene with Martha. I've always suspected that confounded housemaid. So I put a marked sovereign in a drawer this morning, and it was gone at lunch-time. She'd better hook it instantly. Of course I shan't prosecute."

" Martha ! " cried Vera. " Stephen, what on earth are you thinking of ? I wish you would leave the servants to me. If you think you can manage this house in your spare time from the works, you are welcome to try. But don't blame me for the consequences." Glances of triumph flashed in her eyes.

" But I tell you——"

" Nonsense," said Vera. " I took the sovereign. I saw it there and I took it, and just to punish you, I've spent it. It's not at all nice to lay traps for servants like that."

" Then why did you tell me just now you hadn't taken it ? " Stephen demanded crossly.

" I didn't feel well enough to argue with you then," Vera replied.

" You've recovered precious quick," retorted Stephen with grimness.

" Of course, if you want to make a scene before strangers," Vera whimpered (poor Charlie a stranger !), " I'll go to bed."

Stephen knew when he was beaten.

She went to the Hockey dance, though. She and Stephen and Charlie and his young sister, aged seventeen, all descended together to the Town Hall in a brougham. The young girl admired Vera's belt excessively, and looked forward to the moment when she too should be a bewitching and captivating wife like Vera, in short, a woman of the world, worshipped by grave, bearded men. And both the men were under the spell of Vera's incurable charm, capricious, surprising, exasperating, indefinable, indispensable to their lives.

" Stupid superstitions ! " reflected Vera. " But of course I never believed it really."

And she cast down her eyes to gloat over the belt.

POWERS OF THE AIR

I FORESAW the danger that threatened him. He was so ignorant, and his sight had been almost destroyed in the city streets. A trustful ignorance is the beginning of wisdom, but these townspeople are conceited with their foolish book-learning ; and reading darkens the eyes of the mind.

I began to warn him in early October when the gales roar far up in the sky. They are harmless then ; they tear at the ricks and the slate roofs, and waste themselves in stripping the trees ; but we are safe until the darkness comes.

I took him to the crown of the stubble land, and turned him with his back to the dark thread of the sea. I pointed to the rooks tumbling about the sky like scattered leaves that sported in a mounting wind.

"We are past the turn," I said. "The black time is coming."

He stood thoughtlessly watching the ecstatic rooks. "Is it some game they play ? " he asked.

I shook my head. "They belong to the darkness," I told him.

He looked at me in that slightly forbearing way of his, and said, "Another of your superstitions."

I was silent for a moment. I stared down at the texture of black fields ploughed for winter wheat, and thought of all the writing that lay before us under that wild October hill, all the clear signs that he could never be taught to read.

"Knowledge," I said. I was afraid for him, and I wished to save him. He had been penned in that little world of the town like a caged gull. He had been blinded by staring at the boards of his coop.

He smiled condescendingly. " You are charmingly primitive still," he said. " Do you worship the sun in secret, and make propitiatory offerings to the thunder ? "

I sighed, knowing that if I would save him I must try to reach his mind by the ear, by the dull and clumsy means of language. That is the fetish of these townspeople. They have no wisdom, only a little recognition of those things that can be described in printed or spoken words. And I dreaded the effort of struggling with the infirmity of this obstinate blind youth.

" I came out here to warn you," I began.

" Against what ? " he asked.

" The forces that have power in the black time," I said. " Even now they are beginning to gather strength. In a month it will not be safe for you to go out on the cliffs after sunset. You may not believe me, but won't you accept my warning in good faith ? "

He patronized me with his smile. " What are these forces ? " he asked.

That is the manner of these book-folk. They ask always for names. If they can but label a thing in a word or in a volume of description they are satisfied that they have achieved knowledge. They bandy these names of theirs as a talisman.

" Who knows ? " I replied. " We have learnt their power. Call them what you will, you cannot change them by any baptism."

" Well, what do they *do* ? " he said, still tolerant. " Have you ever seen them ? " he added, as if he would trick me.

I had, but how could I describe them to him ? Can one explain the colours of autumn to a man born blind ? Or is there any language which will set out the play of a breaker among the rocks ? How then could I talk to him of that which I had known only in the fear of my soul ?

" Have you ever seen the wind ? " I said.

He laughed. " Well, then, tell me your evidence," he replied.

I searched my mind for something that he might regard as evidence. " Men," I said, " used to believe that the little birds, the finches and the tits, rushed blindly at the lantern of the lighthouses, and dashed themselves to death as a moth will dash itself into the candle. But now they know that the birds only seek a refuge near the light, and that they will rest till dawn on the perches that are built for them."

" Quite true," he agreed. " And what then ? "

" The little birds are prey to the powers of the air when

the darkness comes," I said ; " and their only chance of life is
to come within the beam of the protecting light.   And when
they could find no place to rest, they hovered and fluttered
until they were weak with the ache of flight, and fell a little
into the darkness ; then in panic and despair they fled back
and overshot their mark."

" But gulls . . ." he began.

" A few," I interrupted him.   " A few, although they, also,
belong to the wild and the darkness.   They fall in chasing
the little birds who, like us, are a quarry."

" A pretty fable," he said ; but I saw that the shadow of a
doubt had fallen across him, and when he asked me another
question I would not reply. . . .

I took him to the door at ten o'clock that night and made
him listen to the revels in the upper air.   Below, it was almost
still and very dark, for the moon was near the new, and the
clouds were travelling North in diligent masses that would
presently bring rain.

" Do you hear them ? " I asked.

He shivered slightly, and pretended that the air was
cold. . . .

As the nights drew in, I began to hope that he had taken
my warning to heart.   He did not speak of it, but he took his
walks while the sun edged across its brief arc of the sky.

I took comfort in the thought that some dim sense of
vision was still left to him ; and one afternoon, when the
black time was almost come, I walked with him on the cliffs.
I meant then to test him ; to discover if, indeed, some feeble
remnant of sight was yet his.

The wind had hidden itself that day, but I knew that it
lurked in the grey depths that hung on the sea's horizon.
Its outrunners streaked the falling blue of the sky with driven
spirits of white cloud ; and the long swell of the rising sea
cried out with fear as it fled, breaking, to its death.

I said no word to him, then, of the coming peril.   We
walked to the cliff's edge and watched the thousand runnels
of foam that laced the blackness of Trescore rock with milk-
white threads, as those driven rollers cast themselves against
the land and burst moon-high in their last despair.

We saw the darkness creeping towards us out of the far
distance, and then we turned from the sea and saw how the
coming shadow was already quenching the hills.   All the
earth was hardening itself to await the night.

" God ! what a lonely place ! " he said.

It seemed lonely to him, but I saw the little creeping movements among the black roots of the furze. To me the place seemed over-populous. Nevertheless I took it as a good sign that he had found a sense of loneliness; it is a sense that often precedes the coming of knowledge. . . .

And when the darkness of winter had come I thought he was safe. He was always back in the house by sunset, and he went little to the cliffs. But now and again he would look at me with something of defiance in his face, as if he braced himself to meet an argument.

I gave him no encouragement to speak. I believed that no knowledge could come to him by that way, that no words of mine could help him. And I was right. But he forced speech upon me. He faced me one afternoon in the depths of the black time. He was stiffened to oppose me.

" It's absurd," he said, " to pretend a kind of superior wisdom. If you can't give me some reason for this super-stition of yours I must go out and test it for myself."

I knew my own feebleness, and I tried to prevaricate by saying : " I gave you reasons."

" They will all bear at least two explanations," he said.

" At least wait," I pleaded. " You are so young."

He was a little softened by my weakness, but he was reso-lute. He meant to teach me, to prove that he was right. He lifted his head proudly and smiled.

" Youth is the age of courage and experiment," he boasted.

" Of recklessness and curiosity," was my amendment.

" I am going," he said.

" You will never come back," I warned him.

" But if I do come back," he said, " will you admit that I am right ? "

I would not accept so foolish a challenge. " Some escape," I said.

" I will go every night until you are convinced," he re-turned. " Before the winter is over, you shall come with me. I will cure you of your fear."

I was angry then ; and I turned my back upon him. I heard him go out and made no effort to hinder him. I sat and brooded and consoled myself with the thought that he would surely return at dusk.

I waited until sunset and he had not come back.

I went to the window and saw that a dying yellow still shone feebly in the west ; and I watched it as I have watched the last flicker of a lantern when a friend makes his way home across the hill.

Already the horrified clouds were leaping up in terror from the edge of the sea, coming with outflung arms that sprawled across the hollow sky.

I went into the hall and found my hat ; and then stood there in the twilight listening for the sound of a footstep. I could not believe that he would stay on the cliff after the darkness had come. I hesitated and listened while the shadows crept together in the corners of the hall.

He had taunted me with my cowardice, and I knew that I must go and seek him. But before I opened the door I waited again and strained my ears so eagerly for the click and shriek of the gate that I created the sound in my own mind. And yet, as I heard it, I knew it for a phantasm.

At last I went out suddenly and fiercely.

A gust of wind shook me before I had reached the gate, and the air was full of intimidating sound. I heard the cry of the driven clouds, and the awful shout of the pursuers mingled with the clamouring and thudding of the endless companies that hurried across the width of heaven.

I dared not look up. I clutched my head with my arms, and ran stumbling to the foot of the path that climbs to the height of the undefended cliff.

I tried to call him, but my voice was caught in the rout of air ; my shout was torn from me and dispersed among the atoms of scuttling foam that huddled a moment among the rocks before they leaped to dissolution.

I stooped to the lee of the singing furze. I dared go no farther. Beyond was all the riot, where the mad sport took strange shapes of soaring whirlpools and sudden draughts, and wonderful calms that suckingly enticed the unknowing to the cliff's edge.

I knew that it would be useless to seek him now. The scream of the gale had mounted unendurably ; he could not be still alive up there in the midst of that reeling fury.

I crept back to the road and the shelter of the cutting, and then I fled to my house.

For a long hour I sat over the fire seeking some peace of mind. I blamed myself most bitterly that I had not hindered him. I might have given way ; have pretended conviction, or, at least, some sympathy with his rash and foolish ignorance. But presently I found consolation in the thought that his fate had always been inevitable. What availed any effort of mine against the unquestionable forces that had pronounced his doom ? I listened to the thudding procession that marched through the upper air, and to the shrieking of the spirits that come down to torture and destroy the things of earth ; and I knew that no effort of mine could have saved him. . . .

And when the outer door banged, and I heard his footsteps in the hall, I believed that he was appearing to me at the moment of his death ; but when he came into the room with shining eyes and bright cheeks, laughing and tossing the hair back from his forehead, I was curiously angry.

" Where have you been ? " I asked. " I went out to the cliff to find you, and thought you were dead."

" You came to the cliffs ? " he said.

" To the foot of the cliff," I confessed.

" Ah ! you must never go farther than that in the black time," he said.

" Then you believe me now ? " I asked.

He smiled. " I believe that *you* would be in danger up there to-night," he said, " because you believe in the powers of the air, and you are afraid."

He stood in the doorway, braced by his struggle with the wind ; and his young eyes were glowing with the consciousness of discovery and new knowledge.

Yet he cannot deny that I showed him the way.

KEEPING HIS PROMISE

IT was eleven o'clock at night, and young Marriott was locked into his room, cramming as hard as he could cram. He was a " Fourth Year Man " at Edinburgh University and he had been ploughed for this particular examination so often that his parents had positively declared they could no longer supply the funds to keep him there.

His rooms were cheap and dingy, but it was the lecture fees that took the money. So Marriott pulled himself together at last and definitely made up his mind that he would pass or die in the attempt, and for some weeks now he had been reading as hard as mortal man can read. He was trying to make up for lost time and money in a way that showed conclusively he did not understand the value of either. For no ordinary man—and Marriott was in every sense an ordinary man—can afford to drive the mind as he had lately been driving his, without sooner or later paying the cost.

Among the students he had few friends or acquaintances, and these few had promised not to disturb him at night, knowing he was at last reading in earnest. It was, therefore, with feelings a good deal stronger than mere surprise that he heard his door-bell ring on this particular night and realized that he was to have a visitor. Some men would simply have muffled the bell and gone on quietly with their work. But Marriott was not this sort. He was nervous. It would have bothered and pecked at his mind all night long not to know who the visitor was and what he wanted. The only thing to do, therefore, was to let him in—and out again—as quickly as possible.

The landlady went to bed at ten o'clock punctually, after which hour nothing would induce her to pretend she heard

72

Who was the visitor and what did he want?

the bell, so Marriott jumped up from his books with an exclamation that augured ill for the reception of his caller, and prepared to let him in with his own hand.

The streets of Edinburgh town were very still at this late hour—it was late for Edinburgh—and in the quiet neighbourhood of F—— Street, where Marriott lived on the third floor, scarcely a sound broke the silence. As he crossed the floor, the bell rang a second time, with unnecessary clamour, and he unlocked the door and passed into the little hall-way with considerable wrath and annoyance in his heart at the insolence of the double interruption.

" The fellows all know I'm reading for this exam. Why in the world do they come to bother me at such an unearthly hour ? "

The inhabitants of the building, with himself, were medical students, general students, poor Writers to the Signet, and some others whose vocations were perhaps not so obvious. The stone staircase, dimly lighted at each floor by a gas-jet that would not turn above a certain height, wound down to the level of the street with no pretence at carpet or railing. At some levels it was cleaner than at others. It depended on the landlady of the particular level.

The acoustic properties of a spiral staircase seem to be peculiar. Marriott, standing by the open door, book in hand, thought every moment the owner of the footsteps would come into view. The sound of the boots was so close and so loud that they seemed to travel disproportionately in advance of their cause. Wondering who it could be, he stood ready with all manner of sharp greetings for the man who dared thus to disturb his work. But the man did not appear. The steps sounded almost under his nose, yet no one was visible.

A sudden queer sensation of fear passed over him—a faintness and a shiver down the back. It went, however, almost as soon as it came, and he was just debating whether he would call aloud to his invisible visitor, or slam the door and return to his books, when the cause of the disturbance turned the corner very slowly and came into view.

It was a stranger. He saw a youngish man, short of figure and very broad. His face was the colour of a piece of chalk, and the eyes, which were very bright, had heavy lines underneath them. Though the cheeks and chin were unshaven and the general appearance unkempt, the man was evidently a gentleman, for he was well dressed and bore himself with a certain air. But, strangest of all, he wore no hat, and carried none in his hand, and although rain had been falling steadily all the evening, he appeared to have neither overcoat nor umbrella.

A hundred questions sprang up in Marriott's mind and rushed to his lips, chief among which was something like " Who in the world are you ? " and " What in the name of Heaven do you come to me for ? " But none of these questions found time to express themselves in words, for almost at once the caller turned his head a little so that the gaslight in the hall fell upon his features from a new angle. Then in a flash Marriott recognized him.

" Field ! Man alive ! Is it you ? " he gasped.

The Fourth Year Man was not lacking in intuition, and he perceived at once that here was a case for delicate treat-ment. He divined, without any actual process of thought, that the catastrophe often predicted had come at last, and that this man's father had turned him out of the house. They had been at a private school together years before, and though they had hardly met once since, the news had not failed to reach him from time to time with considerable detail, for the family lived near his own, and between certain of the sisters there was great intimacy. Young Field had gone wild later, he remembered hearing about it all—drink, a woman, opium, or something of the sort—he could not exactly call to mind.

" Come in," he said at once, his anger vanishing. " There's been something wrong, I can see. Come in, and tell me all about it and perhaps I can help——" He hardly knew what to say, and stammered a lot more besides. The dark side of life, and the horror of it, belonged to a world that lay remote from his own select little atmosphere of books and dreamings. But he had a man's heart for all that.

He led the way across the hall, shutting the front door carefully behind him, and noticed as he did so that the other, though certainly sober, was unsteady on his legs, and evidently much exhausted. Marriott might not be able to pass his examinations, but he at least knew the symptoms of starvation —acute starvation, unless he was much mistaken—when they stared him in the face.

" Come along," he said cheerfully, and with genuine sym-pathy in his voice. " I'm glad to see you. I was going to have a bite of something to eat, and you're just in time to join me."

The other made no audible reply, and shuffled so feebly with his feet that Marriott took his arm by way of support. He noticed for the first time that the clothes hung on him with pitiful looseness. The broad frame was literally hardly more than a frame. He was as thin as a skeleton. But, as he touched him, the sensation of faintness and dread returned. It only lasted a moment, and then passed off, and he ascribed it not unnaturally to the distress and shock of seeing a former friend in such a pitiful plight.

" Better let me guide you. It's shamefully dark—this hall. I'm always complaining," he said lightly, recognizing by the weight upon his arm that the guidance was sorely needed, " but the old cat never does anything except promise." He led him to the sofa, wondering all the time where he had come from and how he had found out the address. It must be at least seven years since those days at the private school when they used to be such close friends.

" Now, if you'll forgive me for a minute," he said, " I'll get supper ready—such as it is. And don't bother to talk. Just take it easy on the sofa. I see you're dead tired. You can tell me about it afterwards, and we'll make plans."

The other sat down on the edge of the sofa and stared in silence, while Marriott got out the brown loaf, scones, and a huge pot of marmalade that Edinburgh students always keep in their cupboards. His eyes shone with a brightness that suggested drugs, Marriott thought, stealing a glance at him from behind the cupboard door. He did not like yet to take a full square look. The fellow was in a bad way, and it would have been so like an examination to stare and wait for explanations. Besides, he was evidently almost too exhausted to speak. So, for reasons of delicacy—and for another reason as well which he could not exactly formulate to himself—he let his visitor rest apparently unnoticed, while he busied himself with the supper. He lit the spirit-lamp to make cocoa, and when the water was boiling he drew up the table with the good things to the sofa, so that Field need not have even the trouble of moving to a chair.

" Now, let's tuck in," he said, " and afterwards we'll have a pipe and a chat. I'm reading for an exam, you know, and I always have something about this time. It's jolly to have a companion."

He looked up and caught his guest's eyes directed straight upon his own. An involuntary shudder ran through him from head to foot. The face opposite him was deadly white and wore a dreadful expression of pain and mental suffering.

" By Gad ! " he said, jumping up, " I quite forgot. I've

got some whisky somewhere. What an ass I am. I never touch it myself when I'm working like this."

He went to the cupboard and poured out a stiff glass which the other swallowed at a single gulp and without any water. Marriott watched him while he drank it, and at the same time noticed something else as well—Field's coat was all over dust, and on one shoulder was a bit of cobweb. It was perfectly dry ; Field arrived on a soaking wet night without hat, umbrella, or overcoat, and yet perfectly dry, even dusty. Therefore he had been under cover. What did it all mean ? Had he been hiding in the building ? . . .

It was very strange. Yet he volunteered nothing ; and Marriott had pretty well made up his mind by this time that he would not ask any questions until he had eaten and slept. Food and sleep were obviously what the poor devil needed most and first—he was pleased with his powers of ready diagnosis—and it would not be fair to press him till he had recovered a bit.

They ate their supper together while the host carried on a running one-sided conversation, chiefly about himself and his exams and his " old cat " of a landlady, so that the guest need not utter a single word unless he really wished to— which he evidently did not ! But, while he toyed with his food, feeling no desire to eat, the other ate voraciously. To see a hungry man devour cold scones, stale oatcake, and brown bread laden with marmalade was a revelation to this inexperienced student who had never known what it was to be without at least three meals a day. He watched in spite of himself, wondering why the fellow did not choke in the process.

But Field seemed to be as sleepy as he was hungry. More than once his head dropped and he ceased to masticate the food in his mouth. Marriott had positively to shake him before he would go on with his meal. A stronger emotion will overcome a weaker, but this struggle between the sting of real hunger and the magical opiate of overpowering sleep was a curious sight to the student, who watched it with mingled astonishment and alarm. He had heard of the pleasure it was to feed hungry men, and watch them eat, but he had never actually witnessed it, and he had no idea it was like this. Field ate like an animal—gobbled, stuffed, gorged. Marriott forgot his reading, and began to feel something very much like a lump in his throat.

" Afraid there's been awfully little to offer you, old man," he managed to blurt out when at length the last scone had

disappeared, and the rapid, one-sided meal was at an end.
Field still made no reply, for he was almost asleep in his seat.
He merely looked up wearily and gratefully.

"Now you must have some sleep, you know," he continued, "or you'll go to pieces. I shall be up all night reading
for this blessed exam. You're more than welcome to my bed.
To-morrow we'll have a late breakfast and—and see what
can be done—and make plans—I'm awfully good at making
plans, you know," he added with an attempt at lightness.

Field maintained his "dead sleepy" silence, but appeared
to acquiesce, and the other led the way into the bedroom,
apologizing as he did so to this half-starved son of a baronet
—whose own home was almost a palace—for the size of the
room. The weary guest, however, made no pretence of
thanks or politeness. He merely steadied himself on his
friend's arm as he staggered across the room, and then, with
all his clothes on, dropped his exhausted body on the bed.
In less than a minute he was to all appearances sound asleep.

For several minutes Marriott stood in the open door and
watched him; praying devoutly that he might never find
himself in a like predicament, and then fell to wondering
what he would do with his unbidden guest on the morrow.
But he did not stop long to think, for the call of his books
was imperative, and happen what might, he must see to it
that he passed that examination.

Having again locked the door into the hall, he sat down
to his books and resumed his notes on *materia medica* where
he had left off when the bell rang. But it was difficult for
some time to concentrate his mind on the subject. His
thoughts kept wandering to the picture of that white-faced,
strange-eyed fellow, starved and dirty, lying in his clothes
and boots on the bed. He recalled their schooldays together
before they had drifted apart, and how they had vowed eternal
friendship—and all the rest of it. And now! What horrible
straits to be in. How could any man let the love of dissipation
take such hold upon him?

But one of their vows together Marriott, it seemed, had
completely forgotten. Just now, at any rate, it lay too far in
the background of his memory to be recalled.

Through the half-open door—the bedroom led out of
the sitting-room and had no other door—came the sound of
deep, long-drawn breathing, the regular steady breathing of
a tired man, so tired that, even to listen to it made Marriott
almost want to go to sleep himself.

" He needed it," reflected the student, " and perhaps it came only just in time ! "

Perhaps so ; for outside the bitter wind from across the Forth howled cruelly and drove the rain in cold streams against the window-panes, and down the deserted streets. Long before Marriott settled down again properly to his reading, he heard distinctly, as it were, through the sentences of the book, the heavy, deep breathing of the sleeper in the next room.

A couple of hours later, when he yawned and changed his books, he still heard the breathing, and went cautiously up to the door to look round.

At first the darkness of the room must have deceived him, or else his eyes were confused and dazzled by the recent glare of the reading-lamp. For a minute or two he could make out nothing at all but dark lumps of furniture, the mass of the chest of drawers by the wall, and the white patch where his bath stood in the centre of the floor.

Then the bed came slowly into view. And on it he saw the outline of the sleeping body gradually take shape before his eyes, growing up strangely into the darkness, till it stood out in marked relief—the long black form against the white counterpane.

He could hardly help smiling. Field had not moved an inch. He watched him a moment or two and then returned to his books. The night was full of the singing voices of the wind and rain. There was no sound of traffic ; no hansoms clattered over the cobbles, and it was still too early for the milk-carts. He worked on steadily and conscientiously, only stopping now and again to change a book, or to sip some of the poisonous stuff that kept him awake and made his brain so active, and on these occasions Field's breathing was always distinctly audible in the room. Outside, the storm continued to howl, but inside the house all was stillness. The shade of the reading-lamp threw all the light upon the littered table, leaving the other end of the room in comparative darkness. The bedroom door was exactly opposite him where he sat. There was nothing to disturb the worker, nothing but an occasional rush of wind against the windows, and a slight pain in his arm.

This pain, however, which he was unable to account for, grew once or twice very acute. It bothered him ; and he tried to remember how, and when, he could have bruised himself so severely, but without success.

At length the page before him turned from yellow to grey, and there were sounds of wheels in the street below. It was four o'clock. Marriott leaned back and yawned prodigiously. Then he drew back the curtains. The storm had subsided and the Castle Rock was shrouded in mist. With another yawn he turned away from the dreary outlook and prepared to sleep the remaining four hours till breakfast on the sofa. Field was still breathing heavily in the next room, and he first tiptoed across the floor to take another look at him.

Peering cautiously round the half-opened door his first glance fell upon the bed now plainly discernible in the grey light of morning. He stared hard. Then he rubbed his eyes. Then he rubbed his eyes again and thrust his head farther round the edge of the door. With fixed eyes, he stared harder still, and harder.

But it made no difference at all. He was staring into an empty room.

The sensation of fear he had felt when Field first appeared upon the scene returned suddenly, but with much greater force. He became conscious, too, that his left arm was throbbing violently and causing him great pain. He stood wondering, and staring, and trying to collect his thoughts. He was trembling from head to foot.

By a great effort of the will he left the support of the door and walked forward boldly into the room.

There, upon the bed, was the impress of a body, where Field had lain and slept. There was the mark of the head on the pillow, and the slight indentation at the foot of the bed where the boots had rested on the counterpane. And there, plainer than ever—for he was closer to it—was *the breathing* !

Marriott tried to pull himself together. With a great effort he found his voice and called his friend aloud by name !

" Field ! Is that you ? Where are you ? "

There was no reply ; but the breathing continued without interruption, coming directly from the bed. His voice had such an unfamiliar sound that Marriott did not care to repeat his questions, but he went down on his knees and examined the bed above and below, pulling the mattress off finally, and taking the coverings away separately one by one. But though the sounds continued there was no visible sign of Field, nor was there any space in which a human being, however small, could have concealed itself. He pulled the bed out from the wall, but the sound *stayed where it was*. It did not move with the bed.

Marriott, finding self-control a little difficult in his weary condition, at once set about a thorough search of the room. He went through the cupboard, the chest of drawers, the little alcove where the clothes hung—everything. But there was no sign of any one. The small window near the ceiling was closed ; and, anyhow, was not large enough to let a cat pass. The sitting-room door was locked on the inside ; he could not have got out that way. Curious thoughts began to trouble Marriott's mind, bringing in their train unwelcome sensations. He grew more and more excited ; he searched the bed again till it resembled the scene of a pillow fight ; he searched both rooms, knowing all the time it was useless— and then he searched again. A cold perspiration broke out all over his body ; and the sound of heavy breathing, all this time, never ceased to come from the corner where Field had lain down to sleep.

Then he tried something else. He pushed the bed back exactly into its original position—and himself lay down upon it just where his guest had lain. But the same instant he sprang up again in a single bound. The breathing was close beside him, almost on his cheek, and between him and the wall ! Not even a child could have squeezed into the space.

He went back into his sitting-room, opened the windows, welcoming all the light and air possible, and tried to think the whole matter over quietly and clearly. Men who read too hard, and slept too little, he knew were sometimes troubled with very vivid hallucinations. Again he calmly reviewed every incident of the night : his accurate sensations ; the vivid details ; the emotions stirred in him ; the dreadful feast—no single hallucination could ever combine all these and cover so long a period of time. But with less satisfaction he thought of the recurring faintness, and curious sense of horror that had once or twice come over him, and then of the violent pains in his arm. These were quite unaccountable.

Moreover, now that he began to analyse and examine, there was one other thing that fell upon him like a sudden revelation : *During the whole time Field had not actually uttered a single word !* Yet, as though in mockery upon his reflections, there came ever from that inner room the sound of the breathing, long-drawn, deep, and regular. The thing was incredible. It was absurd.

Haunted by visions of brain fever and insanity, Marriott put on his cap and mackintosh and left the house. The morning air on Arthur's Seat would blow the cobwebs from his brain ; the scent of the heather, and above all, the sight of the sea. He roamed over the wet slopes above Holyrood for a couple of hours, and did not return until the exercise had shaken some of the horror out of his bones, and given him a ravening appetite into the bargain.

As he entered he saw that there was another man in the room, standing against the window with his back to the light. He recognized his fellow-student, Greene, who was reading for the same examination.

" Read hard all night, Marriott," he said, " and thought I'd drop in here to compare notes and have some breakfast. You're out early ? " he added, by way of a question. Marriott said he had a headache and a walk had helped it, and Greene nodded and said, " Ah ! " But when the girl had set the steaming porridge on the table and gone out again, he went on with rather a forced tone, " Didn't know you had any friends who drank, Marriott ? "

This was obviously tentative, and Marriott replied dryly that he did not know it either.

" Sounds just as if some chap were ' sleeping it off ' in there, doesn't it, though ? " persisted the other, with a nod in the direction of the bedroom, and looking curiously at his friend. The two men stared steadily at each other for several seconds, and then Marriott said earnestly :

" Then you hear it too, thank God ! "

" Of course I hear it. The door's open. Sorry if I wasn't meant to."

" Oh, I don't mean that," said Marriott, lowering his voice. " But I'm awfully relieved. Let me explain. Of course, if you hear it too, then it's all right ; but really it frightened me more than I can tell you. I thought I was going to have brain fever, or something, and you know what a lot depends on this exam. It always begins with sounds, or visions, or some sort of beastly hallucination, and I——"

" Rot ! " ejaculated the other impatiently. " What *are* you talking about ? "

" Now, listen to me, Greene," said Marriott, as calmly as he could, for the breathing was still plainly audible, " and I'll tell you what I mean, only don't interrupt." And thereupon he related exactly what had happened during the night, telling everything, even down to the pain in his arm. When it was over he got up from the table and crossed the room.

" You hear the breathing now plainly, don't you ? " he said. Greene said he did. " Well, come with me, and we'll search

the room together." The other, however, did not move from
his chair.

" I've been in already," he said sheepishly ; " I heard the
sounds and thought it was you. The door was ajar—so I
went in."

Marriott made no comment, but pushed the door open
as wide as it would go. As it opened, the sound of breathing
grew more and more distinct.

" *Some one* must be in there," said Greene under his
breath.

" *Some one* is in there, but *where* ? " said Marriott. Again
he urged his friend to go in with him. But Greene refused
point-blank ; said he had been in once and had searched the
room and there was nothing there. He would not go in
again for a good deal.

They shut the door and retired into the other room to
talk it all over with many pipes. Greene questioned his
friend very closely, but without illuminating result, since
questions cannot alter facts.

" The only thing that ought to have a proper, a logical
explanation is the pain in my arm," said Marriott, rubbing
that member with an attempt at a smile. " It hurts so infernally and aches all the way up. I can't remember bruising it,
though."

" Let me examine it for you," said Greene. " I'm awfully
good at bones in spite of the examiners' opinion to the contrary." It was a relief to play the fool a bit, and Marriott
took his coat off and rolled up his sleeve.

" By George, though, I'm bleeding ! " he exclaimed.
" Look here ! What on earth's this ? "

On the forearm, quite close to the wrist, was a thin red
line. There was a tiny drop of apparently fresh blood on it.
Greene came over and looked closely at it for some minutes.
Then he sat back in his chair, looking curiously at his friend's
face.

" You've scratched yourself without knowing it," he said
presently.

" There's no sign of a bruise. It must be something else
that made the arm ache."

Marriott sat very still, staring silently at his arm as though
the solution of the whole mystery lay there actually written
upon the skin.

" What's the matter ? I see nothing very strange about
a scratch," said Greene, in an unconvincing sort of voice.

" It was your cuff-links probably. Last night in your excitement——"

But Marriott, white to the very lips, was trying to speak.
The sweat stood in great beads on his forehead. At last he
leaned forward close to his friend's face.

" Look," he said, in a low voice that shook a little. . " Do
you see that red mark ? I mean *underneath* what you call the
scratch ? "

Greene admitted he saw something or other, and Marriott
wiped the place clean with his handkerchief and told him to
look again more closely.

" Yes, I see," returned the other, lifting his head after a
moment's careful inspection. " It looks like an old scar."

" It *is* an old scar," whispered Marriott, his lips trembling.
" *Now* it all comes back to me."

" All what ? " Greene fidgeted on his chair. He tried to
laugh, but without success. His friend seemed bordering on
collapse.

" Hush ! Be quiet, and—I'll tell you," he said. " *Field
made that scar.*"

For a whole minute the two men looked each other full in
the face without speaking.

" Field made that scar ! " repeated Marriott at length in a
louder voice.

" Field ! You mean—last night ? "

" No, not last night. Years ago—at school, with his knife.
And I made a scar in his arm with mine." Marriott was talking
rapidly now.

" We exchanged drops of blood in each other's cuts. He
put a drop into my arm and I put one into his——"

" In the name of Heaven, what for ? "

" It was a boys' compact. We made a sacred pledge, a
bargain. I remember it all perfectly now. We had been
reading some dreadful book and we swore to appear to one
another—I mean, whoever died first swore to show himself
to the other. And we sealed the compact with each other's
blood. I remember it all so well—the hot summer afternoon
in the playground, seven years ago—and one of the masters
caught us and confiscated the knives—and I have never
thought of it again to this day——"

" And you mean——" stammered Greene.

But Marriott made no answer. He got up and crossed
the room and lay down wearily upon the sofa, hiding his
face in his hands.

Greene himself was a bit nonplussed. He left his friend alone for a little while, thinking it all over again. Suddenly an idea seemed to strike him. He went over to where Marriott still lay motionless on the sofa and roused him. In any case it was better to face the matter, whether there was an explanation or not. Giving in was always the silly exit.

" I say, Marriott," he began, as the other turned his white face up to him. " There's no good being so upset about it. I mean—if it's all a hallucination we know what to do. And if it isn't—well, we know what to think, don't we ? "

" I suppose so. But it frightens me horribly for some reason," returned his friend in a hushed voice. " And that poor devil——"

" But, after all, if the worst is true and—and that chap *has* kept his promise—well, he has, that's all, isn't it ? "

Marriott nodded.

" There's only one thing that occurs to me," Greene went on, " and that is, are you quite sure that—that he really ate like that—I mean that he actually *ate anything at all* ? " he finished, blurting out all his thought.

Marriott stared at him for a moment and then said he could easily make certain. He spoke quietly. After the main shock no lesser surprise could affect him.

" I put the things away myself," he said, " after we had finished. They are on the third shelf in that cupboard. No one's touched 'em since."

He pointed without getting up, and Greene took the hint and went over to look.

" Exactly," he said, after a brief examination ; " just as I thought. It was partly hallucination, at any rate. The things haven't been touched. Come and see for yourself."

Together they examined the shelf. There was the brown loaf, the plate of stale scones, the oatcake, all untouched. Even the glass of whisky Marriott had poured out stood there with the whisky still in it.

" You were feeding—no one," said Greene. " Field ate and drank nothing. He was not there at all ! "

" But the breathing ? " urged the other in a low voice, staring with a dazed expression on his face.

Greene did not answer. He walked over to the bedroom, while Marriott followed him with his eyes. He opened the door, and listened. There was no need for words. The sound of deep, regular breathing came floating through the air. There was no hallucination about that, at any rate.

Marriott could hear it where he stood on the other side of the room.

Greene closed the door and came back. " There's only one thing to do," he declared with decision. " Write home and find out about him, and meanwhile come and finish your reading in my rooms. I've got an extra bed."

" Agreed," returned the Fourth Year Man ; " there's no hallucination about that exam ; I must pass that whatever happens."

And this was what they did.

It was about a week later when Marriott got the answer from his sister. Part of it he read out to Greene :

" It is curious," she wrote, " that in your letter you should have inquired after Field. It seems a terrible thing, but you know only a short while ago Sir John's patience became exhausted, and he turned him out of the house, they say without a penny. Well, what do you think ? He has killed himself. At least, it looks like suicide. Instead of leaving the house, he went down into the cellar and simply starved himself to death. . . . They're trying to suppress it, of course, but I heard it all from my maid, who got it from their footman. . . . They found the body on the 14th, and the doctor said he had died about twelve hours before. . . . He was dreadfully thin. . . ."

" Then he died on the 13th," said Greene.

Marriott nodded.

" That's the very night he came to see you."

Marriott nodded again.

DEARTH'S FARM

IT is really not far : our fast train does it in eighty minutes. But so sequestered is the little valley in which I have made my solitary home that I never go to town without the delicious sensation of poising my hand over a lucky-bag full of old memories. In the train I amuse myself by summoning up some of those ghosts of the past, a past not distant, but sufficiently remote in atmosphere from my present to be invested with a certain sentimental glamour. "Perhaps I shall meet you—or you." But never yet have I succeeded in guessing what London held up her sleeve for me. She has that happiest of tricks—without which Paradise will be dull indeed—the trick of surprise. In London, if in no other place, it is the unexpected that happens. For me Fleet Street is the scene *par excellence* of these adventurous encounters, and it was in Fleet Street, three months ago, that I ran across Bailey, of Queens', whom I hadn't seen for five years. Bailey is not his name, nor Queens' his college, but these names will serve to reveal what is germane to my purpose and to conceal the rest.

His recognition of me was instant ; mine of him more slow. He told me his name twice ; we stared at each other, and I struggled to disguise the blankness of my memory. The situation became awkward. I was the more embarrassed because I feared lest he should too odiously misinterpret my non-recognition of him, for the man was shabby and unshaven enough to be suspicious of an intentional slight. Bailey, Bailey . . . now who the devil was Bailey? And then, when he had already made a gesture of moving on, memory stirred to activity.

"Of course, I remember. Bailey. Theosophy. You

used to talk to me about theosophy, didn't you ? I remember
perfectly now." I glanced at my watch. " If you're not
busy let's go and have tea somewhere."

He smiled, with a hint of irony in his eyes, as he answered :
" I'm not busy." I received the uncomfortable impression
that he was hungry and with no ordinary hunger, and the idea
kept me silent, like an awkward schoolboy, while we walked
together to a teashop that I knew.

Seated on opposite sides of the tea-table, we took stock
of each other. He was thin, and his hair greying ; his complexion had a soiled unhealthy appearance ; the cheeks had
sunk in a little, throwing into prominence the high cheekbones above which his sensitive eyes glittered with a new
light, a light not of heaven. Compared with the Bailey I now
remembered so well, a rather sleek young man with an almost
feline love of luxury blossoming like a tropical plant in the
exotic atmosphere of his Cambridge rooms, compared with that
man this was but a pale wraith. In those days he had been a
flaming personality, suited well—too well, for my plain taste—
to the highly coloured orientalism that he affected in his mural
decorations. And co-existent in him with this lust for soft
cushions and chromatic orgies, which repelled me, there was
an imagination that attracted me : an imagination delighting
in highly coloured metaphysical theories of the universe. These
theories, which were as fantastic as *The Arabian Nights*, and
perhaps as unreal, proved his academic undoing : he came
down badly in his Tripos, and had to leave without a degree.
Many a man has done that and yet prospered, but Bailey,
it was apparent, hadn't prospered. I made the conventional
inquiries, adding, " It must be six or seven years since we met
last."

" More than that," said Bailey morosely, and lapsed into
silence. " Look here," he burst out suddenly, " I'm going
to behave like a cad. I'm going to ask you to lend me a pound
note. And don't expect it back in a hurry."

We both winced a little as the note changed hands.
" You've had bad luck," I remarked, without, I hope, a hint
of pity in my voice. " What's wrong ? "

He eyed me over the rim of his teacup. " I look a lot
older to you, I expect ? "

" You don't look very fit," I conceded.

" No, I don't." His cup came down with a nervous
slam upon the saucer. " Going grey, too, aren't I ? " I was
forced to nod agreement. " Yet, do you know, a month ago

there wasn't a grey hair in my head.   You write stories, don't
you ?   I saw your name somewhere.   I wonder if you could
write my story.   You may get your money back after all. . . .
By God, that would be funny, wouldn't it ! "

I couldn't see the joke, but I was curious about his story.
And after we had lit our cigarettes he told it to me, to the
accompaniment of a driving storm of rain that tapped like a
thousand idiot fingers upon the plate-glass windows of the
shop.

II

A FEW weeks ago, said Bailey, I was staying at the house
of a cousin of mine.   I never liked the woman, but I
wanted free board and lodging, and hunger soon blunts the
edge of one's delicacy.   She's at least ten years my senior, and
all I could remember of her was that she had bullied me
when I was a child into learning to read.   Ten years ago
she married a man named Dearth—James Dearth, the resident
owner of a smallish farm in Norfolk, not far from the coast.
All her relatives opposed the marriage.   Relatives always
do.   If people waited for the approval of relatives before
marrying, the world would be depopulated in a generation.
This time it was religion.   My cousin's people were primitive
and methodical in their religion, as the name of their sect
confessed ;   whereas Dearth professed a universal toleration
that they thought could only be a cloak for indifference.   I
have my own opinion about that, but it doesn't matter now.
When I met the man I forgot all about religion :   I was simply
repelled by the notion of any woman marrying so odd a being.
Rather small in build, he possessed the longest and narrowest
face I have ever seen on a man of his size.   His eyes were set
exceptionally wide apart, and the nose, culminating in large
nostrils, made so slight an angle with the rest of the face that,
seen in profile, it was scarcely human.   Perhaps I exaggerate a
little, but I know no other way of explaining the peculiar
revulsion he inspired in me.   He met me at the station in his
dogcart, and wheezed a greeting at me.   " You're Mr. Bailey,
aren't you ?   I hope you've had an agreeable journey.   Monica
will be delighted."   This seemed friendly enough, and my
host's conversation during that eight-mile drive did much to
make me forget my first distaste of his person.   He was
evidently a man of wide reading, and he had a habit of polite
deference that was extremely flattering, especially to me who
had had more than my share of the other thing.   I was cashiered

during the war, you know. Never mind why. Whenever he
laughed, which was not seldom, he exhibited a mouthful of
very large regular teeth.

Dearth's Farm, to give it the local name, is a place with a
personality of its own. Perhaps every place has that. Sometimes I fancy that the earth itself is a personality, or a community of souls locked fast in a dream from which at any
moment they may awake, like volcanoes, into violent action.
Anyhow, Dearth's Farm struck me as being peculiarly personal, because I found it impossible not to regard its climatic
changes as changes of mood. You remember my theory that
chemical action is only physical action seen from without?
Well, I'm inclined to think in just the same way of every manifestation of natural energy. But you don't want to hear
about my fancies. The farmhouse, which is approached by
a narrow winding lane from the main road, stands high up
in a kind of shallow basin of land, a few acres ploughed, but
mostly grass. The countryside has a gentle prettiness more
characteristic of the south-eastern counties. On three sides
wooded hills slope gradually to the horizon ; on the fourth
side grassland rises a little for twenty yards and then curves
abruptly down. To look through the windows that give out
upon this fourth side is to have the sensation of being on
the edge of a steep cliff, or at the end of the world. On a still
day, when the sun is shining, the place has a languid beauty,
an afternoon atmosphere. You remember Tennyson's Lotus
Isles, " in which it seemed always afternoon " : Dearth's Farm
has something of that flavour on a still day. But such days are
rare ; the two or three I experienced shine like jewels in the
memory. Most often that stretch of fifty or sixty acres is a
gathering-ground for all the bleak winds of the earth. They
seem to come simultaneously from the land and from the sea,
which is six miles away, and they swirl round in that shallow
basin of earth, as I have called it, like maddened devils seeking
escape from a trap. When the storms were at their worst I
used to feel as though I were perched insecurely on a gigantic
saucer held a hundred miles above the earth. But I am not a
courageous person. Monica, my cousin, found no fault with
the winds. She had other fears, and I had not been with her
three days before she began to confide them to me. Her
overtures were as surprising as they were unwelcome, for that
she was not a confiding person by nature I was certain. Her
manners were reserved to the point of diffidence, and we had
nothing in common save a detestation of the family from which

we had both sprung. I suppose you will want to know something of her looks. She was a tall, full-figured woman, handsome for her years, with jet-black hair, a sensitive face, and a
complexion almost Southern in its dark colouring. I love
beauty and I found pleasure in her mere presence, which did
something to lighten for me the gloom that pervaded the
house ; but my pleasure was innocent enough, and Dearth's
watchdog airs only amused me. Monica's eyes—unfathom-
able pools—seemed troubled whenever they rested on me :
whether by fear or by some other emotion I didn't at first
know.

She chose her moment well, coming to me when Dearth
was out of the house, looking after his men, and I, pleading a
headache, had refused to accompany him. The malady was
purely fictitious, but I was bored with the fellow's company,
and sick of being dragged at his heels like a dog for no better
reason than his too evident jealousy afforded.

" I want to ask a kindness of you," she said. " Will you
promise to answer me quite frankly ? " I wondered what
the deuce was coming, but I promised, seeing no way out of it.
" I want you to tell me," she went on, " whether you see anything queer about me, about my behaviour ? Do I say or do
anything that seems to you odd ? "

Her perturbation was so great that I smiled to hide my
perception of it. I answered jocularly : " Nothing at all odd,
my dear Monica, except this question of yours. What makes
you ask it ? "

But she was not to be shaken so easily out of her fears,
whatever they were. " And do you find nothing strange
about this household either ? "

" Nothing strange at all," I assured her. " Your marriage
is an unhappy one, but so are thousands of others. Nothing
strange about that."

" What about him ? " she said. And her eyes seemed to
probe for an answer.

I shrugged my shoulders. " Are you asking for my opinion
of your husband ? A delicate thing to discuss."

" We're speaking in confidence, aren't we ! " She spoke
impatiently, waving my politeness away.

" Well, since you ask, I don't like him. I don't like his
face : it's a parody on mankind. And I can't understand
why you threw yourself away on him."

She was eager to explain. " He wasn't always like this.
He was a gifted man, with brains and an imagination. He

still is, for all I know. You spoke of his face—now how would
you describe his face, in one word ? "

I couldn't help being tickled by the comedy of the situation : a man and a woman sitting in solemn conclave seeking
a word by which to describe another man's face, and that man
her husband. But her air of tragedy, though I thought it
ridiculous, sobered me. I pondered her question for a while,
recalling to my mind's eye the long, narrow physiognomy and
the large teeth of Dearth.

At last I ventured the word I had tried to avoid. " Equine,"
I suggested.

" Ah ! " There was a world of relief in her voice. " You've
seen it, too."

She told me a queer tale. Dearth, it appears, had a love
and understanding of horses that was quite unparalleled. His
wife, too, had loved horses and it had once pleased her to see
her husband's astonishing power over the creatures, a power
which he exercised always for their good. But his bene-
factions to the equine race were made at a hideous cost to himself, of which he was utterly unaware. Monica's theory was
too fantastic even for me to swallow, and I, as you know,
have a good stomach for fantasy. You will have already
guessed what it was. Dearth was growing, by a process too
gradual and subtle for perception, into the likeness of the
horses with whom he had so complete sympathy. This was
Mrs. Dearth's notion of what was happening to her husband.
And she pointed out something significant that had escaped
my notice. She pointed out that the difference between him
and the next man was not altogether, or even mainly, a physical
difference. In effect she said : " If you scrutinize the features
more carefully, you will find them to be far less extraordinary
than you now suppose. The poison is not in his features.
It is in the psychical atmosphere he carries about with him :
something which infects you with the idea of horses and makes
you impose that idea on his appearance, magnifying his facial
peculiarities." Just now I mentioned that in the early days
of her marriage Monica had shared this love of horses. Later,
of course, she came to detest them only one degree less than she
detested her husband. That is saying much. Only a few months
before my visit matters had come to a crisis between the two.
Without giving any definite reason, she had confessed, under
pressure, that he was unspeakably offensive to her ; and since
then they had met only at meals and always reluctantly. She
shuddered to recall that interview, and I shuddered to imagine

it. I was no longer surprised that she had begun to entertain
doubts of her own sanity.

But this wasn't the worst. The worst was Dandy, the white
horse. I found it difficult to understand why a white horse
should alarm her, and I began to suspect that the nervous
strain she had undergone was making her inclined to magnify
trifles. " It's his favourite horse," she said. " That s as
much as saying that he dotes on it to a degree that is unhuman.
It never does any work. It just roams the fields by day, and
at night sleeps in the stable." Even this didn't, to my mind,
seem a very terrible indictment. If the man was mad on
horses, what more natural than this petting of a particular
favourite ?—a fine animal, too, as Monica herself admitted.
" Roams the fields," cried my poor cousin urgently. " Or did
until these last few weeks. Lately it has been kept in its stable,
day in, day out, eating its head off and working up energy
enough to kill us all." This sounded to me like the language
of hysteria, but I waited for what was to follow. " The day
you came, did you notice how pale I looked ? I had had a
fright. As I was crossing the yard with a pail of separated milk
for the calves, that beast broke loose from the stable and sprang
at me. Yes, Dandy. He was in a fury. His eyes burned with
ferocity. I dodged him by a miracle, dropped the pail, and
ran back to the house shrieking for help. When I entered
the living-room my husband feigned to be waking out of sleep.
He didn't seem interested in my story, and I'm convinced
that he had planned the whole thing." It was past my understanding how Dearth could have made his horse spring out of
his stable and make a murderous attack upon a particular
woman, and I said so. " You don't know him yet," retorted
Monica. " And you don't know Dandy. Go and look at the
beast. Go now, while James is out."

The farmyard, with its pool of water covered in green
slime, its manure and sodden straw, and its smell of pigs, was
a place that seldom failed to offend me. But on this occasion I
picked my way across the cobblestones thinking of nothing
at all but the homicidal horse that I was about to spy upon.
I have said before that I'm not a courageous man, and you'll
understand that I stepped warily as I neared the stable. I saw
that the lower of the two doors was made fast and with the
more confidence unlatched the other.

I peered in. The great horse stood, bolt upright but
apparently in a profound sleep. It was, indeed, a fine creature,
with no spot or shadow, so far as I could discern, to mar its

glossy whiteness. I stood there staring and brooding for several minutes, wondering if both Monica and I were the victims of some astounding hallucination. I had no fear at all of Dandy, after having seen him ; and it didn't alarm me when, presently, his frame quivered, his eyes opened, and he turned to look at me. But as I looked into his eyes an indefinable fear possessed me. The horse stared dumbly for a moment, and his nostrils dilated. Although I half-expected him to tear his head out of the halter and prance round upon me, I could not move. I stared, and as I stared, the horse's lips moved back from the teeth in a grin, unmistakably a grin, of malign intelligence. The gesture vividly recalled Dearth to my mind. I had described him as equine, and if proof of the word's aptness were needed, Dandy had supplied that proof.

" He's come back," Monica murmured to me, on my return to the house. " Ill, I think. He's gone to lie down. Have you seen Dandy ? "

" Yes. And I hope not to see him again."

But I was to see him again, twice again. The first time was that same night, from my bedroom window. Both my bedroom and my cousin's looked out upon that grassy hill of which I spoke. It rose for a few yards until almost level with the second storey of the house and then abruptly curved away. Somewhere about midnight, feeling restless and troubled by my thoughts, I got out of bed and went to the window to take an airing.

I was not the only restless creature that night. Standing not twenty yards away, with the sky for background, was a great horse. The moonlight made its white flank gleam like silver, and lit up the eyes that stared fixedly at my window.

III

FOR sixteen days and nights we lived, Monica and I, in the presence of this fear, a fear none the less real for being non-susceptible of definition. The climax came suddenly, without any sort of warning, unless Dearth's idiotic hostility towards myself could be regarded as a warning. The utterly unfounded idea that I was making love to his wife had taken root in the man's mind, and every day his manner to me became more openly vindictive. This was the cue for my departure, with warm thanks for my delightful holiday ; but I didn't choose to take it. I wasn't exactly in love with Monica,

but she was my comrade in danger and I was reluctant to leave
her to face her nightmare terrors alone.

The most cheerful room in that house was the kitchen,
with its red-tiled floor, its oak rafters, and its great open fireplace.   And when in the evenings the lamp was lit and we sat
there, listening in comfort to the everlasting gale that raged
round the house, I could almost have imagined myself happy,
had it not been for the presence of my reluctant host.   He was
a skeleton at a feast, if you like !   By God, we were a genial
party.   From seven o'clock to ten we would sit there, the three
of us, fencing off silence with the most pitiful of small talk.
On this particular night I had been chaffing him gently, though
with intention, about his fancy for keeping a loaded rifle hanging over the kitchen mantelpiece ; but at last I sickened of the
pastime, and the conversation, which had been sustained only
by my efforts, lapsed.   I stared at the red embers in the grate,
stealing a glance now and again at Monica to see how she was
enduring the discomfort of such a silence.   The cheap alarum-
clock ticked loudly, in the way that cheap alarum-clocks have.
When I looked again at Dearth he appeared to have fallen
asleep.   I say " appeared," for I instantly suspected him of
shamming sleep in order to catch us out.   I knew that he
believed us to be in love with each other, and his total lack of
evidence must have occasioned him hours of useless fury.   I
suspected him of the most melodramatic intentions : of
hoping to see a caress pass between us that would justify him
in making a scene.   In that scene, as I figured it, the gun over
the mantelpiece might play an important part.   I don't like
loaded guns.

The sight of his closed lids exasperated me into a bitter
speech designed for him to overhear.   " Monica, your husband
is asleep.   He is asleep only in order that he may wake at the
chosen moment and pour out the contents of his vulgar little
mind upon our heads."

This tirade astonished her, as well it might.   She glanced
up, first at me, then at her husband ; and upon him her eyes
remained fixed.   " He's not asleep," she said, rising slowly
out of her chair.

" I know he's not," I replied.

By now she was at his side, bending over him.   " No,"
she remarked coolly.   " He's dead."

At those words the wind outside redoubled its fury, and
it seemed as though all the anguish of the world was in its wail.
The spirit of Dearth's Farm was crying aloud in a frenzy that

Pressed against the window was the face of the white horse.

shook the house, making all the windows rattle. I shuddered
to my feet. And in the moment of my rising the wail died
away, and in the lull I heard outside the window a sudden
sound of feet, of pawing, horse's feet. My horror found vent
in a sort of desperate mirth.

"No, not dead. James Dearth doesn't die so easily."

Shocked by my levity, she pointed mutely to the body in
the chair. But a wild idea possessed me, and I knew that
my wild idea was the truth. "Yes," I said, "that may be
dead as mutton. But James Dearth is outside, come to spy
on you and me. Can't you hear him ? "

I stretched out my hand to the blind cord. The blind
ran up with a rattle, and, pressed against the window, looking
in upon us, was the face of the white horse, its teeth bared in
a malevolent grin. Without losing sight of the thing for a
moment, I backed towards the fire. Monica, divining my
intention, took down the gun from its hook and yielded it to
my desirous fingers. I took deliberate aim, and shot.

And then, with the crisis over, as I thought, my nerves
went to rags. I sat down limply, Monica huddled at my feet ;
and I knew with a hideous certitude that the soul of James
Dearth, violently expelled from the corpse that lay outside
the window, was in the room with me, seeking to re-enter that
human body in the chair. There was a long moment of agony
during which I trembled on the verge of madness, and then a
flush came back into the dead pallid cheeks, the body breathed,
the eyes opened. . . . I had just enough strength left to drag
myself out of my seat. I saw Monica's eyes raised to mine ; I
can never for a moment stop seeing them. Three hours
later I stumbled into the arms of the stationmaster, who put
me in the London train under the impression that I was drunk.
Yes, I left alone. I told you I wasn't a courageous man. . . .

IV

BAILEY'S voice abruptly ceased. The tension in my listening mind snapped, and I came back with a jerk, as though
released by a spring, to my seat in the teashop. Bailey's queer
eyes glittered across at me for a moment, and then, their light
dying suddenly out, they became infinitely weary of me and
of all the sorry business of living. A rationalist in grain, I find
it impossible to accept the story quite as it stands. Sub-
stantially true it may be, probably is, but that it has been
distorted by the prism of Bailey's singular personality I can

hardly doubt. But the angle of that distortion must remain a matter for conjecture.

No such dull reflections came then to mar my appreciation of the quality of the strange hush that followed his last words. Neither of us spoke. An agitated waitress made us aware that the shop was closing, and we went into the street without a word. The rain was unremitting. I shrank back into the shelter of the porch while I fastened the collar of my mackintosh, and when I stepped out upon the pavement again, Bailey had vanished into the darkness.

I have never ceased to be vexed at losing him, and never ceased to fear that he may have thought the loss not unwelcome to me. My only hope is that he may read this and get into touch with me again, so that I may discharge my debt to him. It is a debt that lies heavily on my conscience—the price of this story, less one pound.

THE HAMMER OF GOD

THE little village of Bohun Beacon was perched on a hill so
steep that the tall spire of its church seemed only like the
peak of a small mountain. At the foot of the church stood
a smithy, generally red with fires and always littered with
hammers and scraps of iron ; opposite to this, over a rude
cross of cobbled paths, was " The Blue Boar," the only inn
of the place. It was upon this crossway, in the lifting of a
leaden and silver daybreak, that two brothers met in the street
and spoke ; though one was beginning the day and the other
finishing it. The Rev. and Hon. Wilfred Bohun was very
devout, and was making his way to some austere exercises of
prayer or contemplation at dawn. Colonel the Hon. Norman
Bohun, his elder brother, was by no means devout, and was
sitting in evening-dress on the bench outside " The Blue
Boar," drinking what the philosophic observer was free to
regard either as his last glass on Tuesday or his first on Wed-
nesday. The colonel was not particular.

The Bohuns were one of the very few aristocratic families
really dating from the Middle Ages, and their pennon had
actually seen Palestine. But it is a great mistake to suppose
that such houses stand high in chivalric tradition. Few except
the poor preserve traditions. Aristocrats live not in traditions
but in fashions. The Bohuns had been Mohocks under
Queen Anne and Mashers under Queen Victoria. But like
more than one of the really ancient houses, they had rotted
in the last two centuries into mere drunkards and dandy
degenerates, till there had even come a whisper of insanity.
Certainly there was something hardly human about the colonel's
wolfish pursuit of pleasure, and his chronic resolution not to
go home till morning had a touch of the hideous clarity of

insomnia. He was a tall, fine animal, elderly, but with hair still startlingly yellow. He would have looked merely blond and leonine, but his blue eyes were sunk so deep in his face that they looked black. They were a little too close together. He had very long yellow moustaches ; on each side of them a fold or furrow from nostril to jaw, so that a sneer seemed cut into his face. Over his evening clothes he wore a curious pale yellow coat that looked more like a very light dressing-gown than an overcoat, and on the back of his head was stuck an extraordinary broad-brimmed hat of a bright green colour, evidently some oriental curiosity caught up at random. He was proud of appearing in such incongruous attires—proud of the fact that he always made them look congruous.

His brother the curate had also the yellow hair and the elegance, but he was buttoned up to the chin in black, and his face was clean-shaven, cultivated, and a little nervous. He seemed to live for nothing but his religion ; but there were some who said (notably the blacksmith, who was a Presbyterian) that it was a love of Gothic architecture rather than of God, and that his haunting of the church like a ghost was only another and purer turn of the almost morbid thirst for beauty which sent his brother raging after women and wine. This charge was doubtful, while the man's practical piety was indubitable. Indeed, the charge was mostly an ignorant misunderstanding of the love of solitude and secret prayer, and was founded on his being often found kneeling, not before the altar, but in peculiar places, in the crypts or gallery, or even in the belfry. He was at the moment about to enter the church through the yard of the smithy, but stopped and frowned a little as he saw his brother's cavernous eyes staring in the same direction. On the hypothesis that the colonel was interested in the church he did not waste any speculations. There only remained the blacksmith's shop, and though the blacksmith was a Puritan and none of his people, Wilfred Bohun had heard some scandals about a beautiful and rather celebrated wife. He flung a suspicious look across the shed, and the colonel stood up laughing to speak to him.

" Good morning, Wilfred," he said. " Like a good landlord I am watching sleeplessly over my people. I am going to call on the blacksmith."

Wilfred looked at the ground, and said : "The blacksmith is out. He is over at Greenford."

" I know," answered the other with silent laughter ; " that is why I am calling on him."

"Norman," said the cleric, with his eye on a pebble in the road, " are you ever afraid of thunderbolts ? "

" What do you mean ? " asked the colonel. " Is your hobby meteorology ? "

" I mean," said Wilfred, without looking up, " do you ever think that God might strike you in the street ? "

" I beg your pardon," said the colonel ; " I see your hobby is folklore."

" I know your hobby is blasphemy," retorted the religious man, stung in the one live place of his nature. " But if you do not fear God, you have good reason to fear man."

The elder raised his eyebrows politely. " Fear man ? " he said.

" Barnes the blacksmith is the biggest and strongest man for forty miles round," said the clergyman sternly. " I know you are no coward or weakling, but he could throw you over the wall."

This struck home, being true, and the lowering line by mouth and nostril darkened and deepened. For a moment he stood with the heavy sneer on his face. But in an instant Colonel Bohun had recovered his own cruel good humour and laughed, showing two dog-like front teeth under his yellow moustache. " In that case, my dear Wilfred," he said quite carelessly, " it was wise for the last of the Bohuns to come out partially in armour."

And he took off the queer round hat covered with green, showing that it was lined within with steel. Wilfred recognized it indeed as a light Japanese or Chinese helmet torn down from a trophy that hung in the old family hall.

" It was the first hat to hand," explained his brother airily ; " always the nearest hat—and the nearest woman."

" The blacksmith is away at Greenford," said Wilfred quietly ; " the time of his return is unsettled."

And with that he turned and went into the church with bowed head, crossing himself like one who wishes to be quit of an unclean spirit. He was anxious to forget such grossness in the cool twilight of his tall Gothic cloisters ; but on that morning it was fated that his still round of religious exercises should be everywhere arrested by small shocks. As he entered the church, hitherto always empty at that hour, a kneeling figure rose hastily to its feet and came towards the full daylight of the doorway. When the curate saw it he stood still with surprise. For the early worshipper was none other than the village idiot, a nephew of the blacksmith, one who neither would nor could care for the church or for anything else. He was always called " Mad Joe," and seemed to have no other name ; he was a dark, strong, slouching lad, with a heavy white face, dark straight hair, and a mouth always open. As he passed the priest, his moon-calf countenance gave no hint of what he had been doing or thinking of. He had never been known to pray before. What sort of prayers was he saying now ? Extraordinary prayers surely.

Wilfred Bohun stood rooted to the spot long enough to see the idiot go out into the sunshine, and even to see his dissolute brother hail him with a sort of avuncular jocularity. The last thing he saw was the colonel throwing pennies at the open mouth of Joe, with the serious appearance of trying to hit it.

This ugly sunlight picture of the stupidity and cruelty of the earth sent the ascetic finally to his prayers for purification and new thoughts. He went up to a pew in the gallery, which brought him under a coloured window which he loved and always quieted his spirit ; a blue window with an angel carrying lilies. There he began to think less about the half-wit, with his livid face and mouth like a fish. He began to think less of his evil brother, pacing like a lean lion in his horrible hunger. He sank deeper and deeper into those cold and sweet colours of silver blossoms and sapphire sky.

In this place half an hour afterwards he was found by Gibbs, the village cobbler, who had been sent for him in some haste. He got to his feet with promptitude, for he knew that no small matter would have brought Gibbs into such a place at all. The cobbler was, as in many villages, an atheist, and his appearance in church was a shade more extraordinary than Mad Joe's. It was a morning of theological enigmas.

" What is it ? " asked Wilfred Bohun rather stiffly, but putting out a trembling hand for his hat.

The atheist spoke in a tone that, coming from him, was quite startlingly respectful, and even, as it were, huskily sympathetic.

" You must excuse me, sir," he said in a hoarse whisper, " but we didn't think it right not to let you know at once. I'm afraid a rather dreadful thing has happened, sir. I'm afraid your brother——"

Wilfred clenched his frail hands. " What devilry has he done now ? " he cried in involuntary passion.

" Why, sir," said the cobbler, coughing, " I'm afraid he's done nothing, and won't do anything. I'm afraid he's done for. You had really better come down, sir."

The curate followed the cobbler down a short winding

stair, which brought them out at an entrance rather higher than the street. Bohun saw the tragedy in one glance, flat underneath him like a plan. In the yard of the smithy were standing five or six men mostly in black, one in an inspector's uniform. They included the doctor, the Presbyterian minister, and the priest from the Roman Catholic chapel, to which the blacksmith's wife belonged. The latter was speaking to her, indeed, very rapidly, in an undertone, as she, a magnificent woman with red-gold hair, was sobbing blindly on a bench. Between these two groups, and just clear of the main heap of hammers, lay a man in evening-dress, spread-eagled and flat on his face. From the height above Wilfred could have sworn to every item of his costume and appearance, down to the Bohun rings upon his fingers ; but the skull was only a hideous splash, like a star of blackness and blood.

Wilfred Bohun gave but one glance, and ran down the steps into the yard. The doctor, who was the family physician, saluted him, but he scarcely took any notice. He could only stammer out : " My brother is dead. What does it mean ? What is this horrible mystery ? " There was an unhappy silence ; and then the cobbler, the most outspoken man present, answered : " Plenty of horror, sir," he said, " but not much mystery."

" What do you mean ? " asked Wilfred, with a white face.

" It's plain enough," answered Gibbs. " There is only one man for forty miles round that could have struck such a blow as that, and he's the man that had most reason to."

" We must not prejudge anything," put in the doctor, a tall, black-bearded man, rather nervously ; " but it is competent for me to corroborate what Mr. Gibbs says about the nature of the blow, sir ; it is an incredible blow. Mr. Gibbs says that only one man in this district could have done it. I should have said myself that nobody could have done it."

A shudder of superstition went through the slight figure of the curate. " I can hardly understand," he said.

" Mr. Bohun," said the doctor in a low voice, " metaphors literally fail me. It is inadequate to say that the skull was smashed to bits like an egg-shell. Fragments of bone were driven into the body and the ground like bullets into a mud wall. It was the hand of a giant."

He was silent a moment, looking grimly through his glasses ; then he added : " The thing has one advantage—that it clears most people of suspicion at one stroke. If you or I or any normally made man in the country were accused of this crime, we should be acquitted as an infant would be acquitted of stealing the Nelson Column."

" That's what I say," repeated the cobbler obstinately ; " there's only one man that could have done it, and he's the man that would have done it. Where's Simeon Barnes, the blacksmith ? "

" He's over at Greenford," faltered the curate.

" More likely over in France," muttered the cobbler.

" No ; he is in neither of those places," said a small and colourless voice, which came from the little Roman priest who had joined the group. " As a matter of fact, he is coming up the road at this moment."

The little priest was not an interesting man to look at, having stubbly brown hair and a round and stolid face. But if he had been as splendid as Apollo no one would have looked at him at that moment. Every one turned round and peered at the pathway which wound across the plain below, along which was indeed walking, at his own huge stride and with a hammer on his shoulder, Simeon the smith. He was a bony and gigantic man, with deep, dark, sinister eyes and a dark chin beard. He was walking and talking quietly with two other men ; and though he was never specially cheerful, he seemed quite at his ease.

" My God ! " cried the atheistic cobbler, " and there's the hammer he did it with."

" No," said the inspector, a sensible-looking man with a sandy moustache, speaking for the first time. " There's the hammer he did it with over there by the church wall. We have left it and the body exactly as they are."

All glanced round, and the short priest went across and looked down in silence at the tool where it lay. It was one of the smallest and the lightest of the hammers, and would not have caught the eye among the rest ; but on the iron edge of it were blood and yellow hair.

After a silence the short priest spoke without looking up, and there was a new note in his dull voice. " Mr. Gibbs was hardly right," he said, " in saying that there is no mystery. There is at least the mystery of why so big a man should attempt so big a blow with so little a hammer."

" Oh, never mind that," cried Gibbs, in a fever. " What are we to do with Simeon Barnes ? "

" Leave him alone," said the priest quietly. " He is coming here of himself. I know those two men with him. They are very good fellows from Greenford, and they have come over about the Presbyterian chapel."

Even as he spoke the tall smith swung round the corner of the church, and strode into his own yard. Then he stood there quite still, and the hammer fell from his hand. The inspector, who had preserved impenetrable propriety, immediately went up to him.

" I won't ask you, Mr. Barnes," he said, " whether you know anything about what has happened here. You are not bound to say. I hope you don't know, and that you will be able to prove it. But I must go through the form of arresting you in the King's name for the murder of Colonel Norman Bohun."

" You are not bound to say anything," said the cobbler in officious excitement. " They've got to prove everything. They haven't proved yet that it is Colonel Bohun, with the head all smashed up like that."

" That won't wash," said the doctor aside to the priest. " That's out of the detective stories. I was the colonel's medical man, and I knew his body better than he did. He had very fine hands, but quite peculiar ones. The second and third fingers were the same in length. Oh, that's the colonel right enough."

As he glanced at the brained corpse upon the ground the iron eyes of the motionless blacksmith followed them and rested there also.

" Is Colonel Bohun dead ? " said the smith quite calmly. " Then he's damned."

" Don't say anything ! Oh, don't say anything," cried the atheist cobbler, dancing about in an ecstasy of admiration of the English legal system. For no man is such a legalist as the good secularist.

The blacksmith turned on him over his shoulder the august face of a fanatic.

" It's well for you infidels to dodge like foxes because the world's law favours you," he said ; " but God guards His own in His pocket, as you shall see this day."

Then he pointed to the colonel and said : " When did this dog die in his sins ? "

" Moderate your language," said the doctor.

" Moderate the Bible's language, and I'll moderate mine. When did he die ? "

" I saw him alive at six o'clock this morning," stammered Wilfred Bohun.

" God is good," said the smith. " Mr. Inspector, I have not the slightest objection to being arrested. It is you who may object to arresting me. I don't mind leaving the court without a stain on my character. You do mind, perhaps, leaving the court with a bad set-back in your career."

The solid inspector for the first time looked at the black-smith with a lively eye ; as did everybody else, except the short, strange priest, who was still looking down at the little hammer that had dealt the dreadful blow.

" There are two men standing outside this shop," went on the blacksmith with ponderous lucidity, " good tradesmen in Greenford whom you all know, who will swear that they saw me from before midnight till daybreak and long after in the committee-room of our Revival Mission, which sits all night, we save souls so fast. In Greenford itself twenty people could swear to me for all that time. If I were a heathen, Mr. Inspector, I would let you walk on to your downfall. But as a Christian man I feel bound to give you your chance, and ask you whether you will hear my alibi now or in court."

The inspector seemed for the first time disturbed, and said, " Of course I should be glad to clear you altogether now."

The smith walked out of his yard with the same long and easy stride, and returned to his two friends from Greenford, who were indeed friends of nearly every one present. Each of them said a few words which no one ever thought of dis-believing. When they had spoken, the innocence of Simeon stood up as solid as the great church above them.

One of those silences struck the group which are more strange and insufferable than any speech. Madly, in order to make conversation, the curate said to the Catholic priest :

" You seem very much interested in that hammer, Father Brown."

" Yes, I am," said Father Brown ; " why is it such a small hammer ? "

The doctor swung round on him.

" By George, that's true," he cried ; " who would use a little hammer with ten larger hammers lying about ? "

Then he lowered his voice in the curate's ear and said : " Only the kind of person that can't lift a large hammer. It is not a question of force or courage between the sexes. It's a question of lifting power in the shoulders. A bold woman could commit ten murders with a light hammer and never turn a hair. She could not kill a beetle with a heavy one."

Wilfred Bohun was staring at him with a sort of hypnotized horror, while Father Brown listened with his head a little on one side, really interested and attentive. The doctor went on with more hissing emphasis :

" Why do these idiots always assume that the only person who hates the wife's lover is the wife's husband ? Nine times out of ten the person who most hates the wife's lover is the wife. Who knows what insolence or treachery he had shown her—look there ? "

He made a momentary gesture towards the red-haired woman on the bench. She had lifted her head at last and the tears were drying on her splendid face. But the eyes were fixed on the corpse with an electric glare that had in it something of idiocy.

The Rev. Wilfred Bohun made a limp gesture as if waving away all desire to know ; but Father Brown, dusting off his sleeve some ashes blown from the furnace, spoke in his indifferent way.

" You are like so many doctors," he said ; " your mental science is really suggestive. It is your physical science that is utterly impossible. I agree that the woman wants to kill the co-respondent much more than the petitioner does. And I agree that a woman will always pick up a small hammer instead of a big one. But the difficulty is one of physical impossibility. No woman ever born could have smashed a man's skull out flat like that." Then he added reflectively, after a pause : " These people haven't grasped the whole of it. The man was actually wearing an iron helmet, and the blow scattered it like broken glass. Look at that woman. Look at her arms."

Silence held them all up again, and then the doctor said rather sulkily : " Well, I may be wrong ; there are objections to everything. But I stick to the main point. No man but an idiot would pick up that little hammer if he could use a big hammer."

With that the lean and quivering hands of Wilfred Bohun went up to his head and seemed to clutch his scanty yellow hair. After an instant they dropped, and he cried : " That was the word I wanted ; you have said the word."

Then he continued, mastering his discomposure : " The words you said were, ' No man but an idiot would pick up the small hammer.' "

" Yes," said the doctor. " Well ? "

" Well," said the curate, " no man but an idiot did." The

rest stared at him with eyes arrested and riveted, and he went on in a febrile and feminine agitation.

" I am a priest," he cried unsteadily, " and a priest should be no shedder of blood. I—I mean that he should bring no one to the gallows. And I thank God that I see the criminal clearly now—because he is a criminal who cannot be brought to the gallows."

" You will not denounce him ? " inquired the doctor.

" He would not be hanged if I did denounce him," answered Wilfred with a wild but curiously happy smile. " When I went into the church this morning I found a madman praying there— that poor Joe, who has been wrong all his life. God knows what he prayed ; but with such strange folk it is not incredible to suppose that their prayers are all upside down. Very likely a lunatic would pray before killing a man. When I last saw poor Joe he was with my brother. My brother was mocking him."

" By Jove ! " cried the doctor, "this is talking at last. But how do you explain——"

The Rev. Wilfred was almost trembling with the excitement of his own glimpse of the truth. " Don't you see ; don't you see," he cried feverishly ; " that is the only theory that covers both the queer things, that answers both the riddles. The two riddles are the little hammer and the big blow. The smith might have struck the big blow, but would not have chosen the little hammer. His wife would have chosen the little hammer, but she could not have struck the big blow. But the madman might have done both. As for the little hammer—why, he was mad and might have picked up any-thing. And for the big blow, have you never heard, doctor, that a maniac in his paroxysm may have the strength of ten men ? "

The doctor drew a deep breath and then said, " By golly, I believe you've got it."

Father Brown had fixed his eyes on the speaker so long and steadily as to prove that his large grey, ox-like eyes were not quite so insignificant as the rest of his face. When silence had fallen he said with marked respect : " Mr. Bohun, yours is the only theory yet propounded which holds water every way and is essentially unassailable. I think, therefore, that you deserve to be told, on my positive knowledge, that it is not the true one." And with that the odd little man walked away and stared again at the hammer.

" That fellow seems to know more than he ought to,"

whispered the doctor peevishly to Wilfred. " Those popish priests are deucedly sly."

" No, no," said Bohun, with a sort of wild fatigue. " It was the lunatic. It was the lunatic."

The group of the two clerics and the doctor had fallen away from the more official group containing the inspector and the man he had arrested. Now, however, that their own party had broken up, they heard voices from the others. The priest looked up quietly and then looked down again as he heard the blacksmith say in a loud voice :

" I hope I've convinced you, Mr. Inspector. I'm a strong man, as you say, but I couldn't have flung my hammer bang here from Greenford. My hammer hasn't any wings that it should come flying half a mile over hedges and fields."

The inspector laughed amicably and said : " No, I think you can be considered out of it, though it's one of the rummiest coincidences I ever saw. I can only ask you to give us all the assistance you can in finding a man as big and strong as yourself. By George ! you might be useful, if only to hold him ! I suppose you yourself have no guess at the man ? "

" I may have a guess," said the pale smith, " but it is not at a man." Then, seeing the scared eyes turn towards his wife on the bench, he put his huge hand on her shoulder, and said : " Nor a woman either."

" What do you mean ? " asked the inspector jocularly. " You don't think cows use hammers, do you ? "

" I think no thing of flesh held that hammer," said the blacksmith in a stifled voice ; " mortally speaking, I think the man died alone."

Wilfred made a sudden forward movement and peered at him with burning eyes.

" Do you mean to say, Barnes," came the sharp voice of the cobbler, " that the hammer jumped up of itself and knocked the man down ? "

" Oh, you gentlemen may stare and snigger," cried Simeon ; " you clergymen who tell us on Sunday in what a stillness the Lord smote Sennacherib. I believe that One who walks invisible in every house defended the honour of mine, and laid the defiler dead before the door of it. I believe the force in that blow was just the force there is in earthquakes, and no force less."

Wilfred said, with a voice utterly undescribable : " I told Norman myself to beware of the thunderbolt."

" That agent is outside my jurisdiction," said the inspector with a slight smile.

" You are not outside His," answered the smith ; " see you to it," and, turning his broad back, he went into the house.

The shaken Wilfred was led away by Father Brown, who had an easy and friendly way with him. " Let us get out of this horrid place, Mr. Bohun," he said. " May I look inside your church ? I hear it's one of the oldest in England. We take some interest, you know," he added with a comical grimace, " in old English churches."

Wilfred Bohun did not smile, for humour was never his strong point. But he nodded rather eagerly, being only too ready to explain the Gothic splendours to some one more likely to be sympathetic than the Presbyterian blacksmith or the atheist cobbler.

" By all means," he said ; " let us go in at this side." And he led the way into the high side entrance at the top of the flight of steps. Father Brown was mounting the first step to follow him when he felt a hand on his shoulder, and turned to behold the dark, thin figure of the doctor, his face darker yet with suspicion.

" Sir," said the physician harshly, " you appear to know some secrets in this black business. May I ask if you are going to keep them to yourself ? "

" Why, doctor," answered the priest, smiling quite pleasantly, " there is one very good reason why a man of my trade should keep things to himself when he is not sure of them, and that is that it is so constantly his duty to keep them to himself when he is sure of them. But if you think I have been discourteously reticent with you or any one, I will go to the extreme limit of my custom. I will give you two very large hints."

" Well, sir ? " said the doctor gloomily.

" First," said Father Brown quietly, " the thing is quite in your own province. It is a matter of physical science. The blacksmith is mistaken, not perhaps in saying that the blow was divine, but certainly in saying that it came by a miracle. It was no miracle, doctor, except in so far as man is himself a miracle, with his strange and wicked and yet half-heroic heart. The force that smashed that skull was a force well known to scientists—one of the most frequently debated of the laws of Nature."

The doctor, who was looking at him with frowning intentness, only said : " And the other hint ? "

" The other hint is this," said the priest. " Do you remember the blacksmith, though he believes in miracles, talking scornfully of the impossible fairy tale that his hammer had wings and flew half a mile across country ? "

" Yes," said the doctor, " I remember that."

" Well," added Father Brown, with a broad smile, " that fairy tale was the nearest thing to the real truth that has been said to-day." And with that he turned his back and stumped up the steps after the curate.

The Reverend Wilfred, who had been waiting for him, pale and impatient, as if this little delay were the last straw for his nerves, led him immediately to his favourite corner of the church, that part of the gallery closest to the carved roof and lit by the wonderful window with the angel. The little Latin priest explored and admired everything exhaustively, talking cheerfully but in a low voice all the time. When in the course of his investigation he found the side exit and the winding stair down which Wilfred had rushed to find his brother dead, Father Brown ran not down but up, with the agility of a monkey, and his clear voice came from an outer platform above.

" Come up here, Mr. Bohun," he called. " The air will do you good."

Bohun followed him, and came out on a kind of stone gallery or balcony outside the building, from which one could see the illimitable plain in which their small hill stood, wooded away to the purple horizon and dotted with villages and farms. Clear and square, but quite small beneath them, was the blacksmith's yard, where the inspector still stood taking notes and the corpse still lay like a smashed fly.

" Might be the map of the world, mightn't it ? " said Father Brown.

" Yes," said Bohun very gravely, and nodded his head.

Immediately beneath and about them the lines of the Gothic building plunged outwards into the void with a sickening swiftness akin to suicide. There is that element of Titan energy in the architecture of the Middle Ages that, from whatever aspect it be seen, it always seems to be rushing away, like the strong back of some maddened horse. This church was hewn out of ancient and silent stone, bearded with old fungoids and stained with the nests of birds. And yet, when they saw it from below, it sprang like a fountain at the stars ; and when they saw it, as now, from above, it poured like a cataract into a voiceless pit. For these two men on the tower were left alone with the most terrible aspect of the Gothic ; the monstrous foreshortening and disproportion, the dizzy perspectives, the glimpses of great things small and small things great ; a topsy-turvydom of stone in the mid-air. Details of stone, enormous by their proximity, were relieved against a pattern of fields and farms, pygmy in their distance. A carved bird or beast at a corner seemed like some vast walking or flying dragon wasting the pastures and villages below. The whole atmosphere was dizzy and dangerous, as if men were upheld in air amid the gyrating wings of colossal genii ; and the whole of that old church, as tall and rich as a cathedral, seemed to sit upon the sunlit country like a cloud-burst.

"I think there is something rather dangerous about standing on these high places even to pray," said Father Brown. "Heights were made to be looked at, not to be looked from."

"Do you mean that one may fall over," asked Wilfred.

"I mean that one's soul may fall if one's body doesn't," said the other priest.

"I scarcely understand you," remarked Bohun indistinctly.

"Look at that blacksmith, for instance," went on Father Brown calmly ; "a good man, but not a Christian—hard, imperious, unforgiving. Well, his Scotch religion was made up by men who prayed on hills and high crags, and learnt to look down on the world more than to look up at heaven. Humility is the mother of giants. One sees great things from the valley ; only small things from the peak."

"But he—he didn't do it," said Bohun tremulously.

"No," said the other in an odd voice ; "we know he didn't do it."

After a moment he resumed, looking tranquilly out over the plain with his pale grey eyes. "I knew a man," he said, "who began by worshipping with others before the altar, but who grew fond of high and lonely places to pray from, corners or niches in the belfry or the spire. And once in one of those dizzy places, where the whole world seemed to turn under him like a wheel, his brain turned also, and he fancied he was God. So that though he was a good man, he committed a great crime."

Wilfred's face was turned away, but his bony hands turned blue and white as they tightened on the parapet of stone.

"He thought it was given to *him* to judge the world and strike down the sinner. He would never have had such a thought if he had been kneeling with other men upon a floor. But he saw all men walking about like insects. He saw one especially strutting just below him, insolent and evident by a bright green hat—a poisonous insect."

Rooks cawed round the corners of the belfry ; but there was no other sound till Father Brown went on.

" This also tempted him, that he had in his hand one of the most awful engines of Nature ; I mean gravitation, that mad and quickening rush by which all earth's creatures fly back to her heart when released. See, the inspector is strutting just below us in the smithy. If I were to toss a pebble over this parapet it would be something like a bullet by the time it struck him. If I were to drop a hammer—even a small hammer——"

Wilfred Bohun threw one leg over the parapet, and Father Brown had him in a minute by the collar.

" Not by that door," he said quite gently ; " that door leads to hell."

Bohun staggered back against the wall, and stared at him with frightful eyes.

" How do you know all this ? " he cried. " Are you a devil ? "

" I am a man," answered Father Brown gravely ; " and therefore have all devils in my heart. Listen to me," he said after a short pause. " I know what you did—at least, I can guess the great part of it. When you left your brother you were racked with no unrighteous rage to the extent even that you snatched up a small hammer, half inclined to kill him with his foulness on his mouth. Recoiling, you thrust it under your buttoned coat instead, and rushed into the church. You pray wildly in many places, under the angel window, upon the platform above, and on a higher platform still, from which you could see the colonel's Eastern hat like the back of a green beetle crawling about. Then something snapped in your soul, and you let God's thunderbolt fall."

Wilfred put a weak hand to his head, and asked in a low voice : " How did you know that his hat looked like a green beetle ? "

" Oh, that," said the other with the shadow of a smile, " that was common sense. But hear me further. I say I know all this ; but no one else shall know it. The next step is for you ; I shall take no more steps ; I will seal this with the seal of confession. If you ask me why, there are many reasons, and only one that concerns you. I leave things to you because you have not yet gone very far wrong, as assassins go. You did not help to fix the crime on the smith when it was easy ;

or on his wife, when that was easy. You tried to fix it on the imbecile because you knew that he could not suffer. That was one of the gleams that it is my business to find in assassins. And now come down into the village, and go your own way as free as the wind ; for I have said my last word."

They went down the winding stairs in utter silence, and came out into the sunlight by the smithy. Wilfred Bohun carefully unlatched the wooden gate of the yard, and going up to the inspector, said : " I wish to give myself up ; I have killed my brother."

THE SECRET SHARER

O N my right hand there were lines of fishing-stakes resembling a mysterious system of half-submerged bamboo fences, incomprehensible in its division of the domain of tropical fishes, and crazy of aspect as if abandoned for ever by some nomad tribe of fishermen now gone to the other end of the ocean ; for there was no sign of human habitation as far as the eye could reach. To the left a group of barren islets, suggesting ruins of stone walls, towers, and blockhouses, had its foundations set in a blue sea that itself looked solid, so still and stable did it lie below my feet ; even the track of light from the westering sun shone smoothly, without that animated glitter which tells of an imperceptible ripple. And when I turned my head to take a parting glance at the tug which had just left us anchored outside the bar, I saw the straight line of the flat shore joined to the stable sea, edge to edge, with a perfect and unmarked closeness, in one levelled floor half brown, half blue under the enormous dome of the sky. Corresponding in their insignificance to the islets of the sea, two small clumps of trees, one on each side of the only fault in the impeccable joint, marked the mouth of the river Meinam we had just left on the first preparatory stage of our homeward journey ; and, far back on the inland level, a larger and loftier mass, the grove surrounding the great Paknam pagoda, was the only thing on which the eye could rest from the vain task of exploring the monotonous sweep of the horizon. Here and there gleams as of a few scattered pieces of silver marked the windings of the great river ; and on the nearest of them, just within the bar, the tug steaming right into the land became lost to my sight, hull and funnel and masts, as though the impassive earth had swallowed her up without an effort, without a tremor. My eye followed the light cloud of her smoke, now here, now there, above the plain, according to the devious curves of the stream, but always fainter and farther away, till I lost it at last behind the mitre-shaped hill of the great pagoda. And then I was left alone with my ship, anchored at the head of the Gulf of Siam.

She floated at the starting-point of a long journey, very still in an immense stillness, the shadows of her spars flung far to the eastward by the setting sun. At that moment I was alone on her decks. There was not a sound in her—and around us nothing moved, nothing lived, not a canoe on the water, not a bird in the air, not a cloud in the sky. In this breathless pause at the threshold of a long passage we seemed to be measuring our fitness for a long and arduous enterprise, the appointed task of both our existences to be carried out, far from all human eyes, with only sky and sea for spectators and for judges.

There must have been some glare in the air to interfere with one's sight, because it was only just before the sun left us that my roaming eyes made out beyond the highest ridge of the principal islet of the group something which did away with the solemnity of perfect solitude. The tide of darkness flowed on swiftly ; and with tropical suddenness a swarm of stars came out above the shadowy earth, while I lingered yet, my hand resting lightly on my ship's rail as if on the shoulder of a trusted friend. But, with all that multitude of celestial bodies staring down at one, the comfort of quiet communion with her was gone for good. And there were also disturbing sounds by this time—voices, footsteps forward ; the steward flitted along the main-deck, a busily ministering spirit ; a hand-bell tinkled urgently under the poop-deck. . . .

I found my two officers waiting for me near the supper table, in the lighted cuddy. We sat down at once, and as I helped the chief mate, I said :

"Are you aware that there is a ship anchored inside the islands ? I saw her mastheads above the ridge as the sun went down."

He raised sharply his simple face, overcharged by a terrible growth of whisker, and emitted his usual ejaculations : " Bless my soul, sir ! You don't say so ! "

My second mate was a round-cheeked, silent young man, grave beyond his years, I thought ; but as our eyes happened to meet I detected a slight quiver on his lips. I looked down at once. It was not my part to encourage sneering on board my ship. It must be said, too, that I knew very little of my officers. In consequence of certain events of no particular significance, except to myself, I had been appointed to the command only a fortnight before. Neither did I know much of the hands forward. All these people had been together for eighteen months or so, and my position was that of the only stranger on board. I mention this because it has some bearing on what is to follow. But what I felt most was my being a stranger to the ship ; and if all the truth must be told, I was somewhat of a stranger to myself. The youngest man on board (barring the second mate), and untried as yet by a position of the fullest responsibility, I was willing to take the adequacy of the others for granted. They had simply to be equal to their tasks ; but I wondered how far I should turn out faithful to that ideal conception of one's own personality every man sets up for himself secretly.

Meantime the chief mate, with an almost visible effect of collaboration on the part of his round eyes and frightful whiskers, was trying to evolve a theory of the anchored ship. His dominant trait was to take all things into earnest consideration. He was of a painstaking turn of mind. As he used to say, he " liked to account to himself " for practically everything that came in his way, down to a miserable scorpion he had found in his cabin a week before. The why and the wherefore of that scorpion—how it got on board and came to select his room rather than the pantry (which was a dark place and more what a scorpion would be partial to), and how on earth it managed to drown itself in the ink-well of his writing-desk—had exercised him infinitely. The ship within the islands was much more easily accounted for ; and just as we were about to rise from table he made his pronouncement. She was, he doubted not, a ship from home lately arrived. Probably she drew too much water to cross the bar, except at the top of spring tides. Therefore she went into that natural harbour to wait for a few days in preference to remaining in an open roadstead.

" That's so," confirmed the second mate suddenly, in his slightly hoarse voice. " She draws over twenty feet. She's the Liverpool ship *Sephora* with a cargo of coal. Hundred and twenty-three days from Cardiff."

We looked at him in surprise.

" The tugboat skipper told me when he came on board for your letters, sir," explained the young man. " He expects to take her up the river the day after to-morrow."

After thus overwhelming us with the extent of his information he slipped out of the cabin. The mate observed regretfully that he " could not account for that young fellow's whims." What prevented him telling us all about it at once ? he wanted to know.

I detained him as he was making a move. For the last two days the crew had had plenty of hard work, and the night before they had very little sleep. I felt painfully that I—a stranger—was doing something unusual when I directed him to let all hands turn in without setting an anchor-watch. I proposed to keep on deck myself till one o'clock or thereabouts. I would get the second mate to relieve me at that hour.

" He will turn out the cook and the steward at four," I concluded, " and then give you a call. Of course at the slightest sign of any sort of wind we'll have the hands up and make a start at once."

He concealed his astonishment. " Very well, sir." Outside the cuddy he put his head in the second mate's door to inform him of my unheard-of caprice to take a five hours' anchor-watch on myself. I heard the other raise his voice incredulously —" What ? The captain himself ? " Then a few more murmurs, a door closed, then another. A few moments later I went on deck.

My strangeness, which had made me sleepless, had prompted that unconventional arrangement, as if I had expected in those solitary hours of the night to get on terms with the ship of which I knew nothing, manned by men of whom I knew very little more. Fast alongside a wharf, littered like any ship in port with a tangle of unrelated things, invaded by unrelated shore people, I had hardly seen her yet properly. Now, as she lay cleared for sea, the stretch of her main-deck seemed to me very fine under the stars. Very fine, very roomy for her size, and very inviting. I descended the poop and paced the waist, my mind picturing to myself the coming passage through the Malay Archipelago, down the Indian Ocean, and up the Atlantic. All its phases were familiar enough to me, every characteristic, all the alternatives which were likely to face me on the high seas—everything ! . . . except the novel responsibility of command. But I took heart from the reasonable thought that the ship was like other ships, the men like other men, and that the sea was not likely to keep any special surprises expressly for my discomfiture.

Arrived at that comforting conclusion, I bethought myself of a cigar and went below to get it. All was still down there.

Everybody at the after end of the ship was sleeping profoundly.
I came out again on the quarter-deck, agreeably at ease in my
sleeping-suit on that warm breathless night, barefooted, a
glowing cigar in my teeth, and, going forward, I was met by
the profound silence of the fore end of the ship.   Only as I
passed the door of the forecastle I heard a deep, quiet, trustful
sigh of some sleeper inside.   And suddenly I rejoiced in the
great security of the sea as compared with the unrest of the
land, in my choice of that untempted life presenting no dis-
quieting problems, invested with an elementary moral beauty
by the absolute straightforwardness of its appeal and by the
singleness of its purpose.

The riding-light in the fore-rigging burned with a clear,
untroubled, as if symbolic, flame, confident and bright in the
mysterious shades of the night.   Passing on my way aft along
the other side of the ship, I observed that the rope side-ladder,
put over, no doubt, for the master of the tug when he came to
fetch away our letters, had not been hauled in as it should
have been.   I became annoyed at this, for exactitude in small
matters is the very soul of discipline.   Then I reflected that I
had myself peremptorily dismissed my officers from duty, and
by my own act had prevented the anchor-watch being formally
set and things properly attended to.   I asked myself whether
it was wise ever to interfere with the established routine of
duties even from the kindest of motives.   My action might
have made me appear eccentric.   Goodness only knew how
that absurdly whiskered mate would " account " for my
conduct, and what the whole ship thought of that informality
of their new captain.   I was vexed with myself.

Not from compunction certainly, but, as it were mechanically, I proceeded to get the ladder in myself.   Now a side-
ladder of that sort is a light affair and comes in easily, yet my
vigorous tug, which should have brought it flying on board,
merely recoiled upon my body in a totally unexpected jerk.
What the devil ! . . . I was so astounded by the immovable-
ness of that ladder that I remained stock-still, trying to account
for it to myself like that imbecile mate of mine.   In the end, of
course, I put my head over the rail.

The side of the ship made an opaque belt of shadow on
the darkling glassy shimmer of the sea.   But I saw at once
something elongated and pale floating very close to the ladder.
Before I could form a guess a faint flash of phosphorescent
light, which seemed to issue suddenly from the naked body of
a man, flickered in the sleeping water with the elusive, silent

play of summer lightning in a night sky. With a gasp I saw revealed to my stare a pair of feet, the long legs, a broad livid back immersed right up to the neck in a greenish cadaverous glow. One hand, awash, clutched the bottom rung of the ladder. He was complete but for the head. A headless corpse ! The cigar dropped out of my gaping mouth with a tiny plop and a short hiss quite audible in the absolute stillness of all things under heaven. At that I suppose he raised up his face, a dimly pale oval in the shadow of the ship's side. But even then I could only barely make out down there the shape of his black-haired head. However, it was enough for the horrid, frost-bound sensation which had gripped me about the chest to pass off. The moment of vain exclamations was past, too. I only climbed on the spare spar and leaned over the rail as far as I could, to bring my eyes nearer to that mystery floating alongside.

As he hung by the ladder, like a resting swimmer, the sea-lightning played about his limbs at every stir ; and he appeared in it ghastly, silvery, fish-like. He remained as mute as a fish, too. He made no motion to get out of the water, either. It was inconceivable that he should not attempt to come on board, and strangely troubling to suspect that perhaps he did not want to. And my first words were prompted by just that troubled incertitude.

" What's the matter ? " I asked in my ordinary tone, speaking down to the face upturned exactly under mine.

" Cramp," it answered, no louder. Then slightly anxious, " I say, no need to call any one."

" I was not going to," I said.

" Are you alone on deck ? "

" Yes."

I had somehow the impression that he was on the point of letting go the ladder to swim away beyond my ken—mysterious as he came. But, for the moment, this being appearing as if he had risen from the bottom of the sea (it was certainly the nearest land to the ship) wanted only to know the time. I told him. And he, down there, tentatively :

" I suppose your captain's turned in ? "

" I am sure he isn't," I said.

He seemed to struggle with himself, for I heard something like the low, bitter murmur of doubt. " What's the good ? " His next words came out with a hesitating effort.

" Look here, my man. Could you call him out quietly ? "

I thought the time had come to declare myself.

" *I* am the captain."

I heard a " By Jove ! " whispered at the level of the water. The phosphorescence flashed in the swirl of the water all about his limbs, his other hand seized the ladder.

" My name's Leggatt."

The voice was calm and resolute. A good voice. The self-possession of that man had somehow induced a corresponding state in myself. It was very quietly that I remarked :

" You must be a good swimmer."

" Yes. I've been in the water practically since nine o'clock. The question for me now is whether I am to let go this ladder and go on swimming till I sink from exhaustion, or—to come on board here."

I felt this was no mere formula of desperate speech, but a real alternative in the view of a strong soul. I should have gathered from this that he was young ; indeed, it is only the young who are ever confronted by such clear issues. But at the time it was pure intuition on my part. A mysterious communication was established already between us two—in the face of that silent, darkened tropical sea. I was young, too ; young enough to make no comment. The man in the water began suddenly to climb up the ladder, and I hastened away from the rail to fetch some clothes.

Before entering the cabin I stood still, listening in the lobby at the foot of the stairs. A faint snore came through the closed door of the chief mate's room. The second mate's door was on the hook, but the darkness in there was absolutely soundless. He, too, was young and could sleep like a stone. Remained the steward, but he was not likely to wake up before he was called. I got a sleeping-suit out of my room and, coming back on deck, saw the naked man from the sea sitting on the main-hatch, glimmering white in the darkness, his elbows on his knees and his head in his hands. In a moment he had concealed his damp body in a sleeping-suit of the same grey-stripe pattern as the one I was wearing and followed me like my double on the poop. Together we moved right aft, barefooted, silent.

" What is it ? " I asked in a deadened voice, taking the lighted lamp out of the binnacle and raising it to his face.

" An ugly business."

He had rather regular features ; a good mouth ; light eyes under somewhat heavy, dark eyebrows ; a smooth, square forehead ; no growth on his cheeks ; a small brown moustache, and a well-shaped, round chin. His expression was concentrated, meditative, under the inspecting light of the lamp I held up to his face ; such as a man thinking hard in solitude might wear. My sleeping-suit was just right for his size. A well-knit young fellow of twenty-five at most. He caught his lower lip with the edge of white, even teeth.

" Yes," I said, replacing the lamp in the binnacle. The warm, heavy tropical night closed upon his head again.

" There's a ship over there," he murmured.

" Yes, I know. The *Sephora*. Did you know of us ? "

" Hadn't the slightest idea. I am the mate of her——" He paused and corrected himself. " I should say I *was*."

" Aha ! Something wrong ? "

" Yes. Very wrong indeed. I've killed a man."

" What do you mean ? Just now ? "

" No, on the passage. Weeks ago. Thirty-nine south. When I say a man——"

" Fit of temper," I suggested, confidently.

The shadowy, dark head, like mine, seemed to nod imperceptibly above the ghostly grey of my sleeping-suit. It was, in the night, as though I had been faced by my own reflection in the depths of a sombre and immense mirror.

" A pretty thing to have to own up to for a Conway boy," murmured my double, distinctly.

" You're a Conway boy ? "

" I am," he said, as if startled. Then, slowly . . . " Perhaps you too——"

It was so ; but being a couple of years older I had left before he joined. After a quick interchange of dates a silence fell ; and I thought suddenly of my absurd mate with his terrific whiskers and the " Bless my soul—you don't say so " type of intellect. My double gave me an inkling of his thoughts by saying :

" My father's a parson in Norfolk. Do you see me before a judge and jury on that charge ? For myself I can't see the necessity. There are fellows that an angel from heaven—— And I am not that. He was one of those creatures that are just simmering all the time with a silly sort of wickedness. Miserable devils that have no business to live at all. He wouldn't do his duty and wouldn't let anybody else do theirs. But what's the good of talking ! You know well enough the sort of ill-conditioned snarling cur——"

He appealed to me as if our experiences had been as identical as our clothes. And I knew well enough the pestiferous danger of such a character where there are no means of legal repression. And I knew well enough also that my double there was no homicidal ruffian. I did not think of asking him for details, and he told me the story roughly in brusque, disconnected sentences. I needed no more. I saw it all going on as though I were myself inside that other sleeping-suit.

" It happened while we were setting a reefed foresail, at dusk. Reefed foresail ! You understand the sort of weather. The only sail we had left to keep the ship running ; so you may guess what it had been like for days. Anxious sort of job, that. He gave me some of his cursed insolence at the sheet. I tell you I was overdone with this terrific weather that seemed to have no end to it. Terrific, I tell you—and a deep ship. I believe the fellow himself was half crazed with funk. It was no time for gentlemanly reproof, so I turned round and felled him like an ox. He up and at me. We closed just as an awful sea made for the ship. All hands saw it coming and took to the rigging, but I had him by the throat, and went on shaking him like a rat, the men above us yelling, Look out ! look out ! ' Then a crash as if the sky had fallen on my head. They say that for over ten minutes hardly anything was to be seen of the ship—just the three masts and a bit of the forecastle head and of the poop all awash driving along in a smother of foam. It was a miracle that they found us, jammed together behind the forebits. It's clear that I meant business, because I was holding him by the throat still when they picked us up. He was black in the face. It was too much for them. It seems they rushed us aft together, gripped as we were, screaming ' Murder ! ' like a lot of lunatics, and broke into the cuddy. And the ship running for her life, touch and go all the time, any minute her last in a sea fit to turn your hair grey only a-looking at it. I understand that the skipper, too, started raving like the rest of them. The man had been deprived of sleep for more than a week, and to have this sprung on him at the height of a furious gale nearly drove him out of his mind. I wonder they didn't fling me overboard after getting the carcase of their precious shipmate out of my fingers. They had rather a job to separate us, I've been told. A sufficiently fierce story to make an old judge and a respectable jury sit up a bit. The first thing I heard when I came to myself was the maddening howling of that endless gale, and on that the voice of the old man. He was hanging on to my bunk, staring into my face out of his sou'-wester.

"'Mr. Leggatt, you have killed a man. You can act no longer as chief mate of this ship.'"

His care to subdue his voice made it sound monotonous. He rested a hand on the end of the skylight to steady himself with, and all that time did not stir a limb, so far as I could see. "Nice little tale for a quiet tea-party," he concluded in the same tone.

One of my hands, too, rested on the end of the skylight; neither did I stir a limb, so far as I knew. We stood less than a foot from each other. It occurred to me that if old "Bless my soul—you don't say so" were to put his head up the companion and catch sight of us, he would think he was seeing double, or imagine himself come upon a scene of weird witchcraft; the strange captain having a quiet confabulation by the wheel with his own grey ghost. I became very much concerned to prevent anything of the sort. I heard the other's soothing undertone.

"My father's a parson in Norfolk," it said. Evidently he had forgotten he had told me this important fact before. Truly a nice little tale.

"You had better slip down into my stateroom now," I said, moving off stealthily. My double followed my movements; our bare feet made no sound; I let him in, closed the door with care, and, after giving a call to the second mate, returned on deck for my relief.

"Not much sign of any wind yet," I remarked when he approached.

"No, sir. Not much," he assented, sleepily, in his hoarse voice, with just enough deference, no more, and barely suppressing a yawn.

"Well, that's all you have to look out for. You have got your orders."

"Yes, sir."

I paced a turn or two on the poop and saw him take up his position face forward with his elbow in the rat-lines of the mizzen-rigging before I went below. The mate's faint snoring was still going on peacefully. The cuddy lamp was burning over the table on which stood a vase with flowers, a polite attention from the ship's provision merchant—the last flowers we should see for the next three months at the very least. Two bunches of bananas hung from the beam symmetrically, one on each side of the rudder-casing. Everything was as before in the ship—except that two of her captain's sleeping-suits were simultaneously in use, one motionless in the cuddy, the other keeping very still in the captain's stateroom.

It must be explained here that my cabin had the form of the capital letter L, the door being within the angle and opening into the short part of the letter. A couch was to the left, the bed-place to the right ; my writing-desk and the chronometers' table faced the door. But any one opening it, unless he stepped right inside, had no view of what I call the long (or vertical) part of the letter. It contained some lockers surmounted by a bookcase ; and few clothes, a thick jacket or two, caps, oilskin coat, and such-like, hung on hooks. There was at the bottom of that part a door opening into my bathroom, which could be entered also directly from the saloon. But that way was never used.

The mysterious arrival had discovered the advantage of this particular shape. Entering my room, lighted strongly by a big bulkhead lamp swung on gimbals above my writing-desk, I did not see him anywhere till he stepped out quietly from behind the coats hung in the recessed part.

" I heard somebody moving about, and went in there at once," he whispered.

I, too, spoke under my breath.

" Nobody is likely to come in here without knocking and getting permission."

He nodded. His face was thin and the sunburn faded, as though he had been ill. And no wonder. He had been, I heard presently, kept under arrest in his cabin for nearly seven weeks. But there was nothing sickly in his eyes or in his expression. He was not a bit like me, really ; yet, as we stood leaning over my bed-place, whispering side by side, with our dark heads together and our backs to the door, anybody bold enough to open it stealthily would have been treated to the uncanny sight of a double captain busy talking in whispers with his other self.

" But all this doesn't tell me how you came to hang on to our side-ladder," I inquired, in the hardly audible murmurs we used, after he had told me something more of the proceedings on board the *Sephora* once the bad weather was over.

" When we sighted Java Head I had had time to think all those matters out several times over. I had six weeks of doing nothing else, and with only an hour or so every evening for a tramp on the quarter-deck."

He whispered, his arms folded on the side of my bed-place, staring through the open port. And I could imagine perfectly the manner of this thinking out—a stubborn if not a steadfast operation; something of which I should have been perfectly incapable.

"I reckoned it would be dark before we closed with the land," he continued, so low that I had to strain my hearing, near as we were to each other, shoulder touching shoulder almost. "So I asked to speak to the old man. He always seemed very sick when he came to see me—as if he could not look me in the face. You know, that foresail saved the ship. She was too deep to have run long under bare poles. And it was I that managed to set it for him. Anyway, he came. When I had him in my cabin—he stood by the door looking at me as if I had the halter round my neck already—I asked him right away to leave my cabin door unlocked at night while the ship was going through Sunda Straits. There would be the Java coast within two or three miles, off Angier Point. I wanted nothing more. I've had a prize for swimming my second year in the Conway."

"I can believe it," I breathed out.

"God only knows why they locked me in every night. To see some of their faces you'd have thought they were afraid I'd go about at night strangling people. Am I a murdering brute? Do I look it? By Jove! if I had been, he wouldn't have trusted himself like that into my room. You'll say I might have chucked him aside and bolted out, there and then—it was dark already. Well, no. And for the same reason I wouldn't think of trying to smash the door. There would have been a rush to stop me at the noise, and I did not mean to get into a confounded scrimmage. Somebody else might have got killed—for I would not have broken out only to get chucked back, and I did not want any more of that work. He refused, looking more sick than ever. He was afraid of the men, and also of that old second mate of his who had been sailing with him for years—a grey-headed old humbug; and his steward, too, had been with him devil knows how long—seventeen years or more—a dogmatic sort of loafer who hated me like poison, just because I was the chief mate. No chief mate ever made more than one voyage in the *Sephora*, you know. Those two old chaps ran the ship. Devil only knows what the skipper wasn't afraid of (all his nerve went to pieces altogether in that hellish spell of bad weather we had)—of what the law would do to him—of his wife, perhaps. Oh yes! she's on board. Though I don't think she would have meddled. She would have been only

too glad to have me out of the ship in any way.   The ' brand of
Cain ' business, don't you see.   That's all right.   I was ready
enough to go off wandering on the face of the earth—and
that was price enough to pay for an Abel of that sort.   Anyhow,
he wouldn't listen to me.   ' This thing must take its course.
I represent the law here.'   He was shaking like a leaf.   ' So
you won't ? '   ' No ! '   ' Then I hope you will be able to
sleep on that,' I said, and turned my back on him.   ' I wonder
that *you* can,' cries he, and locks the door.

     " Well, after that, I couldn't.   Not very well.   That was
three weeks ago.   We have had a slow passage through the
Java Sea ;   drifted about Carimata for ten days.   When we
anchored here they thought, I suppose, it was all right.   The
nearest land (and that's five miles) is the ship's destination ;
the consul would soon set about catching me ;   and there
would have been no object in bolting to these islets there.   I
don't suppose there's a drop of water on them.   I don't know
how it was, but to-night that steward, after bringing me my
supper, went out to let me eat it, and left the door unlocked.
And I ate it—all there was, too.   After I had finished I strolled
out on the quarter-deck.   I don't know that I meant doing
anything.   A breath of fresh air was all I wanted, I believe.
Then a sudden temptation came over me.   I kicked off my
slippers and was in the water before I had made up my mind
fairly.   Somebody heard the splash and they raised an awful
hullabaloo.   ' He's gone ! Lower the boats ! He's committed suicide ! No, he's swimming.'   Certainly I was
swimming.   It's not so easy for a swimmer like me to commit
suicide by drowning.   I landed on the nearest islet before the
boat left the ship's side.   I heard them pulling about in the
dark, hailing, and so on, but after a bit they gave up.   Everything quieted down and the anchorage became as still as death.
I sat down on a stone and began to think.   I felt certain they
would start searching for me at daylight.   There was no place
to hide on those stony things—and if there had been, what
would have been the good ?   But now I was clear of that ship,
I was not going back.   So after a while I took off all my
clothes, tied them up in a bundle with a stone inside, and
dropped them in the deep water on the outer side of that islet.
That was suicide enough for me.   Let them think what they
liked, but I didn't mean to drown myself.   I meant to swim
till I sank—but that's not the same thing.   I stuck out for
another of these little islands, and it was from that one that I
first saw your riding-light.   Something to swim for.   I went

on easily, and on the way I came upon a flat rock a foot or two above water. In the daytime, I dare say, you might make it out with a glass from your poop. I scrambled up on it and rested myself for a bit. Then I made another start. That last spell must have been over a mile."

His whisper was getting fainter and fainter, and all the time he stared straight out through the port-hole, in which there was not even a star to be seen. I had not interrupted him. There was something that made comment impossible in his narrative, or perhaps in himself; a sort of feeling, a quality, which I can't find a name for. And when he ceased, all I found was a futile whisper: " So you swam for our light ? "

" Yes—straight for it. It was something to swim for. I couldn't see any stars low down because the coast was in the way, and I couldn't see the land, either. The water was like glass. One might have been swimming in a confounded thousand-feet deep cistern with no place for scrambling out anywhere ; but what I didn't like was the notion of swimming round and round like a crazed bullock before I gave out ; and as I didn't mean to go back . . . No. Do you see me being hauled back, stark naked, off one of these little islands by the scruff of the neck and fighting like a wild beast ?   Somebody would have got killed for certain, and I did not want any of that. So I went on. Then your ladder——"

" Why didn't you hail the ship ? " I asked, a little louder.

He touched my shoulder lightly. Lazy footsteps came right over our heads and stopped. The second mate had crossed from the other side of the poop and might have been hanging over the rail, for all we knew.

" He couldn't hear us talking—could he ? " my double breathed into my very ear, anxiously.

His anxiety was an answer, a sufficient answer, to the question I had put to him. An answer containing all the difficulty of that situation. I closed the port-hole quietly, to make sure. A louder word might have been overheard.

" Who's that ? " he whispered then.

" My second mate. But I don't know much more of the fellow than you do."

And I told him a little about myself. I had been appointed to take charge while I least expected anything of the sort, not quite a fortnight ago. I didn't know either the ship or the people. Hadn't had the time in port to look about me or size anybody up. And as to the crew, all they knew was that I was appointed to take the ship home. For the rest, I was almost as much of a stranger on board as himself, I said. And at the moment I felt it most acutely. I felt that it would take very little to make me a suspect person in the eyes of the ship's company.

He had turned about meantime ; and we, the two strangers in the ship, faced each other in identical attitudes.

" Your ladder——" he murmured, after a silence. " Who'd have thought of finding a ladder hanging over at night in a ship anchored out here ! I felt just then a very unpleasant faintness. After the life I've been leading for nine weeks, anybody would have got out of condition. I wasn't capable of swimming round as far as your rudder-chains. And, lo and behold ! there was a ladder to get hold of. After I gripped it I said to myself, ' What's the good ? ' When I saw a man's head looking over I thought I would swim away presently and leave him shouting—in whatever language it was. I didn't mind being looked at. I—I liked it. And then you speaking to me so quietly—as if you had expected me—made me hold on a little longer. It had been a confounded lonely time—I don't mean while swimming. I was glad to talk a little to somebody that didn't belong to the *Sephora*. As to asking for the captain, that was a mere impulse. It could have been no use, with all the ship knowing about me and the other people pretty certain to be round here in the morning. I don't know—I wanted to be seen, to talk with somebody, before I went on. I don't know what I would have said. . . . ' Fine night, isn't it ? ' or something of the sort."

" Do you think they will be round here presently ? " I asked with some incredulity.

" Quite likely," he said faintly.

He looked extremely haggard all of a sudden. His head rolled on his shoulders.

" H'm. We shall see then. Meantime get into that bed," I whispered. " Want help ? There."

It was a rather high bed-place with a set of drawers underneath. This amazing swimmer really needed the lift I gave him by seizing his leg. He tumbled in, rolled over on his back, and flung one arm across his eyes. And then, with his face nearly hidden, he must have looked exactly as I used to look in that bed. I gazed upon my other self for a while before drawing across carefully the two green serge curtains which ran on a brass rod. I thought for a moment of pinning them together for greater safety, but I sat down on the couch, and once there I felt unwilling to rise and hunt for a pin. I would do it in a moment. I was extremely tired, in a peculiarly intimate way, by the strain of stealthiness, by the effort of whispering and the general secrecy of this excitement. It was three o'clock by now and I had been on my feet since nine, but I was not sleepy ; I could not have gone to sleep. I sat there, fagged out, looking at the curtains, trying to clear my mind of the confused sensation of being in two places at once, and greatly bothered by an exasperating knocking in my head. It was a relief to discover suddenly that it was not my head at all, but on the outside of the door. Before I could collect myself the words " Come in " were out of my mouth, and the steward entered with a tray, bringing in my morning coffee. I had slept, after all, and I was so frightened that I shouted, " This way ! I am here, steward," as though he had been miles away. He put down the tray on the table next the couch and only then said, very quietly, " I can see you are here, sir." I felt him give me a keen look, but I dared not meet his eyes just then. He must have wondered why I had drawn the curtains of my bed before going to sleep on the couch. He went out, hooking the door open as usual.

I heard the crew washing decks above me. I knew I would have been told at once if there had been any wind. Calm, I thought, and I was doubly vexed. Indeed, I felt dual more than ever. The steward reappeared suddenly in the doorway. I jumped up from the couch so quickly that he gave a start.

" What do you want here ? "

" Close your port, sir—they are washing decks."

" It is closed," I said, reddening.

" Very well, sir." But he did not move from the doorway and returned my stare in an extraordinary, equivocal manner for a time. Then his eyes wavered, all his expression changed, and in a voice unusually gentle, almost coaxingly :

" May I come in to take the empty cup away, sir ? "

" Of course ! " I turned my back on him while he popped in and out. Then I unhooked and closed the door and even pushed the bolt. This sort of thing could not go on very long. The cabin was as hot as an oven, too. I took a peep at my double, and discovered that he had not moved, his arm was still over his eyes ; but his chest heaved ; his hair was wet ; his chin glistened with perspiration. I reached over him and opened the port.

" I must show myself on deck," I reflected.

Of course, theoretically, I could do what I liked, with no one to say nay to me within the whole circle of the horizon ; but to lock my cabin door and take the key away I did not dare. Directly I put my head out of the companion I saw the group of my two officers, the second mate barefooted, the chief mate in long indiarubber boots, near the break of the poop, and the steward half-way down the poop-ladder talking to them eagerly. He happened to catch sight of me and dived, the second ran down on the main-deck shouting some order or other, and the chief mate came to meet me, touching his cap.

There was a sort of curiosity in his eye that I did not like. I don't know whether the steward had told them that I was " queer " only, or downright drunk, but I know the man meant to have a good look at me. I watched him coming with a smile which, as he got into point-blank range, took effect and froze his very whiskers. I did not give him time to open his lips.

" Square the yards by lifts and braces before the hands go to breakfast."

It was the first particular order I had given on board that ship ; and I stayed on deck to see it executed, too. I had felt the need of asserting myself without loss of time. That sneering young cub got taken down a peg or two on that occasion, and I also seized the opportunity of having a good look at the face of every foremast man as they filed past me to go to the afterbraces. At breakfast-time, eating nothing myself, I presided with such frigid dignity that the two mates were only too glad to escape from the cabin as soon as decency permitted ; and all the time the dual working of my mind distracted me almost to the point of insanity. I was constantly watching myself, my secret self, as dependent on my actions as my own personality, sleeping in that bed, behind that door which faced me as I sat at the head of the table. It was very much like being mad, only it was worse because one was aware of it.

I had to shake him for a solid minute, but when at last he opened his eyes it was in the full possession of his senses, with an inquiring look.

" All's well so far," I whispered. " Now you must vanish into the bathroom."

He did so, as noiseless as a ghost, and I then rang for the steward, and facing him boldly, directed him to tidy up my stateroom while I was having my bath—" and be quick about it." As my tone admitted of no excuses, he said, "Yes, sir," and ran off to fetch his dust-pan and brushes. I took a bath and did most of my dressing, splashing, and whistling softly for the steward's edification, while the secret sharer of my life stood drawn up bolt upright in that little space, his face looking very sunken in daylight, his eyelids lowered under the stern, dark line of his eyebrows drawn together by a slight frown.

When I left him there to go back to my room the steward was finishing dusting. I sent for the mate and engaged him in some insignificant conversation. It was, as it were, trifling with the terrific character of his whiskers ; but my object was to give him an opportunity for a good look at my cabin. And then I could at last shut, with a clear conscience, the door of my stateroom and get my double back into the recessed part. There was nothing else for it. He had to sit still on a small folding-stool, half smothered by the heavy coats hanging there. We listened to the steward going into the bathroom out of the saloon, filling the water-bottles there, scrubbing the bath, setting things to rights, whisk, bang, clatter—out again into the saloon—turn the key—click. Such was my scheme for keeping my second self invisible. Nothing better could be contrived under the circumstances. And there we sat ; I at my writing-desk ready to appear busy with some papers, he behind me, out of sight of the door. It would not have been prudent to talk in daytime ; and I could not have stood the excitement of that queer sense of whispering to myself. Now and then, glancing over my shoulder, I saw him far back there, sitting rigidly on the low stool, his bare feet close together, his arms folded, his head hanging on his breast—and perfectly still. Anybody would have taken him for me.

I was fascinated by it myself. Every moment I had to glance over my shoulder. I was looking at him when a voice outside the door said :

" Beg pardon, sir."

" Well ! " . . . I kept my eyes on him, and so, when the voice outside the door announced, " There's a ship's boat coming our way, sir," I saw him give a start—the first movement he had made for hours. But he did not raise his bowed head.

" All right. Get the ladder over."

I hesitated. Should I whisper something to him ? But what ? His immobility seemed to have been never disturbed. What could I tell him he did not know already ? . . . Finally I went on deck.

II

THE skipper of the *Sephora* had a thin red whisker all round his face, and the sort of complexion that goes with hair of that colour ; also the particular, rather smeary shade of blue in the eyes. He was not exactly a showy figure ; his shoulders were high, his stature but middling—one leg slightly more bandy than the other. He shook hands, looking vaguely around. A spiritless tenacity was his main characteristic, I judged. I behaved with a politeness which seemed to disconcert him. Perhaps he was shy. He mumbled to me as if he were ashamed of what he was saying ; gave his name (it was something like Archbold—but at this distance of years I hardly am sure), his ship's name, and a few other particulars of that sort, in the manner of a criminal making a reluctant and doleful confession. He had had terrible weather on the passage out—terrible—terrible—wife aboard, too.

By this time we were seated in the cabin and the steward brought in a tray with a bottle and glasses. " Thanks ! No." Never took liquor. Would have some water, though. He drank two tumblerfuls. Terrible thirsty work. Ever since daylight had been exploring the islands round his ship.

" What was that for—fun ? " I asked, with an appearance of polite interest.

" No ! " He sighed. " Painful duty."

As he persisted in his mumbling and I wanted my double to hear every word, I hit upon the notion of informing him that I regretted to say I was hard of hearing.

" Such a young man, too ! " he nodded, keeping his smeary blue, unintelligent eyes fastened upon me. What was the cause of it—some disease ? he inquired, without the least sympathy and as if he thought that, if so, I'd got no more than I deserved.

" Yes ; disease," I admitted in a cheerful tone which seemed to shock him. But my point was gained, because ᴋe had to raise his voice to give me his tale. It is not worth while to record that version. It was just over two months since all this had happened, and he had thought so much about it that he seemed completely muddled as to its bearings, but still immensely impressed.

" What would you think of such a thing happening on board your own ship ? I've had the *Sephora* for these fifteen years. I am a well-known shipmaster."

He was densely distressed—and perhaps I should have sympathized with him if I had been able to detach my mental vision from the unsuspected sharer of my cabin as though he were my second self. There he was on the other side of the bulkhead, four or five feet from us, no more, as we sat in the saloon. I looked politely at Captain Archbold (if that was his name), but it was the other I saw, in a grey sleeping-suit, seated on a low stool, his bare feet close together, his arms folded, and every word said between us falling into the ears of his dark head bowed on his chest.

"I have been at sea now, man and boy, for seven-and-thirty years, and I've never heard of such a thing happening in an English ship. And that it should be my ship. Wife on board, too."

I was hardly listening to him.

"Don't you think," I said, "that the heavy sea which, you told me, came aboard just then might have killed the man ? I have seen the sheer weight of a sea kill a man very neatly, by simply breaking his neck."

"Good God !" he uttered impressively, fixing his smeary blue eyes on me. "The sea ! No man killed by the sea ever looked like that." He seemed positively scandalized at my suggestion. And as I gazed at him, certainly not prepared for anything original on his part, he advanced his head close to mine and thrust his tongue out at me so suddenly that I couldn't help starting back.

After scoring over my calmness in this graphic way he nodded wisely. If I had seen the sight, he assured me, I would never forget it as long as I lived. The weather was too bad to give the corpse a proper sea burial. So next day at dawn they took it up on the poop, covering its face with a bit of bunting ; he read a short prayer, and then, just as it was, in its oilskins and long boots, they launched it amongst those mountainous seas that seemed ready every moment to swallow up the ship herself and the terrified lives on board of her.

"That reefed foresail saved you," I threw in.

"Under God—it did," he exclaimed fervently. "It was by a special mercy, I firmly believe, that it stood some of those hurricane squalls."

"It was the setting of that sail which——" I began.

"God's own hand in it," he interrupted me. "Nothing less could have done it. I don't mind telling you that I hardly dared give the order. It seemed impossible that we could touch anything without losing it, and then our last hope would have been gone."

The terror of that gale was on him yet. I let him go on for a bit, then said, casually—as if returning to a minor subject :

" You were very anxious to give up your mate to the shore people, I believe ? "

He was. To the law. His obscure tenacity on that point had in it something incomprehensible and a little awful ; something, as it were, mystical, quite apart from his anxiety that he should not be suspected of " countenancing any doings of that sort." Seven-and-thirty virtuous years at sea, of which over twenty of immaculate command, and the last fifteen in the *Sephora*, seemed to have laid him under some pitiless obligation.

" And you know," he went on, groping shamefacedly amongst his feelings, " I did not engage that young fellow. His people had some interest with my owners. I was in a way forced to take him on. He looked very smart, very gentlemanly, and all that. But do you know—I never liked him, somehow. I am a plain man. You see, he wasn't exactly the sort for the chief mate of a ship like the *Sephora*."

I had become so connected in thoughts and impressions with the secret sharer of my cabin, that I felt as if I, personally, were being given to understand that I, too, was not the sort that would have done for the chief mate of a ship like the *Sephora*. I had no doubt of it in my mind.

" Not at all the style of man. You understand," he insisted superfluously, looking hard at me.

I smiled urbanely. He seemed at a loss for a while.

" I suppose I must report a suicide."

" Beg pardon ? "

" Sui-cide ! That's what I'll have to write to my owners directly I get in."

" Unless you manage to recover him before to-morrow," I assented dispassionately. . . . " I mean, alive."

He mumbled something which I really did not catch, and I turned my ear to him in a puzzled manner. He fairly bawled :

" The land—I say, the mainland is at least seven miles off my anchorage."

" About that."

My lack of excitement, of curiosity, of surprise, of any sort of pronounced interest, began to arouse his distrust. But except for the felicitous pretence of deafness I had not tried to pretend anything. I had felt utterly incapable of playing the part of ignorance properly, and therefore was afraid to try. It is also certain that he had brought some ready-made suspicions with him, and that he viewed my politeness as a strange and unnatural phenomenon. And yet how else could I have received him ? Not heartily ! That was impossible for psychological reasons, which I need not state here. My only object was to keep off his inquiries. Surlily ? Yes, but surliness might have provoked a point-blank question. From its novelty to him and from its nature, punctilious courtesy was the manner best calculated to restrain the man. But there was the danger of his breaking through my defence bluntly. I could not, I think, have met him by a direct lie, also for psychological (not moral) reasons. If he had only known how afraid I was of his putting my feeling of identity with the other to the test ! But, strangely enough— I thought of it only afterward—I believe that he was not a little disconcerted by the reverse side of that weird situation, by something in me that reminded him of the man he was seeking —suggested a mysterious similitude to the young fellow he had distrusted and disliked from the first.

However that might have been, the silence was not very prolonged. He took another oblique step.

" I reckon I had no more than a two-mile pull to your ship. Not a bit more."

" And quite enough, too, in this awful heat," I said.

Another pause full of mistrust followed. Necessity, they say, is mother of invention, but fear, too, is not barren of ingenious suggestions. And I was afraid he would ask me point-blank for news of my other self.

" Nice little saloon, isn't it ? " I remarked, as if noticing for the first time the way his eyes roamed from one closed door to the other. " And very well fitted out, too. Here, for instance," I continued, reaching over the back of my seat negligently and flinging the door open, " is my bathroom."

He made an eager movement, but hardly gave it a glance. I got up, shut the door of the bathroom, and invited him to have a look round, as if I were very proud of my accommodation. He had to rise and be shown round, but he went through the business without any raptures whatever.

" And now we'll have a look at my stateroom," I declared, in a voice as loud as I dared to make it, crossing the cabin to the starboard side with purposely heavy steps.

He followed me in and gazed around. My intelligent double had vanished. I played my part.

"Very convenient—isn't it ? "

"Very nice. Very comf . . ." He didn't finish, and went out brusquely as if to escape from some unrighteous wiles of mine. But it was not to be. I had been too frightened not to feel vengeful ; I felt I had him on the run, and I meant to keep him on the run. My polite insistence must have had something menacing in it, because he gave in suddenly. And I did not let him off a single item ; mate's room, pantry, storerooms, the very sail-locker which was also under the poop—he had to look into them all. When at last I showed him out on the quarter-deck he drew a long, spiritless sigh, and mumbled dismally that he must really be going back to his ship now. I desired my mate, who had joined us, to see to the captain's boat.

The man of whiskers gave a blast on the whistle which he used to wear hanging round his neck, and yelled, " *Sephoras* away ! " My double down there in my cabin must have heard, and certainly could not feel more relieved than I. Four fellows came running out from somewhere forward and went over the side, while my own men, appearing on deck too, lined the rail. I escorted my visitor to the gangway ceremoniously, and nearly overdid it. He was a tenacious beast. On the very ladder he lingered, and in that unique, guiltily conscientious manner of sticking to the point :

"I say . . . you . . . you don't think that——"

I covered his voice loudly :

"Certainly not. . . . I am delighted. Good-bye."

I had an idea of what he meant to say, and just saved myself by the privilege of defective hearing. He was too shaken generally to insist, but my mate, close witness of that parting, looked mystified and his face took on a thoughtful cast. As I did not want to appear as if I wished to avoid all communication with my officers, he had the opportunity to address me.

"Seems a very nice man. His boat's crew told our chaps a very extraordinary story, if what I am told by the steward is true. I suppose you had it from the captain, sir ? "

"Yes. I had a story from the captain."

"A very horrible affair—isn't it, sir ? "

"It is."

"Beats all these tales we hear about murders in Yankee ships."

" I don't think it beats them. I don't think it resembles them in the least."

" Bless my soul—you don't say so ! But of course I've no acquaintance whatever with American ships, not I, so I couldn't go against your knowledge. It's horrible enough for me. . . . But the queerest part is that those fellows seemed to have some idea the man was hidden aboard here. They had really. Did you ever hear of such a thing ? "

" Preposterous—isn't it ? "

We were walking to and fro athwart the quarter-deck. No one of the crew forward could be seen (the day was Sunday), and the mate pursued :

" There was some little dispute about it. Our chaps took offence. ' As if we would harbour a thing like that,' they said. ' Wouldn't you like to look for him in our coal-hole ? ' Quite a tiff. But they made it up in the end. I suppose he did drown himself. Don't you, sir ? "

" I don't suppose anything."

" You have no doubt in the matter, sir ? "

" None whatever."

I left him suddenly. I felt I was producing a bad impression, but with my double down there it was most trying to be on deck. And it was almost as trying to be below. Altogether a nerve-trying situation. But on the whole I felt less torn in two when I was with him. There was no one in the whole ship whom I dared take into my confidence. Since the hands had got to know his story, it would have been impossible to pass him off for any one else, and an accidental discovery was to be dreaded now more than ever. . . .

The steward being engaged in laying the table for dinner, we could talk only with our eyes when I first went down. Later in the afternoon we had a cautious try at whispering. The Sunday quietness of the ship was against us ; the stillness of air and water around her was against us ; the elements, the men were against us—everything was against us in our secret partnership ; time itself—for this could not go on for ever. The very trust in Providence was, I suppose, denied to his guilt. Shall I confess that this thought cast me down very much ? And as to the chapter of accidents which counts for so much in the book of success, I could only hope that it was closed. For what favourable accident could be expected ?

" Did you hear everything ? " were my first words as soon as we took up our position side by side, leaning over my bed-place.

He had. And the proof of it was his earnest whisper, " The man told you he hardly dared to give the order."

I understood the reference to be to that saving foresail.

" Yes. He was afraid of it being lost in the setting."

" I assure you he never gave the order. He may think he did, but he never gave it. He stood there with me on the break of the poop after the maintopsail blew away, and whimpered about our last hope—positively whimpered about it and nothing else—and the night coming on ! To hear one's skipper go on like that in such weather was enough to drive any fellow out of his mind. It worked me up into a sort of desperation. I just took it into my own hands and went away from him, boiling, and—— But what's the use telling you ? *You* know ! . . . Do you think that if I had not been pretty fierce with them I should have got the men to do anything ? Not it ! The bo's'n perhaps ? Perhaps ! It wasn't a heavy sea—it was a sea gone mad ! I suppose the end of the world will be something like that ; and a man may have the heart to see it coming once and be done with it—but to have to face it day after day—— I don't blame anybody. I was precious little better than the rest. Only—I was an officer of that old coal-wagon, anyhow——"

" I quite understand," I conveyed that sincere assurance into his ear. He was out of breath with whispering ; I could hear him pant slightly. It was all very simple. The same strung-up force which had given twenty-four men a chance, at least, for their lives, had, in a sort of recoil, crushed an unworthy mutinous existence.

But I had no leisure to weigh the merits of the matter —footsteps in the saloon, a heavy knock. " There's enough wind to get under way with, sir." Here was the call of a new claim upon my thoughts and even upon my feelings.

" Turn the hands up," I cried through the door. " I'll be on deck directly."

I was going out to make the acquaintance of my ship. Before I left the cabin our eyes met—the eyes of the only two strangers on board. I pointed to the recessed part where the little camp-stool awaited him and laid my finger on my lips. He made a gesture—somewhat vague—a little mysterious, accompanied by a faint smile, as if of regret.

This is not the place to enlarge upon the sensations of a man who feels for the first time a ship move under his feet to his own independent word. In my case they were not unalloyed. I was not wholly alone with my command ; for there was that stranger in my cabin. Or rather, I was not completely and wholly with her. Part of me was absent. That mental feeling of being in two places at once affected me physically as if the mood of secrecy had penetrated my very soul. Before an hour had elapsed since the ship had begun to move, having occasion to ask the mate (he stood by my side) to take a compass bearing of the Pagoda, I caught myself reaching up to his ear in whispers. I say I caught myself, but enough had escaped to startle the man. I can't describe it otherwise than by saying that he shied. A grave, pre-occupied manner, as though he were in possession of some perplexing intelligence, did not leave him henceforth. A little later I moved away from the rail to look at the compass with such a stealthy gait that the helmsman noticed it—and I could not help noticing the unusual roundness of his eyes. These are trifling instances, though it's to no commander's advantage to be suspected of ludicrous eccentricities. But I was also more seriously affected. There are to a seaman certain words, gestures, that should in given conditions come as naturally, as instinctively as the winking of a menaced eye. A certain order should spring on to his lips without thinking; a certain sign should get itself made, so to speak, without reflection. But all unconscious alertness had aban-doned me. I had to make an effort of will to recall myself back (from the cabin) to the conditions of the moment. I felt that I was appearing an irresolute commander to those people who were watching me more or less critically.

And, besides, there were the scares. On the second day out, for instance, coming off the deck in the afternoon (I had straw slippers on my bare feet) I stopped at the open pantry door and spoke to the steward. He was doing something there with his back to me. At the sound of my voice he nearly jumped out of his skin, as the saying is, and incidentally broke a cup.

"What on earth's the matter with you?" I asked, astonished.

He was extremely confused. "Beg your pardon, sir. I made sure you were in your cabin."

"You see I wasn't."

"No, sir, I could have sworn I had heard you moving in there not a moment ago. It's most extraordinary . . . very sorry, sir."

I passed on with an inward shudder. I was so identified with my secret double that I did not even mention the fact in those scanty, fearful whispers we exchanged. I suppose he had made some slight noise of some kind or other. It would have been miraculous if he hadn't at one time or another. And yet, haggard as he appeared, he looked always perfectly self-controlled, more than calm—almost invulnerable. On my suggestion he remained almost entirely in the bathroom, which, upon the whole, was the safest place. There could be really no shadow of an excuse for any one ever wanting to go in there, once the steward had done with it. It was a very tiny place. Sometimes he reclined on the floor, his legs bent, his head sustained on one elbow. At others I would find him on the camp-stool, sitting in his grey sleeping-suit and with his cropped dark hair like a patient, unmoved convict. At night I would smuggle him into my bed-place, and we would whisper together, with the regular footfalls of the officer of the watch passing and repassing over our heads. It was an infinitely miserable time. It was lucky that some tins of fine preserves were stowed in a locker in my stateroom ; hard bread I could always get hold of ; and so he lived on stewed chicken, *paté de foie gras*, asparagus, cooked oysters, sardines—on all sorts of abominable .sham delicacies out of tins. My early morning coffee he always drank ; and it was all I dared do for him in that respect.

Every day there was the horrible manœuvring to go through so that my room and then the bathroom should be done in the usual way. I came to hate the sight of the steward, to abhor the voice of that harmless man. I felt that it was he who would bring on the disaster of discovery. It hung like a sword over our heads.

The fourth day out, I think (we were then working down the east side of the Gulf of Siam, tack for tack, in light winds and smooth water)—the fourth day, I say, of this miserable juggling with the unavoidable, as we sat at our evening meal, that man, whose slightest movement I dreaded, after putting down the dishes ran up on deck busily. This could not be dangerous. Presently he came down again ; and then it appeared that he had remembered a coat of mine which I had thrown over a rail to dry after having been wetted in a shower which had passed over the ship in the afternoon. Sitting stolidly at the head of the table I became terrified at the sight of the garment on his arm. Of course he made for my door. There was no time to lose.

" Steward," I thundered. My nerves were so shaken that I could not govern my voice and conceal my agitation.

This was the sort of thing that made my terrifically whiskered mate tap his forehead with his forefinger. I had detected him using that gesture while talking on deck with a confidential air to the carpenter. It was too far to hear a word, but I had no doubt that this pantomime could only refer to the strange new captain.

"Yes, sir," the pale-faced steward turned resignedly to me. It was this maddening course of being shouted at, checked without rhyme or reason, arbitrarily chased out of my cabin, suddenly called into it, sent flying out of his pantry on incomprehensible errands, that accounted for the growing wretchedness of his expression.

"Where are you going with that coat ? "

"To your room, sir."

"Is there another shower coming ? "

"I'm sure I don't know, sir. Shall I go up again and see, sir ? "

"No ! never mind." .

My object was attained, as of course my other self in there would have heard everything that passed. During this interlude my two officers never raised their eyes off their respective plates ; but the lip of that confounded cub, the second mate, quivered visibly.

I expected the steward to hook my coat on and come out at once. He was very slow about it ; but I dominated my nervousness sufficiently not to shout after him. Suddenly I became aware (it could be heard plainly enough) that the fellow for some reason or other was opening the door of the bathroom. It was the end. The place was literally not big enough to swing a cat in. My voice died in my throat and I went stony all over. I expected to hear a yell of surprise and terror, and made a movement, but had not the strength to get on my legs. Everything remained still. Had my second self taken the poor wretch by the throat ? I don't know what I would have done next moment if I had not seen the steward come out of my room, close the door, and then stand quietly by the sideboard.

"Saved," I thought. "But, no ! Lost ! Gone ! He was gone ! "

I laid my knife and fork down and leaned back in my chair. My head swam. After a while, when sufficiently recovered to speak in a steady voice, I instructed my mate to put the ship round at eight o'clock himself.

"I won't come on deck," I went on. "I think I'll turn

in, and unless the wind shifts I don't want to be disturbed before midnight. I feel a bit seedy."

" You did look middling bad a little while ago," the chief mate remarked without showing any great concern.

They both went out, and I stared at the steward clearing the table. There was nothing to be read on that wretched man's face. But why did he avoid my eyes ? I asked myself. Then I thought I should like to hear the sound of his voice.

" Steward ! "

" Sir ! " Startled as usual.

" Where did you hang up that coat ? "

" In the bathroom, sir." The usual anxious tone. " It's not quite dry yet, sir."

For some time longer I sat in the cuddy. Had my double vanished as he had come ? But of his coming there was an explanation, whereas his disappearance would be inexplicable. . . . I went slowly into my dark room, shut the door, lighted the lamp, and for a time dared not turn round. When at last I did I saw him standing bolt upright in the narrow recessed part. It would not be true to say I had a shock, but an irresistible doubt of his bodily existence flitted through my mind. Can it be, I asked myself, that he is not visible to other eyes than mine ? It was like being haunted. Motionless, with a grave face, he raised his hands slightly at me in a gesture which meant clearly, " Heavens ! what a narrow escape ! " Narrow, indeed. I think I had come creeping quietly as near insanity as any man who has not actually gone over the border. That gesture restrained me, so to speak.

The mate with the terrific whiskers was now putting the ship on the other tack. In the moment of profound silence which follows upon the hands going to their stations I heard on the poop his raised voice : " Hard alee ! " and the distant shout of the order repeated on the maindeck. The sails, in that light breeze, made but a faint fluttering noise. It ceased. The ship was coming round slowly ; I held my breath in the renewed stillness of expectation ; one wouldn't have thought that there was a single living soul on her decks. A sudden brisk shout, " Mainsail haul ! " broke the spell, and in the noisy cries and rush overhead of the men running away with the main-brace we two, down in my cabin, came together in our usual position by the bed-place.

He did not wait for my question. " I heard him fumbling here and just managed to squat myself down in the bath," he whispered to me. " The fellow only opened the door

and put his arm in to hang the coat up. All the
same——"

"I never thought of that," I whispered back, even more
appalled than before at the closeness of the shave, and mar-
velling at that something unyielding in his character which
was carrying him through so finely. There was no agitation
in his whisper. Whoever was being driven distracted, it
was not he. He was sane. And the proof of his sanity was
continued when he took up the whispering again.

"It would never do for me to come to life again."

It was something that a ghost might have said. But
what he was alluding to was his old captain's reluctant admission
of the theory of suicide. It would obviously serve his turn—
if I had understood at all the view which seemed to govern the
unalterable purpose of his action.

"You must maroon me as soon as ever you can get amongst
these islands off the Cambodje shore," he went on.

"Maroon you! We are not living in a boy's adventure
tale," I protested. His scornful whispering took me up.

"We aren't indeed! There's nothing of a boy's tale
in this. But there's nothing else for it. I want no more.
You don't suppose I am afraid of what can be done to me?
Prison or gallows or whatever they may please. But you
don't see me coming back to explain such things to an old
fellow in a wig and twelve respectable tradesmen, do you?
What can they know whether I am guilty or not—or of *what*
I am guilty, either? That's my affair. What does the Bible
say? 'Driven off the face of the earth.' Very well. I am
off the face of the earth now. As I came at night so I shall go."

"Impossible!" I murmured. "You can't."

"Can't? . . . Not naked like a soul on the Day of Judgment. I shall freeze on to this sleeping-suit. The Last Day
is not yet — and . . . you have understood thoroughly.
Didn't you?"

I felt suddenly ashamed of myself. I may say truly
that I understood—and my hesitation in letting that man swim
away from my ship's side had been a mere sham sentiment,
a sort of cowardice.

"It can't be done now till next night," I breathed out.
"The ship is on the off-shore tack and the wind may fail us."

"As long as I know that you understand," he whispered.
"But of course you do. It's a great satisfaction to have got
somebody to understand. You seem to have been there on
purpose." And in the same whisper, as if we two whenever

we talked had to say things to each other which were not fit
for the world to hear, he added, " It's very wonderful."

We remained side by side talking in our secret way—but
sometimes silent or just exchanging a whispered word or two
at long intervals. And as usual he stared through the port.
A breath of wind came now and again into our faces. The
ship might have been moored in dock, so gently and on an even
keel she slipped through the water, that did not murmur
even at our passage, shadowy and silent like a phantom sea.

At midnight I went on deck, and to my mate's great
surprise put the ship round on the other tack. His terrible
whiskers flitted round me in silent criticism. I certainly
should not have done it if it had been only a question of getting
out of that sleepy gulf as quickly as possible. I believe he told
the second mate, who relieved him, that it was a great want
of judgment. The other only yawned. That intolerable cub
shuffled about so sleepily and lolled against the rails in such a
slack, improper fashion that I came down on him sharply.

" Aren't you properly awake yet ? "

" Yes, sir ! I am awake."

" Well, then, be good enough to hold yourself as if you
were. And keep a look-out. If there's any current we'll
be closing with some islands before daylight."

The east side of the gulf is fringed with islands, some
solitary, others in groups. On the blue background of the
high coast they seem to float on silvery patches of calm water,
arid and grey, or dark green and rounded like clumps of ever-
green bushes, with the larger ones, a mile or two long, showing
the outlines of ridges, ribs of grey rock under the dank mantle
of matted leafage. Unknown to trade, to travel, almost to
geography, the manner of life they harbour is an unsolved
secret. There must be villages—settlements of fishermen at
least—on the largest of them, and some communication with
the world is probably kept up by native craft. But all that
forenoon, as we headed for them, fanned along by the faintest
of breezes, I saw no sign of man or canoe in the field of the
telescope I kept on pointing at the scattered group.

At noon I gave no orders for a change of course, and the
mate's whiskers became much concerned and seemed to be
offering themselves unduly to my notice. At last I said :

" I am going to stand right in. Quite in—as far as I can
take her."

The stare of extreme surprise imparted an air of ferocity
also to his eyes, and he looked truly terrific for a moment.

"We're not doing well in the middle of the gulf," I continued casually. "I am going to look for the land breezes to-night."

"Bless my soul! Do you mean, sir, in the dark amongst the lot of all them islands and reefs and shoals?"

"Well—if there are any regular land breezes at all on this coast one must get close inshore to find them, mustn't one?"

"Bless my soul!" he exclaimed again under his breath. All that afternoon he wore a dreamy, contemplative appearance which in him was a mark of perplexity. After dinner I went into my stateroom as if I meant to take some rest. There we two bent our dark heads over a half-unrolled chart lying on my bed.

"There," I said. "It's got to be Koh-ring. I've been looking at it ever since sunrise. It has got two hills and a low point. It must be inhabited. And on the coast opposite there is what looks like the mouth of a biggish river—with some town, no doubt, not far up. It's the best chance for you that I can see."

"Anything. Koh-ring let it be."

He looked thoughtfully at the chart as if surveying chances and distances from a lofty height—and following with his eyes his own figure wandering on the blank land of Cochin-China, and then passing off that piece of paper clean out of sight into uncharted regions. And it was as if the ship had two captains to plan her course for her. I had been so worried and restless running up and down that I had not had the patience to dress that day. I had remained in my sleeping-suit, with straw slippers and a soft floppy hat. The closeness of the heat in the gulf had been most oppressive, and the crew were used to see me wandering in that airy attire.

"She will clear the south point as she heads now," I whispered into his ear. "Goodness only knows when, though, but certainly after dark. I'll edge her in to half a mile, as far as I may be able to judge in the dark——"

"Be careful," he murmured warningly—and I realized suddenly that all my future, the only future for which I was fit, would perhaps go irretrievably to pieces in any mishap to my first command.

I could not stop a moment longer in the room. I motioned him to get out of sight and made my way on the poop. That unplayful cub had the watch. I walked up and down for a while thinking things out, then beckoned him over.

" Send a couple of hands to open the two quarter-deck ports," I said mildly.

He actually had the impudence, or else so forgot himself in his wonder at such an incomprehensible order, as to repeat :

" Open the quarter-deck ports ! What for, sir ? "

" The only reason you need concern yourself about is because I tell you to do so. Have them open wide and fastened properly."

He reddened and went off, but I believe made some jeering remark to the carpenter as to the sensible practice of ventilating a ship's quarter-deck. I know he popped into the mate's cabin to impart the fact to him because the whiskers came on deck, as it were by chance, and stole glances at me from below—for signs of lunacy or drunkenness, I suppose.

A little before supper, feeling more restless than ever, I rejoined, for a moment, my second self. And to find him sitting so quietly was surprising, like something against nature, inhuman.

I developed my plan in a hurried whisper.

" I shall stand in as close as I dare and then put her round. I shall presently find means to smuggle you out of here into the sail-locker, which communicates with the lobby. But there is an opening, a sort of square for hauling the sails out, which gives straight on the quarter-deck and which is never closed in fine weather, so as to give air to the sails. When the ship's way is deadened in stays and all the hands are aft at the main-braces you shall have a clear road to slip out and get overboard through the open quarter-deck port. I've had them both fastened up. Use a rope's end to lower yourself into the water so as to avoid a splash—you know. It could be heard and cause some beastly complication."

He kept silent for a while, then whispered, " I understand."

" I won't be there to see you go," I began with an effort. " The rest . . . I only hope I have understood, too."

" You have. From first to last "—and for the first time there seemed to be a faltering, something strained in his whisper. He caught hold of my arm, but the ringing of the supper bell made me start. He didn't, though ; he only released his grip.

After supper I didn't come below again till well past eight o'clock. The faint, steady breeze was loaded with dew ; and the wet, darkened sails held all there was of propelling power in it. The night, clear and starry, sparkled darkly, and the opaque, lightless patches shifting slowly against the low stars were the drifting islets. On the port bow there was a big one more distant and shadowily imposing by the great space of sky it eclipsed.

On opening the door I had a back view of my very own self looking at a chart. He had come out of the recess and was standing near the table.

" Quite dark enough," I whispered.

He stepped back and leaned against my bed with a level, quiet glance. I sat on the couch. We had nothing to say to each other. Over our heads the officer of the watch moved here and there. Then I heard him move quickly. I knew what that meant. He was making for the companion ; and presently his voice was outside my door.

" We are drawing in pretty fast, sir. Land looks rather close."

" Very well," I answered. " I am coming on deck directly."

I waited till he was gone out of the cuddy, then rose. My double moved too. The time had come to exchange our last whispers, for neither of us was ever to hear each other's natural voice.

" Look here ! " I opened a drawer and took out three sovereigns. " Take this, anyhow. I've got six and I'd give you the lot, only I must keep a little money to buy some fruit and vegetables for the crew from native boats as we go through Sunda Straits."

He shook his head.

" Take it," I urged him, whispering desperately. " No one can tell what——"

He smiled and slapped meaningly the only pocket of the sleeping-jacket. It was not safe, certainly. But I produced a large old silk handkerchief of mine, and tying the three pieces of gold in a corner, pressed it on him. He was touched, I suppose, because he took it at last and tied it quickly round his waist under the jacket, on his bare skin.

Our eyes met ; several seconds elapsed, till, our glances still mingled, I extended my hand and turned the lamp out. Then I passed through the cuddy, leaving the door of my room wide open. . . . " Steward ! "

He was still lingering in the pantry in the greatness of his zeal, giving a rub-up to a plated cruet-stand the last thing before going to bed. Being careful not to wake up the mate, whose room was opposite, I spoke in an undertone.

He looked round anxiously. " Sir ! "

" Can you get me a little hot water from the galley ? "

" I am afraid, sir, the galley fire's been out for some time now."

" Go and see."

He fled up the stairs.

" Now," I whispered loudly into the saloon—too loudly, perhaps, but I was afraid I couldn't make a sound. He was by my side in an instant—the double captain slipped past the stairs—through a tiny dark passage . . . a sliding door. We were in the sail-locker, scrambling on our knees over the sails. A sudden thought struck me. I saw myself wandering barefooted, bareheaded, the sun beating on my dark poll. I snatched off my floppy hat and tried hurriedly in the dark to ram it on my other self. He dodged and fended off silently. I wonder what he thought had come to me before he understood and suddenly desisted. Our hands met gropingly, lingered united in a steady, motionless clasp for a second. . . . No word was breathed by either of us when they separated.

I was standing quietly by the pantry door when the steward returned.

" Sorry, sir. Kettle barely warm. Shall I light the spirit-lamp ? "

" Never mind."

I came out on deck slowly. It was now a matter of conscience to shave the land as close as possible—for now he must go overboard whenever the ship was put in stays. Must ! There could be no going back for him. After a moment I walked over to leeward and my heart flew into my mouth at the nearness of the land on the bow. Under any other circumstances I would not have held on a minute longer. The second mate had followed me anxiously.

I looked on till I felt I could command my voice.

" She will weather," I said then in a quiet tone.

" Are you going to try that, sir ? " he stammered out incredulously.

I took no notice of him and raised my tone just enough to be heard by the helmsman.

" Keep her good full."

" Good full, sir."

The wind fanned my cheek, the sails slept, the world was silent. The strain of watching the dark loom of the land grow bigger and denser was too much for me. I had shut my eyes—because the ship must go closer. She must ! The stillness was intolerable. Were we standing still ?

When I opened my eyes the second view started my heart with a thump. The black southern hill of Koh-ring seemed to hang right over the ship like a towering fragment of the everlasting night. On that enormous mass of blackness there was not a gleam to be seen, not a sound to be heard. It was gliding irresistibly toward us and yet seemed already within reach of the hand. I saw the vague figures of the watch grouped in the waist, gazing in awed silence.

"Are you going on, sir ? " inquired an unsteady voice at my elbow.

I ignored it. I had to go on.

" Keep her full. Don't check her way. That won't do now," I said warningly.

" I can't see the sails very well," the helmsman answered me, in strange, quavering tones.

Was she close enough ? Already she was, I won't say in the shadow of the land, but in the very blackness of it, already swallowed up as it were, gone too close to be recalled, gone from me altogether.

" Give the mate a call," I said to the young man who stood at my elbow as still as death. " And turn all hands up."

My tone had a borrowed loudness reverberated from the height of the land. Several voices cried out together : " We are all on deck, sir."

Then stillness again, with the great shadow gliding closer, towering higher, without a light, without a sound. Such a hush had fallen on the ship that she might have been a bark of the dead floating in slowly under the very gate of Erebus.

" My God ! Where are we ? "

It was the mate moaning at my elbow. He was thunder-struck, and as it were deprived of the moral support of his whiskers. He clapped his hands and absolutely cried cut, " Lost ! "

" Be quiet," I said sternly.

He lowered his tone, but I saw the shadowy gesture of his despair. " What are we doing here ? "

" Looking for the land wind."

He made as if to tear his hair, and addressed me recklessly.

" She will never get out. You have done it, sir. I knew it'd end in something like this. She will never weather, and you are too close now to stay. She'll drift ashore before she's round. O my God ! "

I caught his arm as he was raising it to batter his poor devoted head, and shook it violently.

"She's ashore already," he wailed, trying to tear himself away.

"Is she ? . . . Keep good full there ! "

"Good full, sir," cried the helmsman in a frightened, thin, child-like voice.

I hadn't let go the mate's arm and went on shaking it. "Ready about, do you hear ? You go forward "—shake— " and stop there "—shake—" and hold your noise "—shake— " and see these head-sheets properly overhauled "—shake, shake—shake.

And all the time I dared not look toward the land lest my heart should fail me. I released my grip at last and he ran forward as if fleeing for dear life.

I wondered what my double there in the sail-locker thought of this commotion. He was able to hear everything—and perhaps he was able to understand why, on my conscience, it had to be thus close—no less. My first order " Hard alee ! " re-echoed ominously under the towering shadow of Koh-ring as if I had shouted in a mountain gorge. And then I watched the land intently. In that smooth water and light wind it was impossible to feel the ship coming-to. No ! I could not feel her. And my second self was making now ready to slip out and lower himself overboard. Perhaps he was gone already . . . ?

The great black mass brooding over our very mast-heads began to pivot away from the ship's side silently. And now I forgot the secret stranger ready to depart, and remembered only that I was a total stranger to the ship. I did not know her. Would she do it ? How was she to be handled ?

I swung the mainyard and waited helplessly. She was perhaps stopped, and her very fate hung in the balance, with the black mass of Koh-ring like the gate of the everlasting night towering over her taffrail. What would she do now ? Had she way on her yet ? I stepped to the side swiftly, and on the shadowy water I could see nothing except a faint phosphorescent flash revealing the glassy smoothness of the sleeping surface. It was impossible to tell—and I had not learned yet the feel of my ship. Was she moving ? What I needed was something easily seen, a piece of paper, which I could throw overboard and watch. I had nothing on me. To run down for it I didn't dare. There was no time. All at once my strained, yearning stare distinguished a white object floating within a yard of the ship's side. White on the black water. A phosphorescent flash passed under it. What was that thing? . . . I recognized my own floppy hat. It must have fallen off his head . . . and he didn't bother. Now I had what I wanted—the saving mark for my eyes. But I hardly thought of my other self, now gone from the ship, to be hidden for ever from all friendly faces, to be a fugitive and a vagabond on the earth, with no brand of the curse on his sane forehead to stay a slaying hand . . . too proud to explain.

And I watched the hat—the expression of my sudden pity for his mere flesh. It had been meant to save his homeless head from the dangers of the sun. And now—behold—it was saving the ship, by serving me for a mark to help out the ignorance of my strangeness. Ha! It was drifting forward, warning me just in time that the ship had gathered sternway.

"Shift the helm," I said in a low voice to the seaman standing still like a statue.

The man's eyes glistened wildly in the binnacle light as he jumped round to the other side and spun round the wheel.

I walked to the break of the poop. On the overshadowed deck all hands stood by the forebraces waiting for my order. The stars ahead seemed to be gliding from right to left. And all was so still in the world that I heard the quiet remark "She's round" passed in a tone of intense relief between two seamen.

"Let go and haul."

The foreyards ran round with a great noise, amidst cheery cries. And now the frightful whiskers made themselves heard giving various orders. Already the ship was drawing ahead. And I was alone with her. Nothing! no one in the world should stand now between us, throwing a shadow on the way of silent knowledge and mute affection, the perfect communion of a seaman with his first command.

Walking to the taffrail, I was in time to make out, on the very edge of a darkness thrown by a towering black mass like the very gateway of Erebus—yes, I was in time to catch an evanescent glimpse of my white hat left behind to mark the spot where the secret sharer of my cabin and of my thoughts, as though he were my second self, had lowered himself into the water to take his punishment: a free man, a proud swimmer striking out for a new destiny.

THE TIGER

*T*HE *tiger was coming at last ;* the almost fabulous beast, the subject of so much conjecture for so many months, was at the docks twenty miles away. Yak Pedersen had gone to fetch it, and Barnabe Woolf's Menagerie was about to complete its unrivalled collection by the addition of a full-grown Indian tiger of indescribable ferocity, newly trapped in the forest and now for the first time exhibited, and so on, and so on. All of which, as it happened, was true. On the previous day Pedersen the Dane and some helpers had taken a brand new four-horse exhibition waggon, painted and carved with extremely legendary tigers lapped in blood—even the bars were gilded—to convey this unmatchable beast to its new masters. The show had had to wait a long time for a tiger, but it had got a beauty at last, a terror indeed by all accounts, though it is not to be imagined that everything recorded of it by Barnabe Woolf was truth and nothing but truth. Showmen do not work in that way.

Yak Pedersen was the tamer and menagerie manager, a tall, blonde, angular man about thirty-five, of dissolute and savage blood himself, with the very ample kind of moustache that bald men often develop ; yes, bald, intemperate, lewd, and an interminable smoker of Cuban cigarettes, which seemed constantly to threaten a conflagration in that moustache. Marie the Cossack hated him, but Yak loved her with a fierce deep passion. Nobody knew why she was called Marie the Cossack. She came from Canning Town—everybody knew that, and her proper name was Fascota, Mrs Fascota, wife of Jimmy Fascota, who was the architect and carpenter and builder of the show. Jimmy was not much to look at, so little in fact that you couldn't help wondering what it was Marie had seen in him when she could have had the King of Poland, as you might say, almost for the asking. But still Jimmy was the boss ganger of the show, and even that young gentleman in frock coat and silk hat who paraded the platform entrance to the arena and rhodomontadoed you into it, often against your will, by the seductive recital of the seven ghastly wonders of the world, all certainly to be seen, to be seen inside, waiting to be seen, must be seen, roll up—even he was subject to the commands of Jimmy Fascota when the time came to dismantle and pack up the show, although the transfer of his activities involved him temporarily in a change, a horrid change, of attire and language. Marie was not a lady, but she was not for Pedersen anyway. She swore like a factory foreman, or a young soldier, and when she got tipsy she was full of freedoms. By the power of God she was beautiful, and by the same gracious power she was virtuous. Her husband knew it ; he knew all about Master Pedersen's passion, too, and it did not interest him. Marie did feats in the lion cages, whipping poor decrepit beasts, desiccated by captivity, through a hoop or over a stick of wood and other kindergarten disportings ; but there you are, people must live, and Marie lived that way. Pedersen was always wooing her. Sometimes he was gracious and kind, but at other times when his failure wearied him he would be cruel and sardonic, with a suggestive tongue whose vice would have scourged her were it not that Marie was impervious, or too deeply inured to mind it. She always grinned at him or fobbed him off with pleasantries, whether he was amorous or acrid.

" God Almighty ! " he would groan, " she is not good for me, this Marie. What can I do for her ? She is burning me alive and the Skaggerack could not quench me, not all of it. The devil ! What can I do with this ? Some day I shall smash her across the eyes, yes, across the eyes."

So you see the man really loved her.

When Pedersen returned from the docks, the car with its captive was dragged to a vacant place in the arena, and the wooden front panel was let down from the bars The marvellous tiger was revealed. It sprung into a crouching attitude as the light surprised the appalling beauty of its smooth fox-coloured coat, its ebony stripes, and snowy pads and belly. The Dane, who was slightly drunk, uttered a yell and struck the bars of the cage with his whip. The tiger did not blench, but all the malice and ferocity in the world seemed to congregate in its eyes and impress with a pride and ruthless grandeur the colossal brutality of its face. It did not move its body, but its tail gradually stiffened out behind it as stealthily as fire moves in the forest undergrowth, and the hair along the ridge of its back rose in fearful spikes. There was the slightest possible distension of the lips, and it fixed its marvellous baleful gaze upon Pedersen. The show people were hushed into silence, and even Pedersen was startled. He showered a few howls and curses at the tiger, who never ceased to fix him with eyes that had something of contempt in them and something of a horrible presage. Pedersen was thrusting a sharp spike through the bars when a figure stepped from the crowd. It was an old negro, a hunchback with a white beard, dressed in a red fez cap, long tunic of buff cotton, and blue trousers. He laid both his hands on the spike and shook his head deprecatingly, smiling all the while. He said nothing, but there was nothing he could say—he was dumb.

" Let him alone, Yak ; let the tiger alone, Yak ! " cried Barnabe Woolf. " What is this feller ? "

Pedersen, with some reluctance, turned from the cage and said : " He is come with the animal."

" So ? " said Barnabe. " Vell, he can go. Ve do not vant any black feller."

" He cannot speak—no tongue—it is gone," Yak replied.

" No tongue ! Vot, have they cut him out ? "

" I should think it," said the tamer. " There was two of them, a white keeper, but that man fell off the ship one night and they do not see him any more. This chap he feed it and look after it. No information of him, dumb, you see, and a foreigner ; don't understand. He have no letters, no money, no name, nowheres to go. Dumb, you see, he has nothing, nothing but a flote. The captain said to take him away with us. Give a job to him, he is a proposition."

" Vot is he got you say ? "

" Flote." Pedersen imitated with his fingers and lips the actions of a flute-player.

" Oh ya, a vloot ! Vell, ve don't want no vloots now ; ve feeds our own tigers, don't ve, Yak ? " And Mr. Woolf, oily but hearty—and well he might be so for he was beautifully rotund, hair like satin, extravagantly clothed, and rich with jewellery—surveyed first with a contemplative grin, and then compassionately the figure of the old negro, who stood unsmiling with his hands crossed humbly before him. Mr. Woolf was usually perspiring, and usually being addressed by perspiring workmen, upon whom he bellowed orders and such anathemas as reduced each recipient to the importance of a potato, and gave him the aspect of a consumptive sheep. But to-day Mr. Woolf was affable and calm. He took his cigar from his mouth and poured a flood of rich grey air from his lips. " Oh ya, look after him a day, or a couple of days." At that one of the boys began to lead the hunchback away as if he were a horse. " Come on, Pompoon," he cried, and thenceforward the unknown negro was called by that name.

Throughout the day the tiger was the sensation of the show, and the record of its ferocity attached to the cage received thrilling confirmation whenever Pedersen appeared before the bars. The sublime concentration of hatred was so intense that children screamed, women shuddered, and even men held their breath in awe. At the end of the day the beasts were fed. Great hacks of bloody flesh were forked into the bottoms of the cages, the hungry victims pouncing and snarling in ecstasy. But no sooner were they served than the front panel of each cage was swung up, and the inmate in the seclusion of his den slaked his appetite and slept. When the public had departed, the lights were put out and the doors of the arena closed. Outside in the darkness only its great rounded oblong shape could be discerned, built high of painted wood, roofed with striped canvas, and adorned with flags. Beyond this matchbox coliseum was a row of caravans, tents, naphtha flares, and buckets of fire on which suppers were cooking. Groups of the show people sat or lounged about, talking, cackling with laughter, and even singing. No one observed the figure of Pompoon as he passed silently on the grass. The outcast, doubly chained to his solitariness by the misfortune of dumbness and strange nationality, was hungry. He had not tasted food that day. He could not understand it any more than he could understand the speech of these people. In the end caravan, nearest the arena, he heard a woman quietly singing. He drew a shining metal flute from his breast, but stood silently until the singer ceased. Then he repeated the tune very accurately and sweetly on his flute. Marie the Cossack came to the door in her green silk tights and high black boots with gilded fringes ; her black velvet doublet had plenty of gilded buttons upon it. She was a big, finely moulded woman, her dark and splendid features were burned healthily by the sun. In each of her ears two gold discs tinkled and gleamed as she moved. Pompoon opened his mouth very widely and supplicatingly ; he put his hand upon his stomach and rolled his eyes so dreadfully that Mrs.

Fascota sent her little daughter Sophy down to him with a basin of soup and potatoes. Sophy was partly undressed, in bare feet and red petticoat. She stood gnawing the bone of a chicken, and grinning at the black man as he swallowed and dribbled as best he could without a spoon. She cried out : " Here, he's going to eat the bloody basin and all, mum ! " Her mother cheerfully ordered her to " give him those fraggiments, then ! " The child did so, pausing now and again to laugh at the satisfied roll of the old man's eyes. Later on Jimmy Fascota found him a couple of sacks, and Pompoon slept upon them beneath their caravan. The last thing the old man saw was Pedersen, carrying a naphtha flare, unlocking a small door leading into the arena, and closing it with a slam after he had entered. Soon the light went out.

II

AFTER a week the show shifted and Pompoon accompanied it. Mrs. Kavanagh, who looked after the birds, was, a little fortunately for him, kicked in the stomach by a mule and had to be left at an infirmary. Pompoon, who seemed to understand birds, took charge of the parakeets, love birds, and other highly coloured fowl, including the quetzal with green mossy head, pink breast, and flowing tails, and the primrose-breasted toucans, with bills like a butcher's cleaver.

The show was always moving on and moving on. Putting it up and taking it down was a more entertaining affair than the exhibition itself. With Jimmy Fascota in charge, and the young man of the frock coat in an ecstasy of labour, half-clothed husky men swarmed up the rigged frameworks, dismantling poles, planks, floors, ropes, roofs, staging, tearing at bolts and bars, walking at dizzying altitudes on narrow boards, swearing at their mates, staggering under vast burdens, sweating till they looked like seals, packing and disposing incredibly of it all, furling the flags, rolling up the filthy awnings, then Right O ! for a market town twenty miles away.

In the autumn the show would be due at a great gala town in the north, the supreme opportunity of the year, and by that time Mr. Woolf expected to have a startling headline about a new tiger act and the intrepid tamer. But somehow Pedersen could make no progress at all with this. Week after week went by, and the longer he left that initial entry into the cage of the tiger, notwithstanding the comforting support of firearms, and hot irons, the more remote appeared the possibility of its capitulation. The tiger's hatred did not manifest itself in roars and gnashing of teeth, but by its rigid implacable pose and a slight flexion of its protruded claws. It seemed as if endowed with an imagination of blood-lust, Pedersen being the deepest conceivable excitation of this. Week after week went by and the show people became aware that Pedersen, their Pedersen, the unrivalled, the dauntless tamer, had met his match. They were proud of the beast. Some said it was Yak's bald crown that the tiger disliked, but Marie swore it was his moustache, a really remarkable piece of hirsute furniture, that he would not have parted with for a pound of gold—so he said. But whatever it was—crown, moustache, or the whole conglomerate Pedersen — the tiger remarkably loathed it and displayed his loathing, while the unfortunate tamer had no more success with it than he had ever had with Marie the Cossack, though there was at least a good humour in her treatment of him which was horribly absent from the attitude of the beast. For a long time Pedersen blamed the hunchback for it all. He tried to elicit from him by gesticulations in front of the cage the secret of the creature's enmity, but the barriers to their intercourse were too great to be overcome, and to all Pedersen's illustrative frenzies Pompoon would only shake his sad head and roll his great eyes until the Dane would cuff him away with a curse of disgust and turn to find the eyes of the tiger, the dusky, smooth-skinned tiger with bitter bars of ebony, fixed upon him with tenfold malignity. How he longed in his raging impotence to transfix the thing with a sharp spear through the cage's gilded bars, or to bore a hole into its vitals with a red-hot iron! All the traditional treatment in such cases, combined first with starvation and then with rich feeding, proved unavailing. Pedersen always had the front flap of the cage left down at night so that he might, as he thought, establish some kind of working arrangement between them by the force of propinquity. He tried to sleep on a bench just outside the cage, but the horror of the beast so penetrated him that he had to turn his back upon it. Even then the intense enmity pierced the back of his brain and forced him to seek a bench elsewhere out of range of the tiger's vision.

Meanwhile, the derision of Marie was not concealed—it was even blatant—and to the old contest of love between herself and the Dane was now added a new contest of personal courage, for it had come to be assumed, in some undeclarable fashion, that if Yak Pedersen could not tame that tiger, then Marie the Cossack would. As this situation crystallized daily, the passion of Pedersen changed to jealousy and hatred. He began to regard the smiling Marie in much the same way as the tiger regarded him.

" The hell-devil ! May some lightning scorch her like a toasted fish ! "

But in a short while this mood was displaced by one of anxiety ; he became even abject. Then, strangely enough, Marie's feelings underwent some modification. She was proud of the chance to subdue and defeat him, but it might be at a great price—too great a price for her. Addressing herself in turn to the dim understanding of Pompoon, she had come to perceive that he believed the tiger to be not merely quite untamable, but full of mysterious dangers. She could not triumph over the Dane unless she ran the risk he feared to run. The risk was colossal then, and with her realization of this some pity for Yak began to exercise itself in her ; after all, were they not in the same boat ? But the more she sympathized the more she jeered. The thing had to be done somehow.

Meanwhile Barnabe Woolf wants that headline for the big autumn show, and a failure will mean a nasty interview with that gentleman. It may end by Barnabe kicking Yak Pedersen out of the wild beast show. Not that Mr. Woolf is so gross as to suggest that. He senses the difficulty, although his manager in his pride will not confess to any. Mr. Woolf declares that his tiger is a new tiger ; Yak must watch out for him, be careful. He talks as if it were just a question of giving the cage a coat of whitewash. He never hints at contingencies ; but still, there is his new untamed tiger, and there is Mr. Yak Pedersen, his wild beast tamer—at present.

III

ONE day the menagerie did not open. It had finished an engagement, and Jimmy Fascota had gone off to another town to arrange the new pitch. The show folk made holiday about the camp, or flocked into the town for marketing or carousals. Mrs. Fascota was alone in her caravan, clothed in her jauntiest attire. She was preparing to go into the town when Pedersen suddenly came silently in and sat down.

" Marie," he said, after a few moments, " I give up that tiger. To me he has given a spell. It is like a mesmerize." He dropped his hands upon his knees in complete humiliation. Marie did not speak, so he asked : " What you think ? "

She shrugged her shoulders, and put her brown arms

akimbo. She was a grand figure so, in a cloak of black satin and a huge hat trimmed with crimson feathers.

" If you can't trust him," she said, " who can ? "

" It is myself I am not to trust. Shameful ! But that tiger will do me, yes, so I will not conquer him. It's bad, very, very bad, is it not so ? Shameful, but I will not do it ! " he declared excitedly.

" What's Barnabe say ? "

" I do not care. Mr. Woolf can think what he can think ! Damn Woolf ! But for what I do think of my own self. . . . Ah ! " He paused for a moment, dejected beyond speech. " Yes, miserable it is, in my own heart very shameful, Marie. And what you think of me, yes, that too ! "

There was a note in his voice that almost confounded her —why, the man was going to cry ! In a moment she was all melting compassion and bravado.

" You leave the devil to me, Yak. What's come over you, man ? God love us, I'll tiger him ! "

But the Dane had gone as far as he could go. He could admit his defeat, but he could not welcome her all too ready amplification of it.

" Na, na, you are good for him, Marie, but you beware. He is not a tiger ; he is beyond everything, foul—he has got a foul heart and a thousand demons in it. I would not bear to see you touch him ; no, no, I would not bear it ! "

" Wait till I come back this afternoon—you wait ! " cried Marie, lifting her clenched fist. " So help me, I'll tiger him, you'll see ! "

Pedersen suddenly awoke to her amazing attraction. He seized her in his arms. " Na, na, Marie ! God above ! I will not have it."

" Aw, shut up ! " she commanded impatiently, and pushing him from her she sprang down the steps and proceeded to the town alone.

She did not return in the afternoon ; she did not return in the evening. She was not there when the camp closed up for the night. Sophy, alone, was quite unconcerned. Pompoon sat outside the caravan, while the flame of the last lamp was perishing weakly above his head. He now wore a coat of shag-coloured velvet. He was old and looked very wise, often shaking his head, not wearily, but as if in doubt. The flute lay glittering upon his knees and he was wiping his lips with a green silk handkerchief when barefoot Sophy, in her red petticoat, crept behind him, unhooked the lamp, and left him in darkness. Then he departed to an old tent the Fascotas had found for him.

When the mother returned the camp was asleep in its darkness and she was very drunk. Yak Pedersen had got her. He carried her into the arena, and bolted and barred the door.

IV

MARIE FASCOTA awoke the next morning in broad daylight; through chinks and rents in the canvas roof of the arena the brightness was beautiful to behold. She could hear a few early risers bawling outside, while all around her the caged beasts and birds were squeaking, whistling, growling, and snarling. She was lying beside the Dane on a great bundle of straw. He was already awake when she became aware of him, watching her with amused eyes.

" Yak Pedersen ! Was I drunk ? " Marie asked dazedly in low, husky tones, sitting up. " What's this, Yak Pedersen ? Was I drunk ? Have I been here all night ? "

He lay with his hands behind his head, smiling in the dissolute ugliness of his abrupt yellow skull so incongruously bald, his moustache so profuse, his nostrils and ears teeming with hairs.

" Can't you speak ? " cried the wretched woman. " What game do you call this ? Where's my Sophy, and my Jimmy— is he back ? "

Again he did not answer ; he stretched out a hand to caress her. Unguarded as he was, Marie smashed down both her fists full upon his face. He lunged back blindly at her, and they both struggled to their feet, his fingers clawing in her thick strands of hair as she struck at him in frenzy. Down rolled the mass, and he seized it ; it was her weakness, and she screamed. Marie was a rare woman—a match for most men—but the capture of her hair gave her utterly into his powerful hands. Uttering a torrent of filthy oaths, Pedersen pulled the yelling woman backwards to him and, grasping her neck with both hands, gave a murderous wrench and flung her to the ground. As she fell Marie's hands clutched a small cage of fortune-telling birds. She hurled this at the man, but it missed him ; the cage burst against a pillar and the birds scattered in the air.

" Marie ! Marie ! " shouted Yak, " listen ! listen ! "

Remorsefully he flung himself before the raging woman,

who swept at him with an axe, her hair streaming, her eyes blazing with the fire of a thousand angers.

" Drunk, was I ! " she screamed at him. " That's how ye got me, Yak Pedersen ? Drunk, was I ? "

He warded the blow with his arm, but the shock and pain of it was so great that his own rage burst out again, and leaping at the woman he struck her a horrible blow across the eyes. She sank to her knees and huddled there without a sound, holding her hands to her bleeding face, her loose hair covering it like a net. At the pitiful sight the Dane's grief conquered him again, and bending over her imploringly he said : " Marie, my love, Marie ! Listen ! It is not true ! Swear me to God, good woman, it is not true, it is not possible ! Swear me to God ! " he raged distractedly. " Swear me to God ! " Suddenly he stopped and gasped. They were in front of the tiger's cage, and Pedersen was as if transfixed by that fearful gaze. The beast stood with hatred concentrated in every bristling hair upon its hide, and in its eyes a malignity that was almost incandescent. Still as a stone, Marie observed this, and began to creep away from the Dane, stealthily, stealthily. On a sudden, with incredible agility, she sprang up the steps of the tiger's cage, tore the pin from the catch, flung open the door, and, yelling in madness, leapt in. As she did so, the cage emptied. In one moment she saw Pedersen grovelling on his knees, stupid, and the next . . .

All the hidden beasts, stirred by instinctive knowledge of the tragedy, roared and raged. Marie's eyes and mind were opened to its horror. She plugged her fingers into her ears ; screamed ; but her voice was a mere wafer of sound in that pandemonium. She heard vast crashes of some one smashing in the small door of the arena, and then swooned upon the floor of the cage.

The bolts were torn from their sockets at last, the slip door swung back, and in the opening appeared Pompoon, alone, old Pompoon with a flaming lamp and an iron spear. As he stepped forward into the gloom he saw the tiger, dragging something in its mouth, leap back into its cage.

And in the opening appeared Pompoon . . .

THE LOOKING-GLASS

FOR an hour or two in the afternoon, Miss Lennox had always made it a rule to retire to her own room for a little rest, so that for this brief interval, at any rate, Alice was at liberty to do just what she pleased with herself. The " just what she pleased," no doubt, was a little limited in range ; and " with herself " was at best no very vast oasis amid its sands.

She might, for example, like Miss Lennox, rest, too, if she pleased. Miss Lennox prided herself on her justice.

But then, Alice could seldom sleep in the afternoon because of her troublesome cough. She might at a pinch write letters, but they would need to be nearly all of them addressed to imaginary correspondents. And not even the most romantic of young human beings can write on indefinitely to one who vouchsafes *no* kind of an answer. The choice in fact merely amounted to that between being " in " or " out " (in *any* sense), and now that the severity of the winter had abated, Alice much preferred the solitude of the garden to the vacancy of the house.

With rain came an extraordinary beauty to the narrow garden—its trees drenched, refreshed, and glittering at break of evening, its early flowers stooping pale above the darkened earth, the birds that haunted there singing as if out of a cool and happy cloister—the stormcock wildly jubilant. There was one particular thrush on one particular tree which you might say all but yelled messages at Alice, messages which sometimes made her laugh, and sometimes almost ready to cry, with delight.

And yet ever the same vague influence seemed to haunt her young mind. Scarcely so much as a mood ; nothing in

the nature of a thought ; merely an influence—like that of
some impressive stranger met—in a dream, say—long ago, and
now half-forgotten.

This may have been in part because the low and foundering
wall between the empty meadows and her own recess of
greenery had always seemed to her like the boundary between
two worlds. On the one side freedom, the wild ; on this, Miss
Lennox, and a sort of captivity. There Reality ; here (her
" duties " almost forgotten) the confines of a kind of waking
dream. For this reason, if for no other, she at the same time
longed for and yet in a way dreaded the afternoon's regular
reprieve.

It had proved, too, both a comfort and a vexation that the
old servant belonging to the new family next door had speedily
discovered this little habit, and would as often as not lie in
wait for her between a bush of lilac and a bright green chestnut
that stood up like a dense umbrella midway along the wall
that divided Miss Lennox's from its one neighbouring garden.
And since apparently it was Alice's destiny in life to be always
precariously balanced between extremes, Sarah had also
turned out to be a creature of rather peculiar oscillations of
temperament.

Their clandestine talks were, therefore, though frequent,
seldom particularly enlightening. None the less, merely to see
this slovenly ponderous woman enter the garden, self-centred,
with a kind of dull arrogance, her louring face as vacant as
contempt of the Universe could make it, was an event ever
eagerly, though at times vexatiously, looked for, and seldom
missed.

Until but a few steps separated them, it was one of Sarah's
queer habits to make believe, so to speak, that Alice was not
there at all. Then, as regularly, from her place of vantage on
the other side of the wall, she would slowly and heavily lift
her eyes to her face, with a sudden energy which at first considerably alarmed the young girl, and afterwards amused her.
For certainly you *are* amused in a sort of fashion when any
stranger you might suppose to be a little queer in the head
proves perfectly harmless. Alice did not exactly like Sarah.
But she could no more resist her advances than the garden
could resist the coming on of night.

Miss Lennox, too, it must be confessed, was a rather
tedious and fretful companion for wits (like Alice's) always
wool-gathering—wool, moreover, of the shimmering kind that
decked the Golden Fleece. Her own conception of the present

was of a niche in Time from which she was accustomed to look back on the dim, though once apparently garish, panorama of the past ; while with Alice, Time had kept promises enough only for a surety of its immense resources—resources illimitable, even though up till now they had been pretty tightly withheld.

Or, if you so preferred, as Alice would say to herself, you could put it that Miss Lennox had all her eggs in a real basket, and that Alice had all hers in a basket that was *not* exactly real—only problematical. All the more reason, then, for Alice to think it a little queer that it had been Miss Lennox herself and not Sarah who had first given shape and substance to her vaguely bizarre intuitions concerning the garden—a walled-in space in which one might suppose intuition alone could discover anything in the least remarkable.

" When my cousin, Mary Wilson (the Wilsons of Aberdeen, as I may have told you), when my cousin lived in this house," she had informed her young companion one evening over her own milk and oatmeal biscuits, " there was a silly talk with the maids that it was haunted."

" The house ? " Alice had inquired, with a sudden crooked look on a face that Nature, it seemed, had definitely intended to be frequently startled ; " The house ? "

" I didn't say the *house*," Miss Lennox testily replied—it always annoyed her to see anything resembling a flush on her young companion's cheek, " and even if I did, I certainly *meant* the garden. If I had meant the house, I should have used the word house. I meant the garden. It was quite unnecessary to correct or contradict me ; and whether or not, it's all the purest rubbish—just a tale, though not the only one of the kind in the world, I fancy."

" Do you remember any of the other tales ? " Alice had inquired, after a rather prolonged pause.

" No, none " ; was the flat reply.

And so it came about that to Sarah (though she could hardly be described as the Serpent of the situation), to Sarah fell the opportunity of enjoying to the full an opening for her fantastic " lore." By insinuation, by silences, now with contemptuous scepticism, now with enormous warmth, she cast her spell, weaving an eager imagination through and through with the rather gaudy threads of superstition.

" Lor, no, *Crimes*, maybe not, though blood is in the roots for all *I* can say." She had looked up almost candidly in the warm, rainy wind, her deadish-looking hair blown back from her forehead.

" Some'll tell you only the old people have eyes to see the mystery ; and some, old or young, if so be they're ripe. Nothing to me either way ; I'm gone past such things. And *what* it is, 'orror and darkness, or golden like a saint in heaven, or pictures in dreams, or just like dying fireworks in the air, the Lord alone knows, Miss, for I don't. But this I *will* say," and she edged up her body a little closer to the wall, the rain-drops the while dropping softly on bough and grass, " May-day's the day, and midnight's the hour, for such as be wakeful and brazen and stoopid enough to watch it out. And what you've got to look for in a manner of speaking is what comes up out of the darkness from behind them trees there ! "

She drew back cunningly.

The conversation was just like clockwork. It recurred regularly—except that there was no need to wind anything up. It wound itself up overnight, and with such accuracy that Alice soon knew the complete series of question and answer by heart or by rote—as if she had learned them out of the Child's Guide to Knowledge, or the Catechism. Still there were interesting points in it even now.

" *And what you've got to look for* "—the *you* was so absurdly impersonal when muttered in that thick, coarse, privy voice. And Alice invariably smiled at this little juncture ; and Sarah as invariably looked at her and swallowed.

" But have *you* looked for—for what you say, you know ? " Alice would then inquire, still with face a little averted towards the black low-boughed group of broad-leafed chestnuts, positive candelabra in their own season of wax-like speckled blossom.

" Me ? *Me ?* I was old before my time, they used to say. Why, besides my poor sister up in Yorkshire there, there's not a mouth utters my name." Her large flushed face smiled, in triumphant irony. " Besides my bed-rid mistress there, and my old what they call feeble-minded sister, Jane Mary, in Yorkshire, I'm as good as in my grave. I may be dull and hot in the head at times, but I stand *alone*—eat alone, sit alone, sleep alone, think alone. There's never been such a lonely person before. Now, what should such a lonely person as me, Miss, I ask you, or what should you either for that matter, be meddling with your May-days and your haunted gardens for ? " She broke off and stared with angry confusion around her, and, lifting up her open hand a little, she added hotly, " Them birds !—My God, I drats 'em for their squealin' ! "

" But, why ? " said Alice, frowning slightly.

" The Lord only knows, Miss ; I hate the sight of 'em !
If I had what they call a blunderbuss in me hand I'd blow 'em
to ribbings."

And Alice never could quite understand why it was that
the normal pronunciation of the word would have suggested
a less complete dismemberment of the victims.

It was on a bleak day in March that Alice first heard really
explicitly the conditions of the quest.

" Your hows and whys ! What I say is I'm sick of it all.
Not so much of you, Miss, which is all greens to me, but of
the rest of it all ! Anyhow, *fast* you must, like the Cartholics,
and you with a frightful hacking cough and all. Come like a
new-begotten bride you must in a white gown, and a wreath
of lillies or rorringe-blossom in your hair, same pretty much as
I made for my mother's coffin this twenty years ago, and which
I wouldn't do now not for respectability even. And me and
my mother, let me tell you, were as close as hens in a roost.
. . . But I'm off me subject. There you sits, even if the snow
itself comes sailing in on your face, and alone you must be
neither book nor candle, and the house behind you shut up
black abed and asleep. But, there ; you so wan and sickly a
young lady. What ghost would come to you, I'd like to know.
You want some fine dark loveyer for a ghost—that's your ghost.
Oo-ay ! There's not a want in the world but's dust and
ashes. That's my bit of schooling."

She gazed on impenetrably at Alice's slender fingers.
And without raising her eyes she leaned her large hands on
the wall, " Meself, Miss, meself's *my* ghost, as they say. Why,
bless me ! it's all thro' the place now, like smoke."

What was all through the place now like smoke Alice
perceived to be the peculiar clarity of the air discernible in
the garden at times. The clearness as it were of glass, of a
looking-glass, which conceals all behind and beyond it, returning only the looker's wonder, or simply her vanity, or even
her gaiety. Why, for the matter of that, thought Alice smiling,
there are people who look into looking-glasses, actually see
themselves there, and yet never turn a hair.

There *wasn't* any glass, of course. Its sort of mirage sprang
only out of the desire of her eyes, out of a restless hunger of
the mind—just to possess her soul in patience till the first
favourable May evening came along and then once and for all
to set everything at rest. It was a thought which fascinated
her so completely that it influenced her habits, her words,
her actions. She even began to long for the afternoon solely

to be alone with it ; and in the midst of the reverie it charmed into her mind, she would glance up as startled as a Dryad to see the " cook-general's " dark face fixing its still cold gaze on her from over the moss-greened wall.   As for Miss Lennox she became testier and more "rational" than ever as she narrowly watched the day approaching when her need for a new companion would become extreme.

Who, however, the lover might be, and where the trysting-place, was unknown even to Alice, though, maybe, not absolutely unsurmised by her, and with a kind of cunning perspicacity perceived only by Sarah.

" I see my old tales have tickled you up, Miss," she said one day, lifting her eyes from the clothes-line she was carrying to the girl's alert and mobile face. " What they call old wives' tales I fancy, too."

" Oh, I don't think so," Alice answered. " I can hardly tell, Sarah. I am only at peace *here*, I know that. I get out of bed at night to look down from the window and wish myself here. When I'm reading, just as if it were a painted illustration—in the book, you know—the scene of it all floats in between me and the print. Besides, I can do just what I like with it. In my mind, I mean. I just imagine ; and there it all is. So you see I could not bear *now* to go away."

" There's no cause to worry your head about that," said the woman darkly, " and as for picking and choosing I never saw much of it for them that's under of a thumb. Why, when *I* was young, I couldn't have borne to live as I do now with just meself wandering to and fro. Muttering I catch meself, too. And, to be sure, surrounded in the air by shapes, and shadows, and noises, and winds, so as sometimes I can neither see nor hear. It's true, God's gospel, Miss—the body's like a clump of wood, it's that dull. And you can't get t'other side, so to speak."

So lucid a portrayal of her own exact sensations astonished the girl. " Well, but what is it, what is it, Sarah ? "

Sarah strapped the air with the loose end of the clothes-line. " Part, Miss, the hauntin' of the garden. Part as them black-jacketed clergymen would say, because we's we. And part 'cos it's all death the other side—all death."

She drew her head slowly in, her puffy cheeks glowed, her small black eyes gazed as fixedly and deadly as if they were anemones on a rock.

The very fulness of her figure seemed to exaggerate her vehemence. She gloated—a heavy somnolent owl puffing its feathers. Alice drew back, swiftly glancing as she did so over her shoulder. The sunlight was liquid wan gold in the meadow, between the black tree-trunks. They lifted their cumbrous branches far above the brick human house, stooping their leafy twigs. A starling's dark iridescence took her glance as he minced pertly in the coarse grass.

" I can't quite see why *you* should think of death," Alice ventured to suggest.

" Me ? Not me ! Where I'm put, I stay. I'm like a stone in the grass, I am. Not that if I were that old mealy-smilin' bag of bones flat on her back on her bed up there with her bits of beadwork and slops through a spout, I wouldn't make sure overnight of not being waked next mornin'. There's something in me that won't let me rest, what they call a volcano, though no more to eat in that beetle cupboard of a kitchen than would keep a Tom Cat from the mange."

" But, Sarah," said Alice, casting a glance up at the curtained windows of the other house, " she looks such a quiet, *patient* old thing. I don't think I *could* stand having not even enough to eat. Why do you stay ? "

Sarah laughed for a full half-minute in silence, staring at Alice meanwhile. " ' Patient ' ! " she replied at last, " Oo-ay. Nor to my knowledge did I ever breathe the contrary. As for staying ; you'd stay all right if that loveyer of yours come along. You'd stand anything—them pale narrow-chested kind ; though me, I'm neether to bend nor break. And if the old man was to look down out of the blue up there this very minute, ay, and shake his fist at me, I'd say it to his face. I loathe your whining psalm-singers. A trap's a trap. You wait and see ! "

" But how do you mean ? " Alice said slowly, her face stooping.

There came no answer. And, on turning, she was surprised to see the bunchy alpaca-clad woman already disappearing round the corner of the house.

The talk softly subsided in her mind like the dust in an empty room. Alice wandered on in the garden, extremely loath to go in. And gradually a curious happiness at last descended upon her heart, like a cloud of morning dew in a dell of wild-flowers. It seemed in moments like these, as if she had been given the power to think—or rather to be conscious, as it were, of thoughts not her own—thoughts like vivid pictures, following one upon another with extraordinary rapidity and brightness through her mind. As if, indeed, thoughts could be like fragments of glass, reflecting light at their every edge and angle. She stood tiptoe at the meadow wall and gazed greedily into the green fields, and across to the pollard aspens by the waterside. Turning, her eyes recognized clear in the shadow and blue-grey air of the garden her solitude —its solitude. And at once all thinking ceased.

"The Spirit is *me* : *I* haunt this place ! " she said aloud, with sudden assurance, and almost in Sarah's own words. "And I don't mind—not the least bit. It can be only my thankful, thankful self that is here. And that can *never* be lost."

She returned to the house, and seemed as she moved to see—almost as if she were looking down out of the sky on herself—her own dwarf figure walking beneath the trees. Yet there was at the same time a curious individuality in the common things, living and inanimate, that were peeping at her out of their secrecy. The silence hung above them as apparent as their own clear reflected colours above the brief Spring flowers. But when she stood tidying herself for the usual hour of reading to Miss Lennox, she was conscious of an almost unendurable weariness.

That night Alice set to work with her needle upon a piece of sprigged muslin to make her " watch-gown " as Sarah called it. She was excited. She hadn't much time, she fancied. It was like hiding in a story. She worked with extreme pains, and quickly. And not till the whole flimsy thing was finished did she try on or admire any part of it. But, at last, in the early evening of one of the middle days of April, she drew her bedroom blind up close to the ceiling to view herself in her yellow grained looking-glass.

The gown, white as milk in the low sunlight, and sprinkled with even white embroidered nosegays of daisies, seemed to attenuate a girlish figure, already very slender. She had arranged her abundant hair with unusual care, and her own clear, inexplicable eyes looked back upon her beauty, bright it seemed with tidings they could not speak.

She regarded closely that narrow, flushed, intense face in an unforeseen storm of compassion and regret, as if with the conviction that she herself was to blame for the inevitable leave-taking. It seemed to gaze like an animal its mute farewell in the dim discoloured glass.

And when she had folded and laid away the gown in her wardrobe, and put on her everyday clothes again, she felt an extreme aversion for the garden. So, instead of venturing out that afternoon, she slipped off its faded blue ribbon from an old bundle of letters which she had hoarded all these years from a school-friend long since lost sight of, and spent the evening reading them over, till headache and an empty despondency sent her to bed.

Lagging Time brought at length the thirtieth of April. Life was as usual. Miss Lennox had even begun to knit her eighth pair of woollen mittens for the annual Church bazaar. To Alice the day passed rather quickly ; a cloudy, humid day with a furtive continual and enigmatical stir in the air. Her lips were parched ; it seemed at any moment her skull might crack with the pain as she sat reading her chapter of Macaulay to Miss Lennox's sparking and clicking needles. Her mind was a veritable rookery of forebodings, flying and returning. She scarcely ate at all, and kept to the house, never even approaching a window. She wrote a long and rather unintelligible letter, which she destroyed when she had read it over. Then suddenly every vestige of pain left her.

And when at last she went to bed—so breathless that she thought her heart at any moment would jump out of her body, and so saturated with expectancy she thought she would die—her candle was left burning calmly, unnodding, in its socket upon the chest of drawers ; the blind of her window was up, towards the houseless by-road ; her pen stood in the inkpot.

She slept on into the morning of May-day, in a sheet of eastern sunshine, till Miss Lennox, with a peevishness that almost amounted to resolution, decided to wake her. But then, Alice, though unbeknown in any really conscious sense to herself, perhaps, had long since decided not to be awakened.

Not until the evening of that day did the sun in his diurnal course for a while illumine the garden, and then very briefly : to gild, to lull, and to be gone. The stars wheeled on in the thick-sown waste of space, and even when Miss Lennox's small share of the earth's wild living creatures had stirred and sunk again to rest in the ebb of night, there came no watcher—not even the very ghost of a watcher—to the garden, in a watch-gown. So that what peculiar secrets found reflex in its dark mirror no human witness was there to tell.

As for Sarah, she had long since done with looking-glasses

once and for all. A place was a place. There was still the washing to be done on Mondays. Fools and weaklings would continue to come and go. But give her *her* way, she'd have blown them and their looking-glasses all to ribbons—with the birds.

THE HOSTELRY

A T the foot of the glaciers, in those naked and rock-bound *couloirs* which indent the snow-clad ranges of the High Alps, you will find every here and there a guest-house. These little hostelries are constructed of timber and are all built very much to the same pattern. The Schwarenbach Inn was one of them.

The Schwarenbach served as a refuge to travellers attempting the passage of the Gemmi. For the six summer months it remained open, with Jean Hauser's family in residence ; but as soon as the early snows began to accumulate, filling the valley and rendering the descent to Loeche impracticable, Jean Hauser with his three sons and his wife and daughter quitted the house, leaving it in charge of the old guide Gaspard Hari and his companion, together with Sam, the big mountain-bred dog. The two men, with the dog, lived in their prison of snow until the spring arrived. They had nothing to look at, except the vast white slopes of the Balmhorn. Pale glistening mountain peaks rose all round them. They were shut in, blockaded, by the snow ; it lay on them like a shroud, growing ever deeper and deeper until the little house was enveloped, closed in, obliterated. The snow piled itself upon the roof, blinded the windows and walled up the door.

On the day, on which the Hauser family took their departure for Loeche, the winter was close at hand, and the descent was becoming dangerous. The three sons set off on foot leading three mules laden with household belongings. Behind them followed the mother, Jeanne Hauser, and her daughter Louise, both riding the same mule. Next and last came the father and the two caretakers. The latter were to

accompany the family as far as the beginning of the track, that
leads down the mountain-side to Loeche.

The party first skirted the edge of the little lake, already
frozen, in its rocky hollow in front of the inn ; then they
proceeded along the valley, which lay before them, a white
sheet of snow, with icy peaks dominating it on every side. A
flood of sunshine fell across the whiteness of this frozen wilderness, lighting it up with a cold, blinding brilliance. There
was no sign of life in this sea of mountains ; not a movement
could be seen in the limitless solitude ; not a sound disturbed
the profound silence.

Gradually the younger of the guides, Ulrich Kunsi, a tall
long-limbed Swiss, forged ahead of the two older men and
overtook the mule, on which the two women were riding.
The daughter saw him as he approached and there was sadness
in the glance with which she summoned him to her side.

She was a little peasant girl with a complexion like milk.
Her flaxen hair was so pale, that one would fancy it had been
bleached by prolonged residence amongst the snows and
glaciers.

On overtaking the mule on which Louise and her mother
were riding, Ulrich Kunsi placed his hand on the crupper and
slackened his pace. The mother began talking ; she ex-
pounded in infinite detail her instructions for wintering. It
was the first time that Ulrich had stayed behind. Old Hari,
on the other hand, had already accomplished his fourteenth
hibernation, under the snow that covered the Schwarenbach
Inn.

Ulrich listened, but without any appearance of grasping
what was said. He never took his eyes off the daughter.
Every now and then he would reply : " Yes, Madame Hauser."
But his thoughts seemed far away, and his face remained calm
and impassive.

They reached the Daubensee, which lies at the foot of the
valley. Its surface was now a vast level sheet of ice. On the
right, the rocks of the Daubenhorn, dark and precipitous, rose
above the vast moraines of the Lemmern Glacier, and the
Wildstrubel towered over all.

As they approached the Gemmi saddle, from which begins
the descent to Loeche, they suddenly beheld, across the deep
wide valley of the Rhone, the prodigious sky-line of the
Valais Alps, a distant multitude of white peaks of unequal
size, some pointed, some flattened, but all glistening in the
rays of the sun.

There was the two-horned Mischabel, the majestic mass
of the Weisshorn, the lumbering Brunegghorn, the lofty and
fear-inspiring Cervin, which has killed so many men, and the
Dent-Blanche, monstrous yet alluring. Below them, in an
enormous hollow at the foot of terrifying precipices, they
caught sight of Loeche, so far away from them that the houses
seemed like a handful of sand, thrown down into the vast
crevasse, which has at one end the barrier of the Gemmi, and
at the other, a wide exit to the Rhone valley.

They had reached the head of a path, which winds downwards, in serpentine coils, fantastic and extraordinary, along
the mountain-side, until it reaches the almost invisible village
at the foot. The mule stopped and the two women jumped
down into the snow. By this time the two older men had
overtaken the rest of the party.

" Now, friends," said old Hauser, " we must say good-bye
till next year. And keep your hearts up."

" Till next year," replied Hari.

The men embraced. Madame Hauser gave her cheek to
be kissed and her daughter followed her example. When it
was Ulrich Kunsi's turn to kiss Louise, he whispered in her ear:
" Don't forget us up on our heights."

" No," she replied in tones so low that he guessed, rather
than heard, the word.

" Well, well, good-bye," said old Hauser again. " Take
care of yourselves."

He strode on past the women and led the way downwards.
All three were lost to view at the first bend in the track. Gaspard
and Ulrich turned back towards the Schwarenbach Inn. They
walked slowly and in silence, side by side. They had seen the
last of their friends. They were to be alone, with no other
companionship, for four or five months.

Gaspard Hari began to tell Ulrich about the previous
winter. His companion then had been Michael Carol ; but
accidents were likely to happen during the long solitude, and
Michael had grown too old for the job. Still, they had had
a pretty good time together. The secret of the whole thing
was to make up your mind to it from the beginning. Sooner
or later one invented distractions and games and things to
while away the time.

With downcast eyes Ulrich Kunsi listened to his companion,
but his thoughts were following the women, who were making
their way to the village, down the zigzag path on the Gemmi
mountain-side

They soon caught sight of the distant inn.   It looked very tiny, like a black dot at the base of the stupendous mountain of snow.   When they opened the door of the house, Sam, the great curly-haired dog, gambolled round them joyfully.

" Well, Ulrich, my boy," said old Gaspard, " we have no women here now.   We must get dinner ready ourselves.   You can set to and peel the potatoes."

They sat down on wooden stools and began to prepare the soup.   The forenoon of the following day seemed long to Ulrich Kunsi.   Old Hari smoked his pipe and spat into the fireplace.   The younger man looked through the window at the superb mountain, which rose in front of the house.   In the afternoon he went out, and pursuing the road he had taken the previous day, he followed the tracks of the mule on which the two women had ridden.   He arrived at last at the saddle of the Gemmi, and lying prone on the edge of the precipice, gazed down on Loeche.   The village, nestling in its rocky hollow, had not yet been obliterated by the snow.   But there was snow very near it.   Its advance had been arrested by the pine forests which guarded the environs of the hamlet.   Seen from a height, the low houses of the village looked like paving-stones set in a field.

Ulrich reflected that Louise Hauser was now in one of those grey cottages.   Which one was it, he wondered.   They were too remote to be separately distinguished.   He had a yearning to go down there, while it was still possible.   But the sun had disappeared behind the great peak of Wildstrubel, and Ulrich turned homewards.   He found Hari smoking. On Ulrich's return Hari proposed a game of cards and the two men sat down on opposite sides of the table.   They played for a long time at a simple game called brisque.   Then they had supper and went to bed.

Subsequent days were like the first, clear and cold, without any fresh fall of snow.   Gaspard passed his days watching the eagles and other rare birds, which adventure themselves in these frozen altitudes.   For his part, Ulrich went regularly to the *col* to look down at the distant village.   In the evening they played cards, dice, and dominoes, staking small objects to lend an interest to the game.

One morning, Hari, who had been the first to rise, called out to Ulrich.   A drifting cloud of white foam, deep yet ethereal, was sinking down on them and on all around them, spreading over them slowly, silently, a cover which grew ever thicker and heavier.   The snowfall lasted four days and four nights. The door and windows had to be cleared, a passage dug, and steps cut, to enable them to climb out on to the surface of powdery snow, which twelve hours of frost had made harder than the granite of the moraines.

After that, they lived as in a prison, hardly ever venturing outside their dwelling. The household tasks were divided between them and were punctually performed. Ulrich Kunsi undertook the cleaning and washing up and keeping the house neat. He also split the firewood. Hari kept the fire going and did the cooking. These necessary and monotonous tasks were relieved by long contests at dice or cards. Being both of them of calm and placid temperament, they never quarrelled. They never went even as far as to display impatience or peevishness, or to speak sharply to each other, both having determined beforehand to make the best of their wintry sojourn on the heights. Occasionally Gaspard took his gun and went out hunting chamois, and when he had the good luck to kill one, it was high day and holiday in the Schwarenbach Inn and there was great feasting on fresh meat.

One morning Hari set forth on one of these expeditions. The thermometer outside the inn showed thirty degrees of frost. Hari started before sunrise, hoping to take the chamois by surprise on the lower slopes of the Wildstrubel.

Left to himself, Ulrich remained in bed until ten o'clock. He was by nature a good sleeper, but he would not have dared to give way to this proclivity in the presence of the old guide, who was an early riser and always full of energy. He lingered over his breakfast, which he shared with Sam, who passed his days and nights sleeping in front of the fire. After breakfast he felt his spirits oppressed, and almost daunted, by the solitude, and he longed for his daily game of cards with the unconquerable craving that comes of ingrained habit. Later, he went out to meet his comrade, who was due to return at four o'clock.

The whole valley was now of a uniform level under its thick covering of snow. The crevasses were full to the top ; the two lakes could no longer be distinguished ; the rocks lay hid under a snowy quilt. Lying at the foot of the immense peaks, the valley was now one immense basin, symmetrical, frozen, and of a blinding whiteness.

It was three weeks since Ulrich had been to the edge of the precipice from which he looked down at the village. He thought he would go there again, before climbing the slopes that led to the Wildstrubel. The snow had now reached

Loeche, and the houses were lost under their white mantle.

Turning to the right, he reached the Lemmern glacier. He walked with the mountaineer's long stride, driving his iron-pointed stick down on to the snow, which was as hard as stone. With his far-sighted eyes he sought the small black dot which he expected to see moving, in the far distance, over this vast sheet of snow. On reaching the edge of the glacier he stopped, wondering whether old Hari had really come that way. Then, with increasing anxiety and quicker steps, he began to skirt the moraines.

The sun was sinking. The snow was suffused with a tinge of pink, and over its crystalline surface swept sharp gusts of a dry and icy breeze. Ulrich tried to reach his friend with a call, shrill, vibrant, prolonged. His voice took its flight into the deathless silence, in which the mountains slept. It rang far out over the deep motionless undulations of frozen foam, like the cry of a bird over the waves of the sea. Then it died away. And there was no reply.

He walked on and on. The sun had sunk behind the peaks, and the purple glow of sunset still lingered about them, but the depths of the valley were grey and shadowy, and Ulrich was suddenly afraid. He had an idea that the silence, the cold, the solitude were taking possession of him, were about to arrest his circulation and freeze his blood, stiffen his limbs and convert him into a motionless, frozen image. With all speed he could, he ran back towards the Inn. Hari, he thought, must have taken another way and reached home already. He would find him seated by the fire, with a dead chamois at his feet. He soon came in sight of the hostelry. There was no smoke issuing from the chimney. Ulrich ran yet faster, and when he opened the door of the house, Sam leaped up to greet him. But there was no Gaspard Hari.

In consternation Kunsi turned hither and thither, as though expecting to find his comrade hiding in a corner. Then he relighted the fire and made the soup, still hoping that he would look up and see the old man coming in. From time to time he went outside, in case there should be some sign of him. Night had fallen, that wan, livid night of the mountains, illumined only by the slender, yellow crescent of a new moon, which was sinking towards the skyline and would soon disappear behind the ridge.

Returning to the house, Ulrich sat down by the fire and while he was warming his hands and feet, his thoughts ran on possible accidents. Gaspard might have broken a leg, or fallen into a hollow, or made a false step, which had cost him a sprained ankle. He would be lying in the snow, helpless against the benumbing cold, in agony of mind, far from any other human soul, calling out for help, shouting with all the strength of his voice in the silence of the night.

How to discover where he was ? So vast and craggy was the mountain, so dangerous the approaches to it, especially in the winter, that it would take ten or twenty guides searching for a week in all directions, to find a man in that immensity. None the less Ulrich made up his mind to take Sam and set forth to look for Gaspard, if he had not come back by one in the morning.

He made his preparations. He put two days' provisions into a bag, took his cramp-irons, wound round his waist a long, strong, slender rope, and inspected thoroughly his spiked stick and his ice-axes. Then he waited. The fire was burning with a clear flame ; the great dog lay snoring in its warmth ; the steady ticking of the clock, in its resonant wooden case, sounded like the beating of a heart. Still he waited, his ears straining to catch any distant noise. When the light breeze whispered round roof and walls, he shivered.

The clock struck the hour of midnight. Feeling chilled and nervous, he put some water on the fire to boil, so that he might have some steaming coffee before setting out. When the clock struck one, he rose, called Sam, opened the door and struck out in the direction of the Wildstrubel. He climbed for five hours continuously. He scaled the rocks with the help of his irons, and cut steps in the ice with his axe, always advancing steadily and sometimes hauling the dog after him up some steep escarpment. It was about six o'clock when he reached one of the peaks to which Gaspard often came in search of chamois. There he waited for the day to break.

The sky above became gradually paler. Then suddenly that strange radiance, which springs no one knows whence, gleamed over the great ocean of snow-clad peaks, stretching for a hundred leagues around him. The vague light seemed to arise out of the snow itself and to diffuse itself in space. One by one, the highest and farthest pinnacles were suffused by a tender rosy hue and the red sun rose from behind the great masses of the Bernese Alps. Ulrich Kunsi set forth again. Like a hunter, he bent down, searching for tracks and saying to his dog :

" Seek, old man, seek."

He was now on his way down the mountain, investigating
every chasm, and sometimes sending forth a prolonged call,
which quickly died away in the dumb immensity. At times he
put his ear close to the ground to listen. Once he thought he
heard a voice and he ran in the direction of it, shouting as he
ran, but he heard nothing more, and sat down, exhausted and
despairing. About midday he shared some food with Sam,
who was as weary as himself. And again he set out on his
search. When evening came, he was still walking, having
accomplished fifty kilometres among the mountains. He was
too far from his house to think of returning there, and too tired
to drag himself along any farther. Digging a hole in the snow,
he curled up in it with his dog, under cover of a blanket, which
he had brought with him. Man and beast lay together, each
body sharing the warmth of the other, but frozen to the marrow
none the less. Ulrich's mind was haunted by visions, and his
limbs were shaking with cold. He could not sleep at all.
When he rose, day was on the point of breaking. His legs felt
as rigid as bars of iron ; his resolution was so enfeebled, that
he almost sobbed aloud in his distress, and his heart beat so
violently that he nearly collapsed with emotion whenever he
fancied that he heard a sound.

The thought suddenly came to him that he too might
perish of cold amidst these solitudes, and the fear of such a
death whipped up his energy and roused him to fresh vigour.
He was now making the descent towards the Inn, and kept
falling down from weariness and picking himself up again.
His dog Sam, with one paw disabled, followed far behind,
limping. It was four o'clock in the afternoon before they
reached the Schwarenbach. Hari was not there. Ulrich lighted
a fire, had something to eat, and then fell asleep, so utterly
stupefied with fatigue that he could think of nothing. He
slept for a long, a very long time. It seemed as if nothing
could break his repose, when suddenly he heard a voice cry
" Ulrich." He was shaken out of his profound torpor, and
started up. Was it a dream ? Was it one of those strange
summonses that disturb the slumber of uneasy souls ? No.
He could hear it still That quivering hail had pierced his ear,
had taken possession of his body, right to the tips of his nervous
fingers. Beyond all doubt, there had been a cry for help, an
appeal for succour. Some one had called out " Ulrich ! "
Then some one must be in the vicinity of the house. There
could be no question about it. He opened the door and shouted
with all his strength " Gaspard, is that you ? "

There was no reply. The silence was not broken by sound, or whisper, or groan. It was night, and the snow lay all around, ghastly in its whiteness.

The wind had risen. It was that icy wind which splits the rocks and leaves nothing alive on these forsaken altitudes. It blew in sharp, withering gusts, dealing death more surely than even the fiery blasts of the desert. Again Ulrich called out :

" Gaspard, Gaspard, Gaspard ! "

He waited a little, but silence still reigned on the mountainside, and he was forthwith stricken by a terror, which shook him to the very bones. He leaped back into the inn, closed and bolted the door, and with chattering teeth collapsed into a chair. He was now sure that the appeal for help had come from his comrade, at the moment at which he was yielding up the ghost. He was as certain of that as one is of being alive or eating bread. For two days and three nights old Gaspard Hari had been wrestling with death in some hollow in one of those deep unsullied ravines, whose whiteness is more sinister than the darkness of underground caverns. For two days and three nights he had been dying, and at this very moment, while he lay in the article of death, his thoughts had turned to his comrade, and his soul, in the instant of gaining its freedom, had flown to the inn where Ulrich lay sleeping. It had exercised that mysterious and terrible power, possessed by the souls of the dead, to haunt the living. The voiceless spirit had called aloud in the overwrought soul of the sleeper, had uttered its last farewell, or, perhaps, its reproach, its curse on the man, who had not searched diligently enough.

Ulrich felt its presence there, behind the walls of the house, behind the door, which he had just closed. The soul was prowling around. It was like a bird of night fluttering against a lighted window. Ulrich, distraught with terror, was ready to scream. He would have taken to flight, but dared not open the door. And never again, he felt, would he dare to open that door, for the spectre would be hovering, day and night, round the inn, until the corpse of the old guide had been recovered and laid in the consecrated earth of a cemetery.

When day broke, Ulrich regained a little confidence from the brilliance of the returning sun. He prepared his breakfast and made some soup for the dog, but after that, he remained seated motionless in a chair. His heart was in agony ; his thoughts turned ever to the old man, who was lying out there in the snow. When night again descended upon the moun-

tains, new terrors assailed him. He paced to and fro in the
smoke-blackened kitchen, by the dim light of a solitary candle.
Up and down he strode, and always he was listening, listening,
for that cry, which had terrified him the night before. Might
it not ring out again through the mournful silence of the outer
world ? He felt forlorn, poor wretch ; forlorn, as never a
man had been, here in this vast whiteness of snow, all alone,
seven thousand feet above the inhabited world, above the
dwellings of men, above the excitements, the hubbub, the
noise, the thrills of life ; alone in the frozen sky. He was torn
by a mad desire to make his escape in whatsoever direction,
by whatsoever means ; to descend to Loeche, even if he had
to hurl himself over the precipice. But he did not dare so
much as to open the door ; he felt sure that that thing outside,
the dead man, would bar his passage, and prevent him from
leaving his comrade alone upon those heights.

As midnight approached his limbs grew weary, and fear
and distress overcame him. He dreaded his bed, as one dreads
a haunted spot, but yielding at last to drowsiness he sank into
a chair.

Suddenly his ears were pierced by the same strident cry
that he had heard the previous night. It was so shrill that
Ulrich stretched out his hands to ward off the ghost, and
losing his balance fell backwards on to the floor. Aroused by
the noise, the dog began to howl in terror, and ran hither and
thither in the room, trying to find out whence the danger
threatened. When he came to the door, he sniffed at the edge
of it, and began howling, snorting, and snarling, his hair
bristling, his tail erect. Beside himself with terror, Kunsi
rose and grasping a stool by one leg, shouted :

" Don't come in. Don't come in. Don't come in or I'll
kill you."

Excited by his menacing tones, the dog barked furiously
at the invisible enemy, whom his master was challenging.
Gradually Sam calmed down, and went back to lie on the
hearth, but he was still uneasy ; his eyes were gleaming and
he was baring his fangs and growling. Ulrich, too, regained
his wits ; but feeling faint with terror, he took a bottle of
brandy from the sideboard and drank several glasses of it in
quick succession. As his mind became duller, his courage
rose, and a feverish heat coursed along his veins. On the
following day he ate hardly anything, confining himself to
the brandy, and for some days after, he lived in a state of
brutish intoxication. The moment the thought of Gaspard

Hari crossed his mind, he began drinking and he did not leave off until he collapsed to the ground in a drunken torpor, and lay there face downwards, snoring and helpless. Hardly had he recovered from the effects of the burning and maddening liquor, when the cry " Ulrich ! " roused him, as though a bullet had penetrated his skull. He started to his feet staggering to and fro, stretching out his hands to keep himself from falling, and calling to his dog to help him. Sam, too, appeared to be seized with his master's madness. He hurled himself against the door, scratching at it with his claws, gnawing it with his long white teeth, while Ulrich, with his head thrown back, his face turned upwards, swallowed brandy in great gulps, as though he were drinking cool water after a climb. Presently his thoughts, his memory, his terror, would be drowned in drunken oblivion.

In three weeks he had finished his entire stock of spirits. But the only effect of his inebriation was to lull his terror to sleep. When the means for this were no longer available, his fears returned with fresh ferocity. His fixed idea, aggravated by prolonged intoxication, gained force continually in that absolute solitude, and worked its way, like a gimlet, ever deeper into his spirit. Like a wild beast in a cage, he paced his room, every now and then putting his ear to the door to listen for the voice of Gaspard's ghost, and hurling defiance at it through the wall. And when, in utter weariness, he lay down, he would again hear the voice and leap once more to his feet. At last, one night, with the courage of a coward driven to bay, he flung himself at the door and opened it, to see who it was who was calling him, and to compel him to silence. But the cold air struck him full in the face, and froze him to the marrow. He slammed the door to again, and shot the bolts, never noticing that his dog had dashed out into the open. Shivering, he threw some more wood on to the fire and sat down to warm himself. Suddenly he started. There was some one scratching at the wall and moaning.

" Go away," he said, terror-stricken.

The answer was a melancholy wail.

His last remaining vestiges of reason were swept away by fear.

" Go away," he cried again, and he turned hither and thither in an effort to find some corner in which he could hide himself. But the creature outside continued to wail, and passed along the front of the house, rubbing itself against the wall. Ulrich dashed to the oaken sideboard, which was full of provisions and crockery, and with superhuman strength dragged it across the room and set it against the door to act as a barricade. Then he took all the remaining furniture, mattresses, palliasses, chairs, and blockaded the window, as if in a state of siege. But the thing outside went on groaning dismally, and Ulrich himself was soon replying with groans not less lugubrious. Days and nights passed, and still these two continued to answer each other's howls.

The ghost, as it seemed to Ulrich, moved unceasingly round the house, scratching at the walls with its nails in a fierce determination to break a way through. Within the house, Ulrich crouched with his ear close to the masonry, following every movement of the thing outside, and answering all its appeals with horrifying shrieks. Then came a night, when Ulrich heard no more sounds from without. Overcome with fatigue, he dropped into a chair and fell asleep immediately. When he awoke, his mind and memory were a blank. It was as if that sleep of prostration had swept his brain clean of everything. He felt hungry and took some food. . . .

The winter was over. The passage of the Gemmi became practicable ; and the Hauser family set forth on its journey to the inn. At the top of the first long acclivity, the two women clambered up on to their mule. They spoke about the two men, whom they expected presently to meet again. They were surprised that neither of them had descended a few days earlier, as soon as the Loeche road was practicable, to give them the news of their long winter sojourn. When they came in sight of the inn, which was still covered with a thick mantle of snow, they saw that the door and window were closed, but old Hauser was reassured by a thin column of smoke, which was rising from the chimney. As he drew nearer, however, he saw on the outer threshold the skeleton of an animal. It was a large skeleton, lying on its side, and the flesh had been torn off the bones by eagles.

All three examined it.

" That must be Sam," Madame Hauser said.

Then she called out for Gaspard, and from the inside of the house came a shrill cry like that of an animal. Old Hauser, too, shouted Gaspard's name. A second cry came from within. The father and his two sons thereupon endeavoured to open the door, but it resisted their efforts. They took a long beam out of an empty stable, and used it as a battering-ram. They dashed it with all their strength against the door, which gave way with the shriek of splintering planks. The sideboard fell over on the floor with a great crash, which shook the house, and revealed, standing behind it, a man whose hair came down to his shoulders, and whose beard touched his chest. His eyes were bright ; his clothing was in rags.

Louise alone recognized him.

" Mamma ! " she gasped, " it is Ulrich."

And the mother saw that it was indeed Ulrich, although his hair had turned white.

He suffered them to come near him and touch him, but when they asked him questions, he made no reply. He had to be taken down to Loeche, where the doctors certified that he was insane.

The fate of old Gaspard was never known.

During the following summer Louise Hauser came near to dying of a decline, which was attributed to the rigours of the mountain climate.

A LARGE DIAMOND

THERE were several of us sitting before the fire at our club, in the room in which we all gather after lunch ; some of us on the sofa in front of it, others scattered about in chairs. It was a grey, dull winter evening. Evening is the word for it, not afternoon. It seemed to have begun about eleven a.m. ; and now at a quarter to three night was obviously falling. Often on such occasions I've heard such talk there that you would not notice that a cheerless day was dully dying in fog, nor for that matter would you have cared if the smiles of summer were luring all others out into golden air. I've heard talk there as brilliant, and sound as well, as any one could desire. And the variety of it ! And yet this evening, with the fog in our throats, and I suppose deep down in our spirits, this is the kind of conversation we were having, as far as I can remember :

" By gad, that's a big one."

" Big what ? "

" Big diamond."

" Oh, I thought you meant a fish."

" No, a diamond."

" But you can't tell from a picture like that."

" Yes, I can."

" How can you ? "

" It's life-size."

" How do you know ? "

" Why, it says so."

" But do you suppose the editor knows ? "

" Of course he does."

" How ? "

"Why, a stone like that is known all over the world : he has only got to ask."

"Still, I don't see how a flat picture can give one any idea of the size of a solid diamond."

"Don't you ? "

"No, I don't."

"Well, anyway it's a big one."

"Oh yes, it's big."

"Well, that's all I said."

One thing, and one thing alone, relieved for me the tedium of this discussion, and that was that Jorkens, who was in the club that day, was solemnly shaking his head. He began at the first mention of a big diamond, quietly continuing through the whole discussion. I hardly noticed him at first, and perhaps should never have done so at all had he not shaken his head with increasing vigour whenever any one called the diamond big. But for this the monotony of his disagreement might have escaped my attention. I listened then to hear what Jorkens would say, and not a word came from him, but the confidence with which he sat shaking his head made me feel—you could not doubt it—that he really knew something about diamonds that was pretty well hidden from most of us. It wasn't like him to sit silent so long ; and it was I that eventually broke his silence when my curiosity could bear it no longer. In any case it was time these two dull fellows stopped discussing their diagram in an illustrated paper. I glanced at the paper and said directly to Jorkens : "It's a pretty big one, isn't it ? "

"Not really," said Jorkens quietly.

"Why," I said, " have you ever seen a bigger one ? "

"Yes," said Jorkens.

"Where is it ? " I asked.

"Well, people who think a stone like that is specially big," said Jorkens, " will hardly believe in my stone."

It was, if I remember right, a diagram of the Koh-i-noor.

"I'll believe anything," I said.

And one or two other fellows, bored I suppose by the fog, leaned forward and said, " So will we."

Something in that seemed to cheer Jorkens and encourage him a good deal, and without any more ado he started his tale at once.

"It was a long time ago," he said. " Many years ago a meteorite had fallen in the far North of Russia, up in the Esquimaux land, a colossal thing ; and it took a year or so for the news to reach civilized Europe. When it did, it came only as rumour. But what struck me at once, as soon as I heard the rumour, was that the thing must have been as big as a mountain. For one can sift truth out of a rumour as well as out of anything else, if you go the right way about it. It appeared first as a fable of the Esquimaux. A god, they said, had arrived in a flaming car and driven away southwards, and the sky was red all night and all the snow was melted for forty miles.

" It was not a matter of trusting the Esquimaux ; I wouldn't trust them a yard ; but simple people invent tales usually for simple reasons, and where was the reason here ? Their report passed unnoticed ; but to me it seemed that the only reason for its existence was that something like that, something that looked like that, must actually have happened ; in fact, a meteorite, and one vastly larger than any that had hit the world before. In the end I went to look for it.

" I had no difficulty in finding it, either : the Esquimaux had given geographical details. What was difficult was to find out what on earth had happened. I found a mountain of meteoric iron before I had gone a day and a half from the coast, and it seemed to be what I was looking for. It was not on the map, but then very little in those parts was ; so that proved nothing. It was of the right material, and within forty or fifty miles of the right place ; and yet, without shutting one's eyes to a very obvious fact, one could not be satisfied that one had discovered what I was looking for. My expedition was purely scientific, and in science you can't shut your eyes to facts that don't quite fit. I used to be very keen on science in those days. I made many scientific journeys. I may have told you of some of them."

I didn't want Jorkens to wander, because, if he did that, you never got him back.

" What was wrong with your mountain ? " I asked.

" Simply," said Jorkens, " that a colossal thing like that, as big as one of the Alps, could not have hit the earth at the enormous pace those things travel at, plus the pace of our own earth, without having gone right in and utterly buried itself. But here it was sticking up in the air as high as the St. Gothard. Well, I questioned the Esquimaux then. I had three or four with me, running my reindeer sleigh, and you must remember that nothing had come to our end of Europe about this meteorite except Esquimaux's rumours, so that these rumours were the only scientific data that I had on which to work. Well, they stuck to their story that the god in his car had arrived much farther North and had driven away in this direction. And the conflagration had been where he had arrived, not here. That puzzled me for a long time. It seemed simple enough. It seemed so like burning forests. And yet there weren't forests there in the North : it was just snow and ice, except for one month in the year, when the snow melted and enough sparse vegetation appeared to feed a few reindeer. I knew very few dozen words of the Esquimaux language, and I questioned them largely by signs ; but there was no doubt about that conflagration.

"And all of a sudden I got it, an exposed stratum of coal. The meteorite must have hit it and set it flaming.

"There was no sign of any coal round the mountain that I had seen, so it must have struck our earth a glancing blow and ricochetted on. That was what I eventually decided on, and it turned out to be right. You see the meteorite had not merely dropped ; the gravitation of Earth had not been its only influence ; if so it would have come straight ; but it had its own orbit and a movement of its own ; this combined with the pull of the earth had made its slanting course, and it had hit us obliquely and ricochetted.

"When I had worked out this it was easy enough to follow up the course of the meteorite to where it had first struck earth. Theory is the difficult thing : any one can do practice. Well, the mountain had hit the earth in several places, leaving shallow hollows like the beds of old lakes, about a mile apart. But after a while the distances grew greater and the hollows much deeper, more and more of them being partly filled with water. I had had to leave the reindeer behind at the mountain, because the snow was rapidly melting. I had chosen the one month in the year when the snow is gone, so that I could see the ground."

"By the way," said some one, "are there diamonds in Russia ? "

"Are there diamonds in Russia ? " repeated Jorkens with a sort of sad fervour.

"Well, you were telling us about a diamond, weren't you ? " he said.

"You shall hear," said Jorkens. "You shall hear." And then he added, "You know what a diamond is, I suppose ? "

"Well, of course we do," said one or two of us, with the rather irritable confident air that so often goes with ignorance. But one man knew. "Crystallized carbon," he said.

And then Jorkens went on with his tale. " The snow had all melted ; I'd timed my journey just right for that ; and we went on with three donkeys that I bought at a kind of village, if you can give such a name to a cluster of huts that comes one year and goes the next. I had three Esquimaux, one for each donkey. Our kit was on the donkeys and we walked.

" We came to a huge depression in the earth, into which water had come, and frozen. A huge lake without reeds, not yet discovered by wild fowl. A most lonely waste ; cold, empty, and glittering dully, the ice turning to slush. And then no more of these hollows for twenty-five miles. It was in fact the last of the bounces the mountain had made. Or the first, rather ; for I was travelling in the opposite direction. We camped about ten miles North of that vast lake, glad to see the last of its chilly miles of dull loneliness. Next day we packed up our crude little tents and did fifteen miles more. And that brought us to the place where the meteor had first hit our earth, striking a glancing blow. Right on the top of the earth it had fallen, partly pulled by our gravitation, and partly flying on some course of its own, which our arrival must have disturbed. Then, as I have said, it ricochetted away.

" There was no mistaking the place where it had struck : first of all, because I had been right about the coal, and we walked over about a mile of cinders, a fine outcrop of coal burned right down to the bottom of the stratum as far as I could tell. And then we came to a wide, flat, dreary waste, going perfectly level to the horizon ; and cold, it was horribly cold. And the snow still covered it though it was gone everywhere else. I intended to camp that night on it so as to take a few miles off the long journey, next day, to the other side. But the Esquimaux would not come. I asked them why not. Bad ice, they said. I stamped through the snow and it seemed hard as steel. But they repeated, ' Bad ice.' ' What's wrong ? ' I asked so far as I could manage their language. ' Too cold,' they said. ' Very bad ice.'

" ' You don't like ice being cold ? ' I tried to ask. But you can't be ironical with natives, in their language, helped out by signs.

" ' No,' they said. ' Very cold.'

" So in the end I took the donkey that had my own tent, and went on alone through the snow. Being unable to tether the donkey he went off that night after the rest, but I managed to get my tent up, and tried to get some sleep, cold though it was. The silence was measureless, not a sound from the cracking of ice, not a rumble from water. There are hundreds of sounds that come grumbling up through ice ; but there there was not a murmur, not a whisper, and no sounds of animal life but my donkey breathing. And later on, when he went away, I thought I heard him slithering on the hardness for five miles, till he reached the shore, for there was no other sound whatever in all that waste. That silence in the cold kept me awake for a long time. So that when a sort of morning came and I put on my skates, I knew already, as well as the Esquimaux, that there was something odd about it. I put on my skates because the layer of snow had all melted. It had puzzled me to see it there at all ; but I have seen the same on a hard tennis-court when it has gone from everything else. I had trudged overnight in my boots, my snow-shoes having gone back with the reindeer ; but now I put on a pair of skates, and calculated on getting to the other side in a few hours. Yet I saw that there was something odd about it. The queer glitter of the thing was odd if nothing else. Well, I soon found out what was the matter with that ice. It was harder than steel. That was one thing that was the matter with it. My skates wouldn't grip at all, and I sprawled and fell till I was bruised all over. What could that meteorite have done to ice, I thought ? And all of a sudden the right idea struck me. If it was harder than steel it wasn't ice. The idea came to me while I was on my hands and knees, looking down into depths of light. I pulled out my pocket-knife and tried to scratch it. Not a mark would it make. There aren't many things on earth that steel won't scratch, and this was one of them. I had a ring in those days, a stone set in gold, that as a matter of fact was rock crystal. Not the one I am wearing now, of course ; that is perfectly genuine. People used to think it was a diamond, though I didn't buy it with that intention. I don't remember why I bought it : liked the look of it, I suppose : took my fancy. Anyhow, I had this bit of a crystal in a ring, and I tried it now on the cold glittering substance ; and not a scratch would it make either. It would have scratched it if it had been rock crystal too. This left very few things it could be. Well, I sat down on the wet stone and took off my skates. Then I stood up and shaded my eyes from that frightful glare, and tried to think. It was no use going back to the idea that that wide plain was of ice. An unscientific mind might have wasted time considering such things ; but the touch of the steel had proved that that was impossible. I had therefore to think forward to new theories. Well, it was easy enough. The first thing you do when you see a stone—I mean, if you are a scientist—is to consider what stratum you're on. The moment I thought of it it was clear enough. I was on coal ; I had seen the burnt cinders all along the edges. You know what coal is."

" Carbon, by gad," said the man who had spoken last.

" But you don't mean . . ." some one else was beginning ; when Jorkens quietly said to him · " Well, you know what crystallizes carbon, or anything else."

" Pressure, isn't it ? " said the other.

" Pressure beyond anything we can imagine, and heat beyond any fire we have ever lit," said Jorkens. " Well, not quite beyond, because a diamond has been made in a laboratory. Only it was so small, and the requisite pressure was so expensive, that I don't think any one ever tried it again. But imagine a white-hot mountain travelling at, say, a thousand miles a minute : add the pace of our earth, doing about the same, and a bit more for the force of gravity ; and pitch the whole thing full into a field of carbon. Why, the result is so obvious that I might have guessed it, without the trouble of going to look. But now that I had gone to look I decided to go right across it and see the other side. And a weary journey it was. The awful hardness, the cold and that deadly glitter, wearied feet and head and heart. Chiefly I was looking for a flaw, in order to insert a knife-blade, or the edge of my skate, and bring a good slab back. And—would you believe it—there was not a flaw in the whole of it.

" A headache I got from the glare grew worse all the time ; and there was no nightfall to help me at the end of June in those latitudes. I plodded wearily on, and the sight of any considerable display of diamonds has wearied me ever since. That is the true reason why I don't go to Lady Clashion's evening parties any more, and you can tell whom you please. Well, I went on and on ; and at last, late in what would have been evening in any civilized country, I got to the other side. There was nothing much to see, just burnt cinders again ; dusty to walk on, of course, but I came the whole way back over the ashes rather than cross that diamond again. I was wearing furs, so I was able to sleep on the way. I couldn't have done it in one journey, even if I'd started fresh. It was a long way round the shore of that diamond, over the ashes.

"I found my Esquimaux again, but nothing would take them near the diamond. Devils had come there, I gathered from them, after the god had gone, and had enchanted the place with coldness and glare. Whether they had pursued him to Earth, or had merely come to the place that he had vacated, I did not know enough of their language to gather. In any case there are many ways of accounting for anything, and the scientific and the religious are two of them. I was going one way, while the Esquimaux went the other.

"I might with some difficulty, and certainly with much publicity, have got a quantity of dynamite at the coast, and gone back and got enough splinters to have stocked the Rue de la Paix. You know Paris? Yes, yes; of course. But I had bigger ideas than that. I wanted to beautify homes. I wanted to form a company that would bring chandeliers of surpassing beauty within reach of the moderately rich. I had planned gorgeous vases. And I had thought a good deal along the lines of sheer utility.

"And in the end what happened? The very day that I got to London, the very day, I saw placards in the streets saying, 'Big Earthquake In ——.' Just saw those words, the top three lines. I rushed up to a newspaper man. 'Don't tell me,' I said. 'Don't tell me. It's in Russia.' And, sure enough, I was right, though they called it something ending in ' ansk.'

"I knew it was there. You see, I knew what a blow the earth had received. I knew that the strata must have been shattered for miles down, under that frightful blow. I had been thinking of nothing else. You know how, if a friend hurts an ankle badly, or has a groggy knee, and all of a sudden you see his name in the papers, or it might be a her; you know at once what's happened; the ankle or knee has given out, and they have fallen and hurt themselves. It was just the same with our poor old earth: I knew what a blow she had had, and the moment I saw the word Earthquake I knew where it was. And I was perfectly right. They had merely worked it out from the seismograph, but I could have told them the very spot.

"Of course I went back at once to see what had happened. No use forming a company to place a thing like that on the market, until you're sure that it's all right. I went back by the next boat. And I found worse than I'd feared. It had been the hell of an earthquake. And no wonder, considering the frightful blow that the strata there had received. The

wonder is that they had held up so long. Worse than I'd
feared, it was certainly ; a long way worse. The diamond
had tilted sideways. It must have been that : it could never
have gone clean out of sight, as it had, if only it had stayed
level. But that would have been too much to expect, with all
the strata like broken arches after some unimaginable railway
accident. When they went they must have just dropped
in heaps, into subterranean caverns of which we know nothing.
Anyhow the diamond was gone. Not even the cinders were
there, that had been like a shore all round it. It was gone
with every trace, and the earth had closed again over it. It
almost looked as if the right thing had happened, in a kind of
way, after all. We're probably better, in the end, without that
diamond. But I'm not a philosopher. Not that I didn't do
my best to bear my loss as I suppose one ought to. And I
think I do, pretty well ; considering the size of it. Only,
you can understand, when I hear any one talk of big diamonds,
that it upsets me a bit. I can't help it."

"Couldn't you have dug for it ? " The question came
out of the silence that had fallen when Jorkens ceased ; it
came out of the gloom of one of the leather chairs, now dim
with that wintry evening but for the glow from the fire.

"Couldn't we have dug for it ! " exclaimed Jorkens.
"Couldn't we have dug for it ! *Of course* we could. A
couple of thousand men might have done for a start. But I
thought we'd better do the thing properly. Fifty thousand
would have been about the right number, and we could have
easily got them in Russia. Labour is cheap there ; ten shillings
a week would have done for them. That would have been
£25,000 a week. We are sure to have got results in about
ten weeks. That would have been two hundred and fifty
thousand in wages. Say the same again for feeding them,
and about the same for transport. Then, of course, there'd
have been the housing ; quite primitive huts would have done.
We could have done the whole thing for a million to start with.
And what is a million in the City of London ? But do you
think I could get it ? Money in plenty, and imagination
simply not there. I tried talk, I tried everything, and as many
drinks as they wanted ; but not one would put up that million.
Good Lord, when I think of the profits, the hundreds of
thousands per cent. profit on that one miserable million ; and
not a single one of them would touch it. It was enough to
make me tell them what I thought of them. I did tell one of
them : and then I gave it up.

"Waiter," he called, "bring me a very small whisky, with just a dash of soda in it."

There are no very small whiskies in our club. There are small whiskies, of course; but all the waiters know that they must never bring a small one to Jorkens.

THE CUPBOARD

AMONG all the tenants of Clifford's Inn none was more highly esteemed than Mr. John Jarvey, Attorney-at-Law. His clients, as the case might be, confided their woes to him unreservedly, depended with boundless faith upon his astuteness to extricate them from their difficulties, and respected him, each and all, for his eminent and approved worth. As for Mr. Jarvey himself, tall and neat of person, kindly and unobtrusive of manner, he seemed to radiate a mild benevolence, from the crisp curls of his precise wig to the broad buckles of his trim shoes ; in a word, Mr. Jarvey was all that a highly respected Attorney-at-Law could possibly attain unto.

Even Job, the gate porter (whose salutations were in exact ratio to his estimation of the standing and condition of the various residents), would lift knobby fingers to the brim of his hat with gesture slow and unspeakably respectful, while Tom, the bed-maker, a cheery soul, given alternately to whistling and sucking at a noxious clay pipe, checked the one and left the other outside when duty summoned him within the top-floor chambers of Number ——, which was Mr. Jarvey's abode ; and Christopher, the bootblack, who plied his trade within the shadow of Temple Bar, with Mr. Jarvey's leg before him and Mr. Jarvey's comfortable, kindly voice in his ears, scrubbed and rubbed with a gusto to lend worthy Mr. Jarvey's shoes an added sheen.

Such, then, was Mr. John Jarvey, Attorney-at-Law, of Number ——, Clifford's Inn.

Now it was upon a certain blusterous and rainy December night towards eleven of the clock, that Job, the gate porter, nodding comfortably over the fire within his lodge, was aroused by a loud and imperious rapping on the outer door.

Sighing, Job sat up and, having paused awhile to blink at the cosy fire and murmur a plaintive curse or so upon his disturber, got slowly to his feet as the summons was repeated and, stepping forth of his lodge, proceeded to draw bolt and bar, and open the gate.

A tall figure, in a long, rain-sodden, many-caped riding-coat and wide-eaved hat—this much he saw by aid of the dim lamp that flickered in the fitful wind-gusts.

" Mr. John Jarvey ? " inquired a hoarse voice, though somewhat indistinct by reason of upturned coat-collar and voluminous muffler.

" 'Oo ? " demanded Job aggressively, and squaring his elbows.

The stranger raised a large hand to loosen the shawl about his mouth and chin, and Job noticed a small, plain gold ring that gleamed upon the little finger of this hand.

" I said Mr. John Jarvey. He lives here still ? "

" Sure-ly ! " nodded Job. " Five and twenty year to my knowin' ! But if you be come on bizness you be over-late ! Mr. Jarvey never sees nobody arter six o'clock, nohow. Never did—never will, makes it a rule, 'e do."

" And he lives here—at Number ——, I think ? "

" Ay, Number ——, top floor as ever was, but if you be come on bizness it aren't no manner o' good you—Lord love me ! " gasped Job as, swept aside by a long arm, he staggered, and watched the tall figure flit past and vanish in the swirling, gusty darkness of the Inn. For a moment Job meditated pursuit, but, thinking better of it, shook his head and proceeded to bolt and bar the gate.

" By goles ! " said he, addressing the gusty dark. " Of all the body-snatching raskell rogues yon's the body-snatchingest —burn 'im, inn'ards and out'ards ! "

With which malediction Job got back to fire and arm-chair and promptly fell a-dozing, like the watchman he was.

Meantime the stranger, with head bowed to the lashing rain, slipped and stumbled over the uneven pavement, blundered into iron railings, fell foul of unsuspected corners and, often pausing to peer about him in the gloom, found his way at last to the dim-lit doorway of Number —— and stood to read, among divers others, the name of John Jarvey, Attorney-at-Law. He seemed to find some subtle fascination in the name, for he stood there with the rain running off him while he read it over and over again, speaking the words to himself in a soft,

sibilant whisper, suggestive of clenched teeth : " John Jarvey,
Attorney-at-Law ! " while his hands (buried in the deep
side-pockets of his coat hitherto) began to fumble with the
muffler that swathed throat and chin, to loosen the buttons of
his caped coat, and his right hand, gliding into his breast,
seemed to touch and caress something that lay hidden there.
Thus stood he, peering from the shadow of his hat and whispering to himself so long that the rain, dripping from his garments,
formed small, evil-looking pools on the dingy floor.

Suddenly he turned and, with left hand outstretched and
groping in the air before him, and right hand hidden in his
bosom, began to climb the dark stair.

He mounted slowly and very softly, and so at last reached
the topmost landing, where burned a lantern whose feeble light
showed a door whereon was painted the name :

MR. JOHN JARVEY

Clenching his fist the visitor struck this name three resounding blows, tried the latch, found the door unlocked and,
flinging it wide, snatched off his hat and stared upon the man,
who, just risen from the elbow-chair beside the blazing fire,
stood staring back at him.

And surely, surely neither Job, the porter, nor Tom, the
bed-maker, nor any of his many clients, would have recognized
the worthy and estimable Mr. John Jarvey in this grey-visaged,
shaking wretch who wiped the sweat from furrowed brow with
nerveless fingers and peered at the intruder in such wide-eyed,
speechless terror.

" Aha ! " said the stranger, flinging off his sodden coat.
" Aha, John—though twenty years are apt to change a man,
I see you remember me. Ay, I've been buried—damn you !
Buried for nigh twenty years, John, while you—you that sent
me to it, prospered and grew fat—curse you ! But the grave
has given up the dead, and I'm alive again, John ! And a live
man has appetites—I have, many and raging ! So here come
I, John, freed from the hell you sent me to."

" I never did, Maurice, no, not I—never—never——"

" So here come I, John, hasting you-wards to supply all
I lack—my every need. For I mean to live, John, live on
you, by you, with you. I mean to make up for all the wasted
years. I have many needs, and every day these needs shall
grow."

Mr. Jarvey's deep-set eyes, usually so keen and steady,

flickered oddly, his glance wandered, his hands fluttered vaguely.

" I—I am not a rich man—indeed no, Maurice. What would you have of me ? "

" All you possess—and then more ! Your money, your friends, your honour, your cursed self-complacency, your life, your very soul. My wants are infinite."

" If," said Mr. Jarvey, in the same strange, hesitant fashion, " if you will be a little reasonable, Maurice, if you'd be—a little reasonable—if you only would——"

" Bah ! " cried the other, seating himself in Mr. Jarvey's cosy elbow-chair and stretching his long legs to the blaze. " Still the same snivelling coward ! She called you coward twenty-odd years ago, and so she might again were she here and alive. But she's dead, John, dead and forgot by all save you and me. And, being dead, should her ghost haunt your chambers to-night and behold you with her spirit-eyes, shivering and sweating where you stand, she'd name you ' coward ' again ! "

From ashen white to burning red, from burning red to ashen white, and upon his pallid cheek a line of sweat that glittered in the candlelight, with hands clenched to sudden, quivering fists, and head bowed between his shoulders, Mr. Jarvey stood and listened, but under drawn brows his eyes, vague no longer, fixed themselves momentarily on the thin, aquiline face opposite, eyes, these, bright with more than their wonted keenness ere they were hidden beneath sudden, down-drooping lids.

" Her—ghost ? " he mumbled indistinctly, his glance wandering again. " Is—she—dead, indeed ? "

" Years ago, John, and with bitter curses on your memory ! Here's her ring—you'll remember it, I'm sure," and the stranger showed a small, battered gold ring upon his little finger, then reaching out he took up a glass that steamed aromatically on the hob.

" Aha," said he, " what's here, John ? "

" My night-cap, Maurice," answered Mr. Jarvey, his roving gaze now upon the worn carpet beneath his slippered feet—" rum—hot water—sugar and a slice of lemon. I—I didn't know she was dead, Maurice ! "

" Ay, she's dead—and gone, like your rum and water," saying which the speaker emptied the glass and set it down with a crash.

" Dead ? " murmured Mr. Jarvey, blinking down at the empty glass. " Dead ? Poor soul ! "

"Damned hypocrite!" cried the intruder, rising so suddenly and with so wild a gesture that his foot struck the iron fender, dislodging the poker; and Mr. Jarvey, starting to the clatter of its fall, stood with bowed head, staring down where it lay gleaming in the firelight.

"Pah!" exclaimed the other, viewing his immobile figure in pallid disgust. "You were always a repulsive thing, Jarvey! How infinitely loathly you'll be when you're dead!"

"Pray," said Mr. Jarvey heavily, and without removing the fixity of his regard, "pray when—did she—die?"

"'Tis no matter for you—enough of it! I'm hungry—feed me, and while I eat I will tell you how I propose to make you the means of life to me henceforth, how you shall make up to me in some small measure for all those years of hell!"

"You will—blackmail me—Maurice?"

"To your last farthing, John, to the uttermost drop of your blood!"

"And if I—seek the shelter—of the law?"

"You dare not! And to-night you shall sign a confession!"

"And if I—refuse, Maurice?"

"This!"

Mr. Jarvey slowly raised his eyes to the pistol half-drawn from the breast of the threadbare coat.

"You would murder me then, Maurice?"

"Joyfully, if need be. But now I'm hungry, and you keep a well-filled cupboard yonder, I'll warrant!"

"Cupboard?" murmured Mr. Jarvey. "Cupboard—well filled? Ay, to be sure!"

And turning, he glanced at the wide cupboard that stood against the opposite wall, a solid and somewhat singular cupboard this, in that, at some dim period, it had been crowned with a deep cornice, the upper moulding of which had been wedged and firm-fixed to the ceiling; and it was upon this upper part, that is to say, between the true top of the cupboard proper and the ceiling, that Mr. Jarvey's gaze was turned as he crossed the room obedient to his visitor's command.

Very soon he had set forth such edibles as he possessed, together with a bottle of wine, and, standing beside the hearth again, chin on breast, watched while his guest plied knife and fork.

"And you—tell me—Maurice," said he at last, speaking in the same hesitant manner and with his gaze now upon the gleaming poker, " you tell me that—you—would—murder me ? "

" Ay, I would, John—like the vermin you are. But you will be infinitely more useful to me alive. By means of you I shall feed full, lie soft, and enjoy such of life as remains for me—to the uttermost."

" And I," said Mr. Jarvey, turning to stare up at the cupboard with a strange, new interest, " I must slave henceforth for your pleasure, Maurice ? "

" Precisely, John ! "

" An evil destiny, Maurice ! "

And here Mr. Jarvey's glance, roving from his guest's lank form to the top of the cupboard, took on a keen and speculative intensity.

" Your sin hath found you out, John, and come home to roost ! "

" A youthful indiscretion, Maurice ! "

" That killed a woman and sent a man to twenty years of hell ! But that is past, John, and the present being now, you shall fill me another glass of your very excellent wine."

Mr. Jarvey, having dutifully refilled the glass, took up his station by the hearth again, while his guest, holding up the wine to the light of the candles, nodded over it, smiling grimly :

" Twenty years of hell and degradation—a woman's life ! Ha, John, I drink to you—here's misery for you in life and damnation in death ! "

The speaker nodded again and, sinking back luxuriously in the cushioned chair, raised his glass to his lips.

Then, swift and sudden and very silent, Mr. Jarvey stooped, and his twitching fingers closed tight upon that heavy, be-polished, gleaming poker.

II

JOB, the night-watchman, opening slumberous eyes, shivered and cursed and, crouching above his fire, stirred it to a blaze, but, conscious of a chill breath, turned to behold the door of his lodge opening softly and slowly, wider and wider, until he might behold a dim figure standing without, a tall figure clad in a rain-sodden, many-caped riding-coat and a shadowy wide-eaved hat.

" Gate—ho—gate ! " said a hoarse voice, indistinct by reason of upturned collar and muffling shawl.

Very slowly the unwilling Job arose, scowling, and stepped forth into a night of gusty wind and rain.

" Look 'ee now, my master," he growled, slowly drawing bolt and bar, " wi' all respecks doo from one as ain't a genelman, an' don't wanter be, to one as is or oughter be, what I means ter say is—don't 'ee come no more o' them jostlings, pushings, nor yet shovings, lest, as 'twixt man an' man, I should be drawed ter belt ye one for a body-snatchin' thief an' rogue, d'ye see ! "

Hereupon the door swung wide and, with never a word or look, the tall figure flitted away into the driving rain and was swallowed in the dark.

III

" COME in ! " cried Mr. Jarvey, sitting up in bed and straightening his night-cap. " Come in, Tom—Lord bless me, Tom. What is it then ? . . . Come in ! "

Obedient to this summons, the door opened to admit a shock of red hair with two round eyes below that rolled themselves in gruesome manner.

" Lord love 'ee, Mr. Jarvey, sir," quoth Tom. " Good mornin' to 'ee, I'm sure, but Lord bless 'ee—an' you a-layin' there a-sleepin' so innercent as babes an' lambs, an' it a-moanin' an' a-groanin' an' carryin' on as do fair make me flesh creep, sir—ay, creep an' likewise crawl——"

" Tom," sighed Mr. Jarvey gently, " Tom, I fear you've been drinking ! "

" Never a blessed spot, sir. S'elp me, Mr. Jarvey, sir, not one, never so much as—O Lord, theer it be at it again—d'ye 'ear it, sir, don't 'ee ? 'Ark to it ! "

So saying, Tom edged himself suddenly into the bedroom but, with terror-stricken face, turned over his shoulder to peer into the chamber behind him as, dull and soft and low, there came a sound inarticulate and difficult to define, a groaning murmur that seemed to swell upon the air and was gone again. Mr. Jarvey's hands were clenched upon the bedclothes, the tassel of his night-cap quivered strangely, but when he spoke his voice was clear and even, and full of benignant reproof :

" Tom, you are drunk, beyond question."

" Not me, sir—no ! Take me Bible oath on't, I will ! Sober as a howl I be, sir. But you 'eard it a-groanin' an' moanin' ghastly-like ; you 'eard it, Mr. Jarvey, sir ? "

" Nonsense, Thomas. Heard what ? Speak plain ! "

" It were a grewgious, gloopy noise, sir—like a stranglin' cat or a dog in a—there ! Oh love me, there 'tis again, sir ! Listen 'ow it dithers like a phanitom in a churchyard, like a——"

Tom's voice ended in a hoarse gasp, for somewhere in the air about them, there seemed a vague stir and rustle, a scutter of faint movement, lost in a fitful, whining murmur. Tom was upon his knees, cowering against the bed, his head half-buried in the counterpane : thus Mr. Jarvey's fingers, chancing to come upon his shock of hair, tweaked it sharply, albeit he spoke in the same benignantly indulgent tone :

" Tom-fool, you are a drunken fool and a fanciful fool. Have done rolling your eyes and go order my breakfast—a rasher of ham, Tom, and two eggs ! Tell Mrs. Valpy I found the coffee over-weak yesterday and the ham cindery. Off with you, Tom, and bring my breakfast in half an hour."

Obediently Tom rose and, heartened by Mr. Jarvey's urbane serenity, shook himself together, pulled a wisp of hair, made a leg and hurried off on his comfortably commonplace errand.

Left alone, Mr. Jarvey sat up in bed, and, tearing off his night-cap, sat twisting it in restless hands. Then all at once, he was out of bed and, (creeping on naked feet, came where he might behold that cupboard ; very still he stood there, save for the restless hands of him that wrenched and twisted at his night-cap, while he stared up at a crack that ran along the cornice with eyes of dreadful expectancy. Suddenly, dropping the night-cap and setting both hands upon his ears, he backed away, but with his gaze fixed ever in the one direction until, reaching his bedchamber, he clapped to the door and locked it.

When, in due season, Tom returned with the breakfast he found Mr. Jarvey shaved and dressed, as serene and precise as usual, from the crisp curls of his trim wig to the buckles of his shoes.

But as he ate his breakfast the cupboard seemed to obtrude itself on his notice more and more, so that he took to watching it furtively, and seemed almost unwilling to glance otherwhere. Even when he sat giving Tom the usual precise directions for dinner, served always, winter and summer, at six o'clock, his look would go wandering in the one direction, so that it seemed to him at last that the keyholes of the two doors stared back at him like small, malevolent eyes.

" A—steak, Tom—yes, a steak with—ah, yes—mushrooms
—and underdone, Thomas. And a pint of claret—nay—
burgundy : 'tis richer and more comforting, Tom—
burgundy——"

" Very good, sir ! " answered Tom ; and now, even as the
clock of St. Clement Danes chimed the hour of nine, he
tendered Mr. Jarvey his hat and cane, according to immemorial
custom. But, to Tom's gasping astonishment, Mr. Jarvey
waved them aside :

" Not yet, Tom, not yet ! " said he. " I've a letter to write
a—ah—yes, a letter to be sure—the office shall wait—and—ah
—Tom—I am thinking—yes, seriously considering—taking
up—smoking."

" What—you, Mr. Jarvey, sir—Lord love me ! "

" Why not, Thomas ? It is a very innocent vice, sure ? "

" Why, so it be, sir, and comforts a man astonishin' ! "

" To be sure ! Now what tobacco do you use, Tom ? "

" Negro-'ead, sir."

" Is it a—good—strong tobacco ? "

" Fairish, sir."

" What is a *very* strong tobacco, Tom ? "

" Why, theer's black twist for one, sir. My grandmother
smokes it and fair reeks, she do. 'Oly powers, she do so,
sir ! "

" Black twist, Tom—to be sure. You may go, Thomas—
and mind, a steak—underdone, with mushrooms."

When Tom had departed, Mr. Jarvey, taking hat and cane,
crossed to the door, but, going thither, whirled suddenly about
to look at the cupboard, and, sinking into a chair, remained to
stare at it until the two keyholes seemed to blink themselves
at him, one after the other, whereupon he stirred and, shifting
his gaze with an effort, rose to his feet and, taking hat and cane,
glanced once more at the cupboard and began to retreat from
it, walking backwards. Reaching the door he leaned there
and nodded his head :

" Black twist ! " said he, " burned in the fire-shovel ! "

Then, groping behind him, he found and lifted the latch
and, backing swiftly out, clapped to the door and hasted down
the winding stair.

IV

" IT were jest a fortnight agone this here very night, Job ! "
exclaimed Tom, the bed-maker, spitting thoughtfully
into the fire.

" An' to-night be Christmas Heve, Tom."

" As ever was, Job, an' 'twere jest two weeks agone, an' mark that. An' I know, becos' that very day I 'ad noo-painted the gate into Fetter Lane an' some raskell 'ad clomb over an' smeared all the paint off, consequently I 'ad to paint it over again. Two weeks to-night, Job, an' Mr. Jarvey never the same man since ! Changed 'e be, ah—an' changin'."

" 'Ow so, Tom, 'ow so ? "

" Took to smokin' 'e 'ave, for one thing, Job—place fair reeks of it of a mornin'—ah, reeks be the only word."

" Smokes, do 'e ? " quoth Job, puffing at his own pipe. " An' werry proper in 'im, too ! Terbaccer's good for the inn'ards, Tom—comforts the bowels an' mellers the system."

" True enough, Job, but 'tis mighty strange in Mr. Jarvey —'im as never could abide the smell of a pipe all these years ! An' now to take to smokin'—ah, an' uncommon strong ter- baccer, too, judgin' by the smell o' the place of a mornin' ! "

" Why, strong terbaccer's the sweetest, Tom ! Gimme plenty o' body in me beer an' me baccy, says I."

" Well, there's body enough in Mr. Jarvey's ! Lord, fair choked me, it did, 's mornin' when I opened the door—gamey, it were—I never sniffed sech terbaccer in all my days—no; not even my grandmother's—an' she reeks to 'oly 'eavens, she do ! An' then, Job, when I opened the door 's mornin' wi' my key there's Mr. Jarvey 'unched up i' the arm-cheer over the 'earth an' the fire dead out. ' Lord love me, Mr. Jarvey,' I says, ' be ye sick, sir ? ' ' Never better, Tom,' says he. ' Only a little wakeful by reason o' the rats ! ' ' Rats ? ' says I. ' I've never seed none 'ereabouts,' I says. ' Why then,' says 'e, ' you didn't 'appen to see one run out o' the cupboard yonder—did ye—there ! ' 'e shouts, quick an' sharp-like, p'intin' with 'is finger—' down in the corner—don't ye see it, Tom ? ' ' Only this, sir ! ' says I, an' picked up one of 'is very own slippers. Whereupon, Job, 'e lays back in 'is cheer an' laughs an' laughs till I thought 'e'd choke 'isself—the kind o' laugh as makes yer flesh creep."

" An' wherefore must your flesh go a-creepin', Tom ? "

" Because all the time 'e was laughin' 'is eyes was big an' round an' starin'."

" Ah ! " nodded Job, " that's rum, that is. Rum took too frequent 'as a way o' makin' any man's eyes stick out—ah, as round as gooseberries, me lad, an' as for seein' things—rats is nothink. It's snakes as is serious, an' pink toads an' big 'airy

worms as twists an' wriggles ain't to be sneezed at nor treated
disrespectful—but rats—wot's rats ? A rat ain't——"

" What's that ? " exclaimed Tom, starting and glancing
suddenly towards the door.

" Wot's—wot ? " demanded Job, starting also and scowling.

" I thought I 'eard something—outside."

" That's St. Clement a-strikin'. Wot yer got ter shake
and shiver at St. Clement for——"

" I dunno ! " muttered Tom. " I thought I 'eard footsteps
outside a-creepin'——"

" 'Ow could ye, be goles, when theer's six inches o' snow
outside, as you werry well know ? "

" Lord, Job—look ! " whispered Tom, starting up and
letting fall his pipe to point with shaking finger. " Look—
there—there ! "

Following that shaking finger Job espied a small, furtive
shape that, flitting from the shadow of the door, scuttered
across the room and was gone.

" A rat ! " he snorted. " An' then wot ? Theer's a-plenty
'ereabouts, as you werry well——"

" Look—the door, Job—look at the door ! "

As he spoke, very slowly and stealthily the door was
opening inch by inch, until suddenly it swung wide and, as if
borne upon the buffeting wind and flurry of snow, a tall figure
appeared, who, clapping to the door, leaned there and, peering
thitherwards, they recognized Mr. Jarvey.

" It came this way, I think ? " he questioned, in a strange,
high-pitched, querulous voice. " I've followed it a long time
and it came in here."

Suddenly this unknown captious voice gave place to
boisterous laughter and, coming forward, Mr. Jarvey hailed
them in his own kindly, benignant tones.

" God bless us all, what a night ! And still snowing—
frosty and snowing—but seasonable ; yes, very seasonable.
A Merry Christmas to you both and a Happy New Year !
This old Inn hath seen a-many Christmasses and known a-many
New Years, and shall know a-many more when we are dead
—ay, dead an' gone—eh, Job ? "

" Why, sir, to ' die an' go ' is natur' arter all."

" And so it is, Job. Death is the most natural thing—a
good thing and kindly—the weary mayhap find rest at last and
the eyes—ay, the eyes that watch us unseen, that blink upon
us if we do but turn our back—these cruel, unsleeping eyes
shall spy upon us no longer. Here is a joyous thought and

this should make death welcome. Tom, my good Thomas, have you chanced to notice the keyholes of my cupboard— I cover them up sometimes—but they are always there ! "

So saying, Mr. Jarvey, having glanced over his shoulder towards the door, nodded and smiled in his kindly benevolent manner as he leaned forward to warm his hands at the fire, while Tom glanced from him to the fragments of his broken pipe on the hearth, and Job puffed thoughtfully. Suddenly upon the silence stole the soft, mellow chime of St. Clement telling the hour.

" 'Ark to Clem," said Job, stirring uneasily as the last stroke died away—" ten o'clock a'ready."

" Ay," sighed Mr. Jarvey, his glance wandering to the door again. " The hours of a man's life are numbered and quick in passing. I've heard St. Clement's bells chiming my life away these many years, Job."

" Well then, sir, with all respeck doo, axing your pardin', I says dang St. Clement's bells wi' all me 'eart."

" No, Job, no. They are like the voices of old friends. I would wish for none other sounds in my ears when I come to die."

" Lord, Mr. Jarvey, sir," exclaimed Job, wriggling in his chair, " why talk o' dyin' ? And this Christmas Heve, too ! "

" An' I'll be goin' ! " quoth Tom, rising suddenly. " You'll be takin' your breakfast a hour later than usual, 'cordin' to custom, to-morrow bein' Christmas Day, Mr. Jarvey, sir ? " he inquired.

" Why no, Tom," answered Mr. Jarvey thoughtfully, " to-morrow being Christmas Day you may take a holiday, Tom."

" But what about you, sir—your breakfast ? "

" I shall be—very well, Tom."

" Why, thank'ee, Mr. Jarvey, sir, I'm sure—good-night and a Merry Christmas to ye ! " exclaimed Tom, touching an eyebrow. Then with the same good wishes to Job, he departed.

For a while there was silence, Job puffing at his pipe and Mr. Jarvey leaning forward to warm his hands and stare into the fire ; and, watching him as he sat thus, Job presently became aware of two things—firstly, that Mr. Jarvey's lips were moving soundlessly ; and secondly, that ever and anon at sudden and frequent intervals he started and turned to glance swiftly towards the door, very much as though some one standing there had spoken in reply to some soundless question.

He did this so often that Job began to glance at the door also, and more than once thought he saw a small, dark shape that flitted amid the shadows. At last, his pipe being out, Job rubbed his chin, scratched his head, wriggled in his chair, and finally spoke.

"Hexcuse me, Mr. Jarvey, sir, but wot might you be a-watchin' of ? "

"Watching ? " repeated Mr. Jarvey, hitching his chair a little nearer to Job's. "No, no—it is I who am watched, Job, wherever I go, sleeping and waking, night and day—which becomes a—little distressing, Job."

"But 'oo's a-goin' to 'ave the imperance to go a-watchin' of you, Mr. Jarvey, sir ? "

Mr. Jarvey leaned nearer to lay a hand upon Job's arm, turning him so that he faced the shadowy corner by the door !

"I'll show you, Job—look—there ! "

Following the direction of Mr. Jarvey's pointing finger, Job thought once more to espy a small, vague shape crouched in this dark corner, a shape that leapt suddenly and scuttered along the grimy wainscot and was gone.

"By goles ! " exclaimed Job, staring. "It be that theer rat again ! "

"Why, yes," nodded Mr. Jarvey, "it does *look* like a rat, but——"

"And a rat it be, sir—only a rat."

"And yet," sighed Mr. Jarvey, shaking his head, "who ever heard of a rat dogging a man through six inches of snow ? "

"Rats," quoth Job sententiously, "rats is queer hannimiles, sir, and uncommon owdacious at times, but I never 'eard tell of a rat follerin' a man through six inches o' snow afore."

"Why, you see, Job," answered Mr. Jarvey, gently shaking his head, " I didn't say this was a rat, I merely remarked that it looked like one. But it grows late, Job, and rat or no, I must be going ! " So saying, he rose slowly and donned his greatcoat, but, with his hand outstretched toward the door-latch, he shivered and turned back to the fire as if unwilling to face the bleak night.

"The wind's rising, Job," said he, shivering again and reaching his hands towards the fire. "Hark to it ! " he whispered, as, from somewhere without, rose a shrill piping that sank to a wail, a sobbing moan and was gone.

"A dismal sound, Job, dismal and ominous—yes, a very evil noise ! "

All at once there broke from him a strangled cry.

"An' the chimbley-pot's loose on Number Five!" said Job gloomily.

For a while they sat listening to the wind that rumbled in the chimney and wailed mournfully, near and far, that filled the world outside with discordant clamour and passing, left behind a bodeful silence. Suddenly Mr. Jarvey was on his feet and, crossing to the door, paused there to glance back to the cosy hearth.

"A happy Christmas, Job," said he. "A happy Christmas to you and all the world!" And then he strode out into the howling night.

He was met by a buffet of icy wind that stopped his breath, a whirl of driving snowflakes that blinded him, while the vague dimness of the Inn about him echoed with chaotic din, shrieks and cries and shrill, piping laughter that swelled to a bellowing roar as the rioting wind swept by.

Taking advantage of a momentary lull Mr. Jarvey crossed the Inn, ploughing through snow ankle-deep, yet paused suddenly more than once to stoop and peer, now this way, now that, as one who watched something small that leapt and wallowed in the snow.

Reaching Number —— he stood awhile gazing up the dark stair and listening until the pervading quiet was 'whelmed in the tumult of the wind and the rattle of lattice and casement. Then Mr. Jarvey, fumbling in a dark corner, brought thence a candle-end, the which he lighted at the dim lantern, and with this flickering before him began to ascend the winding stair.

And ever, as Mr. Jarvey mounted, his glance roved here and there, now searching the dimness before him and now the gloom behind.

He reached his own stair at last, and, pausing at the foot to snuff his candle with unsteady fingers, he went slowly up and up until, all at once, there broke from him a strangled cry and he stood to stare at the small, grey shape of that which, crouched, glared down at him from the topmost stair.

The candle fell and was extinguished; came a howling wind-gust that roared beneath the eaves, that shook and buffeted at rattling windows, and then in the darkness within rose shriek on shriek that was not of the wind, a rush of feet, a clash of iron, the crash of heavy blows and rending of wooden panels. But outside, the wind, as if wrought to maddened frenzy, roared and shrieked in wild halloo, louder, wilder, till, spent at last, it sank to a doleful whine, a murmur, and was still.

And upon this quiet was the stealthy sound of a closing door, the grind of key in lock and the shooting of heavy bolts.

V

" AND you don't 'ave no rec'lection at all o' seein' 'im go out o' the gate, Job ? "

" Not me, Tom. Nary a glimp of 'un since Christmas Heve ! "

" An' there's 'is door fast-locked an' me knockin' 'eavens 'ard an' no answer—nary a sound. Job—I don't like it."

" Maybe 'e's out o' town, Tom."

" Not 'im ! An' then there's a curious thing about 'is door."

" Wot, Tom, wot ? "

" Top panel be all cracked across. A noo crack, Job."

" W'y then you can look through said crack, Job."

" No, I ain't tall enough, but cracked an' split it be. Come an' see for yourself."

" Why, Tom, the wind brought down the chimbley pot on Number Five t'other night, but I never 'eard o' wind splittin' a door yet."

" Well, come an' see, Job."

With due deliberation Job got into his coat, clapped on his hat and accompanied Tom to the top chambers of Number ——. Arrived on Mr. Jarvey's landing, he beheld the door fast shut and, sure enough, a great crack in one of the upper panels.

With Tom's assistance Job contrived to get his eye to the split in the panel and thus peer into the room, and, doing so, gasped and shrank away and, slipping from Tom's hold, leaned against the wall as if faint.

" What is it, Job—Lord love us, what——? "

" We gotter—open—the door, Tom ! "

" Aye, but why, Job—why ? "

" We gotter—open—the door ! Come now—both together!"

Between them they forced the door at last and then, beholding what was beyond, cowered back, clasping each other, as well they might. For there, sure enough, was Mr. Jarvey, dangling against the cupboard from a hook deep-driven into the roof-beam, while above his dead face, from the broken panelling above the cupboard, was something black and awful, shaped like the talons of a great bird, but upon one of the talons there still gleamed a small, plain gold ring.

THE OTHER SENSE

OCT. 21st.—They have told me to-day, with obvious reluctance, and in the kindest fashion, that I am to go to-morrow to the house of a Dr. Schreiber, in whose care I am to remain until I am restored to health. Restored to health!—my God! I am as healthy a lad of nineteen (I believe) as any one would wish to meet; certainly I have no recollection of any illness beyond a dose of measles when I was seven, and a very slight touch of scarlet fever a few years ago. Restored to health!—no, that is merely their kind way of putting it. What they really mean is : I am to go and live with this Dr. Schreiber, whoever he may be, until he, and they, and the doctors whom they have brought to see me so often lately, think I am—*sane*.

That, of course, is the real truth. I have often wondered, as I have grown up out of my lonely childhood towards manhood, how strange it is that what seems so easy to the child about truth-telling seems so difficult to the man—now I am beginning to understand. All the same, it would have been much more to my taste if my guardian and his wife had said to me, "Angus, we're very, very sorry, but the doctors and we don't think everything is as it should be with your intellect, and Dr. Schreiber is a famous mental specialist, and——" so on.

But then—equally, of course—they couldn't have said that to me if they really believe that I *am* mad. And they *do*. I know—I have seen them not once, but a thousand times since I came here to London from Alt-na-Shiel two years ago (when shall I see it again, and the mists on the mountains!), watching me as country folk watch the freaks at a fair. There is a puzzled look which comes into their faces ; their brows

knit, and their lips are slowly compressed, or pursed up, and—
if they think I do not see them—*they look at each other and
shake their heads and sigh.*

I cannot think of more than three things which should
make them believe me mad. One is that I am very fond
of solitude, liking to be left to myself as much as I can. Another
is that I think a great deal—just as I read a great deal—and
that I sometimes frown at my thoughts, sometimes smile at
them, sometimes laugh, long and loud, at them. Perhaps,
when Major Kennedy and Mrs. Kennedy and I are alone after
dinner, he reading *The Times* and she busied with her knitting,
behaviour of this sort on my part may seem strange—it is only
now occurring to me that it *may.* Certainly I have seen the
Major drop his newspaper and jump—literally *jump*—in his
arm-chair when, thinking of something that amused me, I have
indulged in a sudden peal of laughter—yet why should one
not laugh whenever one sees or thinks of something to laugh
at ? But I have found that a great many of the people whom
I have met in London only laugh when a sort of signal is given.

Those are two reasons. The only other reason I can
think of is that I have told them once or twice—just as I told
the doctors whom they have at times brought to see me—that
I can *see* things which, I find out, most other people do not or
cannot see. The first time I told them, for instance, of the
spirit which I have seen a score or so of times at Alt-na-Shiel,
they stared at me as if I were telling them lies, and they both
looked curiously uncomfortable. Now, my old nurse, Margaret
Lang, never looked uncomfortable when I told her of these
things, neither did Dugald Graeme, my father's old body-
servant. They seemed to realize and to understand my
meaning.

I have been thinking to-day (since I heard what my guardian
and his wife had to tell me—he, poor man, in his stiff military-
modelled sentences, and she more by tears than by words)
about my life as a child and afterwards as a boy. Alt-na-Shiel
is in one of the loneliest glens of the Strathern Mountains—
a very great way indeed from the railways. There my father—
Angus MacIntyre, like myself—went to live just after he was
married to my mother, and there my mother died just after I
was born. My father was a man of books, and after my
mother's death he thought of nothing but books. Margaret
Lang—helped by Dugald Graeme—brought me up, but after
I was able to walk, my real nurse and mother was the open air.
I used to sit out—anywhere—all day long, content to see the

sky, and hear the countryside sounds, and smell the heather and the gorse and the bracken. And I cannot remember, looking back, when it was that I did not see things that other people did not see. I was never afraid of anything that I ever saw.

I have gone on *seeing* ever since—now, usually, at long intervals. When I was seventeen my father died, and it was found that Major Kennedy, a distant connection, was to be my guardian, and that I was to live with him until my twenty-first year. That is why I am now writing this in my journal in my own room in Major Kennedy's house in Bayswater—and why I am to-morrow to take up my residence with Dr. Schreiber at Wimbledon Common. Possibly I am writing it because, for anything I know, this may be my last day of complete liberty. I do not know what the rules are in these private mad-houses—if this to which I am going is such a place.

If I may speak frankly to myself in these pages, I must say that I cannot see why I should be considered at all mentally afflicted. I am, as things go, fairly well educated ; fond as I am of solitude, I am fond of games, especially of football, golf, and tennis ; I am certainly very strong in body, and of rude health. And as for my appetite . . .

However, they say I suffer from occasional delusions. We shall see.

II

OCT. 23rd.—I came here—to Dr. Schreiber's house—yesterday afternoon, accompanied by Dr. Wilkinson, one of the two doctors who have been to see me so often lately. The parting between the Kennedys and myself made me think of the conventional descriptions of boys going to school. Major Kennedy shook hands with me at least six times, and Mrs. Kennedy cried. Dr. Wilkinson and I talked football all the way from Bayswater to Wimbledon, and I found out that he got his Blue at Oxford—I forget in what year.

Just before we got to Wimbledon Common I thought I would have a little straightforward conversation with Dr. Wilkinson.

" Look here, sir," I said. " You, in common with Dr. Gordon and Major and Mrs. Kennedy, think I am a little mad ? "

" I think that a few months' residence with Dr. Schreiber will turn you out as fit as a fiddle," he replied.

" Why do most people give an evasive answer when it would be much simpler to tell the truth in one word ? " I asked him.

" Ah, why don't they ? " he answered. " I've often wondered that myself."

" Or, again," said I, " how is it that people who happen through no fault of their own to possess a certain faculty, or certain faculties, which other people—most people—do not possess, are invariably considered to be—queer ? "

He shook his head, and I relapsed into such a profound and cogitative silence that at last he asked me what I was thinking about.

" I was thinking, sir," I replied, " how admirably you would have filled the *rôle* of those physicians of the Middle Ages who, whenever powerful monarchs or statesmen wanted to get rid of any person inimical to them, were ever ready to testify to their madness and to enclose them within a dungeon or an oubliette, or——"

" Well, you'll not find Dr. Schreiber's place much of a dungeon, my boy ! " he said, laughing. " Here we are, so you can see for yourself."

I got out of the brougham and looked about me. This house is an old-fashioned structure of red brick, covered over with climbing plants, and it stands in the midst of a bright green lawn, the flower-beds and borderings of which are just now cheerful with a profusion of autumn blooms. There is not a suspicion of anything prison-like about it—on the contrary, its appearance suggests freedom and liberty. My first glance at it forced me to set up a comparison between it and Bayswater.

Dr. Schreiber came out to meet us. He is a youngish man—perhaps thirty-five, perhaps forty—tall, muscular, broad-shouldered, bronzed, cheery. I should have taken him for one of the sweller sort of professional cricketers rather than for what I was led to believe him—a private mad-house keeper. He welcomed me in a very friendly way, and after Dr. Wilkinson had gone volunteered to show me round the house and grounds. I was somewhat astonished to find no one about, except servants in the house and a gardener sweeping up fallen leaves on the lawn.

" Where, sir," I asked, " are the rest of us ? "

" The rest of whom ? " he inquired, looking surprised.

" The rest of your other mad folk," I answered. " I am sent here because they think me mad."

He laughed—burst, rather, into laughter—and slapped my shoulders.

"Oh, hang all that, old chap!" he said. "There's no one here but you, myself, my assistant, Pollard, who's a real good sort, and the servants. You're as free as air here, and if I don't give you a first-class time it won't be my fault."

Later we fell to talking about golf. To-day, after he had been to visit his patients—he seems to have a pretty extensive practice—we managed to get a full round in before dusk came on. He beat me by two up and one to play.

III

OCT. 27th.—I have been very happy here so far—much happier, I believe—nay, am sure, than I have ever been since I left Alt-na-Shiel. Life is very pleasant in this house, and with Dr. Schreiber. He is very different, I think, to all other men I have ever met. I have been with him frequently to visit some of his poorer patients—it seemed to me that he *laughs* them out of their complaints. I do not mean that he laughs *at* them, but that his cheeriness is infectious, and lifts them out of themselves. He is certainly a great man—a big *human*.

Last night, after dinner, he and I were playing billiards, and somehow—I do not know how—we reached the question of what those other people call my delusion. We sat down—this was the first time I had ever spoken of it to him—and I told him of some things which I had seen—especially of the ghost (if it is a ghost) of the parish clerk of Ardnashonach. Instead of looking as if he could scarcely believe his ears (as Major Kennedy looks), or shaking his head (as Dr. Wilkinson did), he listened most intently, and asked me a lot of questions. Not questions about myself, which is what I detest, but sensible questions.

"And they aren't delusions, you know," I said at the end. "I *have* seen these things—*seen* them! You believe me?"

"Yes," he said, "I do. Look here—if you ever *see* anything while you're here, just come that minute and tell me. Now, then, we've time for another hundred before bed."

IV

NOV. 4th.—I have been examining this old house inside and out with some interest since Dr. Schreiber told me, a day or two ago, that it was once (a century or more ago)

the residence of a famous statesman. It is, I think, Early
Georgian, and has the most delightful rooms, many of which
are panelled in oak to a considerable height. There is one,
now used as a dining-room, but formerly the library, which
attracts me more than all the rest. It has four high narrow
windows overlooking the garden, and with its quaint old oak
furniture (which Dr. Schreiber took over from his predecessor
in the practice, a man named Turrell, who was, he says, one
of the cleverest men of his day) it makes a picture of colour and
distinction. There is an old oak long settle near the deep
fireplace in which I shall love to sit when the winter really
settles in—if it ever does in this soft-aired, sunny south, so
different to the far-away north.

V

Nov. 17th.—Something has happened.
       That seems a trite enough thing to write down, but
the three words, after all, mean much, followed by an explanation. The truth is, my curious sense (extra sense, I suppose),
has manifested itself again. I believe the last time was five
years ago, when I saw the fairies near the church of Dalnarossie.

Yesterday afternoon, about five o'clock, Dr. Schreiber
having gone to London, and Mr. Pollard to visit a patient
across the Common, I was alone in the dining-room, and sitting
in the corner of the long settle. There was no light in the
room except that of the fire, which had burnt itself down to
that clear glow which fires get on sharp, frosty afternoons of
late autumn. I had spent most of the time since lunch reading
a curious old book which I had found in Dr. Schreiber's study
the day before, and was leaning back against the cushions of
the long settle with my eyes closed—thinking of what I had
read, and enjoying the quiet of the shadowy, scarcely-lighted
room—when I suddenly *felt* that I was not alone. The feeling
was so strong, so acute, that for a full minute I remained
quiescent. At last I opened my eyes, knowing without doubt
that I was going to see something.

What I saw was this :

There stood upon the big, square hearthrug, within a
few feet of me, a young man whom I judged to be of about
my own age—perhaps a little older. He was tall, he stooped
slightly, and he was spare of figure. His attire was modern—
a black morning coat and vest and dark, striped trousers—
and he stood with his hands in his pockets, after the fashion

affected by Eton boys—somewhat slouchingly. His head was
bent forward, and at first I could not see his face, but he
presently turned a little, and the glow of the fire fell on it. I
knew then that I was regarding a ghost.

The face confirmed me in my belief that this was—had
been, I should say—a young man of say, nineteen years of
age. It was a sad, uneasy face—a face whereon were many
signs of anxiety, trouble, perplexity—and it was curiously
old. It was not a strong face—the chin was small and delicate ;
the mouth amiable, but weak ; the eyes, big and blue, were
the eyes of a child—and there was a frightened expression in
them.

I sat perfectly still, watching. The figure remained in
an irresolute position—fidgeting on the hearthrug for a minute
or so—then it walked slowly to the window, stood looking
out into the garden awhile, then came back to the hearthrug,
lingered there a minute more, and finally crossed the room
and opened the door. I followed it through the doorway on
the instant ; the servants had already lighted the hall lamp,
and the hall was clearly illuminated. And the hall was empty.
There was no figure there.

I told Dr. Schreiber all this after we had finished our
usual game of billiards last night. He listened with the
gravest attention to everything I said, and when I had finished
merely remarked :

" Angus, if you should ever see this apparition, or whatever
it may be, again, do not be afraid to tell me at once."

VI

Nov. 22*nd*.—I have seen the ghost of the young man
again.

This afternoon I went out to stroll about the neighbourhood, and in the course of my wanderings turned into Wimbledon churchyard. I was walking aimlessly about the paths,
looking at the tombstones and wondering if they had any
unusual names or quaint epitaphs upon them, when I suddenly
saw the apparition again, standing at the side of a grave which
lay at the chancel end of the church. It was attired exactly as
before, and stood in a similar fashion, slightly slouching, with
its hands in the pockets of its trousers. The face was just as
sad and troubled as ever, and had the same air of perplexity.
The big, blue, childish eyes turned from the grave to the
headstone, and from the headstone to the grave, as if trying to

read something on the one or to see something on the other.
Then they stared all round the churchyard—wonderingly.

I drew nearer, and looked at the inscription on the tomb-
stone by which the ghost stood—in fact, I approached to
within a few feet of the ghost itself.   It seemed to me that it
saw me—but only looked at me in the casual, uninterested
way in which strangers regard each other.

The inscription was short and simple :

> Here lieth the body of Major-General Sir Arthur
> Debenham, K.C.B. ; born January 15th, 1831 ; died
> October 4th, 1892. Also that of Florence Georgiana,
> his wife ; born September 12th, 1834 ; died February 7th,
> 1893. Also in memory of their only child, Everard ;
> born August 12th, 1874 ; died July 20th, 1893, at Hudiks-
> vall, Sweden, where he is interred.

When I looked round again the apparition had disappeared.

I came straight back to Dr. Schreiber's house, and happened
to catch him just coming in.   After I had told him of this
second appearance he remained silent for some time, and at
last, without making any comment, asked me to go with him
into the garden.   He approached the gardener, an oldish man,
who was at work there before Dr. Schreiber took over the
practice.

" Gregson," he said, " you've lived a long time about here,
haven't you ? "

" Man and boy, five-and-fifty years, sir," replied Gregson.

" Did you ever know Major-General Sir Arthur Debenham ? "

" Know the old General, sir ?   I should think I did !—
why, he lived not half a mile from here.   I knew 'em all.
Why, the young gentleman, poor Mr. Everard, he lived here
in this very house with your predecessor, Dr. Turrell, for
some months after Lady Debenham died.   Dr. Turrell and
him was a-travelling on the Continent when Mr. Everard died,
sir."

" What was the matter with him—with Mr. Everard ? "

" Matter, sir ?   Why, what I calls a galloping consumption.
He was a weak, white-faced lad always, and he got a deal worse
after he came to live with the doctor.   That was why they
went to foreign parts—to see if it would do him any good."

" Why did he come to live with Dr. Turrell—had he no
relations of his own that he could go to ? "

" They did say, sir, that he'd neither kith nor kin.   Dr.

Turrell had been the old General's doctor, and Lady Debenham's too—he was about the only friend they had hereabouts,
sir. They were a bit queer, the old gentleman and his wife—
eccentric, as they term it."

" Was the General rich ? "

Gregson scratched his head.

" Well, I should say he was a warm man, sir—always
considered to be so, anyway. Kept his carriage, and so on,"
he answered.

After a few more questions we went away. But I have
since been asking more questions of Gregson and of the housekeeper. Their description of Everard Debenham is that of
the apparition of the young man whose ghost I have now seen
on two occasions.

VII

Nov. 28th.—I think that even Major Kennedy will now
believe that I possess some curious power of seeing the
usually unseen.

Yesterday afternoon, at two o'clock, Dr. Schreiber, Mr.
Pollard, and myself were lunching in the dining-room when
I suddenly saw the ghost enter. It came in very quietly—in
its usual half-slouching attitude, and immediately upon entering the room halted and stood looking about it in an irresolute
manner. The expression of the face was, if anything, more
anxious than ever, and the eyes were almost miserable in their
perplexity.

My companions saw me lay down my knife and fork and
look towards the door with a fixed expression.

" What is it, Angus ? " inquired Dr. Schreiber.

" It is here again," I answered, knowing that Mr. Pollard
was by this time acquainted with the matter.

" Where is it ? "

" Standing between you and the door. It looks as if it
did not know where to go, or what to do, or as if it were seeking
somebody or something."

" Watch it closely, then, and tell us what happens."

Then I began to report the ghost's movements to them.

" It has walked over to the window and is standing there,
looking out into the garden . . . now it has come to the
hearthrug, and is staring into the fire . . . and now it is going
out of the room again. . . ."

" Follow it," said Dr. Schreiber.

The three of us left the table and followed the ghost out of the room. This time it did not disappear—instead, it turned to the right along the hall and went into Dr. Schreiber's study.

"What is it doing ? " asked the doctor, when we got within.

" It is standing in front of your desk, looking at your writing-chair. It seems more perplexed than ever. Now it has gone round to the hearth and is looking all along the mantelpiece as if it wanted to find something . . . now it is leaving the room.

" Follow it."

The ghost went out through the hall into the garden—we three close upon its heels. It stood on the step outside the door for a moment, looking very dejected ; then moved slowly away across the garden and walked round the lawn in the centre once or twice. It now slouched more than ever, and its head hung forward as if it were in trouble or pain. Suddenly it turned away by a side path towards a part of the garden given up to trees and shrubs. I described its further movements to my companions.

" It is walking up that little path which leads to the summer-house . . . now it has entered the summer-house . . . it is standing there looking just as lost, perplexed, troubled as ever . . . now it . . . ah ! "

" What do you see, Angus ? " asked the doctor.

" It has gone—disappeared," I replied.

We turned back to the house.

" What do you think of that, Pollard ? " said Dr. Schreiber.

" Queer ! " replied Mr. Pollard.

Nobody said anything more just then, and very soon afterwards the two doctors went out together. An hour later they returned with a carpenter and his assistant and a couple of men who looked like navvies. Dr. Schreiber asked me to come with them, and then led the way to the summer-house. When we arrived there he addressed the carpenter.

" I want the floor of this place removed, and the soil beneath excavated until I tell the men to stop," he said. " Do it at once."

It did not take much time for the carpenter and his men to take up the floor, which was formed of squares of pine wood, easily detachable.

Then the men began to dig.

There is no necessity to write down the details of this

gruesome search. We found the body of the young man whose ghost I had seen so many times. It was dressed just as the ghost was dressed. Gregson at once identified it as that of Evererd Debenham.

Dr. Schreiber has communicated with the Home Office, the police, and the coroner.

VIII

Nov. 30th.—The coroner's inquest is just over. The expert from the Home Office, a famous doctor, says that Everard Debenham was poisoned, and the jury have returned a verdict of wilful murder against Dr. Turrell, to whom, it seems, all General Debenham's estate was left in the event of Everard's death if that took place previous to his marriage and the birth of children. We hear that Dr. Turrell has been arrested at Edinburgh, where he had gone to live after selling his practice to Dr. Schreiber.

IX

March 21st.—*Alassio, Italy.*—On arriving here this after-noon we found the English newspapers, and learnt from them that Dr. Turrell was hanged at Wandsworth Gaol last week, and that he left a full confession. There are also articles commenting upon the strange circumstances under which the crime was discovered.

But there was nothing strange about them to me.

GHOST OF HONOUR

"OF course, it isn't as nice as it should be," said Mrs. St. Pancreas, as she showed Robertson into the Great Hall; "I mean, restoring's a lost art these days, isn't it? The Dennistouns' place is much more picturesque than this; but then theirs was in better repair and didn't have to be pulled down and shored up. Anyway, we have got a ghost."

"No!" said Robertson.

"But we have! We see him very often."

"And do you," he inquired, "like that?"

"Well," she answered, rather apologetically, "it isn't as if he does any harm—sometimes, in fact, he's quite entertaining—so we have to like it. I don't imagine that he'd go if we didn't. Still, I expect you'll hear him before dinner."

"Hear him?" Robertson turned a little sick.

"Yes. You see—— Oh, here's Henry."

Mr. St. Pancreas shook hands with Robertson. "Nice to meet you again. Have any difficulty finding the way here? How do you like the house? Cost me a bit, but I do like atmosphere."

"You must get it from what your wife was telling me."

Mrs. St. Pancreas gazed into her velvet lap. "I had to mention the ghost to him, Harry, or he'd wonder who was playing the organ."

"Not an organ!" Robertson wished he were dead.

"Yes. You see, he always likes to amuse himself for half an hour or so before dinner by playing little tunes, and people think it odd if we don't explain beforehand."

"Why does he behave like this, and who is he? Is there a legend?"

228

" Oh, of sorts," Mr. St. Pancreas answered deprecatingly. " The Dunbow family weren't aristocrats, or anything like that, so it isn't a very exciting one."

" Please tell me about it," Robertson bowed his head, for he wished to learn the worst. Mr. St. Pancreas looked at his wife. She looked back at her husband, her eyes troubled. " Shall we tell him, Harry ? "

" Go ahead."

" Well, you see, the Dunbows were all successful actors on the comedy stage, and they appear to have been very popular in their day. We have quite a lot of old theatre programmes in the library, mouldering old things, you know, with their names printed on them and the parts they played."

" Shakespeare ? "

" Not exactly. As far as I can gather, they played in farce and sung crude comic songs. You know what they were at that time. Well, as I was telling you, they were all actors. The best of the lot, apparently, was Jeremiah, who is going to play the organ to us before dinner. He was a jolly man, but he had, unfortunately, a very bad temper. He used to dramatize every situation ; I believe his wife and children had to put up with the most appalling scenes, all about nothing. If he hadn't dramatized his own death, we shouldn't . . ."

" . . . Have to endure him now," Mr. St. Pancreas put in, forgetting himself.

" Sh-sh-h ! " His wife glanced up at the minstrels' gallery. " Do be careful, dear. I'd hate to put him out of temper. As I was saying, Mr. Robertson, he dramatized his death. You see, he was a martyr to indigestion. This gave him a very red face—his contemporaries used to call him ' Beefy ' Dunbow, which sounds like somebody in the society papers to-day, doesn't it ?—and if he wasn't very careful with his diet, he got heartburn. You can trace all that in the letters we've found relating to the family. Well, this made a good deal of trouble for his wife. She had to buy him the most delicate foods which cost a great deal—I believe, incidentally, that they were up to their ears in debt—and he had a special leaning towards expensive fish. This had to be personally selected and boned by his wife before he would touch it."

" 'To cut a long story short," said Mr. St. Pancreas, who seemed to be listening for something, " one day Mistress Dunbow had the misfortune to leave quite a large bone in a sole which she had fried for her husband. She might have done it purposely ; if she did, more power to her elbow, but that's all by the way. Of course Jeremiah, who, as I always suspect, ate far too quickly, had to get it stuck in his throat. He started choking and choking, and his face grew so red and blue that they were all scared out of their wits. Staggering away from the table, he managed to gasp out—what exactly was it that he managed to gasp out, Agatha ? "

She fumbled in her evening bag. " Wait a minute, dear ; I've got it down. I always keep it scribbled on an envelope, Mr. Robertson, because people do like to have things accurate, and my memory is so poor. Here we are. He said : ' Mistress, you have taken my life away. My blood be on this roof-tree for evermore. Until the fall of this house I will walk within it, and when the last brick crumbles to dust I will walk the site of it. Only one grain of mercy will I leave with you : never shall living soul behold my face ' ; and as far as I know," she added, " nobody ever has."

" Seems a great deal for a choking man to say, doesn't it ? " said Robertson, with a light laugh. He hoped that they would remember and admire, in after years, his courageous acceptance of the legend of Jeremiah.

Mr. St. Pancreas moistened his lips. " His descendants probably elaborated the story. Anyhow, there it is for what it's worth. Personally, I rather like the fellow. He gives no trouble, except that I'm not keen on organs, and it does add to the atmosphere, don't you agree ? "

Robertson agreed. " Oh, quite. And has he got a special room to haunt ? "

" Certainly not," said Mrs. St. Pancreas cheerfully. " He just goes wherever he likes, bless him ! "

" What does he play, hellish fugues ? "

" Oh no, nothing like that. Quite jolly pieces sometimes, aren't they, Agatha ? He's got a sense of humour, too. He's progressive, anyway—wants to learn, if you know what I mean. For instance, I went into the library last night, and there he was, with his back to me, of course, reading my bound volume of *Punch* ! Can't dislike a fellow who does that, can you ? By the way, do you mind ghosts ? Perhaps I should have asked you before."

" No," answered Robertson, in a little voice.

" That's fine, because I expect you'll see a good bit of him during the week-end. We'd miss old Jerry if he went, wouldn't we, dear ? "

" We would," she answered vaguely, because she, too, was listening.

" What's that ? " cried Robertson. He had heard the rushing of a great wind.

" Oh, that." Mr. St. Pancreas smiled. " He's blowing up the pipes, or whatever you call it. You can't see him ; he's just round the corner of the gallery. Ah, here we go ! "

The music swelled up, filling every corner of the hall.

" Pretty little thing," Robertson said carelessly, bracing himself against the back of his chair ; " song by Lawes, I think. He plays very well. Good technique, if a trifle *rubato*."

" He tried to play some modern stuff last week. Agatha and I left some Gershwin on the organ just to see what he'd do, but he can't sight-read very well. He soon stopped trying, and went back to his ' Up-the-Middle-and-Down-Again ' tunes."

" Would you like to have a look at him ? " asked Mrs. St. Pancreas diffidently. " He won't mind a bit, and you may as well meet him now as later. He never turns round, of course, so there's nothing to be afraid of."

" Not a bit," agreed her husband. " Come along up."

" Perhaps he won't like a stranger to stare at him," Robertson mumbled.

" Silly ! " said Mrs. St. Pancreas, slapping him playfully, with a wink to her husband that he might not be jealous.

Robertson arose. " All right," he said, " lead on."

" We'll go up the stairs to the gallery and round the corner," Mr. St. Pancreas smiled. " Careful of the steps, old man ; they're slippery."

They went up. Robertson hung back a little. " Perhaps he's sensitive. You go. I shouldn't like to make things awkward for you."

" You'd like to meet our friend, wouldn't you, Jerry ? " Mr. St. Pancreas called out.

The music stopped for a second.

" Some one laughed," Robertson said.

" He did, I expect. That means it's O.K. Come on. No need to be scared. Just round this corner and there we are."

But when they had rounded the bend and the music was deafening in their ears, Robertson shut his eyes.

" Go on, look," said Mrs. St. Pancreas. " It's nearly dinner-time, and he'll be off again before we know where we are. I haven't the least idea where he goes to, but it's quite amusing to watch him disappear."

Robertson looked. He saw, seated on the long stool before the instrument, a fattish bundle of grave clothes. There was an old cape on the shoulders and a nightcap on the head. Of the actual body only the feet were visible, soft white feet on the pedals, a little dirty between the toes as if mould still clung to them. The figure rocked and swayed in an ecstasy of abandonment, pressing the keys joyfully with its swaddled fingers.

"Aren't you afraid he'll turn round?" Robertson whispered. Then he felt a terrible dropping in his belly, for the ghost had stopped playing.

"Not he," said Mr. St. Pancreas bluffly, "he's a man of his word," and Robertson fancied that his voice was conciliatory. Then Jeremiah started again, playing with unusual relish a fughetta by John Blow. "Nearly dinner-time," Mrs. St. Pancreas murmured; "this will be the last item."

And so it was. The ghost took his hands from the keyboard. Again there came the sound of a tearing wind, as if a quantity of excess air in the instrument were seeking release. The cape on Jeremiah's shoulders arose to whirl round his head in a cloud of grey dust. Robertson sneezed so violently that his head was jerked down. When he raised it again, the ghost had gone.

"That's that," said Mrs. St. Pancreas. She stopped to examine the pedals. "How I do wish he wouldn't leave his nasty mould about; it makes such a lot of work for the maids! Never mind. I suppose we mustn't complain. He's very nice in all other respects."

The dinner-gong rang.

"Good!" said Mr. St. Pancreas, his face creased with contentment. "I'm hungry, and I haven't got indigestion like Jerry. Come along, Robertson, and I hope you like duck."

They spent a pleasant enough evening. Mr. St. Pancreas told Robertson how he had made all his money, which was very useful to know, and Mrs. St. Pancreas turned the wireless on and off, discovering several strange new stations uncharted in any radio news. Robertson drank a great deal of very excellent Dunbow port, which his host had acquired with the property. After the meal he told a good many humorous stories and related some lengthy reminiscences, for he was not eager to go to bed, but kind Mrs. St. Pancreas, perceiving his reluctance, hastened to reassure him. He might have no fear, she said, because she had seen the ghost in his room the previous night, and Jeremiah seldom visited the same place twice in succession. Mr. St. Pancreas, who was an under-

standing man, gave Robertson a bottle of port to take to bed
with him. " Perhaps we shouldn't have asked you to come
here really, old man, but we've got so used to Jerry Dunbow
that we never imagine anybody being scared."

" I'm not scared," Robertson said. " After all, one can
get used to anything, and I'm having a new experience at
least." The port was mellow within him. " Don't you
imagine I'm scared of you, Massa Dunbow ! " he roared,
hardily cupping his hands to his mouth that Jeremiah, if he
were still in the gallery, might hear him plainly.

" I shouldn't do that if I were you, old boy," murmured
Mr. St. Pancras nervously. " According to the legends he's
a bit touchy. Well, cheerio, and sleep well. Don't forget
your medicine."

Robertson said good night to Mrs. St. Pancreas and went
upstairs with his host. " Oh, by the by," said the latter, as
they turned into the left wing, " you can see Jerry's face even
if he won't show it. Here's his picture." He held up a candle.
He had refused to have the house electrified, for he liked the
atmosphere.

" Oh, this is he, is it ? " remarked Robertson, staring up
at the portrait of a jolly gentleman in lemon-coloured periwig.
" Looks rather fun, doesn't he ? Fat, too. Can't see his eyes
for cheeks. I'll bet he hit the bottle in his day."

Mr. St. Pancreas pushed him gently into his room. " Good
night," he said. " See you to-morrow."

So mellow was the port that Robertson did not even say,
" I hope you will."

He shut the door. His allotted room was pleasant by
night, colourfully furnished by Mrs. St. Pancreas with regard
to no particular period and lavishly candle-lit. He was relieved
to see that there was no four-poster but a low divan bed, and
that there were no portraits on the walls. He examined the
few bad water-colours to reassure himself that none of them
had any sinister intent. Then he finished the port, undressed
himself, and got into bed. He remembered to his annoyance
that he had not blown out the candles. " Let them burn out,"
he thought, and he covered his head with the quilt.

He slept very beautifully until three o'clock in the morning,
when Jeremiah came in and stood by the bed.

Robertson, waking out of a deep sleep, knew that he was
there, but he made no sign. He lay under the sheets, his fists
clenched, his legs stretched stiffly to the bedrail, that he might
feel himself strong. " He will go," he thought. " He must.

He'll be certain to disappear when he thinks he has no power to wake me."

Then he heard a sound in the room. Jeremiah was whistling a merry catch. " I won't stir," Robertson whispered to himself, feeling the sweat on his cheeks. " When he's gone through all his tricks he'll leave me alone."

Jeremiah sang. He sang a song about Clarinda and False Chloe. It was a dubious song, well suited to the fat voice. If he were a little flat, it was no more than might be expected, seeing that the ghost had had no practice for nearly three hundred years.

Jeremiah began to get angry. He had been a popular figure on the stage in his day, and now he was getting no appreciation at all. Also, he disliked the way Robertson had addressed him. He recited a lewd little poem. Robertson knew that his cheeks were so blown out by annoyance that the small eyes were almost invisible.

Jeremiah pulled at the quilt. Robertson cried out. His heart dropped through his stomach, his flesh froze. Then he was suddenly calm, no longer afraid. There was a long silence. He heard the click of the door. After a time the wind rose in the organ, and the drone of a cold Pavane filled the halls and the winding galleries. Mr. and Mrs. St. Pancreas, lying in the west bedrooms, heard nothing.

Jeremiah came back. Robertson raised the quilt. As he opened his eyes, his lashes brushed the folds of the dusty cerements. He got out of the other side of the bed and stood at the foot of it. The candles still burned brightly, spiralling up to the moulded ceiling. He looked at Jeremiah, at his fat red face, at his small, sunken mouth. A streak of yellowish hair blew from under the night-cap to flutter in the draught of the open door.

Master of himself, Robertson bowed. " Mr. Dunbow," he said calmly, triumphantly, " you are not, I fear, a man of your word. I think you promised that never should living soul behold your face. I have you, as I believe they said somewhere around your day or a little before, on the hip."

Walking to the dressing-table, he searched there for cigarettes and matches. He wondered if Jeremiah had been addicted, at any time, to tobacco. If so, he would hand him a pipe and there would be a pretty story to tell to his hosts in the morning. He fumbled under the bed for his slippers, for his feet were very cold.

Then Jeremiah spoke. " So I did," he said, and he smiled happily, for he was dramatizing the moment. " So I did, in truth," he lisped, offering his arm, " and I have not broken it. You died of fright—let me see, some fifteen minutes ago. Shall we proceed, sir ? "

ROADS OF DESTINY

I go to seek on many roads
    What is to be.
True heart and strong, with love to light—
Will they not bear me in the fight
To order, shun or wield or mould
    My Destiny ?
        Unpublished Poems of David Mignot.

THE song was over. The words were David's ; the air, one of the countryside. The company about the inn table applauded heartily, for the young poet paid for the wine. Only the notary, M. Papineau, shook his head a little at the lines, for he was a man of books, and he had not drunk with the rest.

David went out into the village street, where the night air drove the wine vapour from his head. And then he remembered that he and Yvonne had quarrelled that day, and that he had resolved to leave his home that night to seek fame and honour in the great world outside.

" When my poems are on every man's tongue," he told himself, in a fine exhilaration, " she will, perhaps, think of the hard words she spoke this day."

Except the roysterers in the tavern, the village folk were abed. David crept softly into his room in the shed of his father's cottage and made a bundle of his small store of clothing. With this upon a staff he set his face outward upon the road that ran from Vernoy.

He passed his father's herd of sheep huddled in their nightly pen—the sheep he herded daily, leaving them to scatter while he wrote verses on scraps of paper. He saw a light yet shining in Yvonne's window, and a weakness shook his purpose of a sudden. Perhaps that light meant that she rued, sleepless, her anger, and that morning might—— But no ! His decision was made. Vernoy was no place for him. Not one soul there could share his thoughts. Out along that road lay his fate and his future.

Three leagues across the dim, moonlit champaign ran the road, straight as a ploughman's furrow. It was believed in the village that the road ran to Paris, at least ; and this name the poet whispered often to himself as he walked. Never so far from Vernoy had David travelled before.

THE LEFT BRANCH

Three leagues, then, the road ran, and turned into a puzzle. It joined with another and a larger road at right angles. David stood, uncertain, for a while, and then took the road to the left.

Upon this more important highway were, imprinted in the dust, wheel tracks left by the recent passage of some vehicle. Some half an hour later these traces were verified by the sight of a ponderous carriage mired in a little brook at the bottom of a steep hill. The driver and postilions were shouting and tugging at the horses' bridles. On the road at one side stood a huge, black-clothed man and a slender lady wrapped in a long, light cloak.

David saw the lack of skill in the efforts of the servants. He quietly assumed control of the work. He directed the outriders to cease their clamour at the horses and to exercise their strength upon the wheels. The driver alone urged the animals with his familiar voice ; David himself heaved a powerful shoulder at the rear of the carriage, and with one harmonious tug the great vehicle rolled up on solid ground. The outriders climbed to their places.

David stood for a moment upon one foot. The huge gentleman waved a hand. " You will enter the carriage," he said, in a voice large, like himself, but smoothed by art and habit. Obedience belonged in the path of such a voice. Brief as was the young poet's hesitation, it was cut shorter still by a renewal of the command. David's foot went to the step. In the darkness he perceived dimly the form of the lady upon the rear seat. He was about to seat himself opposite, when the voice again swayed him to its will : " You will sit at the lady's side."

The gentleman swung his great weight to the forward seat. The carriage proceeded up the hill. The lady was shrunk, silent, into her corner. David could not estimate whether she was old or young, but a delicate, mild perfume from her clothes stirred his poet's fancy to the belief that there was loveliness beneath the mystery. Here was an adventure such as he had often imagined. But as yet he held no key to it, for no word was spoken while he sat with his impenetrable companions.

In an hour's time David perceived through the window that the vehicle traversed the street of some town. Then it stopped in front of a closed and darkened house, and a postilion alighted to hammer impatiently upon the door. A latticed window above flew wide and a night-capped head popped out.

" Who are ye that disturb honest folk at this time of night ? My house is closed. 'Tis too late for profitable travellers to be abroad. Cease knocking at my door, and be off."

" Open ! " spluttered the postilion loudly ; " open for Monseigneur the Marquis de Beaupertuys."

" Ah ! " cried the above voice. " Ten thousand pardons, my lord. I did not know—the hour is so late—at once shall the door be opened, and the house placed at my lord's disposal."

Inside was heard the clink of chain and bar, and the door was flung open. Shivering with chill and apprehension, the landlord of the Silver Flagon stood, half clad, candle in hand, upon the threshold.

David followed the marquis out of the carriage. " Assist the lady," he was ordered. The poet obeyed. He felt her small hand tremble as he guided her descent. " Into the house," was the next command.

The room was the long dining-hall of the tavern. A great oak table ran down its length. The huge gentleman seated himself in a chair at the nearer end. The lady sank into another against the wall, with an air of great weariness. David stood, considering how best he might now take his leave and continue upon his way.

" My lord," said the landlord, bowing to the floor, " h—had I ex—expected this honour, entertainment would have been ready. T—t—there is wine and cold fowl and m—m—may-be——"

" Candles," said the marquis, spreading the fingers of one plump white hand in a gesture he had.

" Y—yes, my lord." He fetched half a dozen candles, lighted them, and set them upon the table.

" If monsieur would, perhaps, deign to taste a certain Burgundy—there is a cask——"

" Candles," said monsieur, spreading his fingers.

" Assuredly—quickly—I fly, my lord."

A dozen more lighted candles shone in the hall. The great bulk of the marquis overflowed his chair. He was dressed in fine black from head to foot save for the snowy ruffles at his wrists and throat. Even the hilt and scabbard of his sword were black. His expression was one of sneering pride. The ends of an upturned moustache reached nearly to his mocking eyes.

The lady sat motionless, and now David perceived that she was young, and possessed of pathetic and appealing beauty. He was startled from the contemplation of her forlorn loveliness by the booming voice of the marquis.

" What is your name and pursuit ? "

" David Mignot. I am a poet."

The moustache of the marquis curled nearer to his eyes.

" How do you live ? "

" I am also a shepherd ; I guarded my father's flock," David answered, with his head high, but a flush upon his cheek.

" Then listen, master shepherd and poet, to the fortune you have blundered upon to-night. This lady is my niece, Mademoiselle Lucie de Varennes. She is of noble descent and is possessed of ten thousand francs a year in her own right. As to her charms, you have but to observe for yourself. If the inventory pleases your shepherd's heart, she becomes your wife at a word. Do not interrupt me. To-night I conveyed her to the château of the Comte de Villemaur, to whom her hand had been promised. Guests were present ; the priest was waiting ; her marriage to one eligible in rank and fortune was ready to be accomplished. At the altar this demoiselle, so meek and dutiful, turned upon me like a leopardess, charged me with cruelty and crimes, and broke, before the gaping priest, the troth I had plighted for her. I swore there and then, by ten thousand devils, that she should marry the first man we met after leaving the château, be he prince, charcoal-burner, or thief. You, shepherd, are the first. Mademoiselle must be wed this night. If not you, then another. You have ten minutes in which to make your decision. Do not vex me with words or questions. Ten minutes, shepherd ; and they are speeding."

The marquis drummed loudly with his white fingers upon the table. He sank into a veiled attitude of waiting. It was as if some great house had shut its doors and windows against approach. David would have spoken, but the huge man's bearing stopped his tongue. Instead he stood by the lady's chair and bowed.

" Mademoiselle," he said, and he marvelled to find his words flowing easily before so much elegance and beauty. " You have heard me say I was a shepherd. I have also had the fancy, at times, that I am a poet. If it be the test of a poet to adore and cherish the beautiful, that fancy is now strengthened. Can I serve you in any way, mademoiselle ? "

The young woman looked up at him with eyes dry and mournful. His frank, glowing face, made serious by the gravity of the adventure, his strong, straight figure and the liquid sympathy in his blue eyes, perhaps, also, her imminent need of long-denied help and kindness, thawed her to sudden tears.

" Monsieur," she said, in low tones, " you look to be true and kind. He is my uncle, the brother of my father, and my only relative. He loved my mother, and he hates me because I am like her. He has made my life one long terror. I am afraid of his very looks, and never before dared to disobey him. But to-night he would have married me to a man three times my age. You will forgive me for bringing this vexation upon you, monsieur. You will, of course, decline this mad act he tries to force upon you. But let me thank you for your generous words, at least. I have had none spoken to me in so long."

There was now something more than generosity in the poet's eye. Poet he must have been, for Yvonne was forgotten ; this fine, new loveliness held him with its freshness and grace. The subtle perfume from her filled him with strange emotions. His tender look fell warmly upon her. She leaned to it, thirstily.

" Ten minutes," said David, " is given me in which to do what I would devote years to achieve. I will not say I pity you, mademoiselle ; it would not be true—I love you. I cannot ask love for you yet, but let me rescue you from this cruel man, and, in time, love may come. I think I have a future ; I will not always be a shepherd. For the present I will cherish you with all my heart and make your life less sad. Will you trust your fate to me, mademoiselle ? "

" Ah, you would sacrifice yourself from pity ! "

" From love. The time is almost up, mademoiselle."

" You will regret it, and despise me."

" I will live only to make you happy, and myself worthy of you."

Her fine small hand crept into his from beneath her cloak.
" I will trust you," she breathed, " with my life. And—
and love—may not be so far off as you think. Tell him.
Once away from the power of his eyes I may forget."

David went and stood before the marquis. The black
figure stirred, and the mocking eyes glanced at the great hall
clock.

" Two minutes to spare. A shepherd requires eight
minutes to decide whether he will accept a bride of beauty and
income ! Speak up, shepherd, do you consent to become
mademoiselle's husband ? "

" Mademoiselle," said David, standing proudly, " has
done me the honour to yield to my request that she become
my wife."

" Well said ! " said the marquis. " You have yet the
making of a courtier in you, master shepherd. Mademoiselle
could have drawn a worse prize after all. And now to be
done with the affair as quick as the Church and the devil will
allow ! "

He struck the table soundly with his sword hilt. The
landlord came, knee-shaking, bringing more candles in the
hope of anticipating the great lord's whims. " Fetch a
priest," said the marquis, " a priest ; do you understand ?
In ten minutes have a priest here, or——"

The landlord dropped his candles and flew.

The priest came, heavy-eyed and ruffled. He made
David Mignot and Lucie de Varennes man and wife, pocketed
a gold piece that the marquis tossed him, and shuffled out
again into the night.

" Wine," ordered the marquis, spreading his ominous
fingers at the host.

" Fill glasses," he said, when it was brought. He stood
up at the head of the table in the candlelight, a black mountain
of venom and conceit with something like the memory of an old
love turned to poison in his eye, as it fell upon his niece.

" Monsieur Mignot," he said, raising his wineglass,
" drink after I say this to you : You have taken to be your
wife one who will make your life a foul and wretched thing.
The blood in her is an inheritance running black lies and
red ruin. She will bring you shame and anxiety. The
devil that descended to her is there in her eyes and skin and
mouth that stoop even to beguile a peasant. There is your
promise, monsieur poet, for a happy life. Drink your wine.
At last, mademoiselle, I am rid of you."

The marquis drank. A little grievous cry, as if from a sudden wound, came from the girl's lips. David, with his glass in his hand, stepped forward three paces and faced the marquis. There was little of a shepherd in his bearing.

"Just now," he said calmly, "you did me the honour to call me ' monsieur.' May I hope, therefore, that my marriage to mademoiselle has placed me somewhat nearer to you in— let us say, reflected rank—has given me the right to stand more as an equal to monseigneur in a certain little piece of business I have in my mind ? "

"You may hope, shepherd," sneered the marquis.

"Then," said David, dashing his glass of wine into the contemptuous eyes that mocked him, "perhaps you will condescend to fight me."

The fury of the great lord outbroke in one sudden curse like a blast from a horn. He tore his sword from its black sheath ; he called to the hovering landlord : "A sword there, for this lout ! " He turned to the lady, with a laugh that chilled her heart, and said : "You put much labour upon me, madame. It seems I must find you a husband and make you a widow in the same night."

"I know not sword-play," said David. He flushed to make the confession before his lady.

" ' I know not sword-play,' " mimicked the marquis. "Shall we fight like peasants with oaken cudgels ? *Hola !* François, my pistols ! "

A postilion brought two shining great pistols ornamented with carven silver, from the carriage holsters. The marquis tossed one upon the table near David's hand. "To the other end of the table," he cried ; "even a shepherd may pull a trigger. Few of them attain the honour to die by the weapon of a De Beaupertuys."

The shepherd and the marquis faced each other from the ends of the long table. The landlord, in an ague of terror, clutched the air and stammered : "M—M—Monseigneur, for the love of Christ ! not in my house !—do not spill blood —it will ruin my custom——" The look of the marquis, threatening him, paralysed his tongue.

"Coward," cried the lord of Beaupertuys, "cease chattering your teeth long enough to give the word for us, if you can."

Mine host's knees smote the floor. He was without a vocabulary. Even sounds were beyond him. Still, by gestures he seemed to beseech peace in the name of his house and custom.

" I will give the word," said the lady, in a clear voice. She went up to David and kissed him sweetly. Her eyes were sparkling bright, and colour had come to her cheek. She stood against the wall, and the two men levelled their pistols for her count.

" *Un—deux—trois !* "

The two reports came so nearly together that the candles flickered but once. The marquis stood, smiling, the fingers of his left hand resting, outspread, upon the end of the table. David remained erect, and turned his head very slowly, searching for his wife with his eyes. Then, as a garment falls from where it is hung, he sank, crumpled, upon the floor.

With a little cry of terror and despair, the widowed maid ran and stooped above him. She found his wound, and then looked up with her old look of pale melancholy. " Through his heart," she whispered. " Oh, his heart ! "

" Come," boomed the great voice of the marquis, " out with you to the carriage ! Daybreak shall not find you on my hands. Wed you shall be again, and to a living husband, this night. The next we come upon, my lady, highwayman or peasant. If the road yields no other, then the churl that opens my gates. Out with you to the carriage ! "

The marquis, implacable and huge, the lady wrapped again in the mystery of her cloak, the postilion bearing the weapons—all moved out to the waiting carriage. The sound of its ponderous wheels rolling away echoed through the slumbering village. In the hall of the Silver Flagon the distracted landlord wrung his hands above the slain poet's body, while the flames of the four-and-twenty candles danced and flickered on the table.

THE RIGHT BRANCH

Three leagues, then, the road ran, and turned into a puzzle. It joined with another and larger road at right angles. David stood, uncertain, for a while, and then took the road to the right.

Whither it led he knew not, but he was resolved to leave Vernoy far behind that night. He travelled a league and then passed a large château which showed testimony of recent entertainment. Lights shone from every window ; from the great stone gateway ran a tracery of wheel tracks drawn in the dust by the vehicles of the guests.

Three leagues farther and David was weary. He rested

and slept for a while on a bed of pine boughs at the roadside.
Then up and on again along the unknown way.

Thus for five days he travelled the great road, sleeping
upon Nature's balsamic beds or in peasants' ricks, eating of
their black, hospitable bread, drinking from streams or the
willing cup of the goatherd.

At length he crossed a great bridge and set his foot within
the smiling city that has crushed or crowned more poets than
all the rest of the world. His breath came quickly as Paris
sang to him in a little undertone her vital chant of greeting—
the hum of voice and foot and wheel.

High up under the eaves of an old house in the Rue Conti,
David paid for lodging, and set himself, in a wooden chair,
to his poems. The street, once sheltering citizens of import
and consequence, was now given over to those who ever follow
in the wake of decline.

The houses were tall and still possessed of a ruined dignity,
but many of them were empty save for dust and the spider.
By night there was the clash of steel and the cries of brawlers
straying restlessly from inn to inn. Where once gentility
abode was now but a rancid and rude incontinence. But here
David found housing commensurate to his scant purse. Daylight and candlelight found him at pen and paper.

One afternoon he was returning from a foraging trip to
the lower world, with bread and curds and a bottle of thin
wine. Half-way up his dark stairway he met—or rather came
upon, for she rested on the stair—a young woman of a beauty
that should balk even the justice of a poet's imagination. A
loose, dark cloak, flung open, showed a rich gown beneath.
Her eyes changed swiftly with every little shade of thought.
Within one moment they would be round and artless like a
child's, and long and cozening like a gipsy's. One hand
raised her gown, undraping a little shoe, high-heeled, with its
ribbons dangling, untied. So heavenly she was, so unfitted
to stoop, so qualified to charm and command ! Perhaps she
had seen David coming, and had waited for his help there.

Ah, would monsieur pardon that she occupied the stairway, but the shoe !—the naughty shoe ! Alas ! it would not
remain tied. Ah ! if monsieur *would* be so gracious !

The poet's fingers trembled as he tied the contrary ribbons.
Then he would have fled from the danger of her presence,
but the eyes grew long and cozening, like a gipsy's, and held
him. He leaned against the balustrade, clutching his bottle
of sour wine.

"You have been so good," she said, smiling. "Does monsieur, perhaps, live in the house?"

"Yes, madame. I—I think so, madame."

"Perhaps in the third storey, then?"

"No, madame; higher up."

The lady fluttered her fingers with the least possible gesture of impatience.

"Pardon. Certainly I am not discreet in asking. Monsieur will forgive me? It is surely not becoming that I should inquire where he lodges."

"Madame, do not say so. I live in the——"

"No, no, no; do not tell me. Now I see that I erred. But I cannot lose the interest I feel in this house and all that is in it. Once it was my home. Often I come here but to dream of those happy days again. Will you let that be my excuse?"

"Let me tell you, then, for you need no excuse," stammered the poet. "I live in the top floor—the small room where the stairs turn."

"In the front room?" asked the lady, turning her head sidewise.

"The rear, madame."

The lady sighed, as if with relief.

"I will detain you no longer then, monsieur," she said, employing the round and artless eye. "Take good care of my house. Alas! only the memories of it are mine now. Adieu, and accept my thanks for your courtesy."

She was gone, leaving but a smile and a trace of sweet perfume. David climbed the stairs as one in slumber. But he awoke from it, and the smile and the perfume lingered with him and never afterward did either seem quite to leave him. This lady of whom he knew nothing drove him to lyrics of eyes, chansons of swiftly conceived love, odes to curling hair, and sonnets to slippers on slender feet.

Poet he must have been, for Yvonne was forgotten; this fine, new loveliness held him with its freshness and grace. The subtle perfume about her filled him with strange emotions.

On a certain night three persons were gathered about a table in a room on the third floor of the same house. Three chairs and the table and a lighted candle upon it was all the furniture. One of the persons was a huge man, dressed in black. His expression was one of sneering pride. The ends of his upturned moustache reached nearly to his mocking eyes. Another was a lady, young and beautiful, with eyes that could be round and artless, like a child's, or long and cozening, like a gipsy's, but were now keen and ambitious, like any other conspirator's. The third was a man of action, a combatant, a bold and impatient executive, breathing fire and steel. He was addressed by the others as Captain Desrolles.

This man struck the table with his fist, and said, with controlled violence :

" To-night. To-night as he goes to midnight mass. I am tired of the plotting that gets nowhere. I am sick of signals and ciphers and secret meetings and such *baragouin*. Let us be honest traitors. If France is to be rid of him, let us kill in the open, and not hunt with snares and traps. To-night, I say. I back my words. My hand will do the deed. To-night, as he goes to mass."

The lady turned upon him a cordial look. Woman, however wedded to plots, must ever thus bow to rash courage. The big man stroked his upturned moustache.

" Dear captain," he said, in a great voice, softened by habit, " this time I agree with you. Nothing is to be gained by waiting. Enough of the palace guards belong to us to make the endeavour a safe one."

" To-night," repeated Captain Desrolles, again striking the table. " You have heard me, marquis ; my hand will do the deed."

" But now," said the huge man softly, " comes a question. Word must be sent to our partisans in the palace, and a signal agreed upon. Our staunchest men must accompany the royal carriage. At this hour what messenger can penetrate so far as the south doorway ? Ribout is stationed there ; once a message is placed in his hands, all will go well."

" I will send the message," said the lady.

" You, countess ? " said the marquis, raising his eyebrows. " Your devotion is great, we know, but——"

" Listen ! " exclaimed the lady, rising and resting her hands upon the table ; " in a garret of this house lives a youth from the provinces as guileless and tender as the lambs he tended there. I have met him twice or thrice upon the stairs. I questioned him, fearing that he might dwell too near the room in which we are accustomed to meet. He is mine if I will. He writes poems in his garret, and I think he dreams of me. He will do what I say. He shall take the message to the palace."

The marquis rose from his chair and bowed. " You did not permit me to finish my sentence, countess," he said. " I would have said : ' Your devotion is great, but your wit and charm are infinitely greater.' "

While the conspirators were thus engaged, David was polishing some lines addressed to his *amorette d'escalier*. He heard a timorous knock at the door, and opened it, with a great throb, to behold her there, panting as one in straits, with eyes wide open and artless, like a child's.

" Monsieur," she breathed. " I come to you in distress. I believe you to be good and true, and I know of no other help. How I flew through the streets among the swaggering men ! Monsieur, my mother is dying. My uncle is a captain of guards in the palace of the king. Some one must fly to bring him. May I hope——"

" Mademoiselle," interrupted David, his eyes shining with the desire to do her service, " your hopes shall be my wings. Tell me how I may reach him."

The lady thrust a sealed paper into his hand.

" Go to the south gate—the south gate, mind —and say to the guards there, ' The falcon has left his nest.' They will pass you, and you will go to the south entrance to the palace. Repeat the words, and give this letter to the man who will reply ' Let him strike when he will.' This is the password, monsieur, entrusted to me by my uncle, for now when the country is disturbed and men plot against the king's life, no one without it can gain entrance to the palace grounds after nightfall. If you will, monsieur, take him this letter so that my mother may see him before she closes her eyes."

" Give it me," said David eagerly. " But shall I let you return home through the streets alone so late ? I——"

" No, no—fly. Each moment is like a precious jewel. Some time," said the lady, with eyes long and cozening, like a gipsy's, " I will try to thank you for your goodness."

The poet thrust the letter into his breast, and bounded down the stairway. The lady, when he was gone, returned to the room below.

The eloquent eyebrows of the marquis interrogated her.

" He is gone," she said, " as fleet and stupid as one of his own sheep, to deliver it."

The table shook again from the batter of Captain Desrolles's fist.

" Sacred name ! " he cried ; " I have left my pistols behind ! I can trust no others."

"Take this," said the marquis, drawing from beneath his cloak a shining, great weapon, ornamented with carven silver. "There are none truer. But guard it closely, for it bears my arms and crest, and already I am suspected. Me, I must put many leagues between myself and Paris this night. To-morrow must find me in my château. After you, dear countess."

The marquis puffed out the candle. The lady, well cloaked, and the two gentlemen softly descended the stairway and flowed into the crowd that roamed along the narrow pavements of the Rue Conti.

David sped. At the south gate of the king's residence a halberd was laid to his breast, but he turned its point with the words : " The falcon has left his nest."

" Pass, brother," said the guard, " and go quickly."

On the south steps of the palace they moved to seize him, but again the *mot de passe* charmed the watchers. One among them stepped forward and began : " Let him strike——" but a flurry among the guards told of a surprise. A man of keen look and soldierly stride suddenly pressed through them and seized the letter which David held in his hand. " Come with me," he said, and led him inside the great hall. Then he tore open the letter and read it. He beckoned to a man uniformed as an officer of musketeers, who was passing. " Captain Tetreau, you will have the guards at the south entrance and the south gate arrested and confined. Place men known to be loyal in their places." To David he said : " Come with me."

He conducted him through a corridor and an ante-room into a spacious chamber, where a melancholy man, sombrely dressed, sat brooding in a great, leather-covered chair. To that man he said :

" Sire, I have told you that the palace is as full of traitors and spies as a sewer is of rats. You have thought, sire, that it was my fancy. This man penetrated to your very door by their connivance. He bore a letter which I have intercepted. I have brought him here that your majesty may no longer think my zeal excessive."

" I will question him," said the king, stirring in his chair. He looked at David with heavy eyes dulled by an opaque film. The poet bent his knee.

" From where do you come ? " asked the king.

" From the village of Vernoy, in the province of Eure-et-Loir, sire."

He beheld her there with eyes wide open and artless, like a child's.

" What do you follow in Paris ? "

" I—I would be a poet, sire."

" What did you in Vernoy ? "

· " I minded my father's flock of sheep."

The king stirred again, and the film lifted from his eyes.

" Ah ! in the fields ! "

" Yes, sire."

" You lived in the fields ; you went out in the cool of the morning and lay among the hedges in the grass. The flock distributed itself upon the hillside ; you drank of the living stream ; you ate your sweet, brown bread in the shade, and you listened, doubtless, to blackbirds piping in the grove. Is not that so, the shepherd ? "

" It is, sire," answered David, with a sigh ; " and to the bees at the flowers, and, maybe, to the grape gatherers singing on the hill."

" Yes, yes," said the king, impatiently ; " maybe to them ; but surely to the blackbirds. They whistled often in the grove, did they not ? "

" Nowhere, sire, so sweetly as in Eure-et-Loir. I have endeavoured to express their song in some verses that I have written."

" Can you repeat those verses ? " asked the king, eagerly. " A long time ago I listened to the blackbirds. It would be something better than a kingdom if one could rightly construe their song. And at night you drove the sheep to the fold and then sat, in peace and tranquillity, to your pleasant bread. Can you repeat those verses, shepherd ? "

" They run this way, sire," said David, with respectful ardour :

> " ' Lazy shepherd, see your lambkins
> Skip, ecstatic, on the mead ;
> See the firs dance in the breezes,
> Hear Pan blowing at his reed.

> " ' Hear us calling from the tree-tops,
> See us swoop upon your flock ;
> Yield us wool to make our nests warm
> In the branches of the ——— ' "

" If it please your majesty," interrupted a harsh voice, " I will ask a question or two of this rhymester. There is little time to spare. I crave pardon, sire, if my anxiety for your safety offends."

" The loyalty," said the king, " of the Duke d'Aumale

is too well proven to give offence." He sank into his chair, and the film came again over his eyes.

"First," said the duke, "I will read you the letter he brought :

"'To-night is the anniversary of the dauphin's death. If he goes, as is his custom, to midnight mass to pray for the soul of his son, the falcon will strike, at the corner of the Rue Esplanade. If this be his intention, set a red light in the upper room at the south-west corner of the palace, that the falcon may take heed.'"

"Peasant," said the duke sternly, "you have heard these words. Who gave you this message to bring ? "

"My lord duke," said David sincerely, "I will tell you. A lady gave it me. She said her mother was ill, and that this writing would fetch her uncle to her bedside. I do not know the meaning of the letter, but I will swear that she is beautiful and good."

"Describe the woman," commanded the duke, "and how you came to be her dupe."

"Describe her ! " said David, with a tender smile. "You would command words to perform miracles. Well, she is made of sunshine and deep shade. She is slender, like the alders, and moves with their grace. Her eyes change while you gaze into them ; now round, and then half-shut as the sun peeps between two clouds. When she comes, heaven is all about her ; when she leaves, there is chaos and a scent of hawthorn blossoms. She came to me in the Rue Conti, number twenty-nine."

"It is the house," said the duke, turning to the king, "that we have been watching. Thanks to the poet's tongue, we have a picture of the infamous Countess Quebedaux."

"Sire and my lord duke," said David earnestly, "I hope my poor words have done no injustice. I have looked into that lady's eyes. I will stake my life that she is an angel, letter or no letter."

The duke looked at him steadily. "I will put you to the proof," he said alowly. "Dressed as the king, you shall, yourself, attend mass in his carriage at midnight. Do you accept the test ? "

David smiled. "I have looked into her eyes," he said. "I had my proof there. Take yours how you will."

Half an hour before twelve the Duke d'Aumale with his

own hands set a red lamp in a south-west window of the palace. At ten minutes to the hour, David, leaning on his arm, dressed as the king, from top to toe, with his head bowed in his cloak, walked slowly from the royal apartments to the waiting carriage. The duke assisted him inside and closed the door. The carriage whirled away along its route to the cathedral.

On the qui vive at a house at the corner of the Rue Esplanade was Captain Tetreau with twenty men, ready to pounce upon the conspirators when they should appear.

But it seemed that, for some reason, the plotters had slightly altered their plans. When the royal carriage had reached the Rue Christopher, one square nearer than the Rue Esplanade, forth from it burst Captain Desrolles, with his band of would-be regicides, and assailed the equipage. The guards upon the carriage, though surprised at the premature attack, descended and fought valiantly. The noise of conflict attracted the force of Captain Tetreau, and they came pelting down the street to the rescue. But, in the meantime, the desperate Desrolles had torn open the door of the king's carriage, thrust his weapon against the body of the dark figure inside, and fired.

Now, with loyal reinforcements at hand, the street rang with cries and the rasp of steel, but the frightened horses had dashed away. Upon the cushions lay the dead body of the poor mock king and poet, slain by a ball from the pistol of Monseigneur, the Marquis de Beaupertuys.

The Main Road

Three leagues, then, the road ran, and turned into a puzzle. It joined with another and larger road at right angles. David stood, uncertain, for a while, and then sat himself to rest upon its side.

Whither those roads led he knew not. Either way there seemed to lie a great world full of chance and peril. And then, sitting there, his eye fell upon a bright star, one that he and Yvonne had named for theirs. That set him thinking of Yvonne, and he wondered if he had not been too hasty. Why should he leave her and his home because a few hot words had come between them ? Was love so brittle a thing that jealousy, the very proof of it, could break it ? Mornings always brought a cure for the little heartaches of evening. There was yet time for him to return home without any one in the sweetly sleeping village of Vernoy being the wiser. His heart was Yvonne's ; there where he had lived always he could write his poems and find his happiness.

David rose, and shook off his unrest and the wild mood that had tempted him. He set his face steadfastly back along the road he had come. By the time he had re-travelled the road to Vernoy his desire to rove was gone. He passed the sheepfold, and the sheep scurried, with a drumming flutter, at his late footsteps, warming his heart by the homely sound. He crept without noise into his little room and lay there, thankful that his feet had escaped the distress of new roads that night.

How well he knew woman's heart ! The next evening Yvonne was at the well in the road where the young congregated in order that the *curé* might have business. The corner of her eye was engaged in a search for David, albeit her set mouth seemed unrelenting. He saw the look ; braved the mouth, drew from it a recantation, and, later, a kiss as they walked homeward together.

Three months afterward they were married. David's father was shrewd and prosperous. He gave them a wedding that was heard of three leagues away. Both the young people were favourites in the village. There was a procession in the streets, a dance on the green ; they had the marionettes and a tumbler out from Dreux to delight the guests.

Then a year, and David's father died. The sheep and the cottage descended to him. He already had the seemliest wife in the village. Yvonne's milk pails and her brass kettles were bright—*ouf !* they blinded you in the sun when you passed that way. But you must keep your eyes upon her yard, for her flower-beds were so neat and gay they restored to you your sight. And you might hear her sing, aye, as far as the double chestnut tree above Père Gruneau's blacksmith forge.

But a day came when David drew out paper from a long-shut drawer, and began to bite the end of a pencil. Spring had come again and touched his heart. Poet he must have been, for now Yvonne was well-nigh forgotten. This fine new loveliness of earth held him with its witchery and grace. The perfume from her woods and meadows stirred him strangely. Daily had he gone forth with his flock, and brought it safe at night. But now he stretched himself under the hedge and pieced words together on his bits of paper. The sheep strayed, and the wolves, perceiving that difficult poems make easy mutton, ventured from the woods and stole his lambs.

David's stock of poems grew larger and his flock smaller. Yvonne's nose and temper waxed sharp and her talk blunt. Her pans and kettles grew dull, but her eyes had caught their flash. She pointed out to the poet that his neglect was reducing the flock and bringing woe upon the household. David hired a boy to guard the sheep, locked himself in the little room in the top of the cottage, and wrote more poems. The boy, being a poet by nature, but not furnished with an outlet in the way of writing, spent his time in slumber. The wolves lost no time in discovering that poetry and sleep are practically the same; so the flock steadily grew smaller. Yvonne's ill-temper increased at an equal rate. Sometimes she would stand in the yard and rail at David through his high window. Then you could hear her as far as the double chestnut tree above Père Gruneau's blacksmith forge.

M. Papineau, the kind, wise, meddling old notary, saw this, as he saw everything at which his nose pointed. He went to David, fortified himself with a great pinch of snuff, and said :

" Friend Mignot, I affixed the seal upon the marriage certificate of your father. It would distress me to be obliged to attest a paper signifying the bankruptcy of his son. But that is what you are coming to. I speak as an old friend. Now, listen to what I have to say. You have your heart set, I perceive, upon poetry. At Dreux I have a friend, one Monsieur Bril—Georges Bril. He lives in a little cleared space in a household of books. He is a learned man ; he visits Paris each year ; he himself has written books. He will tell you when the catacombs were made, how they found out the names of the stars, and why the plover has a long bill. The meaning and the form of poetry is to him as intelligent as the baa of a sheep is to you. I will give you a letter to him, and you shall take him your poems and let him read them. Then you will know if you shall write more, or give your attention to your wife and business."

" Write the letter," said David, " I am sorry you did not speak of this sooner."

At sunrise next morning he was on the road to Dreux with the precious roll of poems under his arm. At noon he wiped the dust from his feet at the door of Monsieur Bril. That learned man broke the seal of M. Papineau's letter, and sucked up its contents through his gleaming spectacles as the sun draws water. He took David inside to his study and sat him down upon a little island beat upon by a sea of books.

Monsieur Bril had a conscience. He flinched not even at a mass of manuscript the thickness of a finger length and rolled to an incorrigible curve. He broke the back of the roll against his knee and began to read. He slighted nothing ; he bored into the lump as a worm into a nut, seeking for a kernel.

Meanwhile David sat, marooned, trembling in the spray of so much literature. It roared in his ears. He held no chart or compass for voyaging in that sea. Half the world, he thought, must be writing books.

Monsieur Bril bored to the last page of the poems. Then he took off his spectacles and wiped them with his handkerchief.

" My old friend, Papineau, is well ? " he asked.

" In the best of health," said David.

" How many sheep have you, Monsieur Mignot ? "

" Three hundred and nine, when I counted them yesterday. The flock has had ill fortune. To that number it has decreased from eight hundred and fifty."

" You have a wife and a home, and lived in comfort. The sheep brought you plenty. You went into the fields with them and lived in the keen air and ate the sweet bread of contentment. You had but to be vigilant and recline there upon Nature's breast, listening to the whistle of the blackbirds in the grove. Am I right thus far ? "

" It was so," said David.

" I have read all your verses," continued Monsieur Bril, his eyes wandering about his sea of books as if he conned the horizon for a sail. " Look yonder, through that window, Monsieur Mignot ; tell me what you see in that tree."

" I see a crow," said David, looking.

" There is a bird," said Monsieur Bril, " that shall assist me where I am disposed to shirk a duty. You know that bird, Monsieur Mignot ; he is the philosopher of the air. He is happy through submission to his lot. None so merry or full-crawed as he with his whimsical eye and rollicking step. The fields yield him what he desires. He never grieves that his plumage is not gay, like the oriole's. And you have heard, Monsieur Mignot, the notes that Nature has given him ? Is the nightingale any happier, do you think ? "

David rose to his feet. The crow cawed harshly from his tree.

"I thank you, Monsieur Bril," he said slowly. "There was not, then, one nightingale note among all those croaks?"

"I could not have missed it," said Monsieur Bril, with a sigh. "I read every word. Live your poetry, man; do not try to write it any more."

"I thank you," said David again. "And now I will be going back to my sheep."

"If you would dine with me," said the man of books, "and overlook the smart of it, I will give you reasons at length."

"No," said the poet, "I must be back in the fields cawing at my sheep."

Back along the road to Vernoy he trudged with his poems under his arm. When he reached his village he turned into the shop of one Zeigler, a Jew out of Armenia, who sold anything that came to his hand.

"Friend," said David, "wolves from the forest harass my sheep on the hills. I must purchase firearms to protect them. What have you?"

"A bad day, this, for me, friend Mignot," said Zeigler, spreading his hands, "for I perceive that I must sell you a weapon that will not fetch a tenth of its value. Only last week I bought from a peddler a wagon full of goods that he procured at a sale by a *commissionaire* of the crown. The sale was of the château and belongings of a great lord—I know not his title—who has been banished for conspiracy against the king. There are some choice firearms in the lot. This pistol—oh, a weapon fit for a prince!—it shall be only forty francs to you, friend Mignot, if I lose ten by the sale. But perhaps an arquebuse——"

"This will do," said David, throwing the money on the counter. "Is it charged?"

"I will charge it," said Zeigler. "And, for ten francs more, add a store of powder and ball."

David laid his pistol under his coat and walked to his cottage. Yvonne was not there. Of late she had taken to gadding much among the neighbours. But a fire was glowing in the kitchen stove. David opened the door of it and thrust his poems in upon the coals. As they blazed up they made a singing, harsh sound in the flue.

"The song of the crow!" said the poet.

He went up to his attic room and closed the door. So quiet was the village that a score of people heard the roar of the great pistol. They flocked thither, and up the stairs where the smoke, issuing, drew their notice.

The men laid the body of the poet upon his bed, awkwardly arranging it to conceal the torn plumage of the poor black crow. The women chattered in a luxury of zealous pity. Some of them ran to tell Yvonne.

M. Papineau, whose nose had brought him there among the first, picked up the weapon and ran his eye over its silver mountings with a mingled air of connoisseurship and grief.

" The arms," he explained, aside, to the *curé*, " and crest of Monseigneur, the Marquis de Beaupertuys."

THE TRAPDOOR

IT was two months before John Staines—under doctor's orders—found suitable accommodation. He must build up his system, the doctor said, by fresh air and quiet at the week-ends after the strain and stress of his office work.

So John explored the home counties; and then, one Sunday late in April, he stopped to drink at an isolated beer house, "The Fernahan Arms," on the eastern edge of Hertfordshire, not far from the main road to Cambridge. It was quiet, sheltering behind a larchwood on the edge of a hill; it seemed clean and spacious within; and in the pale gold of the spring sunshine it looked a friendly place.

The landlady was dark and stout, and the very fact that her gaze, when she brought his beer, was completely—almost carefully—devoid of interest, made him decide that "The Fernahan Arms" might prove to be the solution of his difficulties.

"Thank you," he said, taking the mug. "Do you have many people staying here during the summer?"

"No," said the landlady.

"You seem to have a pretty large place. I suppose it's rather off the beaten track to catch many casual visitors."

"'Tis," said the landlady.

"I was wondering," he continued, "whether—you see, I'm looking for some place where I could come down to at the week-ends—Saturday to Monday morning—and I was wondering whether we couldn't come to some arrangement. I—I like this place," he added lamely. The landlady was not being very helpful. She looked at him for a minute or two.

" Yes," she said again.

" Well, now "—there was a shade of impatience in his voice—" what are your terms ? "

As if she had been waiting to make quite sure that he was in earnest, the woman became a little more communicative. Her name, it appeared, was Mrs. Palethorpe. They arranged that he should have a room to the front at the top of the house overlooking the road. Yes, she understood that he was after quiet and rest. She assured him that it would be quiet. There was hardly any traffic on the road and none at night. He would have his meals brought up to him. Would he like to see the room ?

It was light and airy and looked across the road over a pleasant vista of wood and meadow. It was furnished with dressing-table and washstand to match, two heavy dining-room chairs upholstered in faded moss-green plush and an immense mahogany commode crowned with an empty carafe upon a mat of crochet in high relief. The pattern of the linoleum was even more astonishing than that of the wallpaper.

It suited John, however, and the following Saturday afternoon found him exploring the place in the sunlight. The village was pleasant without being picturesque, and only a chimney here or a patch of stonework there hinted at its antiquity. There were prehistoric remains of some sort in the meadow beyond the church ; but these, he decided, would keep until Sunday before he examined them. In the meantime the sun was low and the breeze had freshened into a decidedly chilly wind. He would return to the inn.

Outside he paused to examine it. It was uncompromisingly square in outline, and the shallow windows and mean proportions of sill and doorway seemed to emphasize its bareness. On the other side of the road stood the sign, as if trying to dissociate itself from the house. The road itself seemed to twist past the house with an air of haste and plunged down the hill in an abrupt curve, hiding itself between thick hawthorn hedges until it reached the calmer levels below. Above, the roof sloped steeply upwards, black against the sunset, surmounted by two chimney stacks with pots of different heights, like irregular teeth.

And with a slight shock John was aware of a resemblance between the house and its mistress, Mrs. Palethorpe. Both had that blankly disinterested expression and that power of altering their appearance according to their mood. At this moment " The Fernahan Arms " was chilly—and looked it.

How different from the bland invitation it had given him on his first arrival !

That evening he sat in the bar with the gamekeeper from the Big House, a couple of farm labourers, and an old-age pensioner in a corduroy suit. He learned quite a lot about " The Fernahan Arms."

As he had suspected, it had not always been a public house. In the happy days before the war, the house had been inhabited by a man of the name of Weedon with his wife and father-in-law—a very old man he was, and dead these twenty year.

" Thirty," said Mrs. Palethorpe from behind the bar.

The pensioner became confused in calculating the exact number of years. Mrs. Palethorpe retired to the parlour and the keeper took up the history.

After the old man died—Wright his name was—Mr. and Mrs. Weedon lived on there till the war came. Then he joined up and was terrible badly wounded and came back and died, and then she moved and *his* cousin's husband, Mr. Palethorpe, took it over and opened a pub. because t'other was closed during the war, see ! and when he died Mrs. Palethorpe she kept it on and made a good thing of it she did, being the only place for two mile around.

" Whose cousin's husband ? " asked John, vainly attempting to connect the relationship of so many pronouns.

" Why, Weedon, of course. Weedon was Mrs. Palethorpe's cousin. . . ."

That lady suddenly reappeared, and with a guilty feeling of having been overheard discussing her affairs, John ordered another couple of drinks. Her face was as expressionless as usual, but John was conscious of her annoyance. It emanated from her so strongly that the atmosphere seemed almost to darken and turn chill. She turned her back and began to add figures in an account book. Conversation stopped except for a few unintelligible noises from the labourers. A clock intruded its precise, monotonous voice. Mrs. Palethorpe let it have its way for several minutes before she turned again.

" Time," she said, with an air of snubbing them all. Mugs were emptied and replaced with furtive scrapes. The door was opened and remained so, letting in the cold night wind to puff the calendars from the wall and draw the lamp flame cornerwise up its chimney until the last of the heavy boots had rasped and clumped its way out. The evening was over.

"I think I'll go right up now," said John.
"Here's your candle," said Mrs. Palethorpe, pointing to the dresser with her left hand as she unhooked the lamp.

She preceded him upstairs and along the passage. He watched the shadows fly from them as they approached, scattering circles and curves of light on walls and ceiling. He noticed, for the first time, just outside his room, a trapdoor in the ceiling.

"What's up there?" he asked.

She stopped.

"The loft," she said.

"Anything in it?"

"Nothing," she replied and walked on into his room.

.   .   .   .

Next morning appeared in a flurry of cloud and sunshine. As John dressed, a sudden shower drenched the shivering fields and hurried away across the hill to give place to a pale rainbow that planted a tentative foot in a hedge opposite his window and arched up out of sight round to the front of the house, gathering strength as he watched it. He went into the passage to get a better view and followed its shining curve to the zenith with a comforting sense of peace and fulfilment. Scarcely focussing his gaze upon it, he stood, his head thrown back, delighting in the spring and the rain and the sunshine, and the fact that he was John Staines. And as he stood there, his eye was caught by the trapdoor and followed its edge to the bolt. It was shot fast; but what riveted his attention was the fact that the handle had been filed or sawn away so that it would be exceedingly difficult to withdraw. He gazed at it for some moments speculating upon the reason for this. Mr. Wright perhaps, or his son-in-law, had wished to prevent the trapdoor from being opened. But if so, why not a padlock? Anybody with patience and a pair of pliers could stand on a step-ladder and draw back the bar. The hinges on the opposite side indicated that the cover opened inward. One would have to push upward and then. . . .

"Here's your breakfast," said Mrs. Palethorpe, behind him.

John blushed. Once again he experienced a guilty feeling of having been caught investigating her private affairs. It was absurd, but he found himself explaining matters.

"I was looking at the rainbow, and I noticed the trapdoor," he said.

"That's the loft," she said.

" I know, but I noticed that the handle of the bolt's missing —and it seemed queer, somehow . . ."

Mrs. Palethorpe stepped past him into his room, bearing the tray. She set it on the table near the window.

" There's only the loft up there," she said. " It's never used."

" I suppose not," he replied. " It would be fairly difficult to open now. What happens when you want to mend the roof ? "

" They climbs up by the washhouse." She turned at the door and looked at him. " There's nothing up there as I knows of, and no cause to go and look. The bolt was that way before we come here."

He found himself returning to the point.

" But who filed off the handle ? " he asked.

She was almost tart. " How should I know ? "

" Mr. Weedon, perhaps ? "

" Mr. Weedon wouldn't have done such a foolish thing— not as *I* knows," she said. " Mr. Weedon was a respectable man. He took the house as his poor father-in-law left it and lived quiet. And if you want to know," she added angrily, " Mr. Wright was an invalid . . . so it wasn't him."

With that she turned and went out.

John ate his breakfast hastily. Why had she been so annoyed ? Damn it ! He had only looked at the blessed trapdoor. And as he passed under it on his way out, he looked at it again, defiantly. She was right ; it certainly had not been used for a long time. The paint lay in scales and blisters that the least touch would have dislodged. The apparent cause of her annoyance was cobwebbed and rusty. It was firm in its socket. Pincers would definitely be necessary. Oil, perhaps, to soften the rust. But why, he asked himself abruptly, was he bothering about bolts and trapdoors ? He was here to get out into the fresh air. There were prehistoric earthworks to explore. Hertfordshire awaited him. Away with dust and cobwebs ! Out into the sunshine !

On his return to the bar that evening he was greeted as an old acquaintance by the pensioner who took up the conversation at exactly the point where he had left off the previous day.

" She were wrong," he announced triumphantly. " It were twenty-five year come twenty-seventh of this month that old Wright died. I asked my daughter, and she calculated it were twenty-five year exactly."

"Really," said John, with a wary eye for Mrs.
Palethorpe's appearance. "Did Mr. Wright have a long
illness ?"

"No, he did not. Why, he were as strong and 'ealthy as I
be till he was took sudden-like. One day he was a-sitting
sunnin' hisself and the next took to 'is bed and no one to set
eyes on him till his corpse were a-carried out near six months
after."

"But six months is a long time for a man to be ill," said
John.

"My Edith she were bad three year," said the pensioner,
with conclusive emphasis. "Mortal agony all the time she
was. No—six months isn't so very long. Why, we 'ad the
doctor every day for the last year and an narf. *And* a distrik
nurse. It were 'er legs," he added confidentially. "Old
Wright he weren't in no pain as it were. Mr. Weedon called
it a decline."

"And what did the doctor call it ? " asked John.

"Ah ! 'E wouldn't have no doctor. That was just it.
Many's the time Mr. Weedon 'e would come an' tell us how
he'd begged on his bended knee to 'ave the doctor, but old
Wright, he was stubborn, he was. Couldn't abide the sight
of a doctor, he couldn't, Mr. Weedon said. Just wasted away.
'Is coffin was as light as light. Just wasted right away. He
were a cross-grained old chap, he were, *and* a tongue on him.
Always creating about something or other, he were."

At this point Mrs. Palethorpe returned to the bar. The
pensioner turned a bright eye on her.

"This young gentleman was asking about old Wright's
illness," he remarked, to John's embarrassment. "I said he
just wasted away, right away."

"Mr. Staines doesn't need to be interested in sickness.
He's here for his health." Her voice carried a warning.

John laughed. "He was calculating the exact date of
Mr. Wright's death before I came in," he said. "I only——"

Mrs. Palethorpe interruped him.

"What does it matter," she said, "twenty, thirty, forty
years ago—it's all over now. He's dead."

"That's right," said the pensioner.

"Very well, then. There's no call for you all to be discussing it. Death's not such a pleasant subject for an old
man, nor yet a young one."

John looked at his feet.

The pensioner, hurt, mumbled incoherently and finished

his beer. The tension was only broken by the entrance of two or three other customers.

But late that night he lay in bed remembering her voice and expression.

" Death's not such a pleasant subject for an old man, nor yet a young one."

And the subject haunted his dreams.

Indeed, it was the culmination of a nightmare of hurrying footsteps and hushed voices in a low room, and it made him start awake and lie breathless for a moment, staring at the grey square of the window and trying to rationalize the panic fears that swooped and fluttered in his mind.

Then, as he lay, the swirling terrors of his dream stopped short and coalesced into one anguished dread that settled on him and chilled his drowsy consciousness into sharp awakening.

From the ceiling above his head came a soft, irregular thumping. Somebody was up there in the dark loft, knocking on the trapdoor !

He listened. The noise continued for a little while, then stopped ; and just as he was beginning to enjoy a glow of re-assurance that his nightmare was over and the normal world was real and solid about him, it began again.

It was no dream.

So real, so urgent a knocking that he was out of bed and at the door in automatic reaction to the appeal before he became conscious of this sudden transference from one strangeness to another. Why should any one knock at such an hour in such a house ? There was no other sound. Outside the window deep greyness dragged on the fields and lifted them to an unfamiliar horizon where a few dull stars sparked feebly in the cloud-rift. The land was cold and empty and indifferent. Inside was a tepid darkness faintly odorous of cloth and cooking. It, too, was unhelpful. And still resounded above him—but fainter now—the knocking that had hammered wakefulness into his dreams.

Once—twice—twice again—and then silence, a quite absolute silence that rang in John's ears. A small drowsy doubt arose. What a fool he was to stand bemused in the darkness listening to problematic noises ! There was no noise now. Had there ever been a noise in this dark grey world ?

Ashamed and sleepy, he stumbled back to bed. Neverthe-less before he left for the early bus next morning he had gazed for a long time at the trapdoor and satisfied the rational half of his mind that the bolt was really rusted into its socket and that no sane person would ever desire to use it as an exit from the loft if there was any other way of doing so. He determined to discover if there were when next he came to " The Fernahan Arms."

.   .   .   .

And, of course, there was not. While Mrs. Palethorpe presided, safely out of the way, at the bar, he prowled inside and out, and finally, with a half-shamed sense of the fantasy of his action, furtively climbed the stairs that led to a loft at the back of the house. There, behind barriers of chicken-food in sacks and the last remnants of winter apples, he passed through an inner door and found that the greater part of the main loft had been partitioned off uncompromisingly with wood and plaster, and that there was no evidence of aperture or entrance.

With full realization, even the thick stuffiness of sunlight upon stagnant air was not warm enough to prevent a shudder over him. For suddenly he knew that the knocking in the night *had* been real, and it had come from a dark prison under the roof that had been unopened for years. And he did not like to think of the time when he must try to sleep in the room beneath.

He went to view the earthworks after that. But a shower drenched him, and a sudden wind wheeped mournfully through the surrounding thicket. Common sense fought losing battles with his uneasiness all the way home, till at last he decided, as he watched his soles steaming before the fire in Mrs. Palethorpe's room, that he must solve the mystery of the trapdoor before darkness arrived with its panic reinforcements.

But it was dusk before he had thought of a suitable excuse for borrowing a pair of pliers—to extract a nail from his shoe, he said ; and then the house was full of footsteps and movements—so full of watchful noise that it seemed like a challenge to finish matters that evening, however late. He waited, therefore, until the bar was open, and even loitered over a half pint, after his supper, in company with the pensioner and one or two men from the farms. Then, just after nine o'clock, he sauntered into the back room and through towards the staircase and the darkness of the upper floors. The window showed grey. Outside on the road lay an ochreish splash of light from a lower window ; and a bat or a bird, swooping suddenly across the sky, seemed only to emphasize the stillness and immobility of the landscape. Very faintly came a murmur from the bar. Up here the quiet silence lay like midnight along the walls—but a night tense with storm.

Quietly and not without a tingling of half-frightened excitement John brought a chair from his room and placed it in the passage below the trapdoor. Standing on it he discovered that he could easily reach the bolt, but it would be tiring to work on it above his head.

He listened.

There was no other sound save the distant intermittent noise of voices in the bar. He was quite alone up here, with little fear of interruption.

Emboldened, he put back the chair and with infinite precaution edged the heavy commode across the linoleum. When he stood on it his shoulders were thrust against the ceiling with his head bowed like a caryatid's.

He flashed a pocket torch and began to twist the rusty bolt with his pliers.

It was very stiff. The grind of metal on metal sent little rustling tremors across the wood. Flakes of long-dried paint fell and spun round in the thick air, and queer reverberations echoed from within the loft.

The bolt turned. Slowly he forced it back, twisting this way and that, and always with one ear strained, as it were, for the least likelihood of disturbance from downstairs. Once he heard a door shut, and as he stopped and turned, his pliers must have struck the trapdoor with a blow that made him start and caused his heart to beat faster with the remembrance of that interior knocking of the previous night. Sweating, he turned his eyes to the grey circle of woodwork lit by his torch. It was not yet too late. The bolt was not yet free. He could still leave things as they were—get down—put away all evidence of his curiosity and descend to light and warmth and normality. But, swinging back, came the memory of his nightmare (if it had been a nightmare) and the necessity of satisfying himself on that point once and for all.

With a dismal sense of compulsion and an almost despairing recklessness, he twisted the bar through the final quarter of an inch, but the ultimate cessation of noise was no relief.

For a moment he hesitated, then with a sudden push he raised the trapdoor. It was lighter than he had anticipated and flew upwards, balancing for one perilous instant while his torch streamed upwards into dusty emptiness, before it fell back on to the floor of the loft with a crash so loud that for a moment John's unfocussed fears were centred round the embarrassment and shame of his discovery by Mrs. Palethorpe.

Instinctively he switched off his torch and stood motionless, his head and shoulders inside the loft, looking down at the greyness of the carpet beneath.

A tense and absolute silence succeeded the noise of the falling trapdoor. But it did not last for long. With a slithering rustle something moved in the blackness and descended upon his head, resolving itself into a pair of hands, thin and damp, covering his face and groping in a blind, brutish fashion about his mouth and eyes.

An old and filthy smell was in his nostrils. He cried out gaspingly, terror and disgust arching his body in a rigid convulsion. But his strangled shouts were muffled in a frenzied pressure. Weakly he sagged and fell clumsily to the ground.

. . . .

Mrs. Palethorpe, it appeared, had found him and dragged him into another room. Her masterful personality did not desert her, though there is no evidence as to how she explained away her lodger's screams to a bar full of interested countrymen. A doctor came and attended to cuts and bruises occasioned by John's fall. He also prescribed something for his shuddering state of collapse and communicated the necessary information to John's place of business that he was unwell and would need a long holiday. He was a discreet man who asked few questions, and it was probably due to him that Mrs. Palethorpe's letter was not despatched for several months.

"DEAR MR. STAINES" (it ran), "I am sending you some things you left behind. I dont wish to be rude, dear sir, but you ought to have minded your business or this would never have happened. Still I suppose you could not have helped it though I could have told you that nothing would have happened if you had left things as they were. It was always only the knocks and they dont do nobody any harm, but it dont like being disturbed, thats why the bolt was cut, only I did not want to tell you, it being a scandal in the family as you might say. Nothing was ever proved only old Wright, he was a terror, always nagging and too old to be good for much, and Weedon was slow to anger and long to put it by, there's no denying. Dear sir, I havent ever said anything to anybody about this before, so please will you keep mum too, because it would do my place a lot of harm ; but the fact was, they did not give the old man enough to eat, and its my belief they kept him up in the loft till he died. The doctor said he were thin when he signed the certificate, but Weedon said he would not eat and he believed it. Nothing ever has happened except the knocks, but the trap was always like that since before we came, and it's like that now again. Please do not say a word about this to anybody, only it was right you should know. I hope you are feeling quite well again and got over it all.—Yours truly,   ALICE PALETHORPE."

John burned the letter and did his best to forget its contents. But he now lives in a first-floor mansion flat and has a marked distaste for old-fashioned country pubs.

BEN BLOWER'S STORY

"ARE you sure that's the *Flame* over by the shore?"
"Cer*ting*, manny! I could tell her pipes acrost the Mazoura."

"And you will overhaul her?"

"Won't we though! I tell ye, strannger, so sure as my name's Ben Blower, that that last tar-bar'l I hove in the furnace has put jist the smart chance of go-ahead into us to cut off the *Flame* from yonder pint, or send our boat to kingdom come."

"The devil!" exclaimed a bystander who, intensely interested in the race, was leaning the while against the partitions of the boiler-room. "I've chosen a nice place to see the sun, near this infernal powder-barrel."

"Not so bad as if you were in it," coolly observed Ben as the other walked rapidly away.

"As if he were in it! in what? in the boiler?"

"Cer*ting*! Don't folks sometimes go into bilers, manny?"

"I should think there'd be other parts of the boat more comfortable."

"That's right; poking fun at me at once't: but wait till we get through this brush with the old *Flame* and I'll tell ye of a regular fixin scrape that a man may get into. It's true, too, every word of it, as sure as my name's Ben Blower." . . .

"You have seen the *Flame* then afore, strannger? Six year ago, when new upon the river, she was a raal out and outer, I tell ye. I was at that time a hand aboard of her. Yes, I belonged to her at the time of her great race with the *Go-liar*. You've heern, mahap, of the blow-up by which we lost it. They made a great fuss about it; but it was nothing but a mere fiz of hot water after all. Only the springing of a few rivets, which loosened a biler-plate or two, and let out a thin spirting upon some niggers that hadn't sense enough to get out of the way. Well, the *Go-liar* took off our passengers, and we ran into Smasher's Landing to repair damages, and bury the poor fools that were killed. Here we laid for a matter of thirty hours or so, and got things to rights on board for a bran new start. There was some carpenters' work yet to be done, but the captain said that that might be fixed off jist as well when we were under way—we had worked hard—the weather was sour, and we needn't do anything more jist now —we might take that afternoon to ourselves, but the next morning he'd get up steam bright and airly, and we'd all come out *new*. There was no temperance society at Smasher's Landing, and I went ashore upon a lark with some of the hands."

I omit the worthy Benjamin's adventures upon land, and, despairing of fully conveying his language in its original Doric force, will not hesitate to give the rest of his singular narrative in my own words, save where, in a few instances, I can recall his precise phraseology, which the reader will easily recognize.

" The night was raw and sleety when I regained the deck of our boat. The officers, instead of leaving a watch above, had closed up everything, and shut themselves in the cabin. The fire-room only was open. The boards dashed from the outside by the explosion had not yet been replaced. The floor of the room was wet, and there was scarcely a corner which afforded a shelter from the driving storm. I was about leaving the room, resigned to sleep in the open air, and now bent only upon getting under the lee of some bulkhead that would protect me against the wind. In passing out I kept my arms stretched forward to feel my way in the dark, but my feet came in contact with a heavy iron lid ; I stumbled and, as I fell, struck one of my hands into the ' manhole ' (I think this was the name he gave to the oval-shaped opening in the head of the boiler), through which the smith had entered to make his repairs. I fell with my arm thrust so far into the aperture that I received a pretty smart blow in the face as it came in contact with the head of the boiler, and I did not hesitate to drag my body after it the moment I recovered from this stunning effect, and ascertained my whereabouts. In a word, I crept into the boiler, resolved to pass the rest of the night there. The place was dry and sheltered. Had my bed been softer I would have had all that man could desire ; as it was, I slept, and slept soundly.

"I should mention though, that, before closing my eyes, I several times shifted my position. I had gone first to the farthest end of the boiler, then again I had crawled back to the manhole, to put my hand out and feel that it was really still open. The warmest place was at the farther end, where I finally established myself, and that I knew from the first. It was foolish in me to think that the opening through which I had just entered could be closed without my hearing it, and that, too, when no one was astir but myself; but the blow on the side of my face made me a little nervous perhaps; besides, I never could bear to be shut up in any place—it always gives a wild-like feeling about the head.

"You may laugh, stranger, but I believe I should suffocate in an empty church if I once felt that I was shut up in it that I could not get out. I have met men afore now just like me, or worse rather, much worse—men that it made sort of furious to be tied down to anything, yet so soft-like and contradictory in their natures that you might lead them anywhere so long as they didn't feel the string. Stranger, it takes all sorts of people to make a world; and we may have a good many of the worst kind of white men here out west. But I have seen folks upon this river—quiet-looking chaps, too, as ever you see—who were so teetotally *carankterankterous* that they'd shoot the doctor who'd tell them they couldn't live when ailing, and make a die of it, just out of spite, when told they *must* get well. Yes, fellows as fond of the good things of earth as you and I, yet who'd rush like mad right over the gang-plank of life if once brought to believe that they had to stay in this world whether they wanted to leave it or not. Thunder and bees! if such a fellow as that had heard the cocks crow as I did—awakened to find darkness about him—darkness so thick you might cut it with a knife—heard other sounds, too, to tell that it was morning, and scrambling to fumble for that manhole, found it, too, black—closed—black and even as the rest of the iron coffin around him, closed, with not a rivet-hole to let God's light and air in—why—why—he'd a *swounded* right down on the spot, as I did, and I ain't ashamed to own it to no white man."

The big drops actually stood upon the poor fellow's brow, as he now paused for a moment in the recital of his terrible story. He passed his hand over his rough features, and resumed it with less agitation of manner.

"How long I may have remained there senseless I don't know. The doctors have since told me it must have been a sort of fit—more like an apoplexy than a swoon, for the attack finally passed off in sleep. Yes, I slept; I know *that*, for I dreamed—dreamed a heap o' things afore I awoke : there is but one dream, however, that I have ever been able to recall distinctly, and that must have come on shortly before I recovered my consciousness. My resting-place through the night had been, as I have told you, at the far end of the boiler. Well, I now dreamed that the manhole was still open, and, what seems curious, rather than laughable, if you take it in connection with other things, I fancied that my legs had been so stretched in the long walk I had taken the evening before that they now reached the whole length of the boiler, and extended through the opening.

" At first (in my dreaming reflections) it was a comfortable thought, that no one could now shut up the manhole without awakening me. But soon it seemed as if my feet, which were on the outside, were becoming drenched in the storm which had originally driven me to seek this shelter. I felt the chilling rain upon my extremities. They grew colder and colder, and their numbness gradually extended upward to other parts of my body. It seemed, however, that it was only the under side of my person that was thus strangely visited. I lay upon my back, and it must have been a species of nightmare that afflicted me, for I knew at last that I was dreaming, yet felt it impossible to rouse myself. A violent fit of coughing restored at last my powers of volition. The water, which had been slowly rising around me, had rushed into my mouth ; I awoke to hear the rapid strokes of the pump which was driving it into the boiler !

" My whole condition—no—not all of it—not yet—my *present* condition flashed with new horror upon me. But I did not again swoon. The choking sensation which had made me faint when I first discovered how I was entombed gave way to a livelier though less overpowering emotion. I shrieked even as I started from my slumber. The previous discovery of the closed aperture, with the instant oblivion that followed, seemed only a part of my dream, and I threw my arms about and looked eagerly for the opening by which I had entered the horrid place—yes, looked for it, and felt for it, though it was the terrible conviction that it was closed—a second time brought home to me—which prompted my frenzied cry. Every sense seemed to have tenfold acuteness, yet not one to act in unison with another. I shrieked again and again— imploringly—desperately—savagely. I filled the hollow chamber with my cries, till its iron walls seemed to tingle around me. The dull strokes of the accursed pump seemed only to mock at, while they deadened, my screams.

"At last I gave myself up. It is the struggle against our fate which frenzies the mind. We cease to fear when we cease to hope. I gave myself up, and then I grew calm !

"I was resigned to die—resigned even to my mode of death. It was not, I thought, so very new after all, as to awaken unwonted horror in a man. Thousands have been sunk to the bottom of the ocean shut up in the holds of vessels— beating themselves against the battened hatches—dragged down from the upper world shrieking, not for life, but for death only beneath the eye and amid the breath of heaven. Thousands have endured that appalling kind of suffocation. I would die only as many a better man had died before me. I *could* meet such a death. I said so—I thought so—I felt so —felt so, I mean, for a minute—or more ; ten minutes it may have been—or but an instant of time. I know not, nor does it matter if I could compute it. There *was* a time, then, when I was resigned to my fate. But, Heaven ! was I resigned to it in the shape in which next it came to appal ? Stranger, I felt that water growing hot about my limbs, though it was yet mid-leg deep. I felt it, and in the same moment heard the roar of the furnace that was to turn it into steam before it could get deep enough to drown one !

"You shudder. It was hideous. But did I shrink and shrivel, and crumble down upon that iron floor, and lose my senses in that horrid agony of fear ? No ! though my brain swam and the life-blood that curdled at my heart seemed about to stagnate there for ever, still *I knew !* I was too hoarse—too hopeless—from my previous efforts, to cry out more. But I struck—feebly at first, and then strongly— frantically with my clenched fist against the sides of the boiler. There were people moving near who *must* hear my blows ! Could not I hear the grating of chains, the suffling of feet, the very rustle of a rope—hear them all, within a few inches of me ? I did ; but the gurgling water that was growing hotter and hotter around my extremities made more noise within the steaming cauldron than did my frenzied blows against its sides.

"Latterly I had hardly changed my position, but now the growing heat of the water made me plash to and fro ; lifting myself wholly out of it was impossible, but I could not remain quiet. I stumbled upon something ; it was a mallet !—a

" They say, too, that I was conscious when they took me out."

chance tool the smith had left there by accident. With what
wild joy did I seize it—with what eager confidence did I now
deal my first blows with it against the walls of my prison !
But scarce had I intermitted them for a moment when I heard
the clang of the iron door as the fireman flung it wide to feed
the flames that were to torture me. My knocking was un-
heard, though I could hear him toss the sticks into the furnace
beneath me, and drive to the door when his infernal oven was
fully crammed.

" Had I yet a hope ? I had ; but it rose in my mind side
by side with the fear that I might now become the agent of
preparing myself a more frightful death. Yes ; when I thought
of that furnace with its fresh-fed flames curling beneath the
iron upon which I stood—a more frightful death even than
that of being boiled alive ! Had I discovered that mallet but
a short time sooner—but no matter, I would by its aid resort
to the only expedient now left.

" It was this. I remembered having a marline-spike in
my pocket, and in less time than I have taken in hinting at
the consequences of thus using it, I had made an impression
upon the sides of the boiler, and soon succeeded in driving
it through. The water gushed through the aperture—would
they see it ? No ; the jet could only play against a wooden
partition which must hide the stream from view ; it must
trickle down upon the decks before the leakage would be
discovered. Should I drive another hole to make that leakage
greater ? Why, the water within seemed already to be sensibly
diminished, so hot had become that which remained ; should
more escape, would I not hear it bubble and hiss upon the
fiery plates of iron that were already scorching the soles of
my feet ? . . .

" Ah ! there is a movement—voices—I hear them calling
for a crowbar. The bulkhead cracks as they pry off the plank-
ing. They have seen the leak—they are trying to get at it !
Good God ! why do they not first dampen the fire ? why do
they call for the—the—

" Stranger, look at that finger : it can never regain its
natural size ; but it has already done all the service that man
could expect from so humble a member. *Sir, that hole would
have been plugged up on the instant* unless *I had jammed my
finger through !*

" I heard the cry of horror as they saw it without—the
shout to drown the fire—the first stroke of the cold-water
pump. They say, too, that I was conscious when they took

me out—but I—I remember nothing more till they brought
a julep to my bedside arterwards, AND *that julep !*——."

"Cooling, was it?"

"STRANNGER ! ! !"

Ben turned away his head and wept—He could no more.

THE SHADOW OF A SHADE

MY sister Lettie has lived with me ever since I had a home of my own. She was my little housekeeper before I married. Now she is my wife's constant companion, and the " darling auntie " of my children, who go to her for comfort, advice, and aid in all their little troubles and perplexities.

But, though she has a comfortable home, and loving hearts around her, she wears a grave, melancholy look on her face, which puzzles acquaintances and grieves friends.

A disappointment ! Yes, the old story of a lost lover is the reason for Lettie's looks. She has had good offers often ; but since she lost the first love of her heart she has never indulged in the happy dream of loving and being beloved.

George Mason was a cousin of my wife's—a sailor by profession. He and Lettie met one another at our wedding, and fell in love at first sight. George's father had seen service before him on the great mysterious sea, and had been especially known as a good Arctic sailor, having shared in more than one expedition in search of the North Pole and the North-West Passage.

It was not a matter of surprise to me, therefore, when George volunteered to go out in the *Pioneer*, which was being fitted out for a cruise in search of Franklin and his missing expedition. There was a fascination about such an undertaking that I felt I could not have resisted had I been in his place. Of course, Lettie did not like the idea at all, but he silenced her by telling ner that men who volunteered for Arctic search were never lost sight of, and that he should not make as much advance in his profession in a dozen years as he would in a year or so of this expedition. I cannot say that Lettie, even after this, was quite satisfied with the notion of his going, but, at all events, she did not argue against it any longer. But the grave look, which is now habitual with her, but was a rare thing in her young and happy days, passed over her face sometimes when she thought no one was looking.

My younger brother, Harry, was at this time an academy student. He was only a beginner then. Now he is pretty well known in the art world, and his pictures command fair prices. Like all beginners in art, he was full of fancies and theories. He would have been a pre-Raphaelite, only pre-Raphaelism had not been invented then. His peculiar craze was for what he styled the Venetian School. Now, it chanced that George had a fine Italian-looking head, and Harry persuaded him to sit to him for his portrait. It was a fair likeness, but a very moderate work of art. The background was so very dark, and George's naval costume so very deep in colour, that the face came out too white and staring. It was a three-quarter picture ; but only one hand showed in it, leaning on the hilt of a sword. As George said, he looked much more like the commander of a Venetian galley than a modern mate.

However, the picture pleased Lettie, who did not care much about art provided the resemblance was good. So the picture was duly framed—in a tremendously heavy frame, of Harry's ordering—and hung up in the dining-room.

And now the time for George's departure was growing nearer. The *Pioneer* was nearly ready to sail, and her crew only waited orders. The officers grew acquainted with each other before sailing, which was an advantage. George took up very warmly with the surgeon, Vincent Grieve, and, with my permission, brought him to dinner once or twice.

" Poor chap, he has no friends nearer than the Highlands, and it's precious lonely work."

" Bring him by all means, George ! You know that any friends of yours will be welcome here."

So Vincent Grieve came. I am bound to say I was not favourably impressed by him, and almost wished I had not consented to his coming. He was a tall, pale, fair young man, with a hard Scots face and a cold, grey eye. There was something in his expression, too, that was unpleasant—something cruel or crafty, or both.

I considered that it was very bad taste for him to pay such marked attention to Lettie, coming, as he did, as the friend of her fiancé. He kept by her constantly and anticipated

George in all the little attentions which a lover delights to pay. I think George was a little put out about it, though he said nothing, attributing his friend's offence to lack of breeding.

Lettie did not like it at all. She knew that she was not to have George with her much longer, and she was anxious to have him to herself as much as possible. But as Grieve was her lover's friend she bore the infliction with the best possible patience.

The surgeon did not seem to perceive in the least that he was interfering where he had no business. He was quite self-possessed and happy, with one exception. The portrait of George seemed to annoy him. He had uttered a little impatient exclamation when he first saw it which drew my attention to him ; and I noticed that he tried to avoid looking at it. At last, when dinner came, he was told to sit exactly facing the picture. He hesitated for an instant and then sat down, but almost immediately rose again.

" It's very childish and that sort of thing," he stammered, " but I cannot sit opposite that picture."

" It is not high art," I said, " and may irritate a critical eye."

" I know nothing about art," he answered, " but it is one of those unpleasant pictures whose eyes follow you about the room. I have an inherited horror of such pictures. My mother married against her father's will, and when I was born she was so ill she was hardly expected to live. When she was sufficiently recovered to speak without delirious rambling she implored them to remove a picture of my grandfather that hung in the room, and which she vowed made threatening faces at her. It's superstitious, but constitutional—I have a horror of such paintings ! "

I believe George thought this was a ruse of his friend's to get a seat next to Lettie ; but I felt sure it was not, for I had seen the alarmed expression of his face.

At night, when George and his friend were leaving, I took an opportunity to ask the former, half in a joke, if he should bring the surgeon to see us again. George made a very hearty assertion to the contrary, adding that he was pleasant enough company among men at an inn, or on board ship, but not where ladies were concerned.

But the mischief was done. Vincent Grieve took advantage of the introduction and did not wait to be invited again. He called the next day, and nearly every day after. He was a more frequent visitor than George now, for George was obliged to attend to his duties, and they kept him on board the *Pioneer* pretty constantly, whereas the surgeon, having seen to the supply of drugs, etc., was pretty well at liberty. Lettie avoided him as much as possible, but he generally brought, or professed to bring, some little message from George to her, so that he had an excuse for asking to see her.

On the occasion of his last visit—the day before the *Pioneer* sailed—Lettie came to me in great distress. The young cub had actually the audacity to tell her he loved her. He knew, he said, about her engagement to George, but that did not prevent another man from loving her too. A man could no more help falling in love than he could help taking a fever. Lettie stood upon her dignity and rebuked him severely; but he told her he could see no harm in telling her of his passion, though he knew it was a hopeless one.

" A thousand things may happen," he said at last, " to bring your engagement with George Mason to an end. Then perhaps you will not forget that another loves you ! "

I was very angry, and was forthwith going to give him my opinion on his conduct, when Lettie told me he was gone, that she had bade him go and had forbidden him the house. She only told me in order to protect herself, for she did not intend to say anything to George, for fear it should lead to a duel or some other violence.

That was the last we saw of Vincent Grieve before the *Pioneer* sailed.

George came the same evening, and was with us till daybreak, when he had to tear himself away and join his ship.

After shaking hands with him at the door, in the cold, grey, drizzly dawn, I turned back into the dining-room, where poor Lettie was sobbing on the sofa.

I could not help starting when I looked at George's portrait, which hung above her. The strange light of daybreak could hardly account for the extraordinary pallor of the face. I went close to it and looked hard at it. I saw that it was covered with moisture, and imagined that that possibly made it look so pale. As for the moisture, I supposed poor Lettie had been kissing the beloved's portrait, and that the moisture was caused by her tears.

It was not till a long time after, when I was jestingly telling Harry how his picture had been caressed, that I learnt the error of my conjecture. Lettie assured me most solemnly that I was mistaken in supposing she had kissed it.

" It was the varnish blooming, I expect," said Harry.

And thus the subject was dismissed, for I said no more, though I knew well enough, in spite of my not being an artist, that the bloom of varnish was quite another sort of thing.

The *Pioneer* sailed. We received—or, rather, Lettie received—two letters from George, which he had taken the opportunity of sending by homeward-bound whalers. In the second he said it was hardly likely he should have an opportunity of sending another, as they were sailing into high latitudes—into the solitary sea, to which none but expedition ships ever penetrated. They were all in high spirits, he said, for they had encountered very little ice and hoped to find clear water farther north than usual. Moreover, he added, Grieve had held a sinecure so far, for there had not been a single case of illness on board.

Then came a long silence, and a year crept away very slowly for poor Lettie. Once we heard of the expedition from the papers. They were reported as pushing on and progressing favourably by a wandering tribe of Esquimaux with whom the captain of a Russian vessel fell in. They had laid the ship up for the winter, and were taking the boats on sledges, and believed they had met with traces of the lost crews that seemed to show they were on the right track.

The winter passed again, and spring calme. It was a balmy, bright spring such as we get occasionaly, even in this changeable and uncertain climate of ours.

One evening we were sitting in the dining-room with the window open, for, although we had long given up fires, the room was so oppressively warm that we were glad of the breath of the cool evening breeze.

Lettie was working. Poor child, though she never murmured, she was evidently pining at George's long absence. Harry was leaning out of the window, studying the evening effect on the fruit blossom, which was wonderfully early and plentiful, the season was so mild. I was sitting at the table, near the lamp, reading the paper.

Suddenly there swept into the room a chill. It was not a gust of cold wind, for the curtain by the open window did not swerve in the least. But the deathly cold pervaded the room —came, and was gone in an instant. Lettie shuddered, as I did, with the intense icy feeling.

She looked up. " How curiously cold it has got all in a minute," she said.

" We are having a taste of poor George's Polar weather," I said with a smile.

At the same moment I instinctively glanced towards his portrait. What I saw struck me dumb. A rush of blood, at fever heat, dispelled the numbing influence of the chill breath that had seemed to freeze me.

I have said the lamp was lighted ; but it was only that I might read with comfort, for the violet twilight was still so full of sunset that the room was not dark. But as I looked at the picture I saw it had undergone a strange change. I saw it as plainly as possible. It was no delusion, coined for the eye by the brain.

I saw, in the place of George's head, a grinning skull ! I stared at it hard ; but it was no trick of fancy. I could see the hollow orbits, the gleaming teeth, the fleshless cheekbones —it was the head of death !

Without saying a word, I rose from my chair and walked straight up to the painting. As I drew nearer a sort of mist seemed to pass before it ; and as I stood close to it, I saw only the face of George. The spectral skull had vanished.

" Poor George ! " I said unconsciously.

Lettie looked up. The tone of my voice had alarmed her, the expression of my face did not reassure her.

" What do you mean ? Have you heard anything ? Oh, Robert, in mercy tell me ! '

She got up and came over to me and, laying her hands on my arm, looked up into my face imploringly.

" No, my dear ; how should I hear ? Only I could not help thinking of the privation and discomfort he must have gone through. I was reminded of it by the cold——"

" Cold ! " said Harry, who had left the window by this time. " Cold ! what on earth are you talking about ? Cold, such an evening as this ! You must have had a touch of ague, I should think."

" Both Lettie and I felt it bitterly cold a minute or two ago. Did you not feel it ? "

" Not a bit ; and as I was three parts out of the window I ought to have felt it if any one did."

It was curious, but that strange chill had been felt only in the room. It was not the night wind, but some super- natural breath connected with the dread apparition I had seen. It was, indeed, the chill of polar winter—the icy shadow of the frozen North.

" What is the day of the month, Harry ? " I asked.

" To-day—the 23rd, I think," he answered ; then added, taking up the newspaper I had been reading : " Yes, here you are.   Tuesday, February the 23rd, if the *Daily News* tells truth, which I suppose it does.   Newspapers can afford to tell the truth about dates, whatever they may do about art." Harry had been rather roughly handled by the critic of a morning paper for one of his pictures a few days before, and he was a little angry with journalism generally.

Presently Lettie left the room, and I told Harry what I had felt and seen, and told him to take note of the date, for I feared that some mischance had befallen George.

" I'll put it down in my pocket-book, Bob.   But you and Lettie must have had a touch of the cold shivers, and your stomach or fancy misled you—they're the same thing, you know.   Besides, as regards the picture, there's nothing in that !   There is a skull there, of course.   As Tennyson says :

> ' Any face, however full
> Padded round with flesh and fat,
> Is but modelled on a skull.'

The skull's there—just as in every good figure-subject the nude is there under the costumes.   You fancy that is a mere coat of paint.   Nothing of the kind !   Art lives, sir !   That is just as much a real head as yours is with all the muscles and bones, just the same.   That's what makes the difference between art and rubbish."

This was a favourite theory of Harry's, who had not yet developed from the dreamer into the worker.   As I did not care to argue with him, I allowed the subject to drop after we had written down the date in our pocket-books.   Lettie sent down word presently that she did not feel well and had gone to bed.   My wife came down presently and asked what had happened.   She had been up with the children and had gone in to see what was the matter with Lettie.

" I think it was very imprudent to sit with the window open, dear.   I know the evenings are warm, but the night air strikes cold at times—at any rate, Lettie seems to have caught a violent cold, for she is shivering very much.   I am afraid she had got a chill from the open windows."

I did not say anything to her then, except that both Lettie and I had felt a sudden coldness ; for I did not care to enter into an explanation again, for I could see Harry was inclined to laugh at me for being so superstitious.

At night, however, in our own room, I told my wife what had occurred, and what my apprehensions were.   She was so upset and alarmed that I almost repented having done so.

The next morning Lettie was better again, and as we did not either of us refer to the events of the preceding night the circumstance appeared to be forgotten by us all.

But from that day I was ever inwardly dreading the arrival of bad news. And at last it came, as I expected.

One morning, just as I was coming downstairs to breakfast, there came a knock at the door, and Harry made his appearance. It was a very early visit for him, for he generally used to spend his mornings at the studio, and drop in on his way home at night.

He was looking pale and agitated.

" Lettie's not down, is she, yet ? " he asked ; and then, before I could answer, added another question : " What newspaper do you take ? "

" The *Daily News*," I answered. " Why ? "

" She's not down ? "

" No."

" Thank God ! Look here ! "

He took a paper from his pocket and gave it to me, pointing out a short paragraph at the bottom of one of the columns.

I knew what was coming the moment he spoke about Lettie.

The paragraph was headed, " Fatal Accident to one of the Officers of the *Pioneer* Expedition Ship." It stated that news had been received at the Admiralty stating that the expedition had failed to find the missing crews, but had come upon some traces of them. Want of stores and necessaries had compelled them to turn back without following those traces up ; but the commander was anxious, as soon as the ship could be refitted, to go out and take up the trail where he left it. An unfortunate accident had deprived him of one of his most promising officers, Lieutenant Mason, who was precipitated from an iceberg and killed while out shooting with the surgeon. He was beloved by all, and his death had flung a gloom over the gallant little troop of explorers.

" It's not in the *News* to-day, thank goodness, Bob," said Harry, who had been searching that paper while I was reading the one he brought—" but you must keep a sharp look-out for some days and not let Lettie see it when it appears, as it is certain to do sooner or later."

Then we both of us looked at each other with tears in our eyes. " Poor George !—poor Lettie ! " we sighed softly.

" But she must be told at some time or other ? " I said despairingly.

" I suppose so," said Harry ; " but it would kill her to come on it suddenly like this. Where's your wife ? "

She was with the children, but I sent up for her and told her the ill-tidings.

She had a hard struggle to conceal her emotion, for Lettie's sake. But the tears would flow in spite of her efforts.

" How shall I ever find courage to tell her ? " she asked.

" Hush ! " said Harry, suddenly grasping her arm and looking towards the door.

I turned. There stood Lettie, with her face pale as death, with her lips apart, and with a blind look about her eyes. She had come in without our hearing her. We never learnt how much of the story she had overheard ; but it was enough to tell her the worst. We all sprang towards her ; but she only waved us away, turned round, and went upstairs again without saying a word. My wife hastened up after her and found her on her knees by the bed, insensible.

The doctor was sent for, and restoratives were promptly administered. She came to herself again, but lay dangerously ill for some weeks from the shock.

It was about a month after she was well enough to come downstairs again that I saw in the paper an announcement of the arrival of the *Pioneer*. The news had no interest for any of us now, so I said nothing about it. The mere mention of the vessel's name would have caused the poor girl pain.

One afternoon shortly after this, as I was writing a letter, there came a loud knock at the front door. I looked up from my writing and listened ; for the voice which inquired if I was in sounded strange, but yet not altogether unfamiliar. As I looked up, puzzling whose it could be, my eye rested accidentally upon poor George's portrait. Was I dreaming or awake ?

I have told you that the one hand was resting on a sword. I could see now distinctly that the forefinger was raised, as if in warning. I looked at it hard, to assure myself it was no fancy, and then I perceived, standing out bright and distinct on the pale face, two large drops, as if of blood.

I walked up to it, expecting the appearance to vanish, as the skull had done. It did not vanish ; but the uplifted finger resolved itself into a little white moth which had settled on the canvas. The red drops were fluid, and certainly not blood, though I was at a loss for the time to account for them.

The moth seemed to be in a torpid state, so I took it off the picture and placed it under an inverted wineglass on the mantelpiece. All this took less time to do than to describe. As I turned from the mantelpiece the servant brought in a card, saying the gentleman was waiting in the hall to know if I would see him.

On the card was the name of " Vincent Grieve, of the exploring vessel *Pioneer*."

" Thank Heaven, Lettie is out," thought I ; and then added aloud to the servant, " Show him in here ; and Jane, if your mistress and Miss Lettie come in before the gentleman goes, tell them I have some one with me on business and do not wish to be disturbed."

I went to the door to meet Grieve. As he crossed the threshold, and before he could have seen the portrait, he stopped, shuddered, and turned white, even to his thin lips.

" Cover that picture before I come in," he said hurriedly, in a low voice. " You remember the effect it had upon me. Now, with the memory of poor Mason, it would be worse than ever."

I could understand his feelings better now than at first ; for I had come to look on the picture with some awe myself. So I took the cloth off a little round table that stood under the window and hung it over the portrait.

When I had done so Grieve came in. He was greatly altered. He was thinner and paler than ever ; hollow-eyed and hollow-cheeked. He had acquired a strange stoop, too, and his eyes had lost the crafty look for a look of terror, like that of a hunted beast. I noticed that he kept glancing sideways every instant, as if unconsciously. It looked as if he heard some one behind him.

I had never liked the man ; but now I felt an insurmountable repugnance to him—so great a repugnance that, when I came to think of it, I felt pleased that the incident of covering the picture at his request had led to my not shaking hands with him.

I felt that I could not speak otherwise than coldly to him ; indeed, I had to speak with painful plainness.

I told him that, of course, I was glad to see him back, but that I could not ask him to continue to visit us. I should be glad to hear the particulars of poor George's death, but that I could not let him see my sister, and hinted, as delicately as I could, at the impropriety of which he had been guilty when he last visited.

He took it all very quietly, only giving a long, weary sigh when I told him I must beg him not to repeat his visit. He looked so weak and ill that I was obliged to ask him to take a glass of wine—an offer which he seemed to accept with great pleasure.

I got out the sherry and biscuits and placed them on the table between us, and he took a glass and drank it off greedily.

It was not without some difficulty that I could get him to tell me of George's death. He related, with evident reluctance, how they had gone out to shoot a white bear which they had seen on an iceberg stranded along the shore. The top of the berg was ridged like the roof of a house, sloping down on one side to the edge of a tremendous overhanging precipice. They had scrambled along the ridge in order to get nearer the game, when George incautiously ventured on the sloping side.

" I called out to him," said Grieve, " and begged him to come back, but too late. The surface was as smooth and slippery as glass. He tried to turn back, but slipped and fell. And then began a horrible scene. Slowly, slowly, but with ever-increasing motion, he began to slide down towards the edge. There was nothing to grasp at—no irregularity or projection on the smooth face of the ice. I tore off my coat, and hastily attaching it to the stock of my gun, pushed the latter towards him ; but it did not reach far enough. Before I could lengthen it, by tying my cravat to it, he had slid yet farther away, and more quickly. I shouted in agony ; but there was no one within hearing. He, too, saw his fate was sealed ; and he could only tell me to bring his last farewell to you, and—and to her ! "—here Grieve's voice broke—" and it was all over ! He clung to the edge of the precipice instinctively for one second, and was gone ! "

Just as Grieve uttered the last word, his jaw fell ; his eye-balls seemed ready to start from his head ; he sprang to his feet, pointed at something behind me, and then flinging up his arms, fell, with a scream, as if he had been shot. He was seized with an epileptic fit.

I instinctively looked behind me as I hurried to raise him from the floor. The cloth had fallen from the picture, where the face of George, made paler than ever by the gouts of red, looked sternly down.

I rang the bell. Luckily, Harry had come in ; and, when the servant told him what was the matter, he came in and assisted me in restoring Grieve to consciousness. Of course, I covered the painting up again.

When he was quite himself again, Grieve told me he was subject to fits occasionally.

He seemed very anxious to learn if he had said or done anything extraordinary while he was in the fit, and appeared reassured when I said he had not. He apologized for the trouble he had given, and said as soon as he was strong enough he would take his leave. He was leaning on the mantelpiece as he said this. The little white moth caught his eye.

" So you have had some one else from the *Pioneer* here before me ? " he said nervously.

I answered in the negative, asking what made him think so.

" Why, this little white moth is never found in such southern latitudes. It is one of the last signs of life northward. Where did you get it ? "

" I caught it here, in this room," I answered.

" That is very strange. I never heard of such a thing before. We shall hear of showers of blood soon, I should not wonder."

" What do you mean ? " I asked.

" Oh, these little fellows emit little drops of a red-looking fluid at certain seasons, and sometimes so plentifully that the superstitious think it is a shower of blood. I have seen the snow quite stained in places. Take care of it, it is a rarity in the south."

I noticed, after he left, which he did almost immediately, that there was a drop of red fluid on the marble under the wineglass. The blood-stain on the picture was accounted for ; but how came the moth here ?

And there was another strange thing about the man, which I had scarcely been able to assure myself of in the room, where there were cross-lights, but about which there was no possible mistake, when I saw him walking away up the street.

" Harry, here—quick ! " I called to my brother, who at once came to the window. " You're an artist—tell me, is there anything strange about that man ? "

" No ; nothing that I can see," said Harry, but then suddenly, in an altered tone, added, " Yes, there is. By Jove, *he has a double shadow* ! "

That was the explanation of his sidelong glances, of the habitual stoop. There was a something always at his side, which none could see, but which cast a shadow.

He turned presently, and saw us at the window. Instantly, he crossed the road to the shady side of the street. I told Harry all that had passed, and we agreed that it would be as well not to say a word to Lettie.

Two days later, when I returned from a visit to Harry's studio, I found the whole house in confusion.

I learnt from Lettie that while my wife was upstairs, Grieve had called, had not waited for the servant to announce him, but had walked straight into the dining-room, where Lettie was sitting. She noticed that he avoided looking at the picture, and, to make sure of not seeing it, had seated himself on the sofa just beneath it. He had then, in spite of Lettie's angry remonstrances, renewed his offer of love, strengthening it finally by assuring her that poor George with his dying breath had implored him to seek her, and watch over her, and marry her.

" I was so indignant I hardly knew how to answer him," said Lettie. " When, suddenly, just as he uttered the last words, there came a twang like the breaking of a guitar—and—I hardly know how to describe it—but the portrait had fallen, and the corner of the heavy frame had struck him on the head, cutting it open, and rendering him insensible."

They had carried him upstairs, by the direction of the doctor, for whom my wife at once sent on hearing what had occurred. He was laid on the couch in my dressing-room, where I went to see him. I intended to reproach him for coming to the house, despite my prohibition, but I found him delirious. The doctor said it was a queer case ; for, though the blow was a severe one, it was hardly enough to account for the symptoms of brain-fever. When he learnt that Grieve had but just returned in the *Pioneer* from the North, he said it was possible that the privation and hardship had told on his constitution and sown the seeds of the malady.

We sent for a nurse, who was to sit up with him, by the doctor's directions.

The rest of my story is soon told. In the middle of the night I was roused by a loud scream. I slipped on my clothes, and rushed out to find the nurse, with Lettie in her arms, in a faint. We carried her into her room, and then the nurse explained the mystery to us.

It appears that about midnight Grieve sat up in bed, and began to talk. And he said such terrible things that the nurse became alarmed. Nor was she much reassured when she became aware that the light of her single candle flung what seemed to be two shadows of the sick man on the wall.

Terrified beyond measure, she had crept into Lettie's room, and confided her fears to her ; and Lettie, who was a courageous and kindly girl, dressed herself, and said she would sit with her. She, too, saw the double shadow—but what she heard was far more terrible.

Grieve was sitting up in bed, gazing at the unseen figure to which the shadow belonged. In a voice that trembled with emotion, he begged the haunting spirit to leave him, and prayed its forgiveness.

" You know the crime was not premeditated. It was a sudden temptation of the devil that made me strike the blow, and fling you over the precipice. It was the devil tempting me with the recollection of her exquisite face—of the tender love that might have been mine, but for you. But she will not listen to me. See, she turns away from me, as if she knew I was your murderer, George Mason ! "

It was Lettie who repeated in a horrified whisper this awful confession.

I could see it all now ! As I was about to tell Lettie of the many strange things I had concealed from her, the nurse, who had gone to see her patient, came running back in alarm.

Vincent Grieve had disappeared. He had risen in his delirious terror, had opened the window, and leaped out. Two days later his body was found in the river.

A curtain hangs now before poor George's portrait, though it is no longer connected with any supernatural marvels ; and never, since the night of Vincent Grieve's death, have we seen aught of that most mysterious haunting presence—the Shadow of a Shade.

THE DWARFS

THE infant who was destined to become the fourth baronet of the name of Lapith was born in the year 1740. He was a very small baby, weighing not more than three pounds at birth, but from the first he was sturdy and healthy. In honour of his maternal grandfather, Sir Hercules Occam of Bishop's Occam, he was christened Hercules. His mother, like many other mothers, kept a notebook, in which his progress from month to month was recorded. He walked at ten months, and before his second year was out he had learnt to speak a number of words. At three years he weighed but twenty-four pounds, and at six, though he could read and write perfectly and showed a remarkable aptitude for music, he was no larger and heavier than a well-grown child of two. Meanwhile, his mother had borne two other children, a boy and a girl, one of whom died of croup during infancy, while the other was carried off by smallpox before it reached the age of five. Hercules remained the only surviving child.

On his twelfth birthday Hercules was still only three feet and two inches in height. His head, which was very handsome and nobly shaped, was too big for his body, but otherwise he was exquisitely proportioned and, for his size, of great strength and agility. His parents, in the hope of making him grow, consulted all the most eminent physicians of the time. Their various prescriptions were followed to the letter, but in vain. One ordered a very plentiful meat diet ; another exercise ; a third constructed a little rack, modelled on those employed by the Holy Inquisition, on which young Hercules was stretched, with excruciating torments, for half an hour every morning and evening. In the course of the next three years Hercules gained perhaps two inches. After that his growth stopped completely, and he remained for the rest of his life a pigmy of three feet and four inches. His father, who had built the most extravagant hopes upon his son, planning for him in his imagination a military career equal to that of Marlborough, found himself a disappointed man. " I have brought an abortion into the world," he would say, and he took so violent a dislike to his son that the boy dared scarcely come into his presence. His temper, which had been serene, was turned by disappointment to moroseness and savagery. He avoided all company (being, as he said, ashamed to show himself, the father of a *lusus naturæ*, among normal, healthy human beings), and took to solitary drinking, which carried him very rapidly to his grave ; for the year before Hercules came of age his father was taken off by an apoplexy. His mother, whose love for him had increased with the growth of his father's unkindness, did not long survive, but little more than a year after her husband's death succumbed, after eating two dozen of oysters, to an attack of typhoid fever.

Hercules thus found himself at the age of twenty-one alone in the world, and master of a considerable fortune, including the estate and mansion of Crome. The beauty and intelligence of his childhood had survived into his manly age, and, but for his dwarfish stature, he would have taken his place among the handsomest and most accomplished young men of his time. He was well read in the Greek and Latin authors, as well as in all the moderns of any merit who had written in English, French, or Italian. He had a good ear for music, and was no indifferent performer on the violin, which he used to play like a bass viol, seated on a chair with the instrument between his legs. To the music of the harpischord and clavichord he was extremely partial, but the smallness of his hands made it impossible for him ever to perform upon these instruments. He had a small ivory flute made for him, on which, whenever he was melancholy, he used to play a simple country air or jig, affirming that this rustic music had more power to clear and raise the spirits than the most artificial productions of the masters. From an early age he practised the composition of poetry, but, though conscious of his great powers in this art, he would never publish any specimen of his writing. " My stature," he would say, " is reflected in my verses ; if the public were to read them it would not be because I am a poet, but because I am a dwarf." Several MS. books of Sir Hercules's poems survive. A single specimen will suffice to illustrate his qualities as a poet.

" In ancient days, while yet the world was young,
Ere Abram fed his flocks or Homer sung ;
When blacksmith Tubal tamed creative fire,
And Jabal dwelt in tents and Jubal struck the lyre ;
Flesh grown corrupt brought forth a monstrous birth
And obscene giants trod the shrinking earth,
Till God, impatient of their sinful brood,
Gave rein to wrath and drown'd them in the Flood.
Teeming again, repeopled Tellus bore
The lubber Hero and the Man of War ;
Huge towers of Brawn, topp'd with an empty Skull,
Witlessly bold, heroically dull.
Long ages pass'd and Man grown more refin'd,
Slighter in muscle but of vaster Mind,
Smiled at his grandsire's broadsword, bow and bill,
And learn'd to wield the Pencil and the Quill.
The glowing canvas and the written page
Immortaliz'd his name from age to age,
His name emblazon'd on Fame's temple wall ;
For Art grew great as Humankind grew small.
Thus man's long progress step by step we trace ;
The Giant dies, the hero takes his place ;
The Giant vile, the dull heroic Block :
At one we shudder and at one we mock.
Man last appears. In him the Soul's pure flame
Burns brightlier in a not inord'nate frame.
Of old when Heroes fought and Giants swarmed,
Men were huge mounds of matter scarce inform'd ;
Wearied by leavening so vast a mass,
The spirit slept and all the mind was crass.
The smaller carcase of these later days
Is soon inform'd ; the Soul unwearied plays
And like a Pharos darts abroad her mental rays.
But can we think that Providence will stay
Man's footsteps here upon the upward way ?
Mankind in understanding and in grace
Advanc'd so far beyond the Giants' race ?
Hence impious thought ! Still led by GOD's own Hand,
Mankind proceeds towards the Promised Land.
A time will come (prophetic, I descry
Remoter dawns along the gloomy sky),
When happy mortals of a Golden Age
Will backward turn the dark historic page,
And in our vaunted race of Men behold
A form as gross, a Mind as dead and cold,
As we in Giants see, in warriors of old.
A time will come, wherein the soul shall be
From all superfluous matter wholly free ;
When the light body, agile as a fawn's,
Shall sport with grace along the velvet lawns.
Nature's most delicate and final birth,
Mankind perfected shall possess the earth.
But ah, not yet ! For still the Giants' race,
Huge, though diminish'd, tramps the Earth's fair face ;

Gross and repulsive, yet perversely proud,
Men of their imperfections boast aloud.
Vain of their bulk, of all they still retain
Of giant ugliness absurdly vain ;
At all that's small they point their stupid scorn
And, monsters, think themselves divinely born.
Sad is the Fate of those, ah, sad indeed,
The rare precursors of the nobler breed !
Who come man's golden glory to foretell,
But pointing Heav'nwards live themselves in Hell."

As soon as he came into the estate, Sir Hercules set about remodelling his household. For though by no means ashamed of his deformity—indeed, if we may judge from the poem quoted above, he regarded himself as being in many ways superior to the ordinary race of man—he found the presence of full-grown men and women embarrassing. Realizing, too, that he must abandon all ambitions in the great world, he determined to retire absolutely from it and to create, as it were, at Crome a private world of his own, in which all should be proportionable to himself. Accordingly, he discharged all the old servants of the house and replaced them gradually, as he was able to find suitable successors, by others of dwarfish stature. In the course of a few years he had assembled about himself a numerous household, no member of which was above four feet high and the smallest among them scarcely two feet and six inches. His father's dogs, such as setters, mastiffs, greyounds, and a pack of beagles, he sold or gave away as too large and too boisterous for his house, replacing them by pugs and King Charles spaniels and whatever other breeds of dog were the smallest. His father's stable was also sold. For his own use, whether riding or driving, he had six black Shetland ponies, with four very choice piebald animals of New Forest breed.

Having thus settled his household entirely to his own satisfaction, it only remained for him to find some suitable companion with whom to share this paradise. Sir Hercules had a susceptible heart, and had more than once, between the ages of sixteen and twenty, felt what it was to love. But here his deformity had been a source of the most bitter humiliation, for, having once dared to declare himself to a young lady of his choice, he had been received with laughter. On his persisting, she had picked him up and shaken him like an importunate child, telling him to run away and plague her no more. The story soon got about—indeed, the young lady herself used to tell it as a particularly pleasant anecdote—and

the taunts and mockery it occasioned were a source of the
most acute distress to Hercules. From the poems written at
this period we gather that he meditated taking his own life.
In course of time, however, he lived down this humiliation ;
but never again, though he often fell in love, and that very
passionately, did he dare to make any advances to those in
whom he was interested. After coming to the estate and
finding that he was in a position to create his own world as
he desired it, he saw that, if he was to have a wife—which he
very much desired, being of an affectionate and, indeed,
amorous temper—he must choose her as he had chosen his
servants—from among the race of dwarfs. But to find a
suitable wife was, he found, a matter of some difficulty ; for
he would marry none who was not distinguished by beauty
and gentle birth. The dwarfish daughter of Lord Bemboro
he refused on the ground that besides being a pigmy she was
hunchbacked ; while another young lady, an orphan belonging
to a very good family in Hampshire, was rejected by him
because her face, like that of so many dwarfs, was wizened and
repulsive. Finally, when he was almost despairing of success,
he heard from a reliable source that Count Titimalo, a Venetian
nobleman, possessed a daughter of exquisite beauty and great
accomplishments, who was but three feet in height. Setting
out at once for Venice, he went immediately on his arrival to
pay his respects to the count, whom he found living with his
wife and five children in a very mean apartment in one of the
poorer quarters of the town. Indeed, the count was so far
reduced in his circumstances that he was even then negotiating
(so it was rumoured) with a travelling company of clowns and
acrobats, who had had the misfortune to lose their performing
dwarf, for the sale of his diminutive daughter Filomena. Sir
Hercules arrived in time to save her from this untoward fate,
for he was so much charmed by Filomena's grace and beauty,
that at the end of three days' courtship he made her a formal
offer of marriage, which was accepted by her no less joyfully
than by her father, who perceived in an English son-in-law a
rich and unfailing source of revenue. After an unostentatious
marriage, at which the English ambassador acted as one of
the witnesses, Sir Hercules and his bride returned by sea to
England, where they settled down, as it proved, to a life of
uneventful happiness.

Crome and its household of dwarfs delighted Filomena,
who felt herself now for the first time to be a free woman
living among her equals in a friendly world. She had many

tastes in common with her husband, especially that of music. She had a beautiful voice, of a power surprising in one so small, and could touch A in alt without effort. Accompanied by her husband on his fine Cremona fiddle, which he played, as we have noted before, as one plays a bass viol, she would sing all the liveliest and tenderest airs from the operas and cantatas of her native country. Seated together at the harpsichord, they found that they could with their four hands play all the music written for two hands of ordinary size, a circumstance which gave Sir Hercules unfailing pleasure.

When they were not making music or reading together, which they often did, both in English and Italian, they spent their time in healthful outdoor exercises, sometimes rowing in a little boat on the lake, but more often riding or driving, occupations in which, because they were entirely new to her, Filomena especially delighted. When she had become a perfectly proficient rider, Filomena and her husband used often to go hunting in the park, at that time very much more extensive than it is now. They hunted not foxes nor hares, but rabbits, using a pack of about thirty black and fawn-coloured pugs, a kind of dog which, when not overfed, can course a rabbit as well as any of the smaller breeds. Four dwarf grooms, dressed in scarlet liveries and mounted on white Exmoor ponies, hunted the pack, while their master and mistress, in green habits, followed either on the black Shetlands or on the piebald New Forest ponies. A picture of the whole hunt—dogs, horses, grooms, and masters—was painted by William Stubbs, whose work Sir Hercules admired so much that he invited him, though a man of ordinary stature, to come and stay at the mansion for the purpose of executing this picture. Stubbs likewise painted a portrait of Sir Hercules and his lady driving in their green enamelled calash drawn by four black Shetlands. Sir Hercules wears a plum-coloured velvet coat and white breeches ; Filomena is dressed in flowered muslin and a very large hat with pink feathers. The two figures in their gay carriage stand out sharply against a dark background of trees ; but to the left of the picture the trees fall away and disappear, so that the four black ponies are seen against a pale and strangely lurid sky that has the golden-brown colour of thunder-clouds lighted up by the sun.

In this way four years passed happily by. At the end of that time Filomena found herself great with child. Sir Hercules was overjoyed. " If God is good," he wrote in his day-book, " the name of Lapith will be preserved and our

rarer and more delicate race transmitted through the generations until in the fullness of time the world shall recognize
the superiority of those beings whom now it uses to make
mock of." On his wife's being brought to bed of a son he
wrote a poem to the same effect. The child was christened
Ferdinando in memory of the builder of the house.

With the passage of the months a certain sense of disquiet
began to invade the minds of Sir Hercules and his lady. For
the child was growing with an extraordinary rapidity. At a
year he weighed as much as Hercules had weighed when he
was three. " Ferdinando goes *crescendo*," wrote Filomena in
her diary. " It seems not natural." At eighteen months the
baby was almost as tall as their smallest jockey, who was a
man of thirty-six. Could it be that Ferdinando was destined
to become a man of the normal, gigantic dimensions ? It was
a thought to which neither of his parents dared yet give open
utterance, but in the secrecy of their respective diaries they
brooded over it in terror and dismay.

On his third birthday Ferdinando was taller than his mother
and not more than a couple of inches short of his father's
height. " To-day for the first time," wrote Sir Hercules,
" we discussed the situation. The hideous truth can be
concealed no longer : Ferdinando is not one of us. On this,
his third birthday, a day when we should have been rejoicing
at the health, the strength, and beauty of our child, we wept
together over the ruin of our happiness. God give us strength
to bear this cross."

At the age of eight Ferdinando was so large and so ex-
uberantly healthy that his parents decided, though reluctantly,
to send him to school. He was packed off to Eton at the
beginning of the next half. A profound peace settled upon
the house. Ferdinando returned for the summer holidays
larger and stronger than ever. One day he knocked down the
butler and broke his arm. " He is rough, inconsiderate,
unamenable to persuasion," wrote his father. " The only
thing that will teach him manners is corporal chastisement."
Ferdinando, who at this age was already seventeen inches
taller than his father, received no corporal chastisement.

One summer holidays about three years later Ferdinando
returned to Crome accompanied by a very large mastiff dog.
He had bought it from an old man at Windsor who found the
beast too expensive to feed. It was a savage, unreliable animal ;
hardly had it entered the house when it attacked one of Sir
Hercules's favourite pugs, seizing the creature in its jaws and

shaking it till it was nearly dead. Extremely put out by this occurrence, Sir Hercules ordered that the beast should be chained up in the stable-yard. Ferdinando sullenly answered that the dog was his, and he would keep it where he pleased. His father, growing angry, bade him take the animal out of the house at once, on pain of his utmost displeasure. Ferdinando refused to move. His mother at this moment coming into the room, the dog flew at her, knocked her down, and in a twinkling had very severely mauled her arm and shoulder ; in another instant it must infallibly have had her by the throat, had not Sir Hercules drawn his sword and stabbed the animal to the heart. Turning on his son, he ordered him to leave the room immediately, as being unfit to remain in the same place with the mother whom he had nearly murdered. So awe-inspiring was the spectacle of Sir Hercules standing with one foot on the carcase of the gigantic dog, his sword drawn and still bloody, so commanding were his voice, his gestures, and the expression of his face, that Ferdinando slunk out of the room in terror and behaved himself for all the rest of the vacation in an entirely exemplary fashion. His mother soon recovered from the bites of the mastiff, but the effect on her mind of this adventure was ineradicable ; from that time forth she lived always among imaginary terrors.

The two years which Ferdinando spent on the Continent, making the Grand Tour, were a period of happy repose for his parents. But even now the thought of the future haunted them ; nor were they able to solace themselves with all the diversions of their younger days. The Lady Filomena had lost her voice and Sir Hercules was grown too rheumatical to play the violin. He, it is true, still rode after his pugs, but his wife felt herself too old and, since the episode of the mastiff, too nervous for such sports. At most, to please her husband, she would follow the hunt at a distance in a little gig drawn by the safest and oldest of the Shetlands.

The day fixed for Ferdinando's return came round. Filomena, sick with vague dreads and presentiments, retired to her chamber and her bed. Sir Hercules received his son alone. A giant in a brown travelling-suit entered the room. " Welcome home, my son," said Sir Hercules in a voice that trembled a little.

" I hope I see you well, sir." Ferdinando bent down to shake hands, then straightened himself up again. The top of his father's head reached to the level of his hip.

Ferdinando had not come alone. Two friends of his own

age accompanied him, and each of the young men had brought
a servant. Not for thirty years had Crome been desecrated
by the presence of so many members of the common race of
men. Sir Hercules was appalled and indignant, but the laws
of hospitality had to be obeyed. He received the young
gentlemen with grave politeness and sent the servants to the
kitchen, with orders that they should be well cared for.

The old family dining-table was dragged out into the light
and dusted (Sir Hercules and his lady were accustomed to
dine at a small table twenty inches high). Simon, the aged
butler, who could only just look over the edge of the big table,
was helped at supper by the three servants brought by Ferdinando and his guests.

Sir Hercules presided, and with his usual grace supported a
conversation on the pleasures of foreign travel, the beauties
of art and nature to be met with abroad, the opera at Venice,
the singing of the orphans in the churches of the same city,
and on other topics of a similar nature. The young men were
not particularly attentive to his discourses ; they were occupied
in watching the efforts of the butler to change the plates and
replenish the glasses. They covered their laughter by violent
and repeated fits of coughing or choking. Sir Hercules
affected not to notice, but changed the subject of the conversation to sport. Upon this one of the young men asked whether
it was true, as he had heard, that he used to hunt the rabbit
with a pack of pug dogs. Sir Hercules replied that it was, and
proceeded to describe the chase in some detail. The young
men roared with laughter.

When supper was over, Sir Hercules climbed down from
his chair and, giving as his excuse that he must see how his
lady did, bade them good-night. The sound of laughter
followed him up the stairs. Filomena was not asleep ; she
had been lying on her bed listening to the sound of enormous
laughter and the tread of strangely heavy feet on the stairs and
along the corridors. Sir Hercules drew a chair to her bedside
and sat there for a long time in silence, holding his wife's hand
and sometimes gently squeezing it. At about ten o'clock they
were startled by a violent noise. There was a breaking of
glass, a stamping of feet, with an outburst of shouts and laughter.
The uproar continuing for several minutes, Sir Hercules rose
to his feet and, in spite of his wife's entreaties, prepared to
go and see what was happening. There was no light on the
staircase, and Sir Hercules groped his way down cautiously,
lowering himself from stair to stair and standing for a moment

on each tread before adventuring on a new step. The noise was louder here ; the shouting articulated itself into recognizable words and phrases. A line of light was visible under the dining-room door. Sir Hercules tiptoed across the hall towards it. Just as he approached the door there was another terrific crash of breaking glass and jangled metal. What could they be doing ? Standing on tiptoe he managed to look through the keyhole. In the middle of the ravaged table old Simon, the butler, so primed with drink that he could scarcely keep his balance, was dancing a jig. His feet crunched and tinkled among the broken glass, and his shoes were wet with spilt wine. The three young men sat round, thumping the table with their hands or with the empty wine bottles, shouting and laughing encouragement. The three servants leaning against the wall laughed too. Ferdinando suddenly threw a handful of walnuts at the dancer's head, which so dazed and surprised the little man that he staggered and fell down on his back, upsetting a decanter and several glasses. They raised him up, gave him some brandy to drink, thumped him on the back. The old man smiled and hiccoughed. " To-morrow," said Ferdinando, " we'll have a concerted ballet of the whole household." " With father Hercules wearing his club and lion-skin," added one of his companions, and all three roared with laughter.

Sir Hercules would look and listen no further. He crossed the hall once more and began to climb the stairs, lifting his knees painfully high at each degree. This was the end ; there was no place for him now in the world, no place for him and Ferdinando together.

His wife was still awake ; to her questioning glance he answered, " They are making mock of old Simon. To-morrow it will be our turn." They were silent for a time.

At last Filomena said, " I do not want to see to-morrow."

" It is better not," said Sir Hercules. Going into his closet he wrote in his day-book a full and particular account of all the events of the evening. While he was still engaged in this task he rang for a servant and ordered hot water and a bath to be made ready for him at eleven o'clock. When he had finished writing he went into his wife's room, and preparing a dose of opium twenty times as strong as that which she was accustomed to take when she could not sleep, he brought it to her, saying, " Here is your sleeping-draught."

Filomena took the glass and lay for a little time, but did not drink immediately. The tears came into her eyes. " Do you remember the songs we used to sing, sitting out there *sulla terrazza* in summer-time ? " She began singing softly in her ghost of a cracked voice a few bars from Stradella's " *Amor, amor, non dormir piu.*" " And you playing on the violin. It seems such a short time ago, and yet so long, long, long. *Adāio, amore. A rivederti.*" She drank off the draught and, lying back on the pillow, closed her eyes. Sir Hercules kissed her hand and tiptoed away, as though he were afraid of waking her. He returned to his closet, and having recorded his wife's last words to him, he poured into his bath the water that had been brought up in accordance with his orders. The water being too hot for him to get into the bath at once, he took down from the shelf his copy of Suetonius. He wished to read how Seneca had died. He opened the book at random. " But dwarfs," he read, " he held in abhorrence as being *lusus naturæ* and of evil omen." He winced as though he had been struck. This same Augustus, he remembered, had exhibited in the amphitheatre a young man called Lucius, of good family, who was not quite two feet in height and weighed seventeen pounds, but had a stentorian voice. He turned over the pages. Tiberius, Caligula, Claudius, Nero : it was a tale of growing horror. " Seneca his preceptor, he forced to kill himself." And there was Petronius, who had called his friends about him at the last, bidding them talk to him, not of the consolations of philosophy, but of love and gallantry, while the life was ebbing away through his opened veins. Dipping his pen once more in the ink he wrote on the last page of his diary : " He died a Roman death." Then, putting the toes of one foot into the water and finding that it was not too hot, he threw off his dressing-gown and, taking a razor in his hand, sat down in the bath. With one deep cut he severed the artery in his left wrist, then lay back and composed his mind to meditation. The blood oozed out, floating through the water in dissolving wreaths and spirals. In a little while the whole bath was tinged with pink. The colour deepened ; Sir Hercules felt himself mastered by an invincible drowsiness ; he was sinking from vague dream to dream. Soon he was sound asleep. There was not much blood in his small body.

GUESTS FROM GIBBET ISLAND

WHOEVER has visited the ancient and renowned village of Communipaw, may have noticed an old stone building, of most ruinous and sinister appearance. The doors and window-shutters are ready to drop from their hinges ; old clothes are stuffed in the broken panes of glass, while legions of half-starved dogs prowl about the premises, and rush out and bark at every passer-by ; for your beggarly house in a village is most apt to swarm with profligate and ill-conditioned dogs. What adds to the sinister appearance of this mansion, is a tall frame in front, not a little resembling a gallows, and which looks as if waiting to accommodate some of the inhabitants with a well-merited airing. It is not a gallows, however, but an ancient sign-post ; for this dwelling, in the golden days of Communipaw, was one of the most orderly and peaceful of village taverns, where public affairs were talked and smoked over. In fact, it was in this very building that Oloffe the Dreamer, and his companions, concerted that great voyage of discovery and colonization, in which they explored Buttermilk Channel, were nearly shipwrecked in the strait of Hell-gate, and finally landed on the island of Manhattan, and founded the great city of New Amsterdam.

Even after the province had been cruelly wrested from the sway of their High Mightinesses, by the combined forces of the British and the Yankees, this tavern continued its ancient loyalty. It is true, the head of the Prince of Orange disappeared from the sign, a strange bird being painted over it, with the explanatory legend of " DIE WILDE GANS," or, The Wild Goose ; but this all the world knew to be a sly riddle of the landlord's, the worthy Teunis Van Gieson, a knowing man, in a small way, who laid his finger beside his nose and

304

winked when any one studied the signification of his sign, and observed that his goose was hatching, but would join the flock whenever they flew over the water—an enigma which was the perpetual recreation and delight of the loyal but fatheaded burghers of Communipaw.

Under the sway of this patriotic, though discreet and quiet publican, the tavern continued to flourish in primeval tranquillity, and was the resort of true-hearted Nederlanders, from all parts of Pavonia, who met here quietly and secretly, to smoke and drink the downfall of Briton and Yankee, and success to Admiral Van Tromp.

The only drawback on the comfort of the establishment, was a nephew of mine host, a sister's son, Yan Yost Vanderscamp by name, and a real scamp by nature. This unlucky whipster showed an early propensity to mischief, which he gratified in a small way, by playing tricks upon the frequenters of the Wild Goose : putting gunpowder in their pipes, or squibs in their pockets, and astonishing them with an explosion, while they sat nodding round the fireplace in the bar-room ; and if perchance a worthy burgher from some distant part of Pavonia lingered until dark over his potation, it was odds but young Vanderscamp would slip a brier under his horse's tail as he mounted, and send him clattering along the road, in neck-or-nothing style, to the infinite astonishment and discomfiture of the rider.

It may be wondered at, that mine host of the Wild Goose did not turn such a graceless varlet out of doors ; but Teunis Van Gieson was an easy-tempered man, and, having no child of his own, looked upon his nephew with almost parental indulgence. His patience and good nature were doomed to be tried by another inmate of his mansion. This was a cross-grained curmudgeon of a negro, named Pluto, who was a kind of enigma in Communipaw. Where he came from, nobody knew. He was found one morning after a storm, cast like a sea-monster on the strand, in front of the Wild Goose, and lay there, more dead than alive. The neighbours gathered round, and speculated on this production of the deep ; whether it were fish or flesh, or a compound of both, commonly yclept a merman. The kind-hearted Teunis Van Gieson, seeing that he wore the human form, took him into his house, and warmed him into life. By degrees, he showed signs of intelligence, and even uttered sounds very much like language, but which no one in Communipaw could understand. Some thought him a negro just from Guinea, who had either fallen overboard, or escaped from a slave-ship. Nothing, however, could ever draw from him any account of his origin. When questioned on the subject, he merely pointed to Gibbet Island, a small rocky islet, which lies in the open bay, just opposite Communipaw, as if that were his native place, though everybody knew it had never been inhabited.

In the process of time, he acquired something of the Dutch language—that is to say, he learnt all its vocabulary of oaths and maledictions, with just words sufficient to string them together. " Donder en blicksem ! "—thunder and lightning—was the gentlest of his ejaculations. For years he kept about the Wild Goose, more like one of those familiar spirits, or household goblins, we read of, than like a human being. He acknowledged allegiance to no one, but performed various domestic offices, when it suited his humour : waiting occasionally on the guests ; grooming the horses, cutting wood, drawing water ; and all this without being ordered. Lay any command on him, and the stubborn sea-urchin was sure to rebel. He was never so much at home, however, as when on the water, plying about in skiff or canoe, entirely alone, fishing, crabbing, or grabbing for oysters, and would bring home quantities for the larder of the Wild Goose, which he would throw down at the kitchen door, with a growl. No wind nor weather deterred him from launching forth on his favourite element : indeed, the wilder the weather, the more he seemed to enjoy it. If a storm was brewing, he was sure to put off from shore ; and would be seen far out in the bay, his light skiff dancing like a feather on the waves, when sea and sky were in a turmoil, and the stoutest ships were fain to lower their sails. Sometimes, on such occasions, he would be absent for days together. How he weathered the tempest, and how and where he subsisted, no one could divine, nor did any one venture to ask, for all had an almost superstitious awe of him. Some of the Communipaw oystermen declared they had more than once seen him suddenly disappear, canoe and all, as if plunged beneath the waves, and after a while come up again, in quite a different part of the bay ; whence they concluded that he could live under water like that notable species of wild duck commonly called the hell-diver. All began to consider him in the light of a foul-weather bird, like the Mother Carey's Chicken or stormy petrel ; and whenever they saw him putting far out in his skiff, in cloudy weather, made up their minds for a storm.

The only being for whom he seemed to have any liking

was Yan Yost Vanderscamp, and him he liked for his very
wickedness. He in a manner took the boy under his tutelage,
prompted him to all kinds of mischief, aided him in every
wild harum-scarum freak, until the lad became the complete
scapegrace of the village ; a pest to his uncle, and to every one
else. Nor were his pranks confined to the land : he soon
learned to accompany old Pluto on the water. Together these
worthies would cruise about the broad bay, and all the neighbouring straits and rivers ; poking around in skiffs and canoes ;
robbing the set nets of the fishermen ; landing on remote
coasts, and laying waste orchards and water-melon patches ;
in short, carrying on a complete system of piracy, on a small
scale. Piloted by Pluto, the youthful Vanderscamp soon
became acquainted with all the bays, rivers, creeks, and inlets
of the watery world around him ; could navigate from the
Hook to Spitting-devil on the darkest night, and learned to
set even the terrors of Hell-gate at defiance.

At length, negro and boy suddenly disappeared, and days
and weeks elapsed, but without tidings of them. Some said
they must have run away and gone to sea ; others jocosely
hinted that old Pluto, being no other than his namesake in
disguise, had spirited away the boy to the nether regions. All,
however, agreed in one thing—that the village was well rid of
them.

In the process of time, the good Teunis Van Gieson slept
with his fathers, and the tavern remained shut up, waiting for
a claimant, for the next heir was Yan Yost Vanderscamp, and
he had not been heard of for years. At length, one day, a
boat was seen pulling for shore, from a long, black, rakish-
looking schooner, that lay at anchor in the bay. The boat's
crew seemed worthy of the craft from which they debarked.
Never had such a set of noisy, roistering, swaggering varlets
landed in peaceful Communipaw. They were outlandish
in garb and demeanour, and were headed by a rough, burly,
bully ruffian, with fiery whiskers, a copper nose, a scar across
his face, and a great Flaunderish beaver slouched on one side
of his head, in whom, to their dismay, the quiet inhabitants
were made to recognize their early pest, Yan Yost Vanderscamp. The rear of this hopeful gang was brought up by old
Pluto, who had lost an eye, grown grizzly-headed, and looked
more like a devil than ever. Vanderscamp renewed his
acquaintance with the old burghers, much against their will,
and in a manner not at all to their taste. He slapped them
familiarly on the back, gave them an iron grip of the hand, and

was hail fellow well met. According to his own account, he had been all the world over; had made money by bagsful; had ships in every sea, and now meant to turn the Wild Goose into a country-seat, where he and his comrades, all rich merchants from foreign parts, might enjoy themselves in the interval of their voyages.

Sure enough, in a little while there was a complete metamorphose of the Wild Goose. From being a quiet, peaceful Dutch public-house, it became a most riotous, uproarious private dwelling; a complete rendezvous for boisterous men of the seas, who came here to have what they called a "blow out" on dry land, and might be seen at all hours, lounging about the door, or lolling out of the windows; swearing among themselves, and cracking rough jokes on every passer-by. The house was fitted up, too, in so strange a manner: hammocks slung to the walls, instead of bedsteads; odd kinds of furniture, of foreign fashion; bamboo couches, Spanish chairs; pistols, cutlasses, and blunderbusses, suspended on every peg; silver crucifixes on the mantel-pieces, silver candlesticks and porringers on the tables, contrasting oddly with the pewter and Delf ware of the original establishment. And then the strange amusements of these sea-monsters! Pitching Spanish dollars, instead of quoits; firing blunderbusses out of the window; shooting at a mark, or at any unhappy dog, or cat, or pig, or barn-door fowl, that might happen to come within reach.

The only being who seemed to relish their rough waggery was old Pluto; and yet he led but a dog's life of it; for they practised all kinds of manual jokes upon him; kicked him about like a football; shook him by his grizzly mop of wool, and never spoke to him without coupling a curse by way of adjective to his name, and consigning him to the infernal regions. The old fellow, however, seemed to like them the better the more they cursed him, though his utmost expression of pleasure never amounted to more than the growl of a petted bear, when his ears are rubbed.

Old Pluto was the ministering spirit at the orgies of the Wild Goose; and such orgies as took place there! Such drinking, singing, whooping, swearing; with an occasional interlude of quarrelling and fighting. The noisier grew the revel, the more old Pluto plied the potations, until the guests would become frantic in their merriment, smashing everything to pieces, and throwing the house out of the windows. Sometimes, after a drinking bout, they sallied forth and scoured the

village, to the dismay of the worthy burghers, who gathered
their women within doors, and would have shut up the house.
Vanderscamp, however, was not to be rebuffed. He insisted on
renewing acquaintance with his old neighbours, and on intro-
ducing his friends, the merchants, to their families ; swore
he was on the look-out for a wife, and meant, before he stopped,
to find husbands for all their daughters. So, will-ye, nill-ye,
sociable he was ; swaggered about their best parlours, with his
hat on one side of his head ; sat on the good wife's nicely
waxed mahogany table, kicking his heels against the carved
and polished legs ; kissed and tousled the young *vrouws* ;
and, if they frowned and pouted, gave them a gold rosary, or a
sparkling cross, to put them in good humour again.

Sometimes nothing would satisfy him, but he must have
some of his old neighbours to dinner at the Wild Goose.
There was no refusing him, for he had the complete upper
hand of the community, and the peaceful burghers all stood
in awe of him. But what a time would the quiet, worthy men
have, among these rake-hells, who would delight to astound
them with the most extravagant gunpowder tales, embroidered
with all kinds of foreign oaths ; clink the can with them ;
pledge them in deep potations ; bawl drinking-songs in their
ears ; and occasionally fire pistols over their heads, or under
the table, and then laugh in their faces, and ask them how they
liked the smell of gunpowder.

Thus was the little village of Communipaw for a time
like the unfortunate wight possessed with devils ; until
Vanderscamp and his brother merchants would sail on another
trading voyage, when the Wild Goose would be shut up, and
everything relapse into quiet, only to be disturbed by his next
visitation.

The mystery of all these proceedings gradually dawned
upon the tardy intellects of Communipaw. These were the
times of the notorious Captain Kidd, when the American
harbours were the resorts of piratical adventurers of all kinds,
who, under pretext of mercantile voyages, scoured the West
Indies, made plundering descents upon the Spanish Main,
visited even the remote Indian Seas, and then came to dispose
of their booty, have their revels, and fit out new expeditions,
in the English colonies.

Vanderscamp had served in this hopeful school, and,
having risen to importance among the buccaneers, had pitched
upon his native village and early home, as a quiet, out-of-the-
way, unsuspected place, where he and his comrades, while

anchored at New York, might have their feasts, and concert their plans, without molestation.

At length the attention of the British Government was called to these piratical enterprises, that were becoming so frequent and outrageous. Vigorous measures were taken to check and punish them. Several of the most noted free-booters were caught and executed, and three of Vanderscamp's chosen comrades, the most riotous swashbucklers of the Wild Goose, were hanged in chains on Gibbet Island, in full sight of their favourite resort. As to Vanderscamp himself, he and his man Pluto again disappeared, and it was hoped by the people of Communipaw that he had fallen in some foreign brawl, or been swung on some foreign gallows.

For a time, therefore, the tranquillity of the village was restored ; the worthy Dutchmen once more smoked their pipes in peace, eyeing, with peculiar complacency, their old pests and terrors, the pirates, dangling and drying in the sun, on Gibbet Island.

This perfect calm was doomed at length to be ruffled. The fiery persecution of the pirates gradually subsided. Justice was satisfied with the examples that had been made, and there was no more talk of Kidd, and the other heroes of like kidney. On a calm summer evening, a boat, somewhat heavily laden, was seen pulling into Communipaw. What was the surprise and disquiet of the inhabitants, to see Yan Yost Vanderscamp seated at the helm, and his man Pluto tugging at the oar ! Vanderscamp, however, was apparently an altered man. He brought home with him a wife, who seemed to be a shrew, and to have the upper hand of him. He no longer was the swaggering, bully ruffian, but affected the regular merchant, and talked of retiring from business, and settling down quietly, to pass the rest of his days in his native place.

The Wild Goose mansion was again opened, but with diminished splendour, and no riot. It is true, Vanderscamp had frequent nautical visitors, and the sound of revelry was occasionally overheard in his house ; but everything seemed to be done under the rose ; and old Pluto was the only servant that officiated at these orgies. The visitors, indeed, were by no means of the turbulent stamp of their predecessors ; but quiet, mysterious traders, full of nods, and winks, and hieroglyphic signs, with whom, to use their cant phrase, "everything was smug." Their ships came to anchor at night, in the lower bay ; and, on a private signal, Vanderscamp would launch his boat, and, accompanied solely by his man Pluto, would make them mysterious visits. Sometimes boats pulled in at night, in front of the Wild Goose, and various articles of merchandise were landed in the dark, and spirited away, nobody knew whither. One of the more curious of the inhabitants kept watch, and caught a glimpse of the features of some of these night visitors, by the casual glance of a lantern, and declared that he recognized more than one of the free-booting frequenters of the Wild Goose, in former times; whence he concluded that Vanderscamp was at his old game, and that this mysterious merchandise was nothing more nor less than piratical plunder. The more charitable opinion, however, was, that Vanderscamp and his comrades, having been driven from their old line of business, by the " oppressions of Government," had resorted to smuggling to make both ends meet.

Be that as it may : I come now to the extraordinary fact, which is the butt-end of this story. It happened late one night, that Yan Yost Vanderscamp was returning across the broad bay, in his light skiff, rowed by his man Pluto. He had been carousing on board of a vessel, newly arrived, and was somewhat obfuscated in intellect by the liquor he had imbibed. It was a still, sultry night ; a heavy mass of lurid clouds was rising in the west, with the low muttering of distant thunder. Vanderscamp called on Pluto to pull lustily, that they might get home before the gathering storm. The old negro made no reply, but shaped his course so as to skirt the rocky shores of Gibbet Island. A faint creaking overhead caused Vanderscamp to cast up his eyes, when, to his horror, he beheld the bodies of his three pot companions and brothers in iniquity dangling in the moonlight, their rags fluttering, and their chains creaking, as they were slowly swung backward and forward by the rising breeze.

" What do you mean, you blockhead ! " cried Vanderscamp, " by pulling so close to the island ? "

" I thought you'd be glad to see your old friends once more," growled the negro. " You were never afraid of a living man ; what do you fear from the dead ? "

" Who's afraid ? " hiccupped Vanderscamp, partly heated by liquor, partly nettled by the jeer of the negro ; " who's afraid ? Hang me, but I would be glad to see them once more, alive or dead, at the Wild Goose. Come, my lads in the wind ! " continued he, taking a draught, and flourishing the bottle above his head, " here's fair weather to you in the other world ; and if you should be walking the rounds to-night, odd's fish ! but I'll be happy if you will drop in to supper."

A dismal creaking was the only reply. The wind blew loud and shrill, and, as it whistled round the gallows and among the bones, sounded as if they were laughing and gibbering in the air. Old Pluto chuckled to himself, and now pulled for home. The storm burst over the voyagers, while they were yet far from shore. The rain fell in torrents, the thunder crashed and pealed, and the lightning kept up an incessant blaze. It was stark midnight before they landed at Communipaw.

Dripping and shivering, Vanderscamp crawled homeward. He was completely sobered by the storm ; the water soaked from without having diluted and cooled the liquor within. Arrived at the Wild Goose, he knocked timidly and dubiously at the door, for he dreaded the reception he was to experience from his wife. He had reason to do so. She met him at the threshold, in a precious ill-humour.

" Is this a time," said she, " to keep people out of their beds, and to bring home company, to turn the house upside down ? "

" Company ? " said Vanderscamp meekly ; " I have brought no company with me, wife."

" No indeed ! they have got here before you, but by your invitation ; and blessed-looking company they are, truly ! "

Vanderscamp's knees smote together. " For the love of Heaven, where are they, wife ? "

" Where ?—why, in the blue room upstairs, making themselves as much at home as if the house were their own."

Vanderscamp made a desperate effort, scrambled up to the room, and threw open the door. Sure enough, there at a table, on which burned a light as blue as brimstone, sat the three guests from Gibbet Island, with halters round their necks, and bobbing their cups together, as if they were hob-or-nobbing, and trolling the old Dutch freebooter's glee, since translated into English :

> ' For three merry lads be we,
> And three merry lads be we ;
> I on the land, and thou on the sand,
> And Jack on the gallows-tree.'

Vanderscamp saw and heard no more. Starting back with horror, he missed his footing on the landing-place, and fell from the top of the stairs to the bottom. He was taken up speechless, and, either from the fall or the fright, was buried in the yard of the little Dutch church at Bergen, on the following Sunday.

From that day forward, the fate of the Wild Goose was sealed. It was pronounced a *haunted house*, and avoided accordingly. No one inhabited it but Vanderscamp's shrew of a widow, and old Pluto, and they were considered but little better than its hobgoblin visitors. Pluto grew more and more haggard and morose, and looked more like an imp of darkness than a human being. He spoke to no one, but went about muttering to himself; or, as some hinted, talking with the devil, who, though unseen, was ever at his elbow. Now and then he was seen pulling about the bay alone, in his skiff, in dark weather, or at the approach of nightfall; nobody could tell why, unless on an errand to invite more guests from the gallows. Indeed, it was affirmed that the Wild Goose still continued to be a house of entertainment for such guests, and that, on stormy nights, the blue chamber was occasionally illuminated, and sounds of diabolical merriment were overheard, mingling with the howling of the tempest. Some treated these as idle stories, until on one such night—it was about the time of the equinox—there was a horrible uproar in the Wild Goose, that could not be mistaken. It was not so much the sound of revelry, however, as strife, with two or three piercing shrieks, that pervaded every part of the village. Nevertheless, no one thought of hastening to the spot. On the contrary, the honest burghers of Communipaw drew their nightcaps over their ears, and buried their heads under the bed-clothes, at the thoughts of Vanderscamp and his gallows companions.

The next morning, some of the bolder and more curious undertook to reconnoitre. All was quiet and lifeless at the Wild Goose. The door yawned wide open, and had evidently been open all night, for the storm had beaten into the house. Gathering more courage from the silence and apparent desertion, they gradually ventured over the threshold. The house had indeed the air of having been possessed by devils. Everything was topsy-turvy; trunks had been broken open, and chests of drawers and corner cupboards turned inside out, as in a time of general sack and pillage; but the most woeful sight was the widow of Yan Yost Vanderscamp, extended a corpse on the floor of the blue chamber, with the marks of a deadly gripe on the windpipe.

All now was conjecture and dismay at Communipaw;

and the disappearance of old Pluto, who was nowhere to be found, gave rise to all kinds of wild surmises. Some suggested that the negro had betrayed the house to some of Vander-scamp's buccaneering associates, and that they had decamped together with the booty ; others surmised that the negro was nothing more nor less than a devil incarnate, who had now accomplished his ends, and made off with his dues.

Events, however, vindicated the negro from this last imputation. His skiff was picked up, drifting about the bay, bottom upward, as if wrecked in a tempest ; and his body was found, shortly afterward, by some Communipaw fishermen, stranded among the rocks of Gibbet Island, near the foot of the pirates' gallows. The fishermen shook their heads, and observed that old Pluto had ventured once too often to invite Guests from Gibbet Island.

THE MEZZOTINT

SOME time ago I believe I had the pleasure of telling you the story of an adventure which happened to a friend of mine by the name of Dennistoun, during his pursuit of objects of art for the museum at Cambridge.

He did not publish his experiences very widely upon his return to England ; but they could not fail to become known to a good many of his friends, and among others to the gentleman who at that time presided over an art museum at another University. It was to be expected that the story should make a considerable impression on the mind of a man whose vocation lay in lines similar to Dennistoun's, and that he should be eager to catch at any explanation of the matter which tended to make it seem improbable that he should ever be called upon to deal with so agitating an emergency. It was, indeed, somewhat consoling to him to reflect that he was not expected to acquire ancient MSS. for his institution ; that was the business of the Shelburnian Library. The authorities of that institution might, if they pleased, ransack obscure corners of the Continent for such matters. He was glad to be obliged at the moment to confine his attention to enlarging the already unsurpassed collection of English topographical drawings and engravings possessed by his museum. Yet, as it turned out, even a department so homely and familiar as this may have its dark corners, and to one of these Mr. Williams was unexpectedly introduced.

Those who have taken even the most limited interest in the acqusition of topographical pictures are aware that there is one London dealer whose aid is indispensable to their researches. Mr. J. W. Britnell publishes at short intervals very admirable catalogues of a large and constantly changing stock of engravings, plans, and old sketches of mansions, churches, and towns in England and Wales. These catalogues were, of course, the ABC of his subject to Mr. Williams : but as his museum already contained an enormous accumulation of topographical pictures, he was a regular, rather than a copious, buyer ; and he rather looked to Mr. Britnell to fill up gaps in the rank and file of his collection than to supply him with rarities.

Now, in February of last year there appeared upon Mr. Williams's desk at the museum a catalogue from Mr. Britnell's emporium, and accompanying it was a typewritten communication from the dealer himself. This latter ran as follows :

DEAR SIR,—We beg to call your attention to No. 978 in our accompanying catalogue, which we shall be glad to send on approval.—Yours faithfully,

J. W. BRITNELL.

To turn to No. 978 in the accompanying catalogue was with Mr. Williams (as he observed to himself) the work of a moment, and in the place indicated he found the following entry :

978.—*Unknown.* Interesting mezzotint : View of a manor-house, early part of the century. 15 by 10 inches ; black frame. £2, 2s.

It was not specially exciting, and the price seemed high. However, as Mr. Britnell, who knew his business and his customer, seemed to set store by it, Mr. Williams wrote a postcard asking for the article to be sent on approval, along with some other engravings and sketches which appeared in the same catalogue. And so he passed without much excitement of anticipation to the ordinary labours of the day.

A parcel of any kind always arrives a day later than you expect it, and that of Mr. Britnell proved, as I believe the right phrase goes, no exception to the rule. It was delivered at the museum by the afternoon post of Saturday, after Mr. Williams had left his work, and it was accordingly brought round to his rooms in college by the attendant, in order that he might not have to wait over Sunday before looking through it and returning such of the contents as he did not propose to keep. And here he found it when he came in to tea, with a friend.

The only item with which I am concerned was the rather large, black-framed mezzotint of which I have already quoted the short description given in Mr. Britnell's catalogue. Some more details of it will have to be given, though I cannot hope to put before you the look of the picture as clearly as it is present to my own eye. Very nearly the exact duplicate of it may be seen in a good many old inn parlours, or in the passages of undisturbed country mansions at the present moment. It was a rather indifferent mezzotint, and an indifferent mezzotint is, perhaps, the worst form of engraving known. It presented a full-face view of a not very large manor-house of the last century, with three rows of plain sashed windows with rusticated masonry about them, a parapet with balls or vases at the angles, and a small portico in the centre. On either side were trees, and in front a considerable expanse of lawn. The legend " A. W. F. sculpsit " was engraved on the narrow margin ; and there was no further inscription. The whole thing gave the impression that it was the work of an amateur. What in the world Mr. Britnell could mean by affixing the price of £2, 2s. to such an object was more than Mr. Williams could imagine. He turned it over with a good deal of contempt ; upon the back was a paper label, the left-hand half of which had been torn off. All that remained were the ends of two lines of writing : the first had the letters —*ngley Hall ;* the second, —*ssex.*

It would, perhaps, be just worth while to identify the place represented, which he could easily do with the help of a gazetteer, and then he would send it back to Mr. Britnell, with some remarks reflecting upon the judgment of that gentleman.

He lighted the candles, for it was now dark, made the tea, and supplied the friend with whom he had been playing golf (for I believe the authorities of the University I write of indulge in that pursuit by way of relaxation) ; and tea was taken to the accompaniment of a discussion which golfing persons can imagine for themselves, but which the conscientious writer has no right to inflict upon any non-golfing persons.

The conclusion arrived at was that certain strokes might have been better, and that in certain emergencies neither player had experienced that amount of luck which a human being has a right to expect. It was now that the friend—let us call him Professor Binks—took up the framed engraving, and said :

" What's this place, Williams ? "

" Just what I am going to try to find out," said Williams,

going to the shelf for a gazetteer. " Look at the back. Something-ley Hall, either in Sussex or Essex. Half the name's gone, you see. You don't happen to know it, I suppose ? "
" It's from that man Britnell, I suppose, isn't it ? " said Binks. " Is it for the museum ? "
" Well, I think I should buy it if the price was five shillings," said Williams ; " but for some unearthly reason he wants two guineas for it. I can't conceive why. It's a wretched engraving, and there aren't even any figures to give it life."
" It's not worth two guineas, I should think," said Binks ; " but I don't think it's so badly done. The moonlight seems rather good to me ; and I should have thought there *were* figures, or at least a figure, just on the edge in front."
" Let's look," said Williams. " Well, it's true the light is rather cleverly given. Where's your figure ? Oh yes ! Just the head, in the very front of the picture."
And indeed there was—hardly more than a black blot on the extreme edge of the engraving—the head of a man or woman, a good deal muffled up, the back turned to the spectator, and looking towards the house.
Williams had not noticed it before.
" Still," he said, " though it's a cleverer thing than I thought, I can't spend two guineas of museum money on a picture of a place I don't know."
Professor Binks had his work to do, and soon went ; and very nearly up to Hall time Williams was engaged in a vain attempt to identify the subject of his picture. " If the vowel before the *ng* had only been left, it would have been easy enough," he thought ; " but as it is, the name may be anything from Guestingley to Langley, and there are many more names ending like this than I thought ; and this rotten book has no index of terminations."
Hall in Mr. Williams's college was at seven. It need not be dwelt upon ; the less so as he met there colleagues who had been playing golf during the afternoon, and words with which we have no concern were freely bandied across the table—merely golfing words, I would hasten to explain.
I suppose an hour or more to have been spent in what is called common-room after dinner. Later in the evening some few retired to Williams's rooms, and I have little doubt that whist was played and tobacco smoked. During a lull in these operations Williams picked up the mezzotint from the table without looking at it, and handed it to a person mildly

interested in art, telling him where it had come from, and the other particulars which we already know.

The gentleman took it carelessly, looked at it, then said, in a tone of some interest :

" It's really a very good piece of work, Williams ; it has quite a feeling of the romantic period. The light is admirably managed, it seems to me, and the figure, though it's rather too grotesque, is somehow very impressive."

" Yes, isn't it ? " said Williams, who was just then busy giving whisky and soda to others of the company, and was unable to come across the room to look at the view again.

It was by this time rather late in the evening, and the visitors were on the move. After they went Williams was obliged to write a letter or two and clear up some odd bits of work. At last, some time past midnight, he was disposed to turn in, and he put out his lamp after lighting his bedroom candle. The picture lay face upwards on the table where the last man who looked at it had put it, and it caught his eye as he turned the lamp down. What he saw made him very nearly drop the candle on the floor, and he declares now that if he had been left in the dark at that moment he would have had a fit. But, as that did not happen, he was able to put down the light on the table and take a good look at the picture. It was indubitable—rankly impossible, no doubt, but absolutely certain. In the middle of the lawn in front of the unknown house there was a figure where no figure had been at five o'clock that afternoon. It was crawling on all-fours towards the house, and it was muffled in a strange black garment with a white cross on the back.

I do not know what is the ideal course to pursue in a situation of this kind. I can only tell you what Mr. Williams did. He took the picture by one corner and carried it across the passage to a second set of rooms which he possessed. There he locked it up in a drawer, sported the doors of both sets of rooms, and retired to bed ; but first he wrote out and signed an account of the extraordinary change which the picture had undergone since it had come into his possession.

Sleep visited him rather late ; but it was consoling to reflect that the behaviour of the picture did not depend upon his own unsupported testimony. Evidently the man who had looked at it the night before had seen something of the same kind as he had, otherwise he might have been tempted to think that something gravely wrong was happening either to his eyes or his mind. This possibility being fortunately precluded, two matters awaited him on the morrow. He must take stock of the picture very carefully, and call in a witness for the purpose, and he must make a determined effort to ascertain what house it was that was represented. He would therefore ask his neighbour Nisbet to breakfast with him, and he would subsequently spend a morning over the gazetteer.

Nisbet was disengaged, and arrived about 9.30. His host was not quite dressed, I am sorry to say, even at this late hour. During breakfast nothing was said about the mezzotint by Williams, save that he had a picture on which he wished for Nisbet's opinion. But those who are familiar with University life can picture for themselves the wide and delightful range of subjects over which the conversation of two Fellows of Canterbury College is likely to extend during a Sunday morning breakfast. Hardly a topic was left unchallenged, from golf to lawn-tennis. Yet I am bound to say that Williams was rather distraught; for his interest naturally centred in that very strange picture which was now reposing, face downwards, in the drawer in the room opposite.

The morning pipe was at last lighted, and the moment had arrived for which he looked. With very considerable—almost tremulous—excitement, he ran across, unlocked the drawer, and, extracting the picture—still face downwards—ran back, and put it into Nisbet's hands.

" Now," he said, " Nisbet, I want you to tell me exactly what you see in that picture. Describe it, if you don't mind, rather minutely. I'll tell you why afterwards."

" Well," said Nisbet, " I have here a view of a country-house—English, I presume—by moonlight."

" Moonlight ? You're sure of that ? "

" Certainly. The moon appears to be on the wane, if you wish for details, and there are clouds in the sky."

" All right. Go on. I'll swear," added Williams in an aside, " there was no moon when I saw it first."

" Well, there's not much more to be said," Nisbet continued. " The house has one—two—three rows of windows, five in each row, except at the bottom, where there's a porch instead of the middle one, and——"

" But what about figures ? " said Williams, with marked interest.

" There aren't any," said Nisbet ; " but——"

" What ! No figure on the grass in front ? "

" Not a thing."

" You'll swear to that ? "

" Certainly I will. But there's just one other thing."

" What ? "

" Why, one of the windows on the ground-floor—left of the door—is open."

" Is it really so ? My goodness ! he must have got in," said Williams, with great excitement ; and he hurried to the back of the sofa on which Nisbet was sitting, and, catching the picture from him, verified the matter for himself. It was quite true. There was no figure, and there was the open window. Williams, after a moment of speechless surprise, went to the writing-table and scribbled for a short time. Then he brought two papers to Nisbet, and asked him first to sign one—it was his own description of the picture, which you have just heard—and then to read the other which was Williams's statement written the night before.

" What can it all mean ? " said Nisbet.

" Exactly," said Williams. " Well, one thing I must do— or three things, now I think of it. I must find out from Garwood "—this was his last night's visitor—" what he saw, and then I must get the thing photographed before it goes further, and then I must find out what the place is."

" I can do the photographing myself," said Nisbet, " and I will. But, you know, it looks very much as if we were assisting at the working out of a tragedy somewhere. The question is, Has it happened already, or is it going to come off ? You must find out what the place is. Yes," he said, looking at the picture again, " I expect you're right : he has got in. And if I don't mistake there'll be the devil to pay in one of the rooms upstairs."

" I'll tell you what," said Williams : " I'll take the picture across to old Green " (this was the senior Fellow of the College, who had been Bursar for many years). " It's quite likely he'll know it. We have property in Essex and Sussex, and he must have been over the two counties a lot in his time."

" Quite likely he will," said Nisbet ; " but just let me take my photograph first. But look here, I rather think Green isn't up to-day. He wasn't in Hall last night, and I think I heard him say he was going down for the Sunday."

" That's true, too," said Williams ; " I know he's gone to Brighton. Well, if you'll photograph it now, I'll go across to Garwood and get his statement, and you keep an eye on it while I'm gone. I'm beginning to think two guineas is not a very exorbitant price for it now."

In a short time he had returned, and brought Mr. Garwood
with him. Garwood's statement was to the effect that the
figure, when he had seen it, was clear of the edge of the picture,
but had not got far across the lawn. He remembered a white
mark on the back of its drapery, but could not have been sure
it was a cross. A document to this effect was then drawn up
and signed, and Nisbet proceeded to photograph the picture.

"Now what do you mean to do?" he said. "Are you
going to sit and watch it all day?"

"Well, no, I think not," said Williams. "I rather imagine
we're meant to see the whole thing. You see, between the time
I saw it last night and this morning there was time for lots
of things to happen, but the creature only got into the house.
It could easily have got through its business in the time and
gone to its own place again ; but the fact of the window being
open, I think, must mean that it's in there now. So I feel
quite easy about leaving it. And, besides, I have a kind of
idea that it wouldn't change much, if at all, in the daytime.
We might go out for a walk this afternoon, and come in to
tea, or whenever it gets dark. I shall leave it out on the table
here, and sport the door. My skip can get in, but no one
else."

The three agreed that this would be a good plan ; and,
further, that if they spent the afternoon together they would
be less likely to talk about the business to other people ; for
any rumour of such a transaction as was going on would bring
the whole of the Phasmatological Society about their ears.

We may give them a respite until five o'clock.

At or near that hour the three were entering Williams's
staircase. They were at first slightly annoyed to see that the
door of his rooms was unsported ; but in a moment it was
remembered that on Sunday the skips came for orders an
hour or so earlier than on week-days. However, a surprise
was awaiting them. The first thing they saw was the picture
leaning up against a pile of books on the table, as it had been
left, and the next thing was Williams's skip, seated on a chair
opposite, gazing at it with undisguised horror. How was
this? Mr. Filcher (the name is not my own invention) was
a servant of considerable standing, and set the standard of
etiquette to all his own college and to several neighbouring
ones, and nothing could be more alien to his practice than to
be found sitting on his master's chair, or appearing to take
any particular notice of his master's furniture or pictures.
Indeed, he seemed to feel this himself. He started violently

. . . Seated on a chair opposite, gazing at it with undisguised horror.

when the three men were in the room, and got up with a marked effort. Then he said :

" I ask your pardon, sir, for taking such a freedom as to set down."

" Not at all, Robert," interposed Mr. Williams. " I was meaning to ask you some time what you thought of that picture."

" Well, sir, of course I don't set up my opinion again yours, but it ain't the pictur I should 'ang where my little girl could see it, sir."

" Wouldn't you, Robert ? Why not ? "

" No, sir. Why, the pore child, I recollect once she see a Door Bible, with pictures not 'alf what that is, and we 'ad to set up with her three or four nights afterwards, if you'll believe me ; and if she was to ketch a sight of this skelinton here, or whatever it is, carrying off the pore baby, she would be in a taking. You know 'ow it is with children ; 'ow nervish they git with a little thing and all. But what I should say, it don't seem a right pictur to be laying about, sir, not where any one that's liable to be startled could come on it. Should you be wanting anything this evening, sir ? Thank you, sir."

With these words the excellent man went to continue the round of his masters, and you may be sure the gentlemen whom he left lost no time in gathering round the engraving. There was the house, as before, under the waning moon and the drifting clouds. The window that had been open was shut, and the figure was once more on the lawn : but not this time crawling cautiously on hands and knees. Now it was erect and stepping swiftly, with long strides, towards the front of the picture. The moon was behind it, and the black drapery hung down over its face so that only hints of that could be seen, and what was visible made the spectators profoundly thankful that they could see no more than a white dome-like forehead and a few straggling hairs. The head was bent down, and the arms were tightly clasped over an object which could be dimly seen and identified as a child, whether dead or living it was not possible to say. The legs of the appearance alone could be plainly discerned, and they were horribly thin.

From five to seven the three companions sat and watched the picture by turns. But it never changed. They agreed at last that it would be safe to leave it, and that they would return after Hall and await further developments.

When they assembled again, at the earliest possible moment, the engraving was there, but the figure was gone, and the

house was quiet under the moonbeams. There was nothing
for it but to spend the evening over gazetteers and guide-
books. Williams was the lucky one at last, and perhaps he
deserved it. At 11.30 p.m. he read from Murray's *Guide to
Essex* the following lines :

> 16½ miles, *Anningley*. The church has been an interest-
> ing building of Norman date, but was extensively classicized
> in the last century. It contains the tomb of the family of
> Francis, whose mansion, Anningley Hall, a solid Queen
> Anne house, stands immediately beyond the churchyard
> in a park of about 80 acres. The family is now extinct,
> the last heir having disappeared mysteriously in infancy
> in the year 1802. The father, Mr. Arthur Francis, was
> locally known as a talented amateur engraver in mezzotint.
> After his son's disappearance he lived in complete retire-
> ment at the Hall, and was found dead in his studio on the
> third anniversary of the disaster, having just completed
> an engraving of the house, impressions of which are of
> considerable rarity.

This looked like business, and, indeed, Mr. Green on his
return at once identified the house as Anningley Hall.

" Is there any kind of explanation of the figure, Green ? "
was the question which Williams naturally asked.

" I don't know, I'm sure, Williams. What used to be
said in the place when I first knew it, which was before I came
up here, was just this : old Francis was always very much
down on these poaching fellows, and whenever he got a chance
he used to get a man whom he suspected of it turned off the
estate, and by degrees he got rid of them all but one. Squires
could do a lot of things then that they daren't think of now.
Well, this man that was left was what you find pretty often
in that country—the last remains of a very old family. I
believe they were Lords of the Manor at one time. I recollect
just the same thing in my own parish."

" What, like the man in *Tess o' the Durbervilles* ? " Williams
put in.

" Yes, I dare say ; it's not a book I could ever read myself.
But this fellow could show a row of tombs in the church there
that belonged to his ancestors, and all that went to sour him
a bit ; but Francis, they said, could never get at him—he
always kept just on the right side of the law—until one night
the keepers found him at it in a wood right at the end of the
estate. I could show you the place now ; it marches with

some land that used to belong to an uncle of mine. And you can imagine there was a row ; and this man Gawdy (that was the name, to be sure—Gawdy ; I thought I should get it—Gawdy), he was unlucky enough, poor chap ! to shoot a keeper. Well, that was what Francis wanted, and grand juries —you know what they would have been then—and poor Gawdy was strung up in double-quick time ; and I've been shown the place he was buried in, on the north side of the church— you know the way in that part of the world : any one that's been hanged or made away with themselves, they bury them that side. And the idea was that some friend of Gawdy's— not a relation, because he had none, poor devil ! he was the last of his line : kind of *spes ultima gentis*—must have planned to get hold of Francis's boy and put an end to *his* line, too. I don't know—it's rather an out-of-the-way thing for an Essex poacher to think of—but, you know, I should say now it looks more as if old Gawdy had managed the job himself. Booh ! I hate to think of it ! have some whisky, Williams ! "

The facts were communicated by Williams to Dennistoun, and by him to a mixed company, of which I was one, and the Sadducean Professor of Ophiology another. I am sorry to say that the latter, when asked what he thought of it, only remarked : " Oh, those Bridgeford people will say anything " —a sentiment which met with the reception it deserved.

I have only to add that the picture is now in the Ashleian Museum ; that it has been treated with a view to discovering whether sympathetic ink has been used in it, but without effect ; that Mr. Britnell knew nothing of it save that he was sure it was uncommon ; and that, though carefully watched, it has never been known to change again.

THE DANCING PARTNER

" THIS story," commenced MacShaugnassy, " comes from
Furtwangen, a small town in the Black Forest. There
lived there a very wonderful old fellow named
Nicholaus Geibel. His business was the making of mechanical
toys, at which work he had acquired an almost European
reputation. He made rabbits that would emerge from the
heart of a cabbage, flop their ears, smooth their whiskers,
and disappear again ; cats that would wash their faces, and
mew so naturally that dogs would mistake them for real cats,
and fly at them ; dolls, with phonographs concealed within
them, that would raise their hats and say, ' Good morning ;
how do you do ? ' and some that would even sing a song.

" But he was something more than a mere mechanic ;
he was an artist. His work was with him a hobby, almost a
passion. His shop was filled with all manner of strange things
that never would, or could, be sold—things he had made for
the pure love of making them. He had contrived a mechanical
donkey that would trot for two hours by means of stored
electricity, and trot, too, much faster than the live article,
and with less need for exertion on the part of the driver ; a
bird that would shoot up into the air, fly round and round
in a circle, and drop to earth at the exact spot from where it
started ; a skeleton that, supported by an upright iron bar,
would dance a hornpipe ; a life-size lady doll that could play
the fiddle ; and a gentleman with a hollow inside who could
smoke a pipe and drink more lager beer than any three
average German students put together, which is saying
much.

" Indeed, it was the belief of the town that old Geibel could
make a man capable of doing everything that a respectable man

need want to do. One day he made a man who did too much, and it came about in this way :

"Young Doctor Follen had a baby, and the baby had a birthday. Its first birthday put Doctor Follen's household into somewhat of a flurry, but on the occasion of its second birthday, Mrs. Doctor Follen gave a ball in honour of the event. Old Geibel and his daughter Olga were among the guests.

"During the afternoon of the next day some three or four of Olga's bosom friends, who had also been present at the ball, dropped in to have a chat about it. They naturally fell to discussing the men, and to criticizing their dancing. Old Geibel was in the room, but he appeared to be absorbed in his newspaper, and the girls took no notice of him.

"'There seem to be fewer men who can dance at every ball you go to,' said one of the girls.

"'Yes, and don't the ones who can give themselves airs,' said another ; 'they make quite a favour of asking you.'

"'And how stupidly they talk,' added a third. 'They always say exactly the same things : "How charming you are looking to-night." "Do you often go to Vienna ? Oh, you should, it's delightful." "What a charming dress you have on." "What a warm day it has been." "Do you like Wagner ?" I do wish they'd think of something new.'

"'Oh, I never mind how they talk,' said a fourth. 'If a man dances well he may be a fool for all I care.'

"'He generally is,' slipped in a thin girl, rather spitefully.

"'I go to a ball to dance,' continued the previous speaker, not noticing the interruption. 'All I ask of a partner is that he shall hold me firmly, take me round steadily, and not get tired before I do.'

"'A clockwork figure would be the thing for you,' said the girl who had interrupted.

"'Bravo!' cried one of the others, clapping her hands, 'what a capital idea !'

"'What's a capital idea ? ' they asked.

"'Why, a clockwork dancer, or, better still, one that would go by electricity and never run down.'

"The girls took up the idea with enthusiasm.

"'Oh, what a lovely partner he would make,' said one ; 'he would never kick you, or tread on your toes.'

"'Or tear your dress,' said another.

"'Or get out of step.'

"'Or get giddy and lean on you.'

" ' And he would never want to mop his face with his handkerchief. I do hate to see a man do that after every dance.'

" ' And wouldn't want to spend the whole evening in the supper-room.'

" ' Why, with a phonograph inside him to grind out all the stock remarks, you would not be able to tell him from a real man,' said the girl who had first suggested the idea.

" ' Oh yes, you would,' said the thin girl, ' he would be so much nicer.'

" Old Geibel had laid down his paper, and was listening with both his ears. On one of the girls glancing in his direction, however, he hurriedly hid himself again behind it.

" After the girls were gone, he went into his workshop, where Olga heard him walking up and down, and every now and then chuckling to himself ; and that night he talked to her a good deal about dancing and dancing men—asked what they usually said and did—what dances were most popular—what steps were gone through, with many other questions bearing on the subject.

" Then for a couple of weeks he kept much to his factory, and was very thoughtful and busy, though prone at unexpected moments to break into a quiet low laugh, as if enjoying a joke that nobody else knew of.

" A month later another ball took place in Furtwangen. On this occasion it was given by old Wenzel, the wealthy timber merchant, to celebrate his niece's betrothal, and Geibel and his daughter were again among the invited.

" When the hour arrived to set out, Olga sought her father. Not finding him in the house, she tapped at the door of his workshop. He appeared in his shirt-sleeves, looking hot but radiant.

" ' Don't wait for me,' he said, ' you go on, I'll follow you. I've got something to finish.'

" As she turned to obey he called after her, ' Tell them I'm going to bring a young man with me—such a nice young man, and an excellent dancer. All the girls will like him.' Then he laughed and closed the door.

" Her father generally kept his doings secret from everybody, but she had a pretty shrewd suspicion of what he had been planning, and so, to a certain extent, was able to prepare the guests for what was coming. Anticipation ran high, and the arrival of the famous mechanist was eagerly awaited.

" At length the sound of wheels was heard outside, followed

by a great commotion in the passage, and old Wenzel himself, his jolly face red with excitement and suppressed laughter, burst into the room and announced in stentorian tones :

" ' Herr Geibel—and a friend.'

" Herr Geibel and his ' friend ' entered, greeted with shouts of laughter and applause, and advanced to the centre of the room.

" ' Allow me, ladies and gentlemen,' said Herr Geibel, ' to introduce you to my friend, Lieutenant Fritz. Fritz, my dear fellow, bow to the ladies and gentlemen.'

" Geibel placed his hand encouragingly on Fritz's shoulder, and the Lieutenant bowed low, accompanying the action with a harsh clicking noise in his throat, unpleasantly suggestive of a death-rattle. But that was only a detail.

" ' He walks a little stiffly ' (old Geibel took his arm and walked him forward a few steps. He certainly did walk stiffly), ' but then, walking is not his forte. He is essentially a dancing man. I have only been able to teach him the waltz as yet, but at that he is faultless. Come, which of you ladies may I introduce him to as a partner. He keeps perfect time ; he never gets tired ; he won't kick you or tread on your dress ; he will hold you as firmly as you like, and go as quickly or as slowly as you please ; he never gets giddy ; and he is full of conversation. Come, speak up for yourself, my boy.'

" The old gentleman twisted one of the buttons at the back of his coat, and immediately Fritz opened his mouth, and in thin tones that appeared to proceed from the back of his head, remarked suddenly, ' May I have the pleasure ? ' and then shut his mouth again with a snap.

" That Lieutenant Fritz had made a strong impression on the company was undoubted, yet none of the girls seemed inclined to dance with him. They looked askance at his waxen face, with its staring eyes and fixed smile, and shuddered. At last old Geibel came to the girl who had conceived the idea.

" ' It is your own suggestion, carried out to the letter,' said Geibel, ' an electric dancer. You owe it to the gentleman to give him a trial.'

" She was a bright, saucy little girl, fond of a frolic. Her host added his entreaties, and she consented.

" Herr Geibel fixed the figure to her. Its right arm was screwed round her waist, and held her firmly ; its delicately jointed left hand was made to fasten itself upon her right. The old toymaker showed her how to regulate its speed, and how to stop it, and release herself.

" ' It will take you round in a complete circle,' he explained ; ' be careful that no one knocks against you, and alters its course.'

" The music struck up. Old Geibel put the current in motion, and Annette and her strange partner began to dance.

" For a while every one stood watching them. The figure performed its purpose admirably. Keeping perfect time and step, and holding its little partner tight clasped in an unyielding embrace, it revolved steadily, pouring forth at the same time a constant flow of squeaky conversation, broken by brief intervals of grinding silence.

" ' How charming you are looking to-night,' it remarked in its thin, far-away voice. ' What a lovely day it has been. Do you like dancing ? How well our steps agree. You will give me another, won't you ? Oh, don't be so cruel. What a charming gown you have on. Isn't waltzing delightful ? I could go on dancing for ever—with you. Have you had supper ? '

" As she grew more familiar with the uncanny creature, the girl's nervousness wore off, and she entered into the fun of the thing.

" ' Oh, he's just lovely,' she cried, laughing; ' I could go on dancing with him all my life.'

" Couple after couple now joined them, and soon all the dancers in the room were whirling round behind them. Nicholaus Geibel stood looking on, beaming with childish delight at his success.

" Old Wenzel approached him, and whispered something in his ear. Geibel laughed and nodded, and the two worked their way quietly towards the door.

" ' This is the young people's house to-night,' said Wenzel, as soon as they were outside ; ' you and I will have a quiet pipe and a glass of hock, over in the counting-house.'

" Meanwhile the dancing grew more fast and furious. Little Annette loosened the screw regulating her partner's rate of progress, and the figure flew round with her swifter and swifter. Couple after couple dropped out exhausted, but they only went the faster, till at length they remained dancing alone.

" Madder and madder became the waltz. The music lagged behind : the musicians, unable to keep pace, ceased, and sat staring. The younger guests applauded, but the older faces began to grow anxious.

" ' Hadn't you better stop, dear,' said one of the women, ' you'll make yourself so tired.'

" But Annette did not answer.

" ' I believe she's fainted,' cried out a girl who had caught sight of her face as it was swept by.

" One of the men sprang forward and clutched at the figure, but its impetus threw him down on to the floor, where its steel-cased feet laid bare his cheek. The thing evidently did not intend to part with its prize easily.

" Had any one retained a cool head, the figure, one cannot help thinking, might easily have been stopped. Two or three men acting in concert might have lifted it bodily off the floor, or have jammed it into a corner. But few human heads are capable of remaining cool under excitement. Those who are not present think how stupid must have been those who were ; those who are reflect afterwards how simple it would have been to do this, that, or the other, if only they had thought of it at the time.

" The women grew hysterical. The men shouted contradictory directions to one another. Two of them made a bungling rush at the figure, which had the result of forcing it out of its orbit in the centre of the room, and sending it crashing against the walls and furniture. A stream of blood showed itself down the girl's white frock, and followed her along the. floor. The affair was becoming horrible. The women rushed screaming from the room. The men followed them.

" One sensible suggestion was made : ' Find Geibel—fetch Geibel.'

" No one had noticed him leave the room, no one knew where he was. A party went in search of him. The others, too unnerved to go back into the ballroom, crowded outside the door and listened. They could hear the steady whir of the wheels upon the polished floor as the thing spun round and round ; the dull thud as every now and again it dashed itself and its burden against some opposing object and ricochetted off in a new direction.

" And everlastingly it talked in that thin ghostly voice, repeating over and over the same formula : ' How charming you are looking to-night. What a lovely day it has been. Oh, don't be so cruel. I could go on dancing for ever—with you. Have you had supper ? '

" Of course they sought for Geibel everywhere but where he was. They looked in every room in the house, then they rushed off in a body to his own place, and spent precious minutes in waking up his deaf old housekeeper. At last it occurred to one of the party that Wenzel was missing also, and then the idea of the counting-house across the yard presented itself to them, and there they found him.

" He rose up, very pale, and followed them ; and he and old Wenzel forced their way through the crowd of guests gathered outside, and entered the room, and locked the door behind them.

" From within there came the muffled sound of low voices and quick steps, followed by a confused scuffling noise, then silence, then the low voices again.

" After a time the door opened, and those near it pressed forward to enter, but old Wenzel's broad shoulders barred the way.

" ' I want you—and you, Bekler,' he said, addressing a couple of the elder men.   His voice was calm, bu. his face was deadly white.   ' The rest of you, please go—get the women away as quickly as you can.'

" From that day old Nicholaus Geibel confined himself to the making of mechanical rabbits, and cats that mewed and washed their faces."

THE WOMAN
WHO RODE AWAY

SHE had thought that this marriage, of all marriages,
would be an adventure. Not that the man himself was
exactly magical to her. A little, wiry, twisted fellow,
twenty years older than herself, with brown eyes and greying
hair, who had come to America a scrap of a wastrel, from
Holland, years ago, as a tiny boy, and from the gold-mines of
the west had been kicked south into Mexico, and now was
more or less rich, owning silver-mines in the wilds of the
Sierra Madre : it was obvious that the adventure lay in his
circumstances, rather than his person. But he was still a
little dynamo of energy, in spite of accidents survived, and
what he had accomplished he had accomplished alone. One
of those human oddments there is no accounting for.

When she actually *saw* what he had accomplished, her
heart quailed. Great green-covered, unbroken mountain-
hills, and in the midst of the lifeless isolation, the sharp pinkish
mounds of the dried mud from the silver-works. Under the
nakedness of the works, the walled-in, one-storey adobe house,
with its garden inside, and its deep inner verandah with
tropical climbers on the sides. And when you looked up
from this shut-in flowered patio, you saw the huge pink cone
of the silver-mud refuse, and the machinery of the extracting
plant against heaven above. No more.

To be sure, the great wooden doors were often open. And
then she could stand outside, in the vast open world. And
see great, void, tree-clad hills piling behind one another,
from nowhere into nowhere. They were green in autumn
time. For the rest, pinkish, stark dry, and abstract.

And in his battered Ford car her husband would take her
into the dead, thrice-dead little Spanish town forgotten among

335

the mountains. The great, sundried dead church, the dead portales, the hopeless covered market-place, where, the first time she went, she saw a dead dog lying between the meat stalls and the vegetable array, stretched out as if for ever, nobody troubling to throw it away. Deadness within deadness.

Everybody feebly talking silver, and showing bits of ore. But silver was at a standstill. The Great War came and went. Silver was a dead market. Her husband's mines were closed down. But she and he lived on in the adobe house under the works, among the flowers that were never very flowery to her.

She had two children, a boy and a girl. And her eldest, the boy, was nearly ten years old before she aroused from her stupor of subjected amazement. She was now thirty-three, a large, blue-eyed, dazed woman, beginning to grow stout. Her little, wiry, tough, twisted, brown-eyed husband was fifty-three, a man as tough as wire, tenacious as wire, still full of energy, but dimmed by the lapse of silver from the market, and by some curious inaccessibility on his wife's part.

He was a man of principles, and a good husband. In a way, he doted on her. He never quite got over his dazzled admiration of her. But essentially, he was still a bachelor. He had been thrown out on the world, a little bachelor, at the age of ten. When he married he was over forty, and had enough money to marry on. But his capital was all a bachelor's. He was boss of his own works, and marriage was the last and most intimate bit of his own works.

He admired his wife to extinction, he admired her body, all her points. And she was to him always the rather dazzling Californian girl from Berkeley whom he had first known. Like any sheik, he kept her guarded among those mountains of Chihuahua. He was jealous of her as he was of his silver-mine : and that is saying a lot.

At thirty-three she really was still the girl from Berkeley, in all but physique. Her conscious development had stopped mysteriously with her marriage, completely arrested. Her husband had never become real to her, neither mentally nor physically. In spite of his late sort of passion for her, he never meant anything to her, physically. Only morally he swayed her, downed her, kept her in an invincible slavery.

So the years went by, in the adobe house strung round the sunny patio, with the silver-works overhead. Her husband was never still. When the silver went dead, he ran a ranch lower down, some twenty miles away, and raised pure-bred

hogs, splendid creatures. At the same time, he hated pigs.
He was a squeamish waif of an idealist, and really hated the
physical side of life. He loved work, work, work, and making
things. His marriage, his children, were something he was
making, part of his business, but with a sentimental income
this time.

Gradually her nerves began to go wrong : she must get
out. She must get out. So he took her to El Paso for three
months. And at least it was the United States.

But he kept his spell over her. The three months ended :
back she was, just the same, in her adobe house among those
eternal green or pinky-brown hills, void as only the undiscovered
is void. She taught her children, she supervised the Mexican
boys who were her servants. And sometimes her husband
brought visitors, Spaniards or Mexicans or occasionally white
men.

He really loved to have white men staying on the place.
Yet he had not a moment's peace when they were there. It
was as if his wife were some peculiar secret vein of ore in his
mines, which no one must be aware of except himself. And
she was fascinated by the young gentlemen, mining engineers,
who were his guests at times. He, too, was fascinated by a
real gentleman. But he was an old-timer miner with a wife,
and if a gentleman looked at his wife, he felt as if his mine
were being looted, the secrets of it pryed out.

It was one of these young gentlemen who put the idea into
her mind. They were all standing outside the great wooden
doors of the patio, looking at the outer world. The eternal,
motionless hills were all green, it was September, after the
rains. There was no sign of anything, save the deserted mine,
the deserted works, and a bunch of half-deserted miner's
dwellings.

" I wonder," said the young man, " what there is behind
those great blank hills."

" More hills," said Lederman. " If you go that way,
Sonora and the coast. This way is the desert—you came from
there. And the other way, hills and mountains."

" Yes, but what *lives* in the hills and the mountains ?
Surely there is something wonderful ? It looks *so* like nowhere
on earth : like being on the moon."

" There's plenty of game, if you want to shoot. And
Indians, if you call *them* wonderful."

" Wild ones ? "

" Wild enough."

" But friendly ? "

" It depends. Some of them are quite wild, and they don't let anybody near. They kill a missionary at sight. And where a missionary can't get, nobody can."

" But what does the government say ? "

" They're so far from everywhere, the government leaves 'em alone. And they're wily ; if they think there'll be trouble, they send a delegation to Chihuahua and make a formal submission. The government is glad to leave it at that."

" And do they live quite wild, with their own savage customs and religion ? "

" Oh yes. They use nothing but bows and arrows. I've seen them in town, in the Plaza, with funny sort of hats with flowers round them, and a bow in one hand, quite naked except for a sort of shirt, even in cold weather—striding round with their savage's bare legs."

" But don't you suppose it's wonderful, up there in their secret villages ? "

" No. What would there be wonderful about it ? Savages are savages, and all savages behave more or less alike : rather low-down and dirty, unsanitary, with a few cunning tricks, and struggling to get enough to eat."

" But surely they have old, old religions and mysteries —it *must* be wonderful, surely it must."

" I don't know about mysteries—howling and heathen practices, more or less indecent. No, I see nothing wonderful in that kind of stuff. And I wonder that you should, when you have lived in London or Paris or New York——"

" Ah, *everybody* lives in London or Paris or New York," said the young man, as if this were an argument.

And his peculiar vague enthusiasm for unknown Indians found a full echo in the woman's heart. She was overcome by a foolish romanticism more unreal than a girl's. She felt it was her destiny to wander into the secret haunts of these timeless, mysterious, marvellous Indians of the mountains.

She kept her secret. The young man was departing, her husband was going with him down to Torreon, on business :— would be away for some days. But before the departure, she made her husband talk about the Indians : about the wandering tribes, resembling the Navajo, who were still wandering free ; and the Yaquis of Sonora : and the different groups in the different valleys of Chihuahua State.

There was supposed to be one tribe, the Chilchuis, living in a high valley to the south, who were the sacred tribe of all the Indians. The descendants of Montezuma and of the old Aztec or Totonac kings still lived among them, and the old priests still kept up the ancient religion, and offered human sacrifices—so it was said. Some scientists had been to the Chilchui country, and had come back gaunt and exhausted with hunger and bitter privation, bringing various curious, barbaric objects of worship, but having seen nothing extraordinary in the hungry, stark village of savages.

Though Lederman talked in this off-hand way, it was obvious he felt some of the vulgar excitement at the idea of ancient and mysterious savages.

" How far away are they ? " she asked.

" Oh—three days on horseback—past Cuchitee and a little lake there is up there."

Her husband and the young man departed. The woman made her crazy plans. Of late, to break the monotony of her life, she had harassed her husband into letting her go riding with him, occasionally, on horseback. She was never allowed to go out alone. The country truly was not safe, lawless and crude.

But she had her own horse, and she dreamed of being free, as she had been as a girl, among the hills of California.

Her daughter, nine years old, was now in a tiny convent in the little half-deserted Spanish mining-town five miles away.

" Manuel," said the woman to her house-servant, " I'm going to ride to the convent to see Margarita, and take her a few things. Perhaps I shall stay the night in the convent. You look after Freddy and see everything is all right till I come back."

" Shall I ride with you on the master's horse, or shall Juan ? " asked the servant.

" Neither of you. I shall go alone."

The young man looked her in the eyes, in protest. Absolutely impossible that the woman should ride alone !

" I shall go alone," repeated the large, placid-seeming, fair-complexioned woman, with peculiar overbearing emphasis. And the man silently, unhappily yielded.

" Why are you going alone, mother ? " asked her son, as she made up parcels of food.

" Am I *never* to be let alone ? Not one moment of my life ? " she cried, with sudden explosion of energy. And the child, like the servant, shrank into silence.

She set off without a qualm, riding astride on her strong

roan horse, and wearing a riding suit of coarse linen, a riding
skirt over her linen breeches, a scarlet neck-tie over her white
blouse, and a black felt hat on her head. She had food in her
saddle-bags, an army canteen with water, and a large, native
blanket tied on behind the saddle. Peering into the distance,
she set off from home. Manuel and the little boy stood in
the gateway to watch her go. She did not even turn to wave
them farewell.

But when she had ridden about a mile, she left the wild
road and took a small trail to the right, that led into another
valley, over steep places and past great trees, and through
another deserted mining-settlement. It was September, the
water was running freely in the little stream that had fed the
now-abandoned mine. She got down to drink, and let the
horse drink too.

She saw natives coming through the trees, away up the
slope. They had seen her, and were watching her closely.
She watched in turn. The three people, two women and a
youth, were making a wide détour, so as not to come too
close to her. She did not care. Mounting, she trotted ahead
up the silent valley, beyond the silver-works, beyond any
trace of mining. There was still a rough trail, that led over
rocks and loose stones into the valley beyond. This trail she
had already ridden, with her husband. Beyond that she knew
she must go south.

Curiously she was not afraid, although it was a frightening
country, the silent, fatal-seeming mountain-slopes, the occasional distant, suspicious, elusive natives among the trees, the
great carrion birds occasionally hovering, like great flies, in
the distance, over some carrion or some ranch house or some
group of huts.

As she climbed, the trees shrank and the trail ran through
a thorny scrub, that was trailed over with blue convolvulus
and an occasional pink creeper. Then these flowers lapsed.
She was nearing the pine trees.

She was over the crest, and before her another silent, void,
green-clad valley. It was past midday. Her horse turned to
a little runlet of water, so she got down to eat her midday meal.
She sat in silence looking at the motionless unliving valley,
and at the sharp-peaked hills, rising higher to rock and pine
trees, southwards. She rested two hours in the heat of the
day, while the horse cropped around her.

Curious that she was neither afraid nor lonely. Indeed,
the loneliness was like a drink of cold water to one who is.

very thirsty. And a strange elation sustained her from within.

She travelled on, and camped at night in a valley beside a stream, deep among the bushes. She had seen cattle and had crossed several trails. There must be a ranch not far off. She heard the strange wailing shriek of a mountain-lion, and the answer of dogs. But she sat by her small camp fire in a secret hollow place and was not really afraid. She was buoyed up always by the curious, bubbling elation within her.

It was very cold before dawn. She lay wrapped in her blanket looking at the stars, listening to her horse shivering, and feeling like a woman who has died and passed beyond. She was not sure that she had not heard, during the night, a great crash at the centre of herself, which was the crash of her own death. Or else it was a crash at the centre of the earth, and meant something big and mysterious.

With the first peep of light she got up, numb with cold, and made a fire. She ate hastily, gave her horse some pieces of oil-seed cake, and set off again. She avoided any meeting— and since she met nobody, it was evident that she in turn was avoided. She came at last in sight of the village of Cuchitee, with its black houses with their reddish roofs, a sombre, dreary little cluster below another silent, long-abandoned mine. And beyond, a long, great mountain-side, rising up green and light to the darker, shaggier green of pine trees. And beyond the pine trees stretches of naked rock against the sky, rock slashed already and brindled with white stripes of snow. High up, the new snow had already begun to fall.

And now, as she neared, more or less, her destination, she began to go vague and disheartened. She had passed the little lake among yellowing aspen trees whose white trunks were round and suave like the white round arms of some woman. What a lovely place ! In California she would have raved about it. But here she looked and saw that it was lovely, but she didn't care. She was weary and spent with her two nights in the open, and afraid of the coming night. She didn't know where she was going, or what she was going for. Her horse plodded dejectedly on, towards that immense and forbidding mountain-slope, following a stony little trail. And if she had had any will of her own left, she would have turned back to the village, to be protected and sent home to her husband.

But she had no will of her own. Her horse splashed through a brook, and turned up a valley, under immense yellowing cotton-wood trees. She must have been near nine thousand feet above sea-level, and her head was light with the altitude and with weariness. Beyond the cotton-wood trees she could see, on each side, the steep sides of mountain-slopes hemming her in, sharp-plumaged with overlapping aspen, and, higher up, with sprouting, pointed spruce and pine tree. Her horse went on automatically. In this tight valley, on this slight trail, there was nowhere to go but ahead, climbing.

Suddenly her horse jumped, and three men in dark blankets were on the trail before her.

" Adios ! " came the greeting, in the full, restrained Indian voice.

" Adios ! " she replied, in her assured, American woman's voice.

" Where are you going ? " came the quiet question, in Spanish.

The men in the dark sarapes had come closer, and were looking up at her.

" On ahead," she replied coolly, in her hard, Saxon Spanish.

These were just natives to her : dark-faced, strongly built men in dark sarapes and straw hats. They would have been the same as the men who worked for her husband, except, strangely, for the long black hair that fell over their shoulders. She noted this long black hair with a certain distaste. These must be the wild Indians she had come to see.

" Where do you come from ? " the same man asked. It was always the one man who spoke. He was young, with quick, large, bright black eyes that glanced sideways at her. He had a soft black moustache on his dark face, and a sparse tuft of beard, loose hairs on his chin. His long black hair, full of life, hung unrestrained on his shoulders. Dark as he was, he did not look as if he had washed lately.

His two companions were the same, but older men, powerful and silent. One had a thin black line of moustache, but was beardless. The other had the smooth cheeks and the sparse dark hairs marking the lines of his chin with the beard characteristic of the Indians.

" I come from far away," she replied, with half-jocular evasion.

This was received in silence.

" But where do you live ? " asked the young man, with that same quiet insistence.

" In the north," she replied airily.

Again there was a moment's silence. The young man conversed quietly, in Indian, with his two companions.

"Where do you want to go, up this way?" he asked suddenly, with challenge and authority, pointing briefly up the trail.

"To the Chilchui Indians," answered the woman laconically.

The young man looked at her. His eyes were quick and black, and inhuman. He saw, in the full evening light, the faint sub-smile of assurance on her rather large, calm, fresh-complexioned face; the weary, bluish lines under her large blue eyes; and in her eyes, as she looked down at him, a half-childish, half-arrogant confidence in her own female power. But in her eyes, also, a curious look of trance.

"*Usted es Señora?* You are a lady?" the Indian asked her.

"Yes, I am a lady," she replied complacently.

"With a family?"

"With a husband and two children, boy and girl," she said.

The Indian turned to his companions and translated, in the low, gurgling speech, like hidden water running. They were evidently at a loss.

"Where is your husband?" asked the young man.

"Who knows?" she replied airily. "He has gone away on business for a week."

The black eyes watched her shrewdly. She, for all her weariness, smiled faintly in the pride of her own adventure and the assurance of her own womanhood, and the spell of the madness that was on her.

"And what do *you* want to do?" the Indian asked her.

"I want to visit the Chilchui Indians—to see their houses and to know their gods," she replied.

The young man turned and translated quickly, and there was a silence almost of consternation. The grave elder men were glancing at her sideways, with strange looks, from under their decorated hats. And they said something to the young man, in deep chest voices.

The latter still hesitated. Then he turned to the woman.

"Good!" he said. "Let us go. But we cannot arrive until to-morrow. We shall have to make a camp to-night."

"Good!" she said. "I can make a camp."

Without more ado, they set off at a good speed up the stony trail. The young Indian ran alongside her horse's head, the other two ran behind. One of them had taken a thick stick, and occasionally he struck her horse a resounding blow on the haunch, to urge him forward. This made the horse jump, and threw her back in the saddle, which, tired as she was, made her angry.

" Don't do that ! " she cried, looking round angrily at the fellow. She met his black, large, bright eyes, and for the first time her spirit really quailed. The man's eyes were not human to her, and they did not see her as a beautiful white woman. He looked at her with a black, bright inhuman look, and saw no woman in her at all. As if she were some strange, unaccountable *thing*, incomprehensible to him, but inimical. She sat in her saddle in wonder, feeling once more as if she had died. And again he struck her horse, and jerked her badly in the saddle.

All the passionate anger of the spoilt white woman rose in her. She pulled her horse to a standstill, and turned with blazing eyes to the man at her bridle.

" Tell that fellow not to touch my horse again," she cried.

She met the eyes of the young man, and in their bright black inscrutability she saw a fine spark, as in a snake's eye, of derision. He spoke to his companion in the rear, in the low tones of the Indian. The man with the stick listened without looking. Then, giving a strange low cry to the horse, he struck it again on the rear, so that it leaped forward spasmodically up the stony trail, scattering the stones, pitching the weary woman in her seat.

The anger flew like a madness into her eyes, she went white at the gills. Fiercely she reined in her horse. But before she could turn, the young Indian had caught the reins under the horse's throat, jerked them forward, and was trotting ahead rapidly, leading the horse.

The woman was powerless. And along with her supreme anger there came a slight thrill of exultation. She knew she was dead.

The sun was setting, a great yellow light flooded the last of the aspens, flared on the trunks of the pine trees, the pineneedles bristled and stood out with dark lustre, the rocks glowed with unearthly glamour. And through this effulgence the Indian at her horse's head trotted unweariedly on, his dark blanket swinging, his bare legs glowing with a strange transfigured ruddiness in the powerful light, and his straw hat with its half-absurd decorations of flowers and feathers shining showily above his river of long black hair. At times he would utter a low call to the horse, and then the other Indian, behind, would fetch the beast a whack with the stick.

The wonder-light faded off the mountains, the world began to grow dark, a cold air breathed down. In the sky, half a moon was struggling against the glow in the west. Huge shadows came down from steep rocky slopes. Water was rushing. The woman was conscious only of her fatigue, her unspeakable fatigue, and the cold wind from the heights. She was not aware how moonlight replaced daylight. It happened while she travelled, unconscious with weariness.

For some hours they travelled by moonlight. Then suddenly they came to a standstill. The men conversed in low tones for a moment.

"We camp here," said the young man.

She waited for him to help her down. He merely stood holding the horse's bridle. She almost fell from the saddle, so fatigued.

They had chosen a place at the foot of rocks that still gave off a little warmth of the sun. One man cut pine-boughs, another erected little screens of pine-boughs against the rock for shelter, and put boughs of balsam pine for beds. The third made a small fire, to heat tortillas. They worked in silence.

The woman drank water. She did not want to eat—only to lie down.

"Where do I sleep?" she asked.

The young man pointed to one of the shelters. She crept in and lay inert. She did not care what happened to her, she was so weary, and so beyond everything. Through the twigs of spruce she could see the three men squatting round the fire on their hams, chewing the tortillas they picked from the ashes with their dark fingers, and drinking water from a gourd. They talked in low, muttering tones, with long intervals of silence. Her saddle and saddle-bags lay not far from the fire, unopened, untouched. The men were not interested in her nor her belongings. There they squatted with their hats on their heads, eating, eating mechanically, like animals, the dark sarape with its fringe falling to the ground before and behind, the powerful dark legs naked and squatting like an animal's, showing the dirty white shirt and the sort of loin-cloth which was the only other garment, underneath. And they showed no more sign of interest in her than if she had been a piece of venison they were bringing home from the hunt, and had hung inside a shelter.

After a while they carefully extinguished the fire, and went inside their own shelter. Watching through the screen of boughs, she had a moment's thrill of fear and anxiety, seeing the dark forms cross and pass silently in the moonlight. Would they attack her now ?

But no ! They were as if oblivious of her. Her horse was hobbled ; she could hear it hopping wearily. All was silent, mountain-silent, cold, deathly. She slept and woke and slept in a semi-conscious numbness of cold and fatigue. A long, long night, icy and eternal, and she aware that she had died.

II

YET when there was a stirring, and a clink of flint and steel, and the form of a man crouching like a dog over a bone at a red splutter of fire, and she knew it was morning coming, it seemed to her the night had passed too soon.

When the fire was going, she came out of her shelter with one real desire left : for coffee. The men were warming more tortillas.

" Can we make coffee ? " she asked.

The young man looked at her, and she imagined the same faint spark of derision in his eyes. He shook his head.

" We don't take it," he said. " There is no time."

And the elder men, squatting on their haunches, looked up at her in the terrible paling dawn, and there was not even derision in their eyes. Only that intense, yet remote, inhuman glitter which was terrible to her. They were inaccessible. They could not see her as a woman at all. As if she *were* not a woman. As if, perhaps, her whiteness took away all her womanhood, and left her as some giant, female white ant. That was all they could see in her.

Before the sun was up, she was in the saddle again, and they were climbing steeply in the icy air. The sun came, and soon she was very hot, exposed to the glare in the bare places. It seemed to her they were climbing to the roof of the world. Beyond against heaven were slashes of snow.

During the course of the morning, they came to a place where the horse could not go farther. They rested for a time with a great slant of living rock in front of them, like the glossy breast of some earth-beast. Across this rock, along a wavering crack, they had to go. It seemed to her that for hours she went in torment, on her hands and knees, from crack to crevice, along the slanting face of this pure rock-mountain.

An Indian in front and an Indian behind walked slowly erect, shod with sandals of braided leather. But she in her riding-boots dared not stand erect.

Yet what she wondered, all the time, was why she per-sisted in clinging and crawling along these mile-long sheets of rock. Why she did not hurl herself down, and have done! The world was below her.

When they emerged at last on a stony slope, she looked back, and saw the third Indian coming carrying her saddle and saddle-bags on his back, the whole hung from a band across his forehead. And he had his hat in his hand, as he stepped slowly, with the slow, soft, heavy tread of the Indian, unwavering in the chinks of rock, as if along a scratch in the mountain's iron shield.

The stony slope led downwards. The Indians seemed to grow excited. One ran ahead at a slow trot, disappearing round the curve of stones. And the track curved round and down, till at last in the full blaze of the mid-morning sun, they could see a valley below them, between walls of rock, as in a great wide chasm let in the mountains. A green valley, with a river, and trees, and clusters of low flat sparkling houses. It was all tiny and perfect, three thousand feet below. Even the flat bridge over the stream, and the square with the houses around it, the bigger buildings piled up at opposite ends of the square, the tall cotton-wood trees, the pastures and stretches of yellow-sere maize, the patches of brown sheep or goats in the distance, on the slopes, the railed enclosures by the stream-side. There it was, all small and perfect, looking magical, as any place will look magical, seen from the mountains above. The unusual thing was that the low houses glittered white, whitewashed, looking like crystals of salt, or silver. This frightened her.

They began the long, winding descent at the head of the barranca, following the stream that rushed and fell. At first it was all rocks : then the pine trees began, and soon, the silver-limbed aspens. The flowers of autumn, big pink daisy-like flowers, and white ones, and many yellow flowers, were in profusion. But she had to sit down and rest, she was so weary. And she saw the bright flowers shadowily, as pale shadows hovering, as one who is dead must see them.

At length came grass and pasture-slopes between mingled aspen and pine trees. A shepherd, naked in the sun save for his hat and his cotton loin-cloth, was driving his brown sheep away. In a grove of trees they sat and waited, she and the young Indian. The one with the saddle had also gone forward.

They heard a sound of some one coming. It was three men, in fine sarapes of red and orange and yellow and black, and with brilliant feather head-dresses. The oldest had his grey hair braided with fur, and his red and orange-yellow sarape was covered with curious black markings, like a leopard-skin. The other two were not grey-haired, but they were elders too. Their blankets were in stripes, and their head-dresses not so elaborate.

The young Indian addressed the elders in a few quiet words. They listened without answering or looking at him or at the woman, keeping their faces averted and their eyes turned to the ground, only listening. And at length they turned and looked at the woman.

The old chief, or medicine-man, whatever he was, had a deeply wrinkled and lined face of dark bronze, with a few sparse grey hairs round' the mouth. Two long braids of grey hair, braided with fur and coloured feathers, hung on his shoulders. And yet, it was only his eyes that mattered. They were black and of extraordinary piercing strength, without a qualm of misgiving in their demonish, dauntless power. He looked into the eyes of the white woman with a long, piercing look, seeking she knew not what. She summoned all her strength to meet his eyes and keep up her guard. But it was no good. He was not looking at her as one human being looks at another. He never even perceived her resistance or her challenge, but looked past them both, into she knew not what.

She could see it was hopeless to expect any human communication with this old being.

He turned and said a few words to the young Indian.

" He asks what do you seek here ? " said the young man in Spanish.

" I ? Nothing ! I only came to see what it was like."

This was again translated, and the old man turned his eyes on her once more. Then he spoke again, in his low muttering tone, to the young Indian.

" He says, why does she leave her house with the white men ? Does she want to bring the white man's God to the Chilchui ? "

" No," she replied, foolhardy. " I came away from the white man's God myself. I came to look for the god of the Chilchui."

Profound silence followed, when this was translated. Then the old man spoke again, in a small voice almost of weariness.

" Does the white woman seek the gods of the Chilchui because she is weary of her own God ? " came the question.

" Yes, she does. She is tired of the white man's God," she replied, thinking that was what they wanted her to say. She would like to serve the gods of the Chilchui.

She was aware of an extraordinary thrill of triumph and exultance passing through the Indians, in the tense silence that followed when this was translated. Then they all looked at her with piercing black eyes, in which a steely covetous intent glittered incomprehensible. She was the more puzzled, as there was nothing sensual or sexual in the look. It had a terrible glittering purity that was beyond her. She was afraid, she would have been paralysed with fear, had not something died within her, leaving her with a cold, watchful wonder only.

The elders talked a little while, then the two went away, leaving her with the young man and the oldest chief. The old man now looked at her with a certain solicitude.

" He says are you tired ? " asked the young man.

" Very tired," she said.

" The men will bring you a carriage," said the young Indian.

The carriage, when it came, proved to be a litter consisting of a sort of hammock of dark woollen frieze, slung on to a pole which was borne on the shoulders of two long-haired Indians. The woollen hammock was spread on the ground, she sat down on it, and the two men raised the pole to their shoulders. Swinging rather as if she were in a sack, she was carried out of the grove of trees, following the old chief, whose leopard-spotted blanket moved curiously in the sunlight.

They had emerged in the valley-head. Just in front were the maize fields, with ripe ears of maize. The corn was not very tall, in this high altitude. The well-worn path went between it, and all she could see was the erect form of the old chief, in the flame and black sarape, stepping soft and heavy and swift, his head forward, looking to neither right nor left. Her bearers followed, stepping rhythmically, the long blue-black hair glistening like a river down the naked shoulders of the man in front.

They passed the maize, and came to a big wall or earthwork made of earth and adobe bricks. The wooden doors were open. Passing on, they were in a network of small gardens, full of flowers and herbs and fruit trees, each garden watered by a tiny ditch of running water. Among each cluster of trees and flowers was a small, glittering white house, windowless, and with closed door. The place was a network of little paths, small streams, and little bridges among square, flowering gardens.

Following the broadest path—a soft narrow track between leaves and grass, a path worn smooth by centuries of human feet, no hoof of horse nor any wheel to disfigure it—they came to the little river of swift bright water, and crossed on a log bridge. Everything was silent—there was not human being anywhere. The road went on under magnificent cottonwood trees. It emerged suddenly outside the central plaza or square of the village.

This was a long oblong of low white houses with flat roofs, and two bigger buildings, having as it were little square huts piled on top of bigger long huts, stood at either end of the oblong, facing each other rather askew. Every little house was a dazzling white, save for the great round beam-ends which projected under the flat eaves, and for the flat roofs. Round each of the bigger buildings, on the outside of the square, was a stockyard fence, inside which was garden with trees and flowers, and various small houses.

Not a soul was in sight. They passed silently between the houses into the central square. This was quite bare and arid, the earth trodden smooth by endless generations of passing feet, passing across from door to door. All the doors of the windowless houses gave on to this blank square, but all the doors were closed. The firewood lay near the threshold, a clay oven was still smoking, but there was no sign of moving life.

The old man walked straight across the square to the big house at the end, where the two upper stories, as in a house of toy bricks, stood each one smaller than the lower one. A stone staircase, outside, led up to the roof of the first story.

At the foot of this staircase the litter-bearers stood still, and lowered the woman to the ground.

"You will come up," said the young Indian who spoke Spanish.

She mounted the stone stairs to the earthen roof of the first house, which formed a platform round the wall of the second story. She followed around this platform to the back of the big house. There they descended again, into the garden at the rear.

So far they had seen no one. But now two men appeared, bare-headed, with long braided hair, and wearing a sort of white shirt gathered into a loin-cloth. These went along with the three newcomers, across the garden where red flowers and yellow flowers were blooming, to a long, low white house. There they entered without knocking.

It was dark inside. There was a low murmur of men's voices. Several men were present, their white shirts showing in the gloom, their dark faces invisible. They were sitting on a great log of smooth old wood, that lay along the far wall. And save for this log, the room seemed empty. But no, in the dark at one end was a couch, a sort of bed, and some one lying there, covered with furs.

The old Indian in the spotted sarape, who had accompanied the woman, now took off his hat and his blanket and his sandals. Laying them aside, he approached the couch, and spoke in a low voice. For some moments there was no answer. Then an old man with the snow-white hair hanging round his darkly visible face, roused himself like a vision, and leaned on one elbow, looking vaguely at the company, in tense silence.

The grey-haired Indian spoke again, and then the young Indian, taking the woman's hand, led her forward. In her linen riding habit, and black boots and hat, and her pathetic bit of a red tie, she stood there beside the fur-covered bed of the old, old man, who sat reared up, leaning on one elbow, remote as a ghost, his white hair streaming in disorder, his face almost black, yet with a far-off intentness, not of this world, leaning forward to look at her.

His face was so old, it was like dark glass, and the few curling hairs that sprang white from his lips and chin were quite incredible. The long white locks fell unbraided and disorderly on either side of the glassy dark face. And under a faint powder of white eyebrows, the black eyes of the old chief looked at her as if from the far, far dead, seeing something that was never to be seen.

At last he spoke a few deep, hollow words, as if to the dark air.

" He says, do you bring your heart to the god of the Chilchui ? " translated the young Indian.

" Tell him yes," she said automatically.

There was a pause. The old Indian spoke again, as if to the air. One of the men present went out. There was a silence as if of eternity, in the dim room that was lighted only through the open door.

The woman looked round. Four old men with grey hair sat on the log by the wall facing the door. Two other men, powerful and impassive, stood near the door. They all had long hair, and wore white shirts gathered into a loin-cloth. Their powerful legs were naked and dark. There was a silence like eternity.

At length the man returned, with white and dark clothing on his arm. The young Indian took them, and holding them in front of the woman, said :

" You must take off your clothes, and put these on."

" If all you men will go out," she said.

" No one will hurt you," he said quietly.

" Not while you men are here," she said.

He looked at the two men by the door. They came quickly forward, and suddenly gripped her arms as she stood, without hurting her, but with great power. Then two of the old men came, and with curious skill slit her boots down with keen knives, and drew them off, and slit her clothing so that it came away from her. In a few moments she stood there white and uncovered. The old man on the bed spoke, and they turned her round for him to see. He spoke again, and the young Indian deftly took the pins and comb from her fair hair, so that it fell over her shoulders in a bunchy tangle.

Then the old man spoke again. The Indian led her to the bedside. The white-haired, glassy-dark old man moistened his finger-tips at his mouth, and most delicately touched her on the breasts and on the body, then on the back. And she winced strangely each time, as the finger-tips drew along her skin, as if Death itself were touching her.

And she wondered, almost sadly, why she did not feel shamed in her nakedness. She only felt sad and lost. Because nobody felt ashamed. The elder men were all dark and tense with some other deep, gloomy, incomprehensible emotion, which suspended all her agitation, while the young Indian had a strange look of ecstasy on his face. And she, she was only utterly strange and beyond herself, as if her body were not her own.

They gave her the new clothing : a long white cotton shift, that came to her knees : then a tunic of thick blue woollen stuff, embroidered with scarlet and green flowers. It was fastened over one shoulder only, and belted with a braid sash of scarlet and black wool.

When she was thus dressed, they took her away, barefoot, to a little house in the stockaded garden. The young Indian told her she might have what she wanted. She asked for water to wash herself. He brought it in a jar, together with a long wooden bowl. Then he fastened the gate-door of her house, and left her a prisoner. She could see through the bars of the gate-door of her house, the red flowers of the garden, and a humming-bird. Then from the roof of the big house she heard the long, heavy sound of a drum, unearthly to her in its summons, and an uplifted voice calling from the house-top in a strange language, with a far-away emotionless intonation, delivering some speech or message. And she listened as if from the dead.

But she was very tired. She lay down on a couch of skins, pulling over her the blanket of dark wool, and she slept, giving up everything.

When she woke it was late afternoon, and the young Indian was entering with a basket-tray containing food, tortillas and corn-mush with bits of meat, probably mutton, and a drink made of honey, and some fresh plums. He brought her also a long garland of red and yellow flowers with knots of blue buds at the end. He sprinkled the garland with water from a jar, then offered it to her, with a smile. He seemed very gentle and thoughtful, and on his face and in his dark eyes was a curious look of triumph and ecstasy, that frightened her a little. The glitter had gone from the black eyes, with their curving dark lashes, and he would look at her with this strange soft glow of ecstasy that was not quite human, and terribly impersonal, and which made her uneasy.

" Is there anything you want ? " he said, in his low, slow, melodious voice, that always seemed withheld, as if he were speaking aside to somebody else, or as if he did not want to let the sound come out to her.

" Am I going to be kept a prisoner here ? " she asked.

" No, you can walk in the garden to-morrow," he said softly. Always this curious solicitude.

" Do you like that drink ? " he said, offering her a little earthenware cup. " It is very refreshing."

She sipped the liquor curiously. It was made with herbs and sweetened with honey, and had a strange, lingering flavour. The young man watched her with gratification.

" It has a peculiar taste," she said.

" It is very refreshing," he replied, his black eyes resting on her always with that look of gratified ecstasy. Then he went away. And presently she began to be sick, and to vomit violently, as if she had no control over herself.

Afterwards she felt a great soothing languor steal over her, her limbs felt strong and loose and full of languor, and she lay on her couch listening to the sounds of the village, watching the yellowing sky, smelling the scent of burning cedar-wood or pine-wood. So distinctly she heard the yapping of tiny dogs, the shuffle of far-off feet, the murmur of voices, so keenly she detected the smell of smoke, and flowers, and evening falling, so vividly she saw the one bright star, infinitely remote, stirring above the sunset, that she felt as if all her senses were diffused on the air, that she could distinguish the sound of evening flowers unfolding, and the actual crystal sound of the heavens, as the vast belts of the world-atmosphere slid past one another, and as if the moisture ascending and the moisture descending in the air resounded like some harp in the cosmos.

She was a prisoner in her house and in the stockaded garden, but she scarcely minded. And it was days before she realized that she never saw another woman. Only the men, the elderly men of the big house, that she imagined must be some sort of temple, and the men priests of some sort. For they always had the same colours, red, orange, yellow, and black, and the same grave, abstracted demeanour.

Sometimes an old man would come and sit in her room with her, in absolute silence. None spoke any language but Indian, save the one younger man. The older men would smile at her, and sit with her for an hour at a time, sometimes smiling at her when she spoke in Spanish, but never answering save with this slow, benevolent-seeming smile. And they gave off a feeling of almost fatherly solicitude. Yet their dark eyes, brooding over her, had something away in their depths that was awesomely ferocious and relentless. They would cover it with a smile, at once, if they felt her looking. But she had seen it.

Always they treated her with this curious impersonal solicitude, this utterly impersonal gentleness, as an old man treats a child. But underneath it she felt there was something else, something terrible. When her old visitor had gone away, in his silent, insidious, fatherly fashion, a shock of fear would come over her ; though of what she knew not.

The young Indian would sit and talk with her freely, as if with great candour. But with him, too, she felt that everything real was unsaid. Perhaps it was unspeakable. His big dark eyes would rest on her almost cherishingly, touched with ecstasy, and his beautiful, slow, languorous voice would trail out its simple, ungrammatical Spanish. He told her he was the grandson of the old, old man, son of the man in the spotted sarape : and they were caciques, kings from the old, old days, before even the Spaniards came. But he himself had been in Mexico City, and also in the United States. He had worked as a labourer, building the roads in Los Angeles. He had travelled as far as Chicago.

" Don't you speak English, then ? " she asked.

His eyes rested on her with a curious look of duplicity and conflict, and he mutely shook his head.

" What did you do with your long hair, when you were in the United States ? " she asked. " Did you cut it off ? "

Again, with the look of torment in his eyes, he shook his head.

" No," he said, in a low, subdued voice, " I wore a hat, and a handkerchief tied round my head."

And he relapsed into silence, as if of tormented memories.

" Are you the only man of your people who has been to the United States ? " she asked him.

" Yes. I am the only one who has been away from here for a long time. The others come back soon, in one week. They don't stay away. The old men don't let them"

" And why did you go ? "

" The old men want me to go—because I shall be the Cacique——"

He talked always with the same naiveté, an almost childish candour. But she felt that this was perhaps just the effect of his Spanish. Or perhaps speech altogether was unreal to him. Anyhow, she felt that all the real things were kept back.

He came and sat with her a good deal—sometimes more than she wished—as if he wanted to be near her. She asked him if he was married. He said he was—with two children.

" I should like to see your children," she said.

But he answered only with that smile, a sweet, almost ecstatic smile, above which the dark eyes hardly changed from their enigmatic abstraction.

It was curious, he would sit with her by the hour, without ever making her self-conscious, or sex-conscious. He seemed to have no sex, as he sat there so still and gentle and apparently submissive, with his head bent a little forward, and the river of glistening black hair streaming maidenly over his shoulders.

Yet when she looked again, she saw his shoulders broad

and powerful, his eyebrows black and level, the short, curved, obstinate black lashes over his lowered eyes, the small, fur-like line of moustache above his blackish, heavy lips, and the strong chin, and she knew that in some other mysterious way he was darkly and powerfully male. And he, feeling her watching him, would glance up at her swiftly with a dark, lurking look in his eyes, which immediately he veiled with that half-sad smile.

The days and the weeks went by, in a vague kind of contentment. She was uneasy sometimes, feeling she had lost the power over herself. She was not in her own power, she was under the spell of some other control. And at times she had moments of terror and horror. But then these Indians would come and sit with her, casting their insidious spell over her by their very silent presence, their silent, sexless, powerful physical presence. As they sat they seemed to take her will away, leaving her will-less and victim to her own indifference. And the young man would bring her sweetened drink, often the same emetic drink, but sometimes other kinds. And after drinking, the languor filled her heavy limbs, her senses seemed to float in the air, listening, hearing. They had brought her a little female dog, which she called Flora. And once, in the trance of her senses, she felt she *heard* the little dog conceive, in her tiny womb, and begin to be complex, with young. And another day she could hear the vast sound of the earth going round, like some immense arrow-string booming.

But as the days grew shorter and colder, when she was cold, she would get a sudden revival of her will, and a desire to go out, to go away. And she insisted to the young man, she wanted to go out.

So one day, they let her climb to the topmost roof of the big house where she was, and look down the square. It was the day of the big dance, but not everybody was dancing. Women with babies in their arms stood in their doorways, watching. Opposite, at the other end of the square, there was a throng before the other big house, and a small, brilliant group on the terrace-roof of the first story, in front of wide open doors of the upper story. Through these wide open doors she could see fire glinting in darkness and priests in headdresses of black and yellow and scarlet feathers, wearing robe-like blankets of black and red and yellow, with long green fringe, were moving about. A big drum was beating slowly and regularly, in the dense, Indian silence. The crowd below waited—

Then a drum started on a high beat, and there came the deep, powerful burst of men singing a heavy, savage music, like a wind roaring in some timeless forest, many mature men singing in one breath, like the wind ; and long lines of dancers walked out from under the big house. Men with naked, golden-bronze bodies and streaming black hair, tufts of red and yellow feathers on their arms, and kilts of white frieze with a bar of heavy red and black and green embroidery round their waists, bending slightly forward and stamping the the earth in their absorbed, monotonous stamp of the dance, a fox-fur, hung by the nose from their belt behind, swaying with the sumptuous swaying of a beautiful fox-fur, the tip of the tail writhing above the dancer's heels. And after each man, a woman with a strange elaborate head-dress of feathers and sea-shells, and wearing a short black tunic, moving erect, holding up tufts of feathers in each hand, swaying her wrists rhythmically and subtly beating the earth with her bare feet.

So, the long line of the dance unfurling from the big house opposite. And from the big house beneath her, strange scent of incense, strange tense silence, then the answering burst of inhuman male singing, and the long line of the dance unfurling.

It went on all day, the insistence of the drum, the cavernous, roaring, storm-like sound of male singing, the incessant swinging of the fox-skins behind the powerful, gold-bronze, stamping legs of the men, the autumn sun from a perfect blue heaven pouring on the rivers of black hair, men's and women's, the valley all still, the walls of rock beyond, the awful huge bulking of the mountain against the pure sky, its snow seething with sheer whiteness.

For hours and hours she watched, spell-bound, and as if drugged. And in all the terrible persistence of the drumming and the primeval, rushing deep singing, and the endless stamping of the dance of fox-tailed men, the tread of heavy, bird-erect women in their black tunics, she seemed at last to feel her own death ; her own obliteration. As if she were to be obliterated from the field of life again. In the strange towering symbols on the heads of the changeless, absorbed women she seemed to read once more the *Mene Mene Tekel Upharsin*. Her kind of womanhood, intensely personal and individual, was to be obliterated again, and the great primeval symbols were to tower once more over the fallen individual independence of woman. The sharpness and the quivering nervous consciousness of the highly bred white woman was to be destroyed again, womanhood was to be cast once more into the great stream of impersonal sex and impersonal passion. Strangely, as if clairvoyant, she saw the immense sacrifice prepared. And she went back to her little house in a trance of agony.

After this, there was always a certain agony when she heard the drums at evening, and the strange uplifted savage sound of men singing round the drum, like wild creatures howling to the invisible gods of the moon and the vanished sun. Something of the chuckling, sobbing cry of the coyote, something of the exultant bark of the fox, the far-off wild melancholy exultance of the howling wolf, the torment of the puma's scream, and the insistence of the ancient fierce human male, with his lapses of tenderness and his abiding ferocity.

Sometimes she would climb the high roof after nightfall, and listen to the dim cluster of young men round the drum on the bridge just beyond the square, singing by the hour. Sometimes there would be a fire, and in the fire-glow, men in their white shirts or naked save for a loin-cloth, would be dancing and stamping like spectres, hour after hour in the dark cold air, within the fire-glow, forever dancing and stamping like turkeys, or dropping squatting by the fire to rest, throwing their blankets round them.

" Why do you all have the same colours ? " she asked the young Indian. " Why do you all have red and yellow and black, over your white shirts ? And the women have black tunics ? "

He looked into her eyes, curiously, and the faint, evasive smile came on to his face. Behind the smile lay a soft, strange malignancy.

"Because our men are the fire and the daytime, and our women are the spaces between the stars at night," he said.

" Aren't the women even stars ? " she said.

" No. We say they are the spaces between the stars, that keep the stars apart."

He looked at her oddly, and again the touch of derision came into his eyes.

" White people," he said, " they know nothing. They are like children, always with toys. We know the sun, and we know the moon. And we say, when a white woman sacrifice herself to our gods, then our gods will begin to make the world again, and the white man's gods will fall to pieces."

" How sacrifice herself ? " she asked quickly.

And he, as quickly covered, covered himself with a subtle smile.

" She sacrifice her own gods and come to our gods, I mean that," he said soothingly.

But she was not reassured. An icy pang of fear and certainty was at her heart.

" The sun he is alive at one end of the sky," he continued, " and the moon lives at the other end. And the man all the time have to keep the sun happy in his side of the sky, and the woman have to keep the moon quiet at her side of the sky. All the time she have to work at this. And the sun can't ever go into the house of the moon, and the moon can't ever go into the house of the sun, in the sky. So the woman, she asks the moon to come into her cave, inside her. And the man, he draws the sun down till he has the power of the sun. All the time he do this. Then when the man gets a woman, the sun goes into the cave of the moon, and that is how everything in the world starts."

She listened, watching him closely, as one enemy watches another who is speaking with double meaning.

" Then," she said, " why aren't you Indians masters of the white men ? "

" Because," he said, " the Indian got weak, and lost his power with the sun, so the white men stole the sun. But they can't keep him—they don't know how. They got him, but they don't know what to do with him, like a boy who catch a big grizzly bear, and can't kill him, and can't run away from him. The grizzly bear eats the boy that catch him, when he want to run away from him. White men don't know what they are doing with the sun, and white women don't know what they do with the moon. The moon she got angry with white women, like a puma when someone kills her little ones. The moon, she bites white women—here inside," and he pressed his side. " The moon, she is angry in a white woman's cave. The Indian can see it—And soon," he added, " the Indian women get the moon back and keep her quiet in their house. And the Indian men get the sun, and the power over all the world. White men don't know what the sun is. They never know."

He subsided into a curious exultant silence.

" But," she faltered, " why do you hate us so ? Why do you hate me ? "

He looked up suddenly with a light on his face, and a startling flame of a smile.

" No, we don't hate," he said softly, looking with a curious glitter into her face.

" You do," she said, forlorn and hopeless.
And after a moment's silence, he rose and went away.

III

WINTER had now come, in the high valley, with snow that melted in the day's sun, and nights that were bitter cold. She lived on, in a kind of daze, feeling her power ebbing more and more away from her, as if her will were leaving her. She felt always in the same relaxed, confused, victimised state, unless the sweetened herb drink would numb her mind altogether, and release her senses into a sort of heightened, mystic acuteness and a feeling as if she were diffusing out deliciously into the harmony of things. This at length became the only state of consciousness she really recognized : this exquisite sense of bleeding out into the higher beauty and harmony of things. Then she could actually hear the great stars in heaven, which she saw through her door, speaking from their motion and brightness, saying things perfectly to the cosmos, as they trod in perfect ripples, like bells on the floor of heaven, passing one another and grouping in the timeless dance, with the spaces of dark between. And she could hear the snow on a cold, cloudy day twittering and faintly whistling in the sky, like birds that flock and fly away in autumn, suddenly calling farewell to the invisible moon, and slipping out of the plains of the air, releasing peaceful warmth. She herself would call to the arrested snow to fall from the upper air. She would call to the unseen moon to cease to be angry, to make peace again with the unseen sun like a woman who ceases to be angry in her house. And she would smell the sweetness of the moon relaxing to the sun in the wintry heaven, when the snow fell in a faint, cold-perfumed relaxation, as the peace of the sun mingled again in a sort of unison with the peace of the moon.

She was aware too of the sort of shadow that was on the Indians of the valley, a deep, stoical disconsolation, almost religious in its depth.

" We have lost our power over the sun, and we are trying to get him back. But he is wild with us, and shy like a horse that has got away. We have to go through a lot." So the young Indian said to her, looking into her eyes with a strained meaning. And she, as if bewitched, replied :

" I hope you will get him back."

The smile of triumph flew over his face.

" Do you hope it ? " he said.

" I do," she answered fatally.

" Then all right," he said. " We shall get him."

And he went away in exultance.

She felt she was drifting on some consummation, which she had no will to avoid, yet which seemed heavy and finally terrible to her.

It must have been almost December, for the days were short, when she was taken again before the aged man, and stripped of her clothing, and touched with the old finger-tips.

The aged cacique looked her in the eyes, with his eyes of lonely, far-off, black intentness, and murmured something to her.

" He wants you to make the sign of peace," the young man translated, showing her the gesture. " Peace and farewell to him."

She was fascinated by the black, glass-like, intent eyes of the old cacique, that watched her without blinking, like a basilisk's, overpowering her. In their depths also she saw a certain fatherly compassion, and pleading. She put her hand before her face, in the required manner, making the sign of peace and farewell. He made the sign of peace back again to her, then sank among his furs. She thought he was going to die, and that he knew it.

There followed a day of ceremonial, when she was brought out before all the people, in a blue blanket with white fringe, and holding blue feathers in her hands. Before an altar of one house, she was perfumed with incense and sprinkled with ash. Before the altar of the opposite house she was fumigated again with incense by the gorgeous, terrifying priests in yellow and scarlet and black, their faces painted with scarlet paint. And then they threw water on her. *Meanwhile she was faintly aware of the fire on the altar, the heavy, heavy sound of a drum, the heavy sound of men beginning powerfully, deeply, savagely to sing, the swaying of the crowd of faces in the plaza below, and the formation for a sacred dance.

But at this time her commonplace consciousness was numb, she was aware of her immediate surroundings as shadows, almost immaterial. With refined and heightened senses she could hear the sound of the earth winging on its journey, like a shot arrow, the ripple-rustling of the air, and the boom of the great arrow-string. And it seemed to her there were two great influences in the upper air, one golden towards the sun, and one invisible silver ; the first travelling like rain ascending to the gold presence sunwards, the second like rain silverily descending the ladders of space towards the hovering, lurking clouds over the snowy mountain-top. Then between them, another presence, waiting to shake himself free of moisture, of heavy white snow that had mysteriously collected about him. And in summer, like a scorched eagle, he would wait to shake himself clear of the weight of heavy sunbeams. And he was coloured like fire. And he was always shaking himself clear, of snow or of heavy heat, like an eagle rustling.

Then there was a still stranger presence, standing watching from the blue distance, always watching. Sometimes running in upon the wind, or shimmering in the heat-waves. The blue wind itself, rushing as it were out of the holes in the earth into the sky, rushing out of the sky down upon the earth. The blue wind, the go-between, the invisible ghost that belonged to two worlds, that played upon the ascending and the descending chords of the rains.

More and more her ordinary personal consciousness had left her, she had gone into that other state of passional cosmic consciousness, like one who is drugged. The Indians, with their heavily religious natures, had made her succumb to their vision.

Only one personal question she asked the young Indian :
" Why am I the only one that wears blue ? "
" It is the colour of the wind. It is the colour of what goes away and is never coming back, but which is always here, waiting like death among us. It is the colour of the dead. And it is the colour that stands away off, looking at us from the distance, that cannot come near to us. When we go near, it goes farther. It can't be near. We are all brown and yellow and black hair, and white teeth and red blood. We are the ones that are here. You with blue eyes, you are the messengers from the far-away, you cannot stay, and now it is time for you to go back."
" Where to ? " she asked.
" To the way-off things like the sun and the blue mother of rain, and tell them that we are the people on the world again, and we can bring the sun to the moon again, like a red horse to a blue mare ; we are the people. The white women have driven back the moon in the sky, won't let her come to the sun. So the sun is angry. And the Indian must give the moon to the sun."
" How ? " she said.
" The white woman got to die and go like a wind to the

sun, tell him the Indians will open the gate to him. And the Indian women will open the gate to the moon. The white women don't let the moon come down out of the blue coral. The moon used to come down among the Indian women, like a white goat among the flowers. And the sun want to come down to the Indian men, like an eagle to the pine-trees. The sun, he is shut out behind the white man, and the moon she is shut out behind the white woman, and they can't get away. They are angry, everything in the world gets angrier. The Indian says, he will give the white woman to the sun, so the sun will leap over the white man and come to the Indian again. And the moon will be surprised, she will see the gate open, and she not know which way to go. But the Indian woman will call to the moon, *Come! Come! Come back into my grasslands. The wicked white woman can't harm you any more.* Then the sun will look over the heads of the white men, and see the moon in the pastures of our women, with the Red Men standing around like pine-trees. Then he will leap over the heads of the white men, and come running past to the Indians through the spruce-trees. And we, who are red and black and yellow, we who stay, we shall have the sun on our right hand and the moon on our left. So we can bring the rain down out of the blue meadows, and up out of the black ; and we can call the wind that tells the corn to grow, when we ask him, and we shall make the clouds to break, and the sheep to have twin lambs. And we shall be full of power, like a spring day. But the white people will be a hard winter, without snow——"

" But," said the white woman, " I don't shut out the moon —how can I ? "

" Yes," he said, " you shut the gate, and then laugh, think you have it all your own way."

She could never quite understand the way he looked at her. He was always so curiously gentle, and his smile was so soft. Yet there was such a glitter in his eyes, and an unrelenting sort of hate came out of his words, a strange, profound, impersonal hate. Personally he liked her, she was sure. He was gentle with her, attracted by her in some strange,-soft, passionless way. But impersonally he hated her with a mystic hatred. He would smile at her, winningly. Yet if, the next moment, she glanced round at him unawares, she would catch that gleam of pure after-hate in his eyes.

" Have I got to die and be given to the sun ? " she asked.

" Sometime," he said, laughing evasively. " Sometime we all die."

They were gentle with her, and very considerate with her. Strange men, the old priests and the young cacique alike, they watched over her and cared for her like women. In their soft, insidious understanding, there was something womanly. Yet their eyes, with that strange glitter, and their dark, shut mouths that would open to the broad jaw, the small, strong, white teeth, had something very primitively male and cruel.

One wintry day, when snow was falling, they took her to a great dark chamber in the big house. The fire was burning in a corner on a high raised dais under a sort of hood or canopy of adobe-work. She saw in the fire-glow the glowing bodies of the almost naked priests, and strange symbols on the roof and walls of the chamber. There was no door or window in the chamber, they had descended by a ladder from the roof. And the fire of pinewood danced continually, showing walls painted with strange devices, which she could not understand, and a ceiling of poles making a curious pattern of black and red and yellow, and alcoves or niches in which were curious objects she could not discern.

The older priests were going through some ceremony near the fire, in silence, intense Indian silence. She was seated on a low projection of the wall, opposite the fire, two men seated beside her. Presently they gave her a drink from a cup, which she took gladly, because of the semi-trance it would induce.

In the darkness and in the silence she was accurately aware of everything that happened to her : how they took off her clothes, and, standing her before a great, weird device on the wall, coloured blue and white and black, washed her all over with water and the amole infusion ; washed even her hair, softly, carefully, and dried it on white cloths, till it was soft and glistening. Then they laid her on a couch under another great indecipherable image of red and black and yellow, and now rubbed all her body with sweet-scented oil, and massaged all her limbs, and her back, and her sides, with a long, strange, hypnotic massage. Their dark hands were incredibly powerful, yet soft with a watery softness she could not understand. And the dark faces, leaning near her white body, she saw were darkened with red pigment, with lines of yellow round the cheeks. And the dark eyes glittered absorbed, as the hands worked upon the soft white body of the woman.

They were so impersonal, absorbed in something that was beyond her. They never saw her as a personal woman : she could tell that. She was some mystic object to them, some vehicle of passions too remote for her to grasp. Herself in a state of trance, she watched their faces bending over her, dark, strangely glistening with the transparent red paint, and lined with bars of yellow. And in this weird, luminous-dark mask of living face, the eyes were fixed with an unchanging steadfast gleam, and the purplish-pigmented lips were closed in a full, sinister, sad grimness. The immense fundamental sadness, the grimness of ultimate decision, the fixity of revenge, and the nascent exultance of those that are going to triumph— these things she could read in their faces, as she lay and was rubbed into a misty glow, by their uncanny dark hands. Her limbs, her flesh, her very bones at last seemed to be diffusing into a roseate sort of mist, in which her consciousness hovered like some sun-gleam in a flushed cloud.

She knew the gleam would fade, the cloud would go grey. But at present she did not believe it. She knew she was a victim ; that all this elaborate work upon her was the work of victimising her. But she did not mind. She wanted it.

Later, they put a short blue tunic on her and took her to the upper terrace, and presented her to the people. She saw the plaza below her full of dark faces and of glittering eyes. There was no pity : only the curious hard exultance. The people gave a subdued cry when they saw her, and she shuddered. But she hardly cared.

Next day was the last. She slept in a chamber of the big house. At dawn they put on her a big blue blanket with a fringe, and led her out into the plaza, among the throng of silent, dark-blanketed people. There was pure white snow on the ground, and the dark people in their dark-brown blankets looked like inhabitants of another world.

A large drum was slowly pounding, and an old priest was declaring from a housetop. But it was not till noon that a litter came forth, and the people gave that low, animal cry which was so moving. In the sack-like litter sat the old, old cacique, his white hair braided with black braid and large turquoise stones. His face was like a piece of obsidian. He lifted his hand in token, and the litter stopped in front of her. Fixing her with his old eyes, he spoke to her for a few moments, in his hollow voice. No one translated.

Another litter came, and she was placed in it. Four priests moved ahead, in their scarlet and yellow and black, with plumed head-dresses. Then came the litter of the old cacique. Then the light drums began, and two groups of singers burst simultaneously into song, male and wild. And the golden-red, almost naked men, adorned with ceremonial feathers and kilts, the rivers of black hair down their backs, formed into two files and began to tread the dance. So they threaded out of the snowy plaza, in two long, sumptuous lines of dark red-gold and black and fur, swaying with a faint tinkle of bits of shell and flint, winding over the snow between the two bee-clusters of men who sang around the drum.

Slowly they moved out, and her litter, with its attendance of feathered, lurid, dancing priests, moved after. Everybody danced the tread of the dance-step, even, subtly, the litter-bearers. And out of the plaza they went, past smoking ovens, on the trail to the great cotton-wood trees, that stood like grey-silver lace against the blue sky, bare and exquisite above the snow. The river, diminished, rushed among fangs of ice. The chequer-squares of gardens within fences were all snowy, and the white houses now looked yellowish.

The whole valley glittered intolerably with pure snow, away to the walls of the standing rock. And across the flat cradle of snow-bed wound the long thread of the dance, shaking slowly and sumptuously in its orange and black motion. The high drums thudded quickly, and on the crystalline frozen air the swell and roar of the chant of savages was like an obsession.

She sat looking out of her litter with big, transfixed blue eyes, under which were the wan markings of her drugged weariness. She knew she was going to die, among the glisten of this snow, at the hands of this savage, sumptuous people. And as she stared at the blaze of blue sky above the slashed and ponderous mountain, she thought : " I am dead already. What difference does it make, the transition from the dead I am to the dead I shall be very soon ! " Yet her soul sickened and felt wan.

The strange procession trailed on, in perpetual dance, slowly across the plain of snow, and then entered the slopes between the pine-trees. She saw the copper-dark men dancing the dance-tread, onwards, between the copper-pale tree trunks. And at last she, too, in her swaying litter, entered the pine-trees.

They were travelling on and on, upwards, across the snow under the trees, past the superb shafts of pale, flaked copper, the rustle and shake and tread of the threading dance, pene-trating into the forest, into the mountain. They were following a stream-bed : but the stream was dry, like summer, dried up by the frozenness of the head-waters. There were dark, red-bronze willow bushes with wattles like wild hair, and pallid

. . . Till the red sun should send his ray through the column of ice.

aspen trees looking like cold flesh against the snow. Then jutting dark rocks.

At last she could tell that the dancers were moving forward no more. Nearer and nearer she came upon the drums, as to a lair of mysterious animals. Then through the bushes she emerged into a strange amphitheatre. Facing was a great wall of hollow rock, down the front of which hung a great, dripping, fang-like spoke of ice. The ice came pouring over the rock from the precipice above, and then stood arrested, dripping out of high heaven, almost down to the hollow stones where the stream-pool should be below. But the pool was dry.

On either side the dry pool, the lines of dancers had formed, and the dance was continuing without intermission, against a background of bushes.

But what she felt was that fanged inverted pinnacle of ice, hanging from the lip of that dark precipice above. And behind the great rope of ice, she saw the leopard-like figures of priests climbing the hollow cliff face to the cave that, like a dark socket, bored a cavity, an orifice, half way up the crag.

Before she could realize, her litter-bearers were staggering in the footholds, climbing the rock. She, too, was behind the ice. There it hung, like a curtain that is not spread, but hangs like a great fang. And near above her was the orifice of the cave sinking dark into the rock. She watched it as she swayed upwards.

On the platform of the cave stood the priests, waiting in all their gorgeousness of feathers and fringed robes, watching her ascent. Two of them stooped to help her litter-bearer. And at length she was on the platform of the cave, far in behind the shaft of ice, above the hollow amphitheatre among the bushes below, where men were dancing, and the whole populace of the village was clustered in silence.

The sun was sloping down the afternoon sky, on the left. She knew that this was the shortest day of the year, and the last day of her life. They stood her facing the iridescent column of ice, which fell down marvellously arrested, away in front of her.

Some signal was given, and the dance below stopped. There was now absolute silence. She was given a little to drink, then two priests took off her mantle and her tunic, and in her strange pallor she stood there, between the lurid robes of the priests, beyond the pillar of ice, beyond and above the dark-faced people. The throng below gave the low, wild cry. Then the priests turned her round, so she stood with her back to the open world, her long blonde hair to the people below. And they cried again.

She was facing the cave, inwards. A fire was burning and flickering in the depths. Four priests had taken off their robes, and were almost as naked as she was. They were powerful men in the prime of life, and they kept their dark, painted faces lowered.

From the fire came the old, old priest, with an incense-pan. He was naked and in a state of barbaric ecstasy. He fumigated his victim, reciting at the same time in a hollow voice. Behind him came another robeless priest, with two flint knives.

When she was fumigated, they laid her on a large flat stone, the four powerful men holding her by the outstretched arms and legs. Behind stood the aged man, like a skeleton covered with dark glass, holding a knife and transfixedly watching the sun ; and behind him again was another naked priest, with a knife.

She felt little sensation, though she knew all that was happening. Turning to the sky, she looked at the yellow sun. It was sinking. The shaft of ice was like a shadow between her and it. And she realized that the yellow rays were filling half the cave, though they had not reached the altar where the fire was, at the far end of the funnel-shaped cavity.

Yes, the rays were creeping round slowly. As they grew ruddier, they penetrated farther. When the red sun was about to sink, he would shine full through the shaft of ice deep into the hollow of the cave, to the innermost.

She understood now that this was what the men were waiting for. Even those that held her down were bent and twisted round, their black eyes watching the sun with a glittering eagerness, and awe, and craving. The black eyes of the aged cacique were fixed like black mirrors on the sun, as if sightless, yet containing some terrible answer to the reddening winter planet. And all the eyes of the priests were fixed and glittering on the sinking orb, in the reddening, icy silence of the winter afternoon.

They were anxious, terribly anxious, and fierce. Their ferocity wanted something, and they were waiting the moment. And their ferocity was ready to leap out into a mystic exultance, of triumph. But still they were anxious.

Only the eyes of that oldest man were not anxious. Black, and fixed, and as if sightless, they watched the sun, seeing beyond the sun. And in their black, empty concentration there was power, power intensely abstract and remote, but deep, deep to the heart of the earth, and the heart of the sun. In absolute motionlessness he watched till the red sun should send his ray through the column of ice. Then the old man would strike, and strike home, accomplish the sacrifice and achieve the power.

The mastery that man must hold, and that passes from race to race.

HONOLULU

THE wise traveller travels only in imagination. An old
Frenchman (he was really a Savoyard) once wrote a
book called *Voyage autour de ma Chambre*. I had not
read it and do not even know what it is about, but the title
stimulates my fancy. In such a journey I could circum-
navigate the globe. An eikon by the chimneypiece can take
me to Russia with its great forests of birch and its white, domed
churches. The Volga is wide, and at the end of a straggling
village, in the wineshop, bearded men in rough sheepskin coats
sit drinking. I stand on the little hill from which Napoleon
first saw Moscow and I look upon the vastness of the city. I
will go down and see the people whom I know more intimately
than so many of my friends—Alyosha, and Vronsky, and a
dozen more. But my eyes fall on a piece of porcelain and I
smell the acrid odours of China. I am borne in a chair along
a narrow causeway between the padi fields, or else I skirt a
tree-clad mountain. My bearers chat gaily as they trudge
along in the bright morning, and every now and then, distant
and mysterious, I hear the sound of a monastery bell. In the
streets of Peking there is a motley crowd, and it scatters to
allow passage to a string of camels, stepping delicately, that
bring skins and strange drugs from the stony deserts of Mon-
golia. In England, in London, there are certain afternoons
in winter when the clouds hang heavy and low and the light is
so bleak that your heart sinks; but then you can look out of
your window, and you see the coco-nut trees crowded upon
the beach of a coral island. The sand is silvery, and when
you walk along in the sunshine it is so dazzling that you can
hardly bear to look at it. Overhead the mynah birds are
making a great to-do, and the surf beats ceaselessly against the

reef. Those are the best journeys, the journeys that you take at your own fireside, for then you lose none of your illusions.

But there are people who take salt in their coffee. They say it gives it a tang, a savour, which is peculiar and fascinating. In the same way there are certain places, surrounded by a halo of romance, to which the inevitable disillusionment which you must experience on seeing them gives a singular spice. You had expected something wholly beautiful and you get an impression which is infinitely more complicated than any that beauty can give you. It is like the weakness in the character of a great man which may make him less admirable but certainly makes him more interesting.

Nothing had prepared me for Honolulu. It is so far away from Europe, it is reached after so long a journey from San Francisco, so strange and so charming associations are attached to the name, that at first I could hardly believe my eyes. I do not know that I had formed in my mind any very exact picture of what I expected, but what I found caused me a great surprise. It is a typical western city. Shacks are cheek by jowl with stone mansions ; dilapidated frame houses stand next door to smart stores with plate-glass windows ; electric cars rumble noisily along the streets ; and motors, Fords, Buicks, Packards, line the pavement. The shops are filled with all the necessities of American civilization. Every third house is a bank and every fifth the agency of a steamship company.

Along the streets crowd an unimaginable assortment of people. The Americans, ignoring the climate, wear black coats and high, starched collars, straw hats, soft hats, and bowlers. The Kanakas, pale brown, with crisp hair, have nothing on but a shirt and a pair of trousers ; but the half-breeds are very smart with flaring ties and patent-leather boots. The Japanese, with their obsequious smile, are neat and trim in white duck, while their women walk a step or two behind them, in native dress, with a baby on their backs. The Japanese children, in bright-coloured frocks, their little heads shaven, look like quaint dolls. Then there are the Chinese. The men, fat and prosperous, wear their American clothes oddly, but the women are enchanting with their tightly-dressed black hair, so neat that you feel it can never be disarranged, and they are very clean in their tunics and trousers, white, or powder-blue, or black. Lastly, there are the Filipinos, the men in huge straw hats, the women in bright yellow muslin with great puffed sleeves.

It is the meeting-place of East and West. The very new rubs shoulders with the immeasurably old. And if you have not found the romance you expected you have come upon something singularly intriguing. All these strange people live close to each other, with different languages and different thoughts ; they believe in different gods and they have different values ; two passions alone they share, love and hunger. And somehow as you watch them you have an impression of extraordinary vitality. Though the air is so soft and the sky so blue, you have, I know not why, a feeling of something hotly passionate that beats like a throbbing pulse through the crowd. Though the native policeman at the corner, standing on a platform, with a white club to direct the traffic, gives the scene an air of respectability, you cannot but feel that it is a respectability only of the surface ; a little below there is darkness and mystery. It gives you just that thrill, with a little catch at the heart, that you have when at night in the forest the silence trembles on a sudden with the low, insistent beating of a drum. You are all expectant of I know not what.

If I have dwelt on the incongruity of Honolulu, it is because just this, to my mind, gives its point to the story I want to tell. It is a story of primitive superstition, and it startles me that anything of the sort should survive in a civilization which, if not very distinguished, is certainly very elaborate. I cannot get over the fact that such incredible things should happen, or at least be thought to happen, right in the middle, so to speak, of telephones, tramcars, and daily papers. And the friend who showed me Honolulu had the same incongruity which I felt from the beginning was its most striking characteristic.

He was an American named Winter, and I had brought a letter of introduction to him from an acquaintance in New York. He was a man between forty and fifty, with scanty black hair, grey at the temples, and a sharp-featured, thin face. His eyes had a twinkle in them and his large horn spectacles gave him a demureness which was not a little diverting. He was tall rather than otherwise, and very spare. He was born in Honolulu and his father had a large store which sold hosiery and all such goods, from tennis racquets to tarpaulins, as a man of fashion could require. It was a prosperous business and I could well understand the indignation of Winter *père* when his son, refusing to go into it, had announced his determination to be an actor. My friend spent twenty years on the stage, sometimes in New York, but more often on the road,

for his gifts were small ; but at last, being no fool, he came to
the conclusion that it was better to sell sock suspenders in
Honolulu than to play small parts in Cleveland, Ohio. He
left the stage and went into the business. I think after the
hazardous existence he had lived so long, he thoroughly
enjoyed the luxury of driving a large car and living in a beautiful
house near the golf-course, and I am quite sure, since he was a
man of parts, he managed the business competently. But he
could not bring himself entirely to break his connection with
the arts, and since he might no longer act he began to paint. He
took me to his studio and showed me his work. It was not
at all bad, but not what I should have expected from him.
He painted nothing but still life, very small pictures, perhaps
eight by ten ; and he painted very delicately, with the utmost
finish. He had evidently a passion for detail. His fruit
pieces reminded you of the fruit in a picture by Ghirlandajo.
While you marvelled a little at his patience, you could not help
being impressed by his dexterity. I imagine that he failed as
an actor because his effects, carefully studied, were neither
bold nor broad enough to get across the footlights.

I was entertained by the proprietary, yet ironical air with
which he showed me the city. He thought in his heart that
there was none in the United States to equal it, but he saw quite
clearly that his attitude was comic. He drove me round to
the various buildings and swelled with satisfaction when
I expressed a proper admiration for their architecture. He
showed me the houses of rich men.

" That's the Stubbs' house," he said. " It cost a hundred
thousand dollars to build. The Stubbs are one of our best
families. Old man Stubbs came here as a missionary more
than seventy years ago."

He hesitated a little and looked at me with twinkling eyes
through his big round spectacles.

" All our best families are missionary families," he said.
" You're not very much in Honolulu unless your father or
your grandfather converted the heathen."

" Is that so ? "

" Do you know your Bible ? "

" Fairly," I answered.

" There is a text which says : The fathers have eaten sour
grapes and the children's teeth are set on edge. I guess it
runs differently in Honolulu. The fathers brought Christianity to the Kanaka and the children jumped his land."

" Heaven helps those who help themselves," I murmured.

" It surely does. By the time the natives of this island had embraced Christianity they had nothing else they could afford to embrace. The kings gave the missionaries land as a mark of esteem, and the missionaries bought land by way of laying up treasure in heaven. It surely was a good investment. One missionary left the business—I think one may call it a business without offence—and became a land agent, but that is an exception. Mostly it was their sons who looked after the commercial side of the concern. Oh, it's a fine thing to have a father who came here fifty years ago to spread the faith."

But he looked at his watch.

" Gee, it's stopped. That means it's time to have a cocktail."

We sped along an excellent road bordered with red hibiscus, and came back into the town.

" Have you been to the Union Saloon ? "

" Not yet."

" We'll go there."

I knew it was the most famous spot in Honolulu and I entered it with a lively curiosity. You get to it by a narrow passage from King Street, and in the passage are offices, so that thirsty souls may be supposed bound for one of these just as well as for the saloon. It is a large square room, with three entrances, and opposite the bar, which runs the length of it, two corners have been partitioned off into little cubicles. Legend states that they were built so that King Kalakaua might drink there without being seen by his subjects, and it is pleasant to think that in one or other of these he may have sat over his bottle, a coal-black potentate, with Robert Louis Stevenson. There is a portrait of him, in oils, in a rich gold frame ; but there are also two prints of Queen Victoria. On the walls, besides, are old line engravings of the eighteenth century, one of which, and Heaven knows how it got there, is after a theatrical picture by De Wilde ; and there are oleographs from the Christmas supplement of the *Graphic* and the *Illustrated London News* of twenty years ago. Then there are advertisements of whisky, gin, champagne, and beer ; and photographs of baseball teams and of native orchestras.

The place seemed to belong not to the modern, hustling world that I had left in the bright street outside, but to one that was dying. It had the savour of the day before yesterday. Dingy and dimly lit, it had a vaguely mysterious air and you could imagine that it would be a fit scene for shady transactions. It suggested a more lurid time, when ruthless men carried their lives in their hands, and violent deeds diapered the monotony of life.

When I went in the saloon was fairly full. A group of business men stood together at the bar, discussing affairs, and in a corner two Kanakas were drinking. Two or three men who might have been store-keepers were shaking dice. The rest of the company plainly followed the sea ; they were captains of tramps, first mates, and engineers. Behind the bar, busily making the Honolulu cocktail for which the place was famous, served two large half-castes, in white, fat, clean-shaven and dark-skinned, with thick, curly hair and large bright eyes.

Winter seemed to know more than half the company, and when we made our way to the bar a little fat man in spectacles, who was standing by himself, offered him a drink.

" No, you have one with me, Captain," said Winter.

He turned to me.

" I want you to know Captain Butler."

The little man shook hands with me. We began to talk, but, my attention distracted by my surroundings, I took small notice of him, and after we had each ordered a cocktail we separated. When we had got into the motor again and were driving away, Winter said to me :

" I'm glad we ran up against Butler. I wanted you to meet him. What did you think of him ? "

" I don't know that I thought very much of him at all," I answered.

" Do you believe in the supernatural ? "

" I don't exactly know that I do," I smiled.

" A very queer thing happened to him a year or two ago. You ought to have him tell you about it."

" What sort of thing ? "

Winter did not answer my question.

" I have no explanation of it myself," he said. " But there's no doubt about the facts. Are you interested in things like that ? "

" Things like what ? "

" Spells and magic and all that."

" I never met any one who wasn't."

Winter paused for a moment.

" I guess I won't tell you myself. You ought to hear it from his own lips so that you can judge. How are you fixed up for to-night ? "

" I've got nothing on at all."

" Well, I'll get hold of him between now and then and see if we can't go down to his ship."

Winter told me something about him. Captain Butler had spent all his life on the Pacific. He had been in much better circumstances than he was now, for he had been first officer and then captain of a passenger-boat plying along the coast of California, but he had lost his ship and a number of passengers had been drowned.

" Drink, I guess," said Winter.

Of course there had been an inquiry, which had cost him his certificate, and then he drifted farther afield. For some years he had knocked about the South Seas, but he was now in command of a small schooner which sailed between Honolulu and the various islands of the group. It belonged to a Chinese to whom the fact that his skipper had no certificate meant only that he could be had for lower wages, and to have a white man in charge was always an advantage.

And now that I had heard this about him I took the trouble to remember more exactly what he was like. I recalled his round spectacles and the round blue eyes behind them, and so gradually reconstructed him before my mind. He was a little man, without angles, plump, with a round face like the full moon and a little fat round nose. He had fair short hair, and he was red-faced and clean-shaven. He had plump hands, dimpled on the knuckles, and short fat legs. He was a jolly soul, and the tragic experience he had gone through seemed to have left him unscarred. Though he must have been thirty-four or thirty-five he looked much younger. But after all I had given him but a superficial attention, and now that I knew of this catastrophe, which had obviously ruined his life, I promised myself that when I saw him again I would take more careful note of him. It is very curious to observe the differences of emotional response that you find in different people. Some can go through terrific battles, the fear of imminent death and unimaginable horrors, and preserve their soul unscathed, while with others the trembling of the moon on a solitary sea or the song of a bird in a thicket will cause a convulsion great enough to transform their entire being. Is it due to strength or weakness, want of imagination or instability of character ? I do not know. When I called up in my fancy that scene of shipwreck, with the shrieks of the drowning and the terror, and then later, the ordeal of the inquiry, the bitter grief of those who sorrowed for the lost, and the harsh things he must have read to himself in the

papers, the shame and the disgrace, it came to me with a shock
to remember that Captain Butler had talked with the frank
obscenity of a schoolboy of the Hawaiian girls and of Ewelei,
the Red Light district, and of his successful adventures. He
laughed readily, and one would have thought he could never
laugh again. I remembered his shining, white teeth ; they
were his best feature. He began to interest me, and thinking
of him and of his gay insouciance I forgot the particular story,
to hear which I was to see him again. I wanted to see him
rather to find out if I could a little more what sort of man he
was.

Winter made the necessary arrangements, and after dinner
we went down to the waterfront. The ship's boat was waiting
for us and we rowed out. The schooner was anchored some
way across the harbour, not far from the breakwater. We
came alongside, and I heard the sound of a ukulele. We
clambered up the ladder.

" I guess he's in the cabin," said Winter, leading the way.

It was a small cabin, bedraggled and dirty, with a table
against one side and a broad bench all round upon which
slept, I supposed, such passengers as were ill-advised enough
to travel in such a ship. A petroleum lamp gave a dim light.
The ukulele was being played by a native girl and Butler was
lolling on the seat, half lying, with his head on her shoulder
and an arm round her waist.

" Don't let us disturb you, Captain," said Winter facetiously.

" Come right in," said Butler, getting up and shaking
hands with us. " What'll you have ? "

It was a warm night, and through the open door you saw
countless stars in a heaven that was still almost blue. Captain
Butler wore a sleeveless undershirt, showing his fat white
arms, and a pair of incredibly dirty trousers. His feet were
bare, but on his curly head he wore a very old, a very shapeless
felt hat.

" Let me introduce you to my girl. Ain't she a peach ? "

We shook hands with a very pretty person. She was a
good deal taller than the captain, and even the Mother Hubbard,
which the missionaries of a past generation had, in the interests
of decency, forced on the unwilling natives, could not conceal
the beauty of her form. One could not but suspect that age
would burden her with a certain corpulence, but now she was
graceful and alert. Her brown skin had an exquisite trans-
lucency and her eyes were magnificent. Her black hair, very
thick and rich, was coiled round her head in a massive plait.

When she smiled in a greeting that was charmingly natural, she showed teeth that were small, even, and white. She was certainly a most attractive creature. It was easy to see that the captain was madly in love with her. He could not take his eyes off her ; he wanted to touch her all the time. That was very easy to understand ; but what seemed to me stranger was that the girl was apparently in love with him. There was a light in her eyes that was unmistakable, and her lips were slightly parted as though in a sigh of desire. It was thrilling. It was even a little moving, and I could not help feeling somewhat in the way. What had a stranger to do with this lovesick pair ? I wished that Winter had not brought me. And it seemed to me that the dingy cabin was transfigured and now it seemed a fit and proper scene for such an extremity of passion. I thought I should never forget that schooner in the harbour of Honolulu, crowded with shipping, and yet, under the immensity of the starry sky, remote from all the world. I liked to think of those lovers sailing off together in the night over the empty spaces of the Pacific from one green, hilly island to another. A faint breeze of romance softly fanned my cheek.

And yet Butler was the last man in the world with whom you would have associated romance, and it was hard to see what there was in him to arouse love. In the clothes he wore now he looked podgier than ever, and his round spectacles gave his round face the look of a prim cherub. He suggested rather a curate who had gone to the dogs. His conversation was peppered with the quaintest Americanisms, and it is because I despair of reproducing these that, at whatever loss of vividness, I mean to narrate the story he told me a little later in my own words. Moreover, he was unable to frame a sentence without an oath, though a good-natured one, and his speech, albeit offensive only to prudish ears, in print would seem coarse. He was a mirth-loving man, and perhaps that accounted not a little for his successful amours ; since women, for the most part frivolous creatures, are excessively bored by the seriousness with which men treat them, and they can seldom resist the buffoon who makes them laugh. Their sense of humour is crude. Diana of Ephesus is always prepared to fling prudence to the winds for the red-nosed comedian who sits on his hat. I realized that Captain Butler had charm. If I had not known the tragic story of the shipwreck I should have thought he had never had a care in his life.

Our host had rung the bell on our entrance and now a

Chinese cook came in with more glasses and several bottles of soda. The whisky and the captain's empty glass stood already on the table. But when I saw the Chinese I positively started, for he was certainly the ugliest man I had ever seen. He was very short, but thick-set, and he had a bad limp. He wore a singlet and a pair of trousers that had been white, but were now filthy, and, perched on a shock of bristly, grey hair, an old tweed deer-stalker. It would have been grotesque on any Chinese, but on him it was outrageous. His broad, square face was very flat as though it had been bashed in by a mighty fist, and it was deeply pitted with smallpox ; but the most revolting thing in him was a very pronounced hare-lip which had never been operated on, so that his upper lip, cleft, went up in an angle to his nose, and in the opening was a huge yellow fang. It was horrible. He came in with the end of a cigarette at the corner of his mouth, and this, I do not know why, gave him a devilish expression.

He poured out the whisky and opened a bottle of soda.

" Don't drown it, John," said the captain.

He said nothing, but handed a glass to each of us. Then he went out.

" I saw you lookin' at my Chink," said Butler, with a grin on his fat, shining face.

" I should hate to meet him on a dark night," I said.

" He sure is homely," said the captain, and for some reason he seemed to say it with a peculiar satisfaction. " But he's fine for one thing, I'll tell the world ; you just have to have a drink every time you look at him."

But my eyes fell on a calabash that hung against the wall over the table, and I got up to look at it. I had been hunting for an old one and this was better than any I had seen outside the museum.

" It was given me by a chief over on one of the islands," said the captain, watching me. " I done him a good turn and he wanted to give me something good."

" He certainly did," I answered.

I was wondering whether I could discreetly make Captain Butler an offer for it, I could not imagine that he set any store on such an article, when, as though he read my thoughts, he said :

" I wouldn't sell that for ten thousand dollars."

" I guess not," said Winter. " It would be a crime to sell it."

" Why ? " I asked.

" That comes into the story," returned Winter. " Doesn't it, Captain ? "

" It surely does."

" Let's hear it then."

" The night's young yet," he answered.

The night distinctly lost its youth before he satisfied my curiosity, and meanwhile we drank a great deal too much whisky while Captain Butler narrated his experiences of San Francisco in the old days and of the South Seas. At last the girl fell asleep. She lay curled up on the seat, with her face on her brown arm, and her bosom rose and fell gently with her breathing. In sleep she looked sullen, but darkly beautiful.

He had found her on one of the islands in the group among which, whenever there was cargo to be got, he wandered with his crazy old schooner. The Kanakas have little love for work and the laborious Chinese, the cunning Japs, have taken the trade out of their hands. Her father had a strip of land on which he grew taro and bananas, and he had a boat in which he went fishing. He was vaguely related to the mate of the schooner, and it was he who took Captain Butler up to the shabby little frame house to spend an idle evening. They took a bottle of whisky with them and the ukulele. The captain was not a shy man and when he saw a pretty girl he made love to her. He could speak the native language fluently and it was not long before he had overcome the girl's timidity. They spent the evening singing and dancing, and by the end of it she was sitting by his side and he had his arm round her waist. It happened that they were delayed on the island for several days and the captain, at no time a man to hurry, made no effort to shorten his stay. He was very comfortable in the snug little harbour and life was long. He had a swim round his ship in the morning and another in the evening. There was a chandler's shop on the water front where sailormen could get a drink of whisky, and he spent the best part of the day there, playing cribbage with the half-caste who owned it. At night the mate and he went up to the house where the pretty girl lived and they sang a song or two and told stories. It was the girl's father who suggested that he should take her away with him. They discussed the matter in a friendly fashion, while the girl, nestling against the captain, urged him by the pressure of her hands and her soft, smiling glances. He had taken a fancy to her and he was a domestic man. He was a little dull sometimes at sea and it would be very pleasant to have a pretty little creature like that about the old ship. He was of a practical turn too, and he recognized that it would be useful to have someone around to darn his socks and look after his linen. He was tired of having his things washed by a Chink, who tore everything to pieces ; the natives washed much better, and now and then when the captain went ashore at Honolulu he liked to cut a dash in a smart duck suit. It was only a matter of arranging a price. The father wanted two hundred and fifty dollars, and the captain, never a thrifty man, could not put his hand on such a sum. But he was a generous one, and with the girl's soft face against his, he was not inclined to haggle. He offered to give a hundred and fifty dollars there and then and another hundred in three months. There was a good deal of argument and the parties could not come to any agreement that night, but the idea had fired the captain, and he could not sleep as well as usual. He kept dreaming of the lovely girl and each time he awoke it was with the pressure of her soft, sensual lips on his. He cursed himself in the morning because a bad night at poker, the last time he was at Honolulu, had left him so short of ready money. And if the night before he had been in love with the girl, this morning he was crazy about her.

" See here, Bananas," he said to the mate, " I've got to have that girl. You go and tell the old man I'll bring the dough up to-night and she can get fixed up. I figure we'll be ready to sail at dawn."

I have no idea why the mate was known by that eccentric name. He was called Wheeler, but though he had that English surname there was not a drop of white blood in him. He was a tall man, and well made, though inclined to stoutness, but much darker than is usual in Hawaii. He was no longer young, and his crisply curling, thick hair was grey. His upper front teeth were cased in gold. He was very proud of them. He had a marked squint and this gave him a saturnine expression. The captain, who was fond of a joke, found in it a constant source of humour and hesitated the less to rally him on the defect, because he realized that the mate was sensitive about it. Bananas, unlike most of the natives, was a taciturn fellow, and Captain Butler would have disliked him if it had been possible for a man of his good nature to dislike any one. He liked to be at sea with some one he could talk to, he was a chatty, sociable creature, and it was enough to drive a missionary to drink to live there day after day with a chap who never opened his mouth. He did his best to wake the mate up, that is to say, he chaffed him without mercy, but it was poor fun to laugh by oneself, and he came to the conclusion that, drunk or sober, Bananas was no fit companion for a white man. But he was a good seaman and the captain was shrewd enough to know the value of a mate he could trust. It was not rare for him to come aboard, when they were sailing, fit for nothing but to fall into his bunk, and it was worth something to know that he could stay there till he had slept his liquor off, since Bananas could be relied on. But he was an unsociable devil, and it would be a treat to have some one he could talk to. That girl would be fine. Besides, he wouldn't be so likely to get drunk when he went ashore if he knew there was a little girl waiting for him when he came on board again.

He went to his friend the chandler, and over a peg of gin asked him for a loan. There was one or two useful things a ship's captain could do for a ship's chandler, and after a quarter of an hour's conversation in low tones (there is no object in letting all and sundry know your business), the captain crammed a wad of notes in his hip-pocket, and that night, when he went back to his ship, the girl went with him.

What Captain Butler, seeking for reasons to do what he had already made up his mind to, had anticipated, actually came to pass. He did not give up drinking, but he ceased to drink in excess. An evening with the boys, when he had been away from town two or three weeks, was pleasant enough, but it was pleasant too to get back to his little girl ; he thought of her, sleeping so softly, and how, when he got into his cabin and leaned over her, she would open her eyes lazily and stretch out her arms for him : it was as good as a full hand. He found he was saving money, and since he was a generous man he did the right things by the little girl : he gave her some silver-backed brushes for her long hair, and a gold chain, and a reconstructed ruby for her finger. Gee, but it was good to be alive.

A year went by, a whole year, and he was not tired of her yet. He was not a man who analyzed his feelings, but this was so surprising that it forced itself upon his attention. There must be something very wonderful about that girl. He couldn't help seeing that he was more wrapped up in her than ever, and sometimes the thought entered his mind that it might not be a bad thing if he married her.

Then, one day the mate did not come in to dinner or to tea. Butler did not bother himself about his absence at the first meal, but at the second he asked the Chinese cook :

" Where's the mate ? He no come tea ? "

"No wantchee," said the Chink.

"He ain't sick?"

"No savvy."

Next day Bananas turned up again, but he was more sullen than ever, and after dinner the captain asked the girl what was the matter with him. She smiled and shrugged her pretty shoulders. She told the captain that Bananas had taken a fancy to her and he was sore because she had told him off. The captain was a good-humoured man and he was not of a jealous nature; it struck him as exceedingly funny that Bananas should be in love. A man who had a squint like that had a precious poor chance. When tea came round he chaffed him gaily. He pretended to speak in the air, so that the mate should not be certain that he knew anything, but he dealt him some pretty shrewd blows. The girl did not think him as funny as he thought himself, and afterwards she begged him to say nothing more. He was surprised at her seriousness. She told him he did not know her people. When their passion was aroused they were capable of anything. She was a little frightened. This was so absurd to him that he laughed heartily.

"If he comes bothering round you, you just threaten to tell me. That'll fix him."

"Better fire him, I think."

"Not on your sweet life. I know a good sailor when I see one. But if he don't leave you alone I'll give him the worst licking he's ever had."

Perhaps the girl had a wisdom unusual in her sex. She knew that it was useless to argue with a man when his mind was made up, for it only increased his stubbornness, and she held her peace. And now on the shabby schooner, threading her way across the silent sea, among those lovely islands, was enacted a dark, tense drama of which the fat little captain remained entirely ignorant. The girl's resistance fired Bananas so that he ceased to be a man, but was simply blind desire. He did not make love to her gently or gaily, but with a black and savage ferocity. Her contempt now was changed to hatred, and when he besought her she answered him with bitter, angry taunts. But the struggle went on silently, and when the captain asked her after a little while whether Bananas was bothering her, she lied.

But one night, when they were in Honolulu, he came on board only just in time. They were sailing at dawn. Bananas had been ashore, drinking some native spirit, and he was drunk.

The captain, rowing up, heard sounds that surprised him. He scrambled up the ladder. He saw Bananas, beside himself, trying to wrench open the cabin door. He was shouting at the girl. He swore he would kill her if she did not let him in.

" What in hell are you up to ? " cried Butler.

The mate let go the handle, gave the captain a look of savage hate, and without a word turned away.

" Stop here. What are you doing with that door ? "

The mate still did not answer. He looked at him with sullen, bootless rage.

" I'll teach you not pull any of your queer stuff with me, you dirty, cross-eyed nigger," said the captain.

He was a good foot shorter than the mate and no match for him, but he was used to dealing with native crews, and he had his knuckle-duster handy. Perhaps it was not an instrument that a gentleman would use, but then Captain Butler was not a gentleman. Nor was he in the habit of dealing with gentlemen. Before Bananas knew what the captain was at, his right arm had shot out and his fist, with its ring of steel, caught him fair and square on the jaw. He fell like a bull under the pole-axe.

" That'll learn him," said the captain.

Bananas did not stir. The girl unlocked the cabin door and came out.

" Is he dead ? "

" He ain't."

He called a couple of men and told them to carry the mate to his bunk. He rubbed his hands with satisfaction and his round blue eyes gleamed behind his spectacles. But the girl was strangely silent. She put her arms round him as though to protect him from invisible harm.

It was two or three days before Bananas was on his feet again, and when he came out of his cabin his face was torn and swollen. Through the darkness of his skin you saw the livid bruise. Butler saw him slinking along the deck and called him. The mate went to him without a word.

" See here, Bananas," he said to him, fixing his spectacles on his slippery nose, for it was very hot. " I ain't going to fire you for this, but you know now that when I hit, I hit hard. Don't forget it, and don't let me have any more funny business."

Then he held out his hand and gave the mate that good-humoured, flashing smile of his which was his greatest charm. The mate took the outstretched hand and twitched his swollen lips into a devilish grin. The incident in the captain's mind was so completely finished that when the three of them sat at dinner he chaffed Bananas on his appearance. He was eating with difficulty and, his swollen face still more distorted by pain, he looked truly a repulsive object.

That evening, when he was sitting on the upper deck, smoking his pipe, a shiver passed through the captain.

" I don't know what I should be shiverin' for on a night like this," he grumbled. " Maybe I've gotten a dose of fever. I've been feelin' a bit queer all day."

When he went to bed he took some quinine, and next morning he felt better, but a little washed out, as though he were recovering from a debauch.

" I guess my liver's out of order," he said, and he took a pill.

He had not much appetite that day and towards evening he began to feel very unwell. He tried the next remedy he knew, which was to drink two or three hot whiskies, but that did not seem to help him much, and when in the morning he surveyed himself in the glass he thought he was not looking quite the thing.

" If I ain't right by the time we get back to Honolulu I'll just give Dr. Denby a call. He'll sure fix me up."

He could not eat. He felt a great lassitude in all his limbs. He slept soundly enough, but he awoke with no sense of refreshment ; on the contrary he felt a peculiar exhaustion. And the energetic little man, who could not bear the thought of lying in bed, had to make an effort to force himself out of his bunk. After a few days he found it impossible to resist the languor that oppressed him, and he made up his mind not to get up.

" Bananas can look after the ship," he said. " He has before now."

He laughed a little to himself as he thought how often he had lain speechless in his bunk after a night with the boys. That was before he had his girl. He smiled at her and pressed her hand. She was puzzled and anxious. He saw that she was concerned about him, and tried to reassure her. He had never had a day's illness in his life and in a week at the outside he would be as right as rain.

" I wish you'd fire Bananas," she said. " I've got a feeling that he's at the bottom of this."

" Damned good thing I didn't, or there'd be no one to sail the ship. I know a good sailor when I see one." His blue eyes, rather pale now, with the whites all yellow, twinkled. " You don't think he's trying to poison me, little girl ? "

She did not answer, but she had one or two talks with the Chinese cook, and she took great care with the captain's food. But he ate little enough now, and it was only with the greatest difficulty that she persuaded him to drink a cup of soup two or three times a day. It was clear that he was very ill, he was losing weight quickly, and his chubby face was pale and drawn. He suffered no pain, but merely grew every day weaker and more languid. He was wasting away. The round trip on this occasion lasted about four weeks and by the time they came to Honolulu the captain was a little anxious about himself. He had not been out of his bed for more than a fortnight and really he felt too weak to get up and go to the doctor. He sent a message asking him to come on board. The doctor examined him, but could find nothing to account for his condition. His temperature was normal.

" See here, Captain," he said, " I'll be perfectly frank with you. I don't know what's the matter with you, and just seeing you like this don't give me a chance. You come into the hospital so that we can keep you under observation. There's nothing organically wrong with you, I know that, and my impression is that a few weeks in hospital ought to put you to rights."

" I ain't going to leave my ship."

Chinese owners were queer customers, he said ; if he left his ship because he was sick, his owner might fire him, and he couldn't afford to lose his job. So long as he stayed where he was his contract safeguarded him, and he had a first-rate mate. Besides, he couldn't leave his girl. No man could want a better nurse ; if any one could pull him through she would. Every man had to die once, and he only wished to be left in peace. He would not listen to the doctor's expostulations, and finally the doctor gave in.

" I'll write you a prescription," he said doubtfully, " and see if it does you any good. You'd better stay in bed for a while."

" There ain't much fear of my getting up, doc," answered the captain. " I feel as weak as a cat."

But he believed in the doctor's prescription as little as did the doctor himself, and when he was alone amused himself by lighting his cigar with it. He had to get amusement out of something, for his cigar tasted like nothing on earth, and he smoked only to persuade himself that he was not too ill to. That evening a couple of friends of his, masters of tramp steamers, hearing he was sick came over to see him.

They discussed his case over a bottle of whisky and a box of
Philippine cigars. One of them remembered how a mate
of his had been taken queer just like that and not a doctor
in the United States had been able to cure him. He had seen
in the paper an advertisement of a patent medicine, and
thought there'd be no harm in trying it. That man was as
strong as ever he'd been in his life after two bottles. But his
illness had given Captain Butler a lucidity which was new and
strange, and while they talked he seemed to read their minds.
They thought he was dying. And when they left him he was
afraid.

The girl saw his weakness. This was her opportunity.
She had been urging him to let a native doctor see him, and
he had stoutly refused ; but now she entreated him. He
listened with harassed eyes. He wavered. It was very
funny that the American doctor could not tell what was the
matter with him. But he did not want her to think that he
was scared. If he let a damned nigger come along and look
at him, it was to comfort *her*. He told her to do what she
liked.

The native doctor came the next night. The captain
was lying alone, half awake, and the cabin was dimly lit by
an oil lamp. The door was softly opened and the girl came in
on tiptoe. She held the door open and some one slipped in
silently behind her. The captain smiled at this mystery,
but he was so weak now, the smile was no more than a glimmer
in his eyes. The doctor was a little, old man, very thin and
very wrinkled, with a completely bald head, and the face of a
monkey. He was bowed and gnarled like an old tree. He
looked hardly human, but his eyes were very bright, and in
the half darkness, they seemed to glow with a reddish light.
He was dressed filthily in a pair of ragged dungarees, and the
upper part of his body was naked. He sat down on his
haunches and for ten minutes looked at the captain. Then he
felt the palms of his hands and the soles of his feet. The girl
watched him with frightened eyes. No word was spoken.
Then he asked for something that the captain had worn. The
girl gave him the old felt hat which the captain used constantly
and taking it he sat down again on the floor, clasping it firmly
with both hands ; and rocking backwards and forwards slowly
he muttered some gibberish in a very low tone.

At last he gave a little sigh and dropped the hat. He took
an old pipe out of his trouser pocket and lit it. The girl went
over to him and sat by his side. He whispered something to

her, and she started violently. For a few minutes they talked in hurried undertones, and then they stood up. She gave him money and opened the door for him. He slid out as silently as he had come in. Then she went over to the captain and leaned over him so that she could speak into his ear.

" It's an enemy praying you to death."

" Don't talk fool stuff, girlie," he said impatiently.

" It's truth. It's God's truth. That's why the American doctor couldn't do anything. Our people can do that. I've seen it done. I thought you were safe because you were a white man."

" I haven't an enemy."

" Bananas."

" What's he want to pray me to death for ? "

" You ought to have fired him before he had a chance."

" I guess if I ain't got nothing more the matter with me than Bananas' hoodoo I shall be sitting up and taking nourishment in a very few days."

She was silent for a while and she looked at him intently.

" Don't you know you're dying ? " she said to him at last.

That was what the two skippers had thought, but they hadn't said it. A shiver passed across the captain's wan face.

" The doctor says there ain't nothing really the matter with me. I've only to lie quiet for a bit and I shall be all right."

She put her lips to his ear as if she were afraid that the air itself might hear.

" You're dying, dying, dying. You'll pass out with the old moon."

" That's something to know."

" You'll pass out with the old moon unless Bananas dies before."

He was not a timid man and he had recovered already from the shock her words, and still more her vehement, silent manner, had given him. Once more a smile flickered in his eyes.

" I guess I'll take my chance, girlie."

" There's twelve days before the new moon."

There was something in her tone that gave him an idea.

" See here, my girl, this is all bunk. I don't believe a word of it. But I don't want you to try any of your monkey tricks with Bananas. He ain't a beauty, but he's a first-rate mate."

He would have said a good deal more, but he was tired out.

He suddenly felt very weak and faint. It was always at that hour that he felt worse. He closed his eyes. The girl watched him for a minute and then slipped out of the cabin. The moon, nearly full, made a silver pathway over the dark sea. It shone from an unclouded sky. She looked at it with terror, for she knew that with its death the man she loved would die. His life was in her hands. She could save him, she alone could save him, but the enemy was cunning, and she must be cunning too. She felt that some one was looking at her, and without turning, by the sudden fear that seized her, knew that from the shadow the burning eyes of the mate were fixed upon her. She did not know what he could do ; if he could read her thoughts she was defeated already, and with a desperate effort she emptied her mind of all content. His death alone could save her lover, and she could bring his death about. She knew that if he could be brought to look into a calabash in which was water so that a reflection of him was made, and the reflection were broken by hurtling the water, he would die as though he had been struck by lightning ; for the reflection was his soul. But none knew better than he the danger, and he could be made to look only by a guile which had lulled his least suspicion. He must never think that he had an enemy who was on the watch to cause his destruction. She knew what she had to do. But the time was short, the time was terribly short. Presently she realized that the mate had gone. She breathed more freely.

Two days later they sailed, and there were ten now before the new moon. Captain Butler was terrible to see. He was nothing but skin and bone, and he could not move without help. He could hardly speak. But she dared do nothing yet. She knew that she must be patient. The mate was cunning, cunning. They went to one of the smaller islands of the group and discharged cargo, and now there were only seven days more. The moment had come to start. She brought some things out of the cabin she shared with the captain and made them into a bundle. She put the bundle in the deck cabin where she and Bananas ate their meals, and at dinner time, when she went in, he turned quickly and she saw that he had been looking at it. Neither of them spoke, but she knew what he suspected. She was making her preparations to leave the ship. He looked at her mockingly. Gradually, as though to prevent the captain from knowing what she was about, she brought everything she owned into the cabin, and some of the captain's clothes, and made them

all into bundles.   At last Bananas could keep silence no longer.
He pointed to a suit of ducks.

" What are you going to do with that ? " he asked.

She shrugged her shoulders.

" I'm going back to my island."

He gave a laugh that distorted his grim face.   The captain
was dying and she meant to get away with all she could lay
hands on.

" What'll you do if I say you can't take those things ?
They're the captain's."

" They're no use to you," she said.

There was a calabash hanging on the wall.   It was the
very calabash I had seen when I came into the cabin and which
we had talked about.   She took it down.   It was all dusty,
so she poured water into it from the water-bottle, and rinsed
it with her fingers.

" What are you doing with that ? "

" I can sell it for fifty dollars," she said.

" If you want to take it you'll have to pay me."

" What d'you want ? "

" You know what I want."

She allowed a fleeting smile to play on her lips.   She
flashed a quick look at him and quickly turned away.   He gave
a gasp of desire.   She raised her shoulders in a little shrug.
With a savage bound he sprang upon her and seized her
in his arms.   Then she laughed.   She put her arms, her soft,
round arms, about his neck, and surrendered herself to him
voluptuously.

When the morning came she roused him out of a deep sleep.
The early rays of the sun slanted into the cabin.   He pressed
her to his heart.   Then he told her that the captain could not
last more than a day or two, and the owner wouldn't so easily
find another white man to command the ship.   If Bananas
offered to take less money he would get the job and the girl
could stay with him.   He looked at her with love-sick eyes.
She nestled up against him.   She kissed his lips, in the foreign
way, in the way the captain had taught her to kiss.   And she
promised to stay.   Bananas was drunk with happiness.

It was now or never.

She got up and went to the table to arrange her hair.
There was no mirror and she looked into the calabash, seeking
for her reflection.   She tidied her beautiful hair.   Then she
beckoned to Bananas to come to her.   She pointed to the
calabash.

" There's something in the bottom of it," she said.

Instinctively, without suspecting anything, Bananas looked full into the water. His face was reflected in it. In a flash she beat upon it violently, with both her hands, so that they pounded on the bottom and the water splashed up. The reflection was broken in pieces. Bananas started back with a sudden hoarse cry and he looked at the girl. She was standing there with a look of triumphant hatred on her face. A horror came into his eyes. His heavy features were twisted in agony, and with a thud, as though he had taken a violent poison, he crumpled up on to the ground. A great shudder passed through his body and he was still. She leaned over him callously. She put her hand on his heart and then she pulled down his lower eye-lid. He was quite dead.

She went into the cabin in which lay Captain Butler. There was a faint colour in his cheeks and he looked at her in a startled way.

" What's happened ? " he whispered.

They were the first words he had spoken for forty-eight hours.

" Nothing's happened," she said.

" I feel all funny."

Then his eyes closed and he fell asleep. He slept for a day and a night, and when he awoke he asked for food. In a fortnight he was well.

It was past midnight when Winter and I rowed back to shore and we had drunk innumerable whiskies and sodas.

" What do you think of it all ? " asked Winter.

" What a question ! If you mean, have I any explanation to suggest, I haven't."

" The captain believes every word of it."

" That's obvious ; but you know that's not the part that interests me most, whether it's true or not, and what it all means ; the part that interests me is that such things should happen to such people. I wonder what there is in that commonplace little man to arouse such a passion in that lovely creature. As I watched her, asleep there, while he was telling the story I had some fantastic idea about the power of love being able to work miracles."

" But that's not the girl," said Winter.

" What on earth do you mean ? "

" Didn't you notice the cook ? "

" Of course I did. He's the ugliest man I ever saw."

" That's why Butler took him. The girl ran away with the

Chinese cook last year.   This is a new one.   He's only had her there about two months."

"Well, I'm hanged."

"He thinks this cook is safe.   But I wouldn't be too sure in his place.   There's something about a Chink, when he lays himself out to please a woman she can't resist him."

ROOUM

FOR all I ever knew to the contrary it was his own name ;
and something about him, name or man or both, always
put me in mind, I can't tell you how, of negroes. As
regards the name, I dare say it was something huggermugger
in the mere sound—something that I classed, for no particular
reason, with the dark and ignorant sort of words, such as
" Obi " and " Hoo-doo." I only know that after I learned
that his name was Rooum, I couldn't for the life of me have
thought of him as being called anything else.

The first impression that you got of his head was that it
was a patchwork of black and white—black bushy hair and
short white beard or else the other way about. As a matter of
fact, both hair and beard were piebald, so that if you saw him
in the gloom a dim patch of white showed down one side of his
head, and dark tufts cropped up here and there in his beard.
His eyebrows alone were entirely black, with a little sprouting
of hair almost joining them. And perhaps his skin helped to
make me think of negroes, for it was very dark, of the dark
brown that always seems to have more than a hint of green
behind it. His forehead was low, and scored across with deep
horizontal furrows.

We never knew when he was going to turn up on a job. We
might not have seen him for weeks, but his face was always
as likely as not to appear over the edge of a crane-platform
just when that marvellous mechanical intuition of his was
badly needed. He wasn't certificated. He wasn't even
trained, as the rest of us understood training ; and he scoffed
at the drawing-office, and laughed outright at logarithms and
our laborious methods of getting out quantities. But he
could set sheers and tackle in a way that made the rest of us

look silly. I remember once how, through the parting of a chain, a sixty-foot girder had come down and lay under a ruck of other stuff, as the bottom chip lies under a pile of spellikins—a hopeless-looking smash. Myself, I'm certificated twice or three times over ; but I can only assure you that I wanted to kick myself when, after I'd spent a day and a sleepless night over the job, I saw the game of tit-tat-toe that Rooum made of it in an hour or two. Certificated or not, a man isn't a fool who can do that sort of thing. And he was one of these fellows, too, who can " find water "—tell you where water is and what amount of getting it is likely to take, by just walking over the place. We aren't certificated up to that yet.

He was offered good money to stick to us—to stick to our firm—but he always shook his black-and-white piebald head. He'd never be able to keep the bargain if he were to make it, he told us quite fairly. I know there are these chaps who can't endure to be clocked to their work with a patent time-clock in the morning, and released of an evening with a whistle —and it's one of the things no master can ever understand. So Rooum came and went erratically, showing up maybe in Leeds or Liverpool, perhaps next on Plymouth Breakwater, and once he turned up in an out-of-the-way place in Glamorgan-shire just when I was wondering what had become of him.

The way I got to know him (got to know him, I mean, more than just to nod) was that he tacked himself on to me one night down Vauxhall way, where we were setting up some small plant or other. We had knocked off for the day, and I was walking in the direction of the bridge when he came up. We walked along together ; and we had not gone far before it appeared that his reason for joining me was that he wanted to know " what a molecule was."

I stared at him a bit.

" What do you want to know that for ? " I said. " What does a chap like you, who can do it all backwards, want with molecules ? "

Oh, he just wanted to know, he said.

So, on the way across the bridge, I gave it him more or less from the book—molecular theory and all the rest of it. But, from the childish questions he put, it was plain that he hadn't got the hang of it all. Did the molecular theory allow things to pass through one another ? " he wanted to know; " *Could* things pass through one another ? " and a lot of ridiculous things like that. I gave it up.

" You're a genius in your own way, Rooum," I said finally ;
" you know these things without the books we plodders have
to depend on. If I'd luck like that, I think I should be content
with it."

But he didn't seem satisfied, though he dropped the matter
for that time. But I had his acquaintance, which was more
than most of us had. He asked me, rather timidly, if I'd lend
him a book or two. I did so, but they didn't seem to contain
what he wanted to know, and he soon returned them, without
remark.

Now you'd expect a fellow to be specially sensitive, one way
or another, who can tell when there's water a hundred feet
beneath him ; and as you know, the big men are squabbling
yet about this water-finding business. But, somehow, the
water-finding puzzled me less than it did that Rooum should
be extraordinarily sensitive to something far commoner and
easier to understand—ordinary echoes. He couldn't stand
echoes. He'd go a mile round rather than pass a place that he
knew had an echo ; and if he came on one by chance, sometimes
he'd hurry through as quick as he could, and sometimes he'd
loiter and listen very intently. I rather joked about this at
first, till I found it really distressed him ; then, of course, I
pretended not to notice. We're all cranky somewhere, and
for that matter, I can't touch a spider myself.

For the remarkable thing that overtook Rooum—(that,
by the way, is an odd way to put it, as you'll see presently ;
but the words came that way into my head, so let them stand)
—for the remarkable thing that overtook Rooum, I don't think
I can begin better than with the first time, or very soon after
the first time, that I noticed this peculiarity about the echoes.

It was early on a particularly dismal November evening,
and this time we were somewhere out south-east London way,
just beyond what they are pleased to call the building-line—
you know these districts of wretched trees and grimy fields
and market-gardens that are about the same to real country that
a slum is to a town. It rained that night ; rain was the most
appropriate weather for the brickfields and sewage-farms and
yards of old carts and railway-sleepers we were passing. The
rain shone on the black hand-bag that Rooum always carried ;
and I sucked at the dottle of a pipe that it was too much trouble
to fill and light again. We were walking in the direction of
Lewisham (I think it would be), and were still a little way from
that eruption of red-brick houses that . . . but you've doubtless seen them.

You know how, when they're laying out new roads, they lay down the narrow strip of kerb first, with neither setts on the one hand nor flag-stones on the other? We had come upon one of these. (I had noticed how, as we had come a few minutes before under a tall hollow-ringing railway arch, Rooum had all at once stopped talking—it was the echo, of course, that bothered him). The unmade road to which we had come had headless lamp-standards at intervals, and ramparts of grey road-metal ready for use; and save for the strip of kerb, it was a broth of mud and stiff clay. A red light or two showed where the road-barriers were—they were laying the mains; a green railway light showed on an embankment; and the Lewisham lamps made a rusty glare through the rain. Rooum went first, walking along the narrow strip of kerb.

The lamp-standards were a little difficult to see, and when I heard Rooum stop suddenly and draw in his breath sharply, I thought he had walked into one of them.

" Hurt yourself? " I said.

He walked on without replying; but half a dozen yards farther on he stopped again. He was listening again. He waited for me to come up.

" I say," he said, in an odd sort of voice, " go a yard or two ahead, will you? "

" What's the matter? " I asked, as I passed ahead. He didn't answer.

Well, I hadn't been leading for more than a minute before he wanted to change again. He was breathing very quick and short.

" Why, what ails you? " I demanded, stopping.

" It's all right. . . . You're not playing any tricks, are you? . . ."

I saw him pass his hand over his brow.

" Come, get on," I said shortly; and we didn't speak again till we struck the pavement with the lighted lamps. Then I happened to glance at him.

" Here," I said brusquely, taking him by the sleeve, " you're not well. We'll call somewhere and get a drink."

" Yes," he said, again wiping his brow. " I say . . . did you hear? "

" Hear what? "

" Ah, you didn't . . . and, of course, you didn't feel anything. . . ."

" Come, you're shaking."

When presently we came to a brightly lighted public-house or hotel, I saw that he was shaking even worse than I had thought. The shirt-sleeved barman noticed it, too, and watched us curiously. I made Rooum sit down, and got him some brandy.

" What was the matter ? " I asked, as I held the glass to his lips.

But I could get nothing out of him except that it was " All right—all right," with his head twitching over his shoulder almost as if he had a touch of the dance. He began to come round a little. He wasn't the kind of man you'd press for explanations, and presently we set out again. He walked with me as far as my lodgings, refused to come in, but for all that lingered at the gate as if loath to leave. I watched him turn the corner in the rain.

We came home together again the next evening, but by a different way, quite half a mile longer. He had waited for me a little pertinaciously. It seemed he wanted to talk about molecules again.

Well, when a man of his age—he'd be near fifty—begins to ask questions, he's rather worse than a child who wants to know where heaven is, or some such thing—for you can't put him off as you can the child. Somewhere or other he'd picked up the word " osmosis," and seemed to have some glimmering of its meaning. He dropped the molecules, and began to ask me about osmosis.

" It means, doesn't it," he demanded, " that liquids will work their way into one another—through a bladder or something ? Say a thick fluid and a thin : you'll find some of the thick in the thin, and the thin in the thick ? "

" Yes. The thick into the thin is ex-osmosis, and the other end-osmosis. That takes place more quickly. But I don't know a deal about it."

" Does it ever take place with solids ? " he next asked.

What was he driving at ? I thought ; but replied : " I believe that what is commonly called ' adhesion ' is something of the sort, under another name."

" A good deal of this bookwork seems to be finding a dozen names for the same thing," he grunted ; and continued to ask his questions.

But what it was he really wanted to know I couldn't for the life of me make out.

Well, he was due any time now to disappear again, having worked quite six weeks in one place ; and he disappeared.

He disappeared for a good many weeks. I think it would be about February before I saw or heard him again.

It was February weather, anyway, and in an echoing enough place that I found him—the subway of one of the Metropolitan stations. He'd probably forgotten the echoes when he'd taken the train ; but, of course, the railway folk won't let a man who happens to dislike echoes go wandering across the metals where he likes.

He was twenty yards ahead when I saw him. I recognized him by his patched head and black hand-bag. I ran along the subway after him.

It was very curious. He'd been walking close to the white-tiled wall, and I saw him suddenly stop ; but he didn't turn. He didn't even turn when I pulled up, close behind him ; he put out one hand to the wall, as if to steady himself. But, the moment I touched his shoulder, he just dropped— just dropped half on his knees against the white tiling. The face he turned round and up to me was transfixed with fright.

There were half a hundred people about—a train was just in—and it isn't a difficult matter in London to get a crowd for much less than a man crouching terrified against a wall, looking over his shoulder as Rooum looked, at another man almost as terrified. I felt somebody's hand on my own arm. Evidently somebody thought I'd knocked Rooum down.

The terror went slowly from his face. He stumbled to his feet. I shook myself free of the man who held me and stepped up to Rooum.

" What the devil's all this about ? " I demanded, roughly enough.

" It's all right . . . it's all right . . ." he stammered.

" Heavens, man, you shouldn't play tricks like that ! "

" No . . . no . . . but for the love of God don't do it again ! . . ."

" We'll not explain here," I said, still in a good deal of a huff ; and the small crowd melted away—disappointed, I dare say, that it wasn't a fight.

" Now," I said, when we were outside in the crowded street, " you might let me know what all this is about, and what it is that for the love of God I'm not to do again."

He was half apologetic, but at the same time half blustering, as if I had committed some sort of an outrage.

" A senseless thing like that ! " he mumbled to himself. " But there ፡ you didn't know. . . . You *don't* know, do you ? . . . I tell you, d'you hear, *you're not to run at all when 'm about !* You're a nice fellow and all that, and get your quantities somewhere near right, if you do go a long way round to do it—but I'll not answer for myself if you run, d'you hear ? . . . Putting your hand on a man's shoulder like that, just when . . ."

" Certainly I might have spoken," I agreed, a little stiffly.

" Of course you ought to have spoken ! Just you see you don't do it again. It's monstrous ! "

I put a curt question.

" Are you sure you're quite right in your head, Rooum ? "

" Ah," he cried, " don't you think I just fancy it, my lad ! Nothing so easy ! I thought you guessed that other time, on the new road . . . it's as plain as a pikestaff . . . no, no, no ! *I* shall be telling *you* something about molecules one of these days ? "

We walked for a time in silence.

Suddenly he asked : " What are you doing now ? "

" I myself, do you mean ? Oh, the firm. A railway job, past Pinner. But we've a big contract coming on in the West End soon they might want you for. They call it ' alterations,' but it's one of these big shop-rebuildings."

" I'll come along."

" Oh, it isn't for a month or two yet."

" I don't mean that. I mean I'll come along to Pinner with you now, to-night, or whenever you go."

" Oh ! " I said.

I don't know that I specially wanted him. It's a little wearing, the company of a chap like that. You never know what he's going to let you in for next. But, as this didn't seem to occur to him, I didn't say anything. If he really liked catching the last train down, a three-mile walk, and then sharing a double-bedded room at a poor sort of ale-house (which was my own programme), he was welcome. We walked a little farther ; then I told him the time of the train and left him.

He turned up at Euston, a little after twelve. We went down together. It was getting on for one when we left the station at the other end, and then we began the tramp across the Weald to the inn. A little to my surprise (for I had begun to expect unaccountable behaviour from him) we reached the inn without Rooum having dodged about changing places with me, or having fallen cowering under a gorse-bush, or anything of that kind. Our talk, too, was about work, not molecules and osmosis.

The inn was only a roadside beer-house—I have forgotten its name—and all its sleeping accommodation was the one double-bedded room. Over the head of my own bed the ceiling was cut away, following the roof-line ; and the wall-paper was perfectly shocking—faded bouquets that made V's and A's, interlacing everywhere. The other bed was made up, and lay across the room.

I think I only spoke once while we were making ready for bed, and that was when Rooum took from his black hand-bag a brush and a torn nightgown.

" That's what you always carry about, is it ? " I remarked ; and Rooum grunted something : Yes . . . never knew where you'd be next . . . no harm, was it ?   We tumbled into bed.

But, for all the lateness of the hour, I wasn't sleepy ; so from my own bag I took a book, set the candle on the end of the mantel, and began to read. Mark you, I don't say I was much better informed for the reading I did, for I was watching the V's on the wallpaper mostly—that, and wondering what was wrong with the man in the other bed who had fallen down at a touch in the subway. He was already asleep.

Now I don't know whether I can make the next clear to you. I'm quite certain he was sound asleep, so that it wasn't just the fact that he spoke. Even that is a little unpleasant, I always think, any sort of sleep-walking ; but it's a very queer sort of sensation when a man actually answers a question that's put to him, knowing nothing whatever about it in the morning. Perhaps I ought not to have put that question ; having put it, I did the next best thing afterwards, as you'll see in a moment . . . but let me tell you.

He'd been asleep perhaps an hour, and I wool-gathering about the wallpaper, when suddenly, in a far more clear and loud voice than he ever used when awake, he said :

" *What the devil is it prevents me seeing him, then ?* "

That startled me, rather, for the second time that evening ; and I really think I had spoken before I had fully realized what was happening.

" From seeing whom ? " I said, sitting up in bed.

" Whom ? . . . You're not attending. The fellow I'm telling you about, who runs after me," he answered—answered perfectly plainly.

I could see his head there on the pillow, black and white, and his eyes were closed. He made a slight movement with his arm, but that did not wake him. Then it came to me, with a sort of start, what was happening. I slipped half out

of bed. Would he—would he—answer another question ?
. . . I risked it, breathlessly.

" Have you any idea who he is ? "

Well, that, too, he answered.

" Who he is ? The Runner ? . . . Don't be silly. *Who else should it be ?* "

With every nerve in me tingling, I tried again.

" What happens, then, when he catches you ? "

This time, I really don't know whether his words were an answer or not ; they were these :

" To hear him catching you up . . . and then padding away ahead again ! All right, all right . . . but I guess it's weakening *him* a bit, too. . . ."

Without noticing it, I had got out of bed, and had advanced quite to the middle of the floor.

" What did you say his name was ? " I breathed.

But that was a dead failure. He muttered brokenly for a moment, gave a deep troubled sigh, and then began to snore loudly and regularly.

I made my way back to bed ; but I assure you that before I did so I filled my basin with water, dipped my face into it, and then set the candlestick afloat in it, leaving the candle burning. I thought I'd like to have a light. . . . It had burned down by morning. Rooum, I remember, remarked on the silly practice of reading in bed.

Well, it was a pretty kind of obsession for a man to have, wasn't it ? Somebody running after him all the time, and then . . . running on ahead ? And, of course, on a broad pavement there would be plenty of room for this running gentleman to run round ; but on an eight- or nine-inch kerb, such as that of the new road out Lewisham way . . . but perhaps he was a jumping gentleman too, and could jump over a man's head. You'd think he'd have to get past some way, wouldn't you ? . . . I remember vaguely wondering whether the name of that Runner was not Conscience ; but Conscience isn't a matter of molecules and osmosis. . . .

One thing, however, was clear ; I'd got to tell Rooum what I'd learned : for you can't get hold of a fellow's secrets in ways like that. I lost no time about it. I told him, in fact, soon after we'd left the inn the next morning—told him how he'd answered in his sleep.

And—what do you think of this ?—he seemed to think I ought to have guessed it ! *Guessed* a monstrous thing like that !

"You're less clever than I thought, with your books and that, if you didn't," he grunted.

"But . . . Good God, man !"

"Queer, isn't it ? But you don't know the queerest . . ."

He pondered for a moment, and then suddenly put his lips to my ear.

"I'll tell you," he whispered. "*It gets harder every time !* . . . At first, he just slipped through : a bit of a catch at my heart, like when you nod off to sleep in a chair and jerk up awake again ; and away he went. But now it's getting grinding, sluggish ; and the pain. . . . You'd notice, that night on the road, the little check it gave me ; that's past long since ; and last night, when I'd just braced myself up stiff to meet it, and you tapped me on the shoulder . . ." He passed the back of his hand over his brow.

"I tell you," he continued, "it's an agony each time. I could scream at the thought of it. It's oftener, too, now, and he's getting stronger. The end-osmosis is getting to be ex-osmosis—is that right ? Just let me tell you one more thing——"

But I'd had enough. I'd asked questions the night before, but now—well, I knew quite as much as, and more than, I wanted.

"Stop, please," I said. "You're either off your head, or worse. Let's call it the first. Don't tell me any more, please."

"Frightened, what ? Well, I don't blame you. But what would *you* do ?"

"I should see a doctor ; I'm only an engineer," I replied.

"Doctors ? . . . Bah !" he said, and spat.

I hope you see how the matter stood with Rooum. What do you make of it ? Could you have believed it—*do* you believe it ? . . . He'd made a nearish guess when he'd said that much of our knowledge is giving names to things we know nothing about ; only rule-of-thumb Physics thinks everything's explained in the Manual ; and you've always got to remember one thing : You can call it Force or what you like, but it's a certainty that things, solid things of wood and iron and stone, would explode, just go off in a puff into space, if it wasn't for something just as inexplicable as that that Rooum said he felt in his own person. And if you can swallow that, it's a relatively small matter whether Rooum's light-footed Familiar slipped through him unperceived, or had to struggle through obstinately. You see now why I said that " a queer thing overtook Rooum."

More : I saw it. This thing, that outrages reason—I saw it happen. That is to say, I saw its effects, and it was in broad daylight, on an ordinary afternoon, in the middle of Oxford Street, of all places. There wasn't a shadow of doubt about it. People were pressing and jostling about him, and suddenly I saw him turn his head and listen, as I'd seen him before. I tell you, an icy creeping ran all over my skin. I fancied *I* felt it approaching, too, nearer and nearer. . . . The next moment he had made a sort of gathering of himself, as if against a gust. He stumbled and thrust—thrust with his body. He swayed, physically, as a tree sways in a wind ; he clutched my arm and gave a loud scream. Then, after seconds—minutes—I don't know how long—he was free again.

And for the colour of his face when by and by I glanced at it . . . well, I once saw a swarthy Italian fall under a sun-stroke, and *his* face was much the same colour that Rooum's negro face had gone ; a cloudy, whitish green.

" Well—you've seen it—what do you think of it ? " he gasped presently, turning a ghastly grin on me.

But it was night before the full horror of it had soaked into me.

Soon after that he disappeared again. I wasn't sorry.

Our big contract in the West End came on. It was a time-contract, with all manner of penalty clauses if we didn't get through ; and I assure you that we were busy. I myself was far too busy to think of Rooum.

It's a shop now, the place we were working at, or rather one of these huge weldings of fifty shops where you can buy anything ; and if you'd seen us there . . . but perhaps you did see us, for people stood up on the tops of omnibuses as they passed, to look over the mud-splashed hoarding into the great excavation we'd made. It was a sight. Staging rose on staging, tier on tier, with interminable ladders all over the steel structure. Three or four squat Otis lifts crouched like iron turtles on top, and a lattice-crane on a towering three-cornered platform rose a hundred and twenty feet into the air. At one end of the vast quarry was a demolished house, showing flues and fireplaces and a score of thicknesses of old wallpaper ; and at night—they might well have stood up on the tops of the buses. A dozen great spluttering violet arc-lights half-blinded you ; down below were the watchmen's fires ; overhead, the riveters had their fire-baskets ; and in odd corners naphtha-

lights guttered and flared.   And the steel rang with the riveters'
hammers, and the crane-chains rattled and clashed. . . .
There's not much doubt in *my mind*, it's the engineers who are
the architects nowadays.   The chaps who think they're the
architects are only a sort of paperhangers, who hang brick and
terra-cotta on our work and clap a pinnacle or two on top—but
never mind that.   There we were, sweating and clanging and
navvying, till the day shift came to relieve us.

And I ought to say that fifty feet above our great gap, and
from end to end across it, there ran a travelling crane on a
skeleton line, with platform, engine, and wooden cab all compact in one.

It happened that they had pitched in as one of the foremen
some fellow or other, a friend of the firm's, a rank duffer, who
pestered me incessantly with his questions.   I did half his work
and all my own, and it hadn't improved my temper much.   On
this night that I'm telling about, he'd been playing the fool
with his questions as if a time-contract was a sort of summer
holiday ; and he'd filled me up to that point that I really can't
say just when it was that Roomm put in an appearance again.
I think I *had* heard somebody mention his name, but I'd paid
no attention.

Well, our Johnnie Fresh came up to me for the twentieth
time that night, this time wanting to know something about the
overhead crane.   At that I fairly lost my temper.

" What ails the crane ? " I cried.   " It's doing its work,
isn't it ?   Isn't everybody doing their work except you ?   Why
can't you ask Hopkins ?   Isn't Hopkins there ? "

" I don't know," he said.

" Then," I snapped, " in that particular I'm as ignorant as
you, and I hope it's the only one."

But he grabbed my arm.

" Look at it now ! " he cried, pointing ; and I looked up.

Either Hopkins or somebody was dangerously exceeding the
speed-limit.   The thing was flying along its thirty yards of rail
as fast as a tram, and the heavy fall-blocks swung like a ponderous kite-tail, thirty feet below.   As I watched, the engine
brought up within a yard of the end of the way, the blocks
crashed like a ram into the broken house, fetching down
plaster and brick, and then the mechanism was reversed.   The
crane set off at a tear back.

" Who in Hell . . ." I began ; but it wasn't a time to talk.
" *Hi !* " I yelled, and made a spring for a ladder.

The others had noticed it, too, for there were shouts all over

Just how we scrambled on I don't know.

the place. By that time I was half-way up the second stage.
Again the crane tore past, with the massive tackle sweeping
behind it, and again I heard the crash at the other end.   Whoever had the handling of it was managing it skilfully, for there
was barely a foot to spare when it turned again.

On the fourth platform, at the end of the way, I found
Hopkins.   He was white, and seemed to be counting on his
fingers.

" What's the matter here ? " I cried.

" It's Rooum," he answered.   " I hadn't stepped out of
the cab, not a minute, when I heard the lever go.   He's running somebody down, he says ; he'll run the whole shoot down
in a minute—look ! . . ."

The crane was coming back again.   Half out of the cab I
could see Rooum's mottled hair and beard.   His brow was
ribbed like a gridiron, and as he ripped past one of the arcs
his face shone like porcelain with the sweat that bathed it.

" Now . . . you ! . . . *Now*, damn you ! . . ." he was
shouting.

" Get ready to board him when he reverses ! " I shouted
to Hopkins.

Just how we scrambled on I don't know.   I got one arm
over the lifting-gear (which, of course, wasn't going), and heard
Hopkins on the other footplate.   Rooum put the brake down
and reversed ; again came the thud of the fall-blocks ; and we
were speeding back again over the gulf of misty orange light.
The stagings were thronged with gaping men.

" Ready ? Now ! " I cried to Hopkins ; and we sprang
into the cab.

Hopkins hit Rooum's wrist with a spanner.   Then he
seized the lever, jammed the brake down and tripped Rooum,
all, as it seemed, in one movement.   I fell on top of Rooum.
The crane came to a standstill half-way down the line.   I held
Rooum panting.

But either Rooum was stronger than I, or else he took me
very much unawares.   All at once he twisted clear from my
grasp and stumbled on his knees to the rear door of the cab.
He threw up one elbow, and staggered to his feet as I made
another clutch at him.

" Keep still, you fool ! " I bawled.   " Hit him over the
head, Hopkins ! "

Rooum screamed in a high voice.

" Run him down—cut him up with the wheels—down,
you !—down, I say !—Oh, my God ! . . . *Ha !* "

He sprang clear out from the crane door, well-nigh taking me with him.

I told you it was a skeleton line, two rails and a tie or two. He'd actually jumped to the right-hand rail. And he was running along it—running along that iron tight-rope, out over that well of light and watching men. Hopkins had started the travelling-gear, as if with some insane idea of catching him ; but there was only one possible end to it. He'd gone fully a dozen yards, while I watched, horribly fascinated ; and then I saw the turn of his head. . . .

He didn't meet it this time ; he sprang to the other rail, as if to evade it. . . .

Even at the take-off he missed. As far as I could see, he made no attempt to save himself with his hands. He just went down out of the field of my vision. There was an awful silence ; then, from far below. . . .

They weren't the men on the lower stages who moved first. The men above went a little way down, and then they, too, stopped. Presently two of them descended, but by a distant way. They returned, with two bottles of brandy, and there was a hasty consultation. Two men drank the brandy off there and then—getting on for a pint of brandy apiece ; then they went down, drunk.

I, Hopkins tells me, had got down on my knees in the crane cab, and was jabbering away cheerfully to myself. When I asked him what I said, he hesitated, and then said : " Oh, you don't want to know that, sir," and I haven't asked him since.

What do *you* make of it ?

THE GREEN LIGHT

T HE man looked down at the figure of the woman on the couch. The little silver clock on the mantelpiece began to chime; he could not bear the sound of it. He flew at the clock like a madman, and dashed it on the ground, and stamped on it. Then he drew down the blind, and opened the door and listened; there was no one on the staircase. Silence seemed now as intolerable to him as sound had been a moment before. He tried to whistle, but his lips were too dry and made only a ridiculous hissing sound. Closing the door behind him, he ran down the staircase and out into the street. The woman on the couch never moved or spoke. It was late in the afternoon; the light from the low sun penetrated the green blind and took from it a horrible colour that seemed to tint the face of the woman on the couch. Flies came out of the dark corners of the room, sulkily busy, crawling and buzzing. One very little fly passed backwards and forwards over the woman's white ringed hand; it moved rapidly, a black speck.

Outside in the street, the man stepped from the pavement into the roadway; a cabman shouted and swore at him, and some one dragged him back by the arm, and told him roughly to look where he was going. He stood still for a minute, and rubbed his forehead with his hand. This would not do. The critical moment had come, the moment when, above all things, it was necessary that his nerve should be perfect and his thoughts clear; and now, when he tried to think, a picture came before the thought and filled his mind—the picture of the white face with the green light upon it. And his heart was beating too fast, and, it seemed to him, almost audibly. He began to feel his pulse, counting the strokes out loud as he

stood on the kerb ; then he was conscious that two or three
boys and loafers were standing in a little group watching
him and laughing at him.   One of the loafers handed him his
hat ; it had fallen off when he dodged back on to the pavement, and he had not noticed it.   He took the hat, and felt
for some coins to give the man.   He found a half-crown and
a halfpenny ; he held them in his hand, and stared at them,
and forgot why he had wanted them.   Then he suddenly
remembered and gave them.   There was a loud yell of laughter;
the boys and loafers were running away, and he heard one
of them shouting, " Let the old stinker out a bit too soon,
ain't they ? " and another, " Garn ! 'E's tight—that's all's
wrong with 'im."

Again he told himself that this would not do.   He must
not think of the past—the awful past.   He must not think of
the future—of his schemes for escape.   He must concentrate
his thoughts on the present moment, until he could get to some
place where he could be alone.   Yes, Regent's Park would do
well, and it was near.   He brushed his hat with his coat-
sleeve, put it on, and walked.   He thought about the movement of his feet, and the best way to cross the road, and how
to avoid running into people, and how to behave as other
people in the street behaved.   All the things that one generally
does unconsciously and automatically required now for their
conduct a distinct mental effort.

As he walked on, his mind seemed to clear a little.   He
reached a spot in Regent's Park where he could lie down in the
grass with no one near him, out of sight.   " Now," he said to
himself, " I need concentrate my thoughts no longer—I can
let them go."   In a second he had gone rapidly through the
past—the jealousy that had burned in his heart, and the way
that he had quieted himself and made his scheme, and carried
it out slowly.   It had been finished that afternoon, when he had
lost control over himself, and——

Through the transparent leaves of the tree near him the
sun came with a greenish glare.   He shuddered and turned
away, so that he could not see it.

Yes, he was to escape—he had made all arrangements for
that.   He drew from his side-pocket a roll of notes, and
counted them, and entered the numbers in his pocket-book.
He had changed a cheque for fifty pounds at the bank that
morning.   The police would find that out, and endeavour
to trace him by discovering where the notes with those numbers
were changed.   That was one of his means of escape.   He

would see to it that the notes were never changed by himself, or in any town where he had been or was likely to be. He was going to sacrifice those ten bank-notes to put the police on a wrong scent. He had plenty of money ready in gold—in gold that could not be traced—for his own needs. He chuckled to himself. It was brilliant, this scheme for providing a wrong scent, for making the very carefulness and astuteness of the detective the stumbling-block in their way ; and it would be so easy to get the notes changed by others—the dishonesty of ordinary human beings would serve his purpose.

His mood had changed now to one of exultation. He told himself time after time that he was right. The law would condemn him, but morally he was right, and had only punished the woman as she deserved to be punished. Only, he must escape. And—yes—he must not forget.

He looked round. There was still no one near ; but his position did not satisfy him. Not a person must see what he was going to do, next. He went on, and found a spot near the canal, where he seemed to be out of sight, and more secure from interruption. Then he took from his pocket a little looking-glass and a pair of scissors. Very carefully he cut away his beard and moustache, that hid the thin-lipped wide mouth, and the small weak chin. He cut as close as he could, and when he had finished he looked like a man who had neglected to shave for a day or two. A barber would shave him now without suspicion. He was satisfied with the operation. The glass showed him a face so changed that it startled him to look at it. He glanced at his watch—it was time to start for the station, where his luggage had been waiting since the day before, if he meant to get shaved on the way there.

He walked a little way, and sat down again. " How well everything has been thought out ! " he said to himself. All would succeed. With a new name, and in another country, without that drunken, faithless, beautiful woman, he would grow happy again. He had only meant to sit down for a minute or two, but his thoughts rambled and became nonsense, and suddenly he fell into a deep sleep. He had been overtaxed.

An hour passed. The train that he had intended to take steamed out of the station, and still he slept. It grew dusk, and still he slept. When the park-keeper touched him on the shoulder, he half-awoke and spoke querulously. Then consciousness came back, and slowly he realized what had happened.

As he walked slowly out of the park, his mind refreshed

with sleep, he for the first time realized something else. In the awful moment when he had left the woman, he had broken down, and forgotten everything. The bag of gold was still lying on the table of the room with the green blind. He must go back and get it. It would be horrible to re-enter that room, but it could not be helped. He dared not change the notes himself, and in any case that amount would be insufficient. He must have the gold.

It added, he told himself, slightly to the risk of discovery, but only slightly. His servants had all been sent out and were not to return until half-past nine. No one else could have entered the house. He would find everything as he left it—the gold on the table and the figure of the woman on the couch. He would let himself in with his latch-key. No passer-by would take any notice of so ordinary an incident. He had no occasion to hurry now, and he turned into the first barber's shop that he saw. His mind was as alert now as it had been when he first formed his scheme.

"Let me have your best razor," he said; "my skin's tender; in fact, for the last two or three days I haven't been able to shave at all."

He chatted with the barber about horse-racing, and said that he himself had a couple of horses in training. Then he inquired the way to Piccadilly, saying that he was a stranger in London, and seemed to take careful note of the barber's directions.

He walked briskly away from the shop towards his own house. A comfortable-looking, ruddy-faced woman was coming towards him. A shaft of green light from a chemist's shop-window fell full on her face as she passed, and the horror came back upon him. It was with difficulty that he checked himself from crying out. He hurried on, but that hideous light seemed to linger in his eyes and to haunt him.

"Keep quiet!" he kept saying to himself under his breath. "Steady yourself; don't be a fool!"

There was an Italian restaurant near, and he went in and drank a couple of glasses of cognac. Then only was he able to go on.

As he turned the corner where his house came into sight he looked up. All the house was dark but for one great green eye in the centre that looked at him. There were lights in that room.

He stood still close to a lamp-post, just touching it to keep his balance. He spoke to himself aloud:

"It's green . . . it's green . . . some one's there!"
A working man passed him, heard him mumbling, looked at
him curiously, and went on.

The great green eye stared at him and fascinated him.
Then other lights darted about, red lights, white lights. Some
one must be going up and down the staircase and passages.
Had she got off the couch? Was the dead woman walking?
How his head throbbed! There were two nerves that seemed
to sound like two consecutive notes on a piano, struck in slow
alternation, then quickening to a rapid shake—whirr! whirr!
Now the two notes were struck together, a repeated discord,
thumped out—clatter! clatter! No, the sound was outside
in the street, and it was the sound of people running. There
were boys with excited eyes and white faces, and blowsy,
laughing women, and a little old ferret-faced man who coughed
as he ran. A police-whistle screamed.

In front of the door of the house a black mass grew up,
getting quickly bigger and bigger. It was a crowd of people
swaying backwards and forwards, kept back by the police.

The police! He was discovered, then. He must get
away at once, not wait another moment. Only the green light
was looking at him.

"Stop that light!" he called.

No one noticed him. The green light went on glimmering,
and drew him nearer. He had to get there. He was on the
outskirts of the crowd now.

Why would not the crowd let him pass? Could not
they hear that he was being called? He pushed his way,
struggling, dragging people on one side. There were angry
voices, a hum growing louder and louder. He caught a woman
by the neck and flung her aside. She screamed. Some one
struck him in the face, and he tried to strike back. Down!
He was down on the road. The air was stifling and stinking
there. He tried to get up, and was forced back. Ah! now
he was up again, his coat torn off his back, muddy, bleeding,
fighting, spitting, howling like a madman.

"Damn you! damn you all!"

The crowd was a storm all round him, tossing him here
and there. Again and again he was struck. There was blood
streaming over his eyes, and through the blood and mingled
with blood he saw the green light looking.

There came a sudden lull. A couple of policemen stood
by him, and one of them had him by the arm, and asked him
what he was doing. He began to cry, sobbing like a child.

" Take me up there," he said, panting, " where the green light is ; it's the dead woman calling."

The policeman stood for a moment hesitating. For a moment the crowd was motionless and silent. Then one of those white-faced boys shrank further back whispering :

" It's the man ! "

THE IRON PINEAPPLE

IT will comfort me to write it. It comforted me to tell my wife, but that consolation vanished when she refused to believe the story and proposed to send for a medical man.

There may be scientific people who could explain what happened to me ; there may be names for the state, and it is possible that others have suffered similarly, and done equally amazing things, but in my humble position of life one has no time for works on morbid psychology or its therapeutics, and I prefer to explain all differently and directly. I choose rather to assert that it pleased Providence to select me on a unique occasion for its own profound purposes.

That is how I explain it now, but to be the weapon of Providence in a great matter is not a part that any sane small shopkeeper would choose, and none will ever know the extent of my sufferings while the secret forces that control our destinies had their terrible way with me ; none will ever fathom my awful woes and fears as I tottered on the brink of downright madness ; none will ever look into the unutterable chasm that for a season yawned between me and my fellow-creatures.

I was cut off from them ; I lived a hideous life apart. No human eye penetrated those dark fastnesses of the spirit where I wandered, lost ; no friendly voice sounded for me ; no sympathy nor understanding came to my side and heartened me to conquer the appalling tribulation.

Doubtless, in some measure, the fault was my own. There were not a few who respected me, and would have done all they might to help me. My wife—what man ever had better ? She was always ready, and her gentle tact paved a way for me through many a neurotic storm and morbid ecstasy, but the secret thing, the obsession of my life, was hidden from her. For shame I hid it ; even to her I could not confess its nature and the profound and shattering effect it had upon my self-control and my self-respect.

The nature of this curse will best appear in the course of my narrative. John Noy is my name, and I dwell in the Cornish haven of Bude. Hither from Holsworthy I came, twenty years ago, but the prosperity that has of late burst in a grateful shower over Bude, converting it from an obscure hamlet to a prosperous resort, was not shared by me.

I keep a small grocery store, and sell fruit and vegetables also ; while to eke out my modest means I control a branch of the post office, and so add little to my income, but much to my daily labours ; for the paltry remuneration of one pound one shilling a month is all that accrues to me for my service in this great department of the State.

I had hoped that in the rising districts of Flexbury, where new houses were springing up like mushrooms, and often with little more than a mushroom's stability, the post office might have opened a way to increased custom, and added to the importance and popularity of my little business. But it never did so. Occasional notepaper and sealing-wax I disposed of, but no respectable augmentation of my own trade could be chronicled as a result of the post office, while, in holiday time, the work proved—and still proves—too much for one head and one pair of hands. Then my clever wife comes to my assistance ; and, even so, our accounts do not always balance.

Of course, Bude is not what it was when first I wedded Mabel Polglaze and took my shop. Now an enormous summer population pours upon us annually, and the golf-links swarm with men and women, who pursue that sport from dawn till evening ; and the wide sands of the shore are covered with children who, in their picturesque attire, are scattered there, like pink and blue, yellow and white flower-petals blowing over the sands when the tide is out.

I never had any children ; and it was a grief to my wife, but a secret joy to me—not because I do not love them, but because, after marriage, my infatuation dawned upon me, and I quickly felt that to hand on such mysterious traits of character would be criminal in the opinion of any conscientious soul.

The cloud ascended by slow degrees upon my clear horizon, and not until it had assumed some quality of sinister significance did I give it much thought. Indeed, in its earliest manifestation, I took pride in it ; and my wife, even from our betrothal, was wont to compliment me upon a certain quality of mind often associated with ultimate prosperity and worldly success.

" Noy," she said to me on one occasion, " your grasp of details is the most remarkable thing about you. You'll fasten on a thing like a dog on a bone, and nought will shake you off it. Whether 'tis sardines, or dried fruits, or spring vegetables, or a new tea, 'twill grip your mind in a most amazing way, and you'll let everything else slip by, and just go for that one object, and keep it in the front of your thoughts, and live on it, like food. And a very fine quality in a grocer ; and many a time you've pushed a line and made the public take a new thing. But what's queer about it, in my judgment, is that, so often as not, you'll put all your heart and soul into some stupid little matter, like a new mouse-trap or new vermin-killer, that don't pay for the trouble. You'll give just so much thought to a penwiper or bottle-washer, not worth sixpence, as you will to a new drink or new food, or some big thing that might mean good money, and plenty of it."

There she hit the nail on the head. I had a way to take some particular matter into my mind, as the hedge-sparrow takes the cuckoo's egg into her nest, and then, when the thing hatched out, all else had to go down before it, and for a season I was a man of one idea, and only one. Had those ideas been important ; had I conceived brilliant plans for Bude, or even for myself, none could have quarrelled with this power of concentration, or suspected that any infirmity of mind lurked behind it, but, as my wife too faithfully pointed out, I was prone to expend my rich stores of nervous energy upon the most trifling and insignificant matters.

Once I caught a grasshopper in our little garden, and for two years I had no mind to anything but grasshoppers. I purchased works on entomology which I could ill afford ; I collected grasshoppers, and spent long hours in studying their manners and customs ; I tamed a grasshopper, and finally acquired a knowledge of these insects that has probably never been equalled in the history of the world.

I fought this down with my wife's help, but it was the beginning of worse things ; and after she had lost her temper, and expressed her opinion of such puerilities in good set terms, I grew afraid, and began to conceal my mind from her. Then I found that, unconsciously, my frankness in all matters of the soul with Mabel had helped to keep me straight, and been a shield between me and the horrid idiosyncrasies of my nature.

The descent to hell was easy and, after barriers were once raised between my aberration and her common sense, the former grew by leaps and bounds. A change came over my horrid interests. Formerly it was some comestible or contrivance in my shop that had fixed my attention and chained my energies, to the loss of more important things ; for the grasshoppers arrived, as it were, before their time, and for many years after I had struggled free of their influence I suffered no similar lapse. But, having once adopted the practice of simulation with Mabel, having once withheld from her the secrets of my heart, the deterioration proceeded apace : I ceased to be vitally interested in my shop ; I wandered afield, and fastened on subjects and objects altogether outside my own life. These I brought into the very heart of my own mystery, and welcomed and worshipped. They were unconceivably trivial : in that lay the growing horror. `

To give an example : I remembered how for a time one monument in the churchyard arrested and absorbed my receptive faculties. Many nameless dead, victims of the sea, sleep their last sleep in our green churchyard upon the hill, and here, above a ship's company drowned long since at the haven mouth, there stands with a certain propriety the figure-head of their wrecked vessel. As it advanced before them in life, hanging above the ocean and leaping to the wave, so now in death the image keeps guard above their pillows, and stands, tall and white, among the lesser monuments of the mortuary. So it has stood for nearly fifty years, and promises long to continue, for it is preserved carefully and guarded against destruction.

This wooden image of the ill-fated *Bencoolan* exercised a most dreadful fascination over me ; and I cannot tell now how often I visited it, touched it, and poured out my futile thoughts as an offering to it. The figure of the Asiatic chieftain became to me an incubus and exercised a mesmeric power of attraction under which for a season I suffered helplessly. Indeed, I only escaped by abandoning the Church of England and joining the sect of the Primitive Wesleyans. I avoided the church and the grave of the drowned men ; I struggled against the horrible attraction of the figure-head. At night I woke and sweated and fought to keep in my couch, and I locked my arms through the bedstead that I might not be torn away to that solemn effigy above the graves.

The Primitive Wesleyans had a chapel within ten minutes' walk of my shop. It was new ; the foundation-stone had been laid but two years before by that famous Wesleyan philanthropist, financier, and friend of man, Bolsover Barbellion. The building, in the last and most debased form of architecture ever sprung from a mean mind, dominated Flexbury, and stood, a mass of hideous stone and baleful brick, above the pitiful rows of new dwelling-houses. But it saved me from the figure-head of the *Bencoolan*, and for a time the ministrations of the Primitive Wesleyans soothed my soul, and offered peace through the channels of religious novelty. I owe them much, and gladly record my debt.

Instances as grim as the foregoing might be cited, but I hasten to the climax of the tragedy and the events that preceded it. My wife, after a lengthened period, during which too surely we had drifted apart in sympathy and mutual understanding, took me to task, and her acerbity, while well enough deserved, none the less caused me a wide measure of astonishment. Never had she struck this note until this hour.

" Why the mischief can't you turn your attention to keeping a roof over our heads ? " she asked. " Trade's never been worse, and you'll lose the post office afore another summer if you make any more mistakes. And here's things happening in the world that might make angels weep. Look at yesterday's paper—all of them benevolent societies come down like a pack of cards, and that saint of God, as we thought—that Bolsover Barbellion—turns out to be a limb of Satan instead. And your own sister ruined, and widows and orphans face to face with the workhouse from one end of England to the other ! And the scoundrel himself has vanished like the dew upon the fleece, as well he may do. And there's another coal strike, the like of which was never knowed, and there's a murder to Plymouth, and talk of war with Germany, and God knows what beside ! Yet you—you can live in this world as if you was no more than a sheep or a cow, and pour out your wits in secret on some twopenny-halfpenny thing that you be too ashamed even to speak about. Yes ; you can, and you do. I know you—if not me, who should ? I hear you a-tossing like a ship in a storm of a night, and you won't let me comfort you no more. And life's hell to a woman placed like me, and I don't say how much longer I'm going to stand it ! How do I know what's in your mind ? How can I help you and comfort you if I'm kept outside in the dark ? All I can tell is that you're mad on something, for you're always out now—

always walking up and down on the cliffs as if you was a sentry
or a coastguard. And some fine day you'll fall over, and that'll
be a nice scandal ; for there's no smoke without fire, and of
course they'll whisper 'twas me that drove you to it."

Thus she ran on, and I made no attempt to stay the torrent.
My last infatuation differed widely from all others, for it was
human ; and had it been a woman, by evil chance, doubtless
my home had crashed down under it, for Mrs. Noy was not of
the type that tolerates any largeness of view in matters of sex.
But a man had for three months exercised an unconscious
control upon me—a large, bearded, able-bodied artist, who
devoted his attention to our cliff scenery, and who painted
pictures in the open air on Bude sands.

I never spoke to him. He was not even aware that he had
an interested spectator, but from the day I first looked over
the low cliffs near the cricket-ground, and saw the top of the
painter's hat, I was lost, and became concentrated upon the
man. He dominated my thoughts, and I felt ill at ease on the
days that I did not see him. I made no effort to learn his
name or ascertain where he lodged, but I speculated deeply
concerning him and the value of his art, and the workings of
his mind and his ambitions and hopes and fears. He had an
interesting face and a large voice, and rejoiced to watch the
children playing on the beach. He painted ill—so, at least,
I thought.

It seemed to me that he was an impressionist, and I felt
aversion from that school, being ignorant of its principles.
Once he left his seat among the rocks to walk beside the sea
awhile, and I emerged from the cliff above, whence I had been
watching him, and descended and looked at his picture. Something urged me to sit on his campstool, and I did so. He
turned, saw me, and approached. But the tide was out, and
he had to walk nearly a quarter of a mile to his easel. I
hastened away and hid from him, and watched him exhibit
no small surprise when he returned. He examined his picture
closely to see that I had not meddled with it.

From that day I conceived a violent dislike to the artist,
and this emotion increased to loathing ; then waxed from that
until it grew into an acute and homicidal hatred. Why such
an awful passion should have wakened in me against this
harmless painter it was impossible to understand.

I had never hated man or mouse until that moment ; and
now, full-fledged, insistent, tigerish, there awoke within me
an antagonism one would have supposed impossible to so mild

a mannered man. I fought it as I had never fought any previous obsession ; I told myself that rather than do any violence to a fellow-creature I would destroy my own body. Time and again, tramping the cliffs to peep down upon the unconscious painter beneath, I urged myself to take a false step, and do even as my wife had predicted that I might do. To escape from this fiendish premonition, to die and be at peace, grew an ever-increasing temptation. But I lacked physical courage ; I could not kill myself. I would have endured any mental torment rather than do so.

I met the painter face to face sometimes, and a demon might have felt his anti-human passion grow weak before the man's kind, good-natured face, great brown beard, laughing brown eyes, and sonorous, genial voice, but my antipathy only increased. It was, so far as I could analyze, quite without motive—a mere destructive instinct that made me tremble to batter and crush out of living this fellow-soul.

I determined to consult a medical man, but hesitated to do so for fear that he would insist upon my incarceration. I was not mad—save in the particular of my passing infatuations ; and, as all the others until now had persisted only for a season, I wept on my knees and prayed to Heaven through long night watches that this awful and crowning trial might also pass from me, and give place to hallucinations less terrific and less fraught with peril to my fellow-creatures.

As if in answer to this prayer there came sudden and astounding relief ; my aberrations changed their direction ; for a season I forgot the painter as though he had never been born, and every hope, desire, and mental energy became concentrated on the humblest and most insignificant object it is possible to mention. It was the lowest depth that I had reached.

On rising ground, not far distant from my shop, were being erected certain new dwelling-houses, and one of these had always pleased me, because it stood as an oasis in the dreary desert of mean buildings rising round about. It was designed in the Italian style, and possessed a distinction, beauty, and reserve foreign to the neighbourhood of Bude and the architectural spirit of the district. An outer wall encompassed this dwelling, and light metal-work ran along the top of it.

To my horror I discovered that a conventional chain was to be erected, and, at intervals of ten feet, the chain was supported by metal pillars crowned with cast-iron pineapples. Why a pleasing building should thus be spoiled by a piece of gratuitous vulgarity I could not understand. But speculation swiftly ceased, for suddenly, like a bolt from the blue, as such ebullitions always came, there burst upon me a frantic lust for one of these same abortions in iron! My soul poured out upon a metal pineapple; and no general hunger or distributed desire for the vile things took hold upon me, but I found my life's energy focussed and concentrated upon the third pineapple on the north side of the railing. For the rest I entertained no attachment; I even disliked them; but the third on the northern side exercised an absolute mastery.

If one may quote a familiar jest in connection with so abhorrent a circumstance, I felt, concerning this hideous piece of cast-iron, that I should not be happy until I got it. Naked roads stretched about this new house. They ran through fields, presently to be built upon, and they were usually deserted, as they led no whither. I was able, therefore, to haunt the iron pineapple, to stroke it, gloat over it, and gratify in some sort my abnormal desire toward it without exciting attention. Indeed, the cunning of actual lunacy marked each new downfall, and, with the exception of Mabel, no human creature as yet had suspected my infirmity.

The pineapple swiftly became an all-absorbing passion, and I fought against its fascination without avail. The desire for possession made this experience especially difficult, because as a rule the attractive object always drew me to be with it, whereas, in this case, there came a frantic longing to have the pineapple with me. I must have thought of the rubbish as a sentient being; I must have exaggerated it into a creature that could feel and sorrow and understand. On wet nights I conceived that the iron pineapple might suffer cold; on hot days I feared that it was enduring discomfort from the summer sun! From the ease and peace of my bed, I pictured the pineapple perched on its lonely pedestal in outer darkness. When there raged a thunderstorm, I feared that the lightning would strike the pineapple and destroy it for ever.

Then an overwhelming determination to secure the pineapple quite possessed me. Therefore I stole it by night. At an hour when a waning moon silvered that rising district of empty houses and unbounded roads, I set forth, crept into the shadow of the Italian dwelling, and, after working with a file for half an hour, won the valueless treasure. Once, during my operations, a policeman passed upon his beat; and I hid in the porch hard by and wondered what the man would have done had he discovered the postmaster and provision merchant,

John Noy, thus occupied between the morning hours of two and three.

To a sleeping wife I returned, and the pineapple was concealed in a drawer that contained my Sunday clothes.

The mass of metal weighed two pounds, and for a week I racked my brains to find fresh hiding-places for it. Now I concealed it under the earth in my garden ; now I hid it in the shop ; now I took it about with me, wrapped up in a parcel.

The trash was never out of my mind. Moreover, a reward of one guinea had been offered for discovery of the person responsible for its disappearance. The owner of the Italian villa himself brought a printed advertisement to me containing the promise. I stuck it up against my shop window with two blue wafers, and soothed him. He was much annoyed, and declared that a fool capable of such wilful and aimless destruction should be captured and locked up for the benefit of the community. How cordially I agreed with him ! And all the while I looked down at a sack of dried peas at his feet, in which the iron pineapple was hidden.

And now the psychology of the mental situation took a turn, and my last two phases of infatuation ran into each other, as one line of rails merges into the next. The iron pineapple and the artist were inextricably mingled in my distracted mind. The one I loved, the other I hated ; and I told myself that not until these two concrete ideas had come together and completed their diverse destinies might my own soul hope for any sort of peace.

So Providence set my brain to the task of fulfilling its inscrutable designs while I, ignorant of that supernatural purpose, merely looked into the darkness of my own heart and cowered before the lurid phantom of madness that I seemed to see advancing upon me from within it. I believed myself now definitely insane, but I was powerless to save the situation ; indeed, an instinct far stronger than that of self-preservation held me in absolute subjection.

I walked on the cliffs and in the lonely lanes, and babbled my problem to the seagulls and the wayside flowers. By night I submitted it to the stars of heaven. In sleep I uttered it aloud, as my wife testified too surely on an occasion of my waking.

We slept with a night-lamp, and on suddenly returning to consciousness I perceived Mabel sitting up and regarding my prostrate form in dismay. The extremity of concern marked her features. I recollect how the shadow of her head (decorated with curling-pins, or some other metal contrivances which hung from it, glittering in the mild beam of the night-light) was thrown enormous upon the ceiling, in an outline that suggested the map of the continent of Africa.

" Holy angels ! " she began. " What's the matter with you now ? You've been babbling like something out of a child's fairy book—like that there *Alice in Wonderland* Mrs. Hussey lent you, and you thought was funny, and I couldn't for the life of me laugh over. You keep on : ' The pineapple and the painter ; the painter and the pineapple, and quantities of sand ! ' And if I'm going mad, you'd better tell me so ; and if I'm not, then, sure as quarter-day, you are. It can't go on. No woman could stand it ! "

I strove to lead her mind into other channels. I explained that I wanted my signboard repainted, and that I proposed to buy a few West Indian pines from time to time to add to the attractions of our fruit department. We then discussed the advent of my only sister—an elderly spinster ruined by the recent collapse of certain benevolent societies. Between a home under my roof and the union workhouse there was literally no choice for her, and, ill as I could afford to support her, my sense of duty left me no alternative but to do so.

It fell out, however, that the forthcoming day was to witness greater matters than the arrival of Susan Noy at Bude. Of late the terrific problem of how to bring the loved pineapple and the hated painter together had made me more than usually inattentive to business. I wandered much, and chiefly by the sea it was that I passed my time. At low tide I walked upon the sands, or sat and brooded among the gaunt rocks, where purple mussels grew in clusters like grapes. At high tide I tramped the cliffs, and reclining upon them, watched the ships pass by on the horizon of the ocean ; or gazed where Lundy, like a blue cloud, arose from the waves.

Here I was in the company of elemental things, and from them alone at this season did my tortured spirit win any sort of hope. The breaking billows and the broad pathway of light that fell upon them at sunset ; the dark faces of the rocks, that watched from under beetling brows for the coming storm ; the passage of wine-coloured cloud shadows on the sea ; the anthem of the great west wind, that made the precipice his cymbal and the crag his harp—these things alone brought a measure of peace to my soul. But calm it wholly they could not ; solve the grotesque problem, that haunted me like a presence, they could not. I lived only to know how the iron pineapple and the cliff painter should be brought together into one idea—indivisible, corporate, compact.

It was fitting that the problem of a lunatic should be solved by a madman. For mad I most certainly was upon this day —one of God's chosen, to work His will through the dark machinery of a temporary mental alienation, a man deliberately robbed of his reason through certain terrific moments that the Everlasting Will might be manifested upon earth to the vindication of His all-watchfulness and justice !

The hour was after noon, the day one in late August, and I walked out upon the cliffs at a moment when general exodus from shore began ; for the luncheon-time approached, and a long line of children, mothers, and nursemaids began to drift away inland from the pleasures of the beach. At one o'clock cliffs and shore were alike deserted for a season, and a pedestrian might also cross the links with safety. The golfers had ceased from troubling.

Now, upon a high cliff north of the bathing-places I wandered, weighted literally, as well as mentally, by my eternal problem. For in my breast-pocket, bulging and dragging me forward at a more acute angle than usual, was the iron pineapple. Why, I know not. But often now I carried it with me, and, when hidden from gaze of man, would display it as though study of the actual object was likely to help my deliberations.

To-day, at the cliff-edge, I dragged it out, and laid it down where the short turf was already becoming seared under August suns. A dwarf betony, with purple bloom, grew at my elbow, and cushions of pink thrift, their blossoms now reduced to mere empty, silver tufts, clung close at hand on the cliff-faces. One crow's-feather, fallen on the grass, moved two yards away as the wind touched it, and the sun flashed upon its shining black plume ; upon the downs a red sheep or two browsed on the sweet, close herbage. Inland rose the low hills, with their stunted trees and grey church towers ascending above them.

I was as lonely as man might be. The world had been deserted that our holiday folk might eat ; and I realized to the full at this moment how entirely had Bude become a pleasure-resort, how absolutely it depended for prosperity upon those who, when their hours of respite came, hastened to North Cornwall for change of air and a place to play in. Not until the eye passed far south to the breakwater and lock

and little canal running therefrom, not until it marked the
ketches lying there, did one perceive any human enterprises
other than those devoted to amusement and relaxation

The iron pineapple stood upon the turf at my hand. The
lump of iron was polished to brightness by constant handling,
and it flashed back the sunshine from the planes of the
cone.

For a long time I stared at it, and revolved my fatuous
problem. Then suddenly, from far below on the beach, there
arose the sound of a human voice singing a song. It was a
mellow, juicy voice ; it was a mellow, juicy song. The first I
recognized quickly enough ; the second I had never heard
before. To this day I cannot say whence came the words or
tune, but they served well enough to express the singer's
present contentment.

To sing such a pæan of joy with such infinite relish and
abandonment proved beyond possibility of doubt that the
lonely creature below me was happy, hopeful, and contented
with his life and its possibilities. " He must," said I, " have
sold one of his strange pictures at a good profit to himself, or
he must have chanced on a kindred spirit, and met a heart
that beats with his, an eye that sees with him. Life for him
has surely brought some fresh beauty or joy, interest or fair
promise, else he could not thus warble from his very soul with
such bird-like content ! " Needless to add that it was my big,
brown-bearded artist who sang while he painted below.

I crept on my breast to the stark edge of the cliff, and looked
down at him. He sat immediately beneath me, and I had
leisure to note the curious perspective of his figure thus seen
from high above his head. He wore a great grey wide-awake,
and, beneath it, strangely foreshortened, bulged his big body
squatted on a camp-stool. His legs did not appear ; they were
tucked under him. But his arms were visible. One hand held
a palette and brushes ; the other, the brush with which he
was engaged. He accentuated the metre of his music by touches
of paint on the drawing before him.

Then it seemed that the necessary inspiration struck me
like a blow. Here were painter and pineapple in juxta-
position. They had approached each other more nearly than
had ever happened until that moment. Only some two hundred
feet of vertical space separated them. And I felt that these
two entities—the one precious in my esteem, and the other
evil—must now conjoin and complete their predestined state
in contact each with other.

It was at this moment that my own volition left me, and a Thing-not-myself took the helm of my life, and steered me forward. With a power of resolution very different from that possessed by my own, with a decision and grip and masculine vigour remote from my vacillation and fickleness, my brain determined, and my hand leapt to obey the order. The crisis swept me like a storm. I felt as a watcher, chained and gagged, yet free to mark the action of another close at hand. I took the iron pineapple, held it perpendicularly above the head of the happy songster below, steadied my arm, that no tremor should deflect the missile, and dropped it.

The metal fell two hundred feet or more, and struck the exact centre of the grey hat beneath me. I heard the sound of impact—a dull thud muffled by the felt of the hat. But the consequences were terrific. Lightning had not destroyed the happy songster more instantly or more absolutely. His arms shot forth, his song was strangled in his head; his big body gave a convulsive jerk in every limb, and he fell forward upon his easel, and brought it to the ground beneath him.

From the moment that he crashed face down into the sand and shingle he remained motionless. In his hands were still the palette and single brush; his legs were drawn up stiffly in the attitude of a man swimming; as I watched, the blood began to well out of his head and run away into the ground. The iron pineapple had fallen forward, and was now a foot in front of him in the middle of his picture.

I descended to see what I had done. I felt a consciousness of immense relief and satisfaction. I was free—I was sane! The cloud had lifted from my spirit. I knew by an over-whelming conviction that henceforth and for ever I should find myself as other men.

I hastened down the cliff, stood on the deserted shore, and approached the fallen painter. It was not until my foot trampled the blood-stained sand at his ear that I began to apprehend the force of the thing that I had committed. The pathos exhibited by the figure of this stricken wretch impressed itself upon me. He was stout and elderly—older than I had guessed. Yet he had been singing of the joys of love; he had chanted the charm of a lady called " Julia " when my iron pineapple descended, as the bolt of Jove from the sky, and struck him into senseless clay. His beard stuck out at a ridiculous angle from beneath his prone face, and my sense of decency led me to touch him, move him, and bestow his corpse in a manner more orderly.

430

EDEN PHILLPOTTS

I determined to turn him over, straighten out his legs, and not leave him thus, humped up on his belly like a frog that a wheel had crushed in the night.

But my purpose was frustrated, and that happened which cast me into an untold abyss of horror, and sent me flying as one demented from my murdered man. I touched his beard, and the whole mass of it came off in my hand! This incident, while less terrible indeed than other things that happened, yet sufficed to upset my jubilant brain. Its quality of unexpectedness may have caused my revulsion. I cannot say; but whereas I faced the dead without a tremor, and prepared reverently to bestow his palpitating dust, so that no feeling of the indecent or grotesque should grate upon the minds of his discoverers, now this outrageous and bizarre surrender of his beard at a touch struck upon me like the departing shadow of the madness I had dropped away for ever with the dropping of the stolen metal. I shivered, and I screamed aloud. My voice echoed along the cliff-face and climbed it, rang over the rocks, and floated seaward, where the broad foam-belts broke upon the shore. But none heard me save a hawk hovering aloft; none saw my frenzied act as I flung the great mass of hair from me and ran away.

Once, in that retreat, I turned and saw the hair, like some living, amorphous monster—a creature of the deep sea and darkness rather than of earth and light—creeping over the level sands after me. And then, indeed, I shrieked amain, and sped for the cliffs and climbed a gully with such haste that my knees and knuckles were dripping blood before I reached the downs. Once there, I looked below in time to see the mass of hair caught up by the wind and blown afar into the sea.

That night I regained my peace, returned home, and slept as I had not slept for many years.

On the following day a West Country journal contained the following item of news:

"An occurrence fraught with the profoundest horror is reported from the holiday resort of Bude, and a spot associated with innocent pleasure, the happiness of children, and the rest and recuperation of jaded men of business, has suddenly become the sinister focus of an extraordinary and inexplicable crime. For the past six months a gentleman, named Walter Grant, has been residing in Victoria Road, at No. 9. The unfortunate artist—for such was his calling—devoted his attention to cliff scenery, and spent

most of his time on Bude sands or in the immediate neighbourhood. And here he has mysteriously perished."

The crime was then recorded, and the theory advanced
that an iron pineapple found beside the dead man was responsible for his destruction. The fact that he had gone to
paint with a beard, and been discovered a clean-shaven corpse
was also noted. It was added that the man had displayed a
kindly and courteous nature, and become popular among the
few who had made his acquaintance. Inquiry established the
fact that he was quite unknown in art circles, and that he had
proposed to leave Bude on the Saturday that followed his
death.

The incident of the recent robbery of the iron pineapple,
and this, its sensational reappearance, also served to make
exciting " copy " for the papers ; but a discovery which cast
these trifles into the shade was destined next morning to fill
not only our local journals. Then the English-speaking world
discovered to its amazement that Bolsover Barbellion, the
runaway rascal responsible for such widespread misery among
the poor and needy, had been traced and discovered on the
eve of his flight from England, and on the day after his flight
from life. Not only the beard, but also the hair of the slain
artist were discovered to be false, and investigations among
his private papers established his identity beyond doubt.

A woman also came forward to testify it—a person named
Julia Dalby. She and he were to have left England in a
steamer from Plymouth on the Saturday after his departure
from Bude, and she alone in the whole world knew his secret
hiding-place. Their passages were already secured in the
name of Mr. and Mrs. Grant, and they were about to sail for
South America.

Not one shadow of suspicion ever fell upon me, but while
my health was enormously improved, and my mind continued
clear, my conscience was ill at ease, and the fact that my wife
simply refused to credit the truth did not serve to lessen my
unrest. A week after the actual event I visited our minister,
and designed to place the facts before him and invite his
criticism and direction, but on the occasion of our meeting
he was so much concerned about a private anxiety that I
delayed my confession. He had determined that the corner-
stone of our chapel must be extracted, for he held that no
good would attend ministrations from a place of worship
whose foundation had been laid by one of the greatest rascals

recorded in modern history. The architect, however, demurred to this proposal, and submitted that to erase the inscription on the foundation-stone would surely meet the case. In grappling with this problem I forgot my own purpose of confession, and never more returned to it.

And to-day, sane and balanced of mind, I walk in the world of men and fear not the gaze of any fellow-creature. My life has taken a turn for the better ; prosperity promises ; the future never looked so fair. Above all, my mental balance is once more normal, and I enjoy a reputation for sound judgment and trustworthiness that brings my lesser neighbours to me in many of their difficulties.

And now I state the case against myself impartially and in print. I place myself without reserve at the mercy of man, and incidentally unravel a mystery that has puzzled the most astute intellects of our criminal service.

My theory—that for a fearful period I was the tool in Higher Hands, cannot, at least, be disproved, and I do not believe that any jury of my fellow-countrymen will condemn me to suffer for the part I played in the destruction of a most notorious enemy of society. Indeed, any earthly punishment would be an anticlimax and a jest at this hour. Nothing that wit of man might devise could put me again to the tortures of the days that are gone ; or do more than reflect phantasmally the horror of the past.

THE DEMON KING

AMONG the company assembled for Mr. Tom Burt's Grand Annual Pantomime at the old Theatre Royal, Bruddersford, there was a good deal of disagreement. They were not quite " the jolly, friendly party " they pretended to be—through the good offices of " Thespian "—to the readers of *The Bruddersford Herald* and *Weekly Herald Budget*. The Principal Boy told her husband and about fifty-five other people that she could work with anybody, was famous for being able to work with anybody, but that nevertheless the management had gone and engaged, as Principal Girl, the one woman in the profession who made it almost impossible for anybody to work with anybody. The Principal Girl told her friend, the Second Boy, that the Principal Boy and the Second Girl were spoiling everything and might easily ruin the show. The Fairy Queen went about pointing out that she did not want to make trouble, being notoriously easy-going, but that sooner or later the Second Girl would hear a few things that she would not like. Johnny Wingfield had been heard to declare that some people did not realize even yet that what audiences wanted from a panto was some good fast comedy work by the chief comedian, who had to have all the scope he required. Dippy and Doppy, the broker's men, hinted that even if there were two stages, Johnny Wingfield would want them both all the time.

But they were all agreed on one point, namely, that there was not a better demon in provincial panto than Mr. Kirk Ireton, who had been engaged by Mr. Tom Burt for this particular show. The pantomime was *Jack and Jill*, and those people who are puzzled to know what demons have to do with Jack and Jill, those innocent water-fetchers, should pay a visit to the nearest pantomime, which will teach them a lot they did not know about fairy tales. Kirk Ireton was not merely a demon, but the Demon King, and when the curtain first went up, you saw him on a darkened stage standing in front of a little chorus of attendant demons, made up of local baritones at ten shillings a night. Ireton looked the part, for he was tall and rather satanically featured and was known to be very clever with his make-up ; and what was more important, he sounded the part too, for he had a tremendous bass voice, of most demonish quality. He had played Mephistopheles in *Faust* many times with a good touring opera company. He was, indeed, a man with a fine future behind him. If it had not been for one weakness, pantomime would never have seen him. The trouble was that for years now he had been in the habit of " lifting the elbow " too much. That was how they all put it. Nobody said that he drank too much, but all agreed that he lifted the elbow. And the problem now was—would there be trouble because of this elbow-lifting ?

He had rehearsed with enthusiasm, sending his great voice to the back of the empty, forlorn gallery in the two numbers allotted to him, but at the later rehearsals there had been ominous signs of elbow-lifting.

" Going to be all right, Mr. Ireton ? " the stage-manager inquired anxiously.

Ireton raised his formidable and satanic eyebrows. " Of course it is," he replied, somewhat hoarsely. " What's worrying you, old man ? "

The other explained hastily that he wasn't worried. " You'll go well here," he went on. " They'll eat those two numbers of yours. Very musical in these parts. But you know Bruddersford, of course. You've played here before."

" I have," replied Ireton grimly. " And I loathe the dam' place. Bores me stiff. Nothing to do in it."

This was not reassuring. The stage-manager knew only too well Mr. Ireton was already finding something to do in the town, and his enthusiastic description of the local golf courses had no effect. Ireton loathed golf too, it seemed. All very ominous.

They were opening on Boxing Day night. By the afternoon, it was known that Kirk Ireton had been observed lifting the elbow very determinedly in the smoke-room of " The Cooper's Arms," near the theatre. One of the stage-hands had seen him : " And by gow, he wor lapping it up an' all," said this gentleman, no bad judge of anybody's power. of suction. From there, it appeared, he had vanished, along with several other riotous persons, two of them thought to be Leeds men—and in Bruddersford they know what Leeds men are.

The curtain was due to rise at seven-fifteen sharp. Most members of the company arrived at the theatre very early. Kirk Ireton was not one of them. He was still absent at six-thirty, though he had to wear an elaborate make-up, with glittering tinselled eyelids and all the rest of it, and had to be on the stage when the curtain rose. A messenger was dispatched to his lodgings, which were not far from the theatre. Even before the messenger returned, to say that Mr. Ireton had not been in since noon, the stage-manager was desperately coaching one of the local baritones, the best of a stiff and stupid lot, in the part of the Demon King. At six-forty-five, no Ireton ; at seven, no Ireton. It was hopeless.

" All right, that fellow's done for himself now," said the great Mr. Burt, who had come to give his Grand Annual his blessing. " He doesn't get another engagement from me as long as he lives. What's this local chap like ? "

The stage-manager groaned and wiped his brow. " Like nothing on earth except a bow-legged baritone from a Wesleyan choir."

" He'll have to manage somehow. You'll have to cut the part."

" Cut it, Mr. Burt ! I've slaughtered it, and what's left of it, he'll slaughter."

Mr. Tom Burt, like the sensible manager he was, believed in a pantomime opening in the old-fashioned way, with a mysterious dark scene among the supernaturals. Here it was a cavern in the hill beneath the Magic Well, and in these dismal recesses the Demon King and his attendants were to be discovered waving their crimson cloaks and plotting evil in good, round chest-notes. Then the Demon King would sing his number (which had nothing whatever to do with Jack and Jill or demonology either), the Fairy Queen would appear, accompanied by a white spotlight, there would be a little dialogue between them, and then a short duet.

The cavern scene was all set, the five attendant demons were in their places, while the sixth, now acting as King, was receiving a few last instructions from the stage-manager, and the orchestra, beyond the curtain, were coming to the end of the overture, when suddenly, from nowhere, there appeared on the dimly-lighted stage a tall and terrifically imposing figure.

" My God ! There's Ireton," cried the stage-manager, and bustled across, leaving the temporary Demon King, abandoned, a pitiful makeshift now. The new arrival was coolly taking his place in the centre. He looked superb. The costume, a skin-tight crimson affair touched with a baleful green, was far better than the one provided by the management. And the make-up was better still. The face had a greenish phosphorescent glow, and its eyes flashed between glittering lids. When he first caught sight of that face, the stage-manager felt a sudden idiotic tremor of fear, but being a stage-manager first and a human being afterwards (as all stage-managers have to be), he did not feel that tremor long, for it was soon chased away by a sense of elation. It flashed across his mind that Ireton must have gone running off to Leeds or somewhere in search of this stupendous costume and make-up. Good old Ireton ! He had given them all a fright, but it had been worth it.

" All right, Ireton ? " said the stage-manager quickly.

" All right," replied the Demon King, with a magnificent, careless gesture.

" Well, you get back in the chorus then," said the stage-manager to the Wesleyan baritone.

" That'll do me champion," said the gentleman, with a sigh of relief. He was not ambitious.

" All ready ? "

The violins began playing a shivery sort of music, and up the curtain went. The six attendant demons, led by the Wesleyan, who was in good voice now that he felt such a sense of relief, told the audience who they were and hailed their monarch in appropriate form. The Demon King, towering above them, dominating the scene superbly, replied in a voice of astonishing strength and richness. Then he sang the number allotted to him. It had nothing to do with Jack and Jill and very little to do with demons, being a rather commonplace bass song about sailors and shipwrecks and storms, with thunder and lightning effects supplied by the theatre. Undoubtedly this was the same song that had been rehearsed ; the words were the same ; the music was the same. Yet it all seemed different. It was really sinister. As you listened, you saw the great waves breaking over the doomed ships, and the pitiful little white faces disappearing in the dark flood. Somehow, the storm was much stormier. There was one great clap of thunder and flash of lightning that made all the attendant demons, the conductor of the orchestra, and a number of people in the wings, nearly jump out of their skins.

" And how the devil did you do that ? " said the stage-manager, after running round to the other wing.

" That's what I said to 'Orace 'ere," said the man in charge of the two sheets of tin and the cannon ball.

" Didn't touch a thing that time, did we, mate ? " said Horace.

" If you ask me, somebody let off a firework, one o' them big Chinese crackers, for that one," his mate continued. " Somebody monkeying about, that's what it is."

And now a white spotlight had found its way on to the stage, and there, shining in its pure ray, was Miss Dulcie Farrar, the Fairy Queen, who was busy waving a silver wand. She was also busy controlling her emotions, for somehow she felt unaccountably nervous. Opening night is opening night, of course, but Miss Farrar had been playing Fairy Queens for the last ten years (and Principal Girls for the ten years before them), and there was nothing in this part to worry her. She rapidly came to the conclusion that it was Mr. Ireton's sudden reappearance, after she had made up her mind that he was not turning up, that had made her feel so shaky, and this caused her to feel rather resentful. Moreover, as an experienced Fairy Queen who had had trouble with demons before, she was convinced that he was about to take more than his share of the stage. Just because he had hit upon such a good make-up ! And it *was* a good make-up, there could be no question about that. That greenish face, those glittering eyes—really, it was awful. Overdoing it, she called it. After all, a panto *was* a panto.

Miss Farrar, still waving her wand, moved a step or two nearer, and cried :

" I know your horrid plot, you evil thing,
    And I defy you, though you are the Demon King."

" What, you ? " he roared, contemptuously, pointing a long forefinger at her.

Miss Farrar should have replied : " Yes, I, the Queen of Fairyland," but for a minute she could not get out a word. As that horribly long forefinger shot out at her, she had felt a sudden sharp pain and had then found herself unable to move. She stood there, her wand held out at a ridiculous angle, motionless, silent, her mouth wide open. But her mind was active enough. " Is it a stroke ? " it was asking feverishly. " Like Uncle Edgar had that time at Greenwich. Oo, it must be. Oo, whatever shall I do ? Oo. Oo. Ooooo."

" Ho-ho-ho-ho-ho." The Demon King's sinister baying mirth resounded through the theatre.

" Ha-ha-ha-ha-ha." This was from the Wesleyan and his friends, and was a very poor chorus of laughs, dubious, almost apologetic. It suggested that the Wesleyan and his friends were out of their depth, the depth of respectable Bruddersfordian demons.

Their king now made a quick little gesture with one hand, and Miss Farrar found herself able to move and speak again. Indeed, the next second, she was not sure that she had ever been *unable* to speak and move. That horrible minute had vanished like a tiny bad dream. She defied him again, and this time nothing happened beyond an exchange of bad lines of lame verse. There were not many of these, however, for there was the duet to be fitted in, and the whole scene had to be played in as short a time as possible. The duet, in which the two supernaturals only defied one another all over again, was early Verdi by way of the local musical director.

After singing a few bars each, they had a rest while the musical director exercised his fourteen instrumentalists in a most imposing operatic passage. It was during this halt that Miss Farrar, who was now quite close to her fellow-duettist, whispered : " You're in great voice, to-night, Mr. Ireton. Wish I was. Too nervous. Don't know why, but I am. Wish I could get it out like you."

She received, as a reply, a flash of those glittering eyes (it really was an astonishing make-up) and a curious little signal with the long forefinger. There was no time for more, for now the voice part began again.

Nobody in the theatre was more surprised by what happened then than the Fairy Queen herself. She could not believe that the marvellously rich soprano voice that came pealing and soaring belonged to her. It was tremendous. Covent Garden would have acclaimed it. Never before, in all her twenty years of hard vocalism, had Miss Dulcie Farrar sung like that, though she had always felt that *somewhere* inside her there was a voice of that quality only waiting the proper signal to emerge and then astonish the world. Now, in some fantastic fashion, it had received that signal.

Not that the Fairy Queen overshadowed her supernatural colleague. There was no overshadowing *him*. He trolled in a

*She had felt a sudden sharp pain and had then found
herself unable to move.*

diapason bass, and with a fine fury of gesture. The pair of them turned that stolen and botched duet into a work of art and significance. You could hear Heaven and Hell at battle in it. The curtain came down on a good rattle of applause. They are very fond of music in Bruddersford, but unfortunately the people who attend the first night of the pantomime are not the people who are most fond of music, otherwise there would have been a furore.

"Great stuff that," said Mr. Tom Burt, who was on the spot. "Never mind, Jim. Let 'em take a curtain. Go on, you two, take the curtain." And when they had both bowed their acknowledgments, Miss Farrar excited and trembling, the Demon King cool and amused, almost contemptuous, Mr. Burt continued : "That would have stopped the show in some places, absolutely stopped the show. But the trouble here is, they won't applaud, won't get going easily."

"That's true, Mr. Burt," Miss Farrar observed. "They take a lot of warming up here. I wish they didn't. Don't you, Mr. Ireton ? "

"Easy to warm them," said the tall crimson figure.

"Well, if anything could, that ought to have done," the lady remarked.

"That's so," said Mr. Burt condescendingly. "You were great, Ireton. But they won't let themselves go."

"Yes, they will." The Demon King, who appeared to be taking his part very seriously, for he had not yet dropped into his ordinary tones, flicked his long fingers in the air, roughly in the direction of the auditorium, gave a short laugh, turned away, and then somehow completely vanished, though it was not difficult to do that in those crowded wings.

Half an hour later, Mr. Burt, his manager, and the stage-manager, all decided that something must have gone wrong with Bruddersford. Liquor must have been flowing like water in the town. That was the only explanation.

"Either they're all drunk or I am," cried the stage-manager.

"I've been giving 'em pantomimes here for five-and-twenty years," said Mr. Burt, "and I've never known it happen before."

"Well, nobody can say they're not enjoying it."

"Enjoying it ! They're enjoying it too much. They're going daft. Honestly, I don't like it. It's too much of a good thing."

The stage-manager looked at his watch. "It's holding up

the show, that's certain. God knows when we're going to get through at this rate. If they're going to behave like this every night, we'll have to cut an hour out of it."

"Listen to 'em now," said Mr. Burt. "And that's one of the oldest gags in the show. Listen to 'em. Nay, dash it, they must be all half-seas over."

What had happened? Why—this: that the audience had suddenly decided to let itself go in a fashion never known in Bruddersford before. The Bruddersfordians are notoriously difficult to please, not so much because their taste is so exquisite but rather because, having paid out money, they insist upon having their money's worth, and usually arrive at a place of entertainment in a gloomy and suspicious frame of mind. Really tough managers like to open a new show in Bruddersford, knowing very well that if it will go there, it will go anywhere, But for the last half-hour of this pantomime there had been more laughter and applause than the Theatre Royal had known for the past six months. Every entrance produced a storm of welcome. The smallest and stalest gags set the whole house screaming, roaring, and rocking. Every song was determinedly encored. If the people had been specially brought out of jail for the performance, they could not have been more easily pleased.

"Here," said Johnny Wingfield, as he made an exit as a Dame pursued by a cow, "this is frightening me. What's the matter with 'em? Is this a new way of giving the bird?"

"Don't ask me," said the Principal Boy. "I wasn't surprised they gave me such a nice welcome when I went on, because I've always been a favourite here, as Mr. Burt'll tell you, but the way they're carrying on now, making such a fuss over nothing, it's simply ridiculous. Slowing up the show, too."

After another quarter of an hour of this monstrous enthusiasm, this delirium, Mr. Burt could be heard grumbling to the Principal Girl, with whom he was standing in that close proximity which Principal Girls somehow invite. "I'll tell you what it is, Alice," Mr. Burt was saying. "If this goes on much longer, I'll make a speech from the stage, asking 'em to draw it mild. Never known 'em to behave like this. And it's a funny thing, I was only saying to somebody—now who was it I said that to?—anyhow, I was only saying to somebody that I wished this audience would let themselves go a bit more. Well, now I wish they wouldn't. And that's that."

There was a chuckle, not loud, but rich, and distinctly audible.

"Here," cried Mr. Burt. "Who's that? What's the joke?"

It was obviously nobody in their immediate vicinity. "It sounded like Kirk Ireton," said the Principal Girl, "judging by the voice." But Ireton was nowhere to be seen. Indeed, one or two people who had been looking for him, both in his dressing-room and behind, had not been able to find him. But he would not be on again for another hour, and nobody had time to discover whether Ireton was drinking again or not. The odd thing was, though, that the audience lost its wild enthusiasm just as suddenly as it had found it, and long before the interval it had turned itself into the familiar stolid Brudders-ford crowd, grimly waiting for its money's worth. The pantomime went on its way exactly as rehearsed, until it came to the time when the demons had to put in another appearance.

Jack, having found the magic water and tumbled down the hill, had to wander into the mysterious cavern and there rest awhile. At least, he declared that he would rest, but being played by a large and shapely female, and probably having that restless feminine temperament, what he did do was to sing a popular song with immense gusto. At the end of that song, when Jack once more declared that he would rest, the Demon King had to make a sudden appearance through a trap-door. And it was reported from below, where a spring-board was in readiness, that no Demon King had arrived to be shot on to the stage.

"Now where—oh, where—the devil has Ireton got to?" moaned the stage-manager, sending people right and left, up and down, to find him.

The moment arrived, Jack spoke his and her cue, and the stage-manager was making frantic signals to her from the wings.

"Ouh-wer," screamed Jack, and produced the most realistic bit of business in the whole pantomime. For the stage directions read *Shows fright*, and Jack undoubtedly did show fright, as well he (or she) might, for no sooner was the cue spoken than there came a horrible green flash, followed by a crimson glare, and standing before her, having apparently arrived from nowhere, was the Demon King. Jack was now in the power of the Demon King and would remain in those evil clutches until rescued by Jill and the Fairy Queen. And it seemed as if the Principal Boy had suddenly developed a capacity for acting (of which nobody had ever suspected her before), or else that she was thoroughly frightened, for now she behaved like a large rabbit in tights. That unrehearsed appearance of the Demon King seemed to have upset her, and now and then she sent uneasy glances into the wings.

It had been decided, after a great deal of talk and drinks round, to introduce a rather novel dancing scene into this pantomime, in the form of a sort of infernal ballet. The Demon King, in order to show his power and to impress his captive, would command his subjects to dance—that is, after he himself had indulged in a little singing, assisted by his faithful six. They talk of that scene yet in Bruddersford. It was only witnessed in its full glory on this one night, but that was enough, for it passed into civic history, and local landlords were often called in to settle bets about it in the pubs. First, the Demon King sang his second number, assisted by the Wesleyan and his friends. He made a glorious job of it, and after a fumbled opening and a sudden glare from him, the Wesleyan six made a glorious job of it too. Then the Demon King had to call for his dancing subjects, who were made up of the troupe of girls known as Tom Burt's Happy Yorkshire Lasses, daintily but demonishly tricked out in red and green. While the Happy Yorkshire Lasses pranced in the foreground, the six attendants were supposed to make a few rhythmical movements in the background, enough to suggest that, if they wanted to dance, they could dance, a suggestion that the stage-manager and the producer knew to be entirely false. The six, in fact, could not dance and would not try very hard, being not only wooden but also stubborn Bruddersford baritones.

But now, the Happy Yorkshire Lasses having tripped a measure, the Demon King sprang to his full height, which seemed to be about seven feet two inches, swept an arm along the Wesleyan six, and commanded them harshly to dance. And they did dance, they danced like men possessed. The King himself beat time for them, flashing an eye at the conductor now and again to quicken that gentleman's baton, and his faithful six, all with the most grotesque and puzzled expressions on their faces, cut the most amazing capers, bounding high into the air, tumbling over one another, flinging their arms and legs about in an ecstasy, and all in time to the music. The sweat shone on their faces ; their eyes rolled forlornly ; but still they did not stop, but went on in crazier and crazier fashion, like genuine demons at play.

" All dance ! " roared the Demon King, cracking his long fingers like a whip, and it seemed as if something had inspired the fourteen cynical men in the orchestral pit, for they played like madmen grown tuneful, and on came the Happy Yorkshire Lasses again, to fling themselves into the wild sport, not as if they were doing something they had rehearsed a hundred times, but as if they, too, were inspired. They joined the orgy of the bounding six, and now, instead of there being only eighteen Happy Lasses in red and green, there seemed to be dozens and dozens of them. The very stage seemed to get bigger and bigger, to give space to all these whirling figures of demoniac revelry. And as they all went spinning, leaping, cavorting crazily, the audience, shaken at last out of its stolidity, cheered them on, and all was one wild insanity.

Yet when it was done, when the King cried, " Stop ! " and all was over, it was as if it had never been, as if everybody had dreamed it, so that nobody was ready to swear that it had really happened. The Wesleyan and the other five all felt a certain faintness, but each was convinced that he had imagined all that wild activity while he was making a few sedate movements in the background. Nobody could be quite certain about anything. The pantomime went on its way ; Jack was rescued by Jill and the Fairy Queen (who was now complaining of neuralgia) ; and the Demon King allowed himself to be foiled, after which he quietly disappeared again. They were looking for him when the whole thing was over except for that grand entry of all the characters at the very end. It was his business to march in with the Fairy Queen, the pair of them dividing between them all the applause for the supernaturals. Miss Farrar, feeling very miserable with her neuralgia, delayed her entrance for him, but as he was not to be found, she climbed the little ladder at the back alone, to march solemnly down the steps towards the audience. And the extraordinary thing was that when she was actually making her entrance, at the top of those steps, she discovered that she was not alone, that her fellow-supernatural was there too, and that he must have slipped away to freshen his make-up. He was more demonish than ever.

As they walked down between the files of Happy Yorkshire Lasses, now armed to the teeth with tinsel spears and shields, Miss Farrar whispered : " Wish I'd arranged for a bouquet. You never get anything here."

" You'd like some flowers ? " said the fantastic figure at her elbow.

" Think I would ! So would everybody else."

" Quite easy," he remarked, bowing slowly to the footlights. He took her hand and led her to one side, and it is a fact—as Miss Farrar will tell you, within half an hour of your making her acquaintance—that the moment their hands met, her neuralgia completely vanished. And now came the time for the bouquets. Miss Farrar knew what they would be ; there would be one for the Principal Girl, bought by the management, and one for the Principal Boy, bought by herself.

" Oo, look ! " cried the Second Boy. " My gosh !— Bruddersford's gone mad."

The space between the orchestral pit and the front row of stalls had been turned into a hothouse. The conductor was so busy passing up bouquets that he was no longer visible. There were dozens of bouquets, and all of them beautiful. It was monstrous. Somebody must have spent a fortune on flowers. Up they came, while everybody cheered, and every woman with a part had at least two or three. Miss Farrar, pink and wide-eyed above a mass of orchids, turned to her colleague among the supernaturals, only to find that once again he had quietly disappeared. Down came the curtain for the last time, but everybody remained standing there, with arms filled with expensive flowers, chattering excitedly. Then suddenly somebody cried, " Oo ! " and dropped her flowers, and others cried, " Oo ! " and dropped *their* flowers, until at last everybody who had had a bouquet had dropped it and cried, " Oo ! "

" Hot," cried the Principal Girl, blowing on her fingers, " hot as anything, weren't they ? Burnt me properly. That's a nice trick."

" Oo, look ! " said the Second Boy, once more. " Look at 'em all. Withering away." And they were, every one of them, all shedding their colour and bloom, curling, writhing, withering away. . . .

" Message come through for you, sir, an hour since," said the doorkeeper to the manager, " only I couldn't get at yer. From the Leeds Infirmary, it is. Says Mr. Ireton was knocked down in Boar Lane by a car this afternoon, but he'll be all right to-morrow. Didn't know who he was at first, so couldn't let anybody know."

The manager stared at him, made a number of strange noises, then fled, signing various imaginary temperance pledges as he went.

" And another thing," said the stage-hand to the stage-manager. " That's where I saw the bloke last. He was there one minute and next minute he wasn't. And look at the place. All scorched."

" That's right," said his mate, " and what's more, just you take a whiff—that's all, just take a whiff. Oo's started using brimstone in this the-ater ? Not me nor you neither. But I've a good idea who it is."

THE QUEEN OF SPADES

THERE was a card party at the rooms of Naroumoff, a lieutenant in the Horse Guards. A long winter night had passed unnoticed, and it was five o'clock in the morning when supper was served. The winners sat down to table with an excellent appetite ; the losers let their plates remain empty before them. Little by little, however, with the assistance of the champagne, the conversation became animated, and was shared by all.

" How did you get on this evening, Surin ? " said the host to one of his friends.

" Oh, I lost, as usual. I really have no luck. I play *mirandole*. You know that I keep cool. Nothing moves me ; I never change my play, and yet I always lose."

" Do you mean to say that all the evening you did not once back the red ? Your firmness of character surprises me."

" What do you think of Hermann ? " said one of the party, pointing to a young Engineer officer. " That fellow never made a bet or touched a card in his life, and yet he watches us playing until five in the morning."

" It interests me," said Hermann ; " but I am not disposed to risk the necessary in view of the superfluous."

" Hermann is a German, and economical ; that is the whole of the secret," cried Tomski. " But what is really astonishing is the Countess Anna Fedorovna ! "

" How so ? " asked several voices.

" Have you not remarked," said Tomski, " that she never plays ? "

" Yes," said Naroumoff, " a woman of eighty, who never touches a card ; that is indeed something extraordinary ! "

" You do not know why ? "

448

" No ; is there a reason for it ? "

" Just listen. My grandmother, you know, some sixty years ago, went to Paris, and became the rage there. People ran after her in the streets, and called her the ' Muscovite Venus.' Richelieu made love to her, and my grandmother makes out that, by her rigorous demeanour, she almost drove him to suicide. In those days women used to play at faro. One evening at the Court she lost, on *parole*, to the Duke of Orleans, a very considerable sum. When she got home, my grandmother removed her beauty spots, took off her hoops, and in this tragic costume went to my grandfather, told him of her misfortune, and asked him for the money she had to pay. My grandfather, now no more, was, so to say, his wife's steward. He feared her like fire ; but the sum she named made him leap into the air. He flew into a rage, made a brief calculation, and proved to my grandmother that in six months she had got through half a million roubles. He told her plainly that he had no villages to sell in Paris, his domains being situated in the neighbourhood of Moscow and of Saratoff ; and finally refused point blank. You may imagine the fury of my grandmother. She boxed his ears, and passed the night in another room.

" The next day she returned to the charge. For the first time in her life, she condescended to arguments and explanations. In vain did she try to prove to her husband that there were debts and debts, and that she could not treat a Prince of the blood like her coachmaker.

" All this eloquence was lost. My grandfather was inflexible. My grandmother did not know where to turn. Happily she was acquainted with a man who was very celebrated at this time. You have heard of the Count of St. Germain, about whom so many marvellous stories were told. You know that he passed for a sort of Wandering Jew, and that he was said to possess an elixir of life and the philosopher's stone.

" Some people laughed at him as a charlatan. Casanova, in his memoirs, says that he was a spy. However that may be, in spite of the mystery of his life, St. Germain was much sought after in good society, and was really an agreeable man. Even to this day my grandmother has preserved a genuine affection for him, and she becomes quite angry when any one speaks of him with disrespect.

" It occurred to her that he might be able to advance the sum of which she was in need, and she wrote a note begging him to call. The old magician came at once, and found her plunged in the deepest despair. In two or three words she told him everything ; related to him her misfortune and the cruelty of her husband, adding that she had no hope except in his friendship and his obliging disposition.

" ' Madam,' said St. Germain, after a few moments reflection, ' I could easily advance you the money you want, but I am sure that you would have no rest until you had repaid me, and I do not want to get you out of one trouble in order to place you in another. There is another way of settling the matter. You must regain the money you have lost.'

" ' But, my dear friend,' answered my grandmother, ' I have already told you that I have nothing left.'

" ' That does not matter,' answered St. Germain. ' Listen to me, and I will explain.'

" He then communicated to her a secret which any of you would, I am sure, give a good deal to possess."

All the young officers gave their full attention. Tomski stopped to light his Turkish pipe, swallowed a mouthful of smoke, and then went on.

" That very evening my grandmother went to Versailles to play at the Queen's table. The Duke of Orleans held the bank. My grandmother invented a little story by way of excuse for not having paid her debt, and then sat down at the table, and began to stake. She took three cards. She won with the first ; doubled her stake on the second, and won again ; doubled on the third, and still won."

" Mere luck ! " said one of the young officers.

" What a tale ! " cried Hermann.

" Were the cards marked ? " said a third.

" I don't think so," replied Tomski gravely.

" And you mean to say," exclaimed Naroumoff, " that you have a grandmother who knows the names of three winning cards, and you have never made her tell them to you ? "

" That is the very deuce of it," answered Tomski. " She had three sons, of whom my father was one ; all three were determined gamblers, and not one of them was able to extract her secret from her, though it would have been of immense advantage to them, and to me also. Listen to what my uncle told me about it, Count Ivan Ilitch, and he told me on his word of honour.

" Tchaplitzki—the one you remember who died in poverty after devouring millions—lost one day, when he was a young man, to Zoritch about three hundred thousand roubles. He was in despair. My grandmother, who had no mercy for the extravagance of young men, made an exception—I do not know why—in favour of Tchaplitzki. She gave him three cards, telling him to play them one after the other, and exacting from him at the same time his word of honour that he would never afterwards touch a card as long as he lived. Accordingly Tchaplitzki went to Zoritch and staked for his revenge. On the first card he staked fifty thousand roubles. He won, doubled the stake, and won again. Continuing his system he ended by gaining more than he had lost.

" But it is six o'clock ! It is really time to go to bed."

Every one emptied his glass and the party broke up.

II

THE old Countess Anna Fedorovna was in her dressing-room, seated before her looking-glass. Three maids were in attendance. One held her pot of rouge, another a box of black pins, a third an enormous lace cap, with flaming ribbons. The Countess had no longer the slightest pretence to beauty, but she preserved all the habits of her youth. She dressed in the style of fifty years before, and gave as much time and attention to her toilet as a fashionable beauty of the last century. Her companion was working at a frame in a corner of the window.

" Good morning, grandmother," said the young officer, as he entered the dressing-room. " Good morning, Mademoiselle Lise. Grandmother, I have come to ask you a favour.'

" What is it, Paul ? "

" I want to introduce to you one of my friends, and to ask you to give him an invitation to your ball."

" Bring him to the ball and introduce him to me there. Did you go yesterday to the Princess's ? "

" Certainly. It was delightful ! We danced until five o'clock in the morning. Mademoiselle Eletzki was charming."

" My dear nephew, you are really not difficult to please. As to beauty, you should have seen her grandmother, the Princess Daria Petrovna. But she must be very old, the Princess Daria Petrovna ! "

" How do you mean old ? " cried Tomski thoughtlessly ; " she died seven years ago."

The young lady who acted as companion raised her head and made a sign to the officer, who then remembered that it was an understood thing to conceal from the Countess the death of any of her contemporaries. He bit his lips. The Countess, however, was not in any way disturbed on hearing that her old friend was no longer in this world.

"Dead!" she said, "and I never knew it! We were maids of honour in the same year, and when we were presented, the Empress "—and the old Countess related for the hundredth time an anecdote of her young days. "Paul," she said, as she finished her story, "help me to get up. Lisabeta, where is my snuff-box.?"

And, followed by the three maids, she went behind a great screen to finish her toilet. Tomski was now alone with the companion.

"Who is the gentleman you wish to introduce to madame?" asked Lisabeta.

"Naroumoff. Do you know him?"

"No. Is he in the army?"

"Yes."

"In the Engineers?"

"No, in the Horse Guards. Why did you think he was in the Engineers?"

The young lady smiled, but made no answer.

"Paul," cried the Countess from behind the screen, "send me a new novel; no matter what. Only see that it is not in the style of the present day."

"What style would you like, grandmother?"

"A novel in which the hero strangles neither his father nor his mother, and in which no one gets drowned. Nothing frightens me so much as the idea of getting drowned."

"But how is it possible to find you such a book? Do you want it in Russian?"

"Are there any novels in Russian? However, send me something or other. You won't forget?"

"I will not forget, grandmother. I am in a great hurry. Good-bye, Lisabeta. What made you fancy Naroumoff was in the Engineers?" and Tomski took his departure.

Lisabeta, left alone, took out her embroidery, and sat down close to the window. Immediately afterwards, in the street, at the corner of a neighbouring house, appeared a young officer. The sight of him made the companion blush to her ears. She lowered her head, and almost concealed it in the linen. At this moment the Countess returned, fully dressed.

"Lisabeta," she said, "have the horses put in; we will go out for a drive."

Lisabeta rose from her chair, and began to arrange her embroidery.

" Well, my dear child, are you deaf ? Go and tell them to put the horses in at once."

" I am going," replied the young lady, as she went out into the ante-chamber.

A servant now came in, bringing some books from Prince Paul Alexandrovitch.

" Say I am much obliged to him. Lisabeta ! Lisabeta ! Where has she run off to ? "

" I was going to dress."

" We have plenty of time, my dear. Sit down, take the first volume, and read to me."

The companion took the book and read a few lines.

" Louder," said the Countess. " What is the matter with you ? Have you a cold ? Wait a moment, bring me that stool. A little closer ; that will do."

Lisabeta read two pages of the book.

" Throw that stupid book away," said the Countess. " What nonsense ! Send it back to Prince Paul, and tell him I am much obliged to him ; and the carriage, is it never coming ? "

" Here it is," replied Lisabeta, going to the window.

" And now you are not dressed. Why do you always keep me waiting ? It is intolerable ! "

Lisabeta ran to her room. She had scarcely been there two minutes when the Countess rang with all her might. Her maids rushed in at one door and her valet at the other.

" You do not seem to hear me when I ring," she cried. " Go and tell Lisabeta that I am waiting for her."

At this moment Lisabeta entered, wearing a new walking dress and a fashionable bonnet.

" At last, miss," cried the Countess. " But what is that you have got on ? and why ? For whom are you dressing ? What sort of weather is it ? Quite stormy, I believe."

" No, your Excellency," said the valet ; " it is exceedingly fine."

" What do you know about it ? Open the ventilator. Just what I told you ! A frightful wind, and as icy as can be. Unharness the horses. Lisabeta, my child, we will not go out to-day. It was scarcely worth while to dress so much."

" What an existence ! " said the companion to herself.

Lisabeta Ivanovna was, in fact, a most unhappy creature. " The bread of the stranger is bitter," says Dante, " and his staircase hard to climb." But who can tell the torments of a poor little companion attached to an old lady of quality ? The Countess had all the caprices of a woman spoilt by the world. She was avaricious and egotistical, and thought all the more of herself now that she had ceased to play an active part in society. She never missed a ball, and she dressed and painted in the style of a bygone age. She remained in a corner of the room, where she seemed to have been placed expressly to serve as a scarecrow. Every one on coming in went to her and made her a low bow, but this ceremony once at an end no one spoke a word to her. She received the whole city at her house, observing the strictest etiquette, and never failing to give to every one his or her proper name. Her innumerable servants, growing pale and fat in the ante-chamber, did absolutely as they liked, so that the house was pillaged as if its owner was really dead. Lisabeta passed her life in continual torture. If she made tea she was reproached with wasting the sugar. If she read a novel to the Countess she was held responsible for all the absurdities of the author. If she went out with the noble lady for a walk or drive, it was she who was to blame if the weather was bad or the pavement muddy. Her salary, more than modest, was never punctually paid, and she was expected to dress " like every one else " ; that is to say, like very few people indeed. When she went into society her position was sad. Every one knew her ; no one paid any attention. At a ball she sometimes danced ; but only when a *vis-à-vis* was wanted. Women would come up to her, take her by the arm, and lead her out of the room if their dress required attending to. She had her portion of self-respect, and felt deeply the misery of her position. She looked with impatience for a liberator to break her chain. But the young men, prudent in the midst of their affected giddiness, took care not to honour her with their attentions, though Lisabeta Ivanovna was a hundred times prettier than the shameless or stupid girls whom they surrounded with their homage. More than once she slunk away from the splendour of the drawing-room to shut herself up alone in her little bedroom, furnished with an old screen and a pieced carpet, a chest of drawers, a small looking-glass, and a wooden bedstead. There she shed tears at her ease, by the light of a tallow candle in a tin candlestick.

One morning—it was two days after the party at Naroumoff's, and a week before the scene we have just sketched—Lisabeta was sitting at her embroidery before the window, when,

looking carelessly into the street, she saw an officer, in the
uniform of the Engineers, standing motionless with his eyes
fixed upon her. She lowered her head, and applied herself
to her work more attentively than ever. Five minutes afterwards she looked mechanically into the street, and the officer
was still in the same place. Not being in the habit of exchanging glances with young men who passed by her window, she
remained with her eyes fixed on her work for nearly two
hours, until she was told that lunch was ready. She got up to
put her embroidery away, and, while doing so, looked into the
street, and saw the officer still in the same place. This seemed
to her very strange. After lunch she went to the window with
a certain emotion, but the officer of Engineers was no longer
in the street.

She thought no more of him. But two days afterwards,
just as she was getting into the carriage with the Countess, she
saw him once more, standing straight before the door. His
face was half concealed by a fur collar, but his black eyes
sparkled beneath his helmet. Lisabeta was afraid, without
knowing why, and she trembled as she took her seat in the
carriage.

On returning home, she rushed with a beating heart
towards the window. The officer was in his habitual place,
with his eyes fixed ardently upon her. She at once withdrew,
burning at the same time with curiosity, and moved by a
strange feeling, which she now experienced for the first time.

No day now passed but the young officer showed himself
beneath the window. Before long a dumb acquaintance was
established between them. Sitting at her work she felt his
presence, and when she raised her head she looked at him for
a long time every day. The young man seemed full of grati-
tude for these innocent favours.

She observed, with the deep and rapid perceptions of youth,
that a sudden redness covered the officer's pale cheeks as soon
as their eyes met. After about a week she would smile at
seeing him for the first time.

When Tomski asked his grandmother's permission to
present one of his friends, the heart of the poor young girl
beat strongly, and when she heard that it was Naroumoff, she
bitterly repented having compromised her secret by letting
it out to a giddy young man like Paul.

Hermann was the son of a German settled in Russia, from
whom he had inherited a small sum of money. Firmly
resolved to preserve his independence, he had made it a

principle not to touch his private income. He lived on his pay, and did not allow himself the slightest luxury. He was not very communicative ; and his reserve rendered it difficult for his comrades to amuse themselves at his expense.

Under an assumed calm he concealed strong passions and a highly-imaginative disposition. But he was always master of himself, and kept himself free from the ordinary faults of young men. Thus, a gambler by temperament, he never touched a card, feeling, as he himself said, that his position did not allow him to " risk the necessary in view of the super-fluous." Yet he would pass entire nights before a card-table, watching with feverish anxiety the rapid changes of the game. The anecdote of Count St. Germain's three cards had struck his imagination. and he did nothing but think of it all that night.

" If," he said to himself next day as he was walking along the streets of St. Petersburg, " if she would only tell me her secret—if she would only name the three winning cards ! I must get presented to her, that I may pay my court and gain her confidence. Yes ! And she is eighty-seven ! She may die this week—to-morrow perhaps. But after all, is there a word of truth in the story ? No ! Economy, Temperance, Work ; these are my three winning cards. With them I can double my capital ; increase it tenfold. They alone can ensure my independence and prosperity."

Dreaming in this way as he walked along, his attention was attracted by a house built in an antiquated style of architecture. The street was full of carriages, which passed one by one before the old house, now brilliantly illuminated. As the people stepped out of the carriages Hermann saw now the little feet of a young woman, now the military boot of a general. Then came a clocked stocking, then a diplomatic pump. Fur-lined cloaks and coats passed in procession before a gigantic porter.

Hermann stopped. "Who lives here ? " he said to a watchman in his box.

" The Countess Anna Fedorovna." It was Tomski's grandmother.

Hermann started. The story of the three cards came once more upon his imagination. He walked to and fro before the house, thinking of the woman to whom it belonged, of her wealth and her mysterious power. At last he returned to his den. But for some time he could not get to sleep ; and when at last sleep came upon him, he saw, dancing before his eyes, cards, a green table, and heaps of roubles and bank-notes.

He saw himself doubling stake after stake, always winning, and then filling his pockets with piles of coin, and stuffing his pocket-book with countless bank-notes. When he awoke, he sighed to find that his treasures were but creations of a disordered fancy ; and, to drive such thoughts from him, he went out for a walk. But he had not gone far when he found himself once more before the house of the Countess. He seemed to have been attracted there by some irresistible force. He stopped, and looked up at the windows. There he saw a girl's head with beautiful black hair, leaning gracefully over a book or an embroidery-frame. The head was lifted, and he saw a fresh complexion and black eyes.

This moment decided his fate.

III

LISABETA was just taking off her shawl and her bonnet when the Countess sent for her. She had had the horses put in again.

While two footmen were helping the old lady into the carriage, Lisabeta saw the young officer at her side. She felt him take her by the hand, lost her head, and found, when the young officer had walked away, that he had left a paper between her fingers. She hastily concealed it in her glove.

During the whole of the drive she neither saw nor heard. When they were in the carriage together the Countess was in the habit of questioning Lisabeta perpetually.

" Who is that man that bowed to us ? What is the name of this bridge ? What is there written on that signboard ? "

Lisabeta now gave the most absurd answers, and was accordingly scolded by the Countess.

" What is the matter with you, my child ? " she asked. " What are you thinking about ? Or do you really not hear me ? I speak distinctly enough, however, and I have not yet lost my head, have I ? "

Lisabeta was not listening. When she got back to the house she ran to her room, locked the door, and took the scrap of paper from her glove. It was not sealed, and it was impossible, therefore, not to read it. The letter contained protestations of love. It was tender, respectful, and translated word for word from a German novel. But Lisabeta did not read German, and she was quite delighted. She was, however, much embarrassed. For the first time in her life she had a secret. Correspond with a young man ! The idea of

such a thing frightened her.   How imprudent she had been !
She had reproached herself, but knew not now what to do.

Cease to do her work at the window, and by persistent coldness try and disgust the young officer ?   Send him back his
letter ?   Answer him in a firm, decided manner ?   What line
of conduct was she to pursue ?   She had no friend, no one to
advise her.   She at last decided to send an answer.   She sat
down at her little table, took pen and paper, and began to
think.   More than once she wrote a sentence and then tore
up the paper.   What she had written seemed too stiff, or else
it was wanting in reserve.   At last, after much trouble, she
succeeded in composing a few lines which seemed to meet the
case.   " I believe," she wrote, " that your intentions are those
of an honourable man, and that you would not wish to offend
me by any thoughtless conduct.   But you must understand
that our acquaintance cannot begin in this way.   I return
your letter, and trust that you will not give me cause to regret
my imprudence."

Next day as soon as Hermann made his appearance, Lisabeta left her embroidery, and went into the drawing-room,
opened the ventilator, and threw her letter into the street,
making sure that the young officer would pick it up.

Hermann, in fact, at once saw it, and, picking it up, entered
a confectioner's shop in order to read it.   Finding nothing dis-
couraging in it, he went home sufficiently pleased with the first
step in his love adventure.

Some days afterwards, a young person with lively eyes called
to see Miss Lisabeta, on the part of a milliner.   Lisabeta wondered what she could want, and suspected, as she received her,
some secret intention.   She was much surprised, however,
when she recognised, on the letter that was now handed to her,
the writing of Hermann.

" You make a mistake," she said, " this letter is not for me."

" I beg your pardon," said the milliner, with a slight smile ;
" be kind enough to read it."

Lisabeta glanced at it.   Hermann was asking for an
appointment.

" Impossible ! " she cried, alarmed both at the boldness of
the request and at the manner in which it was made.   " This
letter is not for me," she repeated ;   and she tore it into a
hundred pieces.

" If the letter was not for you, why did you tear it up ?
You should have given it me back, that I might take it to the
person it was meant for."

"True," said Lisabeta, quite disconcerted. "But bring me no more letters, and tell the person who gave you this one that he ought to blush for his conduct."

Hermann, however, was not a man to give up what he had once undertaken. Every day Lisabeta received a fresh letter from him—sent now in one way, now in another. They were no longer translated from the German. Hermann wrote under the influence of a commanding passion, and in a language which was his own. Lisabeta could not hold out against such torrents of eloquence. She received the letters, kept them, and at last answered them. Every day her answers were longer and more affectionate, until at last she threw out of the window a letter couched as follows :—

"This evening there is a ball at the Embassy. The Countess will be there. We shall remain until two in the morning. You may manage to see me alone. As soon as the Countess leaves home, that is to say towards eleven o'clock, the servants are sure to go out, and there will be no one left but the porter, who will be sure to be asleep in his box. Enter as soon as it strikes eleven, and go upstairs as fast as possible. If you find any one in the ante-chamber, ask whether the Countess is at home, and you will be told she is out, and, in that case, you must resign yourself, and go away. In all probability, however, you will meet no one. The Countess's women are together in a distant room. When you are once in the ante-chamber, turn to the left, and walk straight on, until you reach the Countess's bedroom. There, behind a large screen, you will see two doors. The one on the right leads to a dark room. The one on the left leads to a corridor at the end of which is a little winding staircase, which leads to my parlour."

At ten o'clock Hermann was already on duty before the Countess's door. It was a frightful night. The winds had been unloosed, and the snow was falling in large flakes ; the lamps gave an uncertain light ; the streets were deserted ; from time to time passed a sleigh, drawn by a wretched hack, on the look-out for a fare. Covered by a thick overcoat, Hermann felt neither the wind nor the snow. At last the Countess's carriage drew up. He saw two huge footmen come forward and take beneath the arms a dilapidated spectre, and place it on the cushions, well wrapped up in an enormous fur cloak. Immediately afterwards, in a cloak of lighter make, her head crowned with natural flowers, came Lisabeta, who sprang into the carriage like a dart. The door was closed, and the carriage rolled on softly over the snow.

The porter closed the street door, and soon the windows of the first floor became dark. Silence reigned throughout the house. Hermann walked backwards and forwards ; then coming to a lamp he looked at his watch. It was twenty minutes to eleven. Leaning against the lamp-post, his eyes fixed on the long hand of his watch, he counted impatiently the minutes which had yet to pass. At eleven o'clock precisely Hermann walked up the steps, pushed open the street door, and went into the vestibule, which was well lighted. As it happened the porter was not there. With a firm and rapid step he rushed up the staircase and reached the ante-chamber. There, before a lamp, a footman was sleeping, stretched out in a dirty greasy dressing-gown. Hermann passed quickly before him and crossed the dining-room and the drawing-room, where there was no light. But the lamp of the ante-chamber helped him to see. At last he reached the Countess's bedroom. Before a screen covered with old icons [sacred pictures] a golden lamp was burning. Gilt arm-chairs, sofas of faded colours, furnished with soft cushions, were arranged symmetrically along the walls, which were hung with China silk. He saw two large portraits, painted by Madame le Brun. One represented a man of forty, stout and full coloured, dressed in a light green coat, with a decoration on his breast. The second portrait was that of an elegant young woman, with an aquiline nose, powdered hair rolled back on the temples, and with a rose over her ear. Everywhere might be seen shepherds and shepherdesses in Dresden china, with vases of all shapes, clocks by Leroy, work-baskets, fans, and all the thousand playthings for the use of ladies of fashion, discovered at the time of Montgolfier's balloons and Mesmer's animal magnetism.

Hermann passed behind the screen, which concealed a little iron bedstead. He saw the two doors ; the one on the right leading to the dark room, the one on the left to the corridor. He opened the latter, saw the staircase which led to the poor little companion's parlour, and then, closing this door, went into the dark room.

The time passed slowly. Everything was quiet in the house. The drawing-room clock struck midnight, and again there was silence. Hermann was standing up, leaning against the stove, in which there was no fire. He was calm ; but his heart beat with quick pulsations, like that of a man determined to brave all dangers he might have to meet, because he knows them to be inevitable. He heard one o'clock strike ; then two ; and soon afterwards the distant roll of a carriage. He now, in spite of himself, experienced some emotion. The carriage approached rapidly and stopped. There was at once a great noise of servants running about the staircases, and a confusion of voices. Suddenly the rooms were all lit up, and the Countess's three antiquated maids came at once into the bedroom. At last appeared the Countess herself.

The walking mummy sank into a large Voltaire armchair. Hermann looked through the crack in the door ; he saw Lisabeta pass close to him, and heard her hurried step as she went up the little winding staircase. For a moment he felt something like remorse ; but it soon passed off, and his heart was once more of stone.

The Countess began to undress before a looking-glass. Her head-dress of roses was taken off, and her powdered wigs separated from her own hair, which was very short and quite white. Pins fell in showers around her. At last she was in her dressing-gown and her night-cap, and in this costume, more suitable to her age, was less hideous than before.

Like most old people, the Countess was tormented by sleeplessness. She had her armchair rolled towards one of the windows, and told her maids to leave her. The lights were put out, and the room was lighted only by the lamp which burned before the holy images. The Countess, sallow and wrinkled, balanced herself gently from right to left. In her dull eyes could be read an utter absence of thought ; and as she moved from side to side, one might have said that she did so not by any action of the will, but through some secret mechanism.

Suddenly this death's-head assumed a new expression ; the lips ceased to tremble, and the eyes became alive. A strange man had appeared before the Countess !

It was Hermann.

" Do not be alarmed, madam," said Hermann, in a low voice, but very distinctly. " For the love of Heaven, do not be alarmed. I do not wish to do you the slightest harm ; on the contrary, I come to implore a favour of you."

The old woman looked at him in silence, as if she did not understand. Thinking she was deaf, he leaned towards her ear and repeated what he had said ; but the Countess still remained silent.

" You can ensure the happiness of my whole life, and without its costing you a farthing. I know that you can name to me three cards——"

The Countess now understood what he required.

" It was a joke," she interrupted. " I swear to you it was only a joke."

" No, madam," replied Hermann in an angry tone. " Remember Tchaplitzki, and how you enabled him to win."

The Countess was agitated. For a moment her features expressed strong emotion ; but they soon resumed their former dulness.

" Cannot you name to me," said Hermann, " three winning cards ? "

The Countess remained silent. " Why keep this secret for your great-grandchildren ? " he continued. " They are rich enough without ; they do not know the value of money. Of what profit would your three cards be to them ? They are debauchees. The man who cannot keep his inheritance will die in want, though he had the science of demons at his command. I am a steady man. I know the value of money. Your three cards will not be lost upon me. Come ! "

He stopped tremblingly, awaiting a reply. The Countess did not utter a word. Hermann went upon his knees.

" If your heart has ever known the passion of love ; if you can remember its sweet ecstasies ; if you have ever been touched by the cry of a new-born babe ; if any human feeling has ever caused your heart to beat, I entreat you by the love of a husband, a lover, a mother, by all that is sacred in life, not to reject my prayer. Tell me your secret ! Reflect ! You are old ; you have not long to live ! Remember that the happiness of a man is in your hands ; that not only myself, but my children and my grandchildren will bless your memory as a saint."

The old Countess answered not a word.

Hermann rose, and drew a pistol from his pocket.

" Hag ! " he exclaimed, " I will make you speak."

At the sight of the pistol the Countess for the second time showed agitation. Her head shook violently ; she stretched out her hands as if to put the weapon aside. Then suddenly she fell back motionless.

" Come, don't be childish ! " said Hermann. " I adjure you for the last time ; will you name the three cards ? "

The Countess did not answer. Hermann saw that she was dead !

IV

LISABETA was sitting in her room, still in her ball dress, lost in the deepest meditation. On her return to the house, she had sent away her maid, and had gone upstairs to her room,

A strange man had appeared before the Countess.

trembling at the idea of finding Hermann there ; desiring, indeed, *not* to find him. One glance showed her that he was not there, and she gave thanks to Providence that he had missed the appointment. She sat down pensively, without thinking of taking off her cloak, and allowed to pass through her memory all the circumstances of the intrigue which had begun such a short time back, and had already advanced so far. Scarcely three weeks had passed since she had first seen the young officer from her window, and already she had written to him, and he had succeeded in inducing her to make an appointment. She knew his name, and that was all. She had received a quantity of letters from him, but he had never spoken to her ; she did not know the sound of his voice, and until that evening, strangely enough, she had never heard him spoken of.

But that very evening Tomski, fancying he had noticed that the young Princess Pauline, to whom he had been paying assiduous court, was flirting, contrary to her custom, with another man, had wished to revenge himself by making a show of indifference. With this noble object he had invited Lisabeta to take part in an interminable mazurka ; but he teased her immensely about her partiality for Engineer officers, and pretending all the time to know much more than he really did, hazarded purely in fun a few guesses which were so happy that Lisabeta thought her secret must have been discovered.

" But who tells you all this ? " she said with a smile.

" A friend of the very officer you know, a most original man."

" And who is this man that is so original ? "

" His name is Hermann."

She answered nothing, but her hands and feet seemed to be of ice.

" Hermann is a hero of romance," continued Tomski. " He has the profile of Napoleon, and the soul of Mephistopheles. I believe he has at least three crimes on his conscience. . . . But how pale you are ! "

" I have a bad headache. But what did this Mr. Hermann tell you ? Is not that his name ? "

" Hermann is very much displeased with his friend, with the Engineer officer who has made your acquaintance. He says that in his place he would behave very differently. But I am quite sure that Hermann himself has designs upon you. At least, he seems to listen with remarkable interest to all that his friend tells him about you."

" And where has he seen me ? "

" Perhaps in church, perhaps in the street ; heaven knows where."

At this moment three ladies came forward according to the custom of the mazurka, and asked Tomski to choose between " forgetfulness and regret." [1]

And the conversation which had so painfully excited the curiosity of Lisabeta came to an end.

The lady who, in virtue of the infidelities permitted by the mazurka, had just been chosen by Tomski, was the Princess Pauline.   During the rapid evolutions which the figure obliged them to make, there was a grand explanation between them, until at last he conducted her to a chair, and returned to his partner.

But Tomski could now think no more, either of Hermann or Lisabeta, and he tried in vain to resume the conversation.   But the mazurka was coming to an end, and immediately afterwards the old Countess rose to go.

Tomski's mysterious phrases were nothing more than the usual platitudes of the mazurka, but they had made a deep impression upon the heart of the poor little companion.   The portrait sketched by Tomski had struck her as very exact ; and with her romantic ideas, she saw in the rather ordinary coun-tenance of her adorer something to fear and admire.   She was now sitting down with her cloak off, with bare shoulders ; her head, crowned with flowers, falling forward from fatigue, when suddenly the door opened and Hermann entered.   She shuddered.

" Where were you ? " she said, trembling all over.

" In the Countess's bedroom.   I have just left her," replied Hermann.   " She is dead."

" Great heavens !   What are you saying ? "

" I am afraid," he said, " that I am the cause of her death."

Lisabeta looked at him in consternation, and remembered Tomski's words :   " He has at least three crimes on his conscience."

Hermann sat down by the window, and told everything. The young girl listened with terror.

So those letters so full of passion, those burning expressions, this daring obstinate pursuit—all this had been inspired by any-thing but love !   Money alone had inflamed the man's soul. She, who had nothing but a heart to offer, how could she make him happy ?   Poor child !   she had been the blind instrument of a robber, of the murderer of her old benefactress.   She wept

[1] The figures and fashions of the mazurka are reproduced in the cotillon of Western Europe.—TRANSLATOR.

bitterly in the agony of her repentance. Hermann watched her in silence ; but neither the tears of the unhappy girl, nor her beauty, rendered more touching by her grief, could move his heart of iron. He had no remorse in thinking of the Countess's death. One sole thought distressed him—the irreparable loss of the secret which was to have made his fortune.

" You are a monster ! " said Lisabeta, after a long silence.

" I did not mean to kill her," replied Hermann coldly. " My pistol was not loaded."

They remained for some time without speaking, without looking at one another. The day was breaking, and Lisabeta put out her candle. She wiped her eyes, drowned in tears, and raised them towards Hermann. He was standing close to the window, his arms crossed, with a frown on his forehead. In this attitude he reminded her involuntarily of the portrait of Napoleon. The resemblance overwhelmed her.

" How am I to get you away ? " she said at last. " I thought you might go out by the back stairs. But it would be necessary to go through the Countess's bedroom, and I am too frightened."

" Tell me how to get to the staircase, and I will go alone."

She went to a drawer, took out a key, which she handed to Hermann, and gave him the necessary instructions. Hermann took her icy hand, kissed her on the forehead, and departed.

He went down the staircase and entered the Countess's bedroom. She was seated quite stiff in her armchair, but her features were in no way contracted. He stopped for a moment, and gazed into her face as if to make sure of the terrible reality. Then he entered the dark room, and, feeling behind the tapestry, found the little door which opened on to a staircase. As he went down it, strange ideas came into his head. " Going down this staircase," he said to himself, " some sixty years ago, at about this time, may have been seen some man in an embroidered coat with powdered wig, pressing to his breast a cocked hat ; some gallant who has long been buried ; and now the heart of his aged mistress has ceased to beat."

At the end of the staircase he found another door, which his key opened, and he found himself in the corridor which led to the street.

V

THREE days after this fatal night, at nine o'clock in the morning, Hermann entered the convent where the last respects were to be paid to the mortal remains of the old Countess. He felt no remorse, though he could not deny to himself that he was the poor woman's assassin. Having no religion, he was, as usual in such cases, very superstitious ; believing that the dead Countess might exercise a malignant influence on his life, he thought to appease her spirit by attending her funeral.

The church was full of people, and it was difficult to get in. The body had been placed on a rich catafalque, beneath a canopy of velvet. The Countess was reposing in an open coffin, her hands joined on her breast, with a dress of white satin, and head-dress of lace. Around the catafalque the family was assembled, the servants in black caftans with a knot of ribbons on the shoulder, exhibiting the colours of the Countess's coat-of-arms. Each of them held a wax candle in his hand. The relations, in deep mourning—children, grandchildren, and great-grandchildren—were all present ; but none of them wept.

To have shed tears would have looked like affectation. The Countess was so old that her death could have taken no one by surprise, and she had long been looked upon as already out of the world. The funeral sermon was delivered by a celebrated preacher. In a few simple, touching phrases he painted the final departure of the just, who had passed long years of contrite preparation for a Christian end. The service concluded in the midst of respectful silence. Then the relations went towards the defunct to take a last farewell. After them, in a long procession, all who had been invited to the ceremony bowed, for the last time, to her who for so many years had been a scarecrow at their entertainments. Finally came the Countess's household ; among them was remarked an old governess, of the same age as the deceased, supported by two women. She had not strength enough to kneel down, but tears flowed from her eyes, as she kissed the hand of her old mistress.

In his turn Hermann advanced towards the coffin. He knelt down for a moment on the flagstones, which were strewed with branches of yew. Then he rose, as pale as death, and walked up the steps of the catafalque. He bowed his head. But suddenly the dead woman seemed to be staring at him ; and with a mocking look she opened and shut one eye. Hermann by a sudden movement started and fell backwards. Several persons hurried towards him. At the same moment, close to the church door, Lisabeta fainted.

Throughout the day, Hermann suffered from a strange indisposition. In a quiet restaurant, where he took his meals, he, contrary to his habit, drank a great deal of wine, with the object of stupefying himself. But the wine had no effect but to excite his imagination, and give fresh activity to the ideas with which he was preoccupied.

He went home earlier than usual ; lay down with his clothes on upon the bed, and fell into a leaden sleep. When he woke up it was night, and the room was lighted up by the rays of the moon. He looked at his watch ; it was a quarter to three. He could sleep no more. He sat up on the bed and thought of the old Countess. At this moment some one in the street passed the window, looked into the room, and then went on. Hermann scarcely noticed it ; but in another minute he heard the door of the ante-chamber open. He thought that his orderly, drunk as usual, was returning from some nocturnal excursion ; but the step was one to which he was not accustomed. Somebody seemed to be softly walking over the floor in slippers.

The door opened, and a woman, dressed entirely in white, entered the bedroom. Hermann thought it must be his old nurse, and he asked himself what she could want at that time of night.

But the woman in white, crossing the room with a rapid step, was now at the foot of his bed, and Hermann recognized the Countess.

" I come to you against my wish," she said in a firm voice. " I am forced to grant your prayer. Three, seven, ace will win, if played one after the other ; but you must not play more than one card in twenty-four hours, and afterwards as long as you live you must never touch a card again. I forgive you my death, on condition of your marrying my companion, Lisabeta Ivanovna."

With these words she walked towards the door, and gliding with her slippers over the floor, disappeared. Hermann heard the door of the ante-chamber open, and soon afterwards saw a white figure pass along the street. It stopped for a moment before his window, as if to look at him.

Hermann remained for some time astounded. Then he got up and went into the next room. His orderly, drunk as usual, was asleep on the floor. He had much difficulty in waking him, and then could not obtain from him the least explanation. The door of the ante-chamber was locked.

Hermann went back to his bedroom, and wrote down all the details of his vision.

VI

Two fixed ideas can no more exist together in the moral world than in the physical two bodies can occupy the same place at the same time ; and " three, seven, ace " soon drove away Hermann's recollection of the old Countess's last moments. " Three, seven, ace " were now in his head to the exclusion of everything else.

They followed him in his dreams, and appeared to him under strange forms. Threes seemed to be spread before him like magnolias, sevens took the form of Gothic doors, and aces became gigantic spiders.

His thoughts concentrated themselves on one single point. How was he to profit by the secret so dearly purchased ? What if he applied for leave to travel ? At Paris, he said to himself, he would find some gambling-house where, with his three cards, he could at once make his fortune.

Chance soon came to his assistance. There was at Moscow a society of rich gamblers, presided over by the celebrated Tchekalinski, who had passed all his life playing at cards, and had amassed millions. For while he lost silver only, he gained banknotes. His magnificent house, his excellent kitchen, his cordial manners had brought him numerous friends and secured for him general esteem.

When he came to St. Petersburg, the young men of the capital filled his rooms, forsaking balls for his card-parties, and preferring the emotions of gambling to the fascinations of flirting. Hermann was taken to Tchekalinski by Naroumoff. They passed through a long suite of rooms, full of the most attentive, obsequious servants. The place was crowded. Generals and high officials were playing at whist ; young men were stretched out on the sofas, eating ices and smoking long pipes. In the principal room at the head of a long table, around which were assembled a score of players, the master of the house held a faro bank.

He was a man of about sixty, with a sweet and noble expression of face, and hair white as snow. On his full, florid countenance might be read good humour and benevolence. His eyes shone with a perpetual smile. Naroumoff introduced Hermann. Tchekalinski took him by the hand, told him that he was glad to see him, that no one stood on ceremony in his house ; and then went on dealing. The deal occupied some time, and stakes were made on more than thirty cards. Tchekalinski waited patiently to allow the winners time to double their stakes, paid what he had lost, listened politely to all observations, and, more politely still, put straight the corners of cards, when in a fit of absence some one had taken the liberty of turning them down. At last, when the game was at an end, Tchekalinski collected the cards, shuffled them again, had them cut, and then dealt anew.

" Will you allow me to take a card ? " said Hermann, stretching out his arms above a fat man who occupied nearly the whole of one side of the table. Tchekalinski, with a gracious smile, bowed in consent. Naroumoff complimented Hermann, with a laugh, on the cessation of the austerity by which his conduct had hitherto been marked, and wished him all kinds of happiness on the occasion of his first appearance in the character of a gambler.

" There ! " said Hermann, after writing some figures on the back of his card.

" How much ? " asked the banker, half closing his eyes. " Excuse me, I cannot see."

" Forty-seven thousand roubles," said Hermann.

Every one's eyes were directed toward the new player.

" He has lost his head," thought Naroumoff.

" Allow me to point out to you," said Tchekalinski, with his eternal smile, " that you are playing rather high. We never put down here, as a first stake, more than a hundred and seventy-five roubles."

" Very well," said Hermann ; " but do you accept my stake or not ? "

Tchekalinski bowed in token of acceptance. " I only wish to point out to you," he said, " that although I am perfectly sure of my friends, I can only play against ready money. I am quite convinced that your word is as good as gold ; but to keep up the rules of the game, and to facilitate calculations, I should be obliged to you if you would put the money on your card."

Hermann took a bank-note from his pocket and handed it to Tchekalinski, who, after examining it with a glance, placed it on Hermann's card.

Then he began to deal. He turned up on the right a ten, and on the left a three.

" I win," said Hermann, exhibiting his three.

A murmur of astonishment ran through the assembly. The banker knitted his eyebrows, but speedily his face resumed its everlasting smile.

" Shall I settle at once ? " he asked.

" If you will be kind enough to do so," said Hermann.

Tchekalinski took a bundle of bank-notes from his pocket-book and paid. Hermann pocketed his winnings and left the table.

Naroumoff was lost in astonishment. Hermann drank a glass of lemonade and went home.

The next evening he returned to the house. Tchekalinski again held the bank. Hermann went to the table, and this time the players hastened to make room for him. Tchekalinski received him with a most gracious bow. Hermann waited, took a card, and staked on it his forty-seven thousand roubles, together with the like sum which he had gained the evening before.

Tchekalinski began to deal. He turned up on the right a knave, and on the left a seven.

Hermann exhibited a seven.

There was a general exclamation. Tchekalinski was evidently ill at ease, but he counted out the ninety-four thousand roubles to Hermann, who took them in the calmest manner, rose from the table, and went away.

The next evening, at the accustomed hour, he again appeared. Every one was expecting him. Generals and high officials had left their whist to watch this extraordinary play. The young officers had quitted their sofas, and even the servants of the house pressed round the table.

When Hermann took his seat, the other players ceased to stake, so impatient were they to see him have it out with the banker, who, still smiling, watched the approach of his antagonist and prepared to meet him. Each of them untied at the same time a pack of cards. Tchekalinski shuffled, and Hermann cut. Then the latter took up a card and covered it with a heap of bank-notes. It was like the preliminaries of a duel. A deep silence reigned through the room.

Tchekalinski took up the cards with trembling hands and dealt. On one side he put down a queen and on the other side an ace.

" Ace wins," said Hermann.

" No. Queen loses," said Tchekalinski.

Hermann looked. Instead of ace, he saw a queen of spades before him. He could not trust his eyes ! And now as he gazed in fascination on the fatal card, he fancied that he saw the queen of spades open and then close her eye, while at the same time she gave a mocking smile. He felt a thrill of nameless horror. The queen of spades resembled the dead Countess !

Hermann is now at the Aboukhoff Asylum, room No. 17—a hopeless madman ! He answers no questions which we put to him. Only he mumbles to himself without cessation, " Three, even, ace ; three, seven, *queen* ! "

THE SEVENTH MAN

IN a one-roomed hut, high within the Arctic Circle, and
only a little south of the eightieth parallel, six men were
sitting—much as they had sat, evening after evening, for
months. They had a clock, and by it they divided the hours
into day and night. As a matter of fact, it was always night.
But the clock said half-past eight, and they called the time
evening.

The hut was built of logs, with an inner skin of rough
match-boarding, daubed with pitch. It measured seventeen
feet by fourteen ; but opposite the door four bunks—two above
and two below—took a yard off the length, and this made the
interior exactly square. Each of these bunks had two doors,
with brass latches on the inner side ; so that the owner, if he
chose, could shut himself up and go to sleep in a sort of cupboard. But as a rule, he closed one of them only—that by
his feet. The other swung back, with its brass latch showing.
The men kept these latches in a high state of polish.

Across the angle of the wall, to the left of the door, and
behind it when it opened, three hammocks were slung, one
above another. No one slept in the uppermost.

But the feature of the hut was its fireplace ; and this was
merely a square hearthstone, raised slightly above the floor,
in the middle of the room. Upon it, and upon a growing
mountain of soft grey ash, the fire burned always. It had no
chimney, and so the men lost none of its warmth. The smoke
ascended steadily and spread itself under the blackened beams
and roof-boards in dense blue layers. But about eighteen
inches beneath the spring of the roof there ran a line of small
trap-doors with sliding panels, to admit the cold air, and
below these the room was almost clear of smoke. A new-

474

comer's eyes might have smarted, but these men stitched their clothes and read in comfort. To keep the up-draught steady they had plugged every chink and crevice in the match-boarding below the trap-doors with moss, and payed the seams with pitch. The fire they fed from a stack of drift and wreck-wood piled to the right of the door, and fuel for the fetching strewed the frozen beach outside—whole trees notched into lengths by lumberers' axes and washed thither from they knew not what continent. But the wreck-wood came from their own ship, the *J. R. MacNeill*, which had brought them from Dundee.

They were Alexander Williamson, of Dundee, better known as the Gaffer ; David Faed, also of Dundee ; George Lashman, of Cardiff ; Long Ede, of Hayle, in Cornwall ; Charles Silchester, otherwise the Snipe, of Ratcliff Highway or thereabouts ; and Daniel Cooney, shipped at Tromso six weeks before the wreck, an Irish-American by birth and of no known address.

The Gaffer reclined in his bunk, reading by the light of a smoky and evil-smelling lamp. He had been mate of the *J. R. MacNeill*, and was now captain as well as patriarch of the party. He possessed three books—the Bible, Milton's *Paradise Lost*, and an odd volume of *The Turkish Spy*. Just now he was reading *The Turkish Spy*. The lamplight glinted on the rim of his spectacles and on the silvery hairs in his beard, the slack of which he had tucked under the edge of his blanket. His lips moved as he read, and now and then he broke off to glance mildly at Faed and the Snipe, who were busy beside the fire with a greasy pack of cards ; or to listen to the peevish grumbling of Lashman in the bunk below him. Lashman had taken to his bed six weeks before with scurvy, and complained incessantly ; and, though they hardly knew it, these complaints were wearing his comrades' nerves to fiddle-strings—doing the mischief that cold and bitter hard work and the cruel loneliness had hitherto failed to do. Long Ede lay stretched by the fire in a bundle of skins, reading in his only book, the Bible, open now at the Song of Solomon. Cooney had finished patching a pair of trousers, and rolled himself in his hammock, whence he stared at the roof and the moonlight streaming up there through the little trap-doors and chivying the layers of smoke. Whenever Lashman broke out into fresh quaverings of self-pity, Cooney's hands opened and shut again, till the nails dug hard into the palm. He groaned at length, exasperated beyond endurance.

" Oh, stow it, George ! Hang it all, man ! . . ."

He checked himself, sharp and short : repentant, and rebuked by the silence of the others. They were good seamen all, and tender dealing with a sick shipmate was part of their code.

Lashman's voice, more querulous than ever, cut into the silence like a knife :

" That's it. You've thought it for weeks, and now you say it. I've knowed it all along. I'm just an encumbrance, and the sooner you're shut of me the better, says you. You needn't to fret. I'll be soon out of it ; out of it—out there, alongside of Bill——"

" Easy there, matey." The Snipe glanced over his shoulder and laid his cards face downward. " Here, let me give the bed a shake up. It'll ease yer."

" It'll make me quiet, you mean. Plucky deal you care about easin' me, any of yer."

" Get out with yer nonsense ! Dan didn't mean it." The Snipe slipped an arm under the invalid's head and rearranged the pillow of skins and gunnybags.

" He didn't, didn't he ? Let him say it then . . ."

The Gaffer read on, his lips moving silently. Heaven knows how he had acquired this strayed and stained and filthy little demi-octavo with the arms of Saumarez on its bookplate—" The Sixth Volume of Letters writ by a Turkish Spy, who liv'd Five-and-Forty Years Undiscovered at Paris : Giving an Impartial Account to the *Divan* at *Constantinople* of the most remarkable Transactions of Europe, And discovering several *Intrigues* and *Secrets* of the *Christian* Courts (especially of that of *France*)," etc., etc. " Written originally in *Arabick*. Translated into *Italian*, and from thence into *English* by the Translator of the First Volume. The Eleventh Edition, London : Printed for G. Strahan, S. Ballard "—and a score of booksellers—" MDCCXLI." Heaven knows why he read it, since he understood about one-half, and admired less than one-tenth. The Oriental reflections struck him as mainly blasphemous. But the Gaffer's religious belief marked down nine-tenths of mankind for perdition : which perhaps made him tolerant. At any rate, he read on gravely between the puffs of his short clay :

" *On the 19th of this Moon, the King and the whole Court were present at a Ballet, representing the grandeur of the* French *monarchy. About the Middle of the Entertainment, there was an Antique Dance perform'd by twelve Masqueraders, in the suppos'd form of* Dæmons. *But before they advanc'd far in their Dance, they found an Interloper amongst 'em, who by encreasing the Number to thirteen, put them quite out of their Measure: For they practise every Step and Motion beforehand, till they are perfect. Being abash'd therefore at the unavoidable Blunders the thirteenth Antique made them commit they stood still like Fools, gazing at one another : None daring to unmask, or speak a Word ; for that would have put all the Spectators into a Disorder and Confusion.* Cardinal Mazarini *(who was the chief Contriver of these Entertainments, to divert the King from more serious Thoughts) stood close by the young Monarch, with the Scheme of the Ballet in his Hand. Knowing therefore that this Dance was to consist but of twelve Antiques, and taking notice that there were actually thirteen, he at first imputed it to some Mistake. But, afterwards, when he perceived the Confusion of the Dancers, he made a more narrow Enquiry into the Cause of this Disorder. To be brief, they convinced the* Cardinal *that it could be no Error of theirs, by a kind of Demonstration, in that they had but twelve Antique Dresses of that sort, which were made on purpose for this particular Ballet. That which made it seem the greater Mystery was, that when they came behind the Scenes to uncase, and examine the Matter, they found but twelve Antiques, whereas on the Stage there were thirteen . . ."*

" Let him say it.   Let him say he didn't mean it, the rotten Irishman ! "

Cooney flung a leg wearily over the side of his hammock, jerked himself out, and shuffled across to the sick man's berth.

" Av coorse I didn' mane it.   It just took me, ye see, lyin' up yondher and huggin' me thoughts in this—wilderness.   I swear to ye, George : and ye'll just wet your throat to show there's no bad blood, and that ye belave me." He took up a pannikin from the floor beside the bunk, pulled a hot iron from the fire, and stirred the frozen drink.   The invalid turned his shoulder pettishly.   " I didn't mane it," Cooney repeated.   He set down the pannikin, and shuffled wearily back to his hammock.

The Gaffer blew a long cloud and stared at the fire ; at the smoke mounting and the grey ash dropping ; at David Faed dealing the cards and licking his thumb between each.   Long Ede shifted from one cramped elbow to another and pushed his Bible near the blaze, murmuring, " Take us the foxes, the little foxes, that spoil our vines."

" Full hand," the Snipe announced.

" Ay," David Faed rolled the quid in his cheek.   The cards

were so thumbed and tattered that by the backs of them each player guessed pretty shrewdly what the other held.   Yet they went on playing night after night ; the Snipe shrilly blessing or cursing his luck, the Scotsman phlegmatic as a bolster.

"Play away, man.   What ails ye ? " he asked.

The Snipe had dropped both hands to his thighs and sat up, stiff and listening.

"Whist !   Outside the door . . ."

All listened.   " I hear nothing," said David, after ten seconds.

"Hush, man—listen !   There, again . . ."

They heard now.   Cooney slipped down from his hammock, stole to the door and listened, crouching, with his ear close to the jamb.   The sound resembled breathing—or so he thought for a moment.   Then it seemed rather as if some creature were softly feeling about the door—fumbling its coating of ice and frozen snow.

Cooney listened.   They all listened.   Usually, as soon as they stirred from the scorching circle of the fire, their breath came from them in clouds.   It trickled from them now in thin wisps of vapour.   They could almost hear the soft grey ash dropping on the hearth.

A log spluttered.   Then the invalid's voice clattered in :

" It's the bears—the bears !   They've come after Bill, and next it'll be my turn.   I warned you—I told you he wasn't deep enough.   O Lord, have mercy . . . mercy . . . ! "   He pattered off into a prayer, his voice and teeth chattering.

" Hush ! " commanded the Gaffer gently ; and Lashman choked on a sob.

" It ain't bears," Cooney reported, still with his ear to the door.   " Leastways . . . we've had bears before.   The foxes, maybe . . . let me listen."

Long Ede murmured : " Take us the foxes, the little foxes . . ."

" I believe you're right," the Gaffer announced cheerfully. " A bear would sniff louder—though there's no telling.   The snow was falling an hour back, and I dessay 'tis pretty thick outside.   If 'tis a bear, we don't want him fooling on the roof, and I misdoubt the drift by the north corner is pretty tall by this time.   Is he there still ? "

" I felt something then . . . through the chink, here . . . like a warm breath.   It's gone now.   Come here, Snipe, and listen."

" ' Breath,' eh ?   Did it *smell* like bear ? "

" I don't know . . . I didn't smell nothing, to notice. Here, put your head down, close."

The Snipe bent his head. And at that moment the door shook gently. All stared ; and saw the latch move up, up . . . and falteringly descend on the staple. They heard the click of it.

The door was secured within by two stout bars. Against these there had been no pressure. The men waited in a silence that ached. But the latch was not lifted again.

The Snipe, kneeling, looked up at Cooney. Cooney shivered and looked at David Faed. Long Ede, with his back to the fire, softly shook his feet free of the rugs. His eyes searched for the Gaffer's face. But the old man had drawn back into the gloom of his bunk, and the lamplight shone only on a grey fringe of beard. He saw Long Ede's look, though, and answered it quietly as ever.

" Take a brace of guns aloft, and fetch us a look round. Wait, if there's a chance of a shot. The trap works. I tried it this afternoon with the small chisel."

Long Ede lit his pipe, tied down the ear-pieces of his cap, lifted a light ladder off its staples, and set it against a roof-beam : then, with the guns under his arm, quietly mounted. His head and shoulders wavered and grew vague to sight in the smoke-wreaths. " Heard anything more ? " he asked. " Nothing since," answered the Snipe. With his shoulder Long Ede pushed up the trap. They saw his head framed in a panel of moonlight, with one frosty star above it. He was wriggling through. " Pitch him up a sleeping-bag somebody," the Gaffer ordered, and Cooney ran with one. " Thank 'ee, mate," said Long Ede, and closed the trap.

They heard his feet stealthily crunching the frozen stuff across the roof. He was working towards the eaves overlapping the door. Their breath tightened. They waited for the explosion of his gun. None came. The crunching began again : it was heard down by the very edge of the eaves. It mounted to the blunt ridge overhead ; then it ceased.

" He will not have seen aught," David Faed muttered.

" Listen, you. Listen by the door again." They talked in whispers. Nothing ; there was nothing to be heard. They crept back to the fire, and stood there warming themselves, keeping their eyes on the latch. It did not move. After a while Cooney slipped off to his hammock ; Faed to his bunk, alongside Lashman's. The Gaffer had picked up his book again. The Snipe laid a couple of logs on the blaze, and remained be-

side it, cowering with his arms stretched out as if to embrace it.
His shapeless shadow wavered up and down on the bunks behind him ; and, across the fire, he still stared at the latch.

Suddenly the sick man's voice quavered out :

" It's not him they want—it's Bill ! They're after Bill, out
there ! That was Bill trying to get in. . . . Why didn't yer open ?
It was Bill, I tell yer ! "

At the first word the Snipe had wheeled right-about-face,
and stood now, pointing, and shaking like a man with ague.

" Matey . . . for the love of God . . ."

" I won't hush. There's something wrong here to-night. I
can't sleep. It's Bill, I tell yer. See his poor hammock up
there shaking. . . ."

Cooney tumbled out with an oath and a thud. " Hush it,
you white-livered swine ! Hush it, or by——" His hand
went behind him to his knife-sheath.

" Dan Cooney "—the Gaffer closed his book and leaned
out—" go back to your bed."

" I won't, Sir. Not unless——"

" Go back."

" Flesh and blood——"

" Go back." And for the third time that night Cooney
went back.

The Gaffer leaned a little farther over the ledge, and addressed the sick man.

" George, I went to Bill's grave not six hours agone. The
snow on it wasn't even disturbed. Neither beast nor man, but
only God, can break up the hard earth he lies under. I tell
you that, and you may lay to it. Now go to sleep."

.   .   .   .

Long Ede crouched on the frozen ridge of the hut, with his
feet in the sleeping-bag, his knees drawn up, and the two guns
laid across them. The creature, whatever its name, that had
tried the door, was nowhere to be seen ; but he decided to wait
a few minutes on the chance of a shot ; that is, until the cold
should drive him below. For the moment the clear tingling air
was doing him good. The truth was Long Ede had begun to be
afraid of himself, and the way his mind had been running for
the last forty-eight hours upon green fields and visions of spring.
As he put it to himself, something inside his head was melting.
Biblical texts chattered within him like running brooks, and as
they fleeted he could almost smell the blown meadow-scent.
" Take us the foxes, the little foxes . . . for our vines have tender
grapes. . . . A fountain of gardens, a well of living waters, and

streams from Lebanon . . . Awake, O north wind, and come, thou south . . . blow upon my garden, that the spices thereof may flow out. . . ." He was light-headed, and he knew it. He must hold out. They were all going mad ; were, in fact, three parts crazed already, all except the Gaffer. And the Gaffer relied on him as his right-hand man. One glimpse of the returning sun—one glimpse only—might save them yet.

He gazed out over the frozen hills, and northward across the ice-pack. A few streaks of pale violet—the ghost of the Aurora—fronted the moon. He could see for miles. Bear or fox, no living creature was in sight. But who could tell what might be hiding behind any one of a thousand hummocks ? He listened. He heard the slow grinding of the ice-pack off the beach : only that. " Take us the foxes, the little foxes . . ."

This would never do. He must climb down and walk briskly, or return to the hut. Maybe there was a bear, after all, behind one of the hummocks, and a shot, or the chance of one, would scatter his head clear of these tom-fooling notions. He would have a search round.

What was that, moving . . . on a hummock, not five hundred yards away ? He leaned forward to gaze.

Nothing now ; but he had seen something. He lowered himself to the eaves by the north corner, and from the eaves to the drift piled there. The drift was frozen solid, but for a treacherous crust of fresh snow. His foot slipped upon this, and down he slid of a heap.

Luckily he had been careful to sling the guns tightly at his back. He picked himself up, and unstrapping one, took a step into the bright moonlight to examine the nipples ; took two steps : and stood stock-still.

There, before him, on the frozen coat of snow, was a footprint. No : two, three, four—many footprints : prints of a naked human foot : right foot, left foot, both naked, and blood in each print—a little smear.

It had come, then. He was mad for certain. He saw them : he put his fingers in them ; touched the frozen blood. The snow before the door was trodden thick with them—some going, some returning.

" The latch . . . lifted. . . ." Suddenly he recalled the figure he had seen moving upon the hummock, and with a groan he set his face northward and gave chase. Oh, he was mad for certain ! He ran like a madman—floundering, slipping, plunging in his clumsy moccasins. " Take us the foxes, the little foxes . . . My beloved put in his hand by the hole of the door, and my bowels were moved for him . . . I charge you, O daughters of Jerusalem . . . I charge you . . . I charge you . . ."

He ran thus for three hundred yards maybe, and then stopped as suddenly as he had started.

His mates—they must not see these footprints, or they would go mad too : mad as he. No, he must cover them up, all within sight of the hut. And to-morrow he would come alone and cover those farther afield. Slowly he retraced his steps. The footprints —those which pointed towards the hut and those which pointed away from it—lay close together ; and he knelt before each, breaking fresh snow over the hollows and carefully hiding the blood. And now a great happiness filled his heart ; interrupted once or twice as he worked by a feeling that some one was following and watching him. Once he turned northwards and gazed, making a telescope of his hands. He saw nothing, and fell again to his long task.

.   .   .   .   .   .

Within the hut the sick man cried softly to himself. Faed, the Snipe, and Cooney slept uneasily, and muttered in their dreams. The Gaffer lay awake, thinking. After Bill, George Lashman ; and after George . . . ? Who next ? And who would be the last—the unburied one ? The men were weakening fast ; their wits and courage coming down at the end with a rush. Faed and Long Ede were the only two to be depended on for a day. The Gaffer liked Long Ede, who was a religious man. Indeed he had a growing suspicion that Long Ede, in spite of some amiable laxities of belief, was numbered among the Elect : or might be, if interceded for. The Gaffer began to intercede for him silently ; but experience had taught him that such " wrestlings," to be effective, must be noisy, and he dropped off to sleep with a sense of failure. . . .

The Snipe stretched himself, yawned, and awoke. It was seven in the morning : time to prepare a cup of tea. He tossed an armful of logs on the fire, and the noise awoke the Gaffer. who at once inquired for Long Ede. He had not returned, " Go you up to the roof. The lad must be frozen." The Snipe climbed the ladder, pushed open the trap, and came back, reporting that Long Ede was nowhere to be seen. The old man slipped a jumper over his suits of clothing—already three deep—reached for a gun, and moved to the door. " Take a cup of something warm to fortify," the Snipe advised. " The kettle won't be five minutes boiling." But the Gaffer pushed up the heavy bolts and dragged the door open.

" What in the . . . ! Here, bear a hand, lads ! "

Long Ede lay prone before the threshold, his outstretched hands almost touching it, his moccasins already covered out of sight by the powdery snow which ran and trickled incessantly —trickled between his long, dishevelled locks, and over the back of his gloves, and ran in a thin stream past the Gaffer's feet.

They carried him in and laid him on a heap of skins by the fire. They forced rum between his clenched teeth and beat his hands and feet, and kneaded and rubbed him. A sigh fluttered on his lips : something between a sigh and a smile, half seen, half heard. His eyes opened, and his comrades saw that it was really a smile.

" Wot cheer, mate ? " It was the Snipe who asked.

" I—I seen . . ." The voice broke off, but he was smiling still.

What had he seen ? Not the sun, surely ! By the Gaffer's reckoning the sun would not be due for a week or two yet : how many weeks he could not say precisely, and sometimes he was glad enough that he did not know.

They forced him to drink a couple of spoonfuls of rum, and wrapped him up warmly. Each man contributed some of his own bedding. Then the Gaffer called to morning prayers, and the three sound men dropped on their knees with him. Now, whether by reason of their joy at Long Ede's recovery, or because the old man was in splendid voice, they felt their hearts uplifted that morning with a cheerfulness they had not known for months. Long Ede lay and listened dreamily while the passion of the Gaffer's thanksgiving shook the hut. His gaze wandered over their bowed forms—" The Gaffer, David Faed, Dan Cooney, the Snipe, and—and George Lashman in his bunk, of course—and me." But, then, *who was the seventh?* He began to count. " There's myself—Lashman, in his bunk— David Faed, the Gaffer, the Snipe, Dan Cooney . . . One, two, three, four—well but that made *seven.* Then who was the seventh ? Was it George who had crawled out of bed and was kneeling there ? Decidedly there were five kneeling. No : there was George, plain enough, in his berth, and not able to move. Then who was the stranger ? Wrong again : there was no stranger. He knew all these men—they were his mates. Was it—Bill ? No, Bill was dead and buried : none of these was Bill, or like Bill. Try again—One, two, three, four, five—and us two sick men, seven. The Gaffer, David Faed, Dan Cooney—have I counted Dan twice ? No, that's Dan, yonder to the right, and only one of him. Five men kneeling, and two on their backs : that makes seven every time. Dear God—suppose——"

The Gaffer ceased, and, in the act of rising from his knees, caught sight of Long Ede's face. While the others fetched their breakfast-cans, he stepped over, and bent and whispered :

" Tell me. Ye've seen what ? "

" Seen ? " Long Ede echoed.

" Ay, seen what ? Speak low—was it the sun ? "

" The s——" But this time the echo died on his lips, and his face grew full of awe uncomprehending. It frightened the Gaffer.

" Ye'll be the better of a snatch of sleep," said he ; and was turning to go, when Long Ede stirred a hand under the edge of his rugs.

" Seven . . . count . . ." he whispered.

" Lord have mercy upon us ! " the Gaffer muttered to his beard as he moved away. " Long Ede ; gone crazed ! "

And yet, though an hour or two ago this had been the worst that could befall, the Gaffer felt unusually cheerful. As for the others, they were like different men, all that day and through the three days that followed. Even Lashman ceased to complain, and, unless their eyes played them a trick, had taken a turn for the better. " I declare, if I don't feel like pitching to sing ! " the Snipe announced on the second evening, as much to his own wonder as to theirs. " Then why in thunder don't you strike up ? " answered Dan Cooney, and fetched his concertina. The Snipe struck up, then and there—" Villikins and his Dinah ! " What is more, the Gaffer looked up from his *Paradise Lost*, and joined in the chorus.

By the end of the second day, Long Ede was up and active again. He went about with a dazed look in his eyes. He was counting, counting to himself, always counting. The Gaffer watched him furtively.

Since his recovery, though his lips moved frequently, Long Ede had scarcely uttered a word. But towards noon on the fourth day he said an extraordinary thing :

" There's that sleeping-bag I took with me the other night. I wonder if 'tis on the roof still. It will be froze pretty stiff by this. You might nip up and see, Snipe, and "—he paused— " if you find it, stow it up yonder on Bill's hammock."

The Gaffer opened his mouth, but shut it again without speaking. The Snipe went up the ladder.

A minute passed ; and then they heard a cry from the roof

—a cry that fetched them all trembling, choking, weeping, cheering, to the foot of the ladder.

" Boys ! boys !—the Sun ! "

.   .   .   .   .   .

Months later—it was June, and even George Lashman had recovered his strength—the Snipe came running with news of the whaling fleet. And on the beach, as they watched the vessels come to anchor, Long Ede told the Gaffer his story : " It was a hall—a hallu—what d'ye call it. I reckon I was crazed, eh ? " The Gaffer's eyes wandered from a brambling hopping about the lichen-covered boulders, and away to the sea-fowl wheeling above the ships : and then came into his mind a tale he had read once in *The Turkish Spy*. " I wouldn't say just that," he answered slowly.

" Anyway," said Long Ede, " I believe the Lord sent a miracle to save us all."

" I wouldn't say just that, either," the Gaffer objected. " I doubt it was meant just for you and me, and the rest were pre-sairved, as you might say incidentally."

LAURA

"YOU are not really dying, are you ? " asked Amanda. " I have the doctor's permission to live till Tuesday," said Laura.

" But to-day is Saturday ; this is serious ! " gasped Amanda.

" I don't know about it being serious ; it is certainly Saturday," said Laura.

" Death is always serious," said Amanda.

" I never said I was going to die. I am presumably going to leave off being Laura, but I shall go on being something. An animal of some kind, I suppose. You see, when one hasn't been very good in the life one has just lived, one re-incarnates in some lower organism. And I haven't been very good, when one comes to think of it. I've been petty and mean and vindictive and all that sort of thing when circumstances have seemed to warrant it."

" Circumstances never warrant that sort of thing," said Amanda hastily.

" If you don't mind my saying so," observed Laura, " Egbert is a circumstance that would warrant any amount of that sort of thing. You're married to him—that's different ; you've sworn to love, honour, and endure him : I haven't."

" I don't see what's wrong with Egbert," protested Amanda.

" Oh, I dare say the wrongness has been on my part," admitted Laura dispassionately ; " he has merely been the extenuating circumstance. He made a thin, peevish kind of fuss, for instance, when I took the collie puppies from the farm out for a run the other day."

" They chased his young broods of speckled Sussex and drove two sitting hens off their nests, besides running all over
486

the flower beds. You know how devoted he is to his poultry
and garden."

"Anyhow, he needn't have gone on about it for the entire
evening and then have said, ' Let's say no more about it ' just
when I was beginning to enjoy the discussion. That's where
one of my petty vindictive revenges came in," added Laura
with an unrepentant chuckle ; " I turned the entire family
of speckled Sussex into his seedling shed the day after the
puppy episode."

"How could you ? " exclaimed Amanda.

"It came quite easy," said Laura ; "two of the hens
pretended to be laying at the time, but I was firm."

"And we thought it was an accident ! "

"You see," resumed Laura, " I really *have* some grounds
for supposing that my next incarnation will be in a lower
organism. I shall be an animal of some kind. On the other
hand, I haven't been a bad sort in my way, so I think I may
count on being a nice animal, something elegant and lively,
with a love of fun. An otter, perhaps."

"I can't imagine you as an otter," said Amanda.

"Well, I don't suppose you can imagine me as an angel,
if it comes to that," said Laura.

Amanda was silent. She couldn't.

"Personally, I think an otter life would be rather enjoy-
able," continued Laura ; " salmon to eat all the year round,
and the satisfaction of being able to fetch the trout in their
own homes without having to wait for hours till they condescend to rise to the fly you've been dangling before them ;
and an elegant svelte figure——"

"Think of the otter hounds," interposed Amanda ; " how
dreadful to be hunted and harried and finally worried to
death ! "

"Rather fun with half the neighbourhood looking on, and
anyhow not worse than this Saturday-to-Tuesday business of
dying by inches ; and then I should go on into something else.
If I had been a moderately good otter I suppose I should get
back into human shape of some sort ; probably something
rather primitive—a little brown, unclothed Nubian boy, I
should think."

"I wish you would be serious," sighed Amanda ; " you
really ought to be if you're only going to live till Tuesday."

As a matter of fact Laura died on Monday.

"So dreadfully upsetting," Amanda complained to her
uncle-in-law, Sir Lulworth Quayne. " I've asked quite a lot

of people down for golf and fishing, and the rhododendrons are just looking their best."

"Laura always was inconsiderate," said Sir Lulworth; "she was born during Goodwood week, with an Ambassador staying in the house who hated babies."

"She had the maddest kind of ideas," said Amanda; "do you know if there was any insanity in her family?"

"Insanity? No, I never heard of any. Her father lives in West Kensington, but I believe he's sane on all other subjects."

"She had an idea that she was going to be reincarnated as an otter," said Amanda.

"One meets with those ideas of reincarnation so frequently, even in the West," said Sir Lulworth, "that one can hardly set them down as being mad. And Laura was such an unaccountable person in this life that I should not like to lay down definite rules as to what she might be doing in an after state."

"You think she really might have passed into some animal form?" asked Amanda. She was one of those who shape their opinions rather readily from the standpoint of those around them.

Just then Egbert entered the breakfast-room, wearing an air of bereavement that Laura's demise would have been insufficient, in itself, to account for.

"Four of my speckled Sussex have been killed," he exclaimed; "the very four that were to go to the show on Friday. One of them was dragged away and eaten right in the middle of that new carnation bed that I've been to such trouble and expense over. My best flower bed and my best fowls singled out for destruction; it almost seems as if the brute that did the deed had special knowledge how to be as devastating as possible in a short space of time."

"Was it a fox, do you think?" asked Amanda.

"Sounds more like a polecat," said Sir Lulworth.

"No," said Egbert, "there were marks of webbed feet all over the place, and we followed the tracks down to the stream at the bottom of the garden; evidently an otter."

Amanda looked quickly and furtively across at Sir Lulworth.

Egbert was too agitated to eat any breakfast, and went out to superintend the strengthening of the poultry yard defences.

"I think she might at least have waited till the funeral was over," said Amanda in a scandalized voice.

"It's her own funeral, you know," said Sir Lulworth; "it's

a nice point in etiquette how far one ought to show respect to
one's own mortal remains."

Disregard for mortuary convention was carried to further
lengths next day ; during the absence of the family at the
funeral ceremony the remaining survivors of the speckled
Sussex were massacred. The marauder's line of retreat
seemed to have embraced most of the flower beds on the lawn,
but the strawberry beds in the lower garden had also suffered.

" I shall get the otter hounds to come here at the earliest
possible moment," said Egbert savagely.

" On no account ! You can't dream of such a thing ! " exclaimed Amanda. " I mean, it wouldn't do, so soon after a
funeral in the house."

" It's a case of necessity," said Egbert ; " once an otter takes
to that sort of thing it won't stop."

" Perhaps it will go elsewhere now that there are no more
fowls left," suggested Amanda.

" One would think you wanted to shield the beast," said
Egbert.

" There's been so little water in the stream lately," objected
Amanda ; " it seems hardly sporting to hunt an animal when
it has so little chance of taking refuge anywhere."

" Good gracious ! " fumed Egbert, " I'm not thinking about
sport. I want to have the animal killed as soon as possible."

Even Amanda's opposition weakened when, during church-
time on the following Sunday, the otter made its way into the
house, raided half a salmon from the larder and worried it
into scaly fragments on the Persian rug in Egbert's studio.

" We shall have it hiding under our beds and biting pieces
out of our feet before long," said Egbert, and from what
Amanda knew of this particular otter she felt that the possibility was not a remote one.

On the evening preceding the day fixed for the hunt
Amanda spent a solitary hour walking by the banks of the
stream, making what she imagined to be hound noises. It was
charitably supposed by those who overheard her performance,
that she was practising for farmyard imitations at the forthcoming village entertainment.

It was her friend and neighbour, Aurora Burret, who
brought her news of the day's sport.

" Pity you weren't out ; we had quite a good day. We
found at once, in the pool just below your garden."

" Did you—kill ? " asked Amanda.

" Rather. A fine she-otter. Your husband got rather

badly bitten in trying to ' tail it.' Poor beast, I felt quite sorry for it, it had such a human look in its eyes when it was killed. You'll call me silly, but do you know who the look reminded me of ? My dear woman, what is the matter ? "

When Amanda had recovered to a certain extent from her attack of nervous prostration Egbert took her to the Nile Valley to recuperate. Change of scene speedily brought about the desired recovery of health and mental balance. The escapades of an adventurous otter in search of a variation of diet were viewed in their proper light. Amanda's normally placid temperament reasserted itself. Even a hurricane of shouted curses, coming from her husband's dressing-room, in her husband's voice, but hardly in his usual vocabulary, failed to disturb her serenity as she made a leisurely toilet one evening in a Cairo hotel.

" What is the matter ? What has happened ? " she asked in amused curiosity.

" The little beast has thrown all my clean shirts into the bath ! Wait till I catch you, you little——"

" What little beast ? " asked Amanda, suppressing a desire to laugh ; Egbert's language was so hopelessly inadequate to express his outraged feelings.

" A little beast of a naked brown Nubian boy," spluttered Egbert.

And now Amanda is seriously ill.

GOAT-CRY, GIRL-CRY

O N the afternoon of the Friday set for my blood baptism, more than fifty friends and relatives gathered at the habitation of Maman Célie. There was no reason to suppose that we might be disturbed, but as an extra precaution a gay *danse Congo* was immediately organized to cover the real purpose of our congregation. Maman Célie had told me that I would get no sleep that night ; so despite the noise I napped until after sunset, when she awakened me and led me across the compound to the *houmfort*.

Through its outer door, which Emanuel stood guarding like a sentinel and unlocked for us, we entered a dim, windowless, cell-like anteroom in which were tethered the sacrificial beasts, a he-goat, two red cocks and two black, an enormous white turkey, and a pair of doves. Huddled there in a corner also was the girl Catherine, Maman Célie's youngest unmarried daughter ; why she was there I did not know, and it is needless to say that I wondered.

From this dim, somewhat sinister ante-chamber we passed through an open doorway into the long, rectangular mystery room, the temple proper, which was lighted with candles and primitive oil-lamps that flickered like torches. Its clay walls were elaborately painted with crude serpent symbols and an-thropomorphic figures. Papa Legba, guardian of the gates, god of the cross-roads, was represented as a venerable old black farmer with a pipe between his teeth ; Ogoun Badagris, the bloody warrior, appeared as an old-time Haitian revolu-tionary general in uniform with a sword ; Wangol, master of the land, drove a yoke of oxen ; Agoué, master of the seas, puffed out his cheeks to blow a wind and held in the hollow of his hand a tiny boat ; the serpent symbols stood for the great Damballa Oueddo, almighty Jove of the Voodoo pantheon, and his consort Ayida Oueddo.

At the near end of the room, close to the doorway through which we had entered, was the wide, low altar, spread over with a white lace tablecloth.   In its centre was a small wooden serpent, elevated horizontally on a little pole as Moses lifted up the serpent in the wilderness ; around this symbol, which was ancient before the Exodus, were grouped thunderstones, Christian crucifixes made in France or Germany, necklaces on which were strung snake vertebræ, others from which hung little medallions of the Virgin Mary.   On the corner of the

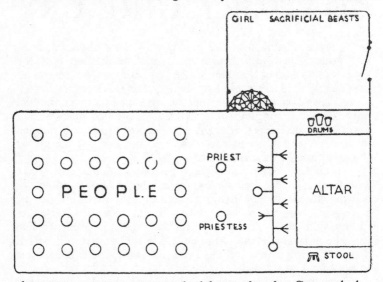

altar nearest me my *ouanga* had been placed.   Grouped also on the altar were earthen jugs containing wine, water, oil ; platters of vegetables and fruits, plates containing common bread, and plates containing elaborate sweet fancy cakes, bought days before down in the plain.   There were bottles of expensive French-labelled grenadine and orgeat, a bottle of rum, kola-champagne, etc.   There were also three cigars, not of the rough sort the peasants smoke, but fat and smooth in their red-gilt bands.   With a naïve but justifiable rationality, these worshippers, whose gods were vitally, utterly real, saw no anachronism in offering to their deities the best of everything that could be procured.   Maman Célie herself, accompanied by Papa Théodore, had gone by narrow trails across mountains and valleys, leading a donkey down to the modern city, shopping there for their celestial guests and returning with the donkey's panniers heavy laden.

On the altar also was a cone-like mound of cornmeal surmounted by an egg, and before the altar candles were burning, and wicks floating in coco-nut shells of oil. At the left were the three *Rada* drums, at the right was a low wooden stool placed for me.

At the other end of the mystery room, so that a ten-foot open space was left before the altar, were seated on the ground the eighteen or twenty people, all close relatives or trusted friends, who were to witness the ceremony. When I entered, they were swaying and singing :

> *Papa Legba, ouvrî barrière pour moins !*
> *Papa Legba, coté petits ou ?*
> *Papa Legba, ou oué yo !*
> *Papa Legba, ouvrî barrière pour li passer !*

> (Father Legba, open wide the gate !
> Father Legba, where are thy children ?
> Father Legba, we are here.
> Father Legba, open wide the gate that he may pass !)

The *papaloi*, a powerful clean-shaven black man of middle age with red turban and a bright-coloured embroidered stole over his shoulders, traced with cornmeal this cabalistic design on the bare earth before the altar :

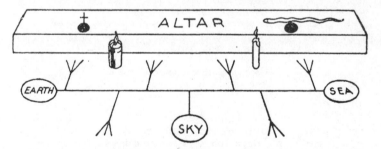

It measured perhaps twelve feet from end to end. The circles, it was afterward explained to me, represented, from left to right, earth, sky, and sea. (Adepts of the esoteric will read here earth, air, and water, or if of a certain school will read earth, air, fire, and water, accepting the central sky-circle as a symbol also of the sun.) All these matters indeed entered into it, but the simpler interpretation was dominant. The forked marks, all connecting, with lines interjoining them with the three circles, thence radiating toward the altar and reversely toward the worshippers, were symbols of tne invisible paths through which the gods and mysteries would move.

Into the earth circle the *papaloi* poured oil, flour, and wine, while the people chanted, " *Wangol maît' la terre* " (Wangol is master of the earth). Into the sky circle he poured rum and ashes, while they chanted, " *Damballa Oueddo, ou maît' la ciel* " (Damballa Oueddo, thou art master of the sky). Into the sea circle he poured water, while they sang, " *Papa Agoué, li maît' la mer* " (Father Agoué, he is master of the sea).

A number of solos interspersed this general chanting. It was impossible to retain them all in memory. I could not make pencil notes there ; not even Maman Célie was able afterward to repeat them all for me, and the next day some of the singers were gone. There was one song to Papa Agoué, however, which I partly remembered because it had seemed to me beautiful, and later I rode to find the singer and transcribe it. It was :

> *Agoué, woyó ! woyó !*
> *Maît' Agoué reter lans la mer;*
> *Li tirer canot.*

> *Bassin blé*
> *Reter toi zilet ;*
> *Nèg coqui' lans mer zorage ;*
> *Li tirer canot là.*

> *Agoué, woyó ! woyó !*

> (Hail to Father Agoué
> Who dwells in the sea !
> He is the Lord of ships.

> In a blue gulf
> There are three little islands.
> The negro's boat is storm-tossed,
> Father Agoué brings it safely in.

> Hail to Father Agoué !)

When this singing and pouring of libations were ended, the *papaloi* sealed the open doorway by tracing thus across its earthen sill :

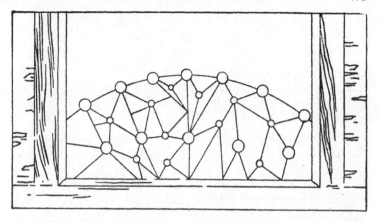

Evil or unwelcome forces which sought to enter would become entangled in the lines and go wandering from circle to circle like lost souls among the stars.

This done, he began the real service, for which all thus far had been but a preparation. He stood with arms raised before the altar and said solemnly, " *Lans nom tout Loi et tout Mystère* " (In the name of all the gods and all the Mysteries).

Maman Célie advanced at a sign from the *papaloi* and was invested by him, with the scarlet robe and headdress of ostrich feathers black and red, as *mamaloi* or priestess. This was accompanied by a shrill chant :

> *Ayida Oueddo, ou couleuvre moins !*
> *Qui lé ou filer ou cou z'éclai !*

> (Ayida Oueddo, my serpent goddess,
> When you come it is like the lightning flash !)

At the same time now I heard through the chanting a sharp long-drawn continuous hissing. It was Maman Célie, hissing like a snake, drawing and expelling the breath through her teeth.

I looked for Maman Célie's familiar sweet, gentle face, but beneath the black and scarlet plumes I saw now only what seemed a rigid mask. I felt that I was looking into the face of a strange, dreadful woman, or into the face of something which I had never seen before. As I watched, the cheeks of this black mask were deeply indrawn so that the face became skull-like, and then alternately puffed out as if the skull had been covered with flesh and come alive.

As the chanting died away, she whirled three times and flung herself prostrate before the altar with her lips pressed against the earth.

Emanuel, without donning sacerdotal garb, but now acting as a sort of altar servant, brought in the two red cocks. Each was handled gently, almost reverently, by the *papaloi*, as he knelt holding it and with white flour traced on its back a cross. One of the small sweet cakes was crumbled, and each cock must peck at it from the *mamaloi's* hand. This was awaited patiently. At the moment when each bird consented to receive the consecrated food, the priestess seized it and rose wildly dancing, whirling with the cock held by its head and feet in her upstretched hands, its wings violently fluttering. Round and round she whirled while the drums throbbed in a quick, tangled, yet steady rhythm. With a sudden twist the cock's head was torn off and as she whirled the blood flew out as if from a sprinkling-pot. The other birds, the black cocks and the dove, were dealt with similarly. As she danced with the white living doves, it was beautiful, and it seemed to me natural also that they should presently die. Blood of the doves was saved in a china cup.

A thing which had a different, a horror-beauty like a mad Goya etching, occurred when the black priestess did her death dance with the huge white turkey. Though far from feeble, possessed of great vitality, she was a slender woman, slightly formed, whose nervous strength lay not in muscular weight. When the turkey's wings spread wide and began to flap frantically above her head as she whirled, the great bird seemed larger and more powerful than she ; it seemed that she would be dragged from her feet, hurled to the ground, or flown away with fabulously into the sky. And as she sought finally to tear off its head, sought to clutch its body between her knees, it attacked her savagely, beating her face and breasts, beating at her so that she was at moments enfolded by the great white wings, so that bird and woman seemed to mingle struggling in a monstrous, mythical embrace. But her fatal hands were still upon its throat, and in that swan-like simulacre of the deed which for the male is always like a little death, it died.

So savage had this scene been that it was almost like an anticlimax when the sacrificial goat was now led through the doorway to the altar, but new and stranger things, contrasting, were yet to happen before other blood was shed. He was a sturdy brown young goat, with big, blue, terrified, almost human eyes, eyes which seemed not only terrified but aware and wondering. At first he bleated and struggled, for the odour of death was in the air, but finally he stood quiet, though still wide-eyed, while red silken ribbons were twined in his little horns, his little hoofs anointed with wine and sweet-scented oils, and an old woman who had come from far over the mountain for this her one brief part in the long ceremony sat down before him and crooned to him alone a song which might have been a baby's lullaby.

When it was finished, the *papaloi* sat down before the little goat and addressed to it a discourse in earnest tones. He told the little goat that it would soon pass through the final gates before us all, instructed it in the mysteries, and pleaded with it concerning its conduct on the other side. But before it passed through the gate, he explained, certain magical changes, making its path easier, would occur on this side. Therefore it need have no fear. Upon its forehead he traced a cross and circle, first with flour and afterward with blood of the doves. Then he presented to it a green, leafy branch to eat.

This goat had by now become inevitably personal to me. I had conceived an affectionate interest in him while the old woman was singing. I recalled what had happened to the other creatures at the moment they touched food, and I had an impulse to cry out to him, " Don't do that, little goat ; Don't touch it ! " But it was a fleeting, purely sentimental impulse. Not for anything, no matter what would happen, could I have seriously wished to stop that ceremony. I believe in such ceremonies. I hope that they will never die out or be abolished. I believe that in some form or another they answer a deep need of the universal human soul. I, who in a sense believe in no religion, believe yet in them all, asking only that they be alive—as religions. Codes of rational ethics and human brotherly love are useful, but they do not touch this thing underneath. Let religion have its bloody sacrifices, yes, even human sacrifices, if thus our souls may be kept alive. Better a black *papaloi* in Haiti with blood-stained hands who believes in his living gods than a frock-coated minister reducing Christ to a solar myth and rationalizing the Immaculate Conception.

And so I did not cry out.

And the goat nibbled the green leaves.

But no knife flashed.

In the dim, bare anteroom with its windowless grey walls, the girl Catherine had remained all this time huddled in a corner, as if drugged or half asleep.

Emanuel had to clutch her tightly by the arm to prevent her from stumbling when they brought her to the altar. Maman Célie hugged her and moaned and shed tears as if they were saying good-bye for ever. The *papaloi* pulled them apart, and some one gave the girl a drink of rum from a bottle. She began to protest in a dull sort of angry, whining way when they forced her down on her knees before the lighted candles. The *papaloi* wound round her forehead red ribbons like those which had been fastened round the horns of the goat, and Maman Célie, no longer as a mourning mother but as an officiating priestess, with rigid face, aided in pouring the oil and wine on the girl's head, feet, hands, and breast.

All this time the girl had been like a fretful, sleepy, annoyed child, but gradually she became docile, sombre, staring with quiet eyes, and presently began a weird song of lamentation. I think she was extemporizing both the words and the melody. She sang :

> *Cochon marron saché chemin caille ;*
> *Moins mandé ça li gagnin.*
> *" Nans Léogane tout moon malade O ! "*

> *Béf marron saché chemin caille.*
> *Moins mandé ça li gagnin.*
> *" Nans gros morne tout moon malade O ! "*

> *Cabrit marron saché chemin caille.*
> *Moins mandé ça li gagnin.*
> *" Nans Guinea tout moon malade O ! "*

> *M'pas malade, m'a p'mourri !*

> (The wild pig came seeking me ;
> I said why have you come ?
> " Every one is sick in Léogane ! "

> The wild bull came seeking me ;
> I said why have you come ?
> " Every one is sick in the mountains ! "

> The wild goat came seeking me ;
> I said why have you come ?
> " Every one is sick in Africa ! "

> So I who am not sick must die !)

And as that black girl sang, and as the inner meaning of her song came to me, I seemed to hear the voice of Jephthah's daughter doomed to die by her own father as a sacrifice to Javeh, going up to bewail her virginity on Israel's lonely mountain. Her plight in actuality was rather that of Isaac bound by Abraham on Mount Moriah ; a horned beast would presently be substituted in her stead ; but the moment for that mystical substitution had not yet come, and as she sang she was a daughter doomed to die.

The ceremony of substitution, when it came, was pure effective magic of a potency which I have never seen equalled in dervish monastery or anywhere. The goat and the girl, side by side before the altar, had been startled, restive, nervous. The smell of blood was in the air, but there was more than that hovering ; it was the eternal, mysterious odour of death itself which both animals and human beings always sense, but not through the nostrils. Yet now the two who were about to die mysteriously merged, the girl symbolically and the beast with a knife in its throat, were docile and entranced, were like automatons. The *papaloi* monotonously chanting, endlessly repeating, " Damballa calls you, Damballa calls you," stood facing the altar with his arms outstretched above their two heads. The girl was now on her hands and knees in the attitude of a quadruped, directly facing the goat, so that their heads and eyes were on a level, less than ten inches apart, and thus they stared fixedly into each other's eyes, while the *papaloi's* hands weaved slowly, ceaselessly above their foreheads, the forehead of the girl and the forehead of the horned beast, each wound with red ribbons, each already marked with the blood of a white dove. By shifting slightly I could see the big, wide, pale-blue, staring eyes of the goat, and the big, black, staring eyes of the girl, and I could have almost sworn that the black eyes were gradually, mysteriously, becoming those of a dumb beast, while a human soul was beginning to peer out through the blue. But dismiss that, and still I tell you that pure magic was here at work, that something very real and fearful was occurring. For as the priest wove his ceaseless incantations, the girl began a low, piteous bleating in which there was nothing, absolutely nothing, human ; and soon a thing infinitely more unnatural occurred ; the goat was moaning and crying like a human child. I believe that through my Druse and Yezidee accounts I have earned a deserved reputation for being not too credulous in the face of marvels. But I was in the presence now of a thing that could not be denied. Old magic was here at work, and it worked appallingly. What difference does it make whether we call it supernatural or merely supernormal ? What difference does it make if we say that the girl was drugged—as I suspect she was—or that both were hypnotized ? Of course they were, if you like. And what then ? We live surrounded by mysteries and imagine that by inventing names we explain them.

Other signs and wonders became manifest. Into this little temple lost among the mountains came in answer to goat-cry girl-cry the Shaggy Immortal One of a thousand names whom the Greeks called Pan. The goat's lingam became erect and rigid, the points of the girl's breasts visibly hardened and were outlined sharply pressing against the coarse, thin, tight-drawn shift that was her only garment. Thus they faced each other motionless as two marble figures on the frieze of some ancient phallic temple. They were like inanimate twin lamps in which a sacred flame burned, steadily yet unconsuming.

While the *papaloi* still wove his spells, his hands moving ceaselessly like an old woman carding wool in a dream, the priestess held a twig green with tender leaves between the young girl and the animal. She held it on a level with their mouths, and neither saw it, for they were staring fixedly into each other's eyes as entranced mediums stare into crystal globes, and with their necks thrust forward so that their foreheads almost touched. Neither could therefore see the leafy branch, but as the old *mamaloi's* hand trembled, the leaves flicked lightly as if stirred by a little breeze against the hairy muzzle of the goat, against the chin and soft lips of the girl. And after moments of breathless watching, it was the girl's lips which pursed out and began to nibble at the leaves. Human beings, normally, when eating, open their mouths and take the food directly in between their teeth. Except for sipping liquids they do not use their lips. But the girl's lips now nibbling at the leaves were like those of a ruminating animal. Her hands, of course, were flat on the ground so that in a sense she perforce must have eaten without using them, somewhat in the manner of a quadruped ; but in a castle near the edge of the Nefud desert I once watched closely a woman eating whose hands were tied behind her back, and that woman, opening her mouth and baring her teeth, took the fragments of food directly between her teeth, as any normal human being would. But this girl now pursed her lips and used them nibbling as horned cattle do. It sounds a slight thing, perhaps, in the describing, but it was weird, unnatural, inhuman.

As she nibbled thus, the *papaloi* said in a hushed but wholly matter-of-fact whisper, like a man who had finished a hard, solemn task and was glad to rest, " *Ça y est* " (There it is).

The *papaloi* was now holding a machete, ground sharp and shining. Maman Célie, priestess, kneeling, held a *gamelle*, a wooden bowl. It was oblong. There was just space enough to thrust it narrowly between the mystically identified pair. Its rim touched the goat's hairy chest and the girl's body, both their heads thrust forward above it. Neither seemed conscious of anything that was occurring, nor did the goat flinch when the *papaloi* laid his hand upon its horns. Nor did the goat utter any sound as the knife was drawn quickly, deeply, across its throat. But at this instant, as the blood gushed like a fountain into the wooden bowl, the girl, with a shrill, piercing, then strangled bleat of agony, leaped, shuddered, and fell senseless before the altar.

At the moment the knife flashed across the goat's throat, the company had begun to chant, not high or loud but with a sort of deep, hushed fervour, across which the girl's inhuman bleating had shrilled sharp as another invisible blade. Now they continued chanting while the celebrants performed their various offices. They chanted :

> *Damballa Oueddo odan q'icit*
> *Mandé ça la ! Oué !*
> *Ayida Oueddo odan q'icit*
> *Mandé ça la ! Oué !*

(Damballa and Ayida, behold the deed we have done as you commanded.)

The body of the goat was thrown as a ritually useless and no longer sacred thing through the door into the ante-room. The body of the unconscious girl, spattered with blood, was lifted carefully into Emanuel's arms and carried away, followed by two old women versed in magic who would attend her recovery. If Maman Célie, her face still like a terrible, inspired mask, bestowed one fleeting glance on either body, I did not see it. She was revolving slowly before the altar with the bowl in her outstretched arms and now held it to the *papaloi*, who received it, drank, then placed it on the altar, and with a little china cup poured libations within each of the three cabalistic circles on the earth. They also sang an invocation to Ybo, another of the ancient gods.

There was a pause, a lull, in which I who had been for
hours too utterly absorbed to give myself a thought, recalled
that all this ceremonial was leading up to an event which
concerned me more deeply than any other present. The time
had now come. A very old black man, deeply wrinkled,
with a beard that was like Spanish moss turned snowy white,
who had been sitting silent all the while, took from a bag
at his feet a white cloth which he wound around his head,
and a white embroidered garment like a cassock which he
put over his shoulders. He invested himself without the aid
of other hands as a black pope or emperor might have done.
He was not of our mountain. He had come riding upon a
donkey from beyond the great Morne. Maman Célie had
summoned him and had paid the expenses from her own
purse. It was a thing for which she would never permit me
to repay her. As he arose and beckoned me to kneel at last
before the altar, there was absolute silence. He was Voodoo
of the Voodoo, but as he laid his hand upon my head it was
neither in creole that he spoke, nor French, nor even the
almost forgotten language of old Guinea. I heard as in a
dream, low, clear, and deep as the voices of old men rarely
are, " *In nomine Patris, et Filii, et Spiritus Sancti. Amen.*"

And when still kneeling there with my eyes closed I heard
as from a great distance and as an echo from years long past
his sure voice intoning that most marvellous and mysterious
of all Latin invocations, " Rosa Mystica . . . Tower of
David . . . Tower of Ivory . . . House of Gold . . . Gate
of Heaven," it seemed to me that I heard too the rolling of
mighty organs beneath vaulted domes. . . .

Oil, wine, and water were poured upon my head, marks
were traced upon my brow with white flour, and then I was
given to eat ritually from the cakes upon the altar, to drink
from the wine, rum, and syrups there. Parts of many cakes
were crumbled together in a little cup and were put into my
mouth with a spoon ; likewise were mingled a few drops
from each of the many bottles.

This, it seemed, had been a preliminary consecration rite
in sincere inclusion of the Christian divinities, saints, and
powers. Now the Voodoo chanting recommenced, and for
the first time my own name was mingled with the creole and
African words. They were beseeching Legba to open wide
the gates for me, Damballa and Ayida to receive me. A sort
of mad fervour was again taking possession of them all. The
old *hougan*, shouting now so that his voice could be heard

above the singing, demanded once more silence, and placing both hands heavily upon my head, pronounced a long mixed African and creole invocation, calling down to witness all the gods and goddesses of ancient Africa. Still commanding silence, he dipped his hand into the wooden bowl and traced on my forehead the bloody Voodoo cross.

Then he lifted the bowl, hesitated for a queer instant as if in courteous doubt—it was a strange, trivial thing to occur at such a moment—and then picked up a clean spoon. Maman Célie interfered angrily. So the bowl itself was held to my lips and three times I drank. The blood had a clean, warm, salty taste. In physical fact, I was drinking the blood of a recently slain goat, but by some mysterious transubstantiation not without its parallels in more than one religion other than Voodoo, I was drinking the blood of the girl Catherine who in the body of the goat had mystically died for me and for all miserable humanity from Léogane to Guinea.

One small thing yet remained to be done. I had been told that it would be done, and its meaning explained to me. I had been told also that for no white man alive or dead had it ever been done before. The *papaloi* took from the altar an egg which had surmounted a little pyramid of cornmeal, and holding it aloft in his cupped hands, pronounced incantation. As the blood had represented the mystery of death, sacrifice, and purification, likewise fertilization as it was poured upon the earth, the egg now represented rebirth, productivity, fertility, re-creation. Maman Célie, the priestess, took it from the hands of the *papaloi*, traced with it a new cross on my forehead, and dashed it to the earth. My knees were spattered. Then the priestess tore off her feathered head-dress, and Maman Célie, the old woman, sank down beside me, put her arms around me, and cried, " Legba, Papa Legba, open wide the gates for this my little one."

THE MAHATMA'S STORY

YOU remember the Grigley's Mahatma, that queer Bengali chap they brought back with them from Bombay? This is one of the tales he told them.

At one time he used to turn up for supper at the Grigleys' every Sunday, dressed in a very long black frock-coat, and a high waistcoat buttoned up to his chin like a clergyman's, and a great white turban wreathed round his head and flopping over one ear. He would arrange himself on Grigley's divan, with his face very meek and his backbone very stiff and his legs very sinuous and curly, like a cross between a blessed Buddha and a boa-constrictor sitting up on its coils. He told his stories in a little quiet, sing-song voice, smiling at the Grigleys all the time, as if they were very young and rather silly children. We would sit before him on the floor, staring at him, the Grigleys with solemn faces full of childlike wonder, and the rest of us rather critical and incredulous—enlightened Westerners, you know.

At first we thought he was pulling all our legs, trying to see what we Westerners would swallow. But no, it was the Grigleys' wonder and our criticism and incredulity that amused him. The things he told us were to him so obvious and of their kind so elementary that he couldn't conceive how any reasonable being could regard them with interest, much less with wonder or suspicion.

I remember at the end of one of his most incredible yarns —about a man, I think, who could be in two places at once— Mrs. Grigley looked up with her little intense face and said :

" Anything—*anything* can happen in the East. The *East is wonderful !* "

She was going on like that, undeterred by the Mahatma's

supple shrug, when George Higgins cut in. He would begin to believe, he said, when things like that began to happen in the West.

The Mahatma looked at him as if he had been a baby and smiled.

"When the East comes to the West they do happen," he said.

It seems that about nine years ago the East came to the West in the person of a certain Rama Dass. He was proclaimed as a Mahatma by the members of a small occult society which lived on the wonder of him for a year or two. Then suddenly and violently it died of Rama Dass. He had caused a sort of scandal that no society, however occult, can be mixed up with and survive. But if the Mahatma's story is as true as he swore it was, Rama Dass must certainly have possessed powers.

To us the remarkable thing about him was, not his powers —the Mahatma had inured us to powers—but the light the whole queer story threw on certain mysterious events involving people whom we all knew. One of them indeed is so well known that I wouldn't give his name if it wasn't that he was under suspicion at the time, and the Mahatma's story clears him.

I mean Augustin Reeve.

You remember he disappeared? Well, we knew things had happened, very queer things, but none of us had ever understood how or why they happened, or how much queerer the real explanation was (if it *is* the real one). Who would have imagined that Augustin Reeve could ever have been mixed up with Rama Dass? But that, of course, was Varley's doing; his contacts were frequently unclean. Not that he had anything to do with the scandal; that was a story none of us were concerned with; I only mention it as proving the Mahatma's point, that the powers of Rama Dass were by no means spiritual. To him they were just the lowest, cheapest sort of magic.

The person who matters is, of course, Augustin Reeve. That's where the mystery comes in. He had everything to lose and nothing in the world to gain, unless you count Delia. Oh, well, I suppose she counted; talking of scandal, she seems to have been at the bottom of his disappearance. The point is—if it was only Delia—he could have had her without disappearing.

Here are the facts as they appeared to us at the time.

Seven years ago Reeve, as I say, vanished. So did Varley's wife, Delia. Muriel Reeve, Reeve's wife, stayed on at the house in Chelsea, which, by the way, was her house. She had the money. When you called there you found Clement Varley in possession. Clement Varley, of all people in the world, who hadn't a decent coat to his back or an address he could own up to, nothing but his beautiful wife Delia, who kept him by sitting for Reeve and, it was said, by complacencies less innocent. Literally we didn't know where they went home at night. They used to receive us at a shabby little club they belonged to. And there he was, as I say, in possession. Oh—of everything : of Reeve's studio, of Muriel's car, of Reeve's servants (till they left), of Reeve's furniture, of Reeve's cellar—and of Muriel. He was quite off his head, suffering from delusions of greatness, imagining that he was a genius, that he had painted Reeve's pictures and that the whole place belonged to him and always had. He was wearing one of Reeve's suits.

And there was Muriel, behaving as if it was all true, humouring him in his madness—actually living with him. But for Muriel, we should simply have supposed that the Reeves had lent him the house while they went abroad somewhere. As it was, it looked like some infamous bargain between Reeve and Varley. That was the incredible thing —that Reeve could lend himself—that Muriel—the angelic Muriel—an inexplicable mystery.

But if you admit Rama Dass and his powers——

Reeve, mind you, had been gone about a year before we heard of him. Then somebody came on him in an opium den down in Limehouse. And it was after that that the stories began to get about. He had taken to drugging, to drink, to every vice you could think of. He did horrible things, things he had to hide for. It looked like it.

Then one day Delia turned up, very shabby, at Grigley's studio and gave him her address as a model. Somewhere in Limehouse. Grigley called there.

Reeve opened the door. He was frightfully shabby too, and very queer. He behaved as if he didn't know Grigley, had never met him, and didn't want to meet him. He was very gentle and very polite about it, but firm. He didn't know Grigley. And Grigley had to go away.

Of course, as bluff it was pitiable, and it seemed to confirm all those stories.

And the mystery of it—if it had been Clement Varley

you could have understood. He had the sort of corrupt beauty which would have lent itself. But Augustin Reeve, with *his* beauty, with his dignity and iron-grey serenity, you couldn't see him playing any part that wasn't noble. Augustin Reeve skulking in awful places to hide a vice, forgetting his old life and repudiating his old friends—it wasn't conceivable ; if you don't believe in Rama Dass.

The next thing was the show of Reeve's Limehouse Scenes (superb masterpieces) at Varley's villainous little club. They sold. Everything he did sold. And we began to hope that he might return to us. Not a bit of it. When he'd made enough money he went over to Paris with Delia and, as you know, he never came back again.

We heard that Varley and Muriel had run across him there. And when Varley was next seen in Chelsea he had Delia with him and Muriel was living again with Reeve in Paris.

Soon after that Varley went smash and disappeared. He couldn't make money and apparently he had spent most of Muriel's. Anyhow he disappeared.

As for Reeve, he must have made pots and pots before he died.

Those were the facts, as far as we knew them. And I say, if you exclude Rama Dass, they are inexplicable.

We only realized him by an accident. We were dining with the Grigleys and the Mahatma was there. We'd been talking about poor Atkinson's death, and Grigley said :

" He would have been a fine man in finer circumstances. The poor devil hadn't a chance."

The Mahatma asked us what we called a chance, and I said, " Well, a decent income and a decent wife. A wife he could have lived *with* and an income he could have lived *on*."

Then the Mahatma said there were no such things as chances. There was nothing but the Karma that each man makes for himself. Then he told his queer story. I shan't attempt to tell it in his words. He had formed his style chiefly on the Bible, and at times he was startling. This is the gist of it.

First of all he said he knew a man who was always saying that we said, that he hadn't a chance. And he asked us if we'd ever heard of Clement Varley ?

Of course we'd heard of him, long before things had begun to happen. Muriel Reeve had taken him up and they were more or less looking after him, and Delia Varley was even then notorious. So was Clement in his way. He had once had a studio and he'd spoiled more canvases than he could afford to pay for, painting the abominations he called portraits. We wondered how on earth the Reeves could put up with the beast, he was so morose and lazy and discontented. I admit he hadn't much to be contented about. But the Reeves were extraordinarily good to him. He wasn't bad at copying and he might have made a decent living that way if he'd stuck to it. Unfortunately, he thought he was a great painter, or at least that he would have been if, as he said, he'd had a chance. He didn't consider himself in the least responsible for his laziness and his vile temper and viler pictures. He believed these things were so because he hadn't an income or a decent place to live in, and because he was tied to a woman he had left off caring about, who had left off caring about him.

The Mahatma was only interested in their case so far as Rama Dass came into it. Still he told us things. He says the two spent most of their time tormenting each other. Delia would fly out at Clement because he didn't earn enough and because he didn't paint like Augustin Reeve. She said he'd no business to marry her when he couldn't keep her, and she'd remind him a dozen times a day that she was keeping *him*.

And Clement would shriek and call on God to witness that nobody could paint within half a mile of a woman like Delia ; and that it was all very well for Reeve. *He* didn't depend on his painting for a living ; *he* hadn't got to prostitute his genius ; he'd had the sense to marry a woman with money, a woman of refinement, a woman who was a perfect angel. But he, Clement, hadn't had a chance.

And Delia would shriek back at him that it was all very well for Muriel. Augustin Reeve was a perfect angel too. But if Muriel had had to live cheek by jowl with a brute like Clement, she wondered what sort of angel she'd have been then. And she would keep on nagging at him to give up trying to paint and find work as a clerk in a bank or something.

Varley's case was complicated by his hideous jealousy of Reeve. And, of course, he fell in love with Muriel.

Those two women were as different as they could well be. Muriel was sombre and intense, black-haired and white, the blonde whiteness of honey. Delia's hair was like a heavy gold helmet clapped on to her head, and her skin was exquisite ; cyclamen-white and pink. Her mouth and eyes glistened as though water ran over them. Her mouth was very red, redder than fair women's mouths generally are, and it had sulky corners. She was beautiful ; but she had the temper of a she-devil. And Muriel really was a heavenly angel. You can't blame Varley for falling in love with her. And you can't blame Delia for falling in love with Reeve. Lots of women were in love with him. But that he should have become infatuated with Delia and Muriel with Varley, that's the uncanny thing ; he wasn't that sort of man and she wasn't that sort of woman ; besides, they hadn't been married a year. This is where the Mahatma's tale comes in.

He said that one evening Varley and his wife brought Rama Dass to Reeve's studio. It would, of course, be Varley that brought him. He'd picked him up in some nasty East End den. And Rama Dass had begun talking, he supposed, about his powers. And then Varley had started grousing as usual, saying he hadn't had a chance, and that if he'd only had what he called Reeve's luck he'd have done something tremendous, and that it was all very well for Reeve, and so on. If only they could change places——

Delia—it must have been Delia—looked at Rama Dass. And Rama Dass made queer Eastern faces at them—you can see him—and said, " Why not ? " He could make them change places in five minutes if they liked. Only they must give him five minutes. And Reeve—it must have been Reeve— said he'd like to see Rama Dass try.

That wasn't a challenge that Rama Dass was likely to let pass. And you can hear the women joining in : " Oh, do try, Mr. Rama Dass, *do* try." You see, Reeve and Muriel didn't believe that anything would happen. It was just their idea of a joke.

And Mr. Rama Dass tried. I've no doubt that was what he'd been brought there for. Varley and Delia were in deadly earnest.

He must have tried for all he was worth. He put them all four to sleep, laid out on Reeve's divan. Then he squatted down by each of them in turn and did some sort of incantation business, mumbling in their ears. And when they came up out of that horrible sleep, they *had* changed places.

That's to say, they had exchanged memories.

Varley found himself completely at home in Reeve's Chelsea house with Reeve's servants and Reeve's furniture and Reeve's bathroom—that must have been the strangest experience of all—and Reeve's wife. He remembered having painted Reeve's pictures. His possession of Reeve's memory entailed most of Reeve's habits, so that his reactions to his surroundings were correct.

You might have thought it would be a bit of a shock to Muriel, finding herself Varley's wife. But the ingenious Mr. Rama Dass had provided for that. His infamous magic poisoned her with Delia's first passion as well as Delia's memory.

In the same way he provided for Reeve's shock when he found himself with Delia. He had done the thing so well— whatever it was he did do—that Reeve drove off peaceably in a taxi-cab with Delia and Rama Dass, and settled down in Varley's rooms in Limehouse—those inconceivably squalid rooms—with every appearance of content. He couldn't remember anything else. His mind behaved exactly as if he had lived in Limehouse for years and years, and before that wherever it was that Varley had happened to be living, down to the room over the tobacconist's shop where he had been born.

Rama Dass had even provided for the case in which these transferred memories should clash. Say, Reeve with Varley's memory, or Muriel with Delia's, remembering each other's original circumstances. At all these points of contradiction Rama Dass had established complete forgetfulness, so that their memories dove-tailed very neatly and nothing destroyed the fourfold illusion. You'll say he couldn't have tampered with the memories of everybody concerned, all the people who had known Varley and Reeve ; but this very exchange of circumstances lessened the chances of contact. Reeve had quite thoroughly disappeared from his circle and Varley from his ; and if any of us did knock up against one of them, why, we were left with our unsolved mystery on our hands. And, naturally, Reeve's friends avoided Varley and Muriel.

I said it was Reeve who mattered most, but as Varley hadn't disappeared yet, whatever else he had done, Varley looms more considerably in this tale. We know, that's to say, the Mahatma seems to have known, more about Varley's behaviour than Reeve's. This because Rama Dass fairly haunted Varley, and the Mahatma was keeping an eye on Rama Dass.

What appears most evident is that Varley had got his chance. He had got *all* the things he had declared were necessary to him if he was to show what was in him. Money, leisure, the right surroundings, and the right woman.

But mark what happened.

When he found himself in Reeve's big studio, he remembered the very pattern of the carpet, he was familiar with the "Salamander" stove and the white-painted pipes of the radiators. Long years of comfort stretched behind him. He remembered with emotion the pictures on the walls and easels. As the Mahatma took care to point out, it was only their memories they had exchanged. They had kept their own bodies, and their own temperaments, and wills. After all, the powers of Rama Dass, though considerable, were not sufficient to cause them to exchange personalities completely. The self, as the Mahatma said, can neither be changed nor exchanged. It was beyond Rama Dass. And as Varley's temperament had always cried out for Persian carpets and voluptuous divans and anthracite stoves and woman's sympathy, it had nothing to say against these illusions of his memory. The presence of the pictures confirmed him in his belief that he was a great painter.

And yet, when at last he had every mortal thing he had ever wanted, when the very scene supported him and invited him to work, for months and months he seems to have simply given himself up to sloth ; driving in Muriel's car, sprawling on Reeve's divans, making love to Reeve's wife ; drinking much too much, and eating frightful quantities of rich food, till he grew so sleek and fat that his own mother wouldn't have known him. Not attempting to work. His bitterest complaint used to be that he couldn't paint because he hadn't enough money to pay for models ; but now, when Reeve's best models turned up on his doormat every morning, he sent them away ; and swore at them for coming, too. In nine months he hadn't done a stroke. He had always some excuse ; he would say the light was bad, or he wasn't in the mood, or Muriel took up all the time he might have worked in. If she put her nose into the studio he would swear at her for always hanging about ; if she left him to himself, he complained that he was neglected and that he might as well never have married her, for all the good she was to him. And again when the angel who, thanks to Rama Dass, must have believed in him as she had believed in Augustin Reeve, when the angel tried encouraging him to paint again he screamed out that he couldn't paint to order and she'd better mind her own business and not come meddling with his. He'd stamp about the studio and call upon God to tell him *how* he could do anything with a woman like that in the house.

And presently they began to hear about Augustin Reeve.

First of all, Delia turned up, imploring Varley to let her sit for him. Then Reeve's pictures began to be shown here and there. And when Muriel praised them—she seems to have retained her judgment—he flew into a rage and swore at her. He said it was all very well for Reeve. *He* had the spur of poverty. He must paint or starve. But as for himself the life he lived was enough to kill all inspiration. He might as well be a grocer. Muriel's money was a drag on him; the house was a drag on him; what did he want with money and houses? Muriel was a drag on him. No artist ought to marry. And then his old cry: He hadn't had a chance.

At last his jealousy of Reeve and that itch of his vanity which he mistook for inspiration, whipped him on to work again.

He must have expected to see, rising up magically under his hand, pictures like those of Augustin Reeve (his old manner) which fairly surrounded him in that house. You see, he thought, poor chap, he had painted them himself. But though he tried his level best to paint in Reeve's old manner he kept on turning out things that were too lamentably in his own. For he had kept his own body, and his body had kept to its own memory, which was much deeper than his mind's memory, and it made his hand move in its old way. It couldn't have moved in any other way. And when he compared what it was doing with what he believed it to have done in the days before he married Muriel, he laid the whole blame of his impotence on her.

" See," he would shout, " what I was before I knew you and what I am now."

And he wished to God he had never married her. He said she had destroyed his soul.

When she reminded him that she had at least given him the sympathy and understanding he had wanted, he said he wanted nothing of the kind and that her business wasn't to understand him—he could understand himself—but to give him pleasure. He was beginning to hanker after Delia's unspiritual beauty.

This didn't seem to us to fit in with Rama Dass and his love-magic. But the Mahatma explained it. Rama Dass had only worked his love-magic on Reeve and Muriel who wouldn't have changed without it. And Varley's will and temperament were stronger than his memory. Memory, the Mahatma said, is only a record; it has no power but that which will and temperament put into it. And Rama Dass hadn't interfered with Varley's temperament and will.

He, Varley, seems to have heard that Reeve and Delia were in Paris; and it occurred to him that here was another chance he hadn't had. So he went to Paris to see what it would do for him.

It did nothing but bring him into touch with Delia again. Meanwhile, whatever it was that Rama Dass had done to Reeve, the effect seems to have worn a bit thin under the friction of Delia's tongue. The Mahatma couldn't tell us much, he seems to have lost track of them after Paris; but I imagine things happened something like this : Reeve would be frightfully sorry for Muriel. The angel's sweetness would show up more beautifully than ever under Varley's treatment. And Muriel would be sorry for Augustin Reeve. I dare say the sight of him was more powerful even than Rama Dass's beastly love-magic. And she worshipped his genius. He seemed greater than ever in his poverty. He *was* greater. Because he kept his own temperament and his own will he had been cheerful and contented even down in Limehouse, the Mahatma says. He trailed behind him the dark tissue of Varley's memory, but when he came to join his own piece on he made it shining.

I ought to tell you that when he took over Varley's three rooms he found any amount of canvases stacked against the wall. When he turned them round and looked at them, though he remembered himself as painting them, he couldn't conceive how he had done anything so vile. And because he never kept his failures he destroyed every one of those abominations, so that of Varley's life nothing remained that could interfere with Reeve's knowledge of his greatness. After that he began painting in what we know as his second manner.

And because he had no money for models he painted Delia over and over again; he painted himself; he painted the people of the house where he lodged; he went out into the streets and along the river and painted what he saw there. Within his range there was nothing paintable he didn't paint. He was a greater artist in the Limehouse days than he was before or since. He stuck to his work all the tighter because it was his only means of getting away from Delia.

And now in Paris, from being sorry for each other, he and Muriel went on to falling in love.

I believe *they* kept pretty straight. But Varley and Delia had no sort of self-control and they fairly gave themselves up to it. And as Muriel's money enabled him to keep her in considerable comfort she was glad enough to live with him this time ; and between them they spent what was left of Muriel's money.　He seems to have sunk lower and lower, and to have painted more and more abominable pictures, till Clement Varley became another name for grotesque incompetence.　These horrors didn't bring him in a cent, so that he was as poor as ever when he and Delia came back to London.

And then, suddenly, he disappeared, and was never heard of again.

We all know what became of Augustin Reeve.　He died three years ago, more famous than he had ever been.　As the Mahatma put it, " each was in the end brought back to that estate he had in the beginning.　For a man's estate is what his self is."

And whenever he hears it said that somebody " hadn't a chance " he tells this tale of Rama Dass and Clement Varley.

He tells it in his quiet, sing-song voice, smiling almost maliciously at the absurdity of our wonder.

Well, I can understand that smile and that supple shrug of his.　What beats me is his attitude to Reeve and Muriel. Nothing more horrible could well have happened to two innocent people.　And he could have saved them.　He could have stopped Rama Dass's little game if he'd liked, or what's the good of being a Mahatma ?　But he took it all as a matter of course or as the fitting punishment of their Western levity.

What's more, that smile suggests that the same thing might happen any day to any of us, if we persist in our scepticism.　And the moral of it seems to be that if you can't despise Rama Dass like a Mahatma, you'd better fear him. In either case you'll keep out of his way.

DEEP IN THE FOREST

MEN will talk and tell you stories if you have the art of listening to them.

In this way you get ideas, but scarcely ever the complete thing such as was given me by Mynheer Andreas Capelmans one day in his tulip loft at Tergou as he sat, looking like a dried bulb, by the long, narrow table littered with cigar boxes holding specimens of mould and small paper bags containing bulbs sent to him from all over Holland for examination.

He is the greatest authority on fungoid diseases and on all diseases affecting the *Liliaceæ* to which natural order the great family of the tulips belong, and the microscope which he had been using stood before him discarded ; he had finished his morning's work, and finding in me a ready and willing listener, he was discoursing on the one subject that was the only subject appealing to his heart and understanding—Plants.

Men are born like that, sometimes ; men to whom women, war, wine, art, cookery, or the chase, are as nothing compared with the one subject appealing to their understandings and their hearts.

This great botanist, for Capelmans is great, I have seen putting salt in his coffee without discovering the error ; but for his housekeeper the condition of his wardrobe would long ere this have made him a guy to be followed by all the boys of Tergou. I doubt if he carries in memory anything of the Great War, and as for love, he had one love affair which I discovered fossilized in the mass of his conversation, but of whose existence as a fresh thing or a fossil I believe him to have been scarcely conscious.

Here is the fossil and with it the story in which it is stuck.

. . . .

There is no doubt to my mind, said the old gentleman, that the Prehistoric held vegetable existences equally strange as those animal existences which are disclosed to us by the bones of the mammoth and the sabre-toothed tiger.

Only the vegetables, being more easily destroyed, have not remained to tell us of themselves or their properties. Of course, many old vegetable forms are still held, to exhibit themselves to the eye of the geologist, but of their finer properties there is nothing in the way of indication.

Yet I believe, and my belief is based on what I came upon near the Javari River in the year 1884, that the old world, the world in which the vegetables reigned supreme, possessed plant forms not without intelligence and power of intelligent movement. Not movement away from the root, but movement of the limbs, tendrils, or leaves.

Indeed, the researches of Sir Chandra Bose on the nervous and arterial systems of plants have revealed a new physiology which denies plants neither movement nor thought, and forestalling him, even in those early days, the conception had come to me that there was a time when there was war between the later plants and the earlier animals.

That there were warrior plants, vaguely represented now by the Venus fly-trap that wars against insects, that the animals by superior intelligence and the power of perfectly free movement obtained the victory, destroyed these warrior plants, all but a few still existing, though maybe in degenerate forms, in the depths of the primæval jungle.

The idea seems fantastic, yet what is there more fantastic than life ; that microscope will show you a whole world of intelligence amidst things without central nervous systems or brains, and are not the peaceful tulips always at war with the spores that would otherwise destroy them ? There is only one true definition of Life—a battle-ground. Well, well, I am wandering from my ground, which is the Javari River.

It was in 1884 that I made my first acquaintance with the upper region of the Amazon, and those vast forests from whence the rubber comes down to Para.

I was travelling for Justus von Beerbohm, collecting plants and making notes of the rubber possibilities of the unexplored regions between the Javari and Marañon.

The Javari, you must know, divides Peru from Brazil, it is more than 2000 miles from where the Amazon disembogues, and of all forest lands and tracts, these vast woods are the least known, the least visited, and the least understood. For there are the rains that bring the floods during which millions of acres of forest are submerged, there is the malaria which fills the air with death, there are the diseases like beri-beri, and the snakes and water reptiles deadly as the diseases.

There is no food here for a white man worth considering owing to the floods that make all attempts at agriculture futile, so that everything has to be imported, yet there are natives, tribes of Indians, inhabiting those higher grounds that are free from water during the flood times.

And, strange to say, these Indians are not of the lowest order of mankind, they possess arts and crafts, are not unpleasing to look on, and show courage of a high order in their wars with the Peruvians.

Louis Teick was my chief man, the same who was killed in the frontier dispute on the Brazilian border in 1906.

He was a keen hunter and a tried explorer, but he was not a botanist, at least, at heart. Under him I had six Seringueros from the rubber plantations below Nazareth, men who had forsaken their work on the plantations, breaking their contracts for the higher pay which I held out as an inducement to them, for such is the ruling passion for money that men, even honourable men of the type that the Seringuero generally is, have all, with few or no exceptions, their price.

We followed the river with a motor launch of the type used in those times, and it was after a journey of six days, and on reaching the great bend above the junction with the Curucu River, that we tied up definitely, using this place as a starting-off point for our exploration of the forest and leaving two men in charge of the boat.

In five minutes from the time of leaving the river bank a veil had fallen behind us, cutting us off from civilization. Tree ferns, palms, vast matamata trees, liantasse festooned with orchids all joined to make this veil, with numberless other forms of vegetable life expressed in leaf, flower, trunk, or tendril.

I confess I was intoxicated. It was my first real experience of what the vegetable world was capable of doing, it was as though I had come into my own kingdom and on a fête day— here in the glasshouse atmosphere where the extraordinary called to the miraculous, and where growth was a passion, a flame burning with sublime fury.

In the botanical garden of Caracas there existed a con-

volvulus that lengthened itself, in the period of growth, at
the rate of an inch an hour, here, without doubt, were lianas
and air shoots capable of exhibiting a linear energy as great
or greater, and pausing to listen, one could hear the voices of
this green multitude and the sounds of the business of this
green commonwealth, the crash of some distant tree felled at
last by the axe of its own rottenness, the drop of a fruit or nut,
the many changing voices of the leaves, for here, as in the
forests of Europe, every tree has its voice, its song, its gesture.

Mynheer Capelmans paused for a moment as if con-
templating the objects of his passion. It seemed to me that
in this inspired moment he grew less like a withered bulb,
swollen yet upheld by the passion of his subject, he seemed,
indeed, as though he might suddenly burst into flower.

He went on :

Striking north, we maintained our way, crossing a small
tributary of the Javari and pausing continuously, as you may
imagine, for the purpose of the collecting box, tree measure-
ments, and so forth.

Teick, who had some knowledge of the coleoptera, asked
permission to add those he found to our collection, but I
would have none of that, these things did not interest me at
all ; as a consequence he sulked and, being a man of moody
disposition, things might have gone badly between us had
we not struck an Indian encampment on the evening of the
third day of our journey through the forest.

The chief of the Seringueros, who could speak the Indian
dialect, went forward to prepare the way for us with these
people, who received us well, giving us of their best and without
fuss or inquiry.

Once satisfied that we were not enemies, they treated us
as friends, and though we must have been of considerable
interest to them, they exhibited a wonderful restraint, asking
few questions and leaving us to our own affairs, which was a
matter of considerable moment to us as we determined to
make the Indian encampment our base of operations, not only
on account of its high position in the forest, but also because
of the fact that the Indian hunters could supply us with food
in exchange for the few small articles of barter which we had
brought with us.

But there was one young girl who did not observe the
reticence and restraint of the rest of the tribe. Her name was
Araya, she was well favoured and plump, with a skin like
polished bronze and a figure whose grace was not lessened

by the fact that her dress consisted only of a few feathers of the mutum bird.

This girl, for some reason hard to seek, was attracted by me and became my unsought-for but very willing slave, she would carry my collecting box in the short expeditions I made by myself into the near-about parts of the forest, and in the camp she was always close to me, insisting on preparing my food and helping in arranging my specimens, and all this without exciting any remark amongst her fellows.

It seemed that amongst these tribes the women have a freedom unknown to the more civilized peoples; they, in fact, do the courting and choose their mates, the man being purely a hunting animal, or at least without any special interest in the business of mating and home-making.

However that may be, Araya had attached herself to me as a wife might attach herself to a husband, and though, of course, there was no feeling of that sort between us, at least on my part, the fidelity was as great, and fortunately so for me, as I will show you in a moment.

II

ONE day Teick, who had been out with Jaos, the head of the Seringueros, prospecting to the west in search of a rubber belt that was supposed to lie in that direction, returned late in the evening and in a state of considerable excitement. He was a different man, in fact, from the man who had started out the day before.

He seemed light-headed and his manner exhibited a sub-dued exaltation which I would have put down to alcohol had I not known that the forest, whilst producing many things, did not produce that.

At supper he scarcely spoke, but afterwards, as we sat smoking by the light of the fire, he broke silence, and in a most surprising manner.

" To-day," said he, " I found something out there—the expedition has come to an end. Here is the spot I have been making for all my life, and I have found that which will make the whole world envy us."

Thinking he referred to some vast tract of rubber forest found by him or to some plant more wonderful than any yet discovered, I questioned him, and at once he fell into one of his fits of moodiness.

· " You cannot think but as a vegetable," said he, " plants,

plants, plants, they are for you as people." Then his mood suddenly changed as though a new thought had come to him. " Let it be so," he said, " it is a plant I have found, the only plant that can confer happiness, the tree that can confer good on those who eat wisely of its fruit and evil on those who do not. I have found this tree of good and evil."

I thought clearly this man is deranged, and fearing to excite him, I pretended to show interest in what he said, and when he asked me would I come with him on the morrow and see this thing for myself, I agreed, hoping that by the morning his mind would have cleared.

But next morning he was just the same and there, talking to him in the light of the day, I saw that whatever affected him it was not madness.

He had evidently found something that had put him into this strange pass, and I must confess that a burning curiosity seized me and that it was I who proposed that we should start at once so that I might see what he had seen.

Jaos was laid up with a bad foot so we started alone, taking provisions enough for two days ; the trail had been blazed by Jaos, still, I took my compass and two hours after sunrise we left the camp, striking our way through the forest.

Scarcely had we gone a hundred yards when I found that I was followed.   Araya had joined us.

" That girl," said Teick, then he laughed, saying, "Well, let her come, she may be of use, who knows ? "

I said nothing and we went forward, a party of three, Araya following, carrying her blow-gun which she always took when journeying in the forest, and a long sharp knife strapped to her waist by a belt.

There are parts of the forest where you cannot move without a knife to cut the lianas, but here and for most of our journey we required nothing in that way, as Jaos had cut our road the day before.

The blaze marks on the trees led us, the toucans and scarlet parrots calling after us and wood beasts rustling away into the thick growths at our approach.

It was getting on for dark when Teick said, " We are now close to the spot. Here is the *tambo* Jaos built, it will shelter us for the night and to-morrow when the sun is up you will see."

In truth, I did. We started at sunrise and, Teick leading, we left the leaf-thatched *tambo* and followed a line of great pachyuba palms that seemed planted with design, so straight

was their row in the midst of the multiform trees of the forest,
then I was aware of a brilliant light ahead and the trees,
tendrils, and leaves fell aside to show an open space where the
ground rose steeply. It was, in fact a hill in the midst of the
forest, a hill of rock on which nothing would grow and whose
side facing us was cut sheer as if with a knife.

Teick led me up to the cliff thus formed.

" This is it," said he.

III

THE rock face, which had the appearance of cement, was
strewn with yellow lumps. Teick took his knife and
attacking one of these lumps dug it out, it was the size of a
musket ball, heavy as lead and yellow. It was gold. Virgin
gold. I bit it and found it dented.

This must have been the bed of some great river in ancient
days, a river that brought the gold down in its wash, and its
mud turning to cement had clung to the nuggets, preserving
them. They were, in fact, like the plums in a pudding or the
almonds in nougat, with this difference, that they varied
vastly in size. Some were only the size of a pea, others big
as an orange. There was enough of the metal here to make
happy the hearts of a hundred men caring for gold, and, musing
on this and the strangeness of the ways of nature that had in
this inaccessible spot set up a cache of that which would satisfy
all men's material desires I forgot the trick that Teick had
played me, but only for a moment. Gold—though a great
thing, was not what my mind had been playing with in imagination, and suddenly, through my sense of wonderment, the
disappointment came on me. I turned to Teick.

" This, then, is all," said I, " this, then, is what you led
me to see ? "

" And what could be better ? " he asked. " It is true I
told you an untruth when I hinted what I did, but what would
you have ? If I had told you I had found gold, you never
would have come with me to see and touch this wonder—
plant-hunter that you are and with a turnip for heart and a
cabbage for head." He laughed in great good humour at this
joke, which I resented.

The gold did not appeal to me at all, and you must understand that in this I was not singular. We who follow science
must so be built that wealth for us is not except in Discovery.
And this is not a virtue, just a law of mind. Quite lately if I

had chosen to leave my researches I could have been wealthy twice over from the artificial manures, the secret of which I have put in the hands of manufacturers—for what ? The State pension which I enjoy suffices for all my needs.

I do not want gold, I have never wanted gold, and so now before this Golconda I stood, not only without desire but filled with disappointment.

The Vegetable Wonder I had been expecting had vanished from my dreams, leaving this !

I have a friend, Mynheer Beerbohm, who is greatly attached to the game of golf, which, as you no doubt know, is played with little balls. He tells me that he often loses these balls, and states as a strange fact that finding them again he often finds two together or close to one another. So it was to happen to-day, and the strange plant which I had hoped to find but had lost, was destined to lead me to a plant, the strangest plant in the world. But I did not know this, else perhaps I would not have quarrelled with Teick.

We in fact came to words, and so hotly that in one of his tempers he left me, striking back to the *tambo* and taking the trail for the camp.

Araya, who had taken her seat on a block of stone, and to whom the gold was as nothing, watched him go with a smile on her face. She seemed pleased that we should be alone together, and as for me I was indifferent, as each carried his own provisions and I had the compass.

Tired, and determined to let him have a good start, as I had no desire for his company, I sat down beside the girl.

" This, Araya," said I, " is what comes from uncontrollable temper joined to an unstable mind." She could not understand me, of course, but so we sometimes talk, when alone, to a dog or cat or just to ourselves. " Here is a man who has forgotten duty and, disturbed in his worship of the golden image, has, in fact, deserted his companion in the wilderness, than which in an explorer there can be no greater sin."

I was meditating on the truth of these words that had escaped from me in the fulness of my feelings when, of a sudden, I felt something around my waist; it was the girl's arm.

Mynheer Capelmans stopped and sighed and seemed looking back into the past, but without regret or any of those emotions that are supposed to accompany the backward glance.

Indeed, from the expression on his face he might have

been watching the antics of two of those infusoria revealed to him by his microscope.

Well, well, he said, going on after a moment. Man is weak and we are all men—especially when we are young men. Suffice it, that we did not hasten to catch up with Teick, in fact we delayed our departure from the *tambo* close to the gold outcrop till the following morning, and when we left I did not even take a specimen of the precious metal with me.

I had determined that Jaos should come back with Teick, not only to take exact bearings of the deposit, but to camouflage the cement cliff so that no stray traveller might come on what we had discovered. I was indifferent to the gold, but not insensible to its value—but even had I been a gold-hunter pure and simple, there was another matter to occupy my mind just now, Araya.

What was I to do about this girl who had suddenly attached herself to me ? Man has been called a hunting animal, it would be more true to name him the hunted animal, for that is indeed what he is where woman is concerned.

Woman, who has reduced defence and retreat into forms of attack and who is never more dangerous than when she is seemingly most docile.

He rubbed his shrivelled hands together in a way he had when making some triumphant point against an antagonist in argument.

" It is true," I said, " she seemed to have hunted you from what you say—all the same——"

I know, said the old gentleman, but we need not debate upon that matter, it is sufficient that I was in a position detrimental to her happiness and my interests. I would have to leave her to return to civilization and she was not of the order of being that is easily left and there was also the tribe.

However, all that was nothing, had I known, for things were to take a sudden and most dramatic turn.

We had deviated from the blazed trail by accident, it did not matter much as I had my compass and could soon find the track again, all the same the going was bad on account of the lianas.

We had reached a clearer space where the trees stood farther apart, when before me I saw a mound scattered with the bones of animals. It was a strange thing to come upon these in the twilight of the woods and with the long liana tendrils hanging down towards it like bell ropes, it looked like some natural altar where sacrifices had been made ; a grim tomb to which animals had come to die.

Then as we stood looking a most surprising thing happened, the body of a bush pig fell from the air above and lay amidst the bones on the mound like a dropped fruit.

A bush pig !

There was only one solution possible. Monkeys must have carried the body up into a tree and dropped it. I looked up. There was nothing to be seen but the tendrils hanging through the gloom and the breaks in the foliage far above. There were no monkeys.

These creatures were thick in the forests, always scampering overhead and springing from bough to bough, there were none here ; there were no scarlet parrots, no loud-voiced toucans, no tree life at all ; nothing but the gloom and the up-rushing tree boles and the down-hanging lianas ; complete silence as though the place were under the spell of some Merlin, some wizard of the trees whose presence had scared away the people of the trees, and this wild idea was not without its basis in truth, for the most fantastic thing in the world is Fact.

Araya was shivering and staring like a fascinated thing, and when I made a step forward towards the mound and for the purpose of examining the body of the pig, she tried to prevent me, talking in her language which I could not understand, even stepping in front of me to block my path. But I pushed her aside.

She followed me as I came like a fool to that terrible midden heap.

Mynheer Capelmans stopped for a moment and took his handkerchief from his pocket and worked it in his hands. He seemed drying the palms of his hands as though sweat had started out on them at the recollection that had risen in his mind.

As I stood, said he, a few feet from the body of the pig, I was suddenly and cruelly seized by the elbow. A down-sweeping and curling tendril had seized me and was lifting me from the ground. I felt in the grip of a monster—then I was free. Araya, springing upwards, had slashed the tendril across with her knife.

I fell on my knees and hands. When I rose she was gone. The tendril, or another, had seized her and winding on her like thread on a bobbin had shortened itself twenty feet or more. She was hanging twenty feet up, motionless, without a sound, evidently crushed or strangled.

This what I am telling you, is true.

The tendril was winding on her like thread on a bobbin

I was paralysed yet fully able to think. I said to myself, "Now, in a moment, I shall be seized again." I saw the down-hanging bell ropes in agitation like the hair of Medusa, yet none of them reached for me.

The horrible, filthy thing was evidently out of action for the moment. Its function had been performed.

Slowly and by degrees movement came back to me and I crept away.

Free of the place, I sat for an hour before I could continue my journey, but I was not blinded to the fact that I had discovered in its lair that which no other white man had ever seen, nor was I incapacitated for performing my duty. I had to return and examine this thing fully.

With the aid of my compass I struck out blazing my way till I met the old trail, and that night I was in camp.

IV

WITH the aid of Jaos I informed the Indians of what had occurred and of the fact that I had marked the way to the spot.

The effect of this news on them was profound.

Jaos said to me, "They are not troubling about the girl, they are rejoicing. They say you have found an O-te-Amoy and they are going to kill it; the last was found and killed ten years ago in a different part of the forest. It is a plant that makes war on men and animals."

Then I said to Jaos and Teick, who was standing by, "I have always felt the possibility that in the old days there were plants like this. It is true. This horrible thing did nothing with the body of the pig, just killed it and dropped it. I have seen, and you will see the last, maybe, of the warriors of a day when the vegetable world did battle against the animal with more weapons than thorns or poison berries."

The next morning we started, every man, woman, and child of the Indians were of the party, and beside the blow-guns which they always carried, the men had armed themselves with the long knives which they used for cutting their way through the forest growths. They also took with them certain leaves gathered from the tree that stood nearest the chief's *tambo*, and also a figure made of bark and dyed a vermilion colour which one of the women had constructed during the night.

Then I knew that I was witnessing something as interesting

as the O-te-Amoy itself—the ceremonious preparations for an attack on it and its destruction.

Something that had come down through the ages, a ritual unknown to all men but these few poor savages who were yet in ancestral touch with the world where once the O-te-Amoy, and perhaps worse fiends of the vegetable world, were frequently to be found.

When we reached the spot we could see from a distance that the body of Araya had been dropped and was lying beside the body of the pig.

Now, a massed attack would have meant that all the tendrils would have fought, reaching instinctively and through a sense that might have been likened to the sense of smell for the individual attackers.

A victim had to be given to quiet the plant and neutralize by satisfaction its fighting powers. This, which I had found out, the Indians well knew from tradition, and they selected an old man whom they had brought with them and who, so far from resisting, seemed pleased at the function he had to perform.

He walked forward to the mound—which I afterwards discovered to be made from the bones of animals piled there through many years and overgrown with plant life—and almost before he reached it, he was seized.

I had the opportunity of watching carefully the seizure. All the hanging tendrils of the O-te-Amoy fell into tremblings and twitchings at his approach and then the nearest one swung towards him as though it were blown by a gentle wind, and then, as though blown by a hurricane, it slashed round him and instantly began to curl on itself with him for a centre or bobbin, shortening itself with amazing rapidity, and lifting the victim as a consequence.

The approach of the tendril reminded me of the comparatively slow approach of a tea-stalk on the surface of a cup of tea to the cup wall, you know that, and the sudden snap with which gravitational attraction ends the business.

Instantly, now that the O-te-Amoy was defenceless because, so to speak, gorged, the attack on it began, men slashing away at the tendrils and others climbing to attack the great central body of the thing.

The attack was of all things I have seen the most interesting.

The fury of the attackers was of the sort that can only be inspired by a living and sentient enemy, yet the thing attacked, could one call it sentient ?

It was a trap, a killer, like the sundew ; like the sundew it exhibited intention, that is all one could say—only this, that, unlike the sundew, its misdeeds were not of the hunting and necessitous kind. It did not feed on its victims. No, it was truly a warrior whose only business was to kill and that constituted the profound interest of the thing, opening as it did a peep at the world's earliest history.

Men climbing cut away the body of the thing and flung it in masses to the ground.

I examined one of these masses, it was composed of vegetable substance convoluted and twisted, and as it lay there before me I thought it moved with a slight expansion and contraction ; I examined portions of the tendrils, they varied from an inch to three inches in diameter, possessed cup-shaped suckers and a tubular structure from which oozed sap mixed with air bubbles, but I could bring nothing away, all had to be burned in a great pyre and on top of the pyre was placed the Ju-Ju stained with vermilion.

Then having buried the girl and the old man we returned to camp—all but Teick, who started alone to get some more specimens of the gold—I may say that though he got up an expedition of his own in the following year he failed to find the gold deposit, a year had obliterated all the blaze marks and the track.

" Tell me," I said, " have you ever published an account of this plant ? "

" No," said Mynheer Capelmans, " I had intended to publish it at a meeting of the Royal Society of London which I attended the following year, but when I saw all those men, those square heads, those practical faces, those convex glasses, I remembered the fate of Du Chailu. My speech on plant life in the Javari district contained nothing of the O-te-Amoy. I wished to retain the respect of my confrères, for there is one golden rule in science, ' Above all things, nothing of the Marvellous.' "

" May I publish it ? "

" With pleasure, it won't hurt *you*."

I tried to get him to speak of the girl again, but the girl seemed to him of no more interest than the old man or the bush pig, and I came away with the feeling that one sometimes comes across animals more extraordinary than even the most extraordinary plants.

THE ISLE OF VOICES

KEOLA was married with Lehua, daughter of Kalamake, the wise man of Molokai, and he kept his dwelling with the father of his wife. There was no man more cunning than that prophet; he read the stars, he could divine by the bodies of the dead, and by the means of evil creatures: he could go alone into the highest parts of the mountain, into the region of the hobgoblins, and there he would lay snares to entrap the spirits of the ancient.

For this reason no man was more consulted in all the kingdom of Hawaii. Prudent people bought, and sold, and married, and laid out their lives by his counsels; and the King had him twice to Kona to seek the treasures of Kamehameha. Neither was any man more feared: of his enemies, some had dwindled in sickness by the virtue of his incantations, and some had been spirited away, the life and the clay both, so that folk looked in vain for so much as a bone of their bodies. It was rumoured that he had the art or the gift of the old heroes. Men had seen him at night upon the mountains, stepping from one cliff to the next; they had seen him walking in the high forest, and his head and shoulders were above the trees.

This Kalamake was a strange man to see. He was come of the best blood in Molokai and Maui, of a pure descent; and yet he was more white to look upon than any foreigner; his hair the colour of dry grass, and his eyes red and very blind, so that "Blind as Kalamake that can see across to-morrow," was a byword in the islands.

Of all these doings of his father-in-law, Keola knew a little by the common repute, a little more he suspected, and the rest he ignored. But there was one thing troubled him. Kalamake was a man that spared for nothing, whether to eat or to drink, or to wear ; and for all he paid in bright new dollars. " Bright as Kalamake's dollars," was another saying in the Eight Isles. Yet he neither sold, nor planted, nor took hire—only now and then from his sorceries—and there was no source conceivable for so much silver coin.

It chanced one day Keola's wife was gone upon a visit to Kaunakakai on the lee side of the island, and the men were forth at the sea-fishing. But Keola was an idle dog, and he lay in the veranda and watched the surf beat on the shore and the birds fly about the cliff. It was a chief thought with him always—the thought of the bright dollars. When he lay down to bed he would be wondering why they were so many, and when he woke at morn he would be wondering why they were all new ; and the thing was never absent from his mind. But this day of all days he made sure in his heart of some discovery. For it seems he had observed the place where Kalamake kept his treasure, which was a lock-fast desk against the parlour wall, under the print of Kamehameha the Fifth, and a photograph of Queen Victoria with her crown ; and it seems again that, no later than the night before, he found occasion to look in, and behold ! the bag lay there empty. And this was the day of the steamer ; he could see her smoke off Kalaupapa ; and she must soon arrive with a month's goods, tinned salmon and gin, and all manner of rare luxuries for Kalamake.

" Now if he can pay for his goods to-day," Keola thought, " I shall know for certain that the man is a warlock, and the dollars come out of the devil's pocket."

While he was so thinking, there was his father-in-law behind him, looking vexed.

" Is that the steamer ? " he asked.

" Yes," said Keola. " She has but to call at Pelekunu, and then she will be here."

" There is no help for it then," returned Kalamake, " and I must take you in my confidence, Keola, for the lack of any one better. Come here within the house."

So they stepped together into the parlour, which was a very fine room, papered and hung with prints, and furnished with a rocking-chair, and a table and a sofa in the European style. There was a shelf of books besides, and a family Bible in the midst of the table, and the lock-fast writing-desk against the wall ; so that any one could see it was the house of a man of substance.

Kalamake made Keola close the shutters of the windows,

while he himself locked all the doors and set open the lid of the desk. From this he brought forth a pair of necklaces hung with charms and shells, a bundle of dried herbs, and the dried leaves of trees, and a green branch of palm.

" What I am about," said he, " is a thing beyond wonder. The men of old were wise ; they wrought marvels, and this among the rest ; but that was at night, in the dark, under the fit stars and in the desert. The same will I do here in my own house, and under the plain eye of day." So saying, he put the Bible under the cushion of the sofa so that it was all covered, brought out from the same place a mat of a wonderfully fine texture, and heaped the herbs and leaves on sand in a tin pan. And then he and Keola put on the necklaces, and took their stand upon the opposite corners of the mat.

" The time comes," said the warlock, " be not afraid."

With that he set flame to the herbs, and began to mutter and wave the branch of palm. At first the light was dim because of the closed shutters ; but the herbs caught strongly afire, and the flames beat upon Keola, and the room glowed with the burning ; and next the smoke rose and made his head swim and his eyes darken, and the sound of Kalamake muttering ran in his ears. And suddenly, to the mat on which they were standing came a snatch or twitch, that seemed to be more swift than lightning. In the same wink the room was gone, and the house, the breath all beaten from Keola's body. Volumes of sun rolled upon his eyes and head, and he found himself transported to a beach of the sea, under a strong sun, with a great surf roaring : he and the warlock standing there on the same mat, speechless, gasping, and grasping at one another, and passing their hands before their eyes.

" What was this ? " cried Keola, who came to himself the first, because he was the younger. " The pang of it was like death."

" It matters not," panted Kalamake. " It is now done."

" And, in the name of God, where are we ? " cried Keola.

" That is not the question," replied the sorcerer. " Being here, we have matter in our hands, and that we must attend to. Go, while I recover my breath, into the borders of the wood, and bring me the leaves of such and such an herb, and such and such a tree, which you will find to grow there plentifully— three handfuls of each. And be speedy. We must be home again before the steamer comes ; it would seem strange if we had disappeared." And he sat on the sand and panted.

Keola went up the beach, which was of shining sand and

coral, strewn with singular shells ; and he thought in his heart :

" How do I not know this beach ? I will come here again and gather shells."

In front of him was a line of palms against the sky ; not like the palms of the Eight Islands, but tall and fresh and beautiful, and hanging out withered fans like gold among the green, and he thought in his heart :

" It is strange I should not have found this grove. I will come here again, when it is warm, to sleep." And he thought, " How warm it has grown suddenly ! " For it was winter in Hawaii, and the day had been chill. And he thought also, " Where are the grey mountains ? And where is the high cliff with the hanging forest and the wheeling birds ? " And the more he considered, the less he might conceive in what quarter of the islands he was fallen.

In the border of the grove, where it met the beach, the herb was growing, but the tree farther back. Now, as Keola went towards the tree, he was aware of a young woman who had nothing on her body but a belt of leaves.

" Well ! " thought Keola, " they are not very particular about their dress in this part of the country." And he paused, supposing she would observe him and escape ; and seeing that she still looked before her, stood and hummed aloud. Up she leaped at the sound. Her face was ashen ; she looked this way and that, and her mouth gaped with terror of her soul. But it was a strange thing that her eyes did not rest upon Keola.

" Good-day," said he. " You need not be so frightened, I will not eat you." And he had scarce opened his mouth before the young woman fled into the bush.

" These are strange manners," thought Keola, and, not thinking what he did, ran after her.

As she ran, the girl kept crying in some speech that was not practised in Hawaii, yet some of the words were the same, and he knew she kept calling and warning others. And presently he saw more people running—men, women, and children, one with another, all running and crying like people at a fire. And with that he began to grow afraid himself, and returned to Kalamake bringing the leaves. Him he told what he had seen.

" You must pay no heed," said Kalamake. " All this is like a dream and shadows. All will disappear and be forgotten."

" It seemed none saw me," said Keola.

" And none did," replied the sorcerer. " We walk here in the broad sun invisible by reason of these charms. Yet they hear us ; and therefore it is well to speak softly, as I do."

With that he made a circle round the mat with stones, and in the midst he set the leaves.

" It will be your part," said he, " to keep the leaves alight, and feed the fire slowly. While they blaze (which is but for a little moment) I must do my errand ; and before the ashes blacken, the same power that brought us carries us away. Be ready now with the match ; and do you call me in good time lest the flames burn out and I be left."

As soon as the leaves caught, the sorcerer leaped like a deer out of the circle, and began to race along the beach like a hound that has been bathing. As he ran, he kept stooping to snatch shells ; and it seemed to Keola that they glittered as he took them. The leaves blazed with a clear flame that consumed them swiftly ; and presently Keola had but a handful left, and the sorcerer was far off, running and stopping.

" Back ! " cried Keola. " Back ! The leaves are near done."

At that Kalamake turned, and if he had run before, now he flew. But fast as he ran, the leaves burned faster. The flame was ready to expire when, with a great leap, he bounded on the mat. The wind of his leaping blew it out ; and with that the beach was gone, and the sun and the sea ; and they stood once more in the dimness of the shuttered parlour and were once more shaken and blinded ; and on the mat betwixt them lay a pile of shining dollars. Keola ran to the shutters ; and there was the steamer tossing in the swell close in.

The same night Kalamake took his son-in-law apart, and gave him five dollars in his hand.

" Keola," said he, " if you are a wise man (which I am doubtful of) you will think you slept this afternoon on the veranda, and dreamed as you were sleeping. I am a man of few words, and I have for my helpers people of short memories.'

Never a word more said Kalamake, nor referred again to that affair. But it ran all the while in Keola's head—if he were lazy before, he would now do nothing.

" Why should I work," thought he, " when I have a father-in-law who makes dollars of sea-shells ? "

Presently his share was spent. He spent it all upon fine clothes. And then he was sorry :

" For," thought he, " I had done better to have bought a

With a great leap, he bounded on the mat.

concertina, with which I might have entertained myself all day long." And then he began to grow vexed with Kalamake.

"This man has the soul of a dog," thought he. "He can gather dollars when he pleases on the beach, and he leaves me to pine for a concertina! Let him beware: I am no child, I am as cunning as he, and hold his secret." With that he spoke to his wife Lehua, and complained of her father's manners.

"I would let my father be," said Lehua. "He is a dangerous man to cross."

"I care that for him!" cried Keola; and snapped his fingers. "I have him by the nose. I can make him do what I please." And he told Lehua the story.

But she shook her head.

"You may do what you like," said she; "but as sure as you thwart my father, you will be no more heard of. Think of this person, and that person; think of Hua, who was a noble of the House of Representatives, and went to Honolulu every year; and not a bone or a hair of him was found. Remember Kamau, and how he wasted to a thread, so that his wife lifted him with one hand. Keola, you are a baby in my father's hands; he will take you with his thumb and finger and eat you like a shrimp."

Now Keola was truly afraid of Kalamake, but he was vain too; and these words of his wife's incensed him.

"Very well," said he, "if that is what you think of me, I will show how much you are deceived." And he went straight to where his father-in-law was sitting in the parlour.

"Kalamake," said he, "I want a concertina."

"Do you, indeed?" said Kalamake.

"Yes," said he, "and I may as well tell you plainly, I mean to have it. A man who picks up dollars on the beach can certainly afford a concertina."

"I had no idea you had so much spirit," replied the sorcerer. "I thought you were a timid, useless lad, and I cannot describe how much pleased I am to find I was mistaken. Now I begin to think I may have found an assistant and successor in my difficult business. A concertina? You shall have the best in Honolulu. And to-night, as soon as it is dark, you and I will go and find the money."

"Shall we return to the beach?" asked Keola.

"No, no!" replied Kalamake; "you must begin to learn more of my secrets. Last time I taught you to pick shells; this time I shall teach you to catch fish. Are you strong enough to launch Pili's boat?"

" I think I am," returned Keola. " But why should we not take your own, which is afloat already ? "

" I have a reason which you will understand thoroughly before to-morrow," said Kalamake. " Pili's boat is the better suited for my purpose. So, if you please, let us meet there as soon as it is dark ; and in the meanwhile, let us keep our own counsel, for there is no cause to let the family into our business."

Honey is not more sweet than was the voice of Kalamake, and Keola could scarce contain his satisfaction.

" I might have had my concertina weeks ago," thought he, " and there is nothing needed in this world but a little courage."

Presently after he spied Lehua weeping, and was half in a mind to tell her all was well.

" But no," thinks he ; " I shall wait till I can show her the concertina ; we shall see what the chit will do then. Perhaps she will understand in the future that her husband is a man of some intelligence."

As soon as it was dark, father and son-in-law launched Pili's boat and set the sail. There was a great sea, and it blew strong from the leeward ; but the boat was swift and light and dry, and skimmed the waves. The wizard had a lantern, which he lit and held with his finger through the ring ; and the two sat in the stern and smoked cigars, of which Kalamake had always a provision, and spoke like friends of magic and the great sums of money which they could make by its exercise, and what they should buy first, and what second ; and Kalamake talked like a father.

Presently he looked all about, and above him at the stars, and back at the island, which was already three parts sunk under the sea, and he seemed to consider ripely his position.

" Look ! " says he, " there is Molokai already far behind us, and Maui like a cloud ; and by the bearing of these three stars I know I am come to where I desire. This part of the sea is called the Sea of the Dead. It is in this place extraordinarily deep, and the floor is all covered with the bones of men, and in the holes of this part gods and goblins keep their habitation. The flow of the sea is to the north, stronger than a shark can swim, and any man who shall here be thrown out of a ship it bears away like a wild horse into the uttermost ocean. Presently he is spent and goes down, and his bones are scattered with the rest, and the gods devour his spirit."

Fear came on Keola at the words, and he looked, and by

the light of the stars and the lantern, the warlock seemed to change.

" What ails you ? " cried Keola, quick and sharp.

" It is not I who am ailing," said the wizard ; " but there is one here very sick."

With that he changed his grasp upon the lantern, and, behold—as he drew his finger from the ring, the finger stuck and the ring was burst, and his hand was grown to be the bigness of three.

At that sight Keola screamed and covered his face.

But Kalamake held up the lantern. " Look rather at my face ! " said he—and his head was huge as a barrel ; and still he grew and grew as a cloud grows on a mountain, and Keola sat before him screaming, and the boat raced on the great seas.

" And now," said the wizard, " what do you think about that concertina ? and are you sure you would not rather have a flute ? No ! says he ; that is well, for I do not like my family to be changeable of purpose. But I begin to think I had better get out of this paltry boat, for my bulk swells to a very unusual degree, and if we are not the more careful, she will presently be swamped."

With that he threw his legs over the side. Even as he did so, the greatness of the man grew thirty-fold and forty-fold as swift as sight or thinking, so that he stood in the deep seas to the armpits, and his head and shoulders rose like a high isle, and the swell beat and burst upon his bosom, as it beats and breaks against a cliff. The boat ran still to the north, but he reached out his hand, and took the gunwale by the finger and thumb, and broke the side like a biscuit, and Keola was spilled into the sea. And the pieces of the boat the sorcerer crushed in the hollow of his hand and flung miles away into the night.

" Excuse me taking the lantern," said he ; " for I have a long wade before me, and the land is far, and the bottom of the sea uneven, and I feel the bones under my toes."

And he turned and went off, walking with great strides ; and as often as Keola sank in the trough he could see him no longer ; but as often as he was heaved upon the crest, there he was striding and dwindling, and he held the lamp high over his head, and the waves broke white about him as he went.

Since first the islands were fished out of the sea, there was never a man so terrified as this Keola. He swam indeed, but he swam as puppies swim when they are cast in to drown, and knew not wherefore. He could but think of the hugeness of the swelling of the warlock, of that face which was great as a mountain, of those shoulders that were broad as an isle, and of the seas that beat on them in vain. He thought, too, of the concertina, and shame took hold upon him ; and of the dead men's bones, and fear shook him.

Of a sudden he was aware of something dark against the stars that tossed, and a light below, and a brightness of the cloven sea ; and he heard speech of men. He cried out aloud and a voice answered ; and in a twinkling the bows of a ship hung above him on a wave like a thing balanced, and swooped down. He caught with his two hands in the chains of her, and the next moment was buried in the rushing seas and the next hauled on board by seamen.

They gave him gin and biscuit and dry clothes, and asked him how he came where they found him, and whether the light which they had seen was the lighthouse, Lae o Ka Laau. But Keola knew white men are like children and only believe their own stories ; so about himself he told them what he pleased, and as for the light (which was Kalamake's lantern) he vowed he had seen none.

This ship was a schooner bound for Honolulu, and then to trade in the low islands ; and by a very good chance for Keola she had lost a man off the bowsprit in a squall. It was no use talking. Keola durst not stay in the Eight Islands. Word goes on quickly, and all men are so fond to talk and carry news, that if he hid in the north end of Kauai or in the south end of Kaü, the wizard would have wind of it before a month, and he must perish. So he did what seemed the most prudent, and shipped sailor in the place of the man who had been drowned.

In some ways the ship was a good place. The food was extraordinarily rich and plenty, with biscuits and salt beef every day, and pea-soup and puddings made of flour and suet twice a week, so that Keola grew fat. The captain also was a good man, and the crew no worse than other whites. The trouble was the mate, who was the most difficult man to please Keola had ever met with, and beat and cursed him daily, both for what he did and what he did not. The blows that he dealt were very sure, for he was strong ; and the words he used were very unpalatable, for Keola was come of a good family and accustomed to respect. And what was the worst of all, whenever Keola found a chance to sleep, there was the mate awake and stirring him up with a rope's end. Keola saw it would never do ; and he made up his mind to run away.

They were about a month out from Honolulu when they made the land. It was a fine starry night, the sea was smooth as well as the sky fair ; it blew a steady trade ; and there was the island on their weather bow, a ribbon of palm trees lying flat along the sea. The captain and the mate looked at it with the night glass, and named the name of it, and talked of it, beside the wheel where Keola was steering. It seemed it was an isle where no traders came. By the captain's way, it was an isle besides where no man dwelt ; but the mate thought otherwise.

" I don't give a cent for the directory," said he. " I've been past here one night in the schooner *Eugenie* : it was just such a night as this ; they were fishing with torches, and the beach was thick with lights like a town."

" Well, well," says the captain, " it's steep-to, that's the great point ; and there ain't any outlying dangers by the chart, so we'll just hug the lee side of it. Keep her ramping full, don't I tell you ! " he cried to Keola, who was listening so hard that he forgot to steer.

And the mate cursed him, and swore that Kanaka was for no use in the world, and if he got started after him with a belaying-pin, it would be a cold day for Keola.

And so the captain and mate lay down on the house together, and Keola was left to himself.

" This island will do very well for me," he thought ; " if no traders deal there, the mate will never come. And as for Kalamake, it is not possible he can ever get as far as this."

With that he kept edging the schooner nearer in. He had to do this quietly, for it was the trouble with these white men, and above all with the mate, that you could never be sure of them ; they would all be sleeping sound, or else pretending, and if a sail shook, they would jump to their feet and fall on you with a rope's end. So Keola edged her up little by little, and kept all drawing. And presently the land was close on board, and the sound of the sea on the sides of it grew loud.

With that, the mate sat up suddenly upon the house.

" What are you doing ? " he roars. " You'll have the ship ashore ! "

And he made one bound for Keola, and Keola made another clean over the rail and plump into the starry sea. When he came up again, the schooner had payed off on her true course, and the mate stood by the wheel himself, and Keola heard him cursing. The sea was smooth under the lee of the island ; it was warm besides, and Keola had his sailor's knife, so he had no fear of sharks. A little way before him the trees stopped ; there was a break in the line of the land like the mouth of a harbour ; and the tide, which was then flowing, took him up and carried him through. One minute he was without, and the next within, had floated there in a wide shallow water, bright with ten thousand stars, and all about him was the ring of the land with its string of palm trees. And he was amazed, because this was a kind of island he had never heard of.

The time of Keola in that place was in two periods—the period when he was alone, and the period when he was there with the tribe. At first he sought everywhere and found no man ; only some houses standing in a hamlet, and the marks of fires. But the ashes of the fires were cold and the rains had washed them away ; and the winds had blown, and some of the huts were overthrown. It was here he took his dwelling ; and he made a fire drill, and a shell hook, and fished and cooked his fish, and climbed after green coco-nuts, the juice of which he drank, for in all the isle there was no water. The days were long to him, and the nights terrifying. He made a lamp of coco-shell, and drew the oil off the ripe nuts, and made a wick of fibre ; and when evening came he closed up his hut, and lit his lamp, and lay and trembled till morning. Many a time he thought in his heart he would have been better in the bottom of the sea, his bones rolling there with the others.

All this while he kept by the inside of the island, for the huts were on the shore of the lagoon, and it was there the palms grew best, and the lagoon itself abounded with good fish. And to the outer side he went once only, and he looked but once at the beach of the ocean, and came away shaking. For the look of it, with its bright sand, and strewn shells, and strong sun and surf, went sore against his inclination.

" It cannot be," he thought, " and yet it is very like. And how do I know ? These white men, although they pretend to know where they are sailing, must take their chance like other people. So that after all we may have sailed in a circle, and I may be quite near to Molokai, and this may be the very beach where my father-in-law gathers his dollars."

So after that he was prudent, and kept to the land side.

It was perhaps a month later, when the people of the place arrived—the fill of six great boats. They were a fine race of men, and spoke a tongue that sounded very different from the tongue of Hawaii, but so many of the words were the same that it was not difficult to understand. The men besides were very courteous, and the women very towardly ; and they made Keola welcome, and built him a house, and gave him a wife ; and what surprised him the most, he was never sent to work with the young men.

And now Keola had three periods. First he had a period of being very sad, and then he had a period when he was pretty merry. Last of all came the third, when he was the most terrified man in the four oceans.

The cause of the first period was the girl he had to wife. He was in doubt about the island, and he might have been in doubt about the speech, of which he had heard so little when he came there with the wizard on the mat. But about his wife there was no mistake conceivable, for she was the same girl that ran from him crying in the wood. So he had sailed all this way, and might as well have stayed in Molokai ; and had left home and wife and all his friends for no other cause but to escape his enemy, and the place he had come to was that wizard's hunting-ground, and the place where he walked invisible. It was at this period when ke kept the most close to the lagoon side, and, as far as he dared, abode in the cover of his hut.

The cause of the second period was talk he had heard from his wife and the chief islanders. Keola himself said little. He was never so sure of his new friends, for he judged they were too civil to be wholesome, and since he had grown better acquainted with his father-in-law the man had grown more cautious. So he told them nothing of himself, but only his name and descent, and that he came from the Eight Islands, and what fine islands they were ; and about the king's palace in Honolulu, and how he was a chief friend of the king and the missionaries. But he put many questions and learned much. The island where he was, was called the Isle of Voices ; it belonged to the tribe, but they made their home upon another, three hours' sail to the southward. There they lived and had their permanent houses, and it was a rich island, where were eggs and chickens and pigs, and ships came trading with rum and tobacco. It was there the schooner had gone after Keola deserted ; there, too, the mate had died, like the fool of a white man as he was. It seems, when the ship came, it was the beginning of the sickly season in that isle, when the fish of the lagoon are poisonous, and all who eat of them swell up and die. The mate was told of it ; he saw the boats preparing, because in that season the people leave that island and sail to the Isle of Voices ; but he was a fool of a white man, who would believe no stories but his own, and he caught one of these fish, cooked it, and ate it, and swelled up and died, which was good news to Keola. As for the Isle of Voices, it lay solitary the most part of the year, only now and then a boat's crew came for copra, and in the bad season, when the fish at the main isle were poisonous, the tribe dwelt there in a body. It had its name from a marvel, for it seemed the sea side of it was all beset with invisible devils ; day and night you heard them talking with one another in strange tongues ; day and night little fires blazed up and were extinguished on the beach ; and what was the cause of these doings no man might conceive. Keola asked them if it were the same in their own island where they stayed, and they told him no, not there ; nor yet in any other of some hundred isles that lay all about them in that sea ; but it was a thing peculiar to the Isle of Voices. They told him also that these fires and voices were ever on the sea side and in the seaward fringes of the wood, and a man might dwell by the lagoon two thousand years (if he could live so long) and never be any way troubled ; and even on the sea side the devils did no harm if let alone. Only once a chief had cast a spear at one of the voices, and the same night he fell out of a coco-nut palm and was killed.

Keola thought a good bit with himself. He saw he would be all right when the tribe returned to the main island, and right enough where he was, if he kept by the lagoon, yet he had a mind to make things righter if he could. So he told the high chief he had once been in an isle that was pestered the same way, and the folk had found a means to cure that trouble.

" There was a tree growing in the bush there," says he, " and it seems these devils came to get the leaves of it. So the people of the isle cut down the tree wherever it was found, and the devils came no more."

They asked what kind of a tree this was, and he showed them the tree of which Kalamake burned the leaves. They found it hard to believe, yet the idea tickled them. Night after night the old men debated it in their councils, but the high chief (though he was a brave man) was afraid of the matter, and reminded them daily of the chief who cast a spear against the voices and was killed, and the thought of that brought all to a stand again.

Though he could not yet bring about the destruction of the trees, Keola was well enough pleased, and began to look about him and take pleasure in his days ; and, among other things, he was the kinder to his wife, so that the girl began to love him greatly. One day he came to the hut, and she lay on the ground lamenting.

" Why ? " said Keola, " what is wrong with you now ? "

She declared it was nothing.

The same night she woke him. The lamp burned very low, but he saw by her face she was in sorrow.

" Keola," she said, " put your ear to my mouth that I may whisper, for no one must hear us. Two days before the boats begin to be got ready, go you to the sea side of the isle and lie in a thicket. We shall choose that place beforehand, you and I ; and hide food ; and every night I shall come near by there singing. So when a night comes and you do not hear me, you shall know we are clean gone out of the island, and you may come forth again in safety."

The soul of Keola died within him.

" What is this ? " he cried. " I cannot live among devils. I will not be left behind upon this isle. I am dying to leave it."

" You will never leave it alive, my poor Keola," said the girl ; " for to tell you the truth, my people are eaters of men ; but this they keep secret. And the reason they will kill you before we leave is because in our island ships come, and Donat-Kimaran comes and talks for the French, and there is a white trader there in a house with a veranda, and a catechist. Oh, that is a fine place indeed ! The trader has barrels filled with flour ; and a French warship once came in the lagoon and gave everybody wine and biscuit. Ah, my poor Keola, I wish I could take you there, for great is my love to you, and it is the finest place in the seas except Papeete."

So now Keola was the most terrified man in the four oceans. He had heard tell of eaters of men in the south islands, and the thing had always been a fear to him ; and here it was knocking at his door. He had heard, besides, by travellers, of their practices, and how when they are in a mind to eat a man, they cherish and fondle him like a mother with a favourite baby. And he saw this must be his own case ; and that was why he had been housed, and fed, and wived, and liberated from all work ; and why the old men and the chiefs discoursed with him like a person of weight. So he lay on his bed and railed upon his destiny ; and the flesh curdled on his bones.

The next day the people of the tribe were very civil, as their way was. They were elegant speakers, and they made beautiful poetry, and jested at meals, so that a missionary must have died laughing. It was little enough Keola cared for their fine ways ; all he saw was the white teeth shining in their mouths, and his gorge rose at the sight ; and when they were done eating, he went and lay in the bush like a dead man.

The next day it was the same, and then his wife followed him.

" Keola," she said, " if you do not eat, I tell you plainly you will be killed and cooked to-morrow. Some of the old chiefs are murmuring already. They think you are fallen sick and must lose flesh."

With that Keola got to his feet, and anger burned in him.

" It is little I care one way or the other," said he. " I am between the devil and the deep sea. Since die I must, let me die the quickest way ; and since I must be eaten at the best of it, let me rather be eaten by hobgoblins than by men. Farewell," said he, and he left her standing, and walked to the sea side of that island.

It was all bare in the strong sun ; there was no sign of man, only the beach was trodden, and all about him as he went, the voices talked and whispered, and the little fires sprang up and burned down. All tongues of the earth were spoken there : the French, the Dutch, the Russian, the Tamil, the Chinese. Whatever land knew sorcery, there were some of its people whispering in Keola's ear. That beach was thick as a cried fair, yet no man seen ; and as he walked he saw the shells vanish before him, and no man to pick them up. I think the devil would have been afraid to be alone in such a company ; but Keola was past fear and courted death. When the fires sprang up, he charged for them like a bull. Bodiless voices called to and fro ; unseen hands poured sand upon the flames ; and they were gone from the beach before he reached them.

" It is plain Kalamake is not here," he thought, " or I must have been killed long since."

With that he sat him down in the margin of the wood, for he was tired, and put his chin upon his hands. The business before his eyes continued ; the beach babbled with voices, and the fires sprang up and sank, and the shells vanished and were renewed again even while he looked.

" It was a by-day when I was here before," he thought, " for it was nothing to this."

And his head was dizzy with the thought of these millions and millions of dollars, and all these hundreds and hundreds of persons culling them upon the beach, and flying in the air higher and swifter than eagles.

" And to think how they have fooled me with their talk of mints," says he, " and that money was made there, when it is clear that all the new coin in all the world is gathered on these sands ! But I will know better the next time ! " said he.

And at last, he knew not very well how or when, sleep fell on Keola, and he forgot the island and all his sorrows.

Early the next day, before the sun was yet up, a bustle woke him. He awoke in fear, for he thought the tribe had caught him napping ; but it was no such matter. Only, on the beach in front of him, the bodiless voices called and shouted one upon another, and it seemed they all passed and swept beside him up the coast of the island.

" What is afoot now ? " thinks Keola. And it was plain to him it was something beyond ordinary, for the fires were not lighted nor the shells taken, but the bodiless voices kept posting up the beach, and hailing and dying away ; and others following, and by the sound of them these wizards should be angry.

" It is not me they are angry at," thought Keola, " for they pass me close."

As when hounds go by, or horses in a race, or city folk coursing to a fire, and all men join and follow after, so it was now with Keola ; and he knew not what he did, nor why he did it, but there, lo and behold ! he was running with the voices.

So he turned one point of the island, and this brought him in view of a second ; and there he remembered the wizard trees to have been growing by the score together in a wood. From this point there went up a hubbub of men crying not to be described ; and by the sound of them, those that he ran with shaped their course for the same quarter. A little nearer, and there began to mingle with the outcry the crash of many axes. And at this a thought came at last into his mind that the high chief had consented ; that the men of the tribe had set to cutting down these trees ; that word had gone about the isle from sorcerer to sorcerer, and these were all now assembling to defend their trees. Desire of strange things swept him on. He posted with the voices, crossed the beach, and came into the borders of the wood, and stood astonished. One tree had fallen, others were part hewed away. There was the tribe clustered. They were back to back, and bodies lay, and blood flowed among their feet. The hue of fear was on all their faces ; their voices went up to heaven shrill as a weasel's cry.

Have you seen a child when he is all alone and has a wooden

sword, and fights, leaping and hewing with the empty air ? Even so the man-eaters huddled back to back and heaved up their axes and laid on, and screamed as they laid on, and behold ! no man to contend with them ! Only here and there Keola saw an axe swinging over against them without hands ; and time and again a man of the tribe would fall before it, clove in twain or burst asunder, and his soul sped howling.

For a while Keola looked upon this prodigy like one that dreams, and then fear took him by the midst as sharp as death, that he should behold such doings. Even in that same flash the high chief of the clan espied him standing, and pointed and called out his name. Thereat the whole tribe saw him also, and their eyes flashed, and their teeth clashed.

" I am too long here," thought Keola, and ran farther out of the wood and down the beach, not caring whither.

" Keola ! " said a voice close by upon the empty sand.

" Lehua ! is that you ? " he cried, and gasped, and looked in vain for her ; but by the eyesight he was stark alone.

" I saw you pass before," the voice answered ; " but you would not hear me. Quick ! get the leaves and the herbs, and let us flee."

" You are there with the mat ? " he asked.

" Here, at your side," said she. And he felt her arms about him. " Quick ! the leaves and the herbs, before my father can get back ! "

So Keola ran for his life, and fetched the wizard fuel ; and Lehua guided him back, and set his feet upon the mat, and made the fire. All the time of its burning, the sound of the battle towered out of the wood ; the wizards and the man-eaters hard at fight ; the wizards, the viewless ones, roaring out aloud like bulls upon a mountain, and the men of the tribe replying shrill and savage out of the terror of their souls. And all the time of the burning, Keola stood there and listened, and shook, and watched how the unseen hands of Lehua poured the leaves. She poured them fast, and the flame burned high, and scorched Keola's hands ; and she speeded and blew the burning with her breath. The last leaf was eaten, the flame fell, and the shock followed, and there were Keola and Lehua in the room at home.

Now, when Keola could see his wife at last he was mighty pleased, and he was mighty pleased to be home again in Molokai and sit down beside a bowl of poi—for they made no poi on board ships, and there was none in the Isle of Voices— and he was out of the body with pleasure to be clean escaped out of the hands of the eaters of men. But there was another matter not so clear, and Lehua and Keola talked of it all night and were troubled. There was Kalamake left upon the isle. If, by the blessing of God, he could but stick there, all were well ; but should he escape and return to Molokai, it would be an ill day for his daughter and her husband. They spoke of his gift of swelling and whether he could wade that distance in the seas. But Keola knew by this time where that island was —and that is to say, in the Low or Dangerous Archipelago. So they fetched the atlas and looked upon the distance in the map, and by what they could make of it, it seemed a far way for an old gentleman to walk. Still, it would not do to make too sure of a warlock like Kalamake, and they determined at last to take counsel of a white missionary.

So the first one that came by Keola told him everything. And the missionary was very sharp on him for taking the second wife in the low island ; but for all the rest, he vowed he could make neither head nor tail of it.

"However," says he, " if you think this money of your father's ill-gotten, my advice to you would be to give some of it to the lepers and some to the missionary fund. And as for this extraordinary rigmarole, you cannot do better than keep it to yourselves."

But he warned the police at Honolulu that, by all he could make out, Kalamake and Keola had been coining false money, and it would not be amiss to watch them.

Keola and Lehua took his advice, and gave many dollars to the lepers and the fund. And no doubt the advice must have been good, for from that day to this, Kalamake has never more been heard of. But whether he was slain in the battle by the trees, or whether he is still kicking his heels upon the Isle of Voices, who shall say ?

THE MAN OF THE NIGHT

THE little instrument on the table by the inspector's desk went "tick-tock." Then it stopped, as though considering how it should word the message it had to give.

It was very still in the charge-room, so still that the big clock above the fireplace was audible. That, and the squeaky scratching of the inspector's quill pen as it moved slowly over the yellow paper on the desk before him, were the only sounds in the room.

Outside it was raining softly, the streets were deserted, and the lines of lamps stretching east and west emphasized the loneliness.

"Tick-tock," said the instrument on the table excitedly, "tick-tock, tick-tock!"

The inspector's high stool creaked as he sat up, listening.

There was a constable at the door, and he, too, heard the frantic call.

"What's that, Gill?" demanded the inspector testily.

The constable came into the charge-room with heavy footsteps.

"Ticketty-ticketty-tick-tock," babbled the instrument, and the constable wrote the message.

> All stations arrest and detain George Thomas, on ticket-of-leave, aged 35, height 5 ft. 8 in., complexion and hair dark, eyes brown, of gentlemanly appearance. Suspected of being concerned in warehouse robbery. Walthamstow and Canning Town especially note this and acknowledge. S.Y.

"In the middle of the night!" exclaimed the inspector

despairingly. " They call me up to tell me what I've told them hours and hours ago ! What a system ! "

He nodded his head hopelessly.

Outside, in the thin rain a man was coming along the street, his hands deep in his pockets, his coat collar turned up, his head on his breast. He shuffled along, his boots squelching in the rain, and slackened his pace as he came up to the station. The policeman he expected to find at the door was absent.

The man stood uneasily at the foot of the steps, set his teeth, and mounted slowly.

He halted again in the passage out of which the charge-room opened. . . .

" It's a rum thing about Thomas," said the inspector's voice. " I thought he was trying to go straight."

" It's his wife, sir," said the constable, and there was a long silence, broken by the loud ticking of the clock.

" Then why did his wife give him away ? " asked the inspector.

" Did she, sir ? "

There was surprise in the constable's voice, but the man in the passage did not hear that. He was leaning against the painted wall, his hand at his throat, his thin, unshaven face a dirty white, his lips trembling.

" She gave him away," said the inspector. He spoke with the deliberation of a man enjoying the sensation of dispensing exclusive news. " Know her ? "

" Slightly, sir," said the policeman's voice.

" Handsome woman—she might have done better than Thomas."

" I think she has," said th constable dryly, and they both laughed.

" That's the reason, is it ? Wants to put him under screw—well, I've heard of such cases . . ."

The man in the passage crept quietly out. He was shaking in every limb ; he almost fell at the last step, and clutched the railings that bordered the station house to keep himself erect.

The rain was pouring down but he did not notice it ; he was shocked, paralysed by his knowledge. He had broken into a warehouse because she had laughed to scorn his attempt at reformation. He had tried to go straight and she had made him go crooked . . . and then, when the job was done, with all the old cleverness so that he left no trace of his identity, she had gone straight away to the police and put him away. But that was nothing. Women had done such things before ; out of jealousy, in a fit of insane anger at some slight, real or fancied, but she had done it deliberately, wickedly, because she loved some man better than she loved him.

He was cool now, seeing things very clearly, and quickened his walk until he was stepping out briskly and lightly, holding his head erect as he had in the days when he was a junioı in a broker's office, and she had been a novel-reading miss of Balham.

The rain streamed down his face, the cuffs of his thin jacket clung to his wrists, his trousers were soaked from thigh to ankle. He knew a little shop off the Commercial Road where they sold cheese and butter and wood. He had purchased for a penny a morsel of bread and cheese ; he remembered that the woman behind the counter had cut the cheese with a heavy knife, newly whetted and pointed . . . he thought the matter out as he turned in the direction of the shop. Such knives are usually kept in a drawer, next to the till, with the bacon saw and the milk tester, and the little rubber stamp which is used for branding margarine in accordance with the law.

He knew the shop would be shuttered, the door locked, and he had no instrument to force an entrance. The " kit " was in the hands of the police—he had wondered how the splits [1] had found them—now he knew.

He gulped down a sob.

Still, there must be a way. The knife was necessary. He was still weak from his last term of penal servitude ; he could not kill her with his hands, she was so strong and beautiful—oh, so beautiful !

Thinking disconnectedly, he came to the shop.

It stood in a little side street. There was one street lamp giving light to the thoroughfare. There was no sound but the dismal drip of rain, nobody in sight. . . . There was a skylight above the shuttered door, it was the only way, he saw that at once. Sometimes these are left unfastened. He stood on tiptoe and felt gingerly along the lower part of the sash. His fingers encountered something that lay on the ledge, and his heart leapt. It was a key. . . . He had guessed this to be a " lock-up " shop ; he knew enough of the casual character of these little shopkeepers not to be surprised at the ease with which an entry might be effected.

[1] Detectives.

He slipped the key into the lock, turned it, and stepped in, closing the door behind him softly.

The air of the shop was hot and stuffy, full of the pungent scent of food-stuffs . . . cheese and ham, and the resinous odour of firewood. He had matches in his pocket, but they were sodden and would not strike. He fumbled round the shelves and came upon a packet. He struck a light, guarding the flame with his hand. The shop had been swept and made tidy for the night. The weights were neatly arranged on either side of the scales, there was a piece of muslin laid over the butter on the slate slab. On the counter, conspicuously displayed, was a note. It contained instructions, written in pencil in a large, uneducated hand, to " Fred." He was to light the fire, put the kettle on, take in the milk, and serve " Mrs. Smith."

Fred was the boy, the early comer in the morning, for whom the key had been placed. It was remarkable that he settled all these particulars to his own satisfaction, as, lighting match after match, he sought the heavy knife with the sharp point and the newly whetted edge. He even felt a certain exultation in the ease with which he had gained admission to the shop, and had an insane desire to whistle and talk.

He found the knife. It was under the counter, with a greatly scarred cutting-board and a steel. He wrapped it up carefully in a sheet of newspaper, then remembered he was hungry. He broke off a wedge of cheese. There was no bread, but an open tin of children's biscuits was handy.

With the food in his hand, with the knife in his pocket, he continued his exploration. Behind the shop was a little parlour. The door was unlocked, and he entered.

He struck match after match, hesitated a moment, then lit the gas. It was a tiny room, cheaply but neatly furnished. There were china ornaments on the mantel-shelf, a few cheap lithographs on the wall, and a loudly ticking clock. There was a clock at the police-station . . . he made a grimace as though he were in pain, felt with his hand for the knife and smiled.

He sat at a little table in the middle of the room and ate the food mechanically, staring hard at the wall ahead of him.

He had done everything for her ; his first crime . . . the few sovereigns extracted from the cash-box. . . . She had inspired that. Her little follies, her little extravagances, her vanities, these had been at the bottom of every step he had taken . . . staring blankly at the wall with wide-opened eyes, he traced his descent.

There was a text on the wall; he had been staring at it all this time, an ill-printed text, black-and-gold, green and vivid crimson, sadly out of register, and bearing in the bottom left-hand corner the conspicuous confession that it was " Printed in Saxony."

His thoughts were elaborate thoughts, but inclined to dive sideways into inconsequent bypaths; insensibly he had fixed his eyes on the text, in a subconscious attempt to concentrate his thoughts. One half of his brain pursued the deadly course of retrospection, the other half grappled half-heartedly with the words on the wall. He read only those that were in capital letters.

> Behold . . . Lamb . . . God . . . taketh Away . . .
> Sins . . . World.

Three years' penal servitude for burglary, two terms of six months for breaking and entering. . . . She had been at his elbow . . . years ago he was a member of a church, sang in the choir, and religious matters had some significance to him. It is strange how such things drop away from a grown man, how the sweet bloom of faith is rubbed off. . . . He married her at a registry office in Marylebone, and they went to Brighton for their honeymoon. She knew well enough that he could not afford to live as they were living; he had never dreamt that she guessed that he was robbing his employer; and when coolly, and with some amusement, she revealed her knowledge, he was shocked, stunned.

" Behold . . . Lamb . . ."

Might religion have helped him had he kept closer to its teachings? He wondered, slowly munching his biscuit and cheese, with his eyes on the garish text.

He found some milk and drank it, then he rose. Where he had sat were two little pools of water, one on the floor, the other on the table where his arm had rested. He turned out the light, walked softly through the shop, listened, and opened the door gently. There was nobody in sight, and he stepped out, closing and locking the door behind him. He put the key on the ledge where he had found it, and went quickly to the main road, the heavy knife, newly whetted and with a sharp point, bumping against his thigh with every step he took.

He had an uneasy feeling, and strove to analyse it down

to a first cause. He decided it was the text, and smiled; then of a sudden the smile froze on his lips. He was not alone.

A man had come from the night, swiftly, silently, and walked with him, step for step.

He stopped dead, his hand wandered down to the pocket where the knife lay.

" What do you want ? " he asked harshly.

The other made no reply; his face was in the shadow. What clothes he wore, what manner of man he was, Thomas could not say, only that, standing there, he was tall, gracefully proportioned, easy of movement.

There was a silence, then :

" Come," said the man from the night, and the burglar accompanied him without question.

They walked in silence, and Thomas observed that the stranger moved in the direction he himself would have taken.

" I shall give myself up—afterwards," he said, speaking feverishly fast. " I will end all this—end it—end it ! "

It did not strike him as curious that he should plunge into most secret depths, revealing the innermost thoughts of his heart; he accepted without wonder the conviction that the stranger knew all.

" She led me down from step to step, down, down ! " sobbed Thomas, as they walked side by side through the narrow streets that led to the river. " It used to worry me at first, but she strangled my conscience—she laughed at my fears. She is a devil, I tell you."

" Other men have said, ' The woman tempted me,' " said the stranger gently. " Yet a man has thought and will of his own."

Thomas shook his head doggedly.

" I had no will where she was," he said. " When I have killed her, I shall be a man again." He tapped his pocket, the knife was still there. " If we had children it might have made a difference, but she hated children."

" If you were free of her, you might be a man," said the stranger. His voice was sweet and deep and sad.

" Yes, yes ! " The other turned on him eagerly. " That is what I mean ; she is in my way. If I kill her, I can start all over again, can't I ? I could go back and face the world and say, ' I've killed the bad part of me, give me another chance '—look ! " He fumbled in his pocket and brought forth the knife. The rain came pitter-patter on the paper wrapping, and his hand trembled in his excited eagerness to display the strong blade, with the silvery edge and the needle-like point.

" I could not kill her with my hands," he said, breathing quickly, " so I got this knife.   I feel I've got to do it, though I hate killing things.   I once killed a rabbit when I was a kiddie, and it haunted me for days."

" If you were free of her, you might be a man," said the stranger again.

" Yes, yes," the thief nodded, " that is what I say—I could go back—back to the old people," his voice broke. " They don't know how far I've gone under."

They turned corner after corner, crossing main thorough-fares, diving through alleys where costers' barrows were stacked, chained wheel to wheel, into mean streets, and across patches of waste ground.

Once, through a little passage they came in sight of the river, saw three barges moored side by side, rising and falling slowly with the tide.   Out in mid-river a steamer lay, three lights glimmering feebly.

" I shall go into the house from the back," Thomas said. " There's nobody else in the house but an old woman—or there oughtn't to be.   My wife sleeps in the front room."

" If you were free of her, you might be a man," said the stranger.

" Yes, yes, yes ! "   The convict was impatient.   " I know that—when I am free . . ."   He laughed happily.

" She dragged you down to the deeps," said the man of the night softly.   " Every step you took for good, she clogged and hindered——"

" That's right—that is the truth," said the other.

" Yet you could never escape her ; you were loyal and faithful and kind."

" God knows that is true," said the man, and wept.

" For better or worse, for richer or poorer," he said, and it seemed to him that the stranger was saying these words at the same time.

At last they reached a street that was more dark, more wretched than any of its neighbours.

The man stopped at a narrow passage which led to the back of the houses.

" I am going in now," he said simply.   " You wait for me here, and when I come back we will start our new life all over again.   I shall kill her quickly."

The man of the night made no reply, and Thomas went

through the passage, turned at right angles along a narrower strip of path between wooden fences, and so came to a rickety back gate.

He opened it and went in. He was in a dirty little yard, littered with the jettison of a poor household. There was a tumbledown fowl run, and as he walked stealthily to the house, a cock crew loudly.

The back room was empty, as he knew. He pushed up the window. It squeaked a little. He waited for the cock to crow again and mask the sound. Then he swung himself up to the window-sill and entered the room.

The point of the knife cut through the thin clothing he wore and he felt a sharp pain in his leg.

He took the knife from his pocket and felt the edge— then he became conscious of the fact that there was somebody in the room.

He gripped the knife tightly and peered through the darkness.

" Who's there ? " he whispered.

" It is I," said a voice he knew, the voice of the man of the night.

" How—how did you get in ? "

He was amazed and bewildered.

" I came with you," said the voice. " Let us free ourselves of this woman—she dragged you down, she is the weed that chokes your soul."

" Yes—yes," Thomas whispered, and reaching out, found the stranger's hand.

Hand in hand they came to the woman's room.

A cheap night-light was burning on the mantel-shelf. She lay with one bare arm thrown out of bed, her breast rose and fell regularly. (He had seen something else that had risen and fallen monotonously ; what was it ? Yes, barges on the river.)

She was handsome in a coarse way, and as she slept she smiled. Some movement of the man disturbed her, for she stirred and murmured a name—it was not the name of him who stood above her, a knife in his shaking hand.

" Do you love her ? "

The stranger's voice was very soft.

The husband shook his head.

" Once—I thought so—now . . ."   He shook his head again.

" Do you hate her ? "

The thief was looking at the sleeping woman earnestly.

" I do not hate her," he said simply. " I served her because it was my duty. . . ."

" Come," said the stranger, and they left the room together.

Thomas unfastened the street door and they passed again into the dreary night.

" I do not love her : I do not hate her," he said again, half to himself. " I went to her because it was my duty— I worked and stole, and she betrayed me—so I thought I would kill her."

The knife was still in his hand.

In silence they traversed the way they came, until they reached a little passage that led to the river.

They turned into this.

At the end of the passage was a flight of stone steps, and they heard the " clug-clug " of water as it washed them.

Thomas raised his hand and sent the knife spinning into the river, and a voice hailed him from the foot of the steps.

" That you, Cole ? "

His heart almost stopped beating. The voice was hard and metallic. He blinked as though awakened from a sleep.

" Is that you, Cole—who is it ? "

Thomas saw a boat at the bottom of the steps. There were four men in it, and one was holding fast with a boat-hook to an iron ring let into the stone.

" Me," said the thief.

" It ain't Cole," said another voice disgustedly. " Cole won't turn up—he's drunk."

There was a whispering in the boat, then an authoritative voice demanded :

" Want a job, my lad ? "

Thomas went down two steps and bent forward.

" Yes—I want a job," he said.

A querulous voice said something about missing the tide.

" Can you cook ? "

" Yes—I can cook."

He had been employed in this capacity in prison.

" Jump in—sign you on to-morrow—we are going to Valparaiso—steam—how does that suit you ? "

Thomas was silent.

" I don't want to come back—here," he said.

" We'll get a better man for the return voyage—jump in."

He got into the boat awkwardly, and the officer at the stern gave an order.

The boat pushed off and then the thief remembered the man of the night.

He could see him plainer than ever he had seen him before. He was a radiant figure standing on the dark edge of the water, his hands outstretched in farewell.

Thomas saw the face, beautiful and benevolent : he saw the faint light that seemed to surround him.

" Behold . . ." muttered the man in the boat. " It's strange how that text . . . Good-bye, good-bye, sir. . . ."

" Who are you talking to, mate ? " asked the sailor who was rowing.

" The—the man who was with me," said Thomas.

" There was no man with you," said the sailor scornfully. " You were by yourself."

MAJOR WILBRAHAM

I AM quite aware that in giving you this story, just as I was told it, I shall incur the charge of downright and deliberate lying.

Especially I shall be told this by any one who knew Wilbraham personally. Wilbraham was not, of course, his real name, but I think that there are certain people who will recognize him from the description of him. I do not know that it matters very much if they do. Wilbraham himself would certainly not mind did he know. (Does he know?) It was the thing, above all, that he wanted those last hours before he died : that I should pass on my conviction of the truth of what he told me to others. What he did not know was that I was not convinced. How could I be? But when the whole comfort of his last hours hung on the simple fact that I was, of course I pretended to the best of my poor ability. I would have done more than that to make him happy.

Most men are conscious at some time in their lives of having felt for a member of their own sex an emotion that is something more than simple companionship. It is a queer feeling quite unlike any other in life, distinctly romantic, and the more so, perhaps, for having no sex feeling in it.

Wilbraham roused just that feeling in me I remember, with the utmost distinctness, at my first meeting with him. It was just after the Boer War, and old Johnny Beaminster gave a dinner-party to some men pals of his at the Phœnix.

There were about fifteen of us, and Wilbraham was the only man present I'd never seen before. He was only a captain then, and neither so red-faced nor so stout as he afterwards became. He was pretty bulky, though, even then, and, with his sandy hair cropped close, his staring blue eyes, his toothbrush moustache, and sharp, alert movements, looked the typical traditional British officer.

There was nothing at all to distinguish him from a thousand other officers of his kind, and yet, from the moment I saw him, I had some especial and personal feeling about him. He was not in type at all the man to whom at that time I should have felt drawn, but the fact remains that I wanted to know him more than any other man in the room, and, although I only exchanged a few words with him that night, I thought of him for quite a long time afterwards.

It did not follow from this, as it ought to have done, that we became great friends. That we never were, although it was myself whom he sent for, three days before his death, to tell me his queer little story. It was then, at the very last, that he confided to me that he, too, had felt something at our first meeting " different " from what one generally feels, that he had always wanted to turn our acquaintance into friendship and had been too shy. I also was shy—and so we missed one another, as I suppose, in this funny, constrained-traditional country of ours, thousands of people miss one another every day.

But although I did not see him very often, and was in no way intimate with him, I kept my ears open for any account of his doings. From one point of view—the club window outlook—he was a very usual figure, one of those stout, rubicund, jolly men, a good polo player, a good man in a house-party, genial-natured, and none-too-brilliantly brained, whom every one liked and no one thought about. All this he was on one side of the report, but, on the other, there were certain stories that were something more than ordinary.

Wilbraham was obviously a sentimentalist and an enthusiast; there was the extraordinary case shortly after I first met him of his championship of X., a man who had been caught card-sharping and received a year's imprisonment for it. On X. leaving prison, Wilbraham championed and defended him, put him up for months in his rooms in Duke Street, walked as often as possible in his company down Piccadilly, and took him over to Paris. It says a great deal for Wilbraham's accepted normality, and his general popularity, that this championship of X. did him no harm. Some men, it is true, did murmur something about " birds of a feather," and one or two kind friends warned Wilbraham in the way kind friends have, and to them he simply said :

" If a feller's a pal he's a pal."

. There followed a year or two later the much more celebrated business of Lady C. I need not go into all that now,
but here again Wilbraham constituted himself her defender,
although she robbed, cheated, and maligned him as she
robbed, cheated, and maligned every one who was good to
her. It was quite obvious that he was not in love with her ;
the obviousness of it was one of the things in him that annoyed
her. He simply felt, apparently, that she had been badly
treated—the very last thing she had been—gave her any
money he had, put his rooms at the disposal of herself and her
friends, and, as I have said, championed her everywhere.

This affair did very nearly finish him socially and in his
regiment. It was not so much that they minded his caring
for Lady C.—after all, any man can be fooled by any woman
—but it was Lady C.'s friends who made the whole thing so
impossible. Well, that affair luckily came to an end just in
time. Lady C. disappeared to Berlin, and was no more seen.

There were other cases, into which I need not go, when
Wilbraham was seen in strange company, always championing
somebody who was not worth the championing. He had no
" social tact," and for them, at any rate, no moral sense. In
himself he was the ordinary normal man about town ; no
prude, but straight as a man can be in his debts, his love
affairs, his friendships, and his sport. Then came the War.
He did brilliantly at Mons, was wounded twice, went out to
Gallipoli, had a touch of Palestine, and returned to France
again to share in Foch's final triumph.

No man can possibly have had more of the War than he
had, and it is my own belief that he had just a little too much
of it.

He had been always perhaps a little " queer," as we are
most of us " queer " somewhere, and the horrors of that
horrible war undoubtedly affected him. Finally he lost, just
a week before the Armistice, one of his best friends, Ross
McLean, a loss from which he certainly never recovered.

I have now, I think, brought together all the incidents
that can throw any kind of light upon the final scene.

In the middle of 1919 he retired from the Army, and it
was from this time to his death that I saw something of him.
He went back to his old rooms at Horton's in Duke Street,
and as I was living at that time in Marlborough Chambers in
Jermyn Street, we were within easy reach of one another.

The early part of 1920 was a " queer time." People had become, I imagine, pretty well accustomed to realizing that those two wonderful hours of Armistice Day had not ushered in the millennium, any more than those first marvellous moments of the Russian revolution produced it.

Every one has always hoped for the millennium, but the trouble since the days of Adam and Eve has always been that people have such different ideas as to what exactly that millennium shall be. The plain facts of the matter simply were that during 1919 and 1920 the world changed from a war of nations to a war of classes, that inevitable change that history has always shown follows on great wars.

As no one ever reads history, it was natural enough that there should be a great deal of disappointment, and a great deal of astonishment. Wilbraham, being a sentimentalist and an idealist, suffered more from this general disappointment than most people. He had had wonderful relations with the men under him throughout the war. He was never tired of recounting how marvellously they had behaved, what heroes they were, and that it was they who would pull the country together.

At the same time he had a naïve horror of Bolshevism and anything unconstitutional, and he watched the transformation of his " brave lads " into discontented and idle workmen with dismay and deep distress. He used sometimes to come round to my rooms and talk to me ; he had the bewildered air of a man walking in his sleep.

During these months I came to love the man. The attraction that I had felt for him from the very first deeply underlay all my relations to him, but as I saw more of him, I found many very positive reasons for my liking. He was the simplest, bravest, purest, most loyal, and most unselfish soul alive. He seemed to me to have no faults at all, unless it were a certain softness towards the wishes of those whom he loved. He could not bear to hurt anybody, but he never hesitated if some principle in which he believed was called in question.

He was the best human being I have ever known, or am ever likely to know.

Well, the crisis arrived with astonishing suddenness. About August 2nd or 3rd I went down to stay with some friends at the little fishing village of Rafiel in Glebeshire.

I saw him just before I left London, and he told me that he was going to stay in town for the first half of August ; that he liked London in August, even though his club would be closed and Horton's delivered over to the painters.

I heard nothing about him for a fortnight, and then I received a most extraordinary letter from Box Hamilton, a fellow-clubman of mine and of Wilbraham's. Had I heard, he said, that poor old Wilbraham had gone right off his " knocker " ? Nobody knew exactly what had happened, but suddenly one day at lunch-time Wilbraham had turned up at Grey's—the club to which our own club was a visitor during its cleaning—had harangued every one about religion in the most extraordinary way, had burst out from there and started shouting in Piccadilly ; had, after collecting a crowd, disappeared and not been seen until the next morning, when he had been found nearly killed after a hand-to-hand fight with the market men in Covent Garden.

It may be imagined how deeply this disturbed me, especially as I felt I was myself to blame. I had noticed that Wilbraham was ill when I had seen him in London, and I should either have persuaded him to come with me to Glebeshire, or stayed with him in London. I was just about to pack up and go to town when I received a letter from a doctor in a nursing-home in South Audley Street, saying that a certain Major Wilbraham was in the home, dying, and asking persistently for myself. I took a motor to Drymouth, and was in London by five o'clock.

I found the South Audley Street nursing-home, and was at once surrounded with the hush, the shaded rooms, the scents of medicine and flowers, and some undefinable cleanliness that belongs to those places.

I waited in a little room, the walls decorated with sporting prints, the green baize centre table laden with volumes of *Punch* and the *Tatler*. Wilbraham's doctor came in to see me, a dapper, smart little man, efficient and impersonal. He told me that Wilbraham had at most only twenty-four hours to live, that his brain was quite clear, and that he was suffering very little pain, that he had been brutally kicked in the stomach by some man in the Covent Garden crowd, and had there received the internal injuries from which he was now dying.

" His brain is quite clear," the doctor said. " Let him talk. It can do him no harm. Nothing can save him. His head is full of queer fancies ; he wants every one to listen to him. He's worrying because there's some message he wants to send—he wants to give it to you."

When I saw Wilbraham he was so little changed that I felt no shock. Indeed, the most striking change in him was the almost exultant happiness in his voice and eyes.

It is true that after talking to him a little I knew that he was dying. He had that strange peace and tranquillity of mind that one saw so often with dying men in the War.

I will try to give an exact account of Wilbraham's narrative ; nothing else is of importance in this little story but that narrative. I can make no comment. I have no wish to do so. I only want to pass it on as he begged me to do.

" If you don't believe me," he said, " give other people the chance of doing so. I know that I am dying. I want as many men and women to have a chance of judging this as is humanly possible. I swear to you that I am telling the truth, and the exact truth in every detail."

I began my account by saying that I was not convinced.

How could I be convinced ?

At the same time I have none of those explanations with which people are so generously forthcoming on these occasions. I can only say that I do not think Wilbraham was insane, nor drunk, nor asleep. Nor do I believe that some one played a practical joke.

Whether Wilbraham was insane between the hours when his visitor left him and his entrance into the nursing-home I must leave to my readers. I myself think he was not.

After all, everything depends upon the relative importance that we place upon ambitions, possessions, emotions—ideas.

Something then suddenly became of so desperate an importance to Wilbraham that nothing else at all mattered. He wanted every one else to see the importance of it as he did. That is all.

It had been a hot and oppressive day ; London had seemed torrid and uncomfortable. The mere fact that Oxford Street was " up " annoyed him. After a slight meal in his flat he went to the promenade concert at Queen's Hall. It was the second night of the season—Monday night—Wagner night.

He had heard no Wagner since August 1914, and was anxious to discover the effect that hearing it again would have upon him. The effect was disappointing.

The *Meistersinger* had always been a great opera for him. The third act music that the orchestra gave to him didn't touch him anywhere. He also discovered that six years' abstinence had not enraptured him any more deeply with the rushing fiddles in the *Tannhäuser* overture, nor with the spinning music in the *Flying Dutchman*. Then came suddenly the prelude to the third act of *Tristan*. That caught him, the peace and tranquillity that he needed lapped him round, he was fully satisfied and could have listened for another hour —a little strange, he told me, because the first half of the third act had always bored him with Tristan's eternal dying. He got up and went away, not caring to stay and listen to the efforts of an inadequate contralto to over-scream the orchestra in the last agonies of *Götterdämmerung*.

He walked home down Regent Street, the quiet melancholy of the pipe music accompanying him, pleasing him, and tranquillizing him. As he reached his flat ten o'clock struck from St. James's Church. He asked the porter whether any one had wanted him during his absence—whether any one was waiting for him now. (Some friend had told him that he might come up and use his spare room one night that week.) No, no one had been. There was no one there waiting.

Great was his surprise, therefore, when opening the door of his flat he found some one standing there, one hand resting on the table. His face turned towards the open door. Stronger, however, than Wilbraham's surprise was his immediate conviction that he knew his visitor well, and this was curious, because the face was undoubtedly strange to him.

" I beg your pardon," Wilbraham said, hesitating.

" I wanted to see you," the stranger said, smiling.

When Wilbraham was telling me this part of his story he seemed to be enveloped—" enveloped " is the word that best conveys my own experience of him—by some quite radiant happiness ; he smiled at me confidentially as though he were telling me something that I had experienced with him, and that must give me the same happiness that it gave him.

" Ought I to have expected—ought I to have known ? " he stammered.

" No, you couldn't have known," the stranger answered. " You're not late. I knew when you would come."

Wilbraham told me that during these moments he was surrendering himself to an emotion of intimacy and companionship that was the most wonderful thing that he had ever known. It was that intimacy and companionship, he told me, for which all his days he had been searching. It was the one thing that life never seemed to give ; even in the greatest love, the deepest friendship, there was that seed of loneliness hidden. He had never found it in man or woman.

Now it was so wonderful that the first thing that he said was :

" And now you're going to stay, aren't you ? You won't go away at once ? "

" Of course I'll stay," he answered, " if you want me."

His guest was dressed in some dark suit ; there was nothing about him in any way odd or unusual. His face thin and pale. His smile kindly.

His English was without accent. His voice was soft and very melodious.

But Wilbraham could notice nothing but his eyes ; they were the most beautiful, tender, gentle eyes that he had ever seen in any human being.

They sat down. Wilbraham's overwhelming fear was lest his guest should leave him. They began to talk, and Wilbraham took it at once as accepted that his friend knew all about him—everything.

He found himself eagerly plunging into details of scenes, episodes that he had long put behind him—put behind him for shame, perhaps, or for regret or for sorrow. He knew at once that there was nothing that he need veil nor hide—nothing. He had no sense that he must consider susceptibilities or avoid self-confession that was humiliating.

But he did find, as he talked on, a sense of shame from another side creep towards him and begin to enclose him. Shame at the smallness, meanness, emptiness of the things that he declared.

He had had always behind his mistakes and sins a sense that he was a rather unusual, interesting person ; if only his friends knew everything about him they would be surprised at the remarkable man that he really was. Now it was exactly the opposite sense that came over him. In the gold-rimmed mirror that was over his mantelpiece he saw himself diminishing, diminishing, diminishing. First himself, large, red-faced, smiling, rotund, lying back in his chair : then the face shrivelling, the limbs shortening, then the face small and peaked, the hands and legs little and mean, then the chair enormous about and around the little trembling animal cowering against the cushion.

He sprang up.

" No, no ! I can't tell you any more—and you've known it all so long. I am mean, small, nothing. I have not even great ambition—nothing."

His guest stood up and put his hand on his shoulder.

They talked, standing side by side, and he said some things
that belonged to Wilbraham alone, that he would not tell me.

Wilbraham asked him why he had come—and to him.

" I will come now to a few of my friends," he said.   " First
one and then another.   Many people have forgotten me behind
my words.   They have built up such a mountain over me with
the doctrines they have attributed to me, the things that they
say that I did.   I am not really," he said, laughing, his hand
on Wilbraham's shoulder, " so dull and gloomy and melancholy
as they have made me.   I loved life ; I loved men ; I loved
laughter and games and the open air.   All things that they have
forgotten.   So from now I shall come back to one or two.   I
am lonely when they see me so solemnly."

Another thing he said : " They are making life complicated
now.   To lead a good life, to be happy, to manage the world,
only the simplest things are needed—love, unselfishness,
tolerance."

" Can I go with you and be with you always ? " Wilbraham
asked.

" Do you really want that ? " he said.

" Yes," said Wilbraham, bowing his head.

" Then you shall come and never leave me again.   In three
days from now."

Then he kissed Wilbraham on the forehead and went
away.

I think that Wilbraham himself became conscious as he
told me this part of his story of the difference between the
seen and remembered figure and the foolish, inadequate
reported words.   Even now, as I repeat a little of what Wilbraham said, I feel the virtue and power slipping away.   But
on that day when I sat beside Wilbraham's bed the conviction
in his voice and eyes held me so that, although my reason kept
me back, my heart told me that he had been in contact with
some power that was a stronger force than anything that I
myself had ever known.

But I have determined to make no personal comment on
this story.   I am here simply as a narrator of fact.

Wilbraham told me that after his guest left him he sat there
for some time in a dream.   Then he sat up, startled as though
some voice, calling, had wakened him, with an impulse that was
like a fire suddenly blazing up and lighting the dark places of
his brain.   I imagine that all Wilbraham's impulses in the past,
chivalrous, idealistic, foolish, had been of that kind—sudden,
of an almost ferocious energy and determination, blind to all

consequences. He must go out at once and tell every one of what had happened to him.

I once read a story somewhere about some town that was expecting a great visitor. Everything was ready, the banners hanging, the music prepared, the crowds waiting in the street.

A man who had once been for some years at the court of the expected visitor, saw him enter the city, sombrely clad, on foot. Meanwhile, his chamberlain entered the town in full panoply with the trumpets blowing and many riders in attendance. The man who knew the real king ran to every one telling the truth, but they laughed at him and refused to listen. And the real king departed quietly as he had come.

It was, I suppose, an influence of this kind that drove Wilbraham now.

What followed might, I think, have been to some extent averted, had his appearance been different. London is a home of madmen, and casually permits any lunacy, so that public peace is not endangered. Had poor Wilbraham looked a fanatic, with pale face, long hair, ragged clothes, much would have been forgiven him, but for a staid, middle-aged gentleman, well-dressed, well-groomed, what could be supposed but insanity, and insanity of a very ludicrous kind?

He put on his coat and went out. From this moment his account was confused. His mind, as he spoke to me, kept returning to that visitor. What happened after his guest's departure was vague and uncertain to him, largely because it was unimportant. He does not know what time it was when he went out, but I gather it must have been about midnight. There were still people in Piccadilly.

Somewhere near the Berkeley Hotel he stopped a gentleman and a lady. He spoke, I am sure, so politely that the man he addressed must have supposed that he was asking for a match, or an address, or something of the kind. Wilbraham told me that very quietly he asked the gentleman whether he might speak to him for a moment, that he had something very important to say ; that he would not, as a rule, dream of interfering in any man's private affairs, but that the importance of his communication outweighed all ordinary conventions ; that he expected that the gentleman had hitherto, as had been his own case, felt much doubt about religious questions, but that now all doubt was once and for ever over, that——

I expect that at that fatal word " religious " the gentleman started as though he had been stung by a snake, felt that this mild-looking man was a dangerous lunatic and tried to move away. It was the lady with him, so far as I can discover, who cried out, " Oh, poor man, he's ill ! " and wanted at once to do something for him.

By this time a crowd was beginning to collect, and as the crowd closed around the central figures more people gathered upon the outskirts and, peering through, wondered what had happened, whether there was an accident, whether it was a " drunk," whether there had been a quarrel, and so on.

Wilbraham, I fancy, began to address them all, telling them his great news, begging them with a desperate urgency to believe him. Some laughed, some stared in wide-eyed wonder, the crowd was increasing, and then, of course, the inevitable policeman, with his " Move on, please," appeared.

How deeply I regret that Wilbraham was not there and then arrested. He would be alive and with us now if that had been done. But the policeman hesitated, I suppose, to arrest any one as obviously a gentleman as Wilbraham, a man, too, as he soon perceived, who was perfectly sober, even though he was not in his right mind.

Wilbraham was surprised at the policeman's interference. He said that the last thing that he wished to do was to create any disturbance, but that he could not bear to let all these people go to their beds without giving them a chance of realizing first that everything was now altered, that he had had the most wonderful news.

The crowd was dispersed, and Wilbraham found himself walking alone with the policeman beside the Green Park.

He must have been a very nice policeman, because, before Wilbraham's death, he called at the nursing-home and was very anxious to know how the poor gentleman was getting on.

He allowed Wilbraham to talk to him, and then did all he could to persuade him to walk home and go to bed. He offered to get him a taxi. Wilbraham thanked him, said he would do so himself, and bade him good-night, and the policeman, seeing that Wilbraham was perfectly composed and sober, left him.

After that the narrative is more confused. Wilbraham apparently walked down Knightsbridge and arrived at last somewhere near the Albert Hall. He must have spoken to a number of different people. One man, a politician apparently, was with him for a considerable time, but only because he was so anxious to emphasize his own views about the Government. Another was a journalist, who continued with him for a while because he scented a story for his newspaper. Some people

*He found himself a little before dawn in the company of a woman
of the town and a broken-down pugilist.*

may remember that there was a garbled paragraph about a " Religious Army Officer " in the *Daily Record.*

He stayed at a cabman's shelter for a time and drank a cup of coffee and told the little gathering there his news. They took it very calmly. They had met so many queer things in their time that nothing seemed odd to them.

His account becomes clearer again when he found himself a little before dawn in the park and in the company of a woman of the town and a drunken, broken-down pugilist. I saw both these persons afterwards and had some talk with them. The pugilist had only the vaguest sense of what had happened. Wilbraham was a " proper old bird," and had given him half a crown to get his breakfast with. They had all slept together under a tree, and he had made some rather voluble protests because the other two would talk so continuously and prevented his sleeping. It was a warm night and the sun had come up behind the tree " surprisin' quick."

The woman was another story. She was quiet and reserved, dressed in black with a neat little black hat with a green feather in it. She had yellow, fluffy hair, and bright, childish, blue eyes, and a simple, innocent expression. She spoke very softly and almost in a whisper. She spoke of her life quite calmly as though she had been a governess or a waitress at a tea-shop. So far as I could discover, she could see nothing odd in Wilbraham, nor in anything that he had said. She was the one person in all the world who had understood him completely and found nothing out of the way in his talk. Strange when you come to think of it. The one person in the world.

She had liked him at once, she said. " I could see that he was kind," she added earnestly, as though to her that was the most important thing in all the world. No, his talk had not seemed odd to her. She had believed every word that he had said. Why not ? You could not look at him and not believe what he said.

Of course, it was true. And why not ? She had known lots of things funnier than that in her sordid life. What was there against it ? She had always thought that there was something in what the parsons said, and now she knew it. It had been a great help to her, what the gentleman had told her. Yes, and he had gone to sleep with his head in her lap—and she had stayed awake all night thinking—and he had woken up just in time to see the sunrise. Some sunrise that was, too !

That was a curious little fact, that all three of them, even the battered pugilist, should have been so deeply struck by that sunrise. Wilbraham on the last day of his life, when he hovered between consciousness and unconsciousness, kept recalling it as though it had been a vision.

" The sun—and the trees suddenly green and bright like glittering swords—and the sky pale like ivory. See, now the sun is rushing up, faster than ever, to take us with him—up, up, leaving the trees like green clouds beneath us—far, far beneath us——"

The woman said it was the finest sunrise she had ever seen ; and, at once, when she saw it, she began to think of a policeman. He'd be moving them on, naturally, and what would he say when he found her there with a gentleman of the highest class ? Say that she had been robbing him, of course. She wanted to move away, but he insisted on going with her, and they woke up the pugilist, and the three of them moved down the park.

He talked to her all the time about his plans. He was looking dishevelled now, and unshaven and dirty. She suggested that he should go back to his flat. No, he wished to waste no time. Who knew how long he had got ? It might be only a day or two. He would go to Covent Garden and talk to the men there.

She was confused as to what happened after that. When they got to the market, the carts were coming in and the men were very busy.

She saw the gentleman speak to one of them very earnestly, but he was very busy and pushed him aside. He spoke to another, who told him to clear out.

Then he jumped on to a box, and almost the last sight she had of him was his standing there in his soiled clothes, a streak of mud on his face, his arms outstretched and crying : " It's true ! It's true ! Stop just a moment ! You must hear me ! "

Some one pushed him off the box. The pugilist rushed in then, cursing them and saying that the man was a gentleman, and had given him half-a-crown, and then some hulking great fellow fought the pugilist and there was a regular mêlée. Wibraham was in the middle of them, was knocked down and trampled upon. No one meant to hurt him, I think. They all seemed very sorry afterwards.

He died two days after being brought into the nursing-home. He was very happy just before he died, pressed my hand, and asked me to look after the girl.

" Isn't it wonderful," were his last words to me, " that it should be true after all ? "

As to Truth, who knows ? Truth is a large order. This is true as far as Wilbraham goes, every word of it. Beyond that ? Well, it must be jolly to be so happy as Wilbraham was.

THE
INEXPERIENCED GHOST

THE scene amidst which Clayton told his story comes back very vividly to my mind. There he sat, for the greater part of the time, in the corner of the authentic settle by the spacious open fire, and Sanderson sat beside him smoking the Broseley clay that bore his name. There was Evans, and that marvel among actors, Wish, who is also a modest man. We had all come down to the Mermaid Club that Saturday morning, except Clayton, who had slept there overnight—which indeed gave him the opening of his story. We had golfed until golfing was invisible ; we had dined, and we were in that mood of tranquil kindliness when men will suffer a story. When Clayton began to tell one, we naturally supposed he was lying. It may be that indeed he was lying —of that the reader will speedily be able to judge as well as I. He began, it is true, with an air of matter-of-fact anecdote, but that we thought was only the incurable artifice of the man.

" I say ! " he remarked, after a long consideration of the upward rain of sparks from the log that Sanderson had thumped, " you know I was alone here last night ? "

" Except for the domestics," said Wish.

" Who sleep in the other wing," said Clayton. " Yes. Well——" he pulled at his cigar for some little time as though he still hesitated about his confidence. Then he said, quite quietly, " I caught a ghost ! "

" Caught a ghost, did you ? " said Sanderson. " Where is it ? "

And Evans, who admires Clayton immensely and has been four weeks in America, shouted, " *Caught* a ghost, did you, Clayton ? I'm glad of it ! Tell us all about it right now."

Clayton said he would in a minute, and asked him to shut the door.

He looked apologetically at me. " There's no eaves-dropping, of course, but we don't want to upset our very excellent service with any rumours of ghosts in the place. There's too much shadow and oak panelling to trifle with that. And this, you know, wasn't a regular ghost. I don't think it will come again—ever.''

" You mean to say you didn't keep it ? " said Sanderson.

" I hadn't the heart to," said Clayton.

And Sanderson said he was surprised.

We laughed, and Clayton looked aggrieved. " I know," he said, with a flicker of a smile, " but the fact is it really *was* a ghost, and I'm as sure of it as I am that I am talking to you now. I'm not joking. I mean what I say."

Sanderson drew deeply at his pipe, with one reddish eye on Clayton, and then emitted a thin jet of smoke more eloquent than many words.

Clayton ignored the comment. " It is the strangest thing that has ever happened in my life. You know I never believed in ghosts or anything of the sort, before, ever ; and then, you know, I bag one in a corner ; and the whole business is in my hands."

He meditated still more profoundly and produced and began to pierce a second cigar with a curious little stabber he affected.

" You talked to it ? " asked Wish.

" For the space, probably, of an hour."

" Chatty ? " I said, joining the party of the sceptics.

" The poor devil was in trouble," said Clayton, bowed over his cigar-end and with the very faintest note of reproof.

" Sobbing ? " some one asked.

Clayton heaved a realistic sigh at the memory. " Good Lord ! " he said ; " yes." And then, " Poor fellow ! yes."

" Where did you strike it ? " asked Evans, in his best American accent.

" I never realized," said Clayton, ignoring him, " the poor sort of thing a ghost might be," and he hung us up again for a time, while he sought for matches in his pocket and lit and warmed to his cigar.

" I took an advantage," he reflected at last.

We were none of us in a hurry. " A character," he said, " remains just the same character for all that it's been dis-embodied. That's a thing we too often forget. People with a certain strength or fixity of purpose may have ghosts of a certain strength and fixity of purpose—most haunting ghosts, you know, must be as one-idea'd as monomaniacs and as obstinate as mules to come back again and again. This poor creature wasn't." He suddenly looked up rather queerly, and his eye went round the room. " I say it," he said, " in all kindliness, but that is the plain truth of the case. Even at the first glance he struck me as weak."

He punctuated with the help of his cigar.

" I came upon him, you know, in the long passage. His back was towards me and I saw him first. Right off I knew him for a ghost. He was transparent and whitish ; clean through his chest I could see the glimmer of the little window at the end. And not only his physique but his attitude struck me as being weak. He looked, you know, as though he didn't know in the slightest whatever he meant to do. One hand was on the panelling and the other fluttered to his mouth. Like—so ! "

" What sort of physique ? " said Sanderson.

" Lean. You know that sort of young man's neck that has two great flutings down the back, here and here—so ! And a little, meanish head with scrubby hair and rather bad ears. Shoulders bad, narrower than the hips ; turn-down collar, ready-made short jacket, trousers baggy and a little frayed at the heels. That's how he took me. I came very quietly up the staircase. I did not carry a light, you know—the candles are on the landing table and there is that lamp—and I was in my list slippers, and I saw him as I came up. I stopped dead at that—taking him in. I wasn't a bit afraid. I think that in most of these affairs one is never nearly so afraid or excited as one imagines one would be. I was surprised and interested. I thought, ' Good Lord ! Here's a ghost at last ! And I haven't believed for a moment in ghosts during the last five-and-twenty years.' "

" Um," said Wish.

" I suppose I wasn't on the landing a moment before he found out I was there. He turned on me sharply, and I saw the face of an immature young man, a weak nose, a scrubby little moustache, a feeble chin. So for an instant we stood— he looking over his shoulder at me—and regarded one another. Then he seemed to remember his high calling. He turned round, drew himself up, projected his face, raised his arms, spread his hands in approved ghost fashion—came towards me. As he did so his little jaw dropped, and he emitted a faint, drawn-out 'Boo.' No, it wasn't—not a bit dreadful. I'd dined. I'd had a bottle of champagne, and being all alone, perhaps two or three—perhaps even four or five—whiskies, so I was as solid as rocks and no more frightened than if I'd been assailed by a frog. 'Boo,' I said. 'Nonsense. You don't belong to *this* place. What are you doing here?'

"I could see him wince. 'Boo—oo,' he said.

"'Boo—be hanged! Are you a member?' I said; and just to show I didn't care a pin for him I stepped through a corner of him and made to light my candle. 'Are you a member?' I repeated, looking at him sideways.

"He moved a little so as to stand clear of me, and his bearing became crestfallen. 'No,' he said, in answer to the persistent interrogation of my eye; 'I'm not a member—I'm a ghost.'

"'Well, that doesn't give you the run of the Mermaid Club. Is there anyone you want to see, or anything of that sort?' And doing it as steadily as possible for fear that he should mistake the carelessness of whisky for the distraction of fear, I got my candle alight. I turned on him, holding it. 'What are you doing here?' I said.

"He had dropped his hands and stopped his booing, and there he stood, abashed and awkward, the ghost of a weak, silly, aimless young man. 'I'm haunting,' he said.

"'You haven't any business to,' I said, in a quiet voice.

"'I'm a ghost,' he said, as if in defence.

"'That may be, but you haven't any business to haunt here. This is a respectable private club; people often stop here with nursemaids and children, and, going about in the careless way you do, some poor little mite could easily come upon you and be scared out of her wits. I suppose you didn't think of that?'

"'No sir,' he said, 'I didn't.'

"'You should have done. You haven't any claim on the place, have you? Weren't murdered here, or anything of that sort?'

"'None, sir; but I thought as it was old and oak-panelled——'

"'That's *no* excuse,' I regarded him firmly. 'Your coming here is a mistake,' I said, in a tone of friendly superiority. I feigned to see if I had my matches, and then looked up at him frankly. 'If I were you I wouldn't wait for cock-crow—I'd vanish right away.'

"He looked embarrassed. 'The fact *is*, sir——' he began.

"' I'd vanish,' I said, driving it home.

"' The fact is, sir, that—somehow—I can't.'

"' You *can't*?'

"' No, sir. There's something I've forgotten. I've been hanging about here since midnight last night, hiding in the cupboards of the empty bedrooms and things like that. I'm flurried. I've never come haunting before, and it seems to put me out.'

"' Put you out?'

"' Yes, sir. I've tried to do it several times, and it doesn't come off. There's some little thing has slipped me, and I can't get back.'

"That, you know, rather bowled me over. He looked at me in such an abject way that for the life of me I couldn't keep up quite the high hectoring vein I had adopted. 'That's queer,' I said, and as I spoke I fancied I heard someone moving about down below. 'Come into my room and tell me more about it,' I said. I didn't, of course, understand this, and I tried to take him by the arm. But, of course, you might as well have tried to take hold of a puff of smoke! I had forgotten my number, I think; anyhow, I remember going into several bedrooms—it was lucky I was the only soul in that wing—until I saw my traps. 'Here we are,' I said, and sat down in the armchair; 'sit down and tell me all about it. It seems to me you have got yourself into a jolly awkward position, old chap.'

"Well, he said he wouldn't sit down; he'd prefer to flit up and down the room if it was all the same to me. And so he did, and in a little while we were deep in a long and serious talk. And presently, you know, something of those whiskies and sodas evaporated out of me, and I began to realize just a little what a thundering rum and weird business it was that I was in. There he was, semi-transparent—the proper conventional phantom, and noiseless except for his ghost of a voice—flitting to and fro in that nice, clean, chintz-hung old bedroom. You could see the gleam of the copper candlesticks through him, and the lights on the brass fender, and the corners of the framed engravings on the wall, and there he was telling me all about this wretched little life of his that had recently ended on earth. He hadn't a particularly honest face, you know, but being transparent, of course, he couldn't avoid telling the truth."

"Eh?" said Wish, suddenly sitting up in his chair.

"What?" said Clayton.

"Being transparent—couldn't avoid telling the truth—I don't see it," said Wish.

" In a little while we were deep in a long and serious talk."

" *I* don't see it," said Clayton, with inimitable assurance. " But it *is* so, I can assure you, nevertheless. I don't believe he got once a nail's breadth off the Bible truth. He told me how he had been killed—he went down into a London basement with a candle to look for a leakage of gas—and described himself as a senior English master in a London private school when that release occurred."

" Poor wretch ! " said I.

" That's what I thought, and the more he talked the more I thought it. There he was, purposeless in life and purposeless out of it. He talked of his father and mother and his schoolmaster, and all who had ever been anything to him in the world, meanly. He had been too sensitive, too nervous ; none of them had ever valued him properly or understood him, he said. He had never had a real friend in the world, I think ; he had never had a success. He had shirked games and failed examinations. ' It's like that with some people,' he said ; ' whenever I got into the examination-room or anywhere everything seemed to go.' Engaged to be married of course —to another over-sensitive person, I suppose—when the indiscretion with the gas escape ended his affairs. ' And where are you now ? ' I asked. ' Not in—— ? '

" He wasn't clear on that point at all. The impression he gave me was of a sort of vague, intermediate state, a special reserve for souls too non-existent for anything so positive as either sin or virtue. *I* don't know. He was much too egotistical and unobservant to give me any clear idea of the kind of place, kind of country, there is on the Other Side of Things. Wherever he was, he seems to have fallen in with a set of kindred spirits : ghosts of weak Cockney young men, who were on a footing of Christian names, and among these there was certainly a lot of talk about ' going haunting ' and things like that. Yes—going haunting ! They seemed to think ' haunting ' a tremendous adventure, and most of them funked it all the time. And so primed, you know, he had come."

" But really ! " said Wish to the fire.

" These are the impressions he gave me, anyhow," said Clayton, modestly. " I may, of course, have been in a rather uncritical state, but that was the sort of background he gave to himself. He kept flitting up and down with his thin voice going—talking, talking about his wretched self, and never a word of clear, firm statement from first to last. He was thinner and sillier and more pointless than if he had been real and alive. Only then, you know, he would not have been in my bedroom here—if he *had* been alive. I should have kicked him out."

"Of course," said Evans, "there *are* poor mortals like that."

"And there's just as much chance of their having ghosts as the rest of us," I admitted.

"What gave a sort of point to him, you know, was the fact that he did seem within limits to have found himself out. The mess he had made of haunting had depressed him terribly. He had been told it would be a ' lark ' ; he had come expecting it to be a ' lark,' and here it was, nothing but another failure added to his record ! He proclaimed himself an utter out-and-out failure. He said, and I can quite believe it, that he had never tried to do anything all his life that he hadn't made a perfect mess of—and through all the wastes of eternity he never would. If he had had sympathy, perhaps—— He paused at that, and stood regarding me. He remarked that, strange as it might seem to me, nobody, not any one, ever had given him the amount of sympathy I was doing now. I could see what he wanted straight away, and I determined to head him off at once. I may be a brute, you know, but being the Only Real Friend, the recipient of the confidences of one of these egotistical weaklings, ghost or body, is beyond my physical endurance. I got up briskly. ' Don't you brood on these things too much,' I said. ' The thing you've got to do is to get out of this—get out of this sharp. You pull yourself together and *try*.' ' I can't,' he said. ' You try,' I said, and try he did."

"Try ! " said Sanderson. " *How* ? "

" Passes," said Clayton.

" Passes ? "

" Complicated series of gestures and passes with the hands. That's how he had come in and that's how he had to get out again. Lord ! what a business I had ! "

" But how could *any* series of passes——" I began.

" My dear man," said Clayton, turning on me and putting a great emphasis on certain words, " you want *everything* clear. I don't know *how*. All I know is that you *do*—that *he* did, anyhow, at least. After a fearful time, you know, he got his passes right and suddenly disappeared."

" Did you," said Sanderson slowly, " observe the passes ? "

" Yes," said Clayton, and seemed to think. " It was tremendously queer," he said. " There we were, I and this thin vague ghost, in that silent room, in this silent, empty inn,

in this silent little Friday-night town. Not a sound except
our voices and a faint panting he made when he swung. There
was the bedroom candle, and one candle òn the dressing-table
alight, that was all—sometimes one or other would flare up
into a tall, lean, astonished flame for a space. And queer
things happened. ' I can't,' he said ; ' I shall never—— ! '
And suddenly he sat down on a little chair at the foot of the
bed and began to sob and sob. Lord ! what a harrowing,
whimpering thing he seemed ! "

" ' You pull yourself together,' I said, and tried to pat
him on the back, and . . . my confounded hand went through
him ! By that time, you know, I wasn't nearly so—massive
as I had been on the landing. I got the queerness of it full.
I remember snatching back my hand out of him, as it were,
with a little thrill, and walking over to the dressing-table.
' You pull yourself together,' I said to him, ' and try.' And
in order to encourage and help him I began to try as well."

" What ! " said Sanderson, " the passes ? "

" Yes, the passes."

" But—— " I said, moved by an idea that eluded me for a
space.

" This is interesting," said Sanderson, with his finger in
his pipe-bowl. " You mean to say this ghost of yours gave
way——"

" Did his level best to give away the whole confounded
barrier ? *Yes*."

" He didn't," said Wish ; " he couldn't. Or you'd have
gone there too."

" That's precisely it," I said, finding my elusive idea put
into words for me.

" That *is* precisely it," said Clayton, with thoughtful eyes
upon the fire.

For just a little while there was silence.

" And at last he did it ? " said Sanderson.

" At last he did it. I had to keep him up to it hard, but he
did it at last—rather suddenly. He despaired, we had a
scene, and then he got up abruptly and asked me to go through
the whole performance, slowly, so that he might see. ' I
believe,' he said, ' if I could *see* I should spot what was wrong
at once.' And he did. ' *I* know,' he said. ' What do you
know ? ' said I. ' *I* know,' he repeated. Then he said,
peevishly, ' I *can't* do it, if you look at me—I really *can't* ;
it's been that, partly, all along. I'm such a nervous fellow
that you put me out.' Well, we had a bit of an argument.

Naturally I wanted to see ; but he was as obstinate as a mule, and suddenly I had come over as tired as a dog—he tired me out. ' All right,' I said, ' *I* won't look at you,' and turned towards the mirror, on the wardrobe, by the bed.

" He started off very fast. I tried to follow him by looking in the looking-glass, to see just what it was had hung. Round went his arms and his hands, so, and so, and so, and then with a rush came to the last gesture of all—you stand erect and open out your arms—and so, don't you know, he stood. And then he didn't ! He didn't ! He wasn't ! I wheeled round from the looking-glass to him. There was nothing ! I was alone, with the flaring candles and a staggering mind. What had happened ? Had anything happened ? Had I been dreaming ? . . . And then, with an absurd note of finality about it, the clock upon the landing discovered the moment was ripe for striking *one*. So !—Ping ! And I was as grave and sober as a judge, with all my champagne and whisky gone into the vast serene. Feeling queer, you know—confoundedly *queer* ! Queer ! Good Lord ! "

He regarded his cigar-ash for a moment. " That's all that happened," he said.

" And then you went to bed ? " asked Evans.

" What else was there to do ? "

I looked Wish in the eye. We wanted to scoff, and there was something, something perhaps in Clayton's voice and manner, that hampered our desire.

" And about these passes ? " said Sanderson.

" I believe I could do them now."

" Oh ! " said Sanderson, and produced a pen-knife and set himself to grub the dottel out of the bowl of his clay.

" Why don't you do them now ? " said Sanderson, shutting his pen-knife with a click.

" That's what I'm going to do," said Clayton.

" They won't work," said Evans.

" If they do——" I suggested.

" You know, I'd rather you didn't," said Wish, stretching ou his legs.

" Why ? " asked Evans.

" I'd rather he didn't," said Wish.

" But he hasn't got 'em right," said Sanderson, plugging too much tobacco into his pipe.

" All the same, I'd rather he didn't," said Wish.

We argued with Wish. He said that for Clayton to go through those gestures was like mocking a serious matter.

" But you don't believe—— ? " I said. Wish glanced at Clayton, who was staring into the fire, weighing something in his mind. " I do—more than half, anyhow, I do," said Wish.

" Clayton," said I, " you're too good a liar for us. Most of it was all right. But that disappearance . . . happened to be convincing. Tell us, it's a tale of cock and bull."

He stood up without heeding me, took the middle of the hearthrug and faced me. For a moment he regarded his feet thoughtfully, and then for all the rest of the time his eyes were on the opposite wall, with an intent expression. He raised his two hands slowly to the level of his eyes and so began. . . .

Now, Sanderson is a Freemason, a member of the lodge of the Four Kings, which devotes itself so ably to the study and elucidation of all the mysteries of Masonry past and present, and among the students of this lodge Sanderson is by no means the least. He followed Clayton's motions with a singular interest in his reddish eye. " That's not bad," he said, when it was done. " You really do, you know, put things together, Clayton, in a most amazing fashion. But there's one little detail out."

" I know," said Clayton. " I believe I could tell you which."

" Well ? "

" This," said Clayton, and did a queer little twist and writhing and thrust of the hands.

" Yes."

" That, you know, was what *he* couldn't get right," said Clayton. " But how do *you*—— ? "

" Most of this business, and particularly how you invented it, I don't understand at all," said Sanderson, " but just that phase—I do." He reflected. " These happen to be a series of gestures—connected with a certain branch of esoteric Masonry— Probably you know. Or else—— *How ?* " He reflected still further. " I do not see I can do any harm in telling you just the proper twist. After all, if you know, you know ; if you don't, you don't."

" I know nothing," said Clayton, " except what the poor devil let out last night."

" Well, anyhow," said Sanderson, and placed his church-warden very carefully upon the shelf over the fireplace. Then very rapidly he gesticulated with his hands.

" So ? " said Clayton, repeating.

" So," said Sanderson, and took his pipe in hand again.

" Ah, *now*," said Clayton, " I can do the whole thing—right."

He· stood up before the waning fire and smiled at us all. But I think there was just a little hesitation in his smile. " If I begin——" he said.

" I wouldn't begin," said Wish.

" It's all right ! " said Evans. " Matter is indestructible. You don't think any jiggery-pokery of this sort is going to snatch Clayton into the world of shades. Not it ! You may try, Clayton, so far as I'm concerned, until your arms drop off at the wrists."

" I don't believe that," said Wish, and stood up and put his arm on Clayton's shoulder. " You've made me half believe in that story somehow, and I don't want to see the thing done."

" Goodness ! " said I, " here's Wish frightened ! "

" I am," said Wish, with real or admirably feigned intensity. " I believe that if he goes through these motions right he'll *go*."

" He'll not do anything of the sort," I cried. " There's only one way out of this world for men, and Clayton is thirty years from that. Besides . . . And such a ghost ! Do you think—— ? "

Wish interrupted me by moving. He walked out from among our chairs and stopped beside the table and stood there. " Clayton," he said, " you're a fool."

Clayton, with a humorous light in his eyes, smiled back at him. " Wish," he said, " is right and all you others are wrong. I shall go. I shall get to the end of these passes, and as the last swish whistles through the air, Presto !—this hearthrug will be vacant, the room will be blank amazement, and a respectably dressed gentleman of fifteen stone will plump into the world of shades. I'm certain. So will you be. I decline to argue further. Let the thing be tried."

" *No*," said Wish, and made a step and ceased, and Clayton raised his hands once more to repeat the spirit's passing.

By that time, you know, we were all in a state of tension— largely because of the behaviour of Wish. We sat all of us with our eyes on Clayton—I, at least, with a sort of tight, stiff feeling about me as though from the back of my skull to the middle of my thighs my body had been changed to steel. And there, with a gravity that was imperturbably serene, Clayton bowed and swayed and waved his hands and arms before us. As he drew towards the end one piled up, one tingled in one's teeth. The last gesture, I have said, was to swing the arms out wide open, with the face held up. And when at last he swung out to this closing gesture I ceased even to breathe. It was ridiculous, of course, but you know that ghost-story feeling. It was after dinner, in a queer, old shadowy house. Would he, after all—— ?

There he stood for one stupendous moment, with his arms open and his upturned face, assured and bright, in the glare of the hanging lamp. We hung through that moment as if it were an age, and then came from all of us something that was half a sigh of infinite relief and half a reassuring " *No !* " For visibly—he wasn't going. It was all nonsense. He had told an idle story, and carried it almost to conviction, that was all ! . . . And then in that moment the face of Clayton changed.

It changed. It changed as a lit house changes when its lights are suddenly extinguished. His eyes were suddenly eyes that were fixed, his smile was frozen on his lips, and he stood there still. He stood there, very gently swaying.

That moment, too, was an age. And then, you know, chairs were scraping, things were falling, and we were all moving. His knees seemed to give, and he fell forward, and Evans rose and caught him in his arms. . . .

It stunned us all. For a minute I suppose no one said a coherent thing. We believed it, yet could not believe it. . . . I came out of a muddled stupefaction to find myself kneeling beside him, and his vest and shirt were torn open, and Sanderson's hand lay on his heart. . . .

Well—the simple fact before us could very well wait our convenience ; there was no hurry for us to comprehend. It lay there for an hour ; it lies athwart my memory, black and amazing still, to this day. Clayton had, indeed, passed into the world that lies so near to and so far from our own, and he had gone thither by the only road that mortal man may take. But whether he did indeed pass there by that poor ghost's incantation, or whether he was stricken suddenly by apoplexy in the midst of an idle tale—as the coroner's jury would have us believe—is no matter for my judging ; it is just one of those inexplicable riddles that must remain unsolved until the final solution of all things shall come. All I certainly know is that, in the very moment, in the very instant, of concluding those passes, he changed, and staggered, and fell down before us— dead !

THE CONFESSION OF
CHARLES LINKWORTH

D<small>R. TEESDALE</small> had occasion to attend the condemned
man once or twice during the week before his execution,
and found him, as is often the case, when the last hope
of life has vanished, quiet and perfectly resigned to his fate,
and not seeming to look forward with any dread to the morning
that each hour that passed brought nearer and nearer. The
bitterness of death appeared to be over for him : it was done
with when he was told that his appeal was refused. But
for those days while hope was not yet quite abandoned, the
wretched man had drunk of death daily. In all his experience
the doctor had never seen a man so wildly and passionately
tenacious of life, nor one so strongly knit to this material
world by the sheer animal lust of living. Then the news
that hope could no longer be entertained was told him, and his
spirit passed out of the grip of that agony of torture and sus-
pense, and accepted the inevitable with indifference. Yet the
change was so extraordinary that it seemed to the doctor rather
that the news had completely stunned his powers of feeling,
and he was below the numbed surface, still knit into material
things as strongly as ever. He had fainted when the result
was told him, and Dr. Teesdale had been called in to attend
him. But the fit was but transient, and he came out of it into
full consciousness of what had happened.

The murder had been a deed of peculiar horror, and there
was nothing of sympathy in the mind of the public towards the
perpetrator. Charles Linkworth, who now lay under capital
sentence, was the keeper of a small stationery store in Sheffield,
and there lived with him his wife and mother. The latter
was the victim of his atrocious crime ; the motive of it being to
get possession of the sum of five hundred pounds, which was

this woman's property. Linkworth, as came out at the trial, was in debt to the extent of a hundred pounds at the time, and during his wife's absence from home, on a visit to relations, he strangled his mother, and during the night buried the body in the small back-garden of his house. On his wife's return, he had a sufficiently plausible tale to account for the elder Mrs. Linkworth's disappearance, for there had been constant jarrings and bickerings between him and his mother for the last year or two, and she had more than once threatened to withdraw herself and the eight shillings a week which she contributed to household expenses, and purchase an annuity with her money. It was true, also, that during the younger Mrs. Linkworth's absence from home, mother and son had had a violent quarrel arising originally from some trivial point in household management, and that in consequence of this, she had actually drawn her money out of the bank, intending to leave Sheffield next day and settle in London where she had friends. That evening she told him this, and during the night he killed her.

His next step, before his wife's return, was logical and sound. He packed up all his mother's possessions and took them to the station, from which he saw them dispatched to town by passenger train, and in the evening he asked several friends in to supper, and told them of his mother's departure. He did not (logically also, and in accordance with what they probably already knew) feign regret, but said that he and she had never got on well together, and that the cause of peace and quietness was furthered by her going. He told the same story to his wife on her return, identical in every detail, adding, however, that the quarrel had been a violent one, and that his mother had not even left him her address. This again was wisely thought of : it would prevent his wife from writing to her. She appeared to accept his story completely : indeed there was nothing strange or suspicious about it.

For a while he behaved with the composure and astuteness which most criminals possess up to a certain point, the lack of which, after that, is generally the cause of their detection. He did not, for instance, immediately pay off his debts, but took into his house a young man as lodger, who occupied his mother's room, and he dismissed the assistant in his shop, and did the entire serving himself. This gave the impression of economy, and at the same time he openly spoke of the great improvement in his trade, and not till a month had passed did he cash any of the bank-notes which he had found in a locked drawer in his mother's room. Then he changed two notes of fifty pounds and paid off his creditors.

At that point his astuteness and composure failed him. He opened a deposit account at a local bank with four more fifty-pound notes, instead of being patient, and increasing his balance at the savings bank pound by pound, and he got uneasy about that which he had buried deep enough for security in the back-garden. Thinking to render himself safer in this regard, he ordered a cartload of slag and stone fragments, and with the help of his lodger employed the summer evenings, when work was over, in building a sort of rockery over the spot. Then came the chance circumstance which really set match to this dangerous train. There was a fire in the lost luggage office at King's Cross Station (from which he ought to have claimed his mother's property) and one of the two boxes was partially burned. The company was liable for compensation, and his mother's name on her linen, and a letter with the Sheffield address on it, led to the arrival of a purely official and formal notice, stating that the company were prepared to consider claims. It was directed to Mrs. Linkworth, and Charles Linkworth's wife received and read it.

It seemed a sufficiently harmless document, but it was endorsed with his death-warrant. For he could give no explanation at all of the fact of the boxes still lying at King's Cross Station, beyond suggesting that some accident had happened to his mother. Clearly he had to put the matter in the hands of the police, with a view to tracing her movements, and if it proved that she was dead, claiming her property, which she had already drawn out of the bank. Such at least was the course urged on him by his wife and lodger, in whose presence the communication from the railway officials was read out, and it was impossible to refuse to take it. Then the silent, uncreaking machinery of justice, characteristic of England, began to move forward. Quiet men lounged about Smith Street, visited banks, observed the supposed increase in trade, and from a house near by looked into the garden where ferns were already flourishing on the rockery. Then came the arrest and the trial, which did not last very long, and on a certain Saturday night the verdict. Smart women in large hats had made the court bright with colour, and in all the crowd there was not one who felt any sympathy with the young athletic-looking man who was condemned. Many of the audience were elderly and respectable mothers, and the crime had been an outrage on motherhood, and they listened to the

unfolding of the flawless evidence with strong approval. They
thrilled a little when the judge put on the awful and ludicrous
little black cap, and spoke the sentence appointed by God.

Linkworth went to pay the penalty for the atrocious deed,
which no one who had heard the evidence could possibly doubt
that he had done, with the same indifference as had marked
his entire demeanour since he knew his appeal had failed.
The prison chaplain who had attended him had done his
utmost to get him to confess, but his efforts had been quite
ineffectual, and to the last he asserted, though without pro-
testation, his innocence. On a bright September morning,
when the sun shone warm on the terrible little procession that
crossed the prison yard to the shed where was erected the
apparatus of death, justice was done, and Dr. Teesdale was
satisfied that life was immediately extinct. He had been
present on the scaffold, had watched the bolt drawn, and the
hooded and pinioned figure drop into the pit. He had heard
the chunk and creak of the rope as the sudden weight came on
to it, and looking down he had seen the queer twitchings of
the hanged body. They had lasted but a second or two ; the
execution had been perfectly satisfactory.

An hour later he made the post-mortem examination, and
found that his view had been correct : the vertebræ of the
spine had been broken at the neck, and death must have been
absolutely instantaneous. It was hardly necessary even to
make that little piece of dissection that proved this, but for
the sake of form he did so. And at that moment he had a very
curious and vivid mental impression that the spirit of the dead
man was close beside him, as if it still dwelt in the broken
habitation of its body. But there was no question at all that
the body was dead : it had been dead an hour. Then followed
another little circumstance that at the first seemed insignificant
though curious also. One of the warders entered, and asked
if the rope which had been used an hour ago, and was the
hangman's perquisite, had by mistake been brought into the
mortuary with the body. But there was no trace of it, and
it seemed to have vanished altogether, though it was a singular
thing to be lost : it was not here ; it was not on the scaffold.
And though the disappearance was of no particular moment,
it was quite inexplicable.

Dr. Teesdale was a bachelor and a man of independent
means, and lived in a tall-windowed and commodious house in
Bedford Square, where a plain cook of surpassing excellence
looked after his food, and her husband his person. There was

no need for him to practise a profession at all, and he performed his work at the prison for the sake of the study of the minds of criminals. Most crime—the transgression, that is, of the rule of conduct which the human race has framed for the sake of its own preservation—he held to be either the result of some abnormality of the brain, or of starvation. Crimes of theft, for instance, he would by no means refer to one head ; often it is true they were the result of actual want, but more often dictated by some obscure disease of the brain. In marked cases it was labelled as kleptomania, but he was convinced there were many others which did not fall directly under the dictation of physical need. More especially was this the case where the crime in question involved also some deed of violence, and he mentally placed underneath this heading, as he went home that evening, the criminal at whose last moments he had been present that morning. The crime had been abominable, the need of money not so very pressing, and the very abomination and unnaturalness of the murder inclined him to consider the murderer as lunatic rather than criminal. He had been, as far as was known, a man of quiet and kindly disposition, a good husband, a sociable neighbour. And then he had committed a crime, just one, which put him outside all pales. So monstrous a deed, whether perpetrated by a sane man or a mad one, was intolerable ; there was no use for the doer of it on this planet at all. But somehow the doctor felt that he would have been more at one with the execution of justice, if the dead man had confessed. It was morally certain that he was guilty, but he wished that when there was no longer any hope for him, he had endorsed the verdict himself.

He dined alone that evening, and after dinner sat in his study which adjoined the dining-room, and feeling disinclined to read, sat in his great red chair opposite the fireplace, and let his mind graze where it would. At once almost, it went back to the curious sensation he had experienced that morning, of feeling that the spirit of Linkworth was present in the mortuary, though life had been extinct for an hour. It was not the first time, especially in cases of sudden death, that he had felt a similar conviction, though perhaps it had never been quite so unmistakable as it had been to-day. Yet the feeling, to his mind, was quite probably formed on a natural and psychical truth. The spirit—it may be remarked that he was a believer in the doctrine of future life, and the non-extinction of the soul with the death of the body—was very likely unable or unwilling to quit at once and altogether the earthly habitation, very likely it lingered there, earth-bound, for a while. In his leisure hours Dr. Teesdale was a considerable student of the occult, for like most advanced and proficient physicians, he clearly recognized how narrow was the boundary of separation between soul and body, how tremendous the influence of the intangible was over material things, and it presented no difficulty to his mind that a disembodied spirit should be able to communicate directly with those who still were bounded by the finite and material.

His meditations, which were beginning to group themselves into definite sequence, were interrupted at this moment. On his desk near at hand stood his telephone, and the bell rang, not with its usual metallic insistence, but very faintly, as if the current was weak, or the mechanism impaired. However, it certainly was ringing, and he got up and took the combined ear and mouthpiece off its hook.

" Yes, yes," he said, " who is it ? "

There was a whisper in reply almost inaudible, and quite unintelligible.

" I can't hear you," he said.

Again the whisper sounded, but with no greater distinctness. Then it ceased altogether.

He stood there, for some half-minute or so, waiting for it to be renewed, but beyond the usual chuckling and croaking, which showed, however, that he was in communication with some other instrument, there was silence. Then he replaced the receiver, rang up the Exchange, and gave his number.

" Can you tell me what number rang me up just now ? " he asked.

There was a short pause, then it was given him. It was the number of the prison, where he was doctor.

" Put me on to it, please," he said.

This was done.

" You rang me up just now," he said down the tube. " Yes, I am Dr. Teesdale. What is it ? I could not hear what you said."

The voice came back quite clear and intelligible.

" Some mistake, sir," it said. " We haven't rang you up."

" But the Exchange tells me you did, three minutes ago."

" Mistake at the Exchange, sir," said the voice.

" Very odd. Well, good-night. Warder Draycott, isn't it ? "

" Yes, sir ; good-night, sir."

Dr. Teesdale went back to his big arm-chair, still less

inclined to read. He let his thoughts wander on for a while, without giving them definite direction, but ever and again his mind kept coming back to that strange little incident of the telephone. Often and often he had been rung up by some mistake, often and often he had been put on to the wrong number by the Exchange, but there was something in this very subdued ringing of the telephone bell, and the unintelligible whisperings at the other end that suggested a very curious train of reflection to his mind, and soon he found himself pacing up and down his room, with his thoughts eagerly feeding on a most unusual pasture.

" But it's impossible," he said aloud.

He went down as usual to the prison next morning and once again he was strangely beset with the feeling that there was some unseen presence there. He had before now had some odd psychical experiences, and knew that he was a " sensitive "—one, that is, who is capable, under certain circumstances, of receiving supernormal impressions, and of having glimpses of the unseen world that lies about us. And this morning the presence of which he was conscious was that of the man who had been executed yesterday morning. It was local, and he felt it most strongly in the little prison yard, and as he passed the door of the condemned cell. So strong was it there that he would not have been surprised if the figure of the man had been visible to him, and as he passed through the door at the end of the passage, he turned round, actually expecting to see it. All the time, too, he was aware of a profound horror at his heart, this unseen presence strangely disturbed him. And the poor soul, he felt, wanted something done for it. Not for a moment did he doubt that this impression of his was objective, it was no imaginative phantom of his own invention that made itself so real. The spirit of Linkworth was there.

He passed into the infirmary, and for a couple of hours busied himself with his work. But all the time he was aware that the same invisible presence was near him, though its force was manifestly less here than in those places which had been more intimately associated with the man. Finally, before he left, in order to test his theory he looked into the execution shed. But next moment with a face suddenly stricken pale, he came out again, closing the door hastily. At the top of the steps stood a figure hooded and pinioned, but hazy of outline and only faintly visible. But it was visible, there was no mistake about it.

Dr. Teesdale was a man of good nerve, and he recovered himself almost immediately, ashamed of his temporary panic. The terror that had blanched his face was chiefly the effect of startled nerves, not of terrified heart, and yet deeply interested as he was in psychical phenomena, he could not command himself sufficiently to go back there. Or rather he commanded himself, but his muscles refused to act on the message. If this poor earth-bound spirit had any communication to make to him, he certainly much preferred that it should be made at a distance. As far as he could understand, its range was circumscribed. It haunted the prison yard, the condemned cell, the execution shed, it was more faintly felt in the infirmary. Then a further point suggested itself to his mind, and he went back to his room and sent for Warder Draycott, who had answered him on the telephone last night.

" You are quite sure," he asked, " that nobody rang me up last night, just before I rang you up ? "

There was a certain hesitation in the man's manner which the doctor noticed.

" I don't see how it could be possible, sir," he said; " I had been sitting close by the telephone for half an hour before, and again before that. I must have seen him, if any one had been to the instrument."

" And you *saw* no one ? " said the doctor with a slight emphasis.

The man became more markedly ill at ease.

" No, sir, I *saw* no one," he said, with the same emphasis.

Dr. Teesdale looked away from him.

" But you had perhaps the impression that there was some one there ? " he asked carelessly, as if it was a point of no interest.

Clearly Warder Draycott had something on his mind, which he found it hard to speak of.

" Well, sir, if you put it like that," he began. " But you would tell me I was half asleep, or had eaten something that disagreed with me at my supper."

The doctor dropped his careless manner.

" I should do nothing of the kind," he said, " any more than you would tell me that I had dropped asleep last night, when I heard my telephone bell ring. Mind you, Draycott, it did not ring as usual, I could only just hear it ringing, though it was close to me. And I could only hear a whisper when I put my ear to it. But when you spoke I heard you quite distinctly. Now I believe there was something—somebody—

at this end of the telephone. You were here, and though you saw no one, you, too, felt there was some one there."

The man nodded.

" I'm not a nervous man, sir," he said, " and I don't deal in fancies. But there was something there. It was hovering about the instrument, and it wasn't the wind, because there wasn't a breath of wind stirring, and the night was warm. And I shut the window to make certain. But it went about the room, sir, for an hour or more. It rustled the leaves of the telephone book, and it ruffled my hair when it came close to me. And it was bitter cold, sir."

The doctor looked him straight in the face.

" Did it remind you of what had been done yesterday morning ? " he asked suddenly.

Again the man hesitated.

" Yes, sir," he said at length. " Convict Charles Link-worth."

Dr. Teesdale nodded reassuringly.

" That's it," he said. " Now, are you on duty to-night ? "

" Yes, sir ; I wish I wasn't."

" I know how you feel, I have felt exactly the same myself. Now whatever this is, it seems to want to communicate with me. By the way, did you have any disturbance in the prison last night ? "

" Yes, sir, there was half a dozen men who had the night-mare. Yelling and screaming they were, and quiet men too, usually. It happens sometimes the night after an execution. I've known it before, though nothing like what it was last night."

" I see. Now, if this—this thing you can't see wants to get at the telephone again to-night, give it every chance. It will probably come about the same time. I can't tell you why, but that usually happens. So unless you must, don't be in this room where the telephone is, just for an hour to give it plenty of time between half-past nine and half-past ten. I will be ready for it at the other end. Supposing I am rung up, I will, when it has finished, ring you up to make sure that I was not being called in—in the usual way."

" And there is nothing to be afraid of, sir ? " asked the man.

Dr. Teesdale remembered his own moment of terror this morning, but he spoke quite sincerely.

" I am sure there is nothing to be afraid of," he said reassuringly.

Dr. Teesdale had a dinner engagement that night, which he broke, and was sitting alone in his study by half-past nine. In the present state of human ignorance as to the law which governs the movements of spirits severed from the body, he could not tell the warder why it was that their visits are so often periodic, timed to punctuality according to our scheme of hours, but in scores of tabulated instances of the appearance of *revenants*, especially if the soul was in sore need of help, as might be the case here, he found that they came at the same hour of day or night. As a rule, too, their power of making themselves seen or heard or felt, grew greater for some little while after death, subsequently growing weaker as they became less earth-bound, or often after that ceasing altogether, and he was prepared to-night for a less indistinct impression. The spirit apparently for the early hours of its disembodiment is weak, like a moth newly broken out from its chrysalis—and then suddenly the telephone bell rang, not so faintly as the night before, but still not with its ordinary imperative tone.

Dr. Teesdale instantly got up, put the receiver to his ears. And what he heard was heart-broken sobbing, strong spasms that seemed to tear the weeper.

He waited for a little before speaking, himself cold with some nameless fear, and yet profoundly moved to help, if he was able.

" Yes, yes," he said at length, hearing his own voice tremble. " I am Dr. Teesdale. What can I do for you ? And who are you ? " he added, though he felt that it was a needless question.

Slowly the sobbing died down, the whispers took its place, still broken by crying.

" I want to tell, sir—I want to tell—I must tell."

" Yes, tell me, what is it ? " said the doctor.

" No, not you—another gentleman, who used to come to see me. Will you speak to him what I say to you ?—I can't make him hear me or see me."

" Who are you ? " asked Dr. Teesdale suddenly.

" Charles Linkworth. I thought you knew. I am very miserable. I can't leave the prison—and it is cold. Will you send for the other gentleman ? "

" Do you mean the chaplain ? " asked Dr. Teesdale.

" Yes, the chaplain. He read the service when I went across the yard yesterday. I shan't be so miserable when I have told."

The doctor hesitated a moment. This was a strange

story that he would have to tell Mr. Dawkins, the prison chaplain, that at the other end of the telephone was the spirit of the man executed yesterday. And yet he soberly believed that it was so that this unhappy spirit was in misery, and wanted to " tell." There was no need to ask what he wanted to tell.

" Yes, I will ask him to come here," he said at length.

" Thank you, sir, a thousand times. You will make him come, won't you ? "

The voice was growing fainter.

" It must be to-morrow night," it said. " I can't speak longer now. I have to go to see—oh, my God, my God."

The sobs broke out afresh, sounding fainter and fainter. But it was in a frenzy of terrified interest that Dr. Teesdale spoke.

" To see what ? " he cried. " Tell me what you are doing, what is happening to you ? "

" I can't tell you ; I mayn't tell you," said the voice very faint. " That is part——" and it died away altogether.

Dr. Teesdale waited a little, but there was no further sound of any kind, except the chuckling and croaking of the instrument. He put the receiver on to its hook again, and then became aware for the first time that his forehead was streaming with some cold dew of horror. His ears sang ; his heart beat very quick and faint, and he sat down to recover himself. Once or twice he asked himself if it was possible that some terrible joke was being played on him, but he knew that could not be so ; he felt perfectly sure that he had been speaking with a soul in torment of contrition for the terrible and irremediable act it had committed. It was no delusion of his senses, either ; here in this comfortable room of his in Bedford Square, with London cheerfully roaring round him, he had spoken with the spirit of Charles Linkworth.

But he had no time (nor indeed inclination, for somehow his soul sat shuddering within him) to indulge in meditation. First of all he rang up the prison.

" Warder Draycott ? " he asked.

There was a perceptible tremor in the man's voice as he answered.

" Yes, sir. Is it Dr. Teesdale ? "

" Yes. Has anything happened here with you ? "

Twice it seemed that the man tried to speak and could not. At the third attempt the words came.

" Yes, sir. He has been here. I saw him go into the room where the telephone is."

" Ah ! Did you speak to him ? "

" No, sir : I sweated and prayed. And there's half a dozen men as have been screaming in their sleep to-night. But it's quiet again now. I think he has gone into the execution shed."

" Yes. Well, I think there will be no more disturbance now. By the way, please give me Mr. Dawkins's home address."

. . . . . .

This was given him, and Dr. Teesdale proceeded to write to the chaplain, asking him to dine with him on the following night. But suddenly he found that he could not write at his accustomed desk, with the telephone standing close to him, and he went upstairs to the drawing-room which he seldom used, except when he entertained his friends. There he recaptured the serenity of his nerves, and could control his hand. The note simply asked Mr. Dawkins to dine with him next night, when he wished to tell him a very strange history and ask his help. " Even if you have any other engagement," he concluded, " I seriously request you to give it up. To-night, I did the same. I should bitterly have regretted it if I had not."

Next night, accordingly, the two sat at their dinner in the doctor's dining-room, and when they were left to their cigarettes and coffee the doctor spoke.

" You must not think me mad, my dear Dawkins," he said, " when you hear what I have got to tell you."

Mr. Dawkins laughed.

" I will certainly promise not to do that," he said.

" Good. Last night and the night before, a little later in the evening than this, I spoke through the telephone with the spirit of the man we saw executed two days ago—Charles Linkworth."

The chaplain did not laugh. He pushed back his chair, looking annoyed.

" Teesdale," he said, " is it to tell me this—I don't want to be rude—but this bogey-tale that you have brought me here this evening ? "

" Yes. You have not heard half of it. He asked me last night to get hold of you. He wants to tell you something. We can guess, I think, what it is."

Dawkins got up.

" Please let me hear no more of it," he said. " The dead do not return. In what state or under what condition they exist has not been revealed to us. But they have done with all material things."

"But I must tell you more," said the doctor. "Two nights ago I was rung up, but very faintly, and could hear only whispers. I instantly inquired where the call came from and was told it came from the prison. I rang up the prison, and Warder Draycott told me that nobody had rung me up. He, too, was conscious of a presence."

"I think that man drinks," said Dawkins sharply.

The doctor paused a moment.

"My dear fellow, you should not say that sort of thing," he said. "He is one of the steadiest men we have got. And if he drinks, why not I also ? "

The chaplain sat down again.

"You must forgive me," he said, "but I can't go into this. These are dangerous matters to meddle with. Besides, how do you know it is not a hoax ? "

"Played by whom ? " asked the doctor. "Hark ! "

The telephone bell suddenly rang. It was clearly audible to the doctor.

"Don't you hear it ? " he said.

"Hear what ? "

"The telephone bell ringing."

"I hear no bell," said the chaplain, rather angrily. "There is no bell ringing."

The doctor did not answer, but went through into his study, and turned on the lights. Then he took the receiver and mouthpiece off its hook.

"Yes ? " he said, in a voice that trembled. "Who is it ? Yes : Mr. Dawkins is here. I will try and get him to speak to you."

He went back into the other room.

"Dawkins," he said, "there is a soul in agony. I pray you to listen. For God's sake come and listen."

The chaplain hesitated a moment.

"As you will," he said.

He took up the receiver and put it to his ear.

"I am Mr. Dawkins," he said.

He waited.

"I can hear nothing whatever," he said at length. "Ah, there was something there. The faintest whisper."

"Ah, try to hear, try to hear ! " said the doctor.

Again the chaplain listened. Suddenly he laid the instrument down, frowning.

"Something—somebody said, ' I killed her, I confess it. I want to be forgiven.' It's a hoax, my dear Teesdale. Somebody knowing your spiritualistic leanings is playing a very grim joke on you. I *can't* believe it."

Dr. Teesdale took up the receiver.

"I am Dr. Teesdale," he said. "Can you give Mr. Dawkins some sign that it is you ? "

Then he laid it down again.

"He says he thinks he can," he said. "We must wait."

The evening was again very warm, and the window into the paved yard at the back of the house was open. For five minutes or so the two men stood in silence, waiting, and nothing happened. Then the chaplain spoke.

"I think that is sufficiently conclusive," he said.

Even as he spoke a very cold draught of air suddenly blew into the room, making the papers on the desk rustle. Dr. Teesdale went to the window and closed it.

"Did you feel that ? " he asked.

"Yes, a breath of air. Chilly."

Once again in the closed room it stirred again.

"And did you feel that ? " asked the doctor.

The chaplain nodded. He felt his heart hammering in his throat suddenly.

"Defend us from all peril and danger of this coming night," he exclaimed.

"Something is coming ! " said the doctor.

As he spoke it came. In the centre of the room not three yards away from them stood the figure of a man with his head bent over on to his shoulder, so that the face was not visible. Then he took his head in both his hands and raised it like a weight, and looked them in the face. The eyes and tongue protruded, a livid mark was round the neck. Then there came a sharp rattle on the boards of the floor, and the figure was no longer there. But on the floor there lay a new rope.

For a long while neither spoke. The sweat poured off the doctor's face, and the chaplain's white lips whispered prayers. Then by a huge effort the doctor pulled himself together. He pointed at the rope.

"It has been missing since the execution," he said.

Then again the telephone bell rang. This time the chaplain needed no prompting. He went to it at once and the ringing ceased. For a while he listened in silence.

"Charles Linkworth," he said at length, " in the sight of

God, in whose presence you stand, are you truly sorry for your sin ? "

Some answer inaudible to the doctor came, and the chaplain closed his eyes. And Dr. Teesdale knelt as he heard the words of the Absolution.

At the close there was silence again.

" I can hear nothing more," said the chaplain, replacing the receiver.

Presently the doctor's man-servant came in with the tray of spirits and syphon. Dr. Teesdale pointed without looking to where the apparition had been.

" Take the rope that is there and burn it, Parker," he said.

There was a moment's silence.

" There is no rope, sir," said Parker.

A VISITOR FROM
DOWN UNDER

" And who will you send to fetch him away ? "

AFTER a promising start, the March day had ended in a
wet evening. It was hard to tell whether rain or fog
predominated. The loquacious bus conductor said " A
foggy evening " to those who rode inside, and " a wet evening "
to such as were obliged to ride outside. But in or on the
buses, cheerfulness held the field, for their patrons, inured to
discomfort, made light of climatic inclemency. All the same,
the weather was worth remarking on : the most scrupulous con-
versationalist could refer to it without feeling self-convicted
of banality. How much more the conductor, who, in common
with most of his kind, had a considerable conversational gift.

The bus was making its last journey through the heart of
London before turning in for the night. Inside it was only
half full. Outside, as the conductor was aware by virtue of
his sixth sense, there still remained a passenger too hardy or
too lazy to seek shelter. And now, as the bus rattled rapidly
down the Strand, the footsteps of this person could be heard
shuffling and creaking upon the metal-shod stairs.

" Any one on top ? " asked the conductor, addressing an
errant umbrella-point and the hem of a mackintosh.

" I didn't notice any one," the man replied.

" It's not that I don't trust you," remarked the conductor,
pleasantly giving a hand to his alighting fare ; " but I think
I'll go up and make sure."

Moments like these, moments of mistrust in the infalli-
bility of his observation, occasionally visited the conductor.
They came at the end of a tiring day, and if he could he with-
stood them. They were signs of weakness, he thought ; and

to give way to them matter for self-reproach. " Going barmy,
that's what you are," he told himself, and he casually took a
fare inside to prevent his mind dwelling on the unvisited
outside. But his unreasoning disquietude survived this
distraction, and murmuring against himself he started to
climb the stairs.

To his surprise, almost stupefaction, he found that his
misgivings were justified. Breasting the ascent, he saw a
passenger sitting on the right-hand front seat ; and the
passenger, in spite of his hat turned down, his collar turned
up, and the creased white muffler that showed between the
two, must have heard him coming ; for though the man was
looking straight ahead, in his outstretched left hand, wedged
between the first and second fingers, he held a coin.

" Jolly evening, don't you think ? " asked the conductor,
who wanted to say something. The passenger made no reply,
but the penny, for such it was, slipped the fraction of an inch
lower in the groove between the pale freckled fingers.

" I said it was a damn wet night," the conductor persisted
irritably, annoyed by the man's reserve. Still no reply.

" Where you for ? " asked the conductor, in a tone suggesting that, wherever it was, it must be a discreditable destination.

" Carrick Street."

" Where ? " the conductor demanded. He had heard all
right, but a slight peculiarity in the passenger's pronunciation
made it appear reasonable to him, and possibly humiliating
to the passenger, that he should not have heard.

" Carrick Street."

" Then why didn't you say Carrick Street ? " the conductor
grumbled as he punched the ticket.

There was a moment's pause, then " Carrick Street," the
passenger repeated.

" Yes, I know, I know ; you needn't go on telling me,"
fumed the conductor, fumbling with the passenger's penny.
He couldn't get hold of it from above, it had slipped too far,
so he passed his hand underneath the other's and drew the
coin from between his fingers.

It was cold, even where it had been held.

" Know ? " said the stranger suddenly, " what do you
know ? "

The conductor was trying to draw his fare's attention to
the ticket, but could not make him look round. " I suppose
I know you are a clever chap," he remarked. " Look here,
now. Where do you want this ticket ? In your buttonhole ? "

"Put it here," said the passenger.

"Where?" asked the conductor. "You aren't a blooming letter-rack."

"Where the penny was," replied the passenger. "Between my fingers."

The conductor felt reluctant, he did not know why, to oblige the passenger in this. The rigidity of the hand disconcerted him : it was stiff, he supposed, or perhaps paralysed. And since he had been standing on the top his own hands were none too warm. The ticket doubled up and grew limp under his repeated efforts to push it in. He bent lower, for he was a good-hearted fellow, and using both hands, one above and one below, he slid the ticket into its bony slot.

"Right you are, Kaiser Bill."

Perhaps the passenger resented this jocular allusion to his physical infirmity ; perhaps he merely wanted to be quiet. All he said was :

"Don't speak to me again."

"Speak to you !" shouted the conductor, losing all self-control. "Catch me speaking to a stuffed dummy !"

Muttering to himself, he withdrew into the bowels of the bus.

.   .   .   .

At the corner of Carrick Street quite a number of people got on board. All wanted to be first, but pride of place was shared by three women, who all tried to enter simultaneously. The conductor's voice made itself audible above the din : "Now then, now then, look where you're shoving ! This isn't a bargain-sale. Gently *please*, lady ; he's only a pore old man." In a moment or two the confusion abated, and the conductor, his hand on the cord of the bell, bethought himself of the passenger on top whose destination Carrick Street was. He had forgotten to get down. Yielding to his good nature, for the conductor was averse to further conversation with his uncommunicative fare, he mounted the stairs, put his head over the top and shouted, "Carrick Street ! Carrick Street !" That was the utmost he could bring himself to do. But his admonition was without effect ; his summons remained unanswered ; nobody came. "Well, if he wants to stay up there he can," muttered the conductor, still aggrieved.

I won't fetch him down, cripple or no cripple." The bus moved on. He slipped by me, thought the conductor, while all that Cup-tie crowd was getting in.

.   .   .   .

The same evening, some five hours earlier, a taxi turned into Carrick Street and pulled up at the door of a small hotel. The street was empty. It looked like a cul-de-sac, but in reality it was pierced at the far end by an alley, like a thin sleeve, which wound its way into Soho.

" That the last, sir ? " inquired the driver, after several transits between the cab and the hotel.

" How many does that make ? "

" Nine packages in all, sir."

" Could you get all your worldly goods into nine packages, driver ? "

" That I could ; into two."

" Well, have a look inside and see if I have left anything."

The cabman felt about among the cushions. " Can't find nothing, sir."

" What do you do with anything you find ? " asked the stranger.

" Take it to New Scotland Yard, sir," the driver promptly replied.

" Scotland Yard ? " said the stranger. " Strike a match, will you, and let me have a look."

But he, too, found nothing, and, reassured, followed his luggage into the hotel.

A chorus of welcome and congratulation greeted him. The manager, the manager's wife, the ministers without portfolio of which all hotels are full, the porters, the liftman, all clustered around him.

" Well, Mr. Rumbold, after all these years ! We thought you'd forgotten us ! And wasn't it odd, the very night your telegram came from Australia we'd been talking about you ! And my husband said, ' Don't you worry about Mr. Rumbold. He'll fall on his feet all right. Some fine day he'll walk in here a rich man.' Not that you weren't always well-off, but my husband meant a millionaire."

" He was quite right," said Mr. Rumbold slowly, savouring his words ; " I am."

" There, what did I tell you ? " the manager exclaimed, as though one recital of his prophecy was not enough. " But I wonder you're not too grand to come to Rossall's Hotel."

" I've nowhere else to go," said the millionaire shortly. " And if I had, I wouldn't. This place is like home to me."

His eyes softened as they scanned the familiar surroundings. They were light-grey eyes, very pale, and seeming paler from their setting in his tanned face. His cheeks were slightly sunken and very deeply lined ; his blunt-ended nose was straight. He had a thin straggling moustache, straw-coloured, which made his age difficult to guess. Perhaps he was nearly fifty, so wasted was the skin on his neck, but his movements, unexpectedly agile and decided, were those of a younger man.

" I won't go up to my room now," he said, in response to the manageress's question. " Ask Clutsam—he's still with you ?—good—to unpack my things. He'll find all I want for the night in the green suit-case. I'll take my despatch-box with me. And tell them to bring me a sherry-and-bitters in the lounge."

As the crow flies, it was not far to the lounge. But by way of the tortuous, ill-lit passages, doubling on themselves, yawning with dark entries, plunging into kitchen stairs—the catacombs so dear to habitués of Rossall's Hotel—it was a considerable distance. Any one posted in the shadow of these alcoves, or arriving at the head of the basement staircase, could not have failed to notice the air of utter content which marked Mr. Rumbold's leisurely progress : the droop of his shoulders, acquiescing in weariness ; the hands turned inwards and swaying slightly, but quite forgotten by their owner ; the chin, always prominent, now pushed forward so far that it looked relaxed and helpless, not at all defiant. The unseen witness would have envied Mr. Rumbold, perhaps even grudged him his holiday airs, his untroubled acceptance of the present and the future.

A waiter whose face he did not remember brought him the *apéritif*, which he drank slowly, his feet propped unconventionally upon a ledge of the chimney-piece ; a pardonable relaxation, for the room was empty. Judge therefore his surprise when, out of a fire-engendered drowsiness, he heard a voice which seemed to come from the wall above his head. A cultivated voice, perhaps too cultivated, slightly husky, yet careful and precise in its enunciation. Even while his eyes searched the room to make sure that no one had come in, he could not help hearing everything the voice said. It seemed to be talking to him, and yet the rather oracular utterance implied a less restricted audience. The utterance of a man who was aware that, though it was a duty for him to speak, for Mr. Rumbold to listen would be both a pleasure and a profit.

" ——A Children's Party," the voice announced in an even, neutral tone, nicely balanced between approval and

distaste, between enthusiasm and boredom ; " six little girls
and six little " (a faint lift in the voice, expressive of tolerant
surprise) " boys. The Broadcasting Company has invited
them to tea, and they are anxious that you should share some
of their fun." (At the last word the voice became almost
positively colourless.) " I must tell you that they have had
tea, and enjoyed it, didn't you, children ? " (A cry of " Yes,"
muffled and timid, greeted this leading question.) " We
should have liked you to hear our table-talk, but there wasn't
much of it, we were so busy eating." For a moment the voice
identified itself with the children. " But we can tell you what
we ate. Now, Percy, tell us what you had."

A piping little voice recited a long list of comestibles ; like
the children in the treacle-well, thought Rumbold, Percy must
have been, or soon will be, very ill. A few others volunteered
the items of their repast. " So you see," said the voice, " we
have not done so badly. And now we are going to have
crackers, and afterwards " (the voice hesitated and seemed to
dissociate itself from the words) " children's games." There
was an impressive pause, broken by the muttered exhortation
of a little girl : " Don't cry, Philip, it won't hurt you."
Fugitive sparks and snaps of sound followed ; more like a fire
being mended, thought Rumbold, than crackers. A murmur
of voices pierced the fusillade. " What have you got, Alec,
what have you got ? " " I've got a cannon." " Give it to
me." " No." " Well, lend it to me." " What do you want
it for ? " " I want to shoot Jimmy."

Mr. Rumbold started. Something had disturbed him.
Was it imagination, or did he hear, above the confused medley
of sound, a tiny click ? The voice was speaking again. " And
now we're going to begin the games." As though to make
amends for past luke-warmness a faint flush of anticipation
gave colour to the decorous voice. " We will commence with
that old favourite, Ring-a-ring-of-Roses."

The children were clearly shy, and left each other to do
the singing. Their courage lasted for a line or two, and then
gave out. But fortified by the Speaker's baritone, powerful
though subdued, they took heart, and soon were singing
without assistance or direction. Their light wavering voices
had a charming effect. Tears stood in Mr. Rumbold's eyes.
" Oranges and Lemons " came next. A more difficult game,
it yielded several unrehearsed effects before it finally got under
way. One could almost see the children being marshalled
into their places, as though for a figure in the Lancers. Some

of them no doubt had wanted to play another game ; children are contrary, and the dramatic side of " Oranges and Lemons," though it appeals to many, always affrights a few. The disinclination of these last would account for the pauses and hesitations which irritated Mr. Rumbold, who, as a child, had always had a strong fancy for this particular game. When, to the tramping and stamping of many small feet, the droning chant began, he leaned back and closed his eyes in ecstasy. He listened intently for the final accelerando which leads up to the catastrophe. Still the prologue maundered on, as though the children were anxious to extend the period of security, the joyous care-free promenade which the great Bell of Bow by his inconsiderate profession of ignorance, was so rudely to curtail. The Bell of Old Bailey pressed their usurers' question ; the Bells of Shoreditch answered with becoming flippancy ; the Bells of Stepney posed their ironical query, when suddenly, before the great Bell of Bow had time to get his word in, Mr. Rumbold's feelings underwent a strange revolution. Why couldn't the game continue, all sweetness and sunshine ? Why drag in the fatal issue ? Let payment be deferred ; let the bells go on chiming and never strike the hour. But heedless of Mr. Rumbold's squeamishness, the game went its way. After the eating comes the reckoning.

> " Here is a candle to light you to bed,
>   And here comes a chopper to chop off your head !
>   Chop, chop, chop . . ."

A child screamed, and there was silence.

Mr. Rumbold felt quite upset, and great was his relief when, after a few more half-hearted rounds of " Oranges and Lemons," the voice announced, " Here we come gathering Nuts and May." At least there was nothing sinister in that. Delicious sylvan scene, comprising in one splendid botanical inexactitude all the charms of winter, spring, and autumn.

What superiority to circumstance was implied in the conjunction of nuts and may ! What defiance of cause and effect ! What a testimony to coincidence ! For cause and effect are against us, as witness the fate of Old Bailey's Debtor ; but coincidence is always on our side, always teaching us how to eat our cake and have it ! The long arm of coincidence ; Mr. Rumbold would have liked to clasp it by the hand.

Meanwhile his own hand conducted the music of the revels and his foot kept time. Their pulses quickened by enjoyment, the children put more heart into the singing ; the game went with a swing ; the ardour and rhythm of it invaded the little room where Mr. Rumbold sat.   Like heavy fumes the waves of the sound poured in, so penetrating, they ravished the sense, so sweet they intoxicated it, so light they fanned it to a flame.   Mr. Rumbold was transported.   His hearing, sharpened by the subjugation and quiescence of his other faculties, began to take in new sounds ; the names, for instance, of the players who were " wanted " to make up each side and of the champions who were to pull them over.   For the listeners-in, the issues of the struggles remained in doubt.   Did Nancy Price succeed in detaching Percy Kingham from his allegiance ? Probably.   Did Alec Wharton prevail against Maisie Drew ? It was certainly an easy win for some one : the contest lasted only a second, and a ripple of laughter greeted it.   Did Violet Kingham make good against Horace Gold ?   This was a dire encounter, punctuated by deep irregular panting.   Mr. Rum-bold could see, in his mind's eye, the two champions straining backwards and forwards across the white motionless hand-kerchief, their faces red and puckered with exertion.   Violet or Horace, one of them had to go : Violet might be bigger than Horace, but then Horace was a boy : they were evenly matched : they had their pride to maintain.   The moment when the will was broken and the body went limp in surrender would be like a moment of dissolution.   Yes, even this game had its stark, uncomfortable side.   Violet or Horace, one of them was smarting now ; crying perhaps, under the humilia-tion of being fetched away.

The game began afresh.   This time there was an eager ring in the children's voic es : two tried antagonists were going to meet : it would be a battle of giants.   The chant throbbed into a war-cry.

> " Who will you have for your Nuts and May,
>   Nuts and May, Nuts and May ?
> Who will you have for your Nuts and May
>   On a cold and frosty morning ? "

They would have Victor Rumbold for Nuts and May, Victor Rumbold, Victor Rumbold ; and from the vindictiveness in their voices they might have meant to have his blood too.

> " And who will you send to fetch him away,
>   Fetch him away, fetch him away ?
> Who will you send to fetch him away
>   On a cold and frosty morning ? "

Like a clarion call, a shout of defiance, came the reply :

> " We'll send Jimmy Hagberd to fetch him away,
>   Fetch him away, fetch him away ;
>   We'll send Jimmy Hagberd to fetch him away,
>   On a wet and foggy evening."

This variation, it might be supposed, was intended to pro-
mote the contest from the realms of pretence into the world
of reality. But Mr. Rumbold probably did not hear that his
abduction had been antedated. He had turned quite green
and his head was lolling against the back of the chair.

.   .   .   .   .   .

" Any wine, sir ? "

" Yes, Clutsam, a bottle of champagne."

" Very good, sir."

Mr. Rumbold drained the first glass at one go.

" Any one coming in to dinner besides me, Clutsam ? " he
presently inquired.

" Not now, sir, it's nine o'clock," replied the waiter, his
voice edged with reproach.

" Sorry, Clutsam, I didn't feel up to the mark before
dinner, so I went and lay down."

The waiter was mollified.

" Thought you weren't looking quite yourself, sir. No bad
news, I hope ? "

" No, nothing. Just a bit tired after the journey."

" And how did you leave Australia, sir ? " inquired the
waiter, to accommodate Mr. Rumbold, who seemed anxious
to talk.

" In better weather than you have here," Mr. Rumbold
replied, finishing his second glass, and measuring with his
eye the depleted contents of the bottle.

The rain kept up a steady patter on the glass roof of the
coffee-room.

" Still, a good climate isn't everything ; it isn't like home,
for instance," the waiter remarked.

" No, indeed."

" There's many parts of the world as would be glad of a
good day's rain," affirmed the waiter.

" There certainly are," said Mr. Rumbold, who found the
conversation sedative.

" Did you do much fishing when you were abroad, sir ? "
the waiter pursued.

" A little."

" Well, you want rain for that," declared the waiter, as one who scores a point. " The fishing isn't preserved in Australia, like what it is here ? "

" No."

" Then there ain't no poaching," concluded the waiter philosophically. " It's every man for himself."

" Yes, that's the rule in Australia."

" Not much of a rule, is it ? " the waiter took him up. " Not much like law, I mean."

" It depends what you mean by law."

" Oh, Mr. Rumbold, sir, you know very well what I mean. I mean the police. Now, if you was to have done a man in out in Australia—murdered him, I mean—they'd hang you for it if they caught you, wouldn't they ? "

Mr. Rumbold teased the champagne with the butt-end of his fork and drank again.

" Probably they would, unless there were special circumstances."

" In which case you might get off ? "

" I might."

" That's what I mean by law," pronounced the waiter. " You know what the law is : you go against it, and you're punished. Of course, I don't mean you, sir ; I only say ' you ' as—as an illustration to make my meaning clear."

" Quite, quite."

" Whereas if there was only what you call a rule," the waiter pursued, deftly removing the remains of Mr. Rumbold's chicken, " it might fall to the lot of any man to round you up. Might be anybody ; might be me."

" Why should you or they," asked Mr. Rumbold, " want to round me up ? I haven't done you any harm, or them."

" Oh, but we should have to, sir."

" Why ? "

" We couldn't rest in our beds, sir, knowing you was at large. You might do it again. Somebody'd have to see to it."

" But supposing there was nobody ? "

" Sir ? "

" Supposing the murdered man hadn't any relatives or friends ; supposing he just disappeared, and no one ever knew that he was dead ? "

" Well, sir," said the waiter, winking portentously, " in that case he'd have to get on your track himself. He wouldn't rest in his grave, sir, no, not he, and knowing what he did."

" Clutsam," said Mr. Rumbold, " bring me another bottle of wine and don't trouble to ice it."

The waiter took the bottle from the table and held it up to the light. " Yes, it's dead, sir."

" Dead ? "

" Yes, sir, finished—empty—dead."

" You're right," Mr. Rumbold agreed. " It's quite dead."

.   .   .   .

It was nearly eleven o'clock. Mr. Rumbold again had the lounge to himself. Clutsam would be bringing his coffee presently. Too bad of Fate to have him haunted by these casual reminders ; too bad, his first day at home. " Too bad, too bad," he muttered, while the fire warmed the soles of his slippers. But it was excellent champagne, he would take no harm from it : the brandy Clutsam was bringing him would do the rest. Clutsam was a good sort, nice, old-fashioned servant . . . nice, old-fashioned house. . . . Warmed by the wine, his thoughts began to pass out of his control.

" Your coffee, sir," said a voice at his elbow.

" Thank you, Clutsam, I'm very much obliged to you," said Mr. Rumbold, with the exaggerated civility of slight intoxication. " You're an excellent fellow. I wish there were more like you."

" I hope so, too, I'm sure," said Clutsam, trying in his muddle-hearted way to deal with both observations at once.

" Don't seem many people about," Mr. Rumbold remarked. " Hotel pretty full ? "

" Oh yes, sir, all the suites are let, and the other rooms too. We're turning people away every day. Why, only to-night a gentleman rang up. Said he would come round late, on the off-chance. But, bless me, he'll find the birds have flown."

" Birds ? " echoed Mr. Rumbold.

" I mean, there ain't any more rooms, not for love nor money."

" Well, I'm sorry for him," said Mr. Rumbold, with ponderous sincerity. " I'm sorry for any man, friend or foe, who has to go tramping about London on a night like this. If I had an extra bed in my room, I'd put it at his disposal."

" You have, sir," the waiter said.

" Why, of course I have. How stupid ! Well, well. I'm sorry for the poor chap. I'm sorry for all homeless ones, Clutsam, wandering on the face of the earth."

" Amen to that," said the waiter devoutly.

" And doctors and such, pulled out of their beds at midnight. It's a hard life. Ever thought about a doctor's life, Clutsam ? "

" Can't say I have, sir."

" Well, well, but it's hard ; you can take that from me."

" What time shall I call you in the morning, sir ? " the waiter asked, seeing no reason why the conversation should ever stop.

" You needn't call me, Clutsam," replied Mr. Rumbold in a sing-song voice, and running the words together as though he were excusing the waiter from addressing him by the waiter's own name. " I'll get up when I'm ready. And that may be pretty late." He smacked his lips over the words. " Nothing like a good lie, eh, Clutsam ? "

" That's right, sir. You have your sleep out," the waiter encouraged him. " You won't be disturbed."

" Good night, Clutsam, you're an excellent fellow, and I don't care who hears me say so."

" Good night, sir."

Mr. Rumbold returned to his chair. It lapped him round, it ministered to his comfort ; he felt at one with it. At one with the fire, the clock, the tables, all the furniture. Their usefulness, their goodness, went out to meet his usefulness, his goodness, met and were friends. Who could bind their sweet influences or restrain them in the exercise of their kind offices ? No one. No one ; certainly not a shadow from the past. The room was perfectly quiet. Street sounds reached it only as a low continuous hum, infinitely reassuring. Mr. Rumbold fell asleep.

He dreamed that he was a boy again, living in his old home in the country. He was possessed, in the dream, by a master-passion ; he must collect firewood whenever and wherever he saw it. He found himself one autumn afternoon in the woodhouse ; that was how the dream began. The door was partly open, admitting a little light, but he could not recall how he got in. The floor of the shed was littered with bits of bark and thin twigs ; but, with the exception of the chopping-block which he knew could not be used, there was nowhere a log of sufficient size to make a fire. Though he did not like being in the woodhouse alone he stayed long enough to make a thorough search. But he could find nothing. The compulsion he knew so well descended on him, and he left the woodhouse and went into the garden. His steps took him to the foot of a high tree, standing by itself in a tangle of long grass at some distance from the house. The tree had been lopped ; for half its height it had no branches, only leafy tufts, sticking out at irregular intervals. He knew what he would see when he looked up into the dark foliage. And there, sure enough it was ; a long dead bough, bare in patches where the bark had peeled off, and crooked in the middle like an elbow.

He began to climb the tree. The ascent proved easier than he expected, his body seemed no weight at all. But he was visited by a terrible oppression, which increased as he mounted. The bough did not want him ; it was projecting its hostility down the trunk of the tree. And every second brought him nearer to an object which he had always dreaded : a growth, people called it. It stuck out from the trunk of the tree, a huge circular swelling thickly matted with twigs. Victor would have rather died than hit his head against it.

By the time he reached the bough twilight had deepened into night. He knew what he had to do : sit astride the bough, since there was none nearby from which he could reach it, and press with his hands until it broke. Using his legs to get what purchase he could, he set his back against the tree, and pushed with all his might downwards. To do this he was obliged to look beneath him, and he saw, far below him on the ground, a white sheet spread out as though to catch him ; and he knew at once that it was a shroud.

Frantically he pulled and pushed at the stiff brittle bough ; a lust to break it took hold of him ; leaning forward his whole length, he seized the bough at the elbow joint and strained it away from him. As it cracked he toppled over and the shroud came rushing upwards. . . .

Mr. Rumbold waked in a cold sweat to find himself clutching the curved arm of the chair on which the waiter had set his brandy. The glass had fallen over, and the spirit lay in a little pool on the leather seat. " I can't let it go like that," he thought, " I must get some more." A man he did not know answered the bell. " Waiter," he said, " bring me a brandy and soda in my room in a quarter of an hour's time. Rumbold, the name is." He followed the waiter out of the room. The passage was completely dark except for a small blue gas-jet, beneath which was huddled a cluster of candlesticks. The hotel, he remembered, maintained an old-time habit of deference towards darkness. As he held the wick to the gas-jet, he heard himself mutter, " Here is a candle to light you to bed." But he recollected the ominous conclusion of the distich, and, fuddled as he was, he left it unspoken.

Shortly after Mr. Rumbold's retirement the door-bell of the hotel rang. Three sharp peals, and no pause between them. " Some one in a hurry to get in," the night porter grumbled to Clutsam, who was on duty till midnight. " Expect he's forgotten his key." He made no haste to answer the summons, it would do the forgetful fellow good to wait : teach him a lesson. So dilatory was he that by the time he reached the hall-door the bell was tinkling again. Irritated by such importunity, he deliberately went back to set straight a pile of newspapers before letting this impatient devil in. To mark his indifference he even kept behind the door while he opened it ; so that his first sight of the visitor only took in his back. But this limited inspection sufficed to show that the man was a stranger and not a guest at the hotel.

In the long black cape which fell almost sheer one side and on the other stuck out as though he had a basket under his arm, he looked like a crow with a broken wing. A bald-headed crow, thought the porter, for there's a patch of bare skin between that white linen thing and his hat.

" Good evening, sir," he said. " what can I do for you ? "

The stranger made no answer, but glided to a side table and began turning over some letters with his right hand.

" Are you expecting a message ? " asked the porter.

" No," the stranger replied. " I want a room for the night."

" Was you the gentleman who telephoned for a room this evening ? "

" Yes."

" In that case I was to tell you we're afraid you can't have one, the hotel's booked right up."

" Are you quite sure?" asked the stranger. " Think again."

" Them's my orders, sir. It don't do me no good to think." At this moment the porter had a curious sensation as though some important part of him, his life maybe, had gone adrift inside him and was spinning round and round. The sensation ceased when he began to speak.

" I'll call the waiter, sir," he said.

But before he called, the waiter appeared, intent on an errand of his own.

" I say, Bill," he began, " what's the number of Mr. Rumbold's room ? He wants a drink taken up, and I forgot to ask him."

" It's thirty-three," said the porter unsteadily. " The double room."

" Why, Bill, what's up ? " the waiter exclaimed. " You look as if you'd seen a ghost."

Both men stared round the hall, and then back at each other. The room was empty.

" God," said the porter. " I must have had the horrors. But he was here a moment ago. Look at this."

On the stone flags lay an icicle, an inch or two long, around which a little pool was fast collecting.

" Why, Bill," cried the waiter, " how did that yet here ? " It's not freezing."

" *He* must have brought it," the porter said.

They looked at each other in consternation, which changed into terror as the sound of a bell made itself heard, coming from the depths of the hotel.

" Clutsam's there," whispered the porter. " He'll have to answer it, whoever it is."

.   .   .   .

Clutsam had taken off his tie, and was getting ready for bed. What on earth could any one want in the lounge at this hour ? He pulled on his coat and went upstairs.

Standing by the fire he saw the same figure whose appearance and disappearance had so disturbed the porter. " Yes, sir," he said.

" I want you to go to Mr. Rumbold," said the stranger, " and ask him if he is prepared to put the other bed in his room at the disposal of a friend."

In a few moments Clutsam returned. " Mr. Rumbold's compliments, sir, and he wants to know who it is." The stranger went to the table in the centre of the room. An Australian newspaper was lying on it, which Clutsam had not noticed before. The aspirant to Mr. Rumbold's hospitality turned over the pages. Then with his finger, which appeared, even to Clutsam standing by the door, unusually pointed, he cut out a rectangular slip, about the size of a visiting card, and, moving away, motioned the waiter to take it.

By the light of the gas-jet in the passage Clutsam read the excerpt. It seemed to be a kind of obituary notice ; but of what possible interest could it be to Mr. Rumbold, to know that the body of Mr. James Hagberd had been discovered in circumstances which suggested that he had met his death by violence ?

After a longer interval Clutsam returned, looking puzzled and a little frightened.

" Mr. Rumbold's compliments, sir, but he knows no one of that name."

" Then take this message to Mr. Rumbold," said the

stranger. " Say ' would he rather that I went up to him, or that he came down to me ? ' "

For the third time Clutsam went to do the stranger's bidding. He did not, however, upon his return open the door of the smoking-room, but shouted through it :

" Mr. Rumbold wishes you to Hell, sir, where you belong, and says ' Come up if you dare.' "

Then he bolted.

A minute later, from his retreat in an underground coal-cellar, he heard a shot fired. Some old instinct, danger-loving or danger-disregarding, stirred in him, and he ran up the stairs quicker than he had ever run up them in his life. In the passage he stumbled over Mr. Rumbold's boots. The bedroom door was ajar. Putting his head down he rushed in. The brightly-lit room was empty. But almost all the movables in it were overturned, and the bed was in a frightful mess. The pillow with its five-fold perforation was the first object on which Clutsam noticed bloodstains. Thenceforward he seemed to see them everywhere. But what sickened him and kept him so long from going down to rouse the others was the sight of an icicle on the window-sill, a thin claw of ice curved like a Chinaman's nail, with a bit of flesh sticking to it.

That was the last he saw of Mr. Rumbold. But a police-man patrolling Carrick Street noticed a man in a long black cape who seemed, from the position of his arm, to be carrying something heavy. He called out to the man and ran after him ; but though he did not seem to be moving very fast the policeman could not overtake him.

THE VOICE IN THE NIGHT

IT was a dark, starless night. We were becalmed in the Northern Pacific. Our exact position I do not know; for the sun had been hidden during the course of a weary, breathless week, by a thin haze which had seemed to float above us, about the height of our mastheads, at whiles descending and shrouding the surrounding sea.

With there being no wind, we had steadied the tiller, and I was the only man on deck. The crew, consisting of two men and a boy, were sleeping forrard in their den; while Will—my friend, and the master of our little craft—was aft in his bunk on the port side of the little cabin.

Suddenly, from out of the surrounding darkness, there came a hail:

" Schooner, ahoy ! "

The cry was so unexpected that I gave no immediate answer, because of my surprise.

It came again—a voice curiously throaty and inhuman, calling from somewhere upon the dark sea away on our port broadside:

" Schooner, ahoy ! "

" Hullo ! " I sung out, having gathered my wits somewhat. " What are you ? What do you want ? "

" You need not be afraid," answered the queer voice, having probably noticed some trace of confusion in my tone. " I am only an old—man."

The pause sounded oddly; but it was only afterwards that it came back to me with any significance.

" Why don't you come alongside, then ? " I queried somewhat snappishly; for I liked not his hinting at my having been a trifle shaken.

622

" I—I—can't. It wouldn't be safe. I——" The voice broke off, and there was silence.

" What do you mean ? " I asked, growing more and more astonished. " Why not safe ? Where are you ? "

I listened for a moment ; but there came no answer. And then, a sudden indefinite suspicion, of I knew not what, coming to me, I stepped swiftly to the binnacle, and took out the lighted lamp. At the same time, I knocked on the deck with my heel to waken Will. Then I was back at the side, throwing the yellow funnel of light out into the silent immensity beyond our rail. As I did so, I heard a slight, muffled cry, and then the sound of a splash as though some one had dipped oars abruptly. Yet I cannot say that I saw anything with certainty ; save, it seemed to me, that with the first flash of the light, there had been something upon the waters, where now there was nothing.

" Hullo, there ! " I called. " What foolery is this ! "

But there came only the indistinct sounds of a boat being pulled away into the night.

Then I heard Will's voice, from the direction of the after scuttle :

" What's up, George ? "

" Come here, Will ! " I said.

" What is it ? " he asked, coming across the deck.

I told him the queer thing which had happened. He put several questions ; then, after a moment's silence, he raised his hands to his lips, and hailed :

" Boat, ahoy ! "

From a long distance away there came back to us a faint reply, and my companion repeated his call. Presently, after a short period of silence, there grew on our hearing the muffled sound of oars ; at which Will hailed again.

This time there was a reply :

" Put away the light."

" I'm damned if I will," I muttered ; but Will told me to do as the voice bade, and I shoved it down under the bulwarks.

" Come nearer," he said, and the oar-strokes continued. Then, when apparently some half-dozen fathoms distant, they again ceased.

" Come alongside," exclaimed Will. " There's nothing to be frightened of aboard here ! "

" Promise that you will not show the light ? "

" What's to do with you," I burst out, " that you're so infernally afraid of the light ? "

" Because——" began the voice, and stopped short.

" Because what ? " I asked quickly.

Will put his hand on my shoulder.

" Shut up a minute, old man," he said, in a low voice. " Let me tackle him."

He leant more over the rail.

" See here, Mister," he said, " this is a pretty queer business, you coming upon us like this, right out in the middle of the blessed Pacific.   How are we to know what sort of a hanky-panky trick you're up to ?   You say there's only one of you. How are we to know, unless we get a squint at you—eh ? What's your objection to the light, anyway ? "

As he finished, I heard the noise of the oars again, and then the voice came ; but now from a greater distance, and sounding extremely hopeless and pathetic.

" I am sorry—sorry ! I would not have troubled you, only I am hungry, and—so is she."

The voice died away, and the sound of the oars, dipping irregularly, was borne to us.

" Stop ! " sung out Will. " I don't want to drive you away. Come back ! We'll keep the light hidden, if you don't like it."

He turned to me :

" It's a damned queer rig, this ; but I think there's nothing to be afraid of ? "

There was a question in his tone, and I replied :

" No, I think the poor devil's been wrecked around here, and gone crazy."

The sound of the oars drew nearer.

" Shove that lamp back in the binnacle," said Will ; then he leaned over the rail and listened.   I replaced the lamp, and came back to his side.   The dipping of the oars ceased some dozen yards distant.

" Won't you come alongside now ? " asked Will in an even voice.   " I have had the lamp put back in the binnacle."

" I—I cannot," replied the voice.   " I dare not come nearer.   I dare not even pay you for the—the provisions."

" That's all right," said Will, and hesitated.   " You're welcome to as much grub as you can take——" Again he hesitated.

" You are very good," exclaimed the voice.   " May God, Who understands everything, reward you——" It broke off huskily.

" The—the lady ? " said Will abruptly.   " Is she——"

" I have left her behind upon the island," came the voice.

" What island ? " I cut in.

" I know not its name," returned the voice. " I would to God—— ! " it began, and checked itself as suddenly.

" Could we not send a boat for her? " asked Will at this point.

" No ! " said the voice, with extraordinary emphasis. " My God ! No ! " There was a moment's pause ; then it added, in a tone which seemed a merited reproach :

" It was because of our want I ventured—because her agony tortured me."

" I am a forgetful brute," exclaimed Will. " Just wait a minute, whoever you are, and I will bring you up something at once."

In a couple of minutes he was back again, and his arms were full of various edibles. He paused at the rail.

" Can't you come alongside for them ? " he asked.

" No—I *dare not*," replied the voice, and it seemed to me that in its tones I detected a note of stifled craving—as though the owner hushed a mortal desire. It came to me then in a flash, that the poor old creature out there in the darkness, was *suffering* for actual need of that which Will held in his arms ; and yet, because of some unintelligible dread, refraining from dashing to the side of our little schooner, and receiving it. And with the lightning-like conviction, there came the knowledge that the Invisible was not mad ; but sanely facing some intolerable horror.

" Damn it, Will ! " I said, full of many feelings, over which predominated a vast sympathy. " Get a box. We must float off the stuff to him in it."

This we did—propelling it away from the vessel, out into the darkness, by means of a boathook. In a minute, a slight cry from the Invisible came to us, and we knew that he had secured the box.

A little later, he called out a farewell to us, and so heartful a blessing, that I am sure we were the better for it. Then, without more ado, we heard the ply of oars across the darkness.

" Pretty soon off," remarked Will, with perhaps just a little sense of injury.

" Wait," I replied. " I think somehow he'll come back. He must have been badly needing that food."

" And the lady," said Will. For a moment he was silent ; then he continued :

" It's the queerest thing ever I've tumbled across, since I've been fishing."

" Yes," I said, and fell to pondering.

And so the time slipped away—an hour, another, and still Will stayed with me ; for the queer adventure had knocked all desire for sleep out of him.

The third hour was three parts through, when we heard again the sound of oars across the silent ocean.

" Listen ! " said Will, a low note of excitement in his voice.

" He's coming, just as I thought," I muttered.

The dipping of the oars grew nearer, and I noted that the strokes were firmer and longer. The food had been needed.

They came to a stop a little distance off the broadside, and the queer voice came again to us through the darkness :

" Schooner, ahoy ! "

" That you ? " asked Will.

" Yes," replied the voice. " I left you suddenly ; but—but there was great need."

" The lady ? " questioned Will.

" The—lady is grateful now on earth. She will be more grateful soon in—in heaven."

Will began to make some reply, in a puzzled voice ; but became confused, and broke off short. I said nothing. I was wondering at the curious pauses, and, apart from my wonder, I was full of a great sympathy.

The voice continued :

" We—she and I, have talked, as we shared the result of God's tenderness and yours——"

Will interposed ; but without coherence.

" I beg of you not to—to belittle your deed of Christian charity this night," said the voice. " Be sure that it has not escaped His notice."

It stopped, and there was a full minute's silence. Then it came again :

" We have spoken together upon that which—which has befallen us. We had thought to go out, without telling any, of the terror which has come into our—lives. She is with me in believing that to-night's happenings are under a special ruling, and that it is God's wish that we should tell to you all that we have suffered since—since——"

" Yes ? " said Will softly.

" Since the sinking of the *Albatross*."

" Ah ! " I exclaimed involuntarily. " She left Newcastle for 'Frisco some six months ago, and hasn't been heard of since."

"Yes," answered the voice. "But some few degrees to the North of the line she was caught in a terrible storm, and dismasted. When the day came, it was found that she was leaking badly, and, presently, it falling to a calm, the sailors took to the boats, leaving—leaving a young lady—my fiancée—and myself upon the wreck.

"We were below, gathering together a few of our belongings, when they left. They were entirely callous, through fear, and when we came up upon the decks, we saw them only as small shapes afar off upon the horizon. Yet we did not despair, but set to work and constructed a small raft. Upon this we put such few matters as it would hold, including a quantity of water and some ship's biscuit. Then, the vessel being very deep in the water, we got ourselves on to the raft, and pushed off.

"It was later, when I observed that we seemed to be in the way of some tide or current, which bore us from the ship at an angle ; so that in the course of three hours, by my watch, her hull became invisible to our sight, her broken masts remaining in view for a somewhat longer period. Then, toward evening, it grew misty, and so through the night. The next day we were still encompassed by the mist, the weather remaining quiet.

"For four days we drifted through this strange haze, until, on the evening of the fourth day, there grew upon our ears the murmur of breakers at a distance. Gradually it became plainer, and, somewhat after midnight, it appeared to sound upon either hand at no very great space. The raft was raised upon a swell several times, and then we were in smooth water, and the noise of the breakers was behind.

"When the morning came, we found that we were in a sort of great lagoon ; but of this we noticed little at the time ; for close before us, through the enshrouding mist, loomed the hull of a large sailing-vessel. With one accord, we fell upon our knees and thanked God ; for we thought that here was an end to our perils. We had much to learn.

"The raft drew near to the ship, and we shouted on them to take us aboard ; but none answered. Presently the raft touched against the side of the vessel, and, seeing a rope hanging downwards, I seized it and began to climb. Yet I had much ado to make my way up, because of a kind of grey, lichenous fungus which had seized upon the rope, and which blotched the side of the ship lividly.

"I reached the rail and clambered over it, on to the deck.

Here I saw that the decks were covered, in great patches, with the grey masses, some of them rising into nodules several feet in height; but at the time I thought less of this matter than of the possibility of there being people aboard the ship. I shouted; but none answered. Then I went to the door below the poop deck. I opened it, and peered in. There was a great smell of staleness, so that I knew in a moment that nothing living was within, and with the knowledge, I shut the door quickly; for I felt suddenly lonely.

" I went back to the side where I had scrambled up. My— my sweetheart was still sitting quietly upon the raft. Seeing me look down she called up to know whether there were any aboard of the ship. I replied that the vessel had the appearance of having been long deserted; but that if she would wait a little I would see whether there was anything in the shape of a ladder by which she could ascend to the deck. Then we would make a search through the vessel together. A little later, on the opposite side of the decks, I found a rope side-ladder. This I carried across, and a minute afterwards she was beside me.

" Together we explored the cabins and apartments in the after part of the ship; but nowhere was there any sign of life. Here and there, within the cabins themselves, we came across odd patches of that queer fungus; but this, as my sweetheart said, could be cleansed away.

" In the end, having assured ourselves that the after portion of the vessel was empty, we picked our ways to the bows, between the ugly grey nodules of that strange growth; and here we made a further search, which told us that there was indeed none aboard but ourselves.

" This being now beyond any doubt, we returned to the stern of the ship and proceeded to make ourselves as comfortable as possible. Together we cleared out and cleaned two of the cabins; and after that I made examination whether there was anything eatable in the ship. This I soon found was so, and thanked God in my heart for His goodness. In addition to this I discovered the whereabouts of the fresh-water pump, and having fixed it I found the water drinkable, though somewhat unpleasant to the taste.

" For several days we stayed aboard the ship, without attempting to get to the shore. We were busily engaged in making the place habitable. Yet even thus early we became aware that our lot was even less to be desired than might have been imagined; for though, as a first step, we scraped away the odd patches of growth that studded the floors and walls of the cabins and saloon, yet they returned almost to their original size within the space of twenty-four hours, which not only discouraged us, but gave us a feeling of vague unease.

" Still we would not admit ourselves beaten, so set to work afresh, and not only scraped away the fungus, but soaked the places where it had been, with carbolic, a can-full of which I had found in the pantry. Yet, by the end of the week the growth had returned in full strength, and, in addition, it had spread to other places, as though our touching it had allowed germs from it to travel elsewhere.

" On the seventh morning, my sweetheart woke to find a small patch of it growing on her pillow, close to her face. At that, she came to me, so soon as she could get her garments upon her. I was in the galley at the time lighting the fire for breakfast.

" ' Come here, John,' she said, and led me aft. When I saw the thing upon her pillow I shuddered, and then and there we agreed to go right out of the ship and see whether we could not fare to make ourselves more comfortable ashore.

" Hurriedly we gathered together our few belongings, and even among these I found that the fungus had been at work ; for one of her shawls had a little lump of it growing near one edge. I threw the whole thing over the side, without saying anything to her.

" The raft was still alongside, but it was too clumsy to guide, and I lowered down a small boat that hung across the stern, and in this we made our way to the shore. Yet, as we drew near to it, I became gradually aware that here the vile fungus, which had driven us from the ship, was growing riot. In places it rose into horrible, fantastic mounds, which seemed almost to quiver, as with a quiet life, when the wind blew across them. Here and there it took on the forms of vast fingers, and in others it just spread out flat and smooth and treacherous. Odd places, it appeared as grotesque stunted trees, seeming extraordinarily kinked and gnarled—— The whole quaking vilely at times.

" At first, it seemed to us that there was no single portion of the surrounding shore which was not hidden beneath the masses of the hideous lichen ; yet, in this, I found we were mistaken ; for somewhat later, coasting along the shore at a little distance, we descried a smooth white patch of what appeared to be fine sand, and there we landed. It was not sand. What it was I do not know. All that I have observed is that upon it the fungus will not grow; while everywhere else, save where the sand-like earth wanders oddly, path-wise, amid the grey desolation of the lichen, there is nothing but that loathsome greyness.

"It is difficult to make you understand how cheered we were to find one place that was absolutely free from the growth, and here we deposited our belongings. Then we went back to the ship for such things as it seemed to us we should need. Among other matters, I managed to bring ashore with me one of the ship's sails, with which I constructed two small tents, which, though exceedingly rough-shaped, served the purposes for which they were intended. In these we lived and stored our various necessities, and thus for a matter of some four weeks all went smoothly and without particular unhappi-ness. Indeed, I may say with much of happiness—for—for we were together.

"It was on the thumb of her right hand that the growth first showed. It was only a small circular spot, much like a little grey mole. My God! how the fear leapt to my heart when she showed me the place. We cleansed it, between us, washing it with carbolic and water. In the morning of the following day she showed her hand to me again. The grey warty thing had returned. For a little while, we looked at one another in silence. Then, still wordless, we started again to remove it. In the midst of the operation she spoke suddenly.

"'What's that on the side of your face, dear?' Her voice was sharp with anxiety. I put my hand up to feel.

"'There! Under the hair by your ear. A little to the front a bit.' My finger rested upon the place, and then I knew.

"'Let us get your thumb done first,' I said. And she submitted, only because she was afraid to touch me until it was cleansed. I finished washing and disinfecting her thumb, and then she turned to my face. After it was finished we sat to-gether and talked awhile of many things; for there had come into our lives sudden, very terrible thoughts. We were, all at once, afraid of something worse than death. We spoke of loading the boat with provisions and water and making our way out on to the sea; yet we were helpless, for many causes, and—and the growth had attacked us already. We decided to stay. God would do with us what was His will. We would wait.

" A month, two months, three months passed and the places grew somewhat, and there had come others. Yet we fought so strenuously with the fear that its headway was but slow, comparatively speaking.

" Occasionally we ventured off to the ship for such stores as we needed. There we found that the fungus grew persistently. One of the nodules on the maindeck became soon as high as my head.

" We had now given up all thought or hope of leaving the island. We had realized that it would be unallowable to go among healthy humans, with the things from which we were suffering.

" With this determination and knowledge in our minds we knew that we should have to husband our food and water ; for we did not know, at that time, but that we should possibly live for many years.

" This reminds me that I have told you that I am an old man. Judged by years this is not so. But—but——"

He broke off ; then continued somewhat abruptly :

" As I was saying, we knew that we should have to use care in the matter of food. But we had no idea then how little food there was left, of which to take care. It was a week later that I made the discovery that all the other bread tanks —which I had supposed full—were empty, and that (beyond odd tins of vegetables and meat, and some other matters) we had nothing on which to depend, but the bread in the tank which I had already opened.

" After learning this I bestirred myself to do what I could, and set to work at fishing in the lagoon ; but with no success. At this I was somewhat inclined to feel desperate until the thought came to me to try outside the lagoon, in the open sea.

" Here, at times, I caught odd fish ; but so infrequently that they proved of but little help in keeping us from the hunger which threatened. It seemed to me that our deaths were likely to come by hunger, and not by the growth of the thing which had seized upon our bodies.

" We were in this state of mind when the fourth month wore out. Then I made a very horrible discovery. One morning, a little before midday, I came off from the ship with a portion of the biscuits which were left. In the mouth of her tent I saw my sweetheart sitting, eating something.

" ' What is it, my dear ? ' I called out as I leapt ashore, Yet, on hearing my voice, she seemed confused, and, turning. slyly threw something towards the edge of the little clearing.

It fell short, and a vague suspicion having arisen within me, I walked across and picked it up. It was a piece of the grey fungus.

" As I went to her with it in my hand, she turned deadly pale ; then a rose red.

" I felt strangely dazed and frightened.

" ' My dear ! My dear ! ' I said, and could say no more. Yet at my words she broke down and cried bitterly. Gradually, as she calmed, I got from her the news that she had tried it the preceding day, and—and liked it. I got her to promise on her knees not to touch it again, however great our hunger. After she had promised she told me that the desire for it had come suddenly, and that, until the moment of desire, she had experienced nothing towards it but the most extreme repulsion.

" Later in the day, feeling strangely restless, and much shaken with the thing which I had discovered, I made my way along one of the twisted paths—formed by the white, sand-like substance—which led among the fungoid growth. I had, once before, ventured along there ; but not to any great distance. This time, being involved in perplexing thought, I went much farther than hitherto.

" Suddenly I was called to myself by a queer hoarse sound on my left. Turning quickly I saw that there was movement among an extraordinarily shaped mass of fungus, close to my elbow. It was swaying uneasily, as though it possessed life of its own. Abruptly, as I stared, the thought came to me that the thing had a grotesque resemblance to the figure of a distorted human creature. Even as the fancy flashed into my brain, there was a slight, sickening noise of tearing, and I saw that one of the branch-like arms was detaching itself from the surrounding grey masses, and coming towards me. The head of the thing—a shapeless grey ball, inclined in my direction. I stood stupidly, and the vile arm brushed across my face. I gave out a frightened cry, and ran back a few paces. There was a sweetish taste upon my lips where the thing had touched me. I licked them, and was immediately filled with an inhuman desire. I turned and seized a mass of the fungus. Then more, and—more. I was insatiable. In the midst of devouring, the remembrance of the morning's discovery swept into my mazed brain. It was sent by God. I dashed the fragment I held to the ground. Then, utterly wretched and feeling a dreadful guiltiness, I made my way back to the little encampment.

" I think she knew, by some marvellous intuition which love must have given, so soon as she set eyes on me. Her quiet sympathy made it easier for me, and I told her of my sudden weakness ; yet omitted to mention the extraordinary thing which had gone before. I desired to spare her all unnecessary terror.

" But, for myself, I had added an intolerable knowledge, to breed an incessant terror in my brain ; for I doubted not but that I had seen the end of one of those men who had come to the island in the ship in the lagoon ; and in that monstrous ending I had seen our own.

" Thereafter we kept from the abominable food, though the desire for it had entered into our blood. Yet our drear punishment was upon us ; for, day by day, with monstrous rapidity, the fungoid growth took hold of our poor bodies. Nothing we could do would check it materially, and so—and so—we who had been human, became—— Well, it matters less each day. Only—only we had been man and maid !

" And day by day, the fight is more dreadful, to withstand the hunger-lust for the terrible lichen.

" A week ago we ate the last of the biscuit, and since that time I have caught three fish. I was out here fishing to-night, when your schooner drifted upon me out of the mist. I hailed you. You know the rest, and may God, out of His great heart, bless you for your goodness to a—a couple of poor outcast souls."

There was the dip of an oar—another. Then the voice came again, and for the last time, sounding through the slight surrounding mist, ghostly and mournful.

" God bless you ! Good-bye."

" Good-bye," we shouted together, hoarsely, our hearts full of many emotions.

I glanced about me. I became aware that the dawn was upon us.

The sun flung a stray beam across the hidden sea ; pierced the mist dully, and lit up the receding boat with a gloomy fire. Indistinctly, I saw something nodding between the oars. I thought of a sponge—a great, grey nodding sponge. The oars continued to ply. They were grey—as was the boat—and my eyes searched a moment vainly for the conjunction of hand and oar. My gaze flashed back to the—head. It nodded forward as the oars went backward for the stroke. Then the oars were dipped, the boat shot out of the patch of light, and the—the thing went nodding into the mist.

BERENICE

" Dicebant mihi sodales, si sepulchrum amicæ visitarem, curas meas aliquantulum fore levatas."—EBN ZAIAT.

MISERY is manifold. The wretchedness of earth is multiform. Overreaching the wide horizon as the rainbow, its hues are as various as the hues of that arch—as distinct too, yet as intimately blended. Over-reaching the wide horizon as the rainbow ! How is it that from beauty I have derived a type of unloveliness ?—from the covenant of peace a simile of sorrow ? But as, in ethics, evil is a consequence of good, so, in fact, out of joy is sorrow born. Either the memory of past bliss is the anguish of to-day, or the agonies which *are* have their origin in the ecstasies which *might have been*.

My baptismal name is Egæus ; that of my family I will not mention. Yet there are no towers in the land more time-honoured than my gloomy, grey, hereditary halls. Our line has been called a race of visionaries ; and in many striking particulars—in the character of the family mansion—in the frescoes of the chief saloon—in the tapestries of the dormitories—in the chiselling of some buttresses in the armoury—but more especially in the gallery of antique paintings—in the fashion of the library chamber—and, lastly, in the very peculiar nature of the library's contents, there is more than sufficient evidence to warrant the belief.

The recollections of my earliest years are connected with that chamber, and with its volumes—of which latter I will say no more. Here died my mother. Herein was I born. But it is mere idleness to say that I had not lived before—that the soul has no previous existence. You deny it ?—let us not argue the matter. Convinced myself, I seek not to convince.

There is, however, a remembrance of aerial forms—of spiritual and meaning eyes—of sounds, musical yet sad—a remembrance which will not be excluded ; a memory like a shadow, vague, variable, indefinite, unsteady ; and like a shadow, too, in the impossibility of my getting rid of it while the sunlight of my reason shall exist.

In that chamber was I born. Thus awaking from the long night of what seemed, but was not, nonentity, at once into the very regions of fairyland—into a palace of imagination—into the wild dominions of monastic thought and erudition—it is not singular that I gazed around me with a startled and ardent eye—that I loitered away my boyhood in books, and dissipated my youth in reverie ; but it *is* singular that as years rolled away, and the noon of manhood found me still in the mansion of my fathers—it is wonderful what stagnation there fell upon the springs of my life—wonderful how total an inversion took place in the character of my commonest thought. The realities of the world affected me as visions, and as visions only, while the wild ideas of the land of dreams became, in turn—not the material of my everyday existence—but in very deed that existence utterly and solely in itself.

Berenice and I were cousins, and we grew up together in my paternal halls. Yet differently we grew—I ill of health, and buried in gloom—she agile, graceful, and overflowing with energy ; hers the ramble on the hill-side—mine the studies of the cloister—I living within my own heart, and addicted body and soul to the most intense and painful meditation—she roaming carelessly through life with no thought of the shadows in her path, or the silent flight of the raven-winged hours. Berenice !—I call upon her name—Berenice !—and from the grey ruins of memory a thousand tumultuous recollections are startled at the sound ! Ah ! vividly is her image before me now, as in the early days of her light-heartedness and joy ! Oh ! gorgeous yet fantastic beauty ! Oh ! sylph amid the shrubberies of Arnheim ! Oh ! naiad among its fountains ! —and then—then all is mystery and terror, and a tale which should not be told. Disease—a fatal disease—fell like the simoon upon her frame, and, even while I gazed upon her, the spirit of change swept over her, pervading her mind, her habits, and her character, and, in a manner the most subtle and terrible, disturbing even the identity of her person ! Alas ! the destroyer came and went, and the victim—where was she ? I knew her not—or knew her no longer as Berenice.

Among the numerous train of maladies superinduced by that fatal and primary one which effected a revolution of so horrible a kind in the moral and physical being of my cousin, may be mentioned as the most distressing and obstinate in its nature, a species of epilepsy not infrequently terminating in *trance* itself—trance very nearly resembling positive dissolution, and from which her manner of recovery was, in most instances, startlingly abrupt. In the meantime my own disease —for I have been told that I should call it by no other appellation—my own disease, then, grew rapidly upon me, and assumed finally a monomaniac character of a novel and extraordinary form—hourly and momently gaining vigour—and at length obtaining over me the most incomprehensible ascendency. This monomania, if I must so term it, consisted in a morbid irritability of those properties of the mind in metaphysical science termed the *attentive*. It is more than probable that I am not understood ; but I fear, indeed, that it is in no manner possible to convey to the mind of the merely general reader, an adequate idea of that nervous *intensity of interest* with which, in my case, the powers of meditation (not to speak technically)'busied and buried themselves, in the contemplation of even the most ordinary objects of the universe.

To muse for long unwearied hours with my attention riveted to some frivolous device on the margin, or in the typography of a book ; to become absorbed for the better part of a summer's day, in a quaint shadow falling aslant upon the tapestry, or upon the floor ; to lose myself for an entire night in watching the steady flame of a lamp, or the embers of a fire ; to dream away whole days over the perfume of a flower ; to repeat monotonously some common word, until the sound, by dint of frequent repetition, ceased to convey any idea whatever to the mind ; to lose all sense of motion or physical existence, by means of absolute bodily quiescence long and obstinately persevered in ;—such were a few of the most common and least pernicious vagaries induced by a condition of the mental faculties, not, indeed, altogether unparalleled, but certainly bidding defiance to anything like analysis or explanation.

Yet let me not be misapprehended.—The undue, earnest, and morbid attention thus excited by objects in their own nature frivolous, must not be confounded in character with that ruminating propensity common to all mankind, and more especially indulged in by persons of ardent imagination. It was not even, as might be at first supposed, an extreme condition, or exaggeration of such propensity, but primarily and essentially distinct and different. In the one instance, the dreamer, or enthusiast, being interested by an object usually *not* frivolous, imperceptibly loses sight of this object in a wilderness of deductions and suggestions issuing therefrom, until at the conclusion of a day-dream, *often replete with luxury*, he finds the *incitamentum* or first cause of his musings entirely vanished and forgotten. In my case the primary object was *invariably frivolous*, although assuming, through the medium of my distempered vision, a refracted and unreal importance. Few deductions, if any, were made ; and those few pertinaciously returning in upon the original object as a centre. The meditations were *never* pleasurable ; and, at the termination of the reverie, the first cause, so far from being out of sight, had attained that supernaturally exaggerated interest which was the prevailing feature of the disease. In a word, the powers of mind more particularly exercised were, with me, as I have said before, the *attentive*, and are, with the day-dreamer, the *speculative*.

My books, at this epoch, if they did not actually serve to irritate the disorder, partook, it will be perceived, largely, in their imaginative and inconsequential nature, of the characteristic qualities of the disorder itself. I well remember, among others, the treatise of the noble Italian Cœlius Secundus Curio, *De Amplitudine Beati Regni Dei ;* St. Austin's great work, *The City of God ;* and Tertullian, *De Carne Christi*, in which the paradoxical sentence, " *Mortuus est Dei filius ; credibile est quia ineptum est : et sepultus resurrexit ; certum est quia impossibile est,*" occupied my undivided time for many weeks of laborious and fruitless investigation.

Thus it will appear that, shaken from its balance only by trivial things, my reason bore resemblance to that ocean-crag spoken of by Ptolemy Hephestion, which, steadily resisting the attacks of human violence, and the fiercer fury of the waters and the winds, trembled only to the touch of the flower called asphodel. And although, to a careless thinker, it might appear a matter beyond doubt, that the alteration produced by her unhappy malady, in the *moral* condition of Berenice, would afford me many objects for the exercise of that intense and abnormal meditation whose nature I have been at some trouble in explaining, yet such was not in any degree the case. In the lucid intervals of my infirmity, her calamity, indeed, gave me pain, and, taking deeply to heart that total wreck of her fair and gentle life, I did not fail to ponder frequently and bitterly upon the wonder-working means by which so strange a revolution had been so suddenly brought to pass. But these reflections partook not of the idiosyncrasy of my disease, and were such as would have occurred, under similar circumstances, to the ordinary mass of mankind. True to its own character, my disorder revelled in the less important but more startling changes wrought in the *physical* frame of Berenice—in the singular and most appalling distortion of her personal identity.

During the brightest days of her unparalleled beauty, most surely I had never loved her. In the strange anomaly of my existence, feelings with me *had never been* of the heart, and my passions *always were* of the mind. Through the grey of the early morning—among the trellised shadows of the forest at noonday—and in the silence of my library at night, she had flitted by my eyes, and I had seen her—not as the living and breathing Berenice, but as the Berenice of a dream not as a being of the earth, earthy, but as the abstraction of such a being—not as a thing to admire, but to analyse—not as an object of love, but as the theme of the most abstruse although desultory speculation. And *now*—now I shuddered in her presence, and grew pale at her approach ; yet bitterly lamenting her fallen and desolate condition, I called to mind that she had loved me long, and, in an evil moment, I spoke to her of marriage.

And at length the period of our nuptials was approaching, when, upon an afternoon in the winter of the year—one of those unseasonably warm, calm, misty days which are the nurse of the beautiful Halcyon,[1]—I sat (and sat, as I thought, alone) in the inner apartment of the library. But uplifting my eyes I saw that Berenice stood before me.

Was it my own excited imagination—or the misty influence of the atmosphere—or the uncertain twilight of the chamber— or the grey draperies which fell around her figure—that caused in it so vacillating and indistinct an outline ? I could not tell. She spoke no word, and I—not for worlds could I have uttered a syllable. An icy chill ran through my frame ; a sense of insufferable anxiety oppressed me ; a consuming curiosity pervaded my soul ; and, sinking back upon the chair, I remained for some time breathless and motionless, with my eyes riveted upon her person. Alas ! its emaciation was excessive, and not one vestige of the former being lurked in any single line of the contour. My burning glances at length fell upon the face.

[1] For as Jove, during the winter season, gives twice seven days of warmth, men have called this clement and temperate time the nurse of the beautiful Halcyon.—SIMONIDES.

The forehead was high, and very pale, and singularly placid ; and the once jetty hair fell partially over it, and overshadowed the hollow temples with innumerable ringlets now of a vivid yellow, and jarring discordantly, in their fantastic character, with the reigning melancholy of the countenance. The eyes were lifeless, and lustreless, and seemingly pupil-less, and I shrank involuntarily from their glassy stare to the contemplation of the thin and shrunken lips. They parted ; and in a smile of peculiar meaning, *the teeth* of the changed Berenice disclosed themselves slowly to my view. Would to God that I had never beheld them, or that, having done so, I had died !

. . . . . .

The shutting of a door disturbed me, and, looking up, I found that my cousin had departed from the chamber. But from the disordered chamber of my brain, had not, alas ! departed, and would not be driven away, the white and ghastly *spectrum* of the teeth. Not a speck on their surface—not a shade on their enamel—not an indenture in their edges—but what that period of her smile had sufficed to brand in upon my memory. I saw them *now* even more unequivocally than I beheld them *then*. The teeth !—the teeth !—they were here, and there, and everywhere, and visibly and palpably before me ; long, narrow, and excessively white, with the pale lips writhing about them, as in the very moment of their first terrible development. Then came the full fury of my *monomania*, and I struggled in vain against its strange and irresistible influence, In the multiplied objects of the external world I had no thoughts but for the teeth. For these I longed with a frenzied desire. All other matters and all different interests became absorbed in their single contemplation. They—they alone were present to the mental eye, and they, in their sole individuality, became the essence of my mental life. I held them in every light. I turned them in every attitude. I surveyed their characteristics. I dwelt upon their peculiarities. I pondered upon their conformation. I mused upon the alteration in their nature. I shuddered as I assigned to them in imagination a sensitive and sentient power, and even when unassisted by the lips, a capability of moral expression. Of Mad'selle Sallé it has been well said, " *que tous ses pas étaient des sentiments,*" and of Berenice I more seriously believed *que toutes ses dents étaient des idées. Des idées !*—ah, here was the idiotic thought that destroyed me ! *Des idées !*—ah, *therefore* it was that I coveted them so madly ! I felt that their possession could alone ever restore me to peace, in giving me back to reason.

And the evening closed in upon me thus—and then the darkness came, and tarried, and went—and the day again dawned—and the mists of a second night were now gathering around—and still I sat motionless in that solitary room ; and still I sat buried in meditation, and still the *phantasma* of the teeth maintained its terrible ascendency as, with the most vivid and hideous distinctness, it floated about amid the changing lights and shadows of the chamber. At length there broke in upon my dreams a cry as of horror and dismay ; and thereunto, after a pause, succeeded the sound of troubled voices, inter-mingled with many low moanings of sorrow, or of pain. I arose from my seat and, throwing open one of the doors of the library, saw standing out in the antechamber a servant maiden, all in tears, who told me that Berenice was—no more. She had been seized with epilepsy in the early morning, and now, at the closing in of the night, the grave was ready for its tenant, and all the preparations for the burial were completed.

.   .   .   .   .   .

I found myself sitting in the library, and again sitting there alone. It seemed that I had newly awakened from a confused and exciting dream. I knew that it was now midnight, and I was well aware that since the setting of the sun Berenice had been interred. But of that dreary period which intervened I had no positive—at least no definite comprehension. Yet its memory was replete with horror—horror more horrible from being vague, and terror more terrible from ambiguity. It was a fearful page in the record of my existence, written all over with dim, and hideous, and unintelligible recollections. I strived to decipher them, but in vain ; while ever and anon, like the spirit of a departed sound, the shrill and piercing shriek of a female voice seemed to be ringing in my ears. I had done a deed—what was it ? I asked myself the question aloud, and the whispering echoes of the chamber answered me, " *What was it ?* "

On the table beside me burned a lamp, and near it lay a little box. It was of no remarkable character, and I had seen it frequently before, for it was the property of the family physician ; but how came it *there*, upon my table, and why did I shudder in regarding it ? These things were in no manner to be accounted for, and my eyes at length dropped to the open pages of a book, and to a sentence underscored therein. The words were the singular but simple ones of the poet Ebn Zaiat, " *Dicebant mihi sodales si sepulchrum amicæ visitarem, curas meas aliquantulum fore levatas.*" Why then, as I perused them, did the hairs of my head erect themselves on end, and the blood of my body become congealed within my veins ?

There came a light tap at the library door, and pale as the tenant of a tomb, a menial entered upon tiptoe. His looks were wild with terror, and he spoke to me in a voice tremulous, husky, and very low. What said he ?—some broken sentences I heard. He told of a wild cry disturbing the silence of the night—of the gathering together of the household—of a search in the direction of the sound ;—and then his tones grew thrillingly distinct as he whispered me of a violated grave—of a disfigured body enshrouded, yet still breathing, still palpitating, still *alive !*

He pointed to my garments ;—they were muddy and clotted with gore. I spoke not, and he took me gently by the hand ;— it was indented with the impress of human nails. He directed my attention to some object against the wall ;—I looked at it for some minutes ;—it was a spade. With a shriek I bounded to the table, and grasped the box that lay upon it. But I could not force it open ; and in my tremor it slipped from my hands, and fell heavily, and burst into pieces ; and from it, with a rattling sound, there rolled out some instruments of dental surgery, intermingled with thirty-two small, white and ivory-looking substances that were scattered to and fro about the floor.